TALES
OF
SNOW

Also by M.J. Haag

Fairy Tale Retellings
(ALL IN THE SAME WORLD)

Beastly Tales
Depravity
Deceit
Devastation

Tales of Cinder
Disowned (prequel) *
Defiant
Disdain
Damnation

Resurrection Chronicles
(hottie demons!)

Demon Ember	*Demon Night*	*Demon Fall*
Demon Flames	*Demon Dawn*	*Demon Kept* *
Demon Ash	*Demon Disgrace*	*Demon Blind* *
Demon Escape	*Demon Design* *	*Demon Defeat - 1*
Demon Deception	*Demon Discord* *	*Demon Defeat - 2*

* novella

TALES
OF
SNOW

M.J. HAAG

Shattered Glass
——PUBLISHING——

To sisters...
Whether by birth
or by choice,
forever there for each other.

DESPAIR

CHAPTER 1

Night hadn't yet given way to dawn as I quietly eased my legs over the edge of my windowsill. My arms strained as I searched for my first foothold.

I wasn't some simpering, useless maid. Yet, I wasn't athletic like Eloise, my twin, either. Where Eloise's hair and skin were kissed by the sun, and she loved to run amok outdoors, seeking any manner of adventure, I, Kellen, was the opposite.

With hair black like the surrounding shadows, pale skin to rival a full moon's glow, and the preference to read about adventures rather than have them, few would guess I possessed the ability to scale the wall of our home without a rope or ladder. Fortunately, when one had an adventurer as a twin, one learned things.

I found a familiar foothold in the stones protruding from the wall and began my descent.

Alone.

No hushed whisper goaded me. No muffled laughter accompanied me. I was utterly without anyone to depend on for the first time in my life.

A pang of sorrow mixed with fear rose, but quickly, I pushed it down. The moment I'd said goodbye to my sister, I'd known there would be no turning back. For my twin—the sole reason for my existence—I would do anything. Even risk death, which was most assuredly what I was doing by escaping the house that had become our prison.

I only hoped Eloise's suffering wouldn't increase because of my actions. While I had no issue with risking myself, I hated the thought that I was risking her as well. However, what Eloise had written in the soot was right.

Without you, there is no control.

If I stayed, Maeve, the woman our father had left to care for us, would use me to control Eloise and would use my sister to control me. Maeve had proven so by chaining my sister to the hearth after having her beaten.

Briefly, the image of Eloise's swollen and bloody face rose in my mind, and rage, unlike anything I'd ever felt, threatened to fill me.

No matter the cost, I would right the wrongs that had been done. To Eloise. To my father. And to my mother.

Even after three weeks, the grief from losing her wanted to consume me. I trembled against the need to feel it, and my fingers slipped on the stone I was gripping. Thankfully, years of keeping up with Eloise saw me correcting my hold with little thought.

Pausing for a moment, I took a steadying breath and listened to the silence in the yard below.

I needed to focus. Too much was at stake to allow the hidden depths of my anger and sorrow to overcome me now. I'd planned my departure to ensure I would be well away before my absence became known and couldn't tarry.

Soundlessly, I scaled down the remainder of the wall and landed lightly on my feet.

As I untied my skirts, I glanced up at the place I'd called my home for sixteen years. The closed window of the room I'd shared with my sister wouldn't indicate how I'd escaped. After all, ladies didn't climb walls. Ladies wouldn't do many of the things I planned to do.

Most would weep or wail and try to find a way to speak the truth of what I'd learned despite the curse binding my tongue. I wasn't the type to give in to her emotions. And absolutely not with emotionally charged theatrics.

I turned and soundlessly started down our rutted drive. My deep red cloak and dark mourning gown beneath blended with the lingering night as I walked softly down our lane. Faint moonlight ushered me to the main road that led into Towdown where, having much to do and very little time to accomplish it, I picked up my skirts and settled into a soundless jog.

Anyone watching me would never suspect the emotions that I'd carefully trapped away. Many thought I was emotionless. Kellen the cold. A boy once said I was made of ice, which supposedly explained my pale skin. Although I felt things as much as any other person—the bitterness of disappointment, the grief of loss, the joy of receiving a gift—it was safer to keep it all locked away and use reason to dictate my actions.

Since agreeing to Eloise's plea to run, I'd given our plight much thought. The kingdom of Drisdall forbade the use of magic. Those who practiced it were cast out, imprisoned, or sentenced to death. Yet, a caster who used blood magic—the worst kind—had come into our home, killed those we loved, and cursed my sister and me so we could never speak of it.

We needed help; however, neither of us could do or say anything to implicate our tormentor. The curse binding us to silence left a single viable route to free us from our current madness—I needed to find our father.

Stricken by grief from the loss of his wife, he had sought to reestablish a trade route between the kingdoms of Drisdall and Turre. However, I saw his plan to enter the Dark Forest for what it was—a means to join his beloved wife. Cursed beasts roamed those forbidden woods, waiting to make a meal of any foolish traveler.

Such as myself.

The sling bag I'd packed bounced lightly against my back, proof of my impending folly. Yet, what other choice did I have?

In my father's mind, arranging for our mother's cousin, Maeve, to stay with Eloise and me had likely been a loving consideration. He could not have known what evil he had invited into our home to sleep in his beloved wife's bed, and I meant to find him before he obtained his permanent escape.

Please don't let it be too late, I thought.

The sun was just beginning to lighten the horizon when I reached the edge of town and slowed to a walk. A few early risers were already making their way to the market district.

Acknowledging no one and keeping my head down under my cloak, I made my way to the bookstore. I knew Eloise would be the first one Maeve questioned once she discovered my absence, which is why I hadn't told her my plans. Yet, I couldn't leave my sister to wonder my fate indefinitely if I should fail. So I planned to leave a clue with Mr. Bentwell that would hopefully lead Eloise to the spellcaster's books we'd found in the attic and the note I'd hidden within them.

Mr. Bentwell answered a good while after my first knock and welcomed me with a surprised smile.

"Kellen Cartwright," he said, stepping aside and gesturing for me to enter. "And without Eloise. This is a surprise."

"I apologize for calling upon you so early."

"Think nothing of it. Your love of the written word delights me, and I understand why you wish to escape to another world."

Since my mother's passing, he'd been sympathetically kind. While the books I'd borrowed from him hadn't dulled the pain, they had provided distraction in ways he would never guess. And because of his help, I felt truly horrible for darkening his doorstep now.

"Do you have another I might borrow?" I asked.

"Of course," he said, leading the way to his desk. "Lady Greylin just returned one that I think you might enjoy. Let's see..."

As he rummaged around his desk, I moved off to select another book from his shelves. It was a children's book I'd read long ago, filled with tales of dangerous magic. I thought it a fitting place to hide a clue for Eloise and slipped the piece of parchment into the barely loose spine.

"Here it is," he said.

I turned and handed him the book of tales as I accepted the one he offered.

"Would you mind holding this one for Eloise? She should finish her current book in a day or two."

I wasn't sure how long it would take for Maeve to unchain Eloise, but something told me the book would be in my sister's hands before the day was done.

"Of course." He set it aside, and we said our farewells.

As I left, I felt the same sense of certainty that would be the last time I ever saw Mr. Bentwell. I forced the sorrow away and carefully tucked away the book he'd loaned me in my bag.

After skirting around the busiest sections of town, I made my way toward the western road that hooked to the north before it reached the Dark Forest. Seeing no wagons along the route, I started jogging once more.

Since Maeve's arrival, our home had settled into a routine. She stayed up late, looking through Father's old documents, and often slept until mid-morning. With the sun cresting the horizon, I needed to move quickly.

My lungs burned for air long before I spotted the road veering north ahead. If not for the bend, I would have missed the old path to the kingdom of Turre altogether.

Leaving the road, I slowed to a walk. My gaze swept over the long grass, searching for any sign of my father's passing. Near a pair of fallen stone pillars, I found it. The remains of an old fire, a saddle, and a pair of empty provisions bags.

The abandoned gear meant that he'd released his horse before going into the Dark Forest. My throat tightened, and I rifled through the abandoned bags, looking for anything I could take with me. The biscuits I found were dotted with mold.

How many days had he lingered here after leaving us over a fortnight ago?

My gaze drifted to the distant trees, and I hoped it had been a good number. I could feel the malevolence waiting in the darkness.

A soft hum danced along my skin, distracting me from the gloom ahead. It wasn't a sound, but a feeling.

Pulling my gaze from the trees, I studied the surrounding area again. Grass, a few stunted trees, my father's camp, and the fallen stones. My gaze lingered on the stones, and I drew closer. The hum grew in pitch yet remained gentle.

Magic.

After Mother's death, I'd discovered books in our attic. They'd detailed many things, such as how to make herbal tinctures to heal and bespelled potions to change one's appearance. But the books also contained other notes. Small, informational sections that had hinted at a larger magical knowledge regarding magic as an energy that existed in nature, beast, and man.

Curious, I set my hand to the stone and *felt* it—an energy that didn't typically belong to a single stone. And each stone in the pillar had it.

I understood I'd found the fabled magic pillars that had once guarded the Dark Forest's winding path to Turre before magic had been banned in Drisdall.

I knew little about the Dark Forest, only what stories my father had shared from his youth when the pillars had still stood. In his time, the road had been safe enough to travel. The pillars had kept the creatures corrupted by magic confined to the darkness of the massive wood that separated the two kingdoms. However, after news spread that Turre's Queen had fallen, the pillars had been destroyed.

Rumors said that the creatures lived in the darkness because they couldn't survive the light, which is why I'd purposely timed my arrival. Logically, every forest had pockets of light. Nature's way to ensure new growth. I simply needed to stay within the pockets and hope I found Father before dark.

Removing my hand from the stone, I straightened the sling bag I wore across my body, took one deep, calming breath, and started forward through the waist-high grass.

At the edge of the forest, I paused and stared ahead at the heavily shadowed trunks. If there was a pocket of light, I couldn't see it.

Once I entered, I knew there would be no turning back.

For Eloise, I thought, stepping into the shadows.

While finding ways to startle my sister had amused me for years, the skills I'd honed in doing so served me well as I moved quickly and quietly through the trees. Even my breathing was soft in the silence, which was a blessing.

How could such a vast place have no birds or small wildlife to fill it with sounds of life?

A twig snapped.

Not close but close enough to hear.

A feeling of danger and the need to hide drove me to the nearest tree, where I pressed my back to the trunk. Heart racing, I looked for the source of danger and spotted a rabbit frozen in fear a few paces away. It wasn't staring at me, though. It was looking to the west, deeper into the woods, the direction I needed to go.

It twitched then bolted to the south, making more noise than an animal its size should. The sound of pursuit was immediate and much louder, punctuated by a savage growl.

Barely breathing, I slid around the trunk of the tree so the creatures wouldn't spot me, waited a few seconds, and slipped to the next tree. Then the next.

Soundlessly, I glided away at a steady pace. The light faded behind me, and my eyes adjusted to the dimness enough that I spotted the old road. Brush and small trees grew in the path, overshadowed by much larger trees to the side. I didn't see any patches of light ahead, but reason said I was most likely to find some along the road.

Would my father have followed the road too?

The sounds behind me stopped.

A familiar tingle ran up my spine. It was something I'd felt with increasing frequency since Father had left us. A sign of danger to come. I hadn't heeded its warning then, but I did now. I strained to listen to the trees around me and heard nothing but silence. The tingle grew stronger. I stepped behind a tree and kept my breath silent and steady.

I saw movement to my left and slowly turned my head to look. Something moved between the trees. It looked like a mix of a bear and a wolf but stood on its disjointed hind legs. Despite its bulky appearance, it moved stealthily, pausing occasionally to sniff the air.

The realization that it might be tracking me barely settled in my mind when it turned slowly, sniffing in my direction. The angle was enough to see the torn remains of the clothes he wore.

"Father." The word escaped in an agonized whisper.

His head swung toward me. I felt no fear. Only anguish that I'd ignored the warning when he'd left. That I hadn't tried to stop him sooner. If I had, Eloise and I might have had a way to rid ourselves of Maeve.

Now...any lingering hope I'd held vanished with the tear that trailed down my cheek.

He stalked toward me, still not making a sound. I didn't try to run. My fate was set.

Another tear, for Eloise, followed the first. And another for my mother.

Even now, facing my own death, I could not speak the name of her killer so my father would know it wasn't his fault. None of this was his fault.

I spoke the only words left to me.

"I'm sorry I failed you."

He stopped before me and reached out to run a claw down my cheek. It scraped my skin painfully as he traced my trail of tears, but I didn't pull away.

He opened his mouth, showing his bloody teeth.

The sound he made was mostly inhuman, but through the growl, I heard what he was trying to say.

"Run."

"I already did," I said. "This is where I am meant to be. You were my last hope."

The feeling of danger intensified a moment before I heard something snap nearby. Father's head whipped toward the sound, and he let out a low snarl.

A second creature emerged from the trees. He moved differently. Less like a man, though he still only walked on his hind legs. Malevolence shone in his eyes as he prowled closer to us.

Father's claws closed over my cloak as he ripped me away from the tree and tossed me aside. I stumbled, trying to keep my feet under me.

"Run," he growled.

The creature leapt toward me at the same time Father launched himself at the beast. Gripping my skirts, I pivoted and ran as they thudded together.

I knew Father had meant for me to leave, but that tingle of warning inside of me whispered the danger outside of these trees was just as great as the dangers within. So, I sprinted along the road, deeper into the forest as their snarls and howls filled the trees behind me.

Ahead, I spotted a sun-dappled circle no bigger than a wagon wheel. A shape moved in the trees not far from it. I ran harder, straight toward the light and the beast. It tensed, ready to pounce. I pulled back at the last moment to skid to a stop within the light.

Instinct screamed to crouch low. I listened immediately and felt something move over my head. Claws snagged my hood, pulling it back and tearing the material as the creature howled in rage. I rocked back with the momentum, almost tumbling out of the light.

The smell of burnt hair filled my nose. When I looked up, I saw the beast in flames. It snarled and yowled as it staggered between the trees, raising a din that others of its kind would hear. I knew I couldn't stay where I was and needed to leave. Yet, I now knew they would track me wherever I went.

I scanned the border of the overgrown road and spotted a cluster of wild onions. Their tops were wilted and brown from the winter. With a quick glance at the burning creature and the surrounding trees, I ran for the onions and clawed at the partially frozen dirt. My fingers squished into the onions. I smeared the mess, dirt and all, on my cloak and face.

Grabbing one last handful, I slipped into the trees and hurried away from the wailing beast. The need to run warred with the whispered warning to move steadily and quietly. I listened to the warning.

Several times, I heard something moving nearby. Each time, I would pause and wait, hoping that the onion was enough to mask my scent.

Fighting broke out several times, and I questioned my sanity often. What did I hope to accomplish by running deeper into the forest? Did I think to reach Turre?

Since the fall of the pillars and the trade route between kingdoms, no one had heard anything from Turre. Rumors circulated, of course. In hushed tones, those old enough to remember spoke of a once beautiful kingdom fallen and in the grasp of dark magic. But no one could substantiate how it had fallen or what magic held it.

Yet, what better way to fight magic than with magic? Perhaps in Turre, I could find a caster to stop Maeve.

If I could reach it.

I'd heard that, on horseback, it would take one the length of a day to reach Turre. With a wagon, one would be hard-pressed and need to bring lanterns to light the way. No one ever spoke of trying to reach Turre using their own two feet.

I glanced up at the dark canopy, trying to estimate the placement of the sun. How long had I been running since entering the forest? Long enough for Maeve to have woken and discover me missing? Was Eloise safe? Would she be beaten again?

Realizing my exhaustion was influencing the dismal spiral of my thoughts, I slowed. I needed to rest, even if just for a moment. The trees were quiet around me. No early spring breeze attempted to stir the air within the dense growth. Silence reigned, and I took several deep but quiet breaths as I scanned for any sign of movement.

My gaze caught on several raised, elongated clumps covered with dead grass and moss on the road. Keeping to the trees, I moved closer to the odd shapes until I saw bones peeking through the decay. Too large to be human. Beasts, then. At least five spread out.

What had killed them?

I froze at the sound of a soft growl.

"Go home."

Father's voice had too much growl, and lips that didn't want to move garbled the words. But I still understood.

Turning slowly, I faced where he waited farther away in the trees. He was bloodied and had gashes across his chest. My heart hurt for him, for I knew the fights I'd heard had been him defending me.

"You know as well as I do—a place does not make a home; the people do. Without you, there is no reason for me to return."

He flinched and slashed his claws angrily through the air.

"Eloise," he panted.

I knew he was asking about her, not telling me to go to her.

"I cannot speak of her fate," I said, rather than saying I last saw her sitting beside the fire.

He moaned softly.

"Father. Please. I—"

One of his ears flicked to the east, and I knew he'd heard something I did not when he held up his claw-tipped hand. I remained silent as he paced a distance in that direction. He stopped and sniffed the air.

A subtle hum, so faint that had I been moving I wouldn't have felt it, teased my senses and drew my gaze from my father to a moss-covered bumpy patch in the road. Something told me I needed whatever lay hidden there.

"Death."

I looked up at my father and saw he was staring at the same spot on the road. I studied him, seeing every similarity to the father I once knew.

"Yours or mine?" I asked softly.

"Mine."

Having already guessed the answer, considering the number of nearby bodies, I simply nodded.

"Take it," he said.

Without protesting, I went to the spot and unearthed an old, waxed leather pouch. The hard lump inside was about the size of a river stone and hummed against my palm. Rather than look at what it might be, I tucked the pouch into my cloak.

"I should keep moving while there's light. Thank you, Father."

He stayed where he was as I turned away and continued moving stealthily down the road.

I didn't look back. I couldn't.

CHAPTER 2

I MOVED SILENTLY AS I WEAVED MY WAY THROUGH THE TREES NEAR the road. Despite the thick canopy overhead, the early spring air began to warm. Nothing unpleasant. But combined with my unending exertion, I began to sweat, and I knew my trick to mask my scent had stopped working when I heard a distant howl.

Instinct told me to run, and I did. The sound of a creature giving chase filled the air around me, pushing me to run faster. Branches and bramble tugged at my hair. I jumped over logs and stumbled down small ravines only to scramble back up the other side.

Something roared behind me. The same sound echoed from all around.

Close.

Too close.

"Father, run!" I yelled, reaching into my cloak.

My labored breathing filled the air as I clawed the pouch open and tore the hard stone free. The emanating light nearly blinded me.

Howls of pain broke loose around me, making my ears ring. What I'd thought was a tree in front of me burst into flames, and I almost tripped on my skirts as I swerved around it and kept running.

I didn't see the log. My foot caught. I went down in a heap, and the warm hum of the stone left my hand. Scrambling to my feet, I grabbed the stone and held it high again. The acrid smell of burnt hair filled the air and my lungs as I panted for breath.

Ignoring the burning mounds toppled around me, I squinted and frantically looked for a direction to run. I'd lost the road.

Where?

After shielding my eyes, I spotted a hint of light through the trees and started my feet moving again. Perhaps it was a burning beast running from me, and I was giving chase. Perhaps not. Either way, I couldn't stand still and wait for the magic of the stone to fail. The screams of the dying were drawing the attention of others.

Distant yips drove me to run faster. The light ahead grew more noticeable.

Pushing myself past the point of breathing, I held my skirts with one hand and the stone aloft behind my head with the other and burst into a sunlit glade.

A trio of men, who had been sitting at a far table playing a game of cards, stood abruptly. I registered their stunned expressions as I wheezed. One started toward me, his brown eyes squinting to see.

My knees gave out as I gasped. Spots danced before my eyes. The world tilted as I fell to my side on the ground.

I heard voices but couldn't make out the words as everything went dark.

A HAND TAPPED MY CHEEK, quite roughly, demanding my attention.

"Sister, cease and let me sleep," I mumbled.

"She's coming around," a deep voice said.

Not Eloise.

I opened my eyes and sat up abruptly. A man close to my age, who'd crouched beside me, leaned away warily. We stared at one another, though for perhaps different reasons.

He was one of the most handsome men I'd ever seen. His soft brown eyes drew one's attention away from his overly long and slightly unkempt brown hair. The proud length of his nose and divot in his chin had likely bespelled many a young miss.

Though momentarily stunned by his handsome visage, I knew not to blindly believe his exterior beauty might reflect an internal beauty. Forcing my gaze from his face, I took in the rest of him with a sweeping glance.

Although both Eloise and I had learned from our parents never to measure a person's worth by the clothing they wore, one could certainly find clues about a person. Despite the shabby quality of the baggy, rough-spun pants and overly large, poorly mended shirt the man wore, they were clean. That proved he had a measure of self-worth regardless of his circumstances, and those who found value in themselves often saw the value in others. It gave me hope this man would not attempt to mistreat me.

Forcing my gaze away, I glanced around the clearing, recalling the man's companions. They remained by the distant table. Like the man beside me, their clothing was oversized and worn. But clean and mended.

They bore a striking resemblance to one another in their high cheekbones and strong jawlines. However, one had blonde hair, and the other a lighter brown than the man beside me. Both were attractively handsome as well. Even the blonde who scowled at me.

The only thing not well-kept about them was their untrimmed, shoulder-length hair. But I didn't find that shocking. Simply normal for their rougher existence.

"I apologize for the intrusion," I said, my gaze again meeting that of the man beside me.

The pair at the table heard. The man with light brown hair made a muffled sound that hinted at humor. The blonde said, "It would have been easier to kill her while she was unconscious."

I gave no reaction to those words. Instead, I watched the man beside me. He made no move to act upon the suggestion. His gaze swept over my face in a way that should have made me wary. Yet, something whispered that I was safe. In the glade or with him, I wasn't sure.

"How high has the sun risen, and how far is Turre from here?" I asked when he remained silent.

He tilted his head slightly. "Where are you from?"

"Towdown in Drisdall," I said. "I entered the forest just after first light."

"Why?" he asked.

"To find my father."

"Did you find him?"

"I did."

"Why isn't he with you, then?"

"Enough, Daemon," the blonde man interrupted. "Stop wasting time, and be rid of her."

Daemon. His name settled into my mind.

"Because he can't be with me," I said, ignoring the blonde one.

Daemon's soft brown gaze swept over me from crown to toe.

"Looks like you ran into trouble. Were you bitten?"

"No. I had—" I stopped and looked around for the stone.

"The bright stone? It fell out of your hand when you fainted. I threw it into the trees."

Masking my disappointment, I met his intent gaze again.

"The light burned them."

"And your father?"

"I told him to run before I used it."

He nodded slowly, still studying me.

"Turre?" I asked. "Can I make it there yet this day?"

"Why do you wish to go there?"

I chose my words carefully. "I wish to see my sister again. I believe I will if I go to Turre."

The man stood and offered his hand to help me to my feet. I hesitated until I noted the rough calluses covering his palm. Those who labored understood hardship. Surely, he wouldn't condemn me for suffering hardships of my own.

The heat of his hand brought my attention to the chill in my own as he helped me upright. Once I stood, I was shocked to realize I was taller than he was by almost a head. I was never taller than anyone. Even my twin rose four inches higher than me. And she wasn't exceptionally tall herself.

I glanced at the other two men and noted they were of similar height to the man before me. The one with blonde hair stood a few inches taller than his light brown-haired partner.

"How long was I unconscious?" I asked as Daemon released my fingers.

"Long enough for your breathing to return to normal," he said.

I nodded.

"Thank you for waking me. I apologize for pressing the issue, but any information you can provide regarding Turre's whereabouts would be most welcome."

"You won't reach it," Daemon said.

"Because you plan to kill me or because the sun is too high?"

He made a small, amused sound.

"Neither. You drew the beasties here. Without your stone, you won't make it more than a few steps outside this glade."

I turned to look at the woods and saw the dim light of the stone through the trees.

"The creatures burst into flames when hit by the light," I said softly as my thoughts churned.

"If you're thinking of trying to reach the stone, I'd advise against it."

"Why?" I asked, facing him again.

"It's too far to safely reach."

Frustration boiled up in me. "Why, then, did you throw it?"

"We don't welcome magic here," the blonde man said.

I glanced at him. "I see. I must be closer to Drisdall than Turre, then. Drisdall doesn't welcome magic either."

"So you admit why you left?" the blonde demanded.

"Enough, Edmund," Daemon said.

The strong name suited the man's temper.

I glanced at the one who hadn't spoken yet, and he averted his gaze.

"You think I'm a magic user?" I asked, looking at Edmund.

"How do you explain the stone?" Edmund asked.

"I found it on the remains of the road." I dug into my cloak and pulled out the still moss-covered pouch. "In this." I tossed it to him. Quite accurately.

He retreated a step and let it fall to the ground rather than catch it. His obvious mistrust and revulsion of me did not hurt. Caring what he thought seemed so trivial with everything else I'd faced.

"My name is Kellen Cartwright. I'm sixteen years old, born after the pillars fell in Drisdall. I have a twin. Eloise. She is the opposite of me in many ways, but I love her without reservation. She is why I risked these woods to find my father. She is why I must travel to Turre.

"Believe me or not. It matters little to me." I looked at Daemon. "To that end, either push me into the woods to let the beasties have me or offer me something to drink and somewhere to rest so I can leave as soon as it is safe."

"You're not staying," Edmund said at the same time Daemon nodded and waved for me to follow him toward the cottage that sat in the center of the unexpectedly large clearing.

"Daemon, you can't be serious!" Edmund raged.

Ignoring him, I followed Daemon.

As we crossed the packed dirt between the tree line and the table, Edmund turned and stormed off. The other one didn't move from his place, but he did finally meet my gaze. Briefly.

Daemon patted his shoulder as he passed him.

Not wishing to make him more uncomfortable, I focused on the unusual, thick beams of wood stuck into the ground beyond the table. Long strips of cloth hung between the posts, connecting them all in a circle. I wondered what they were for.

Behind them sat the cottage, a modest, rough plank structure. The door stood open.

"You can rest inside," Daemon said, stopping at the door. "I'll bring you some water from the well."

"Thank you."

He left me at the door, and after a glance at the other man who hadn't moved, I cautiously entered.

The small space was lit only by a pair of open windows. It was enough to see the bench beside the door and the neat line of worn boots that waited underneath it.

Sitting, I removed mine as well while noting the cozy interior. The plank floors reminded me of the owners' clothing—worn smooth from use but meticulously kept. Remnants of ash dusted the bottom of an otherwise clean, cold hearth. The kettle hung above it and the table set before it hinted at a cooking space seldom used for that purpose. Dust-free cushioned chairs spaced in different groups said the space was used more frequently as a sitting room.

Across from the hearth, a ladder rose to the loft above. From where I stood, I could see the ends of several beds. Thanks to the books from Mr. Bentwell, I understood the risks to my virtue if I chose to rest there.

A closed door set in the wall opposite the hearth piqued my curiosity. Rather than dare to open it without invitation, I considered Edmund's attitude toward me before choosing to sit on the short stool before the hearth. Better an uncomfortable stool than accidentally choosing Edmund's prized chair.

Tiredly, I ran a hand over my face. It came away with a bit of dried onion. I cringed and thought of Eloise. She would have laughed and gently poked fun at my appearance to tease me from the despair clinging to my heart.

"I think she would like to wash." The quiet words drew my attention to the doorway. The other man stood outside the door, watching me. But not with the same scrutiny as Edmund. Once our gazes met, he flushed and hurried away.

Daemon took his place and glanced at me curiously.

"I rubbed last summer's wild onion on my skin to mask my scent. It worked for a short time."

"Ah. I see. I can take your cloak and air it if you'd like."

I rose with less grace than usual and a wince.

"Are you hurt?"

"Sore. My sister is the adventurer who loves to run and climb. I prefer reading."

"I hear that's a suitable pastime for a lady."

The words struck a discordant note in me. A lady. How many times had Maeve lectured about appearances? What good was being a lady when one was beaten and chained?

"You don't look well," Daemon said, surrendering the pail of water he held.

"My mind is unsettled," I answered honestly. "My father was bitten and has become one of those creatures, and I don't know what to do."

"I'm truly sorry."

"You say it as if the matter is settled. Is there no way to save him?" I desperately clung to that hope.

"The creatures of this forest are cursed."

I knew more than I would have liked about curses. One bound me to silence. Another had killed my mother and sent my father to this place.

"Anything made can be broken," I said.

"Anything made by magic can only be broken by magic," Daemon corrected.

"All the more reason to continue to Turre. I heard magic isn't forbidden there."

"You'll find no help in Turre." He nodded toward the ladder beside the door. "In the cupboard, you can find a cup for drinking and a clean cloth for washing. Drink. Wash. Rest."

He started to turn away. The tingle of warning was absent, yet something still felt wrong. The same way it did whenever I caught Eloise in a lie.

"Daemon," I said, stopping him. "I've learned that kindness can be a lie. Don't trouble yourself with the effort of lying to me. I have nothing left and will give no more."

He nodded and left me. I closed the door behind him and removed the sling from around my shoulders to hang it and my cloak on a peg driven into the wall.

The cool water was a welcome relief to my dry throat, and the coarse cloth I'd found in the cupboard behind the ladder helped scrub away the onion from my skin. Nothing could be done for my dirt-stained hem. But I did peel off my muddy stockings to wash them. When I was finished, I hung them over the kettle's rod and carried the dirty water to the door.

Edmund paused his pacing several lengths away and watched me set the bucket outside.

That the men were wary of me was plain and something I understood. I didn't trust them either. Yet, I had very little choice in staying. I wished Daemon hadn't thrown the stone into the trees, but again, I understood his reasoning. I'd used the stone without consideration for the consequence due to my desperation. And magic, like people, couldn't be blindly trusted.

Turning away, I returned to the stool, this time moving it closer to the table where I folded my arms and rested my head.

AN INSISTENT TINGLE in my right leg roused me enough to hear the lower murmur of voices. I opened my eyes and saw the light hadn't yet faded, which meant I hadn't slept long. Through the open door, I glimpsed a group of men—seven—all of a similar height and build, ranging in age from a few years older than me to about my age. Two of them looked exactly the same.

Two Daemons. Twins, but not like me and Eloise.

I straightened with a grimace and used my arms to help myself stand from the stool. My back cracked like Judith's when she worked too long in the kitchen without a break. Thinking of the woman who'd been like a second mother to Eloise threatened to stir emotions I couldn't afford to feel.

One of the men noticed my attention and nodded to the others.

The conversation quieted, and they all turned to look at me. All had a degree of wariness as they stared at me. I couldn't hold them to blame for that after bursting into their clearing while holding a magic stone and promptly fainting. Anyone would be wary having witnessed that.

After a moment, one left the group and strode toward the cottage. His light brown hair was tousled in an endearing disarray, and he had sun creases around his hazel eyes. He looked the most wary, excluding Edmund's angry scowl.

I waited where I was beside the table and watched him pause just outside the door.

Despite striking me as a good-natured man who enjoyed a laugh, he frowned.

"Kellen?" he said.

"Kellen Cartwright, a non-magic using maiden from Towdown in Drisdall."

His lips twitched slightly. "Thank you for the clarification. Are you hurt?"

"I ran until I fainted and am sore and tired but not bitten."

"I see."

"I can imagine what you see. An unwelcome guest, certainly. But most likely someone with a more sinister intent, considering Edmund's initial anger. Though, I struggle to understand why. Only someone foolish and desperate would attempt to travel the Dark Forest."

"Do you believe sinister folk cannot be foolish or desperate?" the man asked.

I considered what I knew of Maeve and the results of all her actions that had led me to that moment. Nothing about her had hinted at foolishness or desperation. She'd been clever and discreet. Manipulating my sister and me so we had remained ignorant of her true nature until it was too late.

If Edmund had encountered someone like Maeve, I could understand his treatment of me. Was it unjust for him to assume I was like her? Perhaps. But would I not now question every woman I met?

My gaze scanned the group of men, and I understood Edmund wasn't the only one who questioned my intent. Likely, they all did. What a sorry lot we were.

"Ah," I said.

"Ah?"

"It isn't something I'd given any thought. But you're right. Anyone can feel desperation. Rather than try to assure you of my non-sinister intent, allow me to speak of how I plan to leave. Although I know nothing of the stone's origins, I do plan to use it to continue on to Turre as soon as the creatures are gone. Perhaps in the morning, they will have lost interest?"

His lips twitched again.

"That is very unlikely."

"Then the next day?"

He slowly shook his head, and I sighed.

"How long must I stay here?" I asked.

"That, I cannot answer. But you're welcome to this cottage until such a time as you wish to leave."

I couldn't help it. I arched a brow at him. "Welcome? I doubt that very much."

He flashed a wry smile. "What if I told you that you're the first outsider we've seen since settling here?"

"That would make you very fortunate."

"Fortunate?"

"You've found a place to remain unbothered by the world. No gossip. No greed. No pressure to be anything but yourselves. If I were not determined to reach Turre, I would ask to stay indefinitely."

If I didn't find help in Turre, perhaps I could free Eloise, and we could return here to hide. Certainly, braving the dangers of the forest a second time could be no less life-threatening than leaving her where she was.

"Daemon mentioned your desire to travel to Turre. There is nothing good there."

"Perhaps not, but there are magic users there. My father was bitten and has turned into one of the creatures. Yet, he didn't hurt me. He protected me so I could reach this glade. I cannot give up hope that there is a way to cure him.

"Why was he bitten?"

My limbs felt heavy with exhaustion again.

"I can see it's an upsetting tale. I apologize for asking."

Surprised, I studied him. No one could read me as well as Eloise. I kept what I felt hidden. Yet, this man had seen my pain.

How? I had kept my expression carefully composed. My limbs hadn't twitched on their own.

"How do you know it's an upsetting tale?"

"I'm good at reading people."

"I thought the same. Then I met a woman who proved appearances can be deceiving. A smile that hid—" I choked, unable to finish my thoughts due to the curse. To hide the fact, I poured a cup of water from a pitcher that now waited on the table.

I sipped until the tightness eased and looked up at him only to see that my dirty cloak had been replaced with a clean, sturdy brown one beside the door.

"How will I know when the creatures have lost interest?" I asked.

"You won't see as many eyes watching us at night."

"And if I decide not to wait, will you attempt to stop me from retrieving the stone?"

He considered me for a long moment. "I think I might."

I set the cup on the table and contemplated what choices were left to me.

"I need time to think," I said. "May I walk around the glade to ease the ache in my legs?"

"Certainly."

He motioned for me to go ahead of him—courtly manners that didn't quite fit his rough clothes. Much like Father's fine clothes never quite hid his humble background. His mannerisms always gave him away. Yet, Maeve had been different. She'd hidden everything with her mannerisms.

Walking out the door without the borrowed cloak, I began to doubt everything I saw around me.

Seven small men hidden in the woods. Homespun clothes and work-roughened hands.

Why come to a place surrounded by cursed creatures? Why throw the stone, which they could have used to leave, out into the woods?

I paused halfway to the others and looked back at the man following me.

"Would you stop me because you truly believe I would not reach Turre or because you think I might?"

"Both. As both would likely mean your death."

CHAPTER 3

THE MAN WATCHED ME AS I CONSIDERED HIS WORDS.

Why would reaching Turre mean my death? I knew very little about the place, only that it had fallen to magic. Were all casters truly bad then? I thought back to the letters I'd found in the attic—correspondence between mother and a caster called Elspeth. Concern for each other had been prominent in all of them. My mother had been a good woman who would never align herself with someone of evil intent.

So then, was his warning based on the people of Turre or the men within this clearing?

I studied his gaze and saw only sincerity. But was it a mask or the truth? Instinct said it was the truth. He and the others meant me no harm.

I hadn't listened to my instincts before and wouldn't make that mistake again. This time, it whispered I was safer where I was.

Nodding, I continued on my way, veering to the right and choosing to walk the border of the trees without speaking to the others. Their gazes tracked me as I paced the perimeter.

Intuition told me I'd stumbled upon more than a clearing. Protected by the Dark Forest on three sides and backed by a rocky outcropping barren of trees and too sheer to climb, few would ever know this glade existed. It was an oasis in an otherwise dangerous world. The breadth of the expanse allowed for a spacious—if trodden—yard in front of the modest cottage and a larger yard in back with a garden.

In the sheer rock face beyond the garden, I saw an opening to a cave. I didn't move closer to inspect it, preferring to follow the trees and let my mind wander once I knew where I was going.

What this place was didn't matter to me. Only how to leave it.

I pondered the choices that were left to me. My father was cursed. I was stuck in this glade for an undetermined amount of time. And Eloise was suffering at home, in my place, until I could resolve Father's current state and return for her.

After several laps, I settled on the best course of action and stopped walking.

The men were no longer in a group by the long table. They were scattered about the glade. One man lounged inside a strip of cloth strung between the posts. While the unique contraption intrigued me, I didn't move closer to inspect it. A pair of them were cutting wood on the side of the cottage. Two more lingered near the cave opening.

"Where's Edmund?" I called.

The one in the odd bed lifted his head to look at me in surprise.

"Edmund? Why do you want him?"

I didn't answer. The man in question came stomping around the side of the cottage, his gaze full of pent up rage. He reminded me a bit of Eloise after someone bullied me. Which is why I wanted to speak to him. Anger loosened tongues.

"I don't want to be here, and you don't want me here," I said before he could speak. His steps slowed, and wariness began to outweigh the anger. That wouldn't do.

"Don't act offended or try to deny the truth. It doesn't suit you."

The anger returned in a flash.

Just like Eloise, I thought.

"The other one told me he would stop me from leaving. He believes I will meet my end either in the woods or in Turre."

"You think I'll go against my brother? You're more foolish than you look," Edmund said.

Brother? Of course. Rather than looking at the others, I pressed forward.

"Against? Never. None of you want me here. He doesn't want me to leave because he thinks I won't survive. But can any of you survive outside of this glade?"

He scoffed. "Do you see sheep around here for us to spin our own cloth? A smithy to make our shovels or—"

A clump of hard dirt hit him in the jaw by the ear.

Edmund's face flushed with his rage as blood bloomed in the remnants of dirt on his face.

"Who did it?" he bellowed.

"Shut your flapping maw, you—"

Edmund roared and head-butted Daemon in his middle, taking him down to the ground.

Annoyed, I marched to the cottage, grabbed up the pitcher of water, and returned to douse the fighting pair with the contents. Edmund sputtered and swung his enraged gaze to me.

"Such behavior is beneath you," I said. "You're an intelligent man able to express himself with words. Use them, or I will fetch more water."

Someone sniggered behind me.

Edmund's face flushed further. I held out the pitcher to whoever stood behind me.

"More please," I said without taking my gaze from Edmund.

He snarled and stood abruptly, leaving Daemon on the ground.

"Your anger robs you of wit, and you revealed things your brother thought you shouldn't."

Edmund's anger immediately vanished. He looked pale and sick with understanding.

"I don't care where you get your cloth and metal from. I only care that you can survive outside this glade. I asked you because I knew I could goad you into an honest answer. If you can survive, so can I. Teach me so I can leave."

I said the last while looking at each of them. They were all there again, watching me.

When no one said anything, I looked at Daemon.

"Your eye is starting to swell. Fetch some water from the well, and place a cool wet cloth on it, or you won't be able to see for a few days. I can't imagine such a disadvantage would be safe here."

I turned to go to the cottage and saw the second Daemon. He was smirking at his twin.

Missing Eloise, I went inside and sat in a more comfortable chair to wait.

My fate, whatever it may be, was now in the hands of seven strangers. They would either teach me to be rid of me or be inconvenienced by my presence forever.

And I would do whatever was necessary to ensure they understood the gravity of the latter.

PATIENCE WAS a virtue that had passed over my twin but graced me. As the light faded from the sky and the men continued to argue quietly outside, I sat in the chair and stared vacantly at the unlit hearth.

I didn't know why the choice to help me or not should require an hours-long debate, but it did. They spoke endlessly, their voices rising and falling with whatever points they were making with one another.

My stomach growled, but I ignored it. Due to the circumstances at home, I'd been unable to take any provisions with me. My sling bag contained another simple dress to change into, along with clean underclothes, some coin, and a letter I'd taken from the attic. Rather than using the coin to purchase a few biscuits at the market, I'd saved them, knowing any help I needed would likely require coin. Only if I managed to reach Turre, though.

The light continued to fade. Outside, I heard the sounds of another escalating scuffle. If they didn't decide soon, they would likely all wake with black eyes, and then no one would be left to help me.

Rising, I went to the door and watched them.

The smiling Daemon noticed me first and elbowed an almost-replica of himself from the brown hair to the brown eyes. The almost-replica was several years younger, though, likely close to my age.

"Excuse the intrusion on your sensible deliberation of my future, but could I trouble you for a respite? I haven't eaten since dinner yesterday."

The youngest lightly kicked the side of one of the pair presently rolling around in the dirt.

"She's hungry."

The fighting stilled.

A blonde with green eyes got off of Edmund and retreated a few steps. He looked very similar to Edmund. Slightly shorter and different colored eyes, but the same chin and nose and hair.

Edmund jumped to his feet. "I don't care one whit if you're hungry or not, you evil spawn of a whore."

I was across the clearing before I recognized my intent and drove my fist right into his wretched mouth. He didn't move much, but his already abused mouth bled anew.

"Be glad I am the weaker sister," I said. "You can call me any manner of name you wish, but do not disparage my mother. She was a good, kind woman. In return for honoring my mother with your silence, I will do the same to your mother. Do we understand one another?"

He slowly inclined his head, watching me guardedly.

"Now, as it's unlikely that you'll resolve your differing opinions with fists, why not set aside your grievances before nightfall and tell me how I can assist in preparing dinner?"

"Have a seat at the table. We will be delighted to serve you," Daemon said with a wink.

"I'll join you," the other Daemon said.

I looked at the one who'd winked. "You're not Daemon. What should I call you?"

His grin widened.

"Darian."

"Hello, Darian," I said, making no mention of the lack of surname.

I looked at the quiet one who'd initially watched me from the door. His light brown hair was a combination of his brothers' brown and blonde.

During the course of my listening, I'd heard a few names mentioned.

"Garron, correct?" I guessed.

He gave a short nod, his bright green eyes meeting mine only briefly before he flushed and looked away.

"And I'm unlikely to forget dear Edmund." I glanced from the scowling brawler to the man who'd been fighting him. They had the same build and looked the same age.

"Identical in almost every way but the eyes. His twin, I presume?" I said.

"Eadric," the man said, holding out his hand. I glanced at it, feeling a measure of surprise.

"Men don't shake women's hands, idiot," Edmund said with a shove.

I captured Eadric's hand and shook it, liking the feeling of his strong fingers around mine. It reminded me of my father. Honest and forthright, treating everyone as an equal. Even women, but more especially my mother.

"It's a rule I never cared for," I said with a small reassuring smile when his glad expression started to fall. "It made me feel even more of an outcast."

"Outcast?" the oldest asked. "Why were you an outcast?"

I glanced at him, again noting the laugh lines. "Because I didn't behave like other maidens. I didn't fawn over the attention the boys my age gave me. I wasn't grateful for their unwanted adoration."

Edmund snorted. "Conceit is a deadly sin."

"I agree, which is why I did not partake in their illusions of me. Who I am should not be a sum of my appearance, and I have no interest in associating with people who would see me as such."

"Then who are you?"

"I am who I am. Who are you, sir, with the brown hair and laugh creases around the eyes?"

They crinkled a little. "You can call me Brandle."

I looked at the last one.

"Liam," he said.

"I am pleased to meet you."

"Are you?" Edmund said, crossing his arms.

"I am. Meeting you is better than meeting my death." I waited a beat. "But only barely."

Darian and Eadric laughed until tears streamed, and I felt the tug of my own humor. It made me miss Eloise more.

"Sit," Brandle said. "I'll fetch the stew from the cold store. Darian, get the dishes."

While he and Darian walked toward the house, Eadric

gestured for me to follow him to the table, which they'd moved closer to the fire near the strung beds.

"Do you sleep in those?" I asked.

"We do," Eadric said, leading me toward one. "They're quite comfortable."

"How do you not fall out?"

He grinned. "It takes practice. Sometimes we still take a tumble."

He demonstrated how he got in and out of it. In seemed more simple than out. At least gracefully. When he set it swinging idly, I understood why he might fall out.

A sound behind me had me glancing over my shoulder to see Brandle set a large pot on the table.

"We cooked the stew this morning," he said.

I readily accepted the helping he ladled for me. Large chunks of meat and root vegetables swam in the watery stew that smelled like smoke. I took my first bite and thanked the years of practice I'd had at keeping a straight face.

"Tastes like shite, doesn't it?" Eadric asked, watching me with a grin.

Garron smacked the back of his head. "Watch your mouth."

"She said we could cuss."

"That's not what she said. She said not to disparage her mother."

"It tastes a bit burnt," I said. "But it's filling, and that's all that matters right now. Thank you for sharing it with me."

My words stopped the brewing fight and set Edmund to scowling again.

"Does it stay like that while you sleep?" I asked him. "Your face," I clarified when he looked confused.

Eadric laughed again. "I like her."

So long as Edmund continued to find issue with my presence, Eadric's fondness for my provocation of his brother likely wouldn't hinder my goal. However, I would need to take care that Eadric didn't grow too fond.

I ate quickly and followed Garron to the well, where he and Liam washed the bowls and pot.

"Who cooked the meal?" I asked.

"Us," Liam said. "Tomorrow it's Eadric and Edmund. Don't expect it to be any better."

"I understand. Allow me to take these back to the cottage."

I carried the clean dishes inside, stowed them in the cabinet behind the ladder, and set the pot on the table.

"You'll find what you need in the loft," Brandle said from the doorway. "If you need anything else, we'll be right outside."

With that, he shut the door, leaving me alone for the first time.

I found a larger bowl to hold water from a pitcher so I could wash. Once my face and feet were clean, I took my sling and spare clothes and climbed the ladder.

Seven neatly made beds waited in the cramped loft. They were narrow, barely wide enough to fit me, but would be more comfortable than sleeping on the plank floor. I set my bundle of things on the bed nearest the ladder and went to the second bed. The blanket covering it was rough and worn. I layered another blanket from the neighboring bed over it and stripped out of my gown.

The first howl filled the night, followed by several more. Outside, I heard the indistinct murmur of the brothers' voices. Edmund's was easy enough to distinguish because of the angry tone. The others were more difficult.

I hoped I wouldn't stay long enough to discern them all.

ELOISE WAS THE EARLY RISER, not me. Yet, I found myself opening my eyes before dawn. I blamed falling asleep so early and the nap the day before.

Warm under the blanket, I stretched languidly then rose. If I wished to eat something that tasted like food today, I knew I couldn't linger.

After dressing in the prior day's soiled gown, I descended the ladder and went to search for the entrance to the cold storage. They'd come inside for the pot, so I knew it had to be there somewhere. The locked door to the left of the ladder seemed the most likely option until I noted the worn groove in the floor in front of the storage cabinet tucked behind the ladder. The cabinet moved rather easily, and a narrow set of stairs descended into darkness.

I found a candle by feel and struck the flint to light it. The weak glow barely cast its light over the sacks of supplies. Grain. Potatoes. Carrots. Dried berries.

Edmund would not be pleased that I'd found their food supply.

Fighting a smile, I moved what I needed, including the hand mill for the grain, up to the kitchen. The glimmer of humor I felt remained even when my arm began to ache after only a few minutes of turning the wheel. I knew I wouldn't be working alone for long. The wheel crushing the grains was too loud not to disturb at least one of them.

A knock sounded at the door several minutes later.

"It's not my home to give permission," I said. "Enter as you please."

The door opened, and from outside, Brandle's gaze swept over everything I'd set out in the kitchen.

"What are you doing?"

"Milling flour. It's harder than it looks." I stopped turning the wheel and stepped back. "If you wouldn't mind taking a turn, we might manage something passable enough to make some biscuits for dinner."

"Biscuits?" He looked from the mill to the other ingredients out on the table to the unlit hearth.

"Biscuits and stew for dinner and boiled oats to break our fast. I'll light the fire and fetch water for those if you're willing to take over the milling."

"I'll get the water," Eadric called from outside.

"It's easier if we cook outside," Brandle said. "There's more workspace for all of us to help."

I hadn't expected a ready offer to help but willingly accepted it. The more of them I could inconvenience, the better. I picked up the bowl of dried berries.

"We'll move it," Brandle said. "It will be more prudent for you to ensure Eadric doesn't add too much water to the pot."

Unsure if I was being kicked out or encouraged to continue, I donned the cloak and left the cottage to find Eadric at the well, where he had two pails of water drawn.

"That is plenty," I said, stopping him from filling a third.

"Are you certain? I heard you say stew and boiled oats."

"Yes, but we can only cook one at a time."

"Ah," he said, shooting me a wry grin. "I should have thought of that."

He had dirt on his cheek and his forehead.

"Were you fighting again?" I asked.

His grin widened. "Edmund heard you. Better he fights with me than antagonize you. A scuffle so he doesn't need to cook is worth it. His cooking tastes like shite too."

"You both remind me of my sister," I said. "Take off your neckcloth."

He clasped his hands to his chest in a true display of shock and prevention.

I shook my head at the hilarity of the situation.

"I vow to leave your manly virtue intact. I only meant to help remove the dirt from your face."

"My neckcloth stays on," he said in all seriousness.

Rather than arguing, I reached into my bodice for the handkerchief I always carried. Stiff from the previous day's perspiration, I doubted it smelled pleasant. So I used one of the buckets of water to rinse it then dabbed Eadric's face as he continued to clutch his neckcloth.

"My sister would find you amusing," I said. "It's typically the maidens that clasp their chest like that."

His green gaze swept over my face as he frowned slightly.

"I can't let you—"

"Eadric, shut your fool mouth," Edmund said a second before he grabbed my shoulder and spun me about.

I wasn't one to grab. The heel of my hand connected with his nose in an upward thrust. I'd meant it for his chin but miscalculated for the height difference. He grunted in pain and thrust me into Eadric, who closed his arms around me as we tipped backward.

My eyes went wide as I realized what was happening. We were going to fall into the well.

My hands whipped out again and gripped the rope. The friction burned my palms, but I didn't ease my hold, squeezing tighter still until I stopped us with the backs of my knees hugging the edge of the well.

Holding his bloody nose, Edmund glared at me. Behind him, Garron came running to help but stopped short and gawked.

"Eadric's holding your…"

"My chest. I know. I can feel it. Perhaps you would be so kind as to help us both so he can release me without falling into your only clean water source."

Garron took a hesitant step forward.

Daemon sprinted around him and grabbed my arms, hauling me and Eadric from the edge of disaster.

"Are you all right?" he asked, prying Eadric's hands off my person.

Ignoring him, I looked at Edmund. "I am amending my previous warning. In addition to neither of us speaking ill of the other's mother, we avoid touching one another. Agreed?"

"He agrees," Brandle said. "We all do."

I stepped around Edmund and strode away, calling over my shoulder, "Dunk his head in a bucket. It'll help with the bruises and stop the bleeding. Might even help with his breathing."

"He's breathing fine," Brandle said.

"I know."

Darian's laugh rang out behind me.

CHAPTER 4

WHEN I REACHED THE TABLE, I GLANCED AT MY RAW PALMS IN frustration.

"I'm sorry I grabbed you," Eadric said, handing me my damp handkerchief.

"It wasn't out of malicious intent, so I'm glad you did. The water wouldn't have tasted the same after we dipped in it."

He smiled crookedly as I wrapped my right palm, the worst one.

"I suppose not. Do you want me to mill?"

"Please."

He milled the flour. Darian came to stoke the fire, and Garron carried the water, pouring in as much as I directed. Liam measured out the oats once the water boiled, and Daemon stirred. I was grateful for all the helping hands since mine burned fiercely each time I moved them. The cold cloth I alternately wrapped around my palms helped soothe some of the pain.

"Let me look," Brandle said when I went to change the material again.

I showed him both hands.

"I'll be back. Don't let her do anything," he called over his shoulder as he walked toward the cottage.

"Kellen, is it supposed to look like this?" Daemon asked, peering into the pot.

I moved to look down at the bubbling mass of oats with him.

"Exactly like that. Haven't you had oats before?" I asked.

"Not in a long while. Since Eadric ate all the honey."

"How long ago was that?" Darian asked with a grin. "Five years now?"

"At least," Daemon said with a laugh.

"It doesn't taste good without the honey," Liam said.

"The berries will help sweeten it," I said. "At home, we often had it with berries and cream."

"We haven't had cream in a very long time," Darian said.

I glanced at him, unsure why such a missed luxury would remove his typical humor.

"Many go without cream. And honey. And soft beds and blankets. That you can remember them at all means your life here is better than most. My mother often reminded my sister and me that hardships are meant to teach us to see beyond our current life circumstances. That there are always those who suffer more." I flashed Darian a wry smile. "Mostly, she reminded Eloise when she whined that there were no sweets to eat because she ate them all."

Darian's smile returned. Daemon, his twin, winked at me.

"Is your mother why you're wearing a mourning gown?" Eadric asked.

Garron reached out to cuff him upside the head.

"You don't ask that, Eadric," he mumbled.

"It's all right. My mother is why I'm in mourning," I said. "She's been gone almost a month now. In many ways, it feels like much longer."

Someone cleared his throat, and I glanced over my shoulder to see Brandle standing nearby.

"I have something that should help your hands." He held up a clay container and gestured to the table.

"Eadric, would you remove the pot from the flames and add the berries, please?" I asked as I sat.

While Eadric did as I'd directed, Brandle uncovered the clay container, and I heard one of the others swear.

"You said we had no more honey," Edmund said angrily.

"I said there was no more honey to eat," Brandle said calmly as he opened my palm and used a carved spoon to drizzle honey on my abraded skin. I saw flecks of something else in it.

"A lie is a lie," Edmund said with more heat.

I kept my attention on my hand, not wanting to provoke him further.

"If you were to eat this honey, your mouth would go numb," Brandle said. "While Darian would likely find your attempts to speak amusing, I doubt you would enjoy the feeling. Would you still care to try some?"

Brandle dipped the spoon again and offered it to his scowling brother.

"No?" Brandle said when Edmund crossed his arms. "Then perhaps I did not lie when I said there was no more honey to eat."

He put the spoon back and carefully wrapped my hands with clean cloth.

"Try not to use them today," he said. "Tomorrow, they should feel better."

I nodded, disappointed that my hands would delay my pursuit to learn how to survive the Dark Forest.

"How long do we need to wait to eat?" Eadric asked. "This smells good."

I turned and saw him inhaling appreciatively over the steaming pot.

"It should be ready," I said.

They moved in a rush, except for Edmund and Brandle. Brandle was closing the honey, and Edmund was glaring at him.

Daemon sat across from me and handed me a full bowl, blocking my view of Edmund's glare.

"Since you're not allowed to use your hands, allow me to feed you, Lamb," Daemon said, reaching for the spoon in my bowl.

"I have table manners and know how to hold a spoon with my fingers, not my palms, Daemon. Focus on your own oats."

Eadric sniggered until he took his first bite.

"If your oats taste like this, I can't wait for dinner," he said around a mouthful.

He got cuffed by Liam *and* Edmund this time. Neither seemed to bother him as he grinned and ate faster. Some of his humor might have been due to Edmund, who was moving closer to his own bowl of oats that someone had served for him.

"How did you make it taste like this? It's not just the berries," Darian said.

"A pinch of salt, the right amount of water and boiling time, and the berries. If one of those is off, it won't taste like this."

"What else do you know how to make?" Liam asked.

"Bread, pastries, oats, soft boiled eggs, meat pies, stews, roasts, vegetables..." I shrugged. "I spent a lot of time in the kitchen."

"You expect us to believe you were a kitchen maid?" Edmund asked. "Dressed like that?"

"I expect nothing from you but your biased hate, Edmund. Eat your oats before they grow cold."

"You don't speak like a kitchen maid," Daemon said.

"Do you know many kitchen maids?" I asked, giving the unpopulated glade a meaningful glance.

Daemon's grin widened.

"You're a stranger to us. It's only natural we're curious," Darian said.

"My mother was a noble woman disowned by her family when she married my father, a merchant. We don't have any titles or own the home in which we'd lived. But we didn't lack for anything. My father was a successful businessman, and my mother was well-educated due to her upbringing. She taught my sister and me to read and write. Father taught us math and trade. Judith and Anne, our help, taught us how to cook and clean. Nothing was above us or beneath us.

"Mother always told us that knowledge was a true wealth that could never be taken away, and the more we knew, the better prepared we would be for whatever hardships we might face in life."

The table rang with their silence until Edmund leaned forward.

"So, you're the daughter of a disowned noble and a rich merchant," Edmund said. "Why would your father come to these woods so soon after losing your mother?"

I set my spoon aside.

"Not everyone brawls to avoid their pain, Edmund. Some run from it."

I stood and left the table, pushing down my own sorrows that wanted to overwhelm me. No one said anything as I went inside and sat in a chair. Staring at the cold hearth but not seeing it, I ran my fingers lightly over my damaged palms.

Many believed that knowledge was power. But it wasn't. It was a tool. How one wielded it determined its use. Some used it to gain wealth and power. Others used it to help.

I wasn't yet certain how I would use the knowledge I'd gained since arriving.

These seven brothers had been here a very long time. Children living in these woods seemed impossible. Yet, they had stories of times past here. And they feared magic and strangers. When faced with the story of my loss, they'd shown true sorrow. Even Edmund, though he'd recovered faster than the others.

What had happened to these men? Why were they here? More importantly, why didn't they want me to leave when I was a stranger they mistrusted?

Certainly, my probable death couldn't stir their compassion enough to outweigh their need to be rid of me. If it did, I would find myself in an impossible situation, for I couldn't stay here an hour more than necessary.

Eloise was counting on me.

LONG AFTER THEY cleared away the morning meal, the faint notes of bird song drew me from my thoughts and to the door. Sunlight filled the otherwise quiet yard in front of the cottage.

Curious where everyone had gone, I left the cottage and wandered to the side yard, enjoying spring's teasing warmth.

Liam sat on a short stool near the well, scrubbing the cooking pot, while Darian stood over him, arms crossed and a smirk on his face.

"I don't need you to tell me how to clean. Go turn the soil in the garden like Brandle said. We need to get the seeds in soon."

Darian's grin widened.

"Admit it. You're willing to wash the pot so you can be the first one she—"

He looked up and stopped speaking when he saw me.

"Kellen," he said with a nod.

"Darian."

He tilted his head at me. "How do you know I'm not Daemon?"

"If Eadric and Edmund had the same eye color, would you mistake them for one another? No. Looking the same doesn't mean you are the same."

"You are right," he said with a laugh. "How do you feel about gardening?"

"It's something of which I have no knowledge."

47

"Would you like to learn?"

I nodded and followed him around the cottage to the garden where last season's growth had already been removed. Small mounds on the far side hinted that something was starting to sprout.

Darian used a long staff with a wedge of flat metal at the end to turn the soil. As he worked, he instructed me on the timing of planting different seeds and the watering and pruning methods for different crops.

"Were your parents farmers?" I asked, marveling at how much he knew.

"No. Henry, a friend of my parents, knew such things. He taught us."

"Will the rest help you?" I asked.

"We take turns doing the chores around here," he said.

"Then what are the others doing today?" I asked.

He shrugged instead of answering, and I looked around the glade.

If they weren't here, then they were out there in the forest with the creatures. If only I hadn't hurt myself, I could have left with them as well and learned how they wandered the trees without attracting attention.

Bird song drew my attention to where the tiny winged friend perched on the roof.

"We don't see them often," Darian said. "We had chickens at one time, but they died during a hard winter. I crave a soft-boiled egg."

"It is not possible to get more?" I asked.

"It's not impossible, but it would be difficult. They are noisy and would draw creatures."

"To the glade?" I asked.

"No, while we travel with them."

"How do you—"

He held up a hand.

"Surviving these woods is not something easily taught." He leaned on the staff and studied me for a moment, his smile fading slightly. "I know you wish to travel to Turre to find a cure for your father, but what will you do if you cannot?"

"Travel there or find a cure?" I asked.

"Both," he said with a slight shrug.

I looked up at the bird happily singing on the roof. It reminded me of my sister. Animals often flocked to her. Nothing quite so obvious, but the trees around our home always rang out with more bird song whenever she went for a walk.

"Then I will find another way," I said.

"Another way?"

"Thank you for teaching me today. I should go start the stew for dinner."

I walked away from him as my thoughts spun.

Eloise was the one who acted without careful consideration. Not me. When I'd left home, I'd thoughtfully weighed each of the potential outcomes that might have resulted from my actions. The most likely outcome had been that I would be caught while trying to leave and Eloise would be punished. Yet, the potential that we would both be treated even worse had I stayed had prompted me to act.

With the spell binding my tongue, I'd been left with only one option—to seek out my father. While I'd known the odds of finding him alive hadn't been in my favor since he'd left us weeks ago, I'd still had hope. Discovering him alive, cursed, yet still aware enough to help me, hadn't been something I'd considered. Yet, all hope wasn't lost. In Turre, I might find help to cure him or perhaps even help to free my sister.

Staying in this glade and idling away time planting gardens and growing crops indefinitely wasn't an option. However, I knew that was what Darian had meant when he'd asked what would happen if I couldn't leave, or worse, could not find the cure for my father in Turre as I hoped.

I paused when the bird stopped singing and looked back at the cottage as it took flight. My feet had found my thinking path from the previous day, and I stood near the border of the glade. It suddenly felt unsafe to be so far from the cottage.

An arm wrapped around my waist from behind and pulled me sharply backward off my feet as another hand covered my mouth. I crashed into a hard chest as I was hauled away from the safety of the glade. But not by a creature. Not with the sun brightly shining. A man. Someone taller than me by almost two heads.

I thrashed in his arms, my own pinned uselessly to my sides.

"Come quietly, and I won't hurt you," the man said softly.

The threat had the opposite effect than what he'd likely intended.

Rather than feeling appropriately subdued, I bit into the fold of skin on his palm. He jerked it away with a curse even as his restraining arm tightened around me. I drew in a large breath as he continued dragging me toward the trees and screamed. Loudly. But the sound wasn't to summon the seven men reluctantly housing me.

"Quiet! The beasts will come," the man whispered, understanding the danger.

I inhaled again.

His fist connected with the side of my head. It hurt like hell and muddled my thoughts. But I thought of all my sister had endured with defiance, and I laughed like a mad woman.

"Let them come!" I yelled, kicking back with my heel. It connected with his shin, but he didn't even flinch. "I would rather the beasts have me."

The clearing's sunlight faded with each step he took.

A twig snapped behind us. My captor stilled.

I laughed again. "Where is your courage now? Is capturing me worth your life?"

He made a sound of frustration and cuffed the side of my head again as he released his hold. The blow knocked me to the side. On my stomach on the forest floor, I didn't have time to react before I heard the angry bellow and the man's grunt.

A scuffle, too close for safety, had me scrambling to stand. Someone stepped on my calf. The weight was there and gone before I could cry out, but it did motivate me to rise faster. My skirts thwarted my first few attempts. I heard fabric tear. Just as I gained my feet, three brawling bodies knocked into me.

I stumbled back, barely keeping upright as my gaze locked on them.

Liam and Darian fought the man. Smaller than him by a good deal, they worked together to keep him down so they could rain blows on his head. Based on the ferocity on Darian's face, my attacker was wise to use his arms to shield himself. But once he regained his feet—as he was trying to do—my saviors would be at a distinct disadvantage.

"I will not be bested by you," the man said, half-rising and swinging out to land a blow to Liam's face.

Deeper in the trees, I caught a glimpse of movement.

If we drove him back, the creatures waiting could deal with him.

I looked around and picked up a hefty branch. When the group turned, I brought the thick rod down on the man's back.

He grunted and fell back to his knees.

Liam grabbed the man's head and wrenched it down to meet his knee with a thud. The man groaned as his eyes rolled back into his head.

Breathing heavily, the three of us looked at one another.

"Who is he?" Darian asked.

"No one I recognize," I said. "He grabbed me and told me that, if I went with him quietly, I wouldn't be hurt."

"So you screamed."

I nodded.

"He won't stay like this for long. Go to the cottage and stay in the cellar until we come for you."

Hesitating, I looked between the two, noting the scratches on Liam's face and Darian's bleeding knuckles. The need to apologize bubbled up. Rather than uttering useless words of regret, I thanked them and hurried to the cottage.

After closing the door, I hid in the cellar.

In the dark, my thoughts dwelled on what had happened. Who was the man? I knew he wasn't simply a random traveler with some misguided attempt at rescue. He would have pulled me toward the light, not the dark trees. And he wouldn't have implied he would hurt me if I didn't remain quiet.

No one entered the Dark Forest without reason. Most entered to die. Considering the way he'd fought, that hadn't been his intent either. So why then risk entering the forest? And why attempt to take me?

I could think of only one reason: Maeve had sent him. Did that then mean Maeve still sought a way to control Eloise?

Tired, I rubbed a hand over my face. The wraps Brandle had used to cover my palms were gritty and damp against my cheeks. I pulled my hands away and sighed, knowing I'd made a mess of my face.

Thoughts of my appearance led to thoughts of what the other brothers would think when they learned of what had happened. Edmund would likely believe I was associated with the man who attempted to take me. And what explanation could I give to explain why someone had appeared to take me only a day after my arrival? None.

For my safety and the safety of the men that lived here, I needed to leave soon. But how? The beasts were still nearby, and I didn't have the glowing stone to keep them at bay.

Frustrated, I carefully paced a few steps in complete darkness and tried to think of a viable solution as I listened for any sounds from above. Minutes passed.

I stopped pacing and stretched my legs to ease the growing ache in my stepped-upon calf. My cheek also stung, but I didn't try to touch it. I needed a cloth, some clean water, and some privacy to erase what had happened. Liam and Darian would likely need the same. Was that what they were doing? Cleaning up? Or were they doing something with the man? Questioning him perhaps? Part of me hoped so. Another part worried that any answers the man gave would only cast more suspicion on me.

My calf suddenly cramped painfully. I lit the candle and looked for somewhere to sit. A stack of old, worn blankets on a shelf offered me a reprieve from the cool dirt floor.

I'd only just sat when the door to the cottage opened above. Footfalls echoed across the floor, and the cabinet quietly slid open, allowing more light to illuminate the supplies around me.

"Kellen, you can come out now," Liam said.

I opened my mouth to answer when a wave of dizziness washed over me. It felt unnatural. An energy just like I'd felt when I'd touched the stone. But wrong.

A tingle of fear raced down my spine.

"Something's wrong," I said just before all the light vanished, and I toppled over onto the blanket.

"Kellen? Are you hurt?"

I could hear the worry in Liam's voice but couldn't respond. I could feel the coarse cloth under my cheek but couldn't open my mouth and lift myself up. Nothing wanted to obey me.

"Close your eyes, Kellen. I'm coming down."

Why couldn't I see if the door was still open above? And why would he want me to close them if I could see?

The stairs creaked as Liam descended, and I fought not to panic. Were my eyes shut? I tried to open my eyes or blink, but neither worked.

"Kellen!"

I heard Liam move near my head and felt my braid move. He swore under his breath then bolted up the stairs. His solid footfalls echoed loudly in the space.

He'd no sooner left than the tingle returned. It didn't feel like it had the last time. It felt more like my limbs were waking as the feeling of wrongness faded.

CHAPTER 5

My eyes opened on their own, and I sat up to look down at myself. Physically, everything seemed the same as before. I struggled to my feet and reassessed how I felt as I straightened the skirts of my mourning dress, which was now ripped in several places. I couldn't say I was sad about it. I hated the dress. But like all my aches and pains, the tears weren't from whatever had just happened.

Favoring my leg, I carefully made my way up the stairs. As I reached the top, I heard Liam urgently speaking outside.

"I'm all right," I called.

However, I didn't feel right. What happened in the cellar had unsettled me more than the man in the woods.

The hushed conversation quieted as I reached the door, and I looked out at Darian and Liam. Their guarded gazes also held concern. For me or themselves?

"I'm not sure what happened. I was below, waiting like you said. One moment, I felt fit and fine; the next, a wave of dizziness brought me low. It wasn't a faint like when I'd arrived in your clearing, exhausted from running. When I fainted then, I knew nothing. This time, I couldn't open my eyes or speak, but I could hear you, Liam." I looked from him to Darian. Both seemed to withdraw further from me. While I knew it was for the best, I found it disappointing.

"The man?" I asked, changing the subject. "Is he gone?"

"Gone and unlikely to survive long," Darian said. "The creatures haven't left yet."

"I know. I saw them when I screamed." My gaze swept over the pair, taking in their injuries. Liam's eye was beginning to swell. "It's not safe for me to linger here. Please help me convince Brandle. I need to leave."

"I pulled some water from the well," Darian said, nodding toward the side yard. "Go wash. Liam and I will take our time to bring up the supplies for dinner. We'll give you a few minutes of privacy before we check on you."

Understanding the dismissal for what it was, I left them at the door and went to wash. Any hope of keeping my bandaged hands dry quickly vanished. The cloth was caked with dirt, and it felt like I had dirt in the herbed-honey.

I unwrapped my hands and washed them. The abrasions from earlier stung as I gently cleaned away the debris. I found new scrapes on the backs of my hands and a few on my face.

Leaning over the bucket, I viewed my reflection in the water. A pale, distorted face. Bright blue eyes outlined by thick black lashes and a single black braid hanging over my shoulder. I looked like myself in only the barest way. Disheveled. Displaced. Desperate.

The laces of my dress didn't cooperate with my fingers. I pulled hard and heard the already ripped fabric rip further. I felt the sound inside of me too. The anger I was trying so hard to keep at bay bubbled up.

I trembled against the volatile energy of it.

I hadn't only learned to hide what I felt to ease my mother's burdens. Containing what I felt kept those around me safe. I couldn't lose control. Not ever.

My moves were rushed and jerky in my haste to pull the gown off. Breathing harder, I tossed it to the ground and stood there in my chemise with my hands fisted and my eyes tightly closed.

Each point of pain became my focus. My raw palms. The stinging places on my face. The scrape on my arm. The ache in my bruised calf. I centered myself around them and slowed my breathing until I regained control.

Then, when the trembling stopped, I calmly picked up the cloth and washed my face.

"Do you have another gown you'd like me to fetch?" Darian asked from behind me.

I glanced over my shoulder and found him and Liam watching me from near the front of the cottage. They didn't look offended or overcome with desire by my lack of clothing. More like wary.

"I would rather not ruin another dress since I still hold hope that I will find my way to Turre," I said. My gaze drifted to the mourning dress I hated. I didn't want to put it back on.

"Do you have any spare clothing I might borrow?" I asked, remembering my conversation with Eloise. We'd bantered about hearing of women who wore men's clothing, and I would much rather do that than wear the mockery of the mourning dress Maeve had made for me.

"You want our clothes?" Liam asked, sounding shocked.

"It needn't be yours," I said. "Any pants and shirt will do. Please. And a cap, if you have one, to hide my hair."

Darian frowned slightly. "You wish to hide that you're a woman."

"Being a woman has brought nothing but hardship and pain to my life," I said. "Perhaps dressing as a man will prevent me from being pulled into the trees again."

He turned to Liam. "Watch over her while I find something that should fit."

Liam nodded, and I faced the well to continue washing. The cool water soothed many of my aches. I had a cut on the back of my leg, which explained why it hurt so fiercely. Thankfully, it had already stopped bleeding.

I glanced over my shoulder at a soft rustle of sound and saw Darian standing there with a bundle in his arms. His gaze was on my calf.

"It will be fine," I said. "I had a similar scrape when I fell out of a tree once."

Darian cleared his throat and met my gaze.

"Brandle will want to look at it when he returns."

"I doubt showing him my injuries will persuade him to help me leave," I said, holding out my hand for the clothes.

Darian's gaze locked onto my raw palm, and a sigh bubbled up inside of me. If I were Eloise, I would let it out, but I'd learned that venting one's emotions rarely led to the desired result. So I swallowed it down and used reason instead.

"I don't need Brandle's attention. Time will heal all my injuries. Now, will you give those clothes to me, or must I wear the torn gown?"

He surrendered the clothes.

"You should change inside," he said.

"Thank you."

They left me alone to change. It felt odd removing the chemise and dressing in a man's tunic and pants. The coarse material made my skin itch, and I debated the wisdom of continuing with such a scheme. Yet, wouldn't wearing men's clothing prove to them that I am serious about learning how to survive the forest?

I set my chemise aside so I would be able to sleep in comfort and twisted my braid up to tuck into the cap Darian had provided. My hands hurt fiercely, and I didn't bother attempting to tie my boots after I slipped them on again.

When I emerged outside, both Liam and Darian were by the table. The cooking fire blazed merrily.

"If you tell us what to do, we'll be your hands," Liam said.

Both followed my instructions well, and soon, the evening's stew simmered over the flames. Once the biscuits were formed, I debated how to cook them.

"I've never cooked biscuits over an open fire before," I said. "But if we use a flat-bottomed pot with a lid, it might act like an oven. Or we could drop them in the stew, and they will cook like large fluffy dumplings."

"Let's put them in the pot," Darian said.

I nodded and cautiously stretched. The aches from earlier were settling in, making everything stiff. Liam's eyes were nearly swollen shut, and Darian had a bruise at the corner of his mouth.

He caught my look and grinned.

"Should we tell Edmund this is from him?" he asked, touching his mouth and wincing.

"I doubt he would feel much guilt," I said. "If that's your intent."

"It would be. Why do you think he wouldn't feel guilt?"

"He's still too angry and afraid to feel anything else."

"Afraid? Why do you think he's afraid?"

"Because I'm here," I said.

"You think Edmund's afraid of you?"

I considered the wariness creeping into Darian's posture.

"I think you all are, which confuses me. Why detain someone you fear?"

I shook my head and looked at the forest. The light of the day was beginning to fade, yet I couldn't see the soft glow of the stone in the trees. The urge to sigh bubbled up again.

"You've either moved the stone, or that man has taken it. Since you did not like me using it and would be unlikely to aid someone who you've fought, I believe one of you moved the stone so neither he nor I could find it."

I glanced at Liam in time to catch his look of surprise. Darian laughed.

"You're as clever as you are pretty, Kellen," he said.

"If I were truly clever, I would know why you're keeping me here."

"What do you mean?" he asked.

"I am an unwanted intruder in your sunlit glade, who desperately wishes to continue her journey; yet, I am unable to do so because those who wish me gone will not assist in my departure. What am I to think of that, Darian? To what purpose does my presence here serve you or your brothers? For it must serve some purpose, or you would have already removed me as you did the man who attacked me."

"Ah, well, the answer to that is simple," he said. "You know how to cook."

I SAT on the bench and leaned back on the table as I stared into the dying fire. The stew cooled to the side in wait for the others' return. In the silence of the yard, I let my mind try to untangle the puzzle of my presence.

Despite Darian's quick answer, I knew it wasn't the truth. They'd allowed me to stay until the creatures were gone before they knew of my ability to fix a passable meal.

A branch snapped in the woods, and I looked up to see the faint glow of red eyes deeper in the trees, far from the day's dying light. I stood and walked closer to the edge, curious. More branches snapped. More eyes blinked into existence.

How could anyone survive the forest with so many creatures prowling?

How had I survived to reach the clearing?

It was luck that I'd found Father first and that he had retained enough sense to want to protect me. And more luck that I'd found the road and the stone when I had. And still more luck that I'd found this glade.

Three chance happenings to bring me to this place? Not likely.

"Luck belongs to the foolish," I said softly.

"Are you calling yourself a fool, then, as well as a man?" Edmund asked from behind me.

I glanced over my shoulder at him and saw the rest of the men returning quietly from the backyard. Their shirts were marked with water drops as if they'd just come from washing at the well. Edmund's expression turned even darker when I looked at him and our gazes met.

Rather than answer him, I resumed my study of the woods.

"Why are you dressed like that? What are you plotting?" he demanded.

"How to survive when I leave," I said. "You should stop fighting with everyone. The blows to your head seemed to be affecting your memory."

Someone snorted. It sounded like Daemon or Eadric.

"Why are you so determined to leave?" Brandle asked.

"Why are you so determined to keep me?" I countered calmly.

"Who was the man that tried to take you?" Edmund asked.

I turned to face them all. Liam flashed me a guilty look, and Darian just grinned. They'd obviously told their brothers what had transpired during their absence.

"Why would you prefer the beasts take you than go with him?" Brandle asked.

It didn't surprise me that Liam and Darian had heard everything I'd said to the man. I had been rather loud about it.

"For me, a known fate is better than an unknown one," I said. "While some may consider my life sheltered, I've seen enough to understand what a man such as he might want to do to me. Would he violate me? Sell me to a workhouse? Perhaps I would wake one day and find myself beaten and chained to a hearth. How long would it take before I began to wish I had never been born? With the beasts, I know exactly what they will do to me."

As I spoke, I met each one of their gazes.

"Your lives are your own, gentlemen. Live them as you see fit, and leave me to live mine as I see fit."

"What are you saying?" Brandle asked.

"When I asked for your help to survive, it wasn't an invitation to control my fate. My fate is my own. Help me or don't. I will leave at first light."

I stepped around the group and made my way to the stew pot. After helping myself to a bowl, I took it inside their home and ate alone while they remained outside.

Since arriving, they'd never entered the cottage while I occupied it.

Initially, I thought it a courtesy to allow me privacy. However, Darian's open appraisal at the well had me reconsidering. With spring's thaw fighting winter's lingering grip, a chill clung to the air once the sun dipped below the canopy. Sleeping inside would be much warmer. Yet, from the moment I'd arrived in the clearing, I'd noted the evidence that they slept outdoors. Why avoid the cottage? Why invite me to stay in it? I glanced at the cabinet that hid their supplies and then at the locked door.

A mystery surrounded this home and these men for certain—but one I did not care to untangle. Finding a way to save Eloise remained my focus. I needed to reach Turre. If I couldn't find someone there to reverse the sickness that gripped Father, then I would find someone with the means to help me free Eloise from Maeve.

Outside, the lower murmur of their conversation came and went in waves. While I hoped that meant they were considering helping me in the morning, I contemplated what I would need to do to survive the forest if they didn't.

Could I count on my father to see me to Turre? Did his

humanity still remain? Unlikely. I wasn't sure why so much of it remained to help me the first time.

Certainly not due to luck.

Three chance happenings.

I let out a slow breath, knowing what I must do but hating it. How long had it been since I'd opened myself to the world around me? Years, for certain. Yet, I'd been tempted when Mother died. If I'd done so, could I have saved us from what happened? Would I have known Maeve for what she was?

Rather than dwell on what might have been, I closed my eyes, leaned back in my chair, and tentatively allowed myself to feel. Just feel.

The pain from losing my mother. The anger from all that had happened since. The unending heartbreak of leaving Eloise behind to bear the consequences of my actions. It all swelled inside of me, straining against the walls of the well I'd carefully built to contain everything. It filled that space within me until the hair on my arms stood up on its own. My skin felt raw. Too sensitive to everything. The coarse fabric of my tunic. The smoke in the air. The hardness of the padded chair underneath me.

I opened myself to it all.

Then my awareness went further. I could feel the cottage. The echo of its history. The joy. The tears. The anger. The frustration. The hope.

So much hope wrapped in desperation.

Beyond that, I could feel *them*. Brandle. Daemon. Darian. Edmund. Eadric. Garron. Liam.

Fear. Worry. Anger—obviously Edmund. And hope…

I brushed past them and focused on the forest and the many beasts surrounding the glade. My skin tingled painfully. The energy threaded around me, tightening.

I quickly closed myself off and opened my eyes. The cottage looked the same. But it wasn't the cottage that would have suffered when I opened myself like that.

Standing, I went to the door and scanned the packed dirt of the yard. It looked the same. So did the seven men who'd stopped speaking at the sight of me. The fire crackled and illuminated Brandle's thoughtful gaze as he watched me.

Beyond them, the light didn't reach the forest, but in the darkness, I saw the red eyes of the beasts I'd sensed. Many, many sets of eyes.

Focusing on the men, I nodded.

"Goodnight."

They said nothing in return as I closed the door.

In the loft, I changed back into my shift and went to sleep. It was fitful at best, filled with dreams of running and calling for Father and Eloise.

Before dawn, I rose and dressed in the pants and tunic once more. When I descended, the closed door didn't surprise me. However, its refusal to open did.

I stared at it. Eloise would have beaten at it and called out obscenities. A waste of time and emotions but likely the reaction they expected. And if I did what they expected, they wouldn't be watching for what they didn't expect.

"What purpose does it serve to keep me here?" I called loudly before banging my fist on the door. "How is it that Edmund is the only one of you with any sense? Release me."

"It's not safe, Kellen," Brandle said from the other side. "Please. Just stay inside for a few days. What happened yesterday called even more of the creatures to this area."

"Let me speak to Edmund," I said.

"He won't help you," Brandle said.

I considered the door. "Won't or can't because he's not here. And if he's not here, that means there's a way to survive these woods even with all the creatures in it. Let me go, Brandle."

"I'm sorry, Kellen. I can't."

"Why?"

"I'll bring you something to eat."

"Don't bother. I'll throw whatever you bring at your head."

I heard a faint chuckle. Daemon? Eadric? Darian? Definitely none of the other three.

Three had lingered in the yard on the day I'd arrived. Two had remained behind with me the day prior. Perhaps five were needed to safely travel with the additional creatures? That likely meant Brandle and another stayed behind. Who, though? Deduction said Eadric since they seemed to be taking turns.

"Hateful men," I said at the door before looking at the cabin's two windows.

Through the one opposite the door, I caught a glimpse of Eadric watching me.

Understanding ·there would be no escape that route, I marched to the ladder and climbed to the loft where I looked up at the thatched roofing.

They brought this upon themselves, I thought as I removed the knife from my bag and began slicing through the thatching. It took some time to see light. I didn't pause my efforts, though, not even when my arms burned and my eyes watered from the falling debris.

The bed beneath me was strewn with thatching fragments by the time I finally made an opening large enough. Straw scraped my face as I pulled myself up onto the roof, and I briefly thought of how much Eloise would have cackled at my current antics. A sad smile tugged at my lips. Likely, my sister was testing limits with her own escapades.

Emerging after much strain, I flattened myself against the roof and scanned the yard. Eadric leaned against a tree at the edge of the clearing on the East side of the cottage. He still watched the window, with no view of what I'd done in the loft. Brandle was near the cooking fire to the West. The sun wasn't yet over the trees, which created long shadows that would work to my advantage. Despite the light, my warm breath still emerged as a small cloud in the chill morning air.

Pants made it easier to creep to the edge of the roof. The distance to the ground, while significant, wasn't anything that concerned me. Subtracting my height, my boots would be no more than four feet from the ground once I hung over the edge.

I lifted my head to check both Eadric and Brandle one last time then carefully extended my arm and let my bag drop to the ground. Neither seemed to hear the soft thump. I waited a bit longer to ensure they were distracted then moved my body so I was parallel with the edge. Swinging my legs over, I held onto the thatching and slowly lowered more of my body. The bite of the thatching burned my already raw palms fiercely, sending jolts of pain through my hands. My fingers slipped. I began to fall.

Strong hands gripped my waist.

"Do you have no sense?" Brandle demanded as he set me on the ground.

I pivoted to glare at him. He was only a few inches shorter than me yet still managed to look rather imposing with his fierce scowl.

"You could have been hurt."

"I'm sorry, Brandle," I said a second before I thrust the heel of my hand into his nose.

He staggered back a step. It allowed me enough space and time to scoop up my bag and sprint toward the trees.

CHAPTER 6

"Eadric!"

Brandle's bellow prompted me to run faster.

Not only would I need to contend with the creatures, but I would also need to worry about—

Arms wrapped around my waist, tackling me from behind but rolling at the last moment so I was spared from falling face first.

One of the hands was gripping a breast.

"Eadric, your hand placement is deplorable," I said.

The hand immediately released me. I drove an elbow into his ribs and bolted off of him.

Brandle was suddenly in front of me. He bent at the knees to catch me around the waist and hoisted me up so I was draped over his shoulder. My braid dragged on the ground, and I thumped his thighs in frustration as he carried me back toward the cottage.

"She's bleeding," Eadric called.

I glanced at the bloody handprint on Brandle's pants.

"It's from his nose," I said.

"No, it's not," Brandle said, sounding calm.

I lifted my head to look at Eadric, who was following us.

"I didn't mean to grab your breast again," he said with a crooked smile and a hint of worry in his gaze.

"I know. That's why *your* nose isn't bleeding."

Brandle carefully righted me once we reached the table so I sat on the surface.

"And what of my nose, Kellen? Was I hit for saving you?"

"Never. I hit you for trying to keep me where I don't belong."

He leaned in. Due to my seat on the table, we were now eye-level with one another.

"That was to save you, Kellen. You will die if you go into the forest."

"That is my choice to make, Brandle. Not yours. Release me."

"You are vexing." He pinched the bridge of his nose and winced.

"And you are in my way. Move, Brandle. Please. I don't want to give Edmund any further reason to hate me."

Brandle considered me for a long moment.

"The beasts will be drawn to the scent of your blood."

"I understand," I said, meeting his gaze.

He tipped his head back and closed his eyes. "Stubborn."

"You shouldn't expose your throat like that when you're annoying," I said. "I'm tempted to hit it next and watch you wheeze."

His gaze snapped to mine. "You say you're annoyed? What of me?"

"The annoyance you feel is of your own making, not mine."

He braced his hands on the table on either side of me, and a glint of something flickered in his gaze, reminding me of Edmund. Then he took a deep, calming breath.

"Why do you care so little for your life?" he asked.

"Thank you for providing me with food and shelter. That is the extent of what I can accept from you, though. Please remove your hands."

He pushed away from the table but surprised me by taking one of my hands and turning it palm up. It was indeed bleeding.

"Can you not feel pain?"

"Of course I feel pain," I said.

"What of fear, Kellen?"

"I feel it as deeply as anyone."

"Yet you never show it. That is why Edmund doubts you."

"Showing my emotions as he does will not endear me to him, Brandle. What is the point of this conversation? Do you seek to bore me until I collapse and become more manageable?"

My voice had remained steadily calm as I spoke; however, I could feel the familiar tingle of warning. Brandle was pushing me too far.

"For your safety, please allow me to leave this place, Brandle." I turned my hand to take both of his in mine. "Please."

He looked down at our hands. "What if I told you that keeping you here would guarantee our safety?"

"What if I told you that keeping me here would jeopardize my sister's safety?"

His gaze met mine. "Will your death help her?" He didn't ask it angrily but with the seriousness of someone who expected an answer.

I released his hands.

"No. She would be forced to face this world's cruelties alone then."

"Do you resent her?"

"Never. Why would you ask such a thing?"

"Because I seek to understand why you wish to kill yourself."

"I wish no such thing."

"Do you not? You asked for our help to survive the forest, yet won't listen to our advice when we say you must wait or you will die."

"You know that is not the help I meant."

"We cannot safely guide you through the trees, Kellen. It was a miracle you arrived at all. Do not doubt that we *are* helping you survive by providing you with a safe place to sleep and food to eat while we wait for the creatures and the tracker to leave."

I frowned slightly.

"Tracker? What do you mean? The man from yesterday?"

Brandle nodded and watched me closely, likely looking for answers I could not give him. The spell that bound me would prevent any damning word from gracing my lips. If the tracker remained, Brandle was right. I couldn't leave now, no matter how desperately I wished to.

When I dropped my gaze, Brandle stepped away from me.

"Help her wash her hands at the well, Eadric, and stop her if she tries to leave. I'll get the honey."

Eadric came close and offered me a consoling smile and help off the table.

"You'll find that Brandle's almost always right. It's annoying at times, but you grow accustomed to it. Do your hands hurt?"

"Dreadfully," I admitted as we walked toward the well.

"I'm sorry I didn't think to grab the rope when we started to fall."

"It's not your fault my hands hurt like this."

He tossed the bucket in and began to draw back up, hand over hand. Every move had a relaxed ease.

"I'm still sorry you were hurt. The honey will make them feel better."

He glanced at me and smiled. It lit his eyes and made him appear even more handsome. With his looks, he could draw many a maid in and press for an advantage, but I realized that Eadric was unlike most people. He had no malice in him. Not a drop of it.

"Thank you, Eadric."

"My pleasure. Now let me help you clean these hands. I don't know everything Brandle does, but I do know how to clean a scrape. I've had my fair share of them."

He rinsed my hands with the fresh water and bent over my palms to gently remove any lingering straw splinters. The care in which he picked out each bit threatened to thaw that place inside of me that I only ever let Eloise see.

"Do you think leaving is foolish too?" I asked.

He glanced at me before returning to his inspection.

"We're all fools for the right reasons, Kellen. I would do anything for my brothers, even attempt to travel the forest alone. It makes sense you feel the same for your sister. But sometimes, we have to ask ourselves if the risk of our immediate death outweighs the risk of waiting." His twinkling gaze met mine. "Brandle made me write 'No risk is worth my life' more times than I can count so it would stick in my head. But it's not necessarily true, is it? For the right thing, my life *is* worth the risk. We just need to be smart about deciding what the right thing is."

"Also, my words," Brandle said behind me.

Eadric's grin widened before he ducked his blonde head and continued cleaning my palms.

I glanced over my shoulder at Brandle.

"I *will* leave. Eventually," I said. "Don't try to lock me in again."

Brandle smiled slightly, and Eadric snorted.

"Since none of us enjoy thatching, we will not lock the door again," Brandle agreed.

"Thank you."

"Rinse it once more," he said, watching Eadric. "I'll dry it and apply the honey."

The water stung, but the soft cloth Brandle used to dab the lingering moisture sent stabbing pain into the palms. Though I didn't flinch away from it or give any other indication, he paused to gently blow on the wounds.

My skin tingled with an awareness I fought not to acknowledge.

"It will take more than a day for this to heal now," he said when he straightened and met my gaze.

71

"Apply the honey, Brandle," I said.

Eadric leaned against the well and watched us closely. Did he see what I did? The way his brother looked at me?

The honey helped the pain almost immediately, and the wraps Brandle wound around my hands weren't too terrible.

"Are you hungry?" Eadric asked once Brandle tucked the end of the cloth in.

"Yes, but I need to use the privy first."

"Come. I'll help you while Brandle hides away the honey."

"Would anyone be foolish enough to eat it after his explanation?" I asked, walking away with Eadric.

"Without a doubt," Eadric said. "Daemon would do anything to avoid work."

I laughed and waited for Eadric to open the door for me.

"Call if you need anything," he said, closing me in.

Flexing my fingers to untie my pants sent spears of pain into my palm. So much so that I struggled with the ties when I finished relieving myself. The strings slipped from my hands, and my pants fell to my ankles.

I should have changed into the dress, I thought.

Pushing aside my annoyance, I bent and pinched the material between two fingers, which seemed to result in the least amount of pain. Working my pants up to my knees, I widened my stance to keep them there and carefully flexed my fingers. Pain shot through my hand again, despite the honey.

If I ever wanted to leave, I needed to heal. Properly.

"Eadric, this isn't going to work," I called through the door.

"The privy doesn't work?"

"These pants. I'm unable to retie them."

"I can tie them for you."

He opened the door...while the pants were still at my knees. I wasn't wearing any underthings.

He didn't notice my wince as I attempted to grab the material.

He was too busy staring at my parted legs until I had my pants pinned against my stomach with my forearm.

Slowly, Eadric's gaze lifted to meet mine.

Neither of us spoke for several seconds.

He cleared his throat. Twice.

"Garron cuffed me after I touched you at the well. I'll probably get another one when Brandle tells them where my hand had landed earlier. This, though, will earn me more than a simple cuffing. Perchance, can we keep this between us?"

"I would prefer to pretend it never happened."

"What happened?" Brandle asked from outside the privy.

"Nothing," Eadric and I said at the same time.

Brandle came to stand behind his brother and looked at me over his shoulder. His gaze flicked to my arm holding my pants, and understanding lit his gaze.

"Perhaps a dress would be more suitable until your hands are better."

"Unless you're familiar with lacing, my shift might be all I can manage."

He nodded and nudged Eadric out of the way to deftly tie my pants.

"The less you use your hands today, the better," he said. "I'll prepare what you need while you eat." He looked at Eadric. "Can you help her without doing anything indecent?"

Eadric's cheeks flushed.

"Any indecency was happenstance," I said quickly, feeling the need to defend him. "He's been nothing but considerate."

Brandle's gaze shifted to me. Something flickered in his expression. Disbelief and perhaps a little hope, which didn't make any sense.

"Then, I will leave you in his considerate care," Brandle said.

When he turned, I felt a small stab of guilt. After all, Brandle had cared for me as well.

"I apologize for hitting your nose," I called.

He waved a hand over his shoulder without pausing. "It was deserved."

I watched Brandle leave and glanced at Eadric.

"Does he get angry?" I asked.

"Often. Usually at Edmund or Daemon, though. I only frustrate him."

A small smile tugged at my lips. "I feel I might do the same."

"Come. I'll feed you."

"This should be interesting," I said, following him. He didn't allow me to use my hands for anything and spoon-fed me the oats they'd kept warm.

"Who cooked?" I asked.

"I did. I paid attention yesterday so we could eat a decent meal today. Not every meal is worth eating."

Once the bowl was empty, he glanced at the door over my shoulder. When I would have turned to look, he placed his hand on my leg just above my knee to keep my attention.

"Do you know any other meals we can make? We have a lot of dried berries that we don't know what to do with. Some went bad last summer. Too old."

"If you don't mind milling flour and being my hands today, we could make some tarts for breakfast."

"Without honey?"

"Without honey or sugar."

He frowned slightly. "We might have sugar and cream later once the others return."

"So you can leave for supplies, but you cannot help me reach Turre."

"Precisely that," Eadric said with a smile. He lifted his hand from my knee and swiped a thumb against the corner of my mouth then brought it to his lips.

"Berry," he said when he caught my stare. "How old are you?"

"Sixteen last fall. Why do you ask?"

"Did your father arrange a marriage for you before he left?"

"No. My mother was strongly opposed to arranged marriages. She said Eloise and I should be free to follow our hearts."

"Interesting that your heart led you here."

I considered his boyish grin.

"Are you flirting with me, Eadric?" I asked.

"I wouldn't dare."

"Why not?"

"I've seen how you hit noses and would prefer not to experience it."

Something dangerous lit inside of me. Affection. I *cared* for Eadric.

"I don't think you ever will," I said sincerely.

His grin widened, and his gaze shifted to somewhere behind me.

"Hear that, Brandle? Kellen doesn't want to hit me!" His gaze shifted back to me. "You're the first one who hasn't wanted to cuff me."

"Give her time, Eadric," Brandle called. "You haven't accidentally poisoned her yet."

I arched a brow at Eadric, and he gave me a sheepish look.

"Henry used to season our food. I remember how it tasted. Better than what we make. That's for certain. I wanted to do the same but didn't add the right herbs. They all look the same." He shrugged slightly.

"What happened?"

"We were sick for days and had to dig a new privy once we all felt better. Who knew a body could hold so much?"

The laugh that escaped me surprised us both. I quickly swallowed it down and watched him for any signs of discomfort.

"You're pretty when you laugh."

"Thank you."

Brandle approached us and looked at me.

"I have everything ready if you'd like to change."

I nodded and stood. He followed but stopped me at the door

where he bent and unlaced my boots so I would be able to kick them off without using my hands.

"Arm over your pants, Kellen," he said, guiding my arm to where it had been in the privy. He tugged the tie loose then reached up to loosen the tie of the tunic. His fingers brushed my neck. If I hadn't been watching him closely, I would have missed the subtle shift in his expression.

Brandle was interested.

In me.

I backed up a step before he finished tugging my neckline loose.

"I can manage the way it is."

His gaze met mine, and he nodded.

"I vow not to lock the door if you choose to close it. Eadric and I will be by the well. Call out if you need anything." He walked away, toward Eadric. I caught Eadric watching me watch his brother. His usual easy smile wasn't tugging at the corner of his mouth.

I closed the door on both of them, and when I faced the room, I saw that Brandle had done more than fetch my shift.

One of the beds from the loft waited in front of the hearth. A small pillow, along with several of the blankets, rested on top of the mattresses. Two of them stacked one on top of the other.

How had we not heard him move those? The bed had to have been difficult with only the ladder to—

The ladder was gone, and a blanket plugged the hole I'd made in the thatching.

My gaze swung to the door as I stepped out of my boots. Though he'd given his word, I wondered if I would find it locked once I finished changing. Rather than check, I went to the bed and let my pants drop to the floor. It took a good deal of wiggling and odd elbow thrusts to work the tunic off without the use of my hands, but I managed.

Bare, I considered the shift Brandle had neatly laid out on the bed. It wouldn't cover much of my person but would enable me to use the privy alone.

With the neckline loose, it didn't take as much effort to put on as the tunic had taken to remove. Once the length of material settled over my legs, I faced the door.

"Eadric?" I called.

"I won't open the door this time. Do you need help?"

His answer made me smile.

"I need help opening the door."

"Oh. Oh!"

It swung open while I was still grinning.

His answering smile faded a little as his gaze swept over me, and his cheeks flushed.

"Er. Uh." He turned his back on me. "I don't think this is decent."

I looked down at myself and fought not to sigh at the gaping neckline.

"Eadric. Just come in here and tie it. Please."

He stepped aside and disappeared from view.

A silent curse echoed in my mind as I hurried after him, only to crash into Brandle. Where the impact should have knocked him back a pace, it sent me reeling instead.

He wrapped an arm around me and steadied me as if he outweighed me. Perhaps he did, despite my extra inches. Father always said that men were born with more muscles. But, I'd always thought he'd said it to stop Eloise from trying to do things she shouldn't.

"You need something tied?" Brandle asked.

My pulse jumped dangerously. Frowning, I tried to take a quick step back, but he held firm.

"Not by you. Eadric can assist me."

"Eadric prefers that I take his place."

I turned my head to look for Eadric, but he was missing.

"Coward," I muttered.

"I think this is the first time I've seen you frown," Brandle said.

I carefully composed my expression. "Release me and tie my neckline without touching me. Please."

He nodded slowly and, watching me closely, did as I asked. His gaze never left my face.

"Did I offend you, Kellen?" he asked as he finished tying.

"No. Thank you for your assistance."

I turned on my bare heel and closed the door on him.

"KELLEN," Daemon called from outside the closed door. "Come see what we've brought."

His voice pulled me from the quiet contemplation of my damaged hands.

Eadric had knocked on the door at midday to offer me a pitcher of water, which I'd accepted. Afterward, I'd left to use the privy—without assistance—and had returned to the cottage as soon as I'd finished, though the day had warmed considerably under the sun and beckoned me.

It was safer for us all if I kept apart, which is why I remained in my seat until a shout rang throughout the cottage. That and it hurt to put on my cloak even without tying it.

"You what?" Edmund yelled.

A moment later, I heard the sound of scuffling.

I told myself not to go. I told myself it didn't matter if Edmund gave Eadric a thrashing. But it did. Eadric hadn't done anything to deserve it.

Drawing my cloak around my shoulders, I stepped into my unlaced boots and used my arm to lift the latch.

Eadric turned from his position near the door to look back at me. In front of him, Edmund and Brandle scuffled about in the dirt while the other brothers quietly watched on.

Imbeciles.

Edmund was landing too many punches to Brandle's face. For the man's continued well-being, I fetched the pitcher despite the pain it caused and tossed the contents on the pair.

Edmund sprang to his feet with an enraged yell. His head swung about in search of the one who'd doused him. When he saw the pitcher in my hand, his gaze narrowed.

Eadric tried to step in front of me. I moved around him to face Edmund directly as Brandle slowly stood.

"Words, Edmund. They should be used before fists, don't you agree? Or should we disregard the pact we've made?"

He breathed out heavily, his anger boiling inside of him.

"You need to leave," he snarled.

"We are of the same mind. Rather than trying to beat that logic into all of your brothers before they are prepared to accept that truth, use your head to find another solution."

"And what solution would that be?" he demanded.

"Brandle believes I will die in the forest. So teach me something useful each day I'm here. Then, once I'm healed and the beasts have dispersed, the rest will have no reason to detain me."

"Useful?" he scoffed. "You think I'll willingly tell you our secrets?"

"Walking silently isn't a secret. Using onion to cover my scent isn't a secret. Yet both are useful bits of knowledge that helped me survive."

"That explains the smell," Daemon said with a laugh. "It clings to the cloak and dress even after we washed them."

"You washed them?" I asked in surprise.

"Does that make us fools in your eyes?" Edmund demanded.

Most any maid in Towdown my age would have run under the weight of his angry glare. Eloise likely would have thrown a rock. I did neither.

I strode toward him with purpose and the pitcher in my hand. He uncrossed his arms and bent his knees slightly.

"Edmund," Brandle said in warning.

But he needn't have bothered. Edmund was bracing for a fight he thought I meant to start. He wouldn't attack me. He was smart enough to know his brothers would never allow it.

When I reached him, I handed him the pitcher.

"You shouldn't worry about your brothers giving away your secrets, Edmund. You do that well enough on your own."

"I haven't told you anything."

"Haven't you? Your actions speak louder than any truth you might utter. A woman has done terrible things to you."

His shocked expression confirmed it.

"Why else carry such a biased rage toward a woman you do not know? Yes, I appeared in your glade while holding a magic stone. But you live between Drisdall and Turre. One forbids magic, and the other welcomes it. In Drisdall, people avoid anything associated with magic, fearing punishment, not the magic itself. But when I appeared, you didn't fear the stone. You feared *me*. The woman who hurt you was a caster, was she not?"

His arms dropped to his sides, and he glanced at Brandle.

"Do not look to your brothers now for help, Edmund. Use your own mind. For the sake of your precious secrets, mask your suspicions and use your words the next time you meet someone new. Your reactions give away more than you know."

His anger slowly melted away from his expression but remained simmering under the surface.

"Unclench your fists before you break the pitcher. Hands give away as much as the eyes," I said. "Remember my helpfulness tomorrow when it is your turn to speak a helpful truth to survive these woods."

He set the pitcher on the table and left the front yard.

I turned to look at the rest of them.

"What do you see in me?" Daemon asked with a wicked grin.

"Trouble," I said.

CHAPTER 7

I looked at Brandle. "Based on Edmund's shout, I thought he was fighting with Eadric. Would you care to tell me what you did to upset Edmund?"

Brandle considered me then shook his head.

"Very well. What goods have you procured?" I asked, looking at Daemon.

"You wish to look at my goods?" He threw his head back and laughed. Brandle cuffed him from the right, and Garron cuffed him from the left.

"Go speak some sense into Edmund," Brandle said.

Daemon nodded and strolled away while Liam gestured to the table.

"You mentioned pastries," he said. "We think we found most everything you should need."

I saw a basket filled with eggs, an earthen jug filled with cream, and a small bag of sugar.

"If used carefully, these supplies should last you a while," I said.

As they had the day before, they all willingly acted as my hands to help prepare the evening meal. Eadric and Garron made another stew while Darian and Liam worked on pastries, and Brandle churned butter with a churner he'd snuck out of the cottage, along with my cloak, when my back was turned.

"You look tired, Princess," Darian said. "I heard you tried escaping through the roof and quite shocked Brandle."

"I believe the blow to his nose shocked him more," I said.

"No, it was the roof," Brandle said.

They all chuckled. I felt a stirring of humor and pushed it down.

"Come sit beside me," Darian said, catching the loose material of my shift between two fingers. He patted the seat beside him with his free hand. "You've had a harrowing day."

I twisted to look back at him and saw a glint in his eyes that didn't bode well for me. It was the same glint Brandle had in his eyes when he'd untied my tunic.

The men in this glade were beginning to remind me of the heroes in the books I'd borrowed from Mr. Bentwell. Headstrong rogues who persisted in their pursuit of the heroine for a single purpose. Ravishment.

My heart gave a dangerous flutter at the idea, and I tugged my shift free from his fingers.

"Unless you wish to feel the heel of my hand against your nose, I suggest you keep to yourself," I said.

"I welcome your hands on me, Princess. Day or night." He had the audacity to wink at me.

For the first time in a long while, I felt a flush creep into my cheeks.

Without answering, I walked toward the cottage. They didn't say anything as I closed the door. Pressing the back of my hand to my heated cheek, I leaned against the wooden panel.

As I'd explained to Brandle, I wasn't impervious to emotions, and being here with these brothers was causing me to feel more than I should. I needed to leave the glade posthaste.

Pushing away from the door, I slipped out of my boots and

cloak and took a seat in the chair to stare at the cold hearth without seeing it. My mind started to dwell on why the men lived in the middle of the forest, but I quickly shook away that riddle and thought of Eloise.

How was she faring? Had Maeve punished her for my disappearance? Three days had already passed. How many more would I need to wait to be reunited with my twin?

The light was almost gone from the sky when someone knocked on the door.

Eadric waited outside with a bowl of stew and a biscuit.

"I saved this for you."

"Thank you, Eadric." I held out my hand, but he didn't surrender the meal.

"This is the first time we've made biscuits. It wasn't something Henry taught us. Could you try it out here and teach us more so we can make other foods once you're gone? Darian burns everything. They won't let me use herbs. Edmund only makes soups, and they don't taste good. Brandle—"

I held up my hand. "I can write down the recipe."

Eadric was already shaking his head.

"No ink or quill or spare paper," he said.

"You're quite persistent."

He grinned widely. "If you had to eat their cooking, you would be persistent too. And probably in the privy."

"Eadric!" Garron scolded from the darkness near the fire.

"If I teach you, will you teach me one thing that will help me survive when I leave?" I asked, looking Eadric in the eye.

His gaze flicked down to the stew he held. After a brief hesitation, he nodded once.

"Very well," I said, stepping into my boots and easing the cloak around my shoulders.

While I ate at the table, I explained how to make a soup that everyone would enjoy. They only interrupted with a few questions. No one flirted or fought. Regardless, I didn't linger.

As soon as I finished the meal, I retreated to the cottage and slept fitfully until dawn.

The pain in my hands had increased through the night, either an indication that the herbs in the honey had lost their potency or that an infection had taken root.

With weak early morning light filling the cottage, I stood and went to the door to step into my boots once more. It mattered not that I wished to avoid the men outside. I needed help.

The door opened with a quiet click. While I thought it was barely noticeable, the brothers stopped what they were doing around the table to turn and look at me.

Darian winked, and it set my heart fluttering again, which I ignored.

My gaze swept over them until I found Brandle.

"My hands hurt," I said.

He nodded. "Would you like Eadric to help you wash them while I fetch more honey?"

"Please."

Eadric followed me to the well.

"I'll use the privy first," I said.

"I'll get the door for you," he said, quickly moving ahead of me. He flashed me a grin as he opened it for me. "I'll wait until you tell me to open it this time."

"I appreciate the courtesy," I said.

The simple act of lifting my shift sent shards of pain through my palms. I pushed the pain away and focused on hurrying. Eadric stayed true to his word and didn't open the door until I said I was ready.

Brandle waited for us at the well. He didn't offer to unwrap my hands but allowed Eadric to do it. However, I wasn't reassured by Brandle's distance. I hadn't mistaken the look in his eyes the previous day. Or in Darian's.

So, my attention remained warily fixed on Brandle as Eadric carefully rinsed my palms with water. His touch was gentle and soothing. Brandle's presence was not. His calm gaze held mine the entire time.

"They don't feel hot," Eadric said. "That's a good sign."

"They hurt fiercely," I said without looking at him. "More than they did yesterday."

Eadric's fingers brushed over the backs of my hands. The gentle caress drew my attention from Brandle.

"I know you said it's not my fault," Eadric said with a sad smile, "But the guilt I feel isn't listening to reason. Would you like to know a secret about the forest?"

"Yes," I said, allowing his continued touch.

"People think it's only filled with creatures, but it's not. Animals live in there too. Many of them."

"I saw a rabbit," I said. "It distracted a creature from finding me."

Eadric nodded. "We had stewed rabbit last night. But there are bigger animals too. Bear. Wolves. Not many, but they're still out there. Sometimes, the creatures will fight with them."

I turned my head to consider the woods.

"Are they equally matched?"

"It depends on the animal and the beast," Eadric said.

When I looked at him, I met his tender smile with one of my own.

"Thank you, Eadric. That is truly helpful."

His bright smile, paired with his blonde hair, reminded me so much of Eloise that it hurt. Without thought, I brushed the backs of my fingers against his cheek. The surprise in his gaze brought me back to the present.

Averting my own gaze, I quickly pulled my hand away.

"I apologize."

Brandle cleared his throat.

"Leave us, Eadric."

I didn't look up at Brandle as he took my first hand and gently applied the honey. It helped the pain almost immediately. He worked quietly and efficiently.

"You're right," he said. "A woman with magic hurt Edmund. She hurt us all. It's hard to trust. But I think you understand that better than most since you don't trust men either."

I finally looked up and met his gaze as he tucked the end of the last wrap into itself.

"No, Brandle. It is not men that I cannot trust but myself. For your safety, do not venture to understand me. Simply help me leave as quickly as possible."

"I think you were meant to appear here, Kellen."

I looked away for a moment and attempted to ignore the tingle of awareness skimming over my skin, but it proved impossible.

"I think so, too," I said softly. "And from a kingdom that forbids magic, I find the idea terrifying." I lifted my gaze to meet his. "As a man hurt by magic, you should find it terrifying, too."

He slowly shook his head. "It wasn't the magic that hurt us but the woman who wielded it. I don't believe you are anything like her."

"In three days' time, you think to know me?" I shook my head and started for the front yard.

The others stood around Eadric, and they all turned to watch me enter the cottage and close the door.

I sat in the chair again to think.

My current circumstance was growing dire due to reasons they would never understand. I needed to act soon. But how? As Eadric had stated the day prior, willfully doing something that would cause my death wouldn't help Eloise or my father.

Someone knocked on the door, and a frustrated sigh escaped me.

I rarely sighed. Things were more serious than I'd first thought then. My control was fraying.

When I opened the door, Edmund stood there, scowling at me.

"Breakfast is ready. You're to join us."

"It would be better if I didn't."

"In that, we agree. However, as the observant woman you are, you'll likely agree that we are outnumbered."

"Tell them I refuse." I moved to close the door, but he reached through, grabbed my wrist, and yanked me sharply forward so I fell into him.

Like his brother, he didn't jostle at the impact.

He righted me and quickly retreated a step. It didn't save him. I struck out, but not with my abused hands.

Unhindered by my skirts, my knee would have nestled between his legs—quite sharply—had he not turned slightly. Instead, it hit his thigh with such strength that he grunted and limped away a step.

From their seats at the table, his brothers witnessed the whole thing.

"She warned you not to touch her," Daemon said with a shake of his head. "I'll bet my next portion of whatever Kellen makes us that Edmund is the first one to feel her knee in full."

"I'll take that bet," Eadric said. "But it won't be Edmund. It will be Brandle."

Brandle frowned and gave Eadric a sharp look. His brother shrugged indifferently.

"You stare at her too much, and she doesn't like it."

"Since when are you observant?" Liam asked, looking at Eadric in disbelief.

Eadric simply gave another shrug.

I focused on Edmund, who was watching me.

"The secret you owe today has increased to two," I said.

"No, the knee makes us even for the wrist."

"Shall we see who sports the larger bruise tomorrow and let your brothers decide?"

Darian stood abruptly. "How hard did you grab her, Edmund?"

Edmund stared at me. His hands remained loose at his sides, but his anger showed in the slight sneer tugging his lip.

"Better," I said. "Relax your mouth."

He let out a snarl and stomped away.

"Provoking him won't see you leaving this glade sooner," Brandle said.

"Perhaps he should stop being so provokable." I shrugged like Eadric had and went inside for my boots and cloak before I joined them at the table.

They'd boiled the eggs.

"Foolish," I said. "They would have kept for weeks."

"We'll get more," Daemon said, setting an egg and a biscuit before me.

Eadric fed me my first bite of each. Both were edible. The egg was cooked through instead of soft in the middle, and the biscuit was chewy.

"The dough was handled too much. Lighter touches and less mixing will yield a more tender biscuit. The egg should have been removed several minutes sooner."

Eadric and Liam nodded.

Edmund returned and joined us at the table, taking the only open spot. Right next to me.

"Covering your scent is a large piece of hiding. Clothes that match the trees is another piece. Brown is broken with white when it snows. Shades of brown for spring and fall. Brown and greens for summer."

"Thank you," I said.

"The creatures are smart. You can't use onions every time. You need to change what you use to hide. A blend of herbs that commonly grow together works too. If it's a combination associated with people, though, you'll give yourself away." His gaze locked with mine. "That was two."

"Thank you, Edmund," I said. "Salt your egg, and it will taste better."

They all reached for the salt at the same time.

"Who is remaining with me today?" I asked.

The fighting for the salt slowed, and they all looked at each other.

"If I have a choice, I would prefer Daemon and Eadric," I said.

"Why?" The heavy suspicion lacing Edmund's tone didn't surprise me.

"They aren't provoked by me in any way."

"What about Garron?" Brandle asked, watching me closely.

"I make Garron uncomfortable."

"I'll stay with Daemon," Garron said.

He didn't look at me but continued eating the simple morning meal they'd made as we all stared at him.

"Well, that's settled then," Brandle said. "Garron and Daemon will stay today." His gaze held mine. "Your word you won't attempt to run?"

I lifted both my wrapped hands.

"That isn't your word, Kellen."

"I liked you better when you underestimated me," I said. "You have my word that I won't foolishly run into the woods before my hands are fully healed. Better?"

"For now." He stood, and the others followed him around the back of the cottage, leaving me with Garron and Daemon.

Daemon grinned at me, folded his hands, and rested his head on them to watch me eat.

"Want me to feed you?"

"No, thank you."

"You're not supposed to be using your hands."

"I think Brandle would have said so."

"He did. Before you came out. But he was afraid you'd retreat into the cottage again if he tried to dictate what you should do."

I paused my effort to grip the spoon and weighed the wisdom

of Daemon's words. By stubbornly refusing help, was I re-injuring my hands and prolonging healing? Likely. Would allowing Daemon's help cause problems? That I couldn't answer until I tried.

While I debated, Garron stood and began to collect the dishes.

Grudgingly, I handed Daemon my spoon. He grinned and pulled my egg and biscuit toward him. Then he fed me. A smirk hovered around his mouth each time he offered me a bite.

"What are you thinking?" I asked.

"I enjoy putting something in your mouth."

Garron cuffed the back of his head so nimbly I barely saw him move.

"Take the dishes," he said, plucking the spoon from Daemon's hands.

Daemon laughed and took away everything Garron had gathered. Garron watched him go then looked down at my spoon.

"I can feed myself," I said.

Rather than surrender the spoon, he sat across from me. With a growing flush, he scooped out a bite of egg and offered it up. He didn't look at me. Just waited for me to take a bite before digging out another one.

"Can I have the biscuit?" I asked. Only one bite remained. He held it up between his fingers. When my lips accidentally brushed them, he jolted out of his seat and walked around to the side yard where I could hear Daemon drawing a bucket from the well.

Twisting in my seat, I stared after him and wondered if he was like me. Feeling things he knew he shouldn't. I'd read in the books in the attic at home that men were sometimes like that too —able to feel the energy around them. But it was more rare in men.

My thoughts drifted from those books to Eloise. This day marked the fourth morning since I'd left her, and I felt a pang of sorrow. It tingled along my skin along with the need to do some-thing. To move.

To...*run.*

A whisper of noise behind me gave warning I wasn't alone a moment before a wad of cloth roughly and deeply filled my mouth.

I let out a muffled yell of rage as I was lifted from the table and carried backward toward the trees. My captor felt and smelled the same as the day before.

Denial filled me. I refused to be the tool they used to control my sister. Thankfully, he'd lifted me high again, likely thinking I would be at a disadvantage if my feet couldn't reach the ground.

Jolting forward in his arms, I flung myself back with all my might and felt my head connect with his nose.

The tracker's pained grunt followed the satisfying crack, but he didn't loosen his hold as he leaned away from me. I twisted and thrashed as I attempted to kick him. Each thump of my heels against his legs brought another grunt, but he didn't release me.

No, he quickly dragged me toward the trees. I lost a boot in my efforts to free myself.

Think, Kellen, I told myself. *You cannot be taken.*

I attempted to force the cloth from my mouth with my tongue and gagged.

Garron rounded the cottage just then. His eyes went wide when he saw me. Desperate, I locked gazes with him and yelled from behind the cloth as I kicked again.

"Daemon!" Garron bellowed as he charged across the clearing.

The man swore, shifted his hold on me while still keeping my arms pinned, and started running. I tried tossing my head back again but only hit the man's shoulder.

The man slammed his fist into the side of my head then dropped me. Dazed from the blow and the sudden impact with the ground, I forgot about my hands and tried to use them as I struggled to lift myself up.

The sounds of a fight didn't register until a boot stomped on my fingers. I quickly jerked my arm to my chest. Hands closed on my shoulders.

I swung out blindly.

"It's me, Kellen," Daemon said, catching my upper arm and using it to pull me to my feet. He leaned me against a nearby tree. "Stay here."

He took a running start and launched himself at the man's back. The chokehold he managed after landing was impressive, as was the way he brought the man to his knees. I could see Garron standing before the man, chest heaving and lip bleeding. He threw a punch that snapped that man's head back into Daemon's.

"Dammit, Garron."

"No cussing," Garron said before rapidly punching the man three more times.

Daemon released him, and the tracker toppled to his side.

Both of the brothers turned to look at me.

"You're bleeding, Lamb," Daemon said. "How many fingers am I holding up?"

"None," I said.

"Well, we know her mind is still sound," he said with a glance at Garron. "You want to deal with him or her?"

"Him," Garron said.

It hurt. I didn't know why. It shouldn't have. Yet, it did.

And Daemon saw it.

"Aw, he doesn't mean it like that," Daemon said, coming to wrap an arm around my waist to support me in place of the tree. "He doubts I'll do the job as well as he can. And rightfully so, Lamb. If you haven't noticed, I tend not to put a lot of effort into things."

He began walking me out of the trees, and I glanced back at Garron. Our gazes met. He quickly looked down at the man.

"Garron," I called.

Daemon paused and turned us.

"Don't let the creatures eat him," I said. "My father is still out there."

Garron nodded, picked up the man's foot, and started dragging him away. A man *twice* his size.

Frowning, I looked up at Daemon.

"I think I might be sick."

I promptly vomited at our feet.

CHAPTER 8

Daemon made consoling sounds and patted my back as I emptied my stomach. When I finished, he asked to carry me, but the ability to agree escaped me. Regardless, I found myself in his arms. He carried me to the well as if I weighed nothing.

"I'm afraid this is going to be cold, Lamb, but it can't be helped. The vomiting is worrisome." He emptied an entire bucket over my head. Then another and another. Gradually, I felt some of my sense returning.

"Enough," I said. "I will drown at this rate."

Shivering, I wrapped my arms around myself as he ran his fingers through my hair to feel my scalp. I winced when he found the tender spot.

"There's the culprit," he said softly. "Stay here. I'll be right back." He ran toward the cottage and returned a few breaths later with one of my blankets.

"If I hold this up, would you trust me enough to remove the shift? I'll wrap you in the blanket without looking. You'll warm faster without it."

I nodded and lifted my hand to tug the neckline loose.

"Wait," Daemon said. He tucked the blanket under his arm

and took one of my hands in his. I saw the blood through the wrap.

"Brandle is not going to be pleased."

"Then don't tell him."

Daemon looked up at me with a small smile. "We tell each other everything, Kellen. Always. For our safety. Let's unwrap it and reapply the honey first. He left it out, not wanting to chance that your hands might pain you while he's gone."

Daemon left me again for the honey. While he was inside, Garron returned. The moment he spotted me, his steps slowed. I shivered and slowly sank to a crouch under his watchful gaze.

"You need to teach your brothers that caution," I said.

He looked down for a moment then quickly closed the distance between us and gently tugged me to my feet.

"You are freezing. Why are you wet?"

"I vomited from the blow to my head. The cold water helped rouse me and settled my stomach. Daemon is getting honey for my hands."

I lifted them to show the bloody wraps.

"Brandle is not going to be pleased."

"Yes, so I've heard. Be sure to tell him it wasn't my idea to be abused yet again."

"I've ensured the tracker won't return for you to suffer a third time."

Garron began unwrapping my hands. He didn't meet my gaze. Not once. So I stopped watching him and focused on his hands. The knuckles were cracked and bleeding, proof of his methods to ensure the tracker left.

"It appears you need some attention too."

Garron's head jerked up. Our gazes locked briefly. He looked shocked.

"Brandle didn't say the honey was only for me, did he? I vow I have no intention of being hurt further. Each time delays when I might finally leave this place."

He dropped his gaze back to my hands.

"The tracker was staying not far from here, using a fire to keep the creatures at bay and a torch to approach our glade. Such a thing won't work for long. Perhaps it's why the beasts are lingering." He tossed aside the first wrap. "I find it peculiar you still wish to leave after learning the tracker waited for you. I believe he had no intention of leaving without you and that you know why."

"I have my suspicions, but I dare not speak them. Regardless, his presence doesn't change my desire to reunite with my sister."

He nodded and tossed the other wrap aside just as Daemon rounded the cottage.

"My poor lamb, look at you shiver," Daemon said. "Garron, hold this blanket while I help her undress."

Garron went to cuff him, but Daemon dodged with a laugh.

"I jest, brother. I'll hold the blanket, and you help her with the tie of her shift. We both know you won't look."

"And you would?" I asked.

"I've been looking since I soaked your shift, Lamb." He lifted the blanket high as my eyes rounded, and I looked down at myself. I could see every detail. My nipples. My belly button. My nether hair.

Heat flooded my cheeks as I looked at Garron. He had his head turned to the side.

"Do you need my assistance?" he asked.

I realized he truly hadn't been looking at anything but my hands or face the entire time.

"I do," I said. "If you could untie the neckline then close your eyes and help me lift it off. I'm too cold, and my fingers refuse to move."

He nodded and did as I asked. Once the shift was off, he turned around and ducked behind the blanket.

"She's ready," I heard him say softly.

"Come, Lamb," Daemon said, wrapping the blanket around

me. It pinned my arms, which I didn't care for, but then he lifted me and sat on the edge of the well with me on his lap. He rubbed my arms through the blanket, attempting to warm me.

"Her feet, Garron," he said. "Check for cuts."

I realized I'd lost both boots at some point, and my feet were so cold I barely felt Garron's touch.

"It's a shame I was the one to hold the blanket, or it would be me washing your feet now," Daemon said softly. "Garron's too shy to look at your pretty ankles."

"Stop attempting to provoke her, Daemon," Garron warned.

Daemon chuckled and held me tighter.

"But Edmund's temper heats him so well."

"It would not benefit you to see me angry," I said.

Daemon hummed a non-answer.

"Her feet are clean and dry. Let me fetch a spare pair of stockings."

"Wait," Daemon said, standing. "Hold her for a moment."

I found myself in Garron's arms as Daemon strode away from us.

"Stay by the well," he called over his shoulder.

"Trouble," I said under my breath.

"Undoubtedly," Garron said, staring after his brother.

I studied Garron's face. He had a scrape on his jaw, which would make shaving uncomfortable. And the corner of his eye was red. It would likely bruise tomorrow. But not a bit of strain showed in his expression.

"Am I not heavy?"

He shook his head, not looking at me. Another hard shiver rocked through me, and I felt his arms tighten around me.

"I'm sorry I stumbled upon your glade. While it saved me, my presence has brought discord and hardship."

"I will not help you leave. So do not ask."

"I won't," I said. "Yet."

Tired and cold, I let my head rest on his broad shoulder.

"Where you see hardship, Kellen, we see hope. And any discord you've noted was there before you appeared. Daemon chooses to sleep rather than acknowledge our reality. Edmund believes his anger will protect him. Eadric purposely overlooks life's hardships and many other things. Darian embraced our fates early on and sees nothing wrong with any of it. Brandle worries for us all, which stifles Liam as the youngest. And I keep my thoughts to myself too often."

"Except now."

He smiled slightly.

"Except now," he said in agreement.

Daemon came jogging around the side of the cottage.

"Everything is ready. I'll take her."

Garron's hold on me tightened briefly before Daemon reached us. Daemon grinned at me as he took me back from his brother.

"Worry not, Lamb. You'll be warm faster in two shakes of your beautiful tail."

His head jerked forward, and I looked over his shoulder at Garron, who was scowling at him.

"You hit each other a lot," I said.

Garron's gaze shifted briefly to me, and a flush slowly tinted his cheeks.

"It's a love tap, nothing more," Daemon said, reclaiming my attention.

We rounded the side of the cottage, and I saw a mattress piled with blankets on top of the table. The nearby fire danced with flames as high as my knees.

It would have been smarter to use the hearth inside, but I was too cold to argue.

Daemon carried me to the table and waited for Garron to pick up the blankets. Rather than place me on the mattress, he stepped up onto the bench and lay down with me, arranging me so I lay facing him.

"Cover us up, Garron," he said, pulling me close so I was pressed against his chest. "And put a few stones by our feet as soon as they're warm."

"No." I stared into Daemon's eyes.

He grinned at me. "Ah, my little lamb, I wish this were for indecent purposes."

Garron pivoted and flicked Daemon's ear.

Daemon chuckled as Garron clarified, "This is the quickest way we know to warm you."

Another shiver racked through me, and I closed my eyes.

"None of that," Daemon said. "Keep looking at me. If you sleep, how will you know your virtue is safe?"

"Garron will keep it safe," I mumbled.

"Not if you close your eyes," Garron said.

Frowning, I opened them to watch Garron. He stood near the fire, staring down at the flames.

"You don't mean that," I said.

"Can you be sure? Stay awake, Lamb," Daemon said.

"Why Lamb?"

His grin widened. "You're rather adorable and obviously need our care. Just like a little lamb."

Daemon was odd. All the brothers were. And I found I didn't mind it. Or them. They were all so beautiful to look at. I found myself staring at Daemon's twinkling eyes and smiling mouth and quickly looked away.

Garron bent down near the fire, disappearing from sight for a moment before standing with a bundle of cloth.

"The stones are hot," he said.

He tucked the bundle under the blankets near our feet. Daemon's hand found my arm trapped under the blanket, and he began to rub it briskly.

"How does your head feel?" he asked.

"It doesn't ache yet."

"And your stomach."

"Settled. For now."

"The water helped then. I don't like the blue tint to your lips, though. Tell me if your head or your stomach begins to ache as you warm."

It took a bit of snuggling against Daemon and several stone changes before the shivers stopped. As I warmed, it became harder to keep my eyes open. I yawned and moved a little closer to Daemon's warmth, which I could finally feel. The hand on my arm moved to wrap around my waist and press me against him.

Without thought, I tried to hold him in return. However, the blanket still trapped me.

"Ah, Lamb, it's better if you do not," Daemon said, understanding my intention. "Garron is watching us closely and will remove me from my place at even a hint of impropriety. And without that blanket separating us, our positions would become very improper."

"Garron said you were the tired one," I mumbled, letting my eyes close. "Stop speaking and go to sleep, Daemon."

He and Garron both chuckled. Neither told me I needed to open my eyes again, so I kept them closed and let myself sleep.

I couldn't be sure how long I stayed like that, warm and safely wrapped in his arms, but it was long enough that my growling stomach and a slight headache woke me. When I opened my eyes, Daemon was gone, and I had a clear view of the pot simmering over the fire. Brandle paused stirring it and looked over at me.

"Stew and biscuits," he said. "Are you hungry?"

"A little. My head aches." I lifted my hand to touch my temple where it hurt the most, but he moved quickly to catch my hand.

"You have a large lump there. It would be best not to touch it."

I nodded and started to sit up. He slid an arm around my back to help me. His hand touched bare skin, and I hesitated only briefly before sitting up and tugging the blanket higher around my shoulders.

"I've laid out your shift inside," he said. "Can you walk on your own?"

"Yes." Holding the blanket to me, I swung my legs over the side of the table. Plain slippers waited for my stockinged feet.

"Garron said you had a few small cuts on your feet," Brandle said, bending to slide the slippers on one foot first, then the other. "We found your boots, but between the cuts and your palms, slippers will be easier for you to put on for now. If your feet hurt, tell me. When you're finished, I'll put more honey on your hands."

I nodded, stood, and carefully made my way to the cottage while ignoring the rest, who watched.

Inside, my shift waited on the chair. It was dry and smelled faintly of wood smoke, which I didn't mind. It wasn't hard to ease it over my head. I didn't bother with the tie at my neck, though.

Covered and alone, I tentatively touched the lump on my head and thought of the man who'd tried to take me twice now.

Brandle and the others would have questions. Of that, I was certain. But what could I say? I refused to lie as Maeve had done to us. Yet, what truth could I tell without implicating her?

A knock sounded at the door.

"Are you well, Lamb?" Daemon asked.

"I'm well enough," I said. "You can open the door."

They were all waiting just beyond the threshold.

"Who in the hell is that man, and why is he determined to take you?" Edmund demanded.

"I would prefer you not hit each other," I said before Brandle could cuff him for swearing. "I understand how much it can hurt."

Garron reached out and flicked Edmund's ear, and a small smile tugged at my lips.

"This amuses you?" Edmund demanded, rubbing his ear.

"Very little does of late, but yes, seeing you get your ear

flicked for uttering a simple curse did bring me a moment of humor.

"You want answers I cannot truthfully give," I said, looking at Edmund. "However, I suspect someone hired the tracker to return me home." My gaze swept over them all, taking in their bruises and scrapes. "I'm sorry I cannot go with him. I know my presence here continues to bring you all hardships."

"We don't wish for you to leave with him," Brandle said. "We've witnessed his treatment of you. Your family should have had more care in choosing the man they sent after you."

"Do you believe a man of good standing virtue would have been willing to enter the forest for coin?" I asked. "I will take more care and stay close to the cottage and whoever remains with me until my hands are healed and I am able to leave."

Garron and Eadric glanced at Brandle.

"Yes, avoiding the edge of the clearing would be wise," he said. "Garron removed the tracker's remaining supplies as well. We hope he'll not remain much longer."

"Thank you," I said to Garron.

"Come," Brandle said. "The stew is ready."

I thought it odd that was the end of their questioning and glanced at Edmund. He watched me with a frown. Darian, who stood beside him, slung his arm around Edmund's shoulders.

"You looked quite comfortable sleeping on the table," Darian said. "Perhaps you'd like to sleep there again tonight."

Edmund only scowled harder and elbowed Darian in the side.

Eadric stepped forward, blocking my view of the pair, and offered his arm. His good cheer had me accepting his escort with a small smile.

"Do the slippers fit?" he asked.

"They do. Where did you find them?"

"In Turre."

Three sets of hands whacked the back of his head. I stopped walking and scowled at the others.

"I already know you are able to go there. Why else do you believe I asked for your help?" I caught Eadric's face between my bandaged hands as he rubbed the back of his head. He stilled and stared at me.

"I cherish your honesty, but you cannot speak every truth that springs into your mind, Eadric. It's dangerous, and I know you're not that thoughtless."

His gaze held mine.

"I'll trade you," he said.

"Trade? For what?"

"One useful thing for a kiss."

Had it been any of the others, I would have retreated into the cottage. However, the glint in Eadric's eyes wasn't lecherous. It was mischievous.

"And why do you want a kiss?"

His smile bloomed brighter than any summer blossom.

"Winning your kiss before any of the rest will prove I'm not as simple as they believe."

"You are clever indeed." I leaned in and brushed my lips against his cheek. "Payment for confirming what I already guessed." I switched to the other cheek and kissed that one as well. "And advance payment for feeding me my dinner."

Eadric smirked as he guided me to the table under his brothers' watchful scowls. To my amusement, he made soft cooing noises as he fed me and wiped the corner of my mouth with his thumb often. I felt cared for and loved in a way that I hadn't felt in a long while. And I liked it.

"You eat like a baby sparrow," he said. "I don't ever want to stop feeding you."

"If you don't, I will surely burst," I said with a laugh.

Everyone at the table stopped eating to stare at me, and I cleared my throat to cover my slip.

"Excuse me." I rose and moved to leave the table.

"Sit, Kellen," Brandle said. "It will be inconvenient to chase after you to apply the honey."

How could such a simple phrase make me bristle? *It wasn't the words but the man who delivered them*, I acknowledged to myself. Brandle-the-worrier provoked me more than Edmund but for an entirely different reason. It was the way he watched me with knowing patience.

I moved toward the fire and sat on the short stool near it. The heat from the embers warmed me, and I felt my skin prickle. A moment later, a blanket wrapped around my shoulders, and I looked up at Liam.

"If you fall ill on top of your existing injuries, Brandle will never let you out of his sight again," Liam said. He slipped his hand under my hair to pull it free of the blanket, and his fingers caressed the back of my neck in the process. I shivered and faced the fire again.

"How long will it take my hands to heal?" I asked without looking at any of them.

"Seven days," Brandle said.

Seven days of their focused attention? I would never last.

"I am a danger to you all," I said. "Edmund saw me for what I was the moment I entered this glade. Don't become complacent. You have already been hurt due to me."

"And what are you?" Edmund asked, standing menacingly.

"Trouble," I said.

He snorted. From the corner of my eye, I saw Garron grab Edmund's shoulder and force him to sit again.

"You don't need to fear us," Brandle said.

"I've already told you. I don't fear you, Brandle. I fear *for* you."

"Liar," he said without malice as he stood. He crouched beside me and set the honey pot on the ground. "Give me your hand."

I hesitated, and the damn man saw it because he chuckled and said, "You have nothing to fear from me, Kitten."

"Kitten?" I echoed, not believing he'd referred to me so.

"You only accept affection on your terms, and you tear things apart when you're unhappy with your circumstance. Do you disagree?"

I turned my head toward the flames again. "Just apply the damn honey, Brandle."

Darian hooted with laughter, and a few of his brothers joined him as Brandle picked up the pot and started applying the mixture to my extended hand. His fingers trailed over my skin as he bound my palms. I knew he was purposely trying to provoke me, so I ignored him and focused on counting embers.

When he finished the second hand, he caught me off guard by kissing my fingertips.

My gaze flew to his.

"We haven't been hurt because of you," he said. "And caring for you isn't a hardship. Before you came, we had very little to look forward to each day."

I tugged my hand free and stood. He remained where he was as I entered the cottage and closed the door on them all.

Silently cursing my damaged hands and the events that brought me to this glade, I paced the small space and struggled to quell the emotions threatening to emerge.

"You will not feel," I whispered to myself. "Think of Eloise. Think of Mother and Father and of home. You are stronger than this."

When I pivoted, I saw Edmund watching me through the far window. I stopped moving and stared at him. He, more than the rest, understood what I wanted to feel. The rage. The frustration. The all-consuming need for revenge.

I inhaled deeply and exhaled slowly. I dropped my shoulders, releasing the tension in them.

Lifting a finger, I traced between my brows and smoothed away all visual traces of my upset. He watched me through it all and tilted his head as he studied my outward calm.

Then he walked away.

CHAPTER 9

I SAT IN A CHAIR AND CONTENTED MYSELF WITH STARING AT THE cold hearth as I recalled better times.

A knock on the door some time later roused me from my wandering thoughts. The sun had set, and Garron waited outside when I opened the door.

"We have your bed ready," he said.

Behind him, the mattress rested on the table.

With spring fighting for its hold, one's breath was easily visible once the sun set. I didn't understand how they managed to sleep outside. Perhaps they were accustomed to it. I was not.

"It's warmer to sleep inside," I said.

"It's easier for us to watch over you out here. We can't all fit inside."

"I don't need watching inside."

"You have a lump on your head," Brandle said from one of the hanging beds. "You need watching."

I turned to go back inside. Garron surprised me by scooping me into his arms.

"If you wish to leave, you need to heal. If you want to heal quickly, you should listen to Brandle's advice," he said as he strode to the table and set me down again.

"I need rest to heal," I said. "And I won't find it out here. Without Daemon, the sun, and heated rocks, I wouldn't have rested comfortably previously."

A flurry of movement came from the hanging beds, and I turned to see Daemon and Darian drop from theirs. Darian grabbed for Daemon, tripping him and shoving him to the ground so he could race to me.

"I'll do it," Darian said. "I'll warm you tonight."

Daemon snorted and rose to his feet as he brushed himself off. He obviously had the same doubts as I did.

"When did I give you the impression that I was simple or naïve?" I asked.

Darian chuckled. The low sound wrapped around me.

"Ah, Princess, you cut me to the quick. Allow me the night to bask in your presence. I vow to be the most honorable of men."

"It's best to agree," Eadric said from his hanging bed. "He won't let any of us sleep until you do, and we're all here to ensure he keeps his word."

"No," I said. "I will not sleep beside you, Darian, simply because you wish it. Go away."

I strode past the pair of men and slid my slippers from my feet before climbing into the bed on the table.

"You are all impossibly obstinate." I pulled the cover over my head and closed my eyes, determined to sleep before I noticed the night's chill.

"Insufferable," I added from under my blanket. "Fretting mother hens."

"Go to sleep, Kitten," I heard Brandle call.

"Ass."

Several of them laughed.

"Your temper is showing, Trouble," Edmund said.

Realizing he was right, I took a deep breath and let it out slowly. Then another. And another.

Curled in a tight ball, I shivered, half-aware but mostly asleep as I drifted in frozen misery. An arm settled on my waist. Heat warmed my back, beckoning me. I inched toward it until my icy backside connected with strong thighs through my shift.

"She's too cold."

I agreed with the assessment.

Warmth enveloped my front, and I pressed my nose to it.

"Damn. She's like ice. Should we wake her?"

"Let her sleep," another said as hands captured my feet and tugged my legs straight. The two bodies on either side pressed close as warm fingers massaged heat into my toes.

Exhaling contentedly, I sank deeper into sleep.

"Wake her and die."

The words were softly spoken, no more than a whisper. But the sincere threat in them wormed its way into my consciousness. I became aware of several things. The warmth surrounding me. How one of my legs rested quite comfortably over someone else's. The hand that rested on my thigh. The way my cheek rested on a shirt-covered, muscled chest. The arm over my waist, anchoring my back to someone else's chest.

I opened my eyes and lifted my head to look down at Darian. His heavy-lidded gaze and the way his fingers started moving on my bare leg pierced me with panic.

"What happened to behaving honorably?" I asked.

"How have I behaved dishonorably?" he asked. "You sought my warmth, and I allowed it without touching you as I wished."

I reached down, removing his hand from my leg so I could straighten. When my fingers brushed his thigh, his gaze heated. The desire turned to surprise in an instant when I pinched the inside of his thigh. He scrambled out of the covers with a muttered curse.

"That felt like a damn bee sting, Princess," he said, rubbing the spot.

A low, soft chuckle sounded near my ear, and I twisted to look back at Daemon.

He grinned. "Good morning, Lamb."

Suppressing the urge to pinch him, too, I got out of bed, donned my slippers, and made my way to the privy. By the time I returned, the mattress was gone and the table set for breakfast. I walked right up to Brandle and held his gaze.

"What do you see?" I asked.

He studied me. "A beautiful woman," he said.

I struggled not to make a face. "Are my pupils irregularly dilated?"

"They are the same size."

I took his hand and touched his fingers to the lump on my head. "The swelling is down, do you agree?"

A wariness crept into his gaze. "It is."

"It is still tender to the touch, but my head does not ache. There is no reason for me to sleep outside tonight."

"I see."

"As do I. Six more days, Brandle."

Rather than eat breakfast, I closed myself in the cottage.

My hands trembled as I went to the wash water. Waking up pressed between Daemon and Darian had been undeniably lovely. I could still feel them—Darian partially under me and Daemon pressed against me—and wanted it back. Badly.

Scooping up the cold water, I washed my flushed face.

Think of Eloise, I reminded myself.

After washing, I unwrapped my raw palms, which had been aching since the moment I opened my eyes. The pain wasn't as consuming as the previous day, though, which was a promising sign.

I left the wraps by the washbowl and opened the door, startling Eadric just outside.

"Are you hungry, Sparrow?" he asked.

Ignoring him, I went to the table and sat in front of the single bowl that remained. I could hear voices from the side of the cottage and surmised one or more of the men were washing their breakfast dishes.

Eadric wandered closer as I fed myself. Moving my hands hurt. The air stung the exposed skin. So I ate quickly, shoveling in the meal in a very unbecoming manner. Eloise would have laughed at the show if I hadn't been in pain. But my twin would have known my pain and silently shared my misery. That's how it felt when Eadric sat across from me with a sad expression. He didn't say anything or offer to help. He understood. Just like Eloise would have. My nose started to tingle.

"Fetch the honey and wraps, please," I said.

He glanced behind me. I followed his gaze and saw Brandle holding both.

"Leave them on the table. I'm wise enough not to eat the honey and, as you can see, can use my hands well enough to apply it."

"Why is it so difficult for you to accept our help?" he asked, surrendering nothing.

"It's not difficult at all. I welcome your help. Tell me...what is Turre like? Would I be better served arriving in a dress or disguised as a man?"

Brandle looked down at his hands.

"It is not that I do not accept help," I said. "It is that you are unwilling to truly give it. Whatever scheme is dwelling in your mind, know that I have no desire to partake in it. My priority remains with my sister and my father. I suggest you not attempt to manipulate me any further. I vow the result will not endear me to any of you."

He lifted his gaze to me. "Is that why you're angry? You thought we were attempting to manipulate you? You were cold, Kellen. Daemon and Darian warmed you the same way Daemon had previously. They did not touch you. You touched them. You pulled Daemon's arm around you and pressed yourself against Darian."

I closed my eyes and fisted my hands, using the pain to keep the torrent of emotions at bay, for I knew he spoke true.

"Then, I apologize and beg forgiveness for my behavior," I said.

Fingers brushed my cheek, and my eyes flew open to look up at Brandle. His heated gaze and the way my pulse sped in response terrified me.

"Please leave the honey and wraps. I can care for myself," I said steadily.

"If not me, then allow Eadric to assist you."

"No."

"Stubborn."

"It's not the first time I've been called that, nor the worst I've been called. I find it sad that holding my ground on what is important to me is viewed as unbecoming; yet, when a man holds to his ideals, he is noble and upright. Think of me as you will. It matters not to me, Brandle. But your insistence to tend to me will not result in me consenting to your help. I will gladly endure without."

He held my gaze for a long moment then put the honey and the wraps on the table.

"We've never been to Drisdall," he said. "So I'm unable to compare Turre to it to help you understand what you will find."

He sat beside me. "Turre is a beautiful kingdom with rocky hills perfect for sheep and goats and the like."

"What of Adele?" I asked, uncovering the honey and smearing a modest amount on my palm. The relief was instant.

"It's known as the most beautiful city in all the kingdoms due to the white spires of the royal family's castle."

I started wrapping the palm. "I'm sure it is lovely. However, I don't care about the beauty of the castle or what grows there. What of the people? Do they welcome strangers? Will I be met with suspicion?"

"The people fear everything," Eadric said. "The current queen has subjugated them for over a decade. Her guards patrol the streets day and night, stopping those who move about to ask their business and inquire where they live."

"The people are taxed heavily. Any attempts at revolt have been met with immediate, unquestioned death," Brandle said. "Adele is beautiful on the outside but rotten to its core on the inside, and the people are so repressed they are more likely to turn you into the Guard for being a stranger than help you."

"I see," I said. "How are you able to trade there?"

"We have a small network of trusted people. However, each time we trade with them, we risk their lives."

I sighed and lifted my hand to Brandle. He tucked the end of the wrap into place without comment and watched me smear honey on my other palm.

"I refuse to risk one life to save another," I said, my thoughts churning. "Are casters like trackers? Can a person hire their services?"

"Casters are exactly like trackers. The upstanding ones would be unlikely to follow you into the forest."

I kept my gaze on the wrap I wound around my palm. When I finished, I lifted it to Brandle for him to secure. Then, I stood without another word and retreated to the cottage.

From the corner of my eye, I saw all the brothers off to the side.

They'd been listening. Now they knew I understood that I would never find the help I needed in Adele.

"You need to eat," Daemon said from the doorway.

"Do I?" I asked absently, staring at the hearth.

In the hours since breakfast, I hadn't yet thought of a solution to my problem. I needed a caster to break my father's curse. If he were too far gone to be saved, I would still need a caster's help to remove Maeve from her position of power. I dreaded that option, though.

"Lamb, please come out and eat."

According to the books in our attic, each caster's abilities varied. Some were stronger than others. I had no idea how strong Maeve was to know what level of caster to hire. The stronger the caster, the more their services would cost. I had very little coin, only an old letter from the king promising help should my family ever need it. Would that be enough to convince a caster of future payment when I wasn't certain that the crown would willingly pay whatever debt I incurred? And even if it were, could I trust any caster I hired if they were willing to traverse the forest?

The safest option was to free Father from his curse. He had the right to remove Maeve, magic or not. He could use the letter, go to the king, and ask for his help removing her. In the course of her removal, she would either give herself away or leave peacefully. Once she was gone, we could all leave. Perhaps Eloise and I could travel with Father and learn about trade.

But how could I free Father without a caster's help?

I stood abruptly and went to the door, interrupting a hushed conversation by the fire as I swept past them.

"Trouble, you forgot your slippers," Edmund called.

As if I cared about slippers or dirty stockings. My hope to save my sister was crumbling with each hour that passed.

Arms closed around my waist before I could reach the trees.

"Kellen, please," Brandle said.

Anger boiled up within me, and I twisted in his arms.

"Release me or suffer," I said.

"Release you to do what? Walk into the woods so either the tracker or the creatures can capture you?"

"As we've already discussed, my death serves no purpose. Now release me."

He reluctantly did so and followed me all the way to the trees.

"Father," I called. "Are you still with me?"

A hand settled on my shoulder and squeezed it lightly.

"If he is not, we are," Brandle said.

I turned and saw all of them standing behind me.

Edmund didn't look as angry as he previously had, and it sent a spike of fear through me. Was he masking as I'd shown him, or was he starting to accept my presence here too?

"Are you ready to learn something?" he asked.

The hope that had been withering bloomed a little.

"Yes."

He nodded his head for me to follow and started for the dirt patch in the center of the yard. I readily trailed behind him, aware that the rest were doing the same. When he reached the center, he looked at me.

"I'll be you. Pick who should attack me."

"Pardon?"

"You've been pulled from the clearing, twice, from behind. Brandle could have easily done the same just now. You should learn how to free yourself if it ever happens again. You can't practice yet, but you can watch. Now, who would you like to see me beat?"

"I would prefer not to choose," I said, even though Brandle's name rose to my mind.

Edmund grinned for the first time. "Brandle then."

I didn't argue and watched Brandle approach Edmund and wrap his arms around his brother's middle. Time after time, Brandle landed on the ground in so many ways. Edmund flipped him over his head once, which the others said I would never be able to manage. It led to a discussion about my strength and how to improve it once I was healed.

"Why does she need to be strong when she has us?" Liam asked at one point.

That stopped the debate on what activities would help me gain strength. Even if their plans meant waiting until my palms would be healed, I was grateful I wouldn't need to chop wood.

The most approved method for me to break an attacker's hold was a pinch to a thigh, if I could manage it. Darian promised it was effective. The next most effective way was to twist and drop from my attacker's arms. It looked a little complicated and would likely only work once on an attacker, but it was something.

At some point during the demonstration, Eadric had appeared beside me and fed me bites of a cold stew. I didn't realize I was eating until he asked if I wanted more.

"No, thank you."

He smiled at me, and it seemed to signal the end of the demonstration.

"Why are you all here today?" I asked.

"In four days, you've been attacked twice and tried to run into the forest once," Edmund said. "Why do you think we're here?"

"What are you not doing by being here?" I asked.

No one answered.

"Keep your secrets. The less I know, the better," I said, starting for the cottage.

Darian caught my arm. "Why?"

"Brandle knows," I said, twisting my arm free.

"If you don't care, you'll be able to leave without guilt," Brandle said.

"Precisely. Leave dinner at the door. I will feed myself."

I didn't know why they were attempting to win my affection and feared learning the reason. However, acknowledging the game they played did not stop their attempts to draw me closer.

Liam arrived at the door first to ask my advice for mending a stocking. But the light was better outside, of course, which meant I needed to join them around the table. I declined and said summer would be upon us soon as he would appreciate the extra air on his feet.

Edmund knocked and asked if I wanted more demonstrations. It tempted me, but I said I would prefer to wait until I could participate.

Eadric asked if I wanted some fresh water. I did pass the pitcher to him simply because he understood not to press for more. He returned it full and left me alone.

Daemon asked if I was tired and wished to nap in one of their swinging beds. I declined.

Darian asked if my feet hurt and needed some honey or his tender touch. I snorted and closed the door in his face.

Brandle knocked just before dinner.

I arched a brow at him and leaned against the doorframe, curious what paltry excuse he might offer to lure me from the cottage.

"I believe your father has sent proof that he's still as much of himself as he can be."

I straightened from the door. "How so?"

He motioned for me to follow and led me to the table where several rabbits and some fowl lay discernibly dead but otherwise unmarred.

"They were tossed into the clearing with their necks broken."

"Could it have been the tracker?" I asked.

"Doubtful. He has no supplies for himself and no reason to

feed us. And they were tossed from the west, where the shadows are already deepest."

"It is wisest not to make any assumptions," I said. "I would like to believe it's my father, but it seems unlikely that he would maintain his humanity when others have not."

"A few have," Eadric said. "It doesn't make them safe, just smarter than the rest."

I fought the need to wrap my arms around myself by closing my eyes and tipping my head back to the darkening sky. How did this information help me? Did it mean my father would never return to himself? I wouldn't know the answer to that until I found a knowledgeable caster. And therein lay the crux of the problem. I still had no way to approach Adele without risking another's life.

"Would you like me to re-braid your hair?"

The unexpected question had me twisting to look at Eadric.

"You went to sleep with wet hair, and it's only tangled more after last night. I wanted to offer my nimble-fingered services this morning, but after you pinched Darian, I thought it wise to remain silent."

"Why did you change your mind?"

"I thought it might help soothe you. It's a soothing memory for me when Henry used to brush our hair."

Edmund snorted. "He was checking for lice, dolt."

Eadric shrugged and flashed his boyish smile at me.

"I could use some soothing," I admitted. "Thank you."

He beamed and told Edmund to fetch the comb and Daemon to clean the game around back. Then he offered his hand to help me sit at the table. I took it. His warm fingers wrapped around mine, and before I considered the consequences, I stepped close and rested my head against his shoulder.

Reckless.

Dangerous.

Step away.

It mattered little what I knew to be the truth or what I told myself. The loneliness I'd felt as I'd stared up at my bedroom window for the last time could no longer be denied.

Exhaling heavily, I closed my eyes, released his hand, and circled my arms around his waist. He ran a hand over my hair, comforting me more than I'd been comforted since mother passed.

"The future is meant to be uncertain, Sparrow," he said softly. "Don't let the fear of that rob you of living in the present."

The others might have thought Eadric a fool simply because his kindness and good nature blinded them to his insight. But I knew better. He was insightfully caring and smart enough to remain silent or silly to put others at ease. And I liked him greatly for those qualities.

"I rather dislike the present," I admitted. "Nothing good has happened."

"Ah, you mean nothing good happened in the past. The present is now. You holding me as you generously allow me to comb and re-braid your hair is pleasant, isn't it?"

"Careful, Eadric. You almost sounded like Brandle and Darian."

"How so?"

"Obnoxiously perceptive and immodestly flirtatious."

Someone snorted nearby.

"How unthoughtful of me."

I pressed my face into his neck to hide my smile, but I knew he felt it when he chuckled. Knowing it was time, I composed myself and retreated. He didn't stop me.

"Feeling better?" he asked.

"I am. Thank you."

"Whenever you need another, I am here to serve."

"The rest of us are willing to line up and continue with these soothing hugs," Darian said from nearby. "I'll go first."

"Would you like another pinch?" I asked.

He scratched his jaw as he considered the question.

"It wasn't an offer," I said.

"I've already told you I'll accept any touch you're willing to give."

"I'll teach you how to throw a punch tomorrow," Edmund said.

I couldn't stop my smile.

"You're all ridiculous."

CHAPTER 10

"Dinner is almost ready," Brandle said. "Sit. Let Eadric try his hands at fixing your hair. He hasn't braided anything in years."

While the stew simmered, Eadric very patiently worked the tangles from my hair. He didn't pull my scalp once as he clumsily attempted a braid. The others watched him closely, poking at his efforts with good-natured comments.

"Please, Princess, I beg you. Let me have a go. I cannot allow you to walk around like that. You look…recently bedded."

I could hear a scuffle behind me.

"He's right that it doesn't look neat," Eadric said. "I apologize."

I patted his hand and caught Liam's expression. It was a mixture of sadness and curiosity, and Brandle's words rang in my head. Before I'd arrived, they'd had nothing to look forward to each day. Could braiding my hair truly be that exciting?

"Liam," I said, holding out the comb. "Let's see if you can do better."

His face lit with anticipation, and Daemon good-naturedly patted his shoulder as he moved toward me. With the hope glinting in all their gazes, I knew they would each want a turn.

Liam's braid wasn't much improved. Garron spent more time combing my hair than attempting to weave it. Edmund waved away his turn. Daemon grinned and elbowed Darian when I called him over for his turn.

"The last thing I braided was rope," he said, smoothing the comb through my hair. "The stiff coarseness helped it stay where I placed it. Your hair slides everywhere."

"Is that why you're running it through your fingers?" Brandle asked.

I could feel Daemon's fingers gently stroking my hair, lending truth to Brandle's words.

"Focus, Daemon," I said.

"Let's have a wager," Darian said. "Whoever provides the tightest braid will be the one to help with our Princess's hair until her hands are better."

"No, thank you," I said.

"Come now, Princess," Darian coaxed.

"I see no advantage to me to allow any of you those liberties."

"While the winner grooms your hair, we will each tell you one thing we've observed in Adele," Brandle said.

Curse the man for offering something I couldn't refuse.

"Each one of you?" I asked, looking at Edmund. He held my gaze and nodded once.

I considered him. His hands were relaxed, and his expression was neutral. Even his eyes were clear.

"So be it," I said.

Daemon stopped playing with my hair and attempted his braid. It was better than the others, but still not very tight.

Darian took the comb from him and unwound the strands. His fingers nimbly twisted the sections while managing to caress my skin often. I reached back to feel the braid and found it to be the best so far.

"I sincerely hope you can braid better, Brandle," I said. "Or my neck will be accosted by Darian's fingers every morning."

Darian tugged my braid from my hold.

"Accosted? You wound me deeply, Princess. I was but checking for a fever."

Brandle snorted and nudged his brother aside.

"I vow not to disappoint you. I've had years more practice."

"You braid women's hair regularly?" I asked. "Perhaps I will be safer with Darian."

Several of the others sniggered.

Brandle said nothing as he deftly braided my hair without caressing my neck. The end result was the same as Darian's.

"I declare you the winner, then," I said.

"I did just as well," Darian said.

"Brandle kept his hands to himself, which places him ahead."

Darian opened his mouth to argue more, but Edmund cut him off.

"I haven't had my chance."

"You?" Liam said, sounding surprised.

I turned to look at Edmund again.

"Is this how you plan to vent your anger then? Tug my hair? Meaner boys than you have already done so, and I've survived. By my leave, do your best."

I faced the table again and waited. He didn't comb my hair first but re-braided it quickly and snuggly in a braid as tight as any I could make.

Darian groaned. "How?"

"Where you played with my hair and worried about tugging the strands, Edmund did not," I said.

"And he didn't hurt me," I quickly added when Garron shot him a dark look. "Now let's eat."

The stew was delicious and tender. As were the biscuits. When everyone finished, Edmund and Garron carried the dishes away to wash, and Liam and Eadric appeared from around back with my mattress, which had been missing since I'd left it this morning.

"Thank you," I said.

However, instead of carrying it inside, they set it on the table.

"No," I said.

"Yes," Brandle said.

I looked at him sharply.

"Please," he added.

"Why?"

He stepped closer and lowered his voice. "He's at the edge of the clearing. I believe he will try one more time before giving up. But it's safer for us to watch over you out here than in there."

I held Brandle's gaze. "I sleep alone, then."

He nodded once.

I went to sit by the fire and contemplated the problem of the tracker as they quietly conversed during their preparation for bed. If the tracker returned to Maeve without me, what would happen to Eloise? What would happen to my twin if he didn't survive the forest?

Brandle sat next to me.

"Are you not tired?" he asked quietly.

"My thoughts are troubled. I worry for my sister and wonder what torment she will feel if the tracker does not return with news of me. Will she think I've perished like we believed my father had?"

Brandle leaned forward, bracing his arms on his knees as he stared into the flames.

"I hesitate to allow him to leave after seeing this place. I considered ensuring he couldn't. However, I had the same troubled thoughts as you. I see how much you care for your sister and don't wish any anguish upon her. Yet, I also have no wish for him to return to try again."

"In that, we agree," I said.

"Would you like to send a message with him?" he asked.

"No. My sister will know that I'm alive for now, and that is enough."

"Very well. We'll ensure he returns with vague news of you, then, and will say nothing on your behalf. You should rest while you're able. I believe our unwanted guest will not let the night pass quietly."

Without the warmth of the fire, I felt the night chill through my shift as I removed my slippers and got into my makeshift bed. I looked beyond the fire at the hanging beds and found seven sets of eyes on me.

"Sleep well, my fierce handmaidens," I said.

Eadric hooted with laughter as I closed my eyes and hid my amusement with my blanket.

IT FELT as if I'd only fallen asleep when I heard a scuffle near the back of the cottage.

"Stay as you are," Liam said softly near my head. "He believes we're sleeping and is attempting to subdue Garron during a visit to the privy. Keep your eyes closed and your hands under those blankets. We'll exhaust the herbed honey if you keep injuring them."

"Your mouth runs like a river," Daemon said. "Hush."

They quieted just as the sounds from the other side of the cottage stopped.

Someone patted my shoulder a breath before I heard a scuff of a boot against dirt nearby. The tracker was coming. But why? I hadn't gone quietly during either of the previous attempts. How did he think he would be able to leave these trees with me now? Did he believe I would sleep through my kidnapping?

"You dare step into our glade again?" Brandle said lowly. "This is our home, and we will defend it with our lives."

The sound of fists hitting flesh echoed around me.

I knew my handmaidens didn't wish for me to watch, but I

wanted to know what was happening. So I peeked through my lashes and saw Brandle fighting a man several heads taller than himself. He moved agilely, dodging blows and landing his own on the tracker's ribs in rapid succession.

The weak moonlight glinted off the metal in the tracker's hand, and I realized why Brandle was dodging blows so earnestly. The man had a knife.

My eyes went wide as Brandle swung upward, hitting the man under the jaw with enough force to snap his head back. The tracker staggered backward. Garron quickly got down on his hands and knees. The man tripped over him and landed hard on his back. Garron bounded to his feet and kicked the tracker in the sides with a level of violence I struggled to associate with the quiet man.

Liam flipped the blanket over my eyes.

"Enough, Garron," he said, no longer quiet.

"Let's remove him," I heard Brandle say. "He's unlikely to make another attempt now."

I tried to remove the blanket, but Liam tugged it back into place.

"I have no wish to be smothered," I said.

"Sorry, Lamb," Daemon said. "Garron was stuck and removed his shirt for Brandle to look. They need the firelight. If you wait a—"

I flipped back the blankets and sat up. Garron stood near the fire with his back to me. Brandle was bent forward as he examined Garron's side. Liam wasn't fast enough to stop me from getting out of bed and closing the distance between us.

"How deep is it?" I asked, coming around to look for myself.

The gash glistened wetly over Garron's ribs.

"Not deep," Brandle said. "The bone stopped it."

"Edmund, fetch the needle and thread Liam was trying to use earlier. Darian, get a fresh pail of water. Daemon, this fire needs to blaze," I said rapidly.

"It will take more than this cut to bring me low, Kellen," Garron said softly. "Please do not fret."

"Fret? I don't fret, Garron. I contemplate scenarios and react appropriately. The cut might not bring you low, but the resulting infection likely will. We need to clean and close the wound properly. From the looks of the scars already gracing your skin, not all your wounds have been."

"Here's the water," Daemon said.

"Get the tea kettle from inside. The water will boil faster in it."

They all moved to do as I said. Brandle heated the needle in the coals while the thread boiled in the water. Garron remained silent as I cleaned the wound. Brandle insisted on stitching it himself, though.

"I'd rather he curse me than you," he said when I tried to deny him.

So I held Garron's hand and rubbed my fingers over his skin to give what comfort I could.

"Think he let himself get stuck on purpose?"

The quiet whisper had me narrowing my eyes on the brothers watching. Each one gave me their most innocent expression.

"I know it was you, Daemon," I said. "I suggest you remain silent, or I'll ask Brandle to sew your mouth closed next."

"Yes, Lamb," he said contritely.

After closing the wound, Brandle snapped the thread off then carefully coiled a long strip of clean cloth around Garron's torso to cover his work.

"Finished." Brandle straightened away and clapped Garron lightly on the shoulder. Edmund thrust a clean shirt over his brother's head and helped him thread his arms through without lifting them too high on his injured side.

"Thank you," Garron said.

I reclaimed Garron's hand. "Come. You can't climb into your swinging bed while stitched together. You can lie with me."

He didn't argue as I led him to the bed. He started to bend to remove his boots.

"No. Not you." I looked at my hands.

"I'll help," Liam said. He removed Garron's boots and lent his arm to help his brother lay back without strain.

I moved to cover him, and Garron shook his head.

"*With* you, or I take my own bed. I won't steal yours."

I let out a sigh, crawled in beside him, and lay on my back to view the stars above. The table and mattress were barely wide enough to accommodate us side by side. It made sense that I'd half-lain on Darian the previous night.

"Never in my life had I thought I would ever sleep beside more than a single man," I said under my breath as Liam covered us.

Garron chuckled. "Never in my life did I think I would sleep beside anyone other than my brothers."

"Fair. Does your side hurt?"

"The sting of the blade lingers, but it is bearable."

"Should we apply some of the honey tincture?"

"No need."

I rolled toward him to study his profile. No pain showed in his expression.

"Will you be able to sleep?"

His lips twitched as he glanced at me. "Not if you keep speaking."

"I should have sewn you myself."

His teeth flashed in a smile, and he closed his eyes.

"I think I'll sleep well, Kellen. Goodnight."

"Does anyone want to stick me?" Darian asked from his swinging bed.

I closed my eyes and ignored the lot of them.

A few moments later, I felt Garron move beside me. His fingers lightly danced over my hair. Understanding he did so to distract himself, I let him be.

Slowly, he lulled me, and on the cusp of sleep, I moved closer and set my hand on his chest just over his heart.

"My life isn't worth yours, Garron. Never forget that."

I woke much like I had the day before, with my leg over another set of legs and my cheek pillowed on a heavily muscled chest. The difference, however, was in the absolute silence of the glade and Garron's steady, even breaths.

The logical side of me said I should quietly remove myself before he woke. The emotional side wanted me to remain as I was, and it provided many reasons to do so. Garron needed rest to heal. No one else was yet awake. They'd sacrificed sleep to keep me safe. I should let them all rest and remain as I was.

I knew I shouldn't stay. Yet, that softer, weaker side of me won.

Moving my cheek slightly, I nuzzled into Garron's warmth and reveled in the feeling of having someone strong and capable beside me. I moved my hand and realized it wasn't over his shirt but under it. My fingers trailed lightly over his left side, tracing his undamaged skin.

He caught my hand in his, stopping my exploration.

I lifted my head to look at him and found him awake and watching me, a flush coloring his cheeks. The apology I'd been about to utter evaporated. I gently tugged my hand free to touch my fingers to his forehead.

He caught my hand again.

"I'm fine, Kellen."

A nearby snort drew my attention to the brothers who were idling around the fire. Each one was watching us.

I tugged my hand free and removed myself from the bed. They said nothing as I put on my slippers and walked away.

When I reached the privy, I paused and looked at Eadric, who had followed to help me with the door.

His smile was slightly sad.

"Why did no one wake me?"

"You looked peaceful."

"I looked wanton, Eadric."

"We thought you looked pretty."

"And viewing a pretty woman makes you sad?"

He looked away for a moment, and I knew he was searching for the right words rather than scanning the trees as he appeared to be doing. When he looked at me, I saw the same thing in his gaze that I'd glimpsed in Brandle and Garron.

"Only you can make me this sad, Kellen. Though I've had the pleasure of knowing you a scant number of days, the idea of continuing our lives in this glade without you strikes me with deep sadness. For I know you mean to leave us."

Where the others had sent me running with their look of interest, I couldn't run from Eadric. Not with those heartfelt words lingering between us. So I stepped closer and placed my bandaged palm on his cheek.

"The thought of leaving this glade fills me with sadness, too," I admitted. "If I had a choice—"

I shook my head, denying the thought of how I would choose to stay if I could. What of my sister? My twin and other half?

I turned away, and he opened the door without comment regarding my sudden withdrawal.

When I emerged again, Brandle was there with the honey and fresh bandages.

"Do they hurt?" he asked.

"Mildly."

"We can wash them at the well and re-bandage them. Or, if you wish, we have a copper tub. You can bathe in the cottage, and we can bandage them after you're finished."

"A real bath?" I asked, hopeful.

He nodded once, watching me warily once more. Did he believe I would strike him for the suggestion? Never. The buckets Daemon had emptied over my head at the well made my scalp itchy, and their attempts at re-braiding my hair had only intensified the growing need to wash it.

"A real bath sounds lovely. Thank you, Brandle."

"It's ready for you, then."

Slightly surprised, I hurried around to the cottage and found the copper tub sitting in front of the lit hearth. A stool sat near it with a sliver of soap and a small stack of towels on top.

"Call out if you need anything," he said before shutting me in.

Someone had thoughtfully covered the windows with a light cloth so I had complete privacy. I stripped out of my shift and eased into the hot water with a sigh. Rather than enjoy the heat idly, I reached back and carefully unwound my braid before ducking under the water.

My hands protested as I curled my fingers to scrub at my scalp, and I reemerged with a wince. I stared at the soaked wraps and debated the wisdom of attempting to soap my hair.

Frustrated, I watched the wisps of steam swirl up from the water. Such a waste. While I slept, they'd hauled water and boiled it. They likely also ensured it wasn't too hot and set out everything I could need.

I hit the water with a splash that made my palm throb and my skin tingle dangerously.

"Kellen? Are you all right?" Brandle asked.

After a few focused breaths, I admitted the truth.

"I'm struggling with frustration over my limitations and am debating the wisdom of washing my hair. I think it will only set back my healing. You wasted your efforts, and I am sincerely sorry for that."

"Cover yourself with a towel. Edmund will come in to assist."

"What?" I turned to look at the door in disbelief. "No. Do not—"

The door started to open, and I scrambled forward to grab a towel to cover myself.

"For the sake of both our sanities, do not turn around, Kellen," Edmund said.

"For the sake of mine, please leave."

"Would you prefer another?"

"I would prefer myself, you dolt."

He chuckled slightly. "I think that's the first time I heard you raise your voice."

Curse the man; he was right.

His hands closed over my hair, lifting it away from my bare back as I clutched the cloth to my chest.

"Lean back and sit lower in the water so your head hangs over the edge. I have another bucket to catch the rinse water. Keep your eyes closed."

I made a face and did as he asked, preferring not to know how he was looking at me. His hands felt huge on my head as he briskly worked the soap into my scalp. His ministrations and the hot water slowly drew the tension from my body. He rinsed my hair with scoops of water from another bucket, which had already begun to cool.

"I think I removed all the soap. You may want to dunk under again, though."

"Thank you, Edmund," I said.

I didn't hear him move closer and was startled when his next words were spoken close to my ear.

"Eadric told us what you said. If you leave, don't ever come back. They would never survive a second abandonment."

My heart beat heavily as his footfalls retreated, and the door closed. I dunked under the water as his words echoed in my head.

Abandonment. Is that how they viewed my leaving? That I

was abandoning them? They didn't know me, nor did I know them. They hadn't welcomed my arrival but now would mourn my departure? It made little sense.

Yet, I felt the same about leaving them.

It was no longer something I looked forward to doing.

CHAPTER 11

I STAYED IN THE WATER UNTIL IT LOST THE REMAINDER OF ITS HEAT, then dried and redressed myself.

When I left the cottage, I saw Brandle waiting by the table. Eadric stirred the pot over the fire. Daemon reclined in his strung-up bed. Garron walked the perimeter of the clearing, pausing occasionally for a small stretch. Edmund and Darian scuffled in the yard, and Liam was absent.

"Come. Let me check your palms," Brandle said.

I sat opposite him. He stood and moved around the table to sit beside me, forcing me to turn toward him.

"Did you sleep well?" he asked as he unwrapped my hands.

"That is an unfair question, Brandle. I did not seek to interrupt Garron's sleep. He should have accepted the bed and let me sleep inside in the chair."

"I only meant to inquire about your sleep, Kellen. Garron's sleep was fine."

"Better than fine," Daemon said. "You have no inkling what it's like to sleep next to your softness, Lamb. If I died today, I would die content."

I frowned at his sleep-relaxed face. "Never utter those words again. No more death."

Brandle caught my chin and turned my face toward him. His astute gaze swept over my face.

"We apologize. You've lost so much, haven't you? Your mother. Your father. And the sister you left behind."

I swallowed hard, trying to contain the fiery emotions that wanted to emerge.

"My father and sister aren't yet lost to me. I haven't given up on them. I *won't* give up on them."

With a nod, he released my chin.

"The question wasn't meant to be unfair. Garron mentioned you shivered a few times. We were worried you weren't warm enough."

I would have been much warmer inside, but I didn't say so. They all knew how I felt about sleeping outside, just as I understood why they'd insisted. And complaining after Garron was hurt defending me would belittle their concern. That was something I would never do.

"If I was cold, I don't recall it. I slept soundly after Garron—" I cleared my throat and focused on Brandle's efforts to coat my palm with honey.

"You shouldn't need the honey tomorrow," Brandle said. "The wrap will be needed for another few days, though."

Once Brandle finished, Eadric took his place and fed me boiled oats and berries. His eyes were once again twinkling with his natural humor.

"Do you think you can teach us something new today?" he asked. "We have the rabbits and fowl from your father in the cold storage."

"Perhaps. Is there a chance for an egg or two?" I asked.

He looked at the others.

"It depends on whether or not your friend has left," Edmund said.

"He is no friend of mine," I said with a trace of annoyance in my tone. "If one of you is willing to help me check the food store under the cottage, I'm sure I can come up with something different."

Eadric glanced at Brandle. I noticed he did that when the answer wasn't something he wanted to deliver himself.

"It would be better if you didn't attempt the ladder for a few more days. However, I can tell you exactly what's down there."

"Are there any root vegetables?"

"Many," he said.

"Do you know what herbs you have?"

He recited a good number of them. Most were meant for cooking, but he also mentioned a few used for different remedies.

"I believe we have what we need to make some hand pies. It's a bit more work, though."

"We're willing," Eadric said quickly.

"Will you help, Daemon?" I asked.

Daemon lifted his head and winked at me. "My hands are your hands."

I told them what I needed from the cellar, including an herb not used for cooking and the tea kettle.

"Are you planning on poisoning us like Eadric?" Brandle asked.

"Tempting, but no," I said. "The tea will help fight infections."

"Ah, so just Garron then," Brandle said. "I think that's fair."

Daemon and Eadric chuckled.

"I'll let you share that glad tidings with Garron yourself," Brandle said as Eadric fed me the last bite of oats.

Liam appeared to take my bowl from him.

"As soon as my hands are healed, I promise to wash my own," I said.

"As soon as your hands are healed, you'll ask to leave," he said. He turned and walked away, leaving me watching after him.

"Garron?" Brandle said. "You were going to tell him you'd like to poison him?"

Understanding he meant to send me away but unsure why, I went to Garron across the clearing.

"May we speak?" I asked when I neared.

He paused his pacing to face me. "Is something wrong?"

"That is the very thing I wished to ask you. Everyone is treating me differently. At the moment of my arrival, I wasn't welcome. Now, no one wishes me to leave. Why?"

He laughed lightly and looked at the ground.

"That is part of why we like you, Kellen. You don't see your own appeal."

I watched the flush creep into his cheeks. The same flush that had colored them when I'd woken.

Frowning slightly, I glanced over my shoulder at the others. Garron grabbed my arms, turning me to face him. More crimson flooded his face.

"When you arrived, we didn't know you. Now that we do, we don't want to let you go."

"You don't know me, Garron. If you did, you would have listened to Edmund and sent me away the moment I arrived."

His gaze swept over my face.

"Would you hit a man sewn together, Kellen?"

"Pardon?"

That was the only warning he gave before he pulled me into his arms and brushed his lips against mine. The touch vanished as quickly as it started. If possible, his face was even more flushed when he pulled back.

"I had to know," he said softly.

"Know what?"

"What it felt like to kiss you before you leave us."

My heart ached. A deep heavy feeling that stole my breath. I brought a hand to my chest, pressing it there in an attempt to ease the pain.

"Why did I have to come here? Why?" I demanded softly.

I turned away from him and ran across the clearing. Darian and Edmund stopped fighting and started toward me. I veered away, around the other side of the cottage, running toward the back, away from them all.

Arms caught me around my waist.

"Don't hit me, I beg you," Darian said. "I don't wish to stop you, but I'm afraid you'll fall and hurt your hands again. If you do, you won't be able to—"

I spun in his arms and clapped my bandaged hand over his mouth. Surprise, then sadness flickered through his expression.

"Not you, too," I said.

His gaze held mine as his hold loosened. He kept one arm around my waist and used the other to gently tug my hand away.

"Then what do you wish to hear from me, Princess?"

"Nothing. Silence is better than hearing how much my presence here will hurt you."

"Your presence doesn't hurt us. Your absence will do that." He released my hand and smoothed back the damp strands of my hair. "You should let Edmund comb and braid this soon."

I could see it in Darian's gaze—the desire to do more than touch my hair.

"You saw Garron kiss me."

"I did," he said. "It drives me mad that he got away with that without even a pinch."

"He asked me if I would hit a sewn man before he did it."

Darian threw his head back and laughed. His hand moved down my back, pressing between my shoulder blades and forcing me closer. He sobered suddenly, his gaze on my mouth.

"If I let Edmund cut me, will you allow me the same privilege?"

"I have no wish to come between brothers."

The corner of his mouth tilted up with amusement.

"That would be impossible, Princess." He moved fast, darting in to brush his lips against mine as he pressed me against his chest. Then he pivoted away, bounding back several paces with a grin.

"You are an odd man, Darian."

"Oddly good-looking?"

I snorted and turned away, continuing toward the garden at a more sedate pace.

Liam was near the well, still washing the breakfast bowls. Ignoring his watchful gaze, I stared at the overturned dirt. Thoughts that needed to come wouldn't. Being kissed by two different men in a handful of minutes had robbed me of rationality.

I wished for my sister or any other female who might guide me through the stunned confusion I felt. It took several moments for the soft bird song to interrupt my reverie. Twisting, I looked up at the roof at the little brown bird that had no qualm in calling out its joy to the world.

"Shameless thing, isn't it?" Brandle said. "It sings so happily about its freedom to soar wherever it pleases while you're trapped here by unhappy circumstances."

"If you speak kind words and attempt to kiss me, too, I will not be responsible for my reaction," I said.

Brandle tucked his hands into his pockets and considered me.

"Daemon repeated his offer to be your hands if you wish to slap either of them. He said he has no qualms hitting a sewn man."

I snorted and immediately attempted to smother my humor.

"I am not angry at either of them," I said. "I'm confused, Brandle. And I have no one to talk to about it. I miss my sister and my mother terribly."

"You can talk to me," he said with sincerity.

"Talk to you? About the men in this glade who are confusing me to the point of madness? About how you all feared me but now suddenly want to kiss me? Is this some game? Which brother can bed the naïve maid first? Have I not suffered enough? Must my heart endure more pain?"

My skin burned, and I closed my eyes and fisted my hands as I breathed through my nose.

"Do not cry," he said a moment before arms encircled me.

"No!" I broke free of his hold and scrambled back several steps.

He looked hurt. *Him.* Because of me.

"Do not look at me as if I am the difficult one here. I have steadfastly remained the same since I arrived. It is all of you who have changed. And why is that, Brandle? Why?"

"Because we realized you are exactly who you say you are. A woman who has recently lost her mother and wishes to find a way to cure her father to return to her sister."

"And believing me gives your brothers leave to suddenly kiss me?"

"No, Kellen."

Brandle reached for me, and I retreated another step. I would have taken more, but the fence stopped me.

"The truth gave us the freedom to dare to hope that we could care for you."

"You were already caring for me."

"To care for you as our own."

I stared at him until movement to the side drew my attention. They all stood there. Watching. Waiting for a reaction that I could not afford to give.

"I would like to go inside. I need time…to think," I said with false calm.

He nodded and indicated I was free to leave. But was I truly? He seemed to read my mind because I only made it a few steps before he called, "Remember your word, Kitten. No running. Your hands aren't yet healed."

"Five more days," I said to myself. I'd repeated the phrase often since escaping into their home. More precisely, every time one of them knocked on the door.

"Dinner is ready. Come eat," Edmund said through the panel.

"I'm afraid I can't do that," I said.

"Why not?"

"I'm much too comfortable to move."

"You need to eat if you want to heal," Edmund said.

"I need rest to heal."

"You can't stay in there all night."

"Ah, so it is not my lack of sustenance but my absence that is the issue. Since I've slept beside Garron, Darian, and Daemon, that leaves four others eager to—how did Darian word it? Feel my softness? No, thank you. I have no wish to force the slumbering wanderings of my hands on anyone else."

A hushed conversation ensued farther away, and I closed my eyes.

The sun had long since set. They'd allowed me to leave the cottage unbothered to use the privy just before the meal had been ready. I'd planned well and had retreated inside for the evening before they understood my intention.

Other than the time Liam discovered me on the floor in the root cellar and Edmund's help washing my hair, they'd never entered the cottage while I was inside, always remaining at the door. Whether due to courtesy or something more, I cared little why they did not forcibly remove me from their home—only that they did not do so.

The conversation quieted, and another knock sounded at the door.

"Five more days," I repeated.

"Brandle needs to check your hands before you sleep," Garron called.

"My hands are well enough that he proclaimed I will not need the honey tomorrow. Thank you for your concern."

Another round of whispered conversation started outside. Their meddling attempts were almost comforting.

"We're not certain that the tracker left," Eadric said.

"Which two will I be sleeping with tonight?" I asked.

"Brandle and Liam," Eadric said.

"Wrong answer."

A scuffle of sound came from just outside the door, and I knew Eadric was being swatted for answering honestly.

"You can choose who sleeps beside you," Brandle said.

"Wrong answer."

"No one," Brandle said quickly. "No one will sleep beside you."

"Even if that had been your first answer, I would not have believed you. Now, be gone from my door and go to sleep."

"It's too early to sleep," Darian said.

"Then read a book, Darian, but cease pestering me."

"But all the books are inside," he said.

"Then plan better tomorrow."

"We will, Kellen," Brandle said. "We will."

THE CRICK in my neck would not ease no matter how many times I stretched it. It felt as if sleeping a single night in the chair had aged me. With a quiet groan, I rose. The blanket that had covered me fell to the floor, and the heavy weight of my neatly braided hair hit my back. I pulled the braid over my shoulder and stared at it. Then I looked from the blanket to the closed door.

Edmund had come in here while I'd slept, covered me, and braided my hair. Vaguely, I recalled feeling someone touching my hair, but it was mixed in with an uncomfortable night in the chair and dreams of running through the forest to escape the creatures chasing me.

What did it mean that he'd entered but hadn't moved me to where I knew they all wanted me?

Frowning, I went to the door and put on my slippers.

It wasn't until I took my cloak from the peg that I realized what I was doing—using my hands.

True to Brandle's prediction, they didn't ache as they had the previous mornings. Which meant I could open the door with very little noise. My gaze swept the yard from the safety of the cottage. In the predawn light, all seven of the occupied beds hung by the central fire remained undisturbed.

Briefly, I wondered how difficult it would be to flip them out of their beds. The imagined sight of their outrage brought a smile to my lips. Rather than give into my desire for a bit of mischief, I decided a trip to the privy took priority.

However, I only managed a single step in that direction before a tingle of awareness had me changing my mind. With light steps, I walked over to Eadric's bed. He snored softly, his face peaceful. I glanced at Darian as he shifted one of his legs over the side of his bed. It proved too tempting.

Silently, I paced around to the other side and pulled up on the edge of the fabric with all my might. His already displaced weight sent him toppling to the ground with a grunt.

Much too alert, he looked up at me in surprise. A glance at the rest proved my suspicion true...that their slumber had been a ruse. They were all awake and watching me.

Ignoring Darian on the other side of his bed, I looked at Eadric.

"I need to use the privy but don't wish to risk another attempted abduction. Will you escort me, please?"

He swung out of his bed with a grin and offered his arm like a practiced gentleman.

"It would be my honor, Sparrow," he said.

"Why was I the one thrown from my bed?" Darian asked, getting to his feet.

"You were more obvious in faking your sleep." I arched a brow at him. "And since you can't keep your hands to yourself, why should I?"

He howled with laughter as Eadric escorted me away.

"What mischief can I expect from your brothers today, Eadric?" I asked quietly.

"You know they don't like when I tell you things," he said.

"It's unlikely you'll tell me something I don't already know. For example, you were all awake waiting for me to go to the privy. Either you meant to corner me, which I doubt, or you meant to remove something from the house while I was away. Perhaps the door so I can't close myself in? Though, that wouldn't make sense since Edmund had no issue with letting himself in while I slept. No, I believe you all mean to remove the chairs so I have no choice but to sleep outside tonight."

With an amused smile, Eadric shook his head. "How could you know that?"

"I saw the lot of you watching me with disapproval through the window. It wasn't a difficult conclusion to reach." I paused as he opened the privy door for me. "I'm struggling to understand why Brandle is so determined, though. It's not fair to any of us to force me to sleep with any of you. I'm keeping my distance to spare us all the pain of separation when I leave. Please try to remind them of that, Eadric. Edmund's voice alone isn't enough."

Eadric nodded and went to draw water from the well for me as I used the privy. After washing my hands, we joined the rest, and I claimed one of the chairs now surrounding the fire without commenting on their removal from the cottage.

"Who will be staying with me today?" I asked.

"All of us," Brandle said.

"Is the man not gone?" I asked, worried.

Brandle held my gaze for a long moment. "He's gone."

Relief coursed through me before I pushed it aside.

"Then there is no reason for all of you to stay. Go do whatever it is you did before I arrived." I looked at Edmund. "And, no, I don't care what it is, Edmund."

"Good," Edmund said, stirring whatever they already had boiling in the pot.

I closed my eyes and focused on banking the frustration that simmered just below the surface. The guilt was next. I was so absorbed in what I was doing that I was unprepared for the gentle brush of lips against mine.

My eyes flew open, and I stared at Brandle. The corner of his mouth tilted up.

"No blow to the nose?"

"I need my hand to heal so I can leave. But I believe Daemon said he was willing to be my hands. A solid blow to Brandle's testicles, please, Daemon."

Eadric crowed and demanded payment for the bet they'd made while Daemon lazily rolled out of his bed.

"I offered my hands," Daemon said, "not my feet. And do not ask me to touch my brother's testicles when *I've* done nothing to offend you."

Brandle's cocky smile grew, and he darted in for another kiss before facing Daemon.

"Let's have a go, then," he said cheerily while my lips tingled dangerously.

The sensation swelled, and I gripped the armrests. My focused breaths did nothing to calm the storm. Likely because Daemon and Brandle were circling each other like they were about to enjoy a lark together, and it annoyed me that they thought this a game.

I stood slowly, shaking with the exertion from my effort to restrain the emotion threatening to break free. The bottoms of my feet ached after two steps. My fingers cramped before I could reach the door.

"Kellen?" Brandle stepped in front of me, his expression filled with worry and confusion.

My gaze dipped to his treacherous mouth. Why had he kissed me twice? My emotions were not a trivial thing with which to be toyed.

I pivoted, seeking to escape, but turned to face Liam.

"You look pale." He reached out and touched my cheek, a gentle caress of his fingers over my over-sensitized skin.

A rush of feeling bubbled out of the fractured well inside me, opening me to the surrounding energy. I could feel the house. The old, steady pulse in the ground. The vibrancy of the brothers.

I struggled to pull it back, to close myself off again. However, my emotions continued to swell as my gaze swung around, looking for an escape.

The brothers stood in a circle around me, watching me with concern.

Light bruises colored Liam and Darian's eyes from their fight with the tracker. Garron's knuckles bore the scrapes. Eadric's compassion-filled gaze met mine, as did Edmund's steady one. But I knew what he was hiding—what they were all hiding. I could feel it all.

I could *feel* them.

Edmund no longer hated or feared me. He feared watching me leave as much as the others, and knowing that cracked the well further.

A thread of panic wrapped tightly around me. I needed to go. Run. I couldn't be this close to them feeling this much—

"Don't run," Edmund said.

How did he know?

A pulse of light flared from under his neck scarf.

For a moment, I thought he had the light rock I'd arrived

with. Then, Garron's scarf did the same. And Liam's. And Eadric's.

I turned slowly, seeing them all glow brightly.

Realization dawned.

Magical amulets.

A memory rose sharply. Painfully. The dinner with Maeve. Her necklace glowing as she controlled the men at our dinner table. Is that what they were doing? Were they controlling me? Controlling my feelings?

Fear consumed me.

I stumbled back a step. Then another.

"No," I whispered desperately.

CHAPTER 12

"KITTEN, IT'S NOT WHAT YOU THINK," BRANDLE SAID, HIS ARMS wrapping around me.

I swung around, striking out violently. My fist hit his throat, and he coughed and choked as he bent over. It was enough. I bolted.

Liam stepped in front of me, blocking my escape to the south. I pivoted.

Daemon blocked me to the west.

I turned again, ran past Brandle into the cottage, and slammed the door shut on them all. The bench scraped against the floor as I pulled it over to block the opening. Would it be enough? I'd witnessed their strength.

The sounds of Brandle's coughing and throat clearing continued as I sank to the floor in front of the bench. My hands shook.

Hadn't I doubted that three coincidences could bring me here? They'd been so wary of me that I never considered I should be wary of them. At least, not for magic. As men, certainly, but never once for magic.

How had I been so naïve?

I wrapped my arms around my legs and set my forehead to my knees. Panic and fear consumed me, pulsing under my skin painfully along with the fear they all felt. It was driving me mad.

A tap came from the window. I jerked my head up and looked at Edmund.

He slowly shook his head then held up a finger. I watched as he ran it between his eyes, smoothing away the frown line there. Then he lifted his other hand and made a show of unfurling his fist.

He was right. I needed to regain control.

Dropping my head to my knees again, I focused on my breathing, calming it and my thoughts so I could think rationally.

Before I could regain control and think of a reason they'd lured me to this place, I was interrupted.

"Lamb," Daemon said from the other side of the door. "I believe we've all learned our lesson. We promise never again to kiss you without permission. Please come out."

"You don't want me to die. You don't want me to leave. What do you want, Daemon?"

"Your help, Lamb. We want your help. No, we need it."

I could *feel* his desperate sincerity. Was it a lie? I'd never let myself feel this openly around Maeve. If I had, what would I have felt? People could lie with their bodies, but what they felt inside rarely lied.

They truly needed my help then. But what kind? I doubted it would be anything simple with his level of desperation.

I lifted my head and saw Eadric and Liam had joined Edmund at the window. They weren't attempting to force their way in, and their expressions of sorrow matched what they felt. If they had lured me here, it wasn't for my death. What then?

"And I need fewer of you here so I can think," I said.

"Will you run, Kitten?" Brandle asked, his voice hoarse.

I closed my eyes and fought not to cry.

"Run to where, Brandle? I have nowhere to go."

"You could go home," he insisted.

"I cannot."

"If you can help us, Kitten, we vow to help you in return. I swear it on my life and the lives of my brothers. Please."

I could no longer deny I had been drawn to this glade for a reason. Were they perhaps the help I needed?

I opened my eyes to look at Eadric, Edmund, and Liam.

"And do your brothers feel the same? Do you believe they would all give their lives to help me once I've helped you?"

I could see by Edmund's expression that he'd heard me. But more than that, I could feel his agreement along with all the others.

"I do."

"Go away, Brandle. I need time to calm...my thoughts. Please."

"Do you see the locked door?" he asked. My gaze shifted to the door beside where the ladder used to be. "The key is on the ledge above it. There's a letter for you on the desk inside. Will you read it?"

Curiosity was always my downfall. I liked *knowing* things. My twin was no different, though a little less driven, depending on the topic. I liked all knowledge, though.

As I went to the door, the three watching me gave no outward indication of their feelings, but I felt their hope. I ran my fingers along the trim just over my head and found the key.

The door unlocked with a rusty click, and I let myself into a very narrow space. A modest desk sat below a small window. It let in enough light that I could see the dust spinning in the air from my disturbance.

I picked up the folded piece of yellowed paper from an open book on the surface of the desk.

Greetings, my dear Maiden,

It is my hope that you are reading this letter

under the direction of my wards. Seven strapping lads who are in desperate need of your assistance. Something dear was taken from them, and they need your help to reclaim it.

It won't be an easy task, and I cannot give you the precise details. If I did, you would then be unable to help them. But know that these complicated circumstances are not of their choosing. They are not meant for this glade. I brought them here to give them what safety I could.

Please care for them. I vow they will return that care to you one hundredfold.

Your most humble supporter, Henry

I stopped reading the letter and looked at the books on the shelf above the window. Books on farming, healing, and several other topics rested in dusty silence, including a set of primers similar to the ones Mother had used to teach Eloise and me reading, writing, and arithmetic.

Taking one down, I opened it and found each of the men's names written neatly inside. I placed it back where I found it and glanced at the letter again. My thoughts tumbled together. I wasn't heartless to their plight, but what of my own? Did my troubles have no meaning in the light of theirs? Neatly refolding the letter, I returned it to its resting place.

When I turned toward the door, I saw the wall behind it was filled with shelves that housed more books. Many of them had no titles written on their spines. Among those were books titled with economics, ethics, mining, and masonry.

Henry, the man I'd heard them mention many times, had been a very knowledgeable man.

I looked back at the book on the desk and moved closer to wipe the dust off the page.

It was a spell to protect the glade from the beasts…written in the same penmanship as the letter. I read it closely, including the warnings for safety if it should ever need to be recast. It had aged Henry twenty years.

With a frown, I turned the pages. Henry had been a caster. A strong one based on the spells he'd noted. Spells for protecting people from being watched. Spells for protecting against magic. With each protection spell I read, I began to calm.

I found one with a spell for protection amulets. It wouldn't allow any spell—good or bad—to touch the wearer. It would glow blue. The spell went on to explain the different types of amulets that were possible, including one that could store life energy, which glowed green.

A tear slowly slid down my cheek. The men here were nothing like Maeve then. Henry, the man who I believed had raised them, had protected them in the best way he was able. I thought of how Eadric had clutched at his shirt when I'd suggested removing it so long ago. They'd been afraid I would discover their protection.

Afraid of me.

Wiping away the tear, I pushed the rest of my emotions back into the well where they belonged.

What the brothers outside felt, along with the persistent tingle crawling under my skin, faded away.

I turned the page back to the spell for the glade and left the room. The door to the cottage stood open. I could see them all waiting for me just outside.

Silent. Watchful. Worried.

"Was magic used to bring me here?" I asked.

"If it was, it wasn't done by us," Brandle said.

"Was it done by someone you know?"

"Not by our knowledge."

"Or with our consent," Garron added.

I inched closer to the door.

"Don't shut us out," Edmund said.

I ignored him and focused on Eadric.

"What did you make for breakfast?" I asked.

He looked surprised and glanced at Darian, who stood beside him.

"We'll make you anything you'd like," Darian said.

"I want pastries like I used to eat at home," I said without hesitation.

"Then you shall have them," Brandle said. "In exchange for sending us away to obtain the ingredients we need, will you please come outside first?"

Damn him for guessing my intent.

"Why?"

"To bid farewell to whoever leaves."

He made me want to stomp my foot. Why was he so stubborn?

"Ah, Lamb, you break my heart when you look at us with those eyes," Daemon said.

I tore my gaze from Brandle to meet Daemon's.

"And how should I view you?"

"Preferably without any cloth—" Garron's elbow jab to Darian's ribs cut his remark short, but not his lazy smile.

"Fine. I'll come out and bid you all farewell so I can have a day of peace."

"Two will need to stay behind," Brandle said.

"So be it. Do I have the freedom to choose who is leaving, or am I not allowed that either?"

Brandle looked down, and I could see he was struggling not to show how much my words hurt him. That, in turn, created an ache in my chest. I didn't want to hurt him. I didn't want to hurt any of them. Yet, my continued presence and their persistence to keep it would do just that. Why couldn't they see I was trying to protect us all?

"You can choose," Brandle said.

"Eadric and Edmund then." Before any of them could respond, I added, "And if I help you, do I have your word that you will do as I ask, regardless of the risk to me, even if what I ask is to reach Adele to secure the help I need to free my family?" I waited for my throat to hurt, but the curse found no issue with saying family. After all, my father was cursed and my family. It didn't incriminate Maeve or what she'd done to bind Eloise to our home.

"You have our word," Brandle said.

"Very well." Vowing to do nothing to cause me to regret my choice, I stepped outside.

Darian caught me up in a hug. I didn't miss the way his head dipped toward my shoulder as he held me tightly. My heart beat painfully at the proximity of his mouth to my chest, and I was already regretting my vow.

"Get off me before I unman you, Darian."

He chuckled and released me with a quick step backward.

"That is how we bid a proper farewell, Princess. An embrace."

Understanding what he meant, my gaze swept over them.

"All of you?" I asked.

"Except Eadric and Edmund," Brandle said.

"Why should I embrace any of you farewell when I didn't even do so to my sister when I left home?" It was technically true, though I had hugged her the prior day.

"We risk our lives each time we leave. It may be the last embrace we ever know."

"If an embrace is too much," Daemon said with a grin, "I'm willing to accept a kiss in its place."

"I believe I've been kissed enough."

"For the morning or the day?" Darian asked. "We need to know how to greet you when we return."

"Silently and without any physical contact," I said, turning to Garron.

He flushed when I stepped close and gently hugged him, careful to avoid where he'd been stitched.

"Return safely," I said.

His arms snapped around me, and he leaned in to press his face against my neck. I felt him breathe in deeply, and a different type of awareness rushed through me. Our faces were equally flushed when he released me.

Liam was next. His gaze danced with anticipation, and I understood why when he set his ear to my breast.

"I have never before appreciated my lack of height as much as in this moment," he said.

"Be careful," Brandle said. "She kicks, hits, and likely bites."

"Please, brother," Darian said. "Stop teasing me with these possibilities."

I heard someone cuff Darian as Liam released me.

Reluctantly, I turned to Daemon.

He opened his arms wide and grinned shamelessly. "Come, Lamb. Show me how much you care for my well-being?"

Face flaming and heart stuttering, I walked into his embrace. He dipped his head to rest it on my shoulder, and I felt his lips brush my neck.

I dug my fingers into his hair and pulled his head back forcefully. He quickly released me and held up his hands in surrender.

"No kissing," I said, pushing him away by his hair.

"Sorry, Lamb," he said, looking completely unrepentant as he smoothed his hair back into place. "You're so soft and smell nice. It's hard to resist showing my affection for you."

"Resist, or receive nothing the next time."

"Understood, Lamb."

Reluctantly, I turned toward Brandle.

He flashed me a small smile. "I was paid in advance and will not ask for more. We will return before nightfall."

I felt an ache in my chest as I watched them leave.

"He has mastered how to incite guilt, hasn't he?" I asked Eadric, who now stood beside me.

"He has," he agreed.

"Guilt about what?" Edmund asked from my other side.

"Not embracing him farewell. Dratted man."

I turned on my heel and would have strode back inside, but my shift caught on something. When I turned to look, I saw it caught between Edmund's fingers.

"How are your hands?" he asked before I could become angry. "Can you make a fist without pain?"

Curious, I tried. "It aches, but it's bearable."

He shook his head and released me.

"It's best not to use them, but there are still some moves I can show you if you're interested."

"Moves?"

"How to strike someone if your hands don't work."

"Edmund, I don't think Brandle wants her to—"

"Hush," I said. "Why do Brandle's wants come before mine? I want to learn. I *like* learning."

I hurried to follow Edmund to the packed ground. He turned toward me, took in my shift, and shook his head again.

"It would be better if you dressed in the tunic and pants for this. You'll likely want to sleep in that tonight, and it will be dirty."

I nodded and eagerly went inside to change. I could hear the indistinct murmur of their conversation and knew I couldn't dally, or Eadric would convince Edmund he was doing something his brothers wouldn't like.

With my pants loosely tied and my tunic almost slipping off my shoulder, I jogged outside in my untied boots.

"Eadric, will you help me?" I asked, forcing him to stop his whispered conversation with Edmund.

Eadric took one step forward then retreated with a worried glance at Edmund.

Edmund snorted and strode toward me.

"After Brandle's talk about touching you inappropriately, Eadric's worried about scaring you off."

"And being hit," Eadric added as Edmund quickly and efficiently tied my pants and boots. When he stood and reached for my tunic, his hand trembled slightly.

"Is that due to anger or fear?" I asked.

"Neither. Or perhaps a little of both. I'm trying not to overthink things."

"That sounds very much like my sister. I prefer to contemplate things carefully."

He finished with the tie and stepped back.

"The letter I read said that I should help you but clearly stated that telling me how would negate any help I might give. So, I won't ask. But how am I to know when I'm being helpful or a nuisance?"

"Trust us to speak up when it's the latter and remain silent when it's the former."

"I thought as much," I said as I followed him back to Eadric.

I spent the morning learning how to use my forearm instead of my palm to break a man's nose. The new technique delighted me, which seemed to concern both Eadric and Edmund.

We took a small break to eat some of the previous night's soup then went to turn over the soil in the garden that hadn't yet been turned. As I watched them work, I asked questions.

"If you can't tell me how to help you, how am I supposed to know what to do?"

"Just keep doing what you've been doing," Edmund said.

"Provoking you and annoying your brothers?"

Eadric flashed a grin at me, but neither answered. Of course they didn't. That would be entirely too helpful to me.

"Will whatever task that's needed take a long time to complete?" I asked.

"Hard to say," Edmund said.

I made a face at him.

"Eadric, you should push him into the dirt."

He pretended like he was going to but didn't.

"How will I know when I've helped you?" I asked.

"You'll know," Eadric said.

"I'd like to help quickly. Can you give me hints?"

Edmund paused what he was doing and leaned on the end of the gardening stick as he considered me.

"A hint is just a segment of explanation. With enough of them, we would be telling you what you would need to do, and that would invalidate everything you have already done."

So I'd already helped? How?

Taking his warning to heart, I didn't ask.

"Will my bed be on the table again tonight?" I asked instead.

Edmund looked a little surprised by the question and then suspicious.

"Why do you ask?"

I shrugged and didn't answer.

"Did you hate sleeping outside?" Eadric asked.

"No. Not even a little. I liked the fresh air and seeing the stars."

"But not the company?" Edmund asked.

"I didn't mind Garron. He kept his hands to himself." I fought not to recall how I'd been unable to do the same.

"Darian and Daemon did as well, Sparrow," Eadric said without censure.

I felt my face heat.

"They didn't mind that your hands wandered, though," he added quickly.

"Shut it, Eadric," Edmund said without sounding angry.

"But she looks upset by what I said."

"Which is why I told you to stop talking," Edmund said, shooting Eadric a warning look.

Eadric sidestepped until he was close to me.

"Do you still remember that elbow thrust?" he asked from the side of his mouth.

He was so innocently mischievous that I couldn't help my smile.

"I do," I said. "I promise to intervene if Edmund begins to look like he wants to deliver a cuffing."

Eadric grinned widely and pulled me into his arms for a hug.

I wrapped my arms around him and returned it willingly.

"If I get to choose my sleeping partners tonight, I'll make sure to choose you for your safety," I said.

He laughed and pulled back from me.

"Hear that, Edmund? I get to sleep next to my little sparrow tonight."

"Maybe I'll knock you out on your way to the privy and pretend to be you," Edmund said. And then he shot me the most ridiculous, Eadric-like smile and added, "Are you hungry, Sparrow?"

He sounded just like Eadric.

Eadric's nervous gaze met mine.

"We'll escort each other to the privy tonight, right?" he asked.

I laughed so hard that I snorted.

CHAPTER 13

THE OTHERS RETURNED LADEN WITH SUPPLIES WELL BEFORE DUSK. I watched them set a crate packed with straw and eggs on the table, along with three crocks of butter and another of cream. Liam carried a wrapped bundle and offered it to me.

"What is this?" I asked.

"Open it."

I untied the bundle and found another shift and a modest dress in a dark blue.

"Even mended, the black one is fancier than most women wear in Turre. I thought this one might—"

I surprised us both by hugging him hard.

"Thank you, Liam."

His arms wrapped around me, and I didn't miss the way he rose up on his toes so he was above my breasts this time.

"You're welcome."

Someone cleared his throat.

"Princess? I chose the color," Darian said. "I knew it would beautifully accent your eyes."

When I released Liam and looked at Darian, he opened his arms expectantly.

Ignoring his invitation, I glanced at Garron, who'd carried the eggs.

"Can I see your side, please?"

He flushed but lifted his shirt so I could inspect his bandages. As I'd suspected, they were dotted with pink.

Turning away from him, I looked at Brandle.

"Did you lie to me?"

His already guarded expression became more so.

"Never."

"Then how did Garron travel to Turre unharmed while bloody?"

Understanding lit Brandle's gaze.

"Because he's not you."

"Haven't you figured it out yet, Trouble?" Edmund asked. "Not every person is bound by the same set of rules."

His comment killed my growing anger. After all, I'd learned that lesson very well already. So had my sister.

A familiar, unnatural wave of dizziness washed over me, followed by a tingle of fear. My gaze flew to Liam's.

"It's happening again."

All the light vanished like before, and I crumpled to the ground amidst their shouts and curses.

"Kellen?" Brandle called.

Like the last time, I couldn't move, but I could feel the dirt under my cheek.

One of them gripped my calf through my pants, shaking me as if to rouse me.

"She did this before in the cellar," Liam said. "I ran to get Darian, but when we returned, she was awake and speaking again."

"Look at your amulet," Edmund said. "Stop touching her."

The hand on my calf disappeared.

"It's still glowing but more faintly," Brandle said. "Whatever this is, a caster is behind it."

I wanted to shout with relief that they were beginning to understand. Maeve thought she was clever in binding me to silence, but she would bring her own downfall.

"Does that mean we've been found?" Eadric asked.

His quiet question brought to light the danger they might be in due to my presence. What was Maeve trying to do? Just find me or something more? Other than being unable to speak or move, I felt fine. Nothing hurt. I thought of the severity with which Maeve had punished my sister and knew that wasn't what this was. What was this, then?

"Look," Garron said.

Several of them swore.

"Someone is trying to see us."

I didn't understand what they meant, but whatever magic had been cast to lock me into place lifted, and I opened my eyes.

"Princess," Darian said, helping me to sit up. "Are you all right?"

"Don't touch her," Brandle said softly.

Darian immediately removed his hands from me, and I looked at Brandle.

"Do you understand now? Why I need to leave? I wish I could help you. Truly, I do, Brandle. But the longer I remain here, the more danger you—" My throat tightened in warning, and I stopped speaking.

Brandle studied me. "What do you think happened just now?"

"I cannot say."

"Because you don't know or because you cannot say."

I smiled slightly, saying nothing.

"I see," he said.

After wiping the dirt from my face, I rose and brushed off my front.

"What harm is there in touching her?" Darian asked.

"None, I should think," I said, answering on Brandle's behalf.

"If someone is trying to see you, as you said, according to the book, your amulets will keep you safe."

They all looked at me with varying expressions of shock.

"You read Henry's books?" Brandle asked.

"The letter was vague at best and resting on the open book. Did you think I wouldn't look for an explanation behind your amulets? Knowing that they are for protection and not to cast is the only reason I am still here."

Eadric clasped his amulet to him like I would attempt to take it. Edmund had taken a step back.

I frowned and looked at Brandle again, annoyed with their reactions.

"I have never met a more capricious group of men in my life. Insist I stay or let me leave. I care not which you choose, but for my sanity, please choose one and commit to it fully." I shook my head, muttered that they were impossible, and gathered up my new clothes.

"If no one has an objection, I'll take my new clothes inside."

They remained silent as I strode into the cottage. I neatly folded the new clothes and tucked them into my sling bag. The crinkle of the king's note stirred my frustration further.

Come morning, would the brothers still feel opposed to my presence and agree to help me leave, or would they again insist I help them first? I could no longer guess.

Eadric's worried question echoed in my mind. *"Does this mean we've been found?"*

Found. That indicated they were hiding here. Was that why they didn't want me to leave? Would my knowledge of their existence bring them danger? I thought of Maeve and the spells she was able to cast and knew it could. She'd forced the truth from me twice before I learned how to speak partial truths to avoid telling her what I didn't want her to know.

Would I be able to keep the presence of these men a secret, though, once I returned to face Maeve?

I wasn't sure.

Sighing, I sat on the floor facing the cold hearth.

"Lamb, come outside," Daemon said from the doorway.

I turned my head and rested it on my knees so I could see him. Eadric and Garron stood behind him.

"We don't like when you stay inside," Eadric said.

"Brandle never intended to let me leave, did he? Meeting you, seeing where you live...I'm a danger to you all now."

"No, Kitten," Brandle said, joining them at the door. "You're not a danger. You're the solution."

I lifted my head to stare at the hearth again for a moment before going to them.

"Does this mean you've fully committed to keeping me here?" I asked, my gaze holding Brandle's.

"I committed days ago when you apologized before hitting me."

"Well, that is a mistake I won't repeat."

He grinned, and the sight of his smile made my heart skip a beat. I averted my gaze and moved to the table where the supplies waited.

"Everything should go to the cellar," I said. "We can leave out a few eggs, though, and I'll teach you how to make pastries after we stuff a fowl for dinner."

For the next hour, I gave directions and tried to focus their enthusiasm on the coming meal. To any outsider, at first glance, they might have believed I led an unruly group of boys. But if they watched closer, they would notice their antics weren't to cause the trouble usually desired by boys. No, they meant to stir another type of trouble—the kind caused by men. They vied for my attention in the most ridiculous manner possible and took every opportunity to accidentally brush against me. They laughed at one another's efforts and goaded each other on.

But they always seemed to know when they pushed too far and quickly apologized—sometimes with a hug, sometimes with a useful tip on surviving the woods—which always distracted me from the emotions attempting to crawl under my skin.

By the time everything was set and cooking, I was ready to retreat to the cottage for some peace. Darian and Daemon wouldn't hear of it.

"Lamb, we faced every danger in that forest with only the memory of your brief embrace to help us endure. Please don't remove your presence. Let us bask in your gracious company until the meal is ready."

"Yes, Princess, tell us what you did to occupy yourself today."

I glanced at Edmund briefly before turning to the pair and holding out my hands.

"I would much rather show you if you're willing."

They latched onto my hands quickly and allowed me to lead them to the packed dirt in the center of the clearing. Daemon's steps grew more hesitant as we neared it. Darian's grin only widened more.

"Edmund showed me something new today," I said, releasing their hands.

I turned my back to them and looked over my shoulder.

"Would either of you like to hold me from behind?"

Darian's gaze lit up, and he dove for me while Daemon took a wary step backward. Darian's arms wrapped around my waist, and his chest pressed against my back as he nuzzled my neck.

"This is a delight, Princess. Why did Edmund—"

I grabbed his hand, wrenched it back, and twisted out of his hold to make enough space to swing my forearm toward Darian's face. Just before my arm connected, I watched Darian's eyes flare with surprise. His head snapped to the side. He grunted as he stumbled back a step and grabbed for his face.

Guilt and fear shot through me.

"Darian? Are you okay? I sincerely apologize," I said, reaching for him.

He straightened with a grin and pulled me into his arms.

"You did so well, Princess." He kissed the side of my neck. "Now, show me what else he taught you."

He released me and waved for me to try again. I looked at Edmund.

"I think I addled him."

Garron shook his head. "He was already addled."

I focused on Darian. "One demonstration is enough. Your lip looks puffy."

His grin grew lopsided, and his gaze became suggestive.

"Do you look at my mouth often, Princess?"

"This glade is the only reason you haven't already been beaten by some maiden's outraged mama," I said.

The rest of them hooted with laughter as Darian held a hand to his heart as if my words had wounded him. However, I could see in his gaze they had not. He was as amused as his brothers.

"I question the sanity of each of you," I said without rancor.

"And you are wise to do so," Darian said, holding out his hand with a courtly bow. "Allow me to demonstrate another indispensable practice."

I tentatively accepted his hand, curious what he would show me.

He swept me into a swirling dance as he hummed a familiar melody.

"You dance?" I asked.

He grinned and moved gracefully through the steps with me. After several sweeping twirls, Daemon stopped him with a hand on his shoulder.

"I believe it's my turn," he said, stealing me away. He hummed a jauntier melody that required a faster pace and had me breathless in moments.

Garron's timely interruption saved me. He held me at a greater distance than the other two and hummed so quietly that his brothers teased him endlessly. His flushed cheeks were endearing as was the way he bowed over my hand and kissed my knuckles before he surrendered me to Eadric.

Eadric, never one to conform easily to another's expectations, began to sing a questionable tune about a baker's wife's job to help his loaf rise as we bounded around the clearing. His hand slipped lower on my waist than it should have as he did his best to evade Liam and Edmund who were both attempting to cut in.

When Edmund swung out to cuff him, I spun Eadric into a dip. He was unrealistically heavy for his size, and I would have dropped him if not for his solid footing and strength.

"I'm not sure how I feel about being on the receiving end of this." He grinned up at me while the others laughed.

"It's the anticipation of what I plan to do next that twists your insides, isn't it?" I asked lightly.

He nodded, and I couldn't resist gracing both his cheeks with a kiss. Darian and Daemon grumbled about the apparent favoritism and asked for equal treatment.

Ignoring them, I faced Liam and bowed deeply instead of curtsying.

Liam grinned and curtsied.

The others hummed together for our song. Liam played along, accepting my lead for a few turns then taking it for his own. He moved more boldly than his brother's before him, his body brushing against mine as we swirled in our dance. While a playful smile lingered around his mouth, it was absent from his gaze.

I knew what he meant to do before he dipped me as I had Eadric.

His lips teased mine as I held his shoulders, and I...enjoyed it. My hands tightened on his shoulders, and he pressed closer to me, weaving a spell around me that didn't require a caster or magic. Just a man and a woman.

When he lifted his head to look at me, my heart beat heavily against its ribbed cage.

"Will you hit me for that?" he asked softly.

"No."

"Does that mean I have permission to do that again?"

"Absolutely not."

He smiled. He had probably noted the breathlessness of my refusal and understood why I'd given it.

Once he righted me, he handed me off to Edmund, who looked ready to cuff Liam for the liberties he'd taken.

"What part of that annoyed you?" I asked as he expertly swung me around the glade. "The part where he kissed me or the part where he asked to do it again?"

He remained silent.

"Come now, Edmund. It isn't like you to hold back your thoughts. If you say nothing, I will fear the worst."

"And what is the worst?" he asked.

"That I will need to sleep beside Liam, too, to protect him from you."

He snorted and glanced at his brothers before spinning me farther away.

"I fear one of them will do something that will cause you to run."

"Ah. I see."

"I doubt you do yet. But I think you will."

I cocked my head at him.

"You sounded very much like Brandle just then."

He made a face and brought us closer to the brother in question.

"Don't tell him that," he said before releasing me.

Still smiling, I turned to Brandle and accepted his hand. Without a word or a tune, he swept me into a dance.

"I'm curious," I said. "How do seven men in the middle of the Dark Forest learn how to dance so well?"

"Henry taught us," he said.

"Henry was a very knowledgeable man," I said.

"He was."

"Is that why Liam was so comfortable being led instead of leading?"

Brandle smiled slightly. "You believe that, as the youngest and shortest, he was often led. But that isn't true. We all took our turns. Henry said it was good for us to know what it felt like to be led as we would experience it again once we marry."

His smile had dimmed slightly at the end, which reminded me of the guilt I'd felt over the way he'd left earlier.

"Well, that explains being led, but what of the curtsey? It was precisely executed."

Brandle's amusement showed in the creased corners of his eyes. Why did I find that so captivating?

"Henry said we should know what a proper curtsy looks like as well," he said.

"So you learned how."

"Precisely."

"How long ago did Henry pass away?" I asked.

The corners of his eyes smoothed out, and he pulled me a little closer.

"He left us three years ago."

"I'm sorry."

"Some things in life are unavoidable."

"The inevitability of losing those we love doesn't make the loss less painful," I said.

His expression softened, and our steps slowed.

"No, it does not. Thank you for dancing with me, Kellen. It was an honor."

He took my hand and bowed low over it with formal precision.

"The honor was mine, Brandle. Thank you."

"Are we done? Does this mean we can eat?" Eadric called.

CHAPTER 14

I RETURNED FROM THE PRIVY—MUTUALLY ESCORTING AND escorted by Eadric—and saw the mattress on the table once again.

"Does the cottage hold bad memories for you?" I asked Eadric.

"Not at all. We have very fond memories of our time in it."

"Then why don't you sleep in it?"

"It gets too crowded with all of us."

It was a modest cottage and would be cozy with all of them inside, but not uncomfortably so.

"Are you worried you will be cold?" Eadric asked. "Brandle was already warming the rocks when we left."

"No, I know I won't be cold."

After dinner, I'd changed back into my shift and slippers as both were more comfortable for sleeping. However, my concern didn't stem from my attire. It stemmed from the liberties I took with my bed companions while I slept. Though I knew they didn't mind it, I did.

With each day, I grew more fond of them. They said they feared my abandonment, but no more than I feared it. It hurt to leave Eloise, my other half. Finding these men had helped distract me from the ache–then to ease it. They were my bandages. What would happen when they were removed? I would be raw and open to the world. I would be dangerous.

"What is it, Sparrow?" Eadric asked gently.

I realized I was holding his arm too tightly and relaxed my grip.

"I'm tired," I said truthfully. Yet no amount of sleep would remedy the exhaustion I felt deep within my bones.

He patted my hand and led me to the makeshift bed where he helped me settle between the covers before joining me.

"Name your second," Eadric said, making choosing my bed partners sound like a duel. Perhaps, in a way, it was.

"Garron. I don't want you hurting your side again," I said.

He moved to join us, and I turned to my side, choosing to face Garron instead of Eadric. Eadric sighed contentedly and snuggled closer to me. As soon as Garron was comfortably settled, I closed my eyes.

"Goodnight, Princess," Darian called. "Dream of me while you sleep."

"Knave," I said without rancor.

"Is that an invitation?"

"In the morning, I cut your hair."

One of the others sniggered.

"In the morning, I shear all of you," I said.

Their groans followed me into my dreams.

"No, don't wake him. I want to see what she does when she discovers him like that."

I lay still against Garron's chest, trying to decipher the meaning behind Darian's gleefully whispered words.

"Think, Darian," Brandle said. "What will you do if she's so outraged that she begins to resent her time here?"

"Brandle's right. You risk upsetting her for entertainment that will not come," Edmund said. "She gave Eadric her word she wouldn't hit him. Just wake him."

The heavy heat of the hand covering my breast over my shift provided the answer as to why they wished to wake Eadric.

Without opening my eyes, I plucked his hand from its perch and dropped it on my waist. Eadric mumbled in his sleep and pressed against me. The weight of his arm lifted, and his hand unerringly settled on my breast again.

"No cuffing or ear tweaks for this," I said, finally opening my eyes and lifting my head.

Watching me fearfully, they stood around the table. Garron, also awake, waited for my reaction as well.

"I apologize for any liberties I've taken in my sleep," I said, removing my hand and making space between us.

Eadric mumbled, holding his prize tightly as I pushed into him.

"Would you like help, Lamb?" Daemon asked. "I can remove him without delivering any form of reprimand."

"Please," I said.

"First, just let me dislodge this." Instead of picking up Eadric's hand, Daemon slid his between my shift and Eadric's palm. Nothing changed in the manner of the hold other than the owner of the hand. Yet, my reaction to it altered. The skin on my arms pebbled, and my breast under his palm began to ache.

Before I could react further, Eadric made an angry sound and shoved Daemon away. Daemon caught Eadric's waist as he fell back and pulled him bodily from the bed, taking the blankets with him.

The cold morning air hit my legs—my shift had ridden up in my sleep due to using Garron as a pillow—and four sets of eyes drifted down to look at the now-exposed limbs.

"Have I not yet suffered enough immodesty for your tastes to allow me to sleep inside like a proper maiden?" I asked with an arched brow.

"Apologies, Princess." Darian scooped up the blanket and covered me.

I untangled myself from Garron and rose to put on my slippers, ignoring Daemon and Eadric, who were discreetly shoving one another.

Standing tall, I faced Brandle. He studied my expression.

"I don't understand why you keep insisting I sleep outdoors. But know that I feel frustration the same as any other. Hiding it does not mean it does not exist. I will try to help you, but do not press too far, Brandle. You will not like the consequences."

He bowed his head in acknowledgment and stepped aside.

If they reacted to how I slammed the cottage door, I couldn't hear it. And I refused to open myself to feel their reactions. It would be too dangerous with the insistent tingle running under my skin. So I closed my eyes and focused on calming the storm raging within.

When I felt in control once more, I took out the homespun dress they'd bought me. The letter from the king fell from the bag, a reminder of what I needed to do. My resolve firmed, and I returned the letter to my sling.

As I dressed normally and unassisted for the first time in days, I considered Brandle's vow to help me in return for my help. If I wished to see Eloise free, I needed to figure out what they needed from me. Edmund said to continue doing as I'd done. However, they didn't like it when I tried to keep myself apart from them. They made it clear they wanted my time and attention.

So be it.

I strode over to the bookcase and picked up the shears from their sewing basket.

When I opened the door, all seven men saw what I held and warily watched me approach.

"Who is first?" I asked.

They all pointed to Liam, who looked between his brothers and the shears with trepidation.

"Very well. Let's go by age then."

"Shoulder-length hair is all the rage in Turre. If we wish to blend, we shouldn't cut it," he said.

"It is common in Drisdall as well. However, you do not have shoulder-length hair. You have a nest, Liam." I picked up the low stool by the fire and moved it several paces away.

Liam reluctantly took his seat, and the others began preparing pastries.

Between my fingers and the comb, I worked through the tangles until his hair hung free in uneven lengths around his shoulders. The snick of the shears quietly echoed in the clearing. Once I finished, I used his leather tie to secure the neatly trimmed length at the base of his skull.

"There. Next."

Liam stood and looked at the others, holding out his arms in question.

"You almost look presentable," Garron said with a smirk as he took a seat.

I repeated the process, running the comb and my fingers through his hair and then trimming it evenly. Standing in front of him, I bent slightly to ensure both sides were level. A whisper of warning tingled along my skin. I straightened abruptly and looked toward the trees.

"What is it?" Garron asked, watching me.

"I don't know."

I turned a slow circle. Nothing seemed out of place, but the quiet whisper of warning remained, reminiscent of what I'd felt the day Mother died. I'd ignored it, and Maeve had arrived to irrefutably change our fates. I would not make the same mistake.

"Stay where you are," I said, moving away from Garron and the others.

They watched me walk to the center of the clearing. After glancing at them to ensure they hadn't followed, I closed my eyes and opened myself. I could feel the forest, the creatures, and the men in the clearing easier than the previous time I'd opened myself. They all felt the same, but something pulsed briefly to the east. Toward Drisdall.

I closed myself to the energy around me and opened my eyes to stare in that direction.

"Kitten?" Brandle called.

Shaking my head, I faced him.

"I think something terrible is about to happen."

He frowned slightly.

"Terrible? Why do you believe that?"

"It's a feeling that I can't explain precisely, but something I felt the day my mother died."

He considered me then looked at the trees. "Was the terrible thing that happened your mother's death?" he asked.

"My mother's death marked the start of the terrible things that have happened." While I spoke, I thought only of Father and me leaving, nothing of what Maeve had done. It enabled me to speak the words without restriction.

"I see." His gaze returned to me. "Have terrible things happened to you since you arrived here?"

"No."

"Then trust us to keep it so."

I glanced over my shoulder at the trees once more then reluctantly nodded. Life had taught me that safety was an idealistic illusion. Those who believed in it suffered horribly when they realized the reality. I held to no such illusion.

Something dangerous would find us soon. Perhaps while I lingered here or perhaps once I left. Preventing it would be impossible. All I could do was brace myself and remember my purpose. Cure my father. Free Eloise. And stop Maeve from misusing her magic ever again.

I returned to Garron and resumed my inspection.

"I'm finished," I said absently after the last snip.

Garron rose so Eadric could take his place.

"Whatever you felt upset you, didn't it?" Eadric asked as I combed through his hair.

"Yes."

"Do you not trust us to keep you safe?" He turned his head to meet my gaze.

"When I was younger, my mother vowed to be my shield against the cruelties in this world. I trusted her. Yet, she died, Eadric. Nothing lasts forever."

His gaze stirred with empathy.

"I do not question your intent with my doubt. I know you and your brothers will stand against those who might wish to harm me. But the world is filled with people who wish harm on others. And no one can stand forever."

He surprised me by standing and pulling me into his arms. I didn't simply allow his hug. I returned it, and I set my head on his shoulder as his brothers watched on.

"You're wrong," Brandle said. "We know from the casters that every living and non-living thing is filled with energy. Death doesn't end the energy; it changes it. So, I don't believe death robbed you of your mother's shield. I think you're still surrounded by it. Protected and guided. I can find no better explanation for your safe arrival in our glade."

I considered his words and finally released Eadric.

"Perhaps," I said. "If it is so, I hope it is enough to keep us safe in the days to come. Sit, Eadric, so I can finish your hair."

His was tangled as badly as Liam and Garron's but not nearly as knotted as Edmund's—since he spent too much time on the ground fighting—or Daemon's, due to how often he'd slept prior to my arrival. When I finished with the pair, they both sported hair closely cropped to their scalps.

"Well, this is sure to stand out," Daemon said, running his hand over it.

"When you next visit Turre, simply scratch your scalp often," I said. "Anyone observing you will assume you have lice and not question the style of your hair."

Daemon sighed and stood. "We try not to call attention to ourselves."

"I would hazard a guess that your height will draw unwanted notice more so than your hair since you always wear caps."

"You wound me, Lamb. I thought you didn't mind my limited height."

"I don't. Your charm makes up for your lack of menacingly towering stature."

"Is that how you view tall men?" Darian asked, taking over the stool.

"With a few exceptions, yes. In my experience, men will use their largess to intimidate those they wish to cow. Especially of the fairer sex."

"Show me." Darian took hold of my skirt and used it to tug me between his legs. "You're bigger than me standing like this. How have others cowed you?"

The slow sardonic smile that curled my lips surprised him.

"You mistake me, Darian. My sister and I witnessed our peers' attempts to intimidate maidens many times. While it might have worked on them, it never worked on us. Our mother raised us to think differently about the world and the people in it. To care for those who are unable to care for themselves and stand against those who would seek to harm those who are weaker." I took his chin in my hand and tipped his head farther back. "Do not mistake me as weak. I am the pliant branch. The switch used to punish the deserving."

"Ah, Princess. You tease me with your honeyed words. What must I do to feel your punishing presence against my backside."

Eadric groaned, and Edmund swore. The scuffle of noise

likely meant that someone was holding him back from giving Darian a beating for being so bold with me.

I tweaked Darian's chin and released it.

"You are a fine-looking man, Darian." I gripped his upper arms and leaned in to loom over him. "But without means, you're unlikely to find a match. I could take pity on you. Take you around back and let you feel what it's like to be with a real woman."

Darian's mouth dropped open in shock.

"Come now. Don't be coy. I've seen the way you look at me. I know you want a good fucking."

He jolted to his feet. I would have been knocked backward had he not caught me around my waist and hoisted me over his shoulder.

He made it two steps before I could no longer hold back my pealing laughter. A moment later, I found myself on my feet, facing his confusion.

"Explain yourself," he commanded.

I laughed harder, doubling over. If only Eloise could have seen—

The thought had me sobering and straightening.

"I apologize, Darian. You asked how other men have attempted to cow me. What I said…it was what has been spoken to me and many others in an effort to intimidate us. I didn't expect you to like it."

He exhaled loudly, rubbed a hand over his face, then looked at his brothers. I glanced over my shoulder at them as well. Garron's face was scarlet. Eadric was grinning like a fool. Edmund scowled at Darian. Daemon was scratching his jaw lightly as he stared at me. Liam covered his mouth and coughed repeatedly. And Brandle studied me with a concerned frown.

"Men spoke to you like that?" he asked.

"They were hardly men if they spoke so coarsely, wouldn't

you agree? Now, are the pastries ready, or should I finish what I've started with Darian?"I asked with a smirk.

I watched Garron and Liam retreat behind the cottage while Eadric laughed like a fool, and Edmund cuffed him.

"If I have a say, I would very much like for you to finish what you've started," Darian said, reclaiming my attention.

Grinning, I motioned for him to return to his stool.

He hummed his pleasure as I combed through his hair and tugged my skirt to move me closer at every opportunity. His hair required very little effort to untangle, and I had it trimmed to length more quickly than the others.

"Brandle," I called, stepping away.

Darian caught me by the waist and pulled me into his lap. Before I knew what he intended, one hand cradled the back of my head, and the other cupped my cheek.

"Payment for such tender care," he said.

Then his lips covered mine. It wasn't the gentle brush he'd given me previously. He caught my bottom lip between his and sucked it gently. I froze as heat burst inside of me, engulfing me and attempting to incinerate the well.

Fueled by fear and desperation, I pushed at Darian's shoulders with force. His mouth left mine. Breathing heavily, he stared at me.

"If you value your life, you will never do such a thing again. Do you understand?" I asked.

For a few beats, he didn't move. Then he gave a single, stiff nod and released me. I stood gracefully, gulped a few breaths to calm myself, and then looked at Brandle.

"If you are willing," I said, motioning to the stool Darian still occupied.

As soon as Brandle strode forward, Darian retreated. Like Liam and Garron, he walked behind the cottage.

"Are you angry with Darian?" Brandle asked.

"No. I feel bad that he misunderstood me. It wasn't my intent to mislead him."

"He knows. We all know that. It was your reaction to his kiss that worries me."

"I have no wish to kill your brother, Brandle. But I did not speak an idle or empty threat. If he continues to push the boundaries I've set in place for everyone's safety, life will be lost."

When he said nothing in response, I began to comb my fingers through his hair.

He exhaled contentedly and closed his eyes. "This isn't a punishment."

"It wasn't meant to be."

"Why did you wish to trim our hair?"

"So you would look more presentable when we go to Turre together."

"Our hair was part of our disguise."

"You wished to look like beggars?"

"We wished to look unworthy of attention."

"It wasn't achieving that goal. You looked worthy of being driven out of any respectable town."

He remained quiet for several minutes as I worked.

"Do you truly wish to help us?" he asked.

"I do."

"Why? Is it only to free your father?"

I paused my work and stepped in front of him to meet his gaze.

"You are full of questions today."

"Today?" Edmund snorted. "He's been like that since I've known him."

"Are you avoiding answering my question?" Brandle asked.

"Are you purposely provoking the woman with the shears?" I countered.

The corners of his mouth lifted briefly.

"What is it you truly wish to ask, Brandle? I know it's not to validate the truth of my need to find a cure for my father."

"You threatened Darian for kissing you. He cares for you. We all do. Do you not care for us? Even if only a crumb?"

I studied his upturned, handsome face and tried to deduce the purpose of his question. His hazel eyes didn't waver under my scrutiny. Rather than the sly calculation I'd seen countless times before, I saw loneliness and despair in his gaze.

My fingers skimmed over his jaw as I reached for his hair.

"Do not mistake the distance I keep for aversion, Brandle. And likewise, do not assume any affection I feel for you or your brothers will keep me in this glade. I made a vow to my sister, and I won't forsake her for a handsome face. Not even for seven of them."

He caught my hand and turned his head to brush his lips against my palm. The contact made my skin tingle dangerously, as did the intensity of his gaze as it held mine.

"We will help you, Kitten. Never doubt that you found your way to us for a reason."

I didn't want to look away from his warm gaze or free my hand. I wanted to kiss him like Darian had kissed me to see what would happen. Would he groan and grip me tighter? Would he lose control? Would I?

My heart began to race at the idea, and I was no longer sure if it was in fear or anticipation.

He didn't miss the twitch in my fingers as I struggled to hold myself back or the hitch in my breathing.

"You will continue to push at my boundaries," I said in sudden understanding.

Rather than answering, Brandle turned his head to grace my palm with another kiss. This time, I felt the tip of his tongue flick against my skin.

I pulled my arm back sharply and scowled at him.

"That handsome nose is wasted on you. You clearly have no concern for its safety."

He grinned.

"Behave yourself and allow me to finish so we might eat before poor Edmund parishes from starvation. I can hear his stomach from here."

Brandle laughed and bent to the side to look around me. "That wasn't an invitation to eat, Edmund."

Edmund grumbled and went to fetch the others while I quickly finished.

Brandle caught my hand when I would have walked away.

"Will you allow me to sleep next to you tonight?" he asked.

"Garron's side—"

"He'll be fine."

"But—"

"No more excuses, Kitten. Choose me. Please."

He kissed the back of my hand and released me just as the others arrived. They went for the pastries that were cooling on the table. A moment of chaos ensued while they light-heartedly fought for the best pastry.

"Here, Princess," Darian said. "I won the best pastry for you." With a smile, he held up the perfectly shaped treat.

Eadric stole it from his palm.

"I'll feed it to you, Sparrow."

Darian whacked the back of Eadric's head. The pastry flew out of his palm. The others scrambled to catch it. Liam came out triumphant and held the pastry aloft.

I plucked it from his hand.

"It is well past time for some of you to leave for the day, is it not?"

CHAPTER 15

EADRIC'S LOOK OF DISAPPOINTMENT SPEARED THROUGH ME AS I took a bite of the pastry.

"I used the shears without issue. Why shouldn't I feed myself?"

"But I like feeding you." His sad words saw me handing over the pastry before I realized my intent.

He grinned widely, led me to the table, and offered me another bite.

"Who would you like to stay with you today?" Edmund asked.

"I'm tired of choosing. Decide amongst yourselves."

Everyone stopped eating and stared at me.

"Do you truly have no preference?" Brandle asked.

"I do not. And I do not like being accused of playing favorites, either. So you may decide."

One by one, they grinned like I'd given them the best gift ever.

"Then we shall," Liam said. "Daemon and Eadric have spent the most time in the glade recently. They need to go."

"Agreed," Brandle said.

"Agreed," Edmund said.

They went around the table, agreeing with Liam. Even Daemon and Eadric.

"Garron should stay today. I don't want to re-sew him," Brandle said.

The others agreed with that as well.

"Liam should stay," Eadric said, feeding me the last bite of pastry and licking his fingers, which had just brushed the corners of my mouth.

The rest agreed. No fighting. No complaining or bitterness.

"It was a pleasure feeding you, Sparrow. I will see you again before dusk." Eadric leaned in and gave me a quick kiss full on the lips. With a grin, he stood, plucked me up from the bench, and turned me around.

Edmund tugged me into his arms and hugged me. "Make sure these two do their chores." He kissed my forehead and released me.

Darian took his place, holding me tightly before I could grasp what was happening.

"I look forward to tonight's demonstration, Princess."

Then Daemon was there, his hand stroking down my back and pressing me into his arms.

"I'll miss you, Lamb."

Heat burst inside of me.

It was too much. Too much touching. Too much emotion.

Darian handed me off to Brandle, who cupped my cheeks and looked into my eyes.

"Will you hug me today, Kitten?"

I needed less contact, not more. But I could see the doubt and worry in his gaze that I would turn him away again. I didn't want to. I wanted him closer. So much closer.

The heat flared stronger. I trembled with it. And with need. I didn't want to feel so alone anymore. I wanted to be wanted, and I wanted to want in return.

Any remaining control I had fractured along with the well inside of me. Emotions came storming out. My skin didn't tingle...it burned. It burned with the need to feel what they were feeling. To know it matched what I felt. That they wanted to stay with me as much as I wanted to stay with them.

But I didn't feel them as much as I felt the energy around me. All of it. The ground. The trees. Each of the seven men.

Panic threaded into the emotions whirling within me. I needed to stop. I needed to close myself off again.

"Kitten?" Brandle frowned and withdrew his hands.

I slowly turned around. Garron was there. He frowned and stepped aside as I started walking that way. The bottoms of my feet ached with the pulse of energy from the ground with each slipper-clad step I took.

"Kellen? What's wrong?" Liam asked.

His fingers dragged against the back of my hand, and I flinched at the rush of his feelings. His worry. His fear that I was leaving because Brandle had asked for his embrace today. His need to do something to make me want to stay again.

The feeling had barely touched me when he caught my hand more firmly and spun me about to pull me into his arms.

"Whatever you need...please, Kellen, don't leave."

"Release me," I managed.

He did, but he didn't move out of my way as he looked up at me to search my gaze.

"Tell us why?"

The well fractured further. I could feel the pulse of life all around me. Beating. Beckoning. Begging to fill that empty place inside of me.

I struggled to breathe and shuffled back a step even as I reached for him.

Liam, the sweet fool, caught my hand.

The hunger grabbed at his energy before I could stop it.

The amulet beneath his shirt flared so brightly it blinded both of us.

"Liam!" Brandle yelled.

I wrenched my hand free of Liam's hold and stumbled back

several steps. Fear that I'd hurt him helped me close myself off again as Brandle rushed forward to grab his brother, who was looking at me in a way that said he understood what had just happened.

Liam understood what I was.

"I'm sorry," I said.

I turned and ran into the cottage, slamming the door behind me. Collapsing to my knees, I closed my eyes and clasped my hands. Shame over what had happened tried to take me, but I pushed it down. I pushed it all down. Anger. Fear. Frustration. Uncertainty.

Emptying my mind, I focused on being calm.

My feet went numb as I sat there, but I didn't attempt to move.

Outside, everything remained quiet.

They knew. They had to know. It was the second time. Would they ask me to leave now?

Tears wanted to well up, but I breathed until the urge passed then opened my eyes to unwrap my hands.

The abrasions from the rope were scabbed and healing well. So were the slivers from clawing my way through the thatching. If need be, I could run again without the creatures scenting my blood. At least until the first time I fell.

A knock sounded on the door.

"Kellen?" Liam called. "Could I trouble you to move to the garden? I was hoping to use the copper tub myself today while the others are gone. I promise not to intrude for too long. The hair from my shearing is making me itch."

The reasonable request robbed me of any reason to deny him. Yet, I knew nothing good would come from opening the door. It was better to keep myself away from them. Better for all of us.

He knocked again.

"Kellen?"

With a small sigh, I stood and lightly stomped some life back into my feet before opening the door for him. He smiled at me.

"Thank you," he said. "I already have the water heating." He waved to the pot on the fire. "I could pull the tub outside, too, if you prefer."

"There is no need to pretend nothing happened, Liam," I said. "I am grateful you had the protection of the charm you wear, but it would be safer if you and your brothers avoided me until I can leave."

Liam considered me. "You're right. Something did happen. But I see no need to avoid you because of it. You know we come from a kingdom that allows magic. We don't fear it as the people of Drisdall do."

"You should fear it," I said. "The cottage is yours for as long as you'd like. Find me by the well once you're finished."

Before I reached the backyard, I heard the scrape of metal against dirt. Garron worked the soil, turning what remained to prepare it for planting.

He looked up at my approach, but he needn't have worried. I carefully kept my distance.

"Should you be doing that?" I asked.

He flashed a small smile at me. "It's this or chop wood. This is easier. I'll leave the chopping to Liam."

"Liam is taking a bath."

Garron frowned, then sighed and propped the stick against the fence near where I stood.

"It looks like I'll be wielding the ax then."

"No. I have no desire to see you sewn together again. One of the others can do it when they return."

He nodded and went to pick up the stick again. I watched him then asked the question burning inside of me.

"Do they fear me now?"

"Fear you? No. We were questioning if it's wise to trust you. But I think we forgot that we come from a place where magic doesn't need to be hidden, and you don't. I can understand why you didn't want to tell us you're a caster."

"I'm not," I said quickly.

"Kellen, there is no shame in being born with the ability to touch the energy around us."

I swallowed hard and took a step back to create more space between us as I said, "There is if you can't control it."

He studied me for a long moment.

"I wasn't born knowing how to speak. Someone had to teach me. Everything I know, I've learned."

His understanding words almost put me at ease, which wasn't something I could afford to be.

I shook my head, silently disagreeing with him.

"Why is controlling your ability any different?" he asked. "If you don't know how to control it, learn how."

"I did learn to control it. It's linked to my emotions. But when they overwhelm me—" I looked away with a slight shrug that belied how much it bothered me that I needed to hide what I wanted to feel in order to control that monstrous thing inside of me.

"You've spoken of your sister often," he said. "Does she know?"

"Not everything," I said. "I believe my mother guessed, but we never spoke of it."

"How could your mother only guess?"

"She was bedridden since I was young and rarely left the estate. Eloise and I were left to manage ourselves by the time we reached our tenth year."

"And when did you know you were a caster?"

"I suspected there was something wrong with me during my twelfth year."

"Tell me."

"I was trying to find Eloise. It was a game of hide and seek in the woods. I grew frustrated. The grass at my feet withered and died. I didn't leave my room for three days after. My mother thought it was due to my first bleeding that happened the following day."

His face flushed.

"I'm sorry. I shouldn't have—"

"Don't. Don't hide things or refrain from speaking the truth out of fear of our reaction. I want to know everything, Kellen. We all do. Nothing that happened has changed our minds. We want your help, and we vow to give ours in return."

"Not many men would want to hear about a woman's first bleeding," I said.

"We're interested in knowing everything about you, Kellen."

I nodded and looked away, unsure what to do or say next.

"Can I ask you more questions?"

"Yes," I said, relieved.

"Why did your emotions overwhelm you earlier?"

I snorted then realized he was entirely serious.

"Are maidens from Turre not typically overwhelmed by the attention of seven men?"

He flushed and smiled shyly.

"I cannot speak for the maidens of Turre. I don't know many, and the ones I know tend to turn the other way when we approach."

"Why?" I asked.

He laughed and shook his head. "Not many females are interested in conversing with men who are a hand shorter than they are."

"Well, that's very small-minded of them."

He shrugged. "Didn't your mother tell you to look for someone tall and strong? Someone whose shoulder you can lean on in times of trouble?"

I thought back and shook my head. "She told me to find someone who would love me without limit or condition. She said nothing about stature or standing."

Garron braced a hand on the fence and vaulted over it agilely. I cringed and reached for his side.

"You shouldn't do that."

"The threads will hold. Brandle knows what he's doing." He caught my hand and tugged it up to place it over his heart. His hand remained over mine.

"Could you trust me to love you, Kellen? Without limit or condition?"

My pulse began to race.

"This is dangerous." I attempted to tug my hand free, but he held fast.

"Breathe, Kellen. Nothing bad will happen."

"Garron, please."

He released my hand only to take me by the arms and draw me closer. My gaze darted from his eyes to his mouth. I recalled how his lips felt against mine. Soft. Warm. Oh, so very tempting.

"Brandle wishes to sleep beside me tonight," I said.

"He's feeling left out," Garron said, his thumb moving over my arm.

Coaxingly or comfortingly? I couldn't be sure.

"Will you allow him to sleep beside you?"

"Should I?"

Garron smiled softly. "I hope you will."

My gaze dipped to Garron's mouth, and I darted in to brush my lips against his. Fleeting, but purposefully done.

"Are you certain?" I asked.

He chuckled and pulled me against his chest to hug me. The feel of his hand smoothing over my hair had me wrapping my arms around his waist so I could rest my head on his shoulder.

"If you are expecting jealousy, you will find none," Garron said. "We all wish for you to stay here. Fighting amongst ourselves over who gets to spend more time with you or sleep beside you will not endear you to us. We know that. So set aside that concern and invite whoever you wish to sleep beside you. Hug whoever you will. Kiss whoever you wish."

I heard his heartbeat speed with each suggestion and lifted my head to look at him.

His gaze swept over my face, lingering on my mouth.

"You are so beautiful, Kellen. Inside and out. Please say you won't hide in the cottage for the remainder of your time here."

I sighed and eased from his hold.

"I won't."

"Thank you."

I TURNED the potatoes sitting at the edge of the coals and gingerly felt if they were soft yet.

"Careful," Liam said. "If you burn yourself—"

"I won't be able to leave. I know, Liam. I will take care."

"Let me do that."

He picked me up and switched places with me.

"How are you so strong?" I asked, watching him turn the remaining potatoes.

"Lots of manual labor," he said.

I studied how his loose shirt molded over his back as he bent forward then glanced at Garron. He watched me openly, and I struggled not to blush.

"I think I'll go inside," I said, taking a step in that direction.

Liam moved quickly, catching me around the waist and depositing me near the fire.

"If you leave, dinner will burn."

"You're exasperatingly persistent."

"If you run inside before the others return, they will think you spent the day there and take their frustration out on us," Garron said.

"Ah." I sat in the nearest chair and glanced at the cottage while my mind pondered the night ahead and Brandle's request. I no longer knew what to think. Of them. Of my place here. Of the help they needed. None of it.

"Did that upset you?" Liam asked.

"No. I'm confused, Liam. By all of this. And weary. I wish to return to my quiet life where the most interesting thing was the current book I borrowed from Mr. Bentwell."

"You like books?" Garron asked. "What kind?"

I flushed scarlet.

"Henry has a few that made me blush," Liam said. "I'm not sure Brandle would approve of you reading them, though."

I glanced at Liam. "And does what Brandle wants have greater importance over what I want?"

"No," Liam said quickly.

"Then if they return while I'm inside, let them know I'm selecting a book to read," I said, rising.

Liam went to step in front of me.

"Leave her be, Liam," Garron said.

I walked inside and went straight to the small study. The door creaked as I partially closed it so I could view the books behind it. With so many lacking titles, I had to take them down and browse the contents to determine the subject.

Spell books.

So many of them.

"Kellen? I think the potatoes are burning."

I set down the book I'd started reading instead of skimming and hurried outside.

Liam and Garron were no longer alone in the yard, and I stopped short at the sight of the others. Sweat stained their clothes, and thick dust coated their skin.

"I sincerely hope you don't expect a welcoming embrace in that state," I said.

Brandle's expression lost its seriousness as his eyes crinkled in the corners.

"If we wash, will we receive a welcoming embrace?"

"If you wash, I will be more open to negotiating what form of welcome is appropriate."

Darian and Daemon tried tripping each other on their way to the well.

"Does anyone want a hot bath? The copper tub is still out in the cottage from earlier," I said.

Darian paused mid-neck-grab for Daemon. "Earlier? We missed you bathing again?"

"Liam bathed. I did not."

"Liam? In the copper tub?" Eadric asked with a growing grin. "Are you still so small?"

Garron cuffed Eadric then gave me an apologetic glance.

"Eadric, don't pick on Liam for his size. It's not kind. And if I can fit in the tub, so can all of you. Now, the stag meat that Garron brought out of cold storage is ready. Go wash so we can eat before dark. Liam, can you remove the potatoes so they can cool? I'll fetch the butter."

By the time I returned, Darian and Daemon were setting plates on the table. Wet hair dripped on their clean clothes.

"Where did you change?" I asked.

"By the well," Darian said. "I believe Eadric and Brandle are still bare if you wish to take a peek."

Garron glanced at me.

"A cuffing is approved for that," I said, setting the butter on the table.

Darian danced out of the way from Garron, but Daemon caught him upside the head.

"Princess, I'm wounded," Darian said.

"Doubtful. You're still speaking."

Daemon chuckled and took a seat at the table as Liam stacked the slightly cooled potatoes on a plate.

"Will you comb my hair for me like you did this morning, Lamb?" Daemon held up the comb I knew I'd returned to its place inside. Yet, I hadn't heard him retrieve it when I'd been in the cellar.

"You have hands. Comb your own hair." I stole a plate from the table and held it out to Liam.

"Hungry?" he asked as he placed a potato on it.

I shrugged and went to the table to cut the hot sphere in half. The butter melted as soon as it touched the steaming center.

"I have hands but no skill," Daemon said, not relenting. "You saw the state of my hair. Please, Lamb?"

"Have Darian comb it. He kept his hair well enough."

Garron removed the kettle with the roast stag and cut me a slice. I scooped out the juice from the bottom and ladled it over my potato before mashing it up with my spoon and knife.

"Eadric is going to be disappointed if you feed yourself," Darian said, watching me.

I paused and wrinkled my nose.

"I want to continue reading before I lose the light."

Brandle and Eadric appeared from around back. Brandle's gaze met mine before it flicked to the cottage. Eadric hurried to me.

"Let me feed you, Sparrow."

I released my utensils and shook my head without censure.

"You have an unusual fascination with feeding me."

He nodded. "It seems I do. I like doing something to care for you."

I opened my mouth to accept the first bite.

"I want to care for you, too," Daemon said. "Eadric feeds you, Garron warms you at night, Edmund braids your hair, Brandle lectures you—"

"I can do without that," I said after hurriedly swallowing.

"And Liam washes your dishes," he continued. "Darian and I feel left out. What can we do to care for you?"

"You amuse me with your frivolous begging for attention," I said.

Darian opened his mouth, and I quickly added, "Both of you."

Eadric grinned as he fed me another bite, and I watched the others serve themselves. Brandle even fixed a plate for Eadric.

"Thank you," Eadric said without looking away from his task.

Why did I let them have their way? Was this truly helping them? My gaze scanned their faces, watching how they glanced at me as they ate quietly. Edmund held my gaze the longest before focusing on his food.

If I were being burdensome, certainly he would have said so.

The sun dipped lower, and with it, the temperature dropped.

"I think I've eaten my fill," I said before I'd finished everything. "Thank you for feeding me, Eadric."

No one tried to stop me as I hurried inside. Rather than close the door, though, I kept it open to let in more light.

"Do you think she found the book?" I heard Liam ask quietly.

"If she hasn't yet, she will," Brandle said.

"Do you think she'll be intrigued?" Darian asked.

"Likely she'll want to kick us all in the bollocks," Edmund said.

Frowning, I glanced at the book I'd been reading. What were the brothers hiding that they thought would either intrigue or anger me? Setting the informative book of spells aside, I returned to my inventory of the small study.

I found a beginner's book to understanding caster energy manipulation, which I set aside, and numerous other spell books that would keep me entranced for hours. In reality, every book would do that; however, the books on farming and animal husbandry called to me less.

Then, I found it—a very thin tome filled with images that explained in precise detail how to couple, bring pleasure to a female, and how the growth of a babe progressed.

Slowly, I backed up to sit in the chair and started from the beginning.

CHAPTER 16

"Kellen?" Brandle called.

I jolted in guilt and hurriedly set the book on the desk.

"Yes?" I returned, trying to fan the heat from my face.

"Can you still read without light? Perhaps you should bring the book to the fire."

I glanced at the book that had held my rapt attention, then grabbed the one beside it—the one about how a caster used energy to cast.

Brandle stood just outside the door as I emerged from the study. His gaze flicked to the book I held, then up to my red face. If he questioned my flush, he didn't do so aloud.

However, he didn't move out of the way as I approached.

"Am I not allowed to read this?" I asked, glancing at the book.

"You can read any book in Henry's study that you wish," he said. "The one you hold might help you understand what happens when you become overwhelmed."

"That is my hope."

Still, Brandle did not move aside.

"Is something troubling you?" I asked.

"It is. We washed, but we did not receive any welcoming embrace."

He wanted me to embrace him? Now? After reading about many other kinds of embraces?

The heat coloring my cheeks grew.

He watched me with a knowing glint in his eyes. Drat the man and his perception.

"Have you changed your mind?" he asked softly.

I understood he wished to know if I was intrigued or angry by what I read. They feared my anger would lead me to leave sooner, and they had made their stance on that quite clear. But he could plainly see I wasn't angry, couldn't he?

"I apologize," I said. "The oversight wasn't intentional, and I will be more mindful when you next return."

"Next return? This day is not yet done."

"You still wish for an embrace?"

"We do," he said.

He studied me as I tried to understand. He knew I wasn't angry. Was he trying to determine if I was intrigued? Why? Did they fear that I would grow too attached to one of them?

"What type of welcome do you wish to receive? And know that whatever you request, I will submit to your brothers. Equally."

He smiled brightly, his eyes dancing with delight. I felt a brief twinge of relief that I had answered in a way that calmed his fears.

"A kiss then," he said, robbing me of relief. "On the lips, please."

"That's very forward of you."

He shrugged. "It's the welcome we all desire."

That dratted word brought to mind the book I'd read, and another memory rose of the last dinner party Maeve had thrown and the wanton behavior of the men in attendance.

"I cannot kiss all of you on the lips," I said firmly.

"Why not?"

I sputtered for a moment.

"I am not some shameless woman, Brandle."

"Kissing us wouldn't make you shameless."

"What would it make me, then?"

"Reasonable," Darian called from his place by the fire.

A bolt of annoyance shot through me, and I felt the walls around the well move.

"For everyone's safety, I need *you* to be more reasonable."

Brandle ran a hand through his hair, showing his frustration.

I opened my mouth to make another suggestion but never made a sound. He moved faster than I thought possible, capturing the back of my head with his raised hand and crashing his mouth against mine. With my lips parted, his tongue met no resistance. It touched mine lightly. Teasing. Coaxing.

I lost the carefully controlled hold on my emotions. The book fell to the ground between us as I gripped his shoulders and tilted my head to grant him better access.

He groaned, and his other hand seized my waist, pressing me against his chest.

The need to possess everything he offered consumed me, and I felt that well inside of me demanding to be filled.

"You'll only prove her point if she notices our amulets, Brandle," Edmund said.

With a growl, Brandle tore his mouth from mine and dug into his tunic to pull out the brightly glowing amulet. Proof that my powers had run wild.

Yet, he looked unharmed. The amulet had protected him. From me.

"Breathe, Lamb," Daemon said. "Nothing terrible happened."

"But if you're still unsure, I would be happy to take Brandle's place," Darian said.

I heard someone cuff his head but didn't take my gaze from Brandle's glowing amulet. Focusing on the well, I slowly closed myself off from what Brandle had made me feel. The glow dimmed by increments. When the amulet finally went dark, my breathing had steadied, and my head had cleared.

"Never do that again," I said. I moved to take a step back and retreat into the cottage, but the arm locked around my waist wouldn't allow it.

Brandle lifted me with ease and turned so he blocked the door.

"You won't hurt us, Kitten. I trust you."

"Then you are a fool, Brandle, who will lead his brothers to an early death."

His jaw tensed.

"Release me."

"I think not."

He bent low and tossed me over his shoulder.

"Brandle! Set me down this instant." He didn't slow his stride.

My face bumped against his backside. The loose material covering his muscled ass filled my mouth as I bit down. His steps faltered as he let out a strangled curse. Another set of arms grabbed me. I found myself upright and staring at a smirking Eadric.

"You almost brought him low, Sparrow. Well done. If you're ever captured again, do that. It appeared quite effective." He turned to look over his shoulder at Edmund. "You should probably teach her how to roll when she hits the ground, though, as I believe any attacker will not restrain himself from throwing her as Brandle had."

I wiped the loose hair away from my forehead and scowled at Eadric.

"I don't want to learn how to fall."

"Then it would be best not to bite your attacker," Brandle said, visibly rubbing his backside.

"Did she break the skin?" Daemon asked.

"Are you offering to check?" Brandle asked.

"I wasn't the one to bite you."

Seven sets of eyes swung toward me.

"And I wasn't the one to toss an unwilling woman over his shoulder? Deal with your sore arse on your own."

Chuckles and laughter rang out around me.

"Here, Princess," Darian said, offering up the book I'd dropped. "Since you're out here, use the firelight to enjoy your book until it's time for bed."

I glanced at Brandle. The sharp rebuke about ruining his chance to sleep beside me died on my tongue at the look in his eyes—closed off yet hinting at anger. He expected rejection. Why did that make me want to comfort him? Perhaps because I understood how alone he felt. How alone they'd all felt out here with only their family to keep them company.

Turning my back on them, I made my way to the fire and opened the book.

Energy exists in everything. The land. The air. All creatures large and small, including humans. Those born with the gift of feeling energy may also have the ability to use energy. It must be said here, within these pages, that one must never use another living creature's energy. Especially not that of another person. To do so is to participate in the use of blood magic.

Blood magic results in premature death. Always.

Likewise, manipulating the energy around us is not without cost. The energy of the land is not infinite and must be drawn with care. The Dark Forest is an example of what happens when proper care is not taken.

During the first war between Turre and Drisdall, both kingdoms called out to the casters of their land to protect their borders. Both sides drew from the land, neither considering the use of the other. And both kingdoms paid heavy prices for the oversight. After peace was struck, the land between the two kingdoms laid dormant for centuries, occupied only by creatures warped by the corruption.

Let the work of casters past be a lesson to future casters.

Cast only when other means to achieve your goal will not work.

Cast with care.

Remain mindful of the well of energy from which you are drawing.

Frowning, I reread the last line then the whole passage. Was this book saying that the wells of energy existed outside a person? It referred to drawing energy several times. Yet, that wasn't what I did.

I never drew anything. I blocked it from flooding me.

My emotions existed within my well, and as long as I blocked myself from feeling them, a lid existed on top of that well to *prevent* the well within me from filling with the energy around me. When I didn't contain my emotions, it felt like I was removing the lid.

Confused, I continued to read and attempted to absorb the explanation of taking energy into one's self and how it was used to feed the spells casters cast.

"I think she'd remain like that all night if we let her," Darian said.

"Can you imagine growing up without knowing who or what you are?" Eadric asked. "I doubt I would be able to set that book aside if I were in her place."

I looked up from the pages to see them sitting in the chairs spread out around the fire.

"May I try something?" I asked.

"If it involves your lips on—" '

Garron smacked the back of Darian's head.

"If you continue to hit him so hard, he will continue to make those remarks," I said. "You are feeding his need for attention."

"Have you considered that I am feeding Garron's need to quietly protect you?" Darian asked with a grin.

Rather than answer, I removed the lid from my well and allowed myself to feel them. Darian wasn't wrong. Garron did want to protect me. They all did. They all wanted a kiss, too.

Ignoring their feelings and the fact that their charms weren't glowing, I focused on the air around us.

The book had described one of the very first spells a caster can easily perform. It had words to help direct the energy in the air so that I could determine the upcoming weather, but before my gaze could dip to the page to speak to them, I *felt* the air. The heavy moisture headed our direction. The crackle of energy in the heavy storm clouds still crawling our way.

"It will storm heavily before sunrise," I said. "Any seeds you've planted in the garden will be washed out."

Edmund muttered a curse.

"We have plenty more seeds," Brandle said.

"Yes, but I have no wish to sow the ground a second time."

"My hands are better," I said, closing myself off again. "I'll help before I leave."

The group fell silent, and I knew they didn't like the reminder.

"Since it's due to rain, I'll return this to the study." I stood and glanced at Brandle. "Will I be made to endure the rain, or shall we sleep indoors?"

"We?" he asked.

"You asked to sleep beside me, and I don't believe any of you wish to face the rain that is coming."

They exchanged glances.

"Allow me to escort you to the privy first," Eadric said, offering his arm and plucking the book from my fingers. "They can arrange the bedding how they see fit."

I took his arm and noted the silence behind us as we walked away.

"Will you truly sleep inside tonight?" I asked.

"We go to the cottage when it rains or snows," he said. "The wind doesn't blow often here, but when it does, we shelter from it as well."

By their own claim, there were no bad memories in the cottage. Yet, they avoided it until they had no choice but to enter. At least, they avoided it while I was inside. Why?

After using the privy and washing, we returned to the cottage, and I saw a fire burning merrily in the hearth. The chairs were stacked to one side near the study to make room for the straw-stuffed mattresses that had been removed from the loft above.

No one waited inside.

I glanced at Eadric, who flashed me an innocent smile.

"The thatching," he said. "If it's to storm, we'll need to fix it. Go rest. We'll join you soon."

I nodded and let myself inside. All seven sleeping mats lined the space before the fire.

After removing my boots, dress, and cloak, I chose the middle one and lay down. The fire had already warmed the space by my feet, and I sighed contentedly. Briefly, I thought of fetching the book then decided against it. If the storm came through in the middle of the night, I would likely lose sleep. Better to get what I could now.

Closing my eyes, I drifted off to the sounds of several of the brothers on the roof and their quiet murmur of conversation.

The cottage was completely dark when I felt someone settle next to me. I rolled toward the warmth, uncaring who it was. An arm wrapped around my shoulders and pulled me close. With a sigh, I settled my head on a heavily muscled chest.

A scuffle broke out nearby.

"You stepped on me, ox," Darian muttered.

"Move over," Liam whispered. "It's my turn to sleep beside her."

I felt someone settle close behind me. A strong torso pressed against my back.

"Shut your mouth," Edmund hissed.

"Wake her and die," Brandle said softly. The sound echoed in my ear, and I moved my hand to pat his chest. A cold hand caressed my back over my shift.

"No more death," I murmured tiredly. "That feels good."

I drifted closer to sleep in the resulting silence until I heard Daemon say, "What are you doing that got her to sound like that?"

"I'm rubbing her back."

I hummed my approval, and they went silent again. Hooking my leg over Brandle's hips, I snuggled closer to his chest and reached back to pull Liam's arm around me. He moved so close it felt like I wore him as a cloak.

Hugging his arm to my chest, I sank further into the comfort of sleep.

THUNDER BOOMED through the cabin and rattled the glass in the window. I jolted in my sleep, and a hand stroked over my hair in the darkness.

"Shh. It's all right, Kitten," Brandle said softly. "You're safe inside."

I snuggled against his chest, blinking heavily against the need to sink back into sleep's embrace.

"The thatching?" I murmured.

"It's holding, Princess. Sleep," Darian said.

Lightning flashed, illuminating the room and the men sleeping in it. With my head pillowed on Brandle's shoulder, the image of Daemon's sleep-relaxed face remained burned into my vision long after the light faded.

His perfectly sculpted cheeks. His long nose with a slight bump in the bridge. His bowed, tempting lips.

All of it was larger than I remembered.

Another flash of light filled the space, showing how his feet extended well past the end of the small mattress.

The sudden crash of thunder startled me, and I jolted against Brandle.

Liam's hand smoothed down my side.

Larger than I remembered.

I had to have seen it wrong. Perhaps this was a dream.

I slowly ran my hand over Brandle's tunic from his chest to the start of his pants, measuring the distance. His torso was not the length of a man of my size but that of a large man. One who matched what I was seeing.

This was no dream.

Brandle's hand caught mine gently and returned it to his chest, where he lightly played with my fingers. My heart fluttered in my chest from his attention and from the pieces that were falling into place in my mind.

Like me, the brothers had been cursed.

I closed my eyes in anguish.

"How did any of you sleep?" Brandle asked softly.

"Eadric is the only one who managed," Darian said.

"I wouldn't have slept if I'd been holding what he held without injury," Daemon said.

"You're all idiots," Edmund said softly. "Stop only focusing on how you feel. How she feels matters more."

"And how does she feel?" Liam asked.

Outside, the rain fell, and the sky rumbled its displeasure, a mere shadow of the turmoil of chaotic emotions I was trying to keep at bay.

"Afraid," Brandle said, trailing his fingers over mine. "Confused. Alone."

His words and the steady beat of his heart helped ease some of everything he knew I was feeling.

"She's not alone. She has us," Eadric said.

"Does she?" Daemon asked, proving himself awake. "We greeted her with hostility and suspicion less than a fortnight ago. And we didn't reassure her the first time we saw her powers slip. We let her run and hide as we debated if we could trust her. The second time, we viewed her with suspicion again. Why would she trust us?"

"We helped rid her of the tracker," Eadric said.

"But she didn't fear the tracker," Brandle said. "She fears her power and hurting others. We've done nothing to help her with that."

They understood me more than any other person ever had. Even Eloise.

And finally, I understood their initial fear of me. Brandle had said they didn't fear magic but the person wielding it. He'd acknowledged a woman had hurt them. She hadn't physically hurt them; she had cursed them.

I thought about how they'd pleaded so earnestly for my help. It had been before they'd learned of my powers, hadn't it? Daemon had mentioned a first time.

While I struggled to remember, another thought rose.

In order to gain their help to reach Turre, I needed to help them break their curse. Without guidance and without answers. Powers or not, it would take time. So much more than I had to spare. Yet, I saw no other viable option.

Forgive me, Eloise, I thought. *I vow to do whatever I must and return quickly. No matter the cost. My life for yours. Always. Without you, I have no reason to exist.*

Brandle's fingers moved over mine, and I questioned if that last vow still rang as true as it had the day I climbed out of my window.

Soon, Eloise. Soon.

THANK YOU FOR READING DESPAIR, Tales of Snow, Book 1! Kellen's story and her struggle denying these seven tempting men continues with Desire, Book 2.

DESIRE

CHAPTER 1

THE FIRE CRACKLED SOFTLY IN THE HEARTH, A COMFORTING SOUND as my thoughts spun with what I'd witnessed the night before during the storm. Tall men with the same features as the men living in this protected glade with me. Cursed men. Like me. Like Eloise.

Lost in thought, I rose from my bed, dressed, and placed the bedding and mattress next to the others already tucked away beneath the window.

Eight days had passed since I'd left my twin. Eight days she had to endure alone. Was she well? Had Maeve hurt her again? I needed to return. Quickly. But to gain the help I needed to free my sister, I needed the help of the seven men protecting me. Help they would give in return for my help. What help they needed, precisely, they could not say. According to the letter, if any of them told me what they required of me, the help I gave would be ineffective. However, I could not afford to waste precious days idly guessing.

Eloise needed me.

But so do they, my intuition whispered.

I stared at the overcast sky through the window and debated

the wisdom of ignoring the warning not to leave. My intuition hadn't yet led me wrong. Ignoring it had, though. That meant staying and attempting to help these cursed men.

Was the help they needed related to the curse I'd witnessed the previous evening? Could it be as simple as finding a way to break that curse?

Simple?

How laughable. Nothing magic-related was ever simple.

My gaze drifted to the door of the study where I'd found the letter asking for help. Should I then start my research there?

The indistinct murmur of voices rose outside before it hushed again, interrupting my thoughts and drawing me away from the study. I considered what I knew of the seven men outside.

They'd lived in this glade since they were children with a man named Henry, who could cast.

They never entered the cabin when I could see them.

They'd obviously been cursed in some way.

And they couldn't speak the truth about how I must help them.

Did that then mean I shouldn't know of their transformation? If I did, would that already negate any help I might give them?

Needing to understand the rules to ensure I did not idly waste time Eloise didn't have, I opened the door and looked out over the rain-soaked yard. The brothers were around the fire, preparing breakfast. They paused at the sound of the latch lifting and turned to look at me.

"Edmund. Could I speak to you for a moment?"

As he started for the cottage, I retreated inside to fetch the comb from the cabinet. Then I stood facing away from the door, careful to avoid the window's reflection.

"Kellen?" Edmund said.

I lifted the comb so he could see it.

"Come. Braid my hair for me."

I thought the following silence meant he was hesitating near the door. However, the tug on the twine holding my hair proved me wrong.

"You move silently," I said.

"It's a learned skill. Necessary here, as you know."

"True."

He plucked the comb from my fingers, and I closed my eyes at the sensation of it gently running through my hair.

"To ensure I make no mistakes, I would like to better understand the rules for the help I can provide," I said.

"I cannot give you any hints."

"And I am not asking for any. If I ask any question that I should not, simply do not answer it."

"All right."

"Could any knowledge I gain through my efforts invalidate the help I give?"

"No."

His answer didn't fully alleviate my concerns as I understood I could not directly ask him if what I saw the night prior was related to the help they needed.

"Am I allowed to read everything that's in the study?"

"Yes. Henry didn't leave anything behind that would hurt us or your chances to help us."

"But did he leave anything that would help?"

"Help you understand the powers you possess? Yes. Brandle believes you're afraid of your abilities. Perhaps the books will help you understand casting more so you will fear it less." His fingers began to twist my hair into a braid.

"I don't fear the power but what it might do to the people around me. I don't want to hurt anyone."

"Can I ask you a question to better help you?" Edmund asked.

"Please."

"Why is Brandle the only one of us who causes you to lose control of your powers?"

"I don't lose control of my powers; I lose control of my

emotions." I would have stopped there, but he tugged at the end of my braid, silently demanding a better explanation. "Brandle is direct and doesn't conceal what he's thinking or feeling when he looks at me.

"With the rest of you, I can lie to myself. Eadric is kind and courteous by nature and the easiest of you to be near. Daemon and Darian are playful and not to be taken too seriously. Liam and Garron are cautious, and you're distant."

"Lie to yourself? In what way?" Edmund asked.

I didn't know he was coiling my braid around his hand until he fisted it and gently tugged my head to the side. I could feel his exhale on my neck, and my eyes popped open.

"Close your eyes, Kellen, and answer me."

Heart thundering, I closed my eyes and focused on controlling the emotions churning inside that well, seeking to escape.

"You are no longer helping me, Edmund. Release me."

"You've lashed out at me several times. You've proven that you have a temper. Yet, you didn't lose control any of those times. Only with Brandle. Why?"

His exhales continued to torture the sensitive skin at my nape. Edmund was no longer distant. He was dangerously close. I shivered, and the walls of the well trembled.

"If you don't wish to be struck again, please release me."

With one hand tangled in my braid, he used the other to cup my chin and tip my head back. His lips skimmed my skin. A soft gasp escaped me at the same time as what I felt slipped free of the well.

My hands closed around his wrists, and I struggled to breathe through what he was making me feel. Heat and need. His and mine. But mostly his.

"Edmund. Please. Stop," I panted.

His tongue darted out, tasting my skin. My knees started to buckle.

"Edmund, enough. You've proven your point," Darian said. "Release her, or I'll kick you in the bollocks myself."

Edmund's lips left my neck to nip the outside of my ear. The feel of his teeth brought me low and robbed me of my last shred of control. The well was wide open, and I felt everything.

The echoes of remembered emotions from within the cottage. The six men gathered around the door, watching their brother slowly unmake me with barely a touch. The land. The rain that had fallen overnight. The beasts in the forest.

One's pulse called to me more than the others. Strong. Familiar. Urgent.

"Father," I gasped, snapping out of the spell Edmund had wrapped around me.

I thrust my head back sharply, connecting with Edmund's nose. He cursed. Daemon laughed. I spun around and darted out the door before any of them could stop me.

Energy from the air and the ground seeped into the well, enabling me to run faster than the men pursuing me.

"Kellen, stop!" Brandle yelled.

An arm circled my waist just before I could reach the trees. We tumbled forward together, but he turned us at the last moment so I landed on him instead of the ground.

"Wait. Don't go. It's too dangerous. Please, Snow."

The pet name he used halted my struggles to be free. I closed myself off from the energy pouring into me and looked up at the overcast sky. The faces of Liam, Darian, Eadric, and Daemon appeared to block the view.

"Are you mad, Princess?" Darian asked, watching me closely.

"Sparrow?" Eadric asked.

"Lamb, you look pale. Tell us what happened. Was it Edmund or something with your father?"

I sat up on Garron's chest and turned to look down at him. The desire to cry was now safely locked away in the well. But I still felt hurt. Deeply.

"You see me as cold?" I asked.

He flushed and shook his head. "Never."

"Why Snow then?"

The scarlet staining his cheeks deepened.

"Snow never stays long."

The sad way he said it almost had me forgetting my purpose.

I rose and offered him my hand.

"I'm not leaving, Garron. I felt my father. He's running this way. Something's wrong."

The words were barely out of my mouth when I heard a growl from within the shadowed depths of the forest.

Father.

His clothes were even more tattered than they had been. Old blood matted the fur on his chest. My heart broke for him, and I moved forward as he extended his hand.

"Kellen. Men come."

"Kellen, don't," Garron said, catching my arm. "It's dangerous."

"Magic," my father growled. The word was barely discernible, unlike the familiar red ribbon my father held in his outstretched hand. My intuition whispered it was dangerous to me.

"How many men?" I asked him.

"Five."

"I understand."

He set the ribbon on the ground and retreated deeper into the shadows.

"The ribbon needs to be destroyed," I said.

"Why?" Daemon asked.

"I cannot give a reason but only assure you that it does."

He strode past me and picked up the ribbon. The beasts in the forest didn't growl at his entry, which I found odd.

"I'll toss it into the flames," he said.

"Thank you."

I yelped when Liam suddenly swept me off my feet.

"What are you doing?" I asked.

His brown eyes danced with amusement as he strode toward the cottage.

"You ran out of the cottage without a cloak or boots, Kellen. We understand your need to speak with your father, but if you cannot take care, then we will."

"I don't understand."

"Your feet, Kellen."

I glanced at my mud-caked feet, feeling the bone-deep chill for the first time.

"I'll warm the water," Darian called as Liam neared the fire.

Edmund sat at the table with a cloth pressed against his nose and a hint of annoyance in his gaze.

"I thought you didn't want to hurt anyone," he said, sounding a bit nasal.

"I don't. Yet, I will defend my person when necessary."

He stood abruptly.

"Edmund," Brandle said with soft warning.

He needn't have bothered. I knew that Edmund had no desire to hurt me. The lingering feel of his teeth against my ear hinted at what he truly desired.

"Defend? Do you believe I would hurt you?" he asked with a scowl.

"Hurt me? No. Take liberties I have not given leave for you to take? Yes."

"Not given leave *yet*," he said. "You won't take me unaware again."

A smile tugged at my lips as I answered, "I bet a copper you make the same mistake before the end of the day."

"I'm betting on Kellen," Darian said.

"I think she's already proven it would be foolish to bet against her," Daemon said.

"A copper?" Brandle asked. "Why do you need coin?"

"What else should I ask for as a prize?" I asked.

"A kiss, Princess," Darian said. "That's always worth winning."

I snorted. This wasn't the first time they requested a kiss. "A copper holds more value. I could buy food, shelter, clothing, or even help with enough of them. What can a kiss do?"

The humor lighting their gazes disappeared, and the emotion that replaced it was one to be wary of. The lot of them were playing some mad game I had no wish to play.

"I would prefer to have my feet clean and appropriately covered before the men Father warned us about arrive," I said. "Please."

Edmund's gaze narrowed on me briefly before he waved Liam toward the cottage. Liam deposited me at the door and caught my chin like his brother had. My heart fluttered.

"I'll return with warm water," he said.

"And a chair, please."

The dangerously playful way his lips tilted at the corners alerted me to the danger of the moment. However, he didn't attempt to kiss me. He simply held my gaze for a few more heart-beats then left.

He and Daemon returned with two pails of tepid water and the short stool.

"The ribbon's been burned to ash," Daemon said, setting the stool just inside the door.

"Thank you."

"Was it yours?"

He watched me closely as Liam handed over the pails.

"It was."

"I thought magic wasn't allowed in Drisdall."

"It's not."

I closed the door on them and washed away the mud. Then I moved the stool closer to the fire to warm my feet.

The knock a few minutes later didn't surprise me.

I found Brandle just outside while the others ate their oats at the table.

"The men your father warned us of have arrived and are

watching from the trees," he said softly. "I believe they're waiting for us to leave."

I nodded and considered our options.

"Rather than wait for them to surprise us, we should surprise them," I said. "Liam and I are closest to the same size in the shoulders. Have him bring me some oats, and we'll switch clothes."

Brandle chuckled.

"I doubt Liam will fit your dress. But your plan is sound. If you're willing to wear his clothes and leave with the rest of us, I believe we can force their hand. The sooner we're rid of them, the better."

Brandle turned to leave, and I caught his arm.

"We'll send them away, won't we?"

He covered my hand with his. "No more death, Kellen. I promise."

With a pat, he left, and I turned my back on the door to begin unlacing my gown.

A throat cleared softly behind me before I finished.

"Come in, and close the door," I said.

I waited for the snick of the latch to speak. "It would be best if I wear what you're wearing now. And a cap. Brandle doesn't believe you can wear my dress, but if you can show a hint of the skirt at the door as we leave, it should convince those watching that I'm still inside."

I let my dress fall to the floor, and standing in only my shift, I stretched my arm behind me.

"Your pants, please, Liam."

"Kellen, you are the most unique woman I have ever met," he said as I listened to the rustle of his clothes.

"The world is filled with interesting women. You've simply been looking in the wrong places."

"Such as this glade filled with my brothers?"

"Precisely." Material weighted my palm, and I took his pants and quickly stepped into them. They fit me just as loosely as they'd fit him, drowning out any hint of femininity I possessed. Without any underthings, the coarser material scratched my inner thighs as I tied the strings. I knew I would grow accustomed to it, though.

Removing my shift, even with my back to him, made my heart race.

"Shirt please," I managed, holding out my hand again.

Instead of placing it in my hand, he brought it over my head. His fingers skimmed down my bare sides as he lowered the tunic and clasped my arms through the material, pinning them. He rested his forehead on the top of my head and exhaled heavily.

I held still, unsure what he meant to do. He released my arms and hugged me from behind. I could feel our size differences then. How the back of my head touched his neck. How his chest met my shoulders. How his bare hips met my back.

His hold didn't feel lewd or wanton but tender and heartfelt.

"Edmund isn't angry that you hit him," Liam said softly, his breath teasing my neck just as his brother's had. "Do you know why?"

I shook my head.

"He said your response to him was worth the pain." Liam's lips brushed my temple. "We all care about you, Kellen. We will keep you safe. Always. And you never need fear us. If Edmund is being an ass, speak it, and we will set him straight. Don't hurt yourself again to reprimand one of us for poor behavior."

His admission of how much they cared wrecked the hold I had on my emotions before I even knew what was happening. Light flared behind me.

"Liam, don't."

"It's okay, Kellen. You're not hurting me. I promise."

He dipped his head and kissed the same spot Edmund had. A soft gasp escaped me, and I cursed myself as a wanton woman as I tilted my head to enjoy the sensation.

"This is wrong," I said.

"Allowing you to dress as a man to keep you safe or asking me to pretend to be a woman?"

I snorted a laugh. He chuckled against my skin then withdrew to simply hold me again. The glow faded as I carefully regained control.

"Be safe, Kellen. That is all we ask of you."

"Are you certain that is all you are asking?" After all, I'd *felt* his desire.

"Well, Edmund and Brandle would be grateful if you stopped abusing their persons, but the rest of us have quietly enjoyed seeing you best them."

"You're as incorrigible as the rest," I said, shaking my head.

Liam kissed my temple again and released me so I could thread my arms through the sleeves of the borrowed tunic.

Once I finished, he turned me toward the door, careful to remain behind me, and handed me a cap.

"Do not forget. You are me," he said.

"I almost wish I could be here to see their faces when they enter the cabin expecting a helpless maid and instead find a naked man."

Liam chuckled. "Their shock will be my advantage."

"Be safe, Liam," I said, tugging the cap on and tucking my hair up.

"I will be. Go to the garden after you leave. The rest will be waiting."

I nodded and opened the door. Darian and Edmund lingered by the fire. They waved farewell indifferently as I left the cottage and went back to cleaning up breakfast. I knew it was an act for those watching, so I returned their half-hearted parting wave and went to join the others by the garden.

When they saw my approach, they started for the cave opening. Daemon lingered to accompany me.

Ahead, the others disappeared one after another into the cave.

When we neared, Daemon gestured to the darkness that had swallowed Garron.

"In you go, Lamb," he said.

Without hesitating, I stepped inside. Garron's large hand wrapped around mine. He led me several paces forward then stopped to whisper in my ear.

"Sound carries in here. Stay where you are."

One of them took my other hand and brought it to his mouth to lightly nibble my fingertips. I tugged my hand free.

"Dolt," I whispered. "No glow."

I heard someone cuff the offender and shook my head at them. In the following silence, a faint shout rose outside.

"Wait for us to return," Brandle whispered.

Then they were gone.

Alone, I listened to the yelling escalate. I heard Edmund's rage-filled roar. Brandle called out. Thumps and cursing rang from the clearing. My feet inched toward the opening.

A tingle of warning whispered that it wasn't safe to leave. However, a moment later, it warned that it wasn't safe to stay either.

"Kellen Cartwright! It's time to return home!"

A shadow filled the opening. Tall. Not one of mine.

"Come out, poppet, and I promise to go easy on you," the man crooned with a laugh.

Edmund's voice filled my head as I stepped forward so the man could see me.

Men see you as small and weak. Use it to your advantage. Hit hard and fast; then run. Show them you're more trouble than they know.

"There you are, poppet," the man said.

He grabbed my left arm. I thrust the heel of my right hand up into his nose. He cursed and jerked my arm, roughly lifting me, bringing me close enough to swing my free hand into his throat. He made a choked sound and dropped me. I thrust my knee up between his legs, and he toppled like a felled tree.

Jumping over his prone body, I bolted out of the cave. Near the garden, I paused long enough to grab the hoe.

"Bitch!"

The word echoed loudly from behind me, spurring me to run.

With my weapon in hand, I raced around the corner of the cottage and straight into the fray. All the times I'd held back when tormented by the boys in town came rushing forward. Edmund's rage became my own as I swung the hoe hard and hit the back of the man beating Garron. The man cried out. So did I when I realized the metal end was stuck in him.

Garron pushed him down and thrust me into the cottage. The door slammed shut, but not before I'd glimpsed another man rising behind Garron.

Breathing heavily, I stared at the planks.

The brothers weren't safe out there. Yet, I wasn't safe in here either. I needed to run. Hide.

The beat of my heart echoed my urgency.

Think, Kellen. Think.

I spun around to face the rest of the space and ran for the cupboard that hid the entrance to their cold storage. Swinging it open, I climbed the shelves like ladder rungs and pulled myself up into the loft.

Lying flat on the floor, I waited. It didn't take long for the door to crash open. I jolted but didn't make a sound as I listened to the grunts and curses that followed. Then everything quieted inside and out.

"That's all of them," Brandle called.

All of them? They'd beaten the trackers?

"Edmund," Darian called.

A whisper of sound came from below.

"Stay hidden, Kellen," Edmund said from inside.

I waited until I heard him moving to lift my head and peer between the bedframes to the space below.

Edmund hoisted one of the unconscious men and threw him

out the door. The second one followed. Corded muscles rippled beneath his now tight, fitted shirt as he moved about the cottage, righting a chair here and bedroll there.

I barely noticed Edmund's efforts to fix the mess they'd made as I stared at him. My memory of the night before hadn't been wrong. He had changed somehow. So much so that he towered over the table and tiny stool. Yet, his features were almost the same. A bit larger and more spread out but still Edmund. A handsome nose, swollen and brushed with blood. Beautifully passionate eyes. A split bottom lip pulled down in a frown as he picked up the broken pitcher.

He stalked toward the door, and I watched him shrink before my eyes the moment he stepped over the threshold.

"It's safe to come out now, Lamb," Daemon called.

I set my forehead on the planks and breathed, struggling not to feel the fear and confusion I wanted to feel.

"Kellen?" Garron called.

"I need a moment," I said.

"Are you hurt?" Brandle asked.

I heard his concern and knew any answer I gave would not be enough to assure him I wasn't. So I picked myself off the floor and climbed down the shelves on shaky limbs.

When I emerged, no trackers remained in the yard. Only my protectors. Garron had his shirt off, and Brandle was looking at his stitches. Darian was holding a cloth to his nose. Liam, now wearing pants, had an eye already swollen shut.

Beaten and bloodied in their efforts to keep and protect me.

Edmund and Eadric strode from the trees together. Eadric was limping.

"None of that," Daemon said, watching me. He lifted his hand and wiped a tear away.

I jerked away and wiped my face in disbelief. I wasn't one to cry. Ever. It was too dangerous.

Yet, the tears continued to fall. A noise escaped me.

"Ah, Lamb." The tender way he said it was my undoing. He held me close as I wept for all that I'd lost and all that I still faced. And I wept for the men who would suffer alongside me, hoping for help I didn't know how to provide.

A hand stroked over my hair.

"Are you hurt, Kitten?" Brandle asked.

"N-no," I said. "I'm angry."

Daemon chuckled. "You have an odd way of showing it."

"You didn't see her swing the hoe," Darian said.

I lifted my head and looked at them. "Did I kill him?"

"It was barely a poke," Liam said.

"Where are they? Do they still breathe?" I insisted.

"Though it would be safer if they did not, they still live," Edmund said.

CHAPTER 2

I dipped the cloth into the bucket of cold water and set it against Liam's eye.

"Hold it there," I said, already taking a second cloth and wetting it.

Darian grinned at me as I came up behind Brandle, who was checking his nose.

"It's broken," Brandle said a moment before he wrenched it. Darian cursed a storm as his eyes watered profusely.

I brushed Brandle aside and gently placed the cold cloth over the bridge of Darian's nose.

"Your brother only sought to protect your handsome visage," I said, running my fingers through Darian's hair to soothe him. He groaned, stole the cloth from my grasp, and tipped his head forward to rest it against my chest.

"I'll brew some tea for the pain," I said.

His arms banded around my waist.

"I'd rather have this," he mumbled.

Brandle chuckled as he moved off to check on Liam.

"If you allow me to leave, you can hold me again once the tea is done."

Darian released me but captured my chin and darted in for a quick kiss.

"Your nose is already broken," I said when he pulled back to wink at me.

"Which is why I know you won't hit it."

Foolish men and their need for affection, I silently grumbled. Yet, I enjoyed grudgingly giving it.

Why?

"Brandle, I believe it still looks a little crooked. You might want to fix it again."

Darian's eyes rounded, and he held up a hand in surrender as he held the cool cloth to his nose once more. The others laughed.

I started for the cottage and called over my shoulder, "Eadric, I want your pants off by the time I return so I can see why you're limping."

Inside, I climbed down into the cold storage and lit the candle to check the herbs for one that would help with swelling and pain. Henry had been thorough in his labeling. I didn't see how Eadric had mistakenly confused them enough to accidentally poison his brothers.

Lost in thought, I yelped when the nearby candle suddenly went out.

I wasn't alone.

"Brandle, now is not the time for your games."

A hand cupped my cheek.

"How did you know it was me?" he asked.

I paused.

"I don't know how. I simply knew."

"Are you afraid?" he asked.

"Of being in the dark with you? Hardly. I know where your nose is."

He chuckled. "You know that's not what I meant. Do you fear staying here...with us?"

I did. And I didn't like thinking about why I was struggling *not* to feel that fear. These men didn't scare me. However, what might happen to them if I stayed did. The trackers they'd fought off weren't their only threat.

"Kellen," Brandle said. "Please. Tell me what you're thinking."

"Yes, I'm afraid. But likely not for the reasons I should be. I'm unpredictable and dangerous.

"My mother was sick for a very long time. Death is part of life. We all know this. Yet..."

"Yet you've always wondered if your mother was weak because of you."

I jerked away from him. He didn't allow my escape but rather pinned me against his chest.

"Edmund's anger gives him away. Your concern reveals more about you," he said. "You've spoken often of your mother and sister. You've risked the forest to save your father. I saw your reaction when you hit the tracker with the hoe. We've seen your fear when you lose control. Why else would you be so afraid of hurting others unless you believe you've already done so?

"Casting doesn't work like that, though, Kellen. If it did, it would have died out long ago. While we're born with the potential, the gift grows as we do. You did not have the power of a caster to hurt your mother at birth. Likely, birthing two babes taxed her as it did my mother."

"Do you truly believe that?" I asked.

"I do."

The tension I'd been holding melted away with his words and his comforting embrace.

"I miss her so much," I admitted. "I miss Eloise, my home, and the life I had. And I hate that I can never go back to the girl I was."

"I don't, Kellen." His fingers brushed over my cheek and down my throat, comforting me. "The girl you were wasn't someone we would have ever had the chance to meet. And we need you right where you are."

I turned in his arms and hugged him. His hand smoothed over my hair as he held me.

"I know," I said. "I won't leave. No matter who comes, I won't leave until I've helped you...or until you ask me to leave."

"That will never happen," he said.

"The trackers will be back, Brandle. You know they will."

"They will. And we'll drive them away again. Eadric wasn't seriously hurt. He merely received a kick to his leg that will leave a bruise and take a few days to heal. Darian's nose is the worst of it. And as long as you assure him he is still handsome, it won't trouble him."

A dry laugh escaped me.

"It's broken, Brandle. If it's hit again before it heals, it will trouble him. Edmund is right. It would be better if those men couldn't return. I just—"

Brandle tipped my head back and kissed me, a gentle brush of his lips against mine. It was comfort and temptation wrapped together. I found myself leaning into it, wanting more. Wanting to lose myself in the feel of him instead of the doubts plaguing my thoughts.

When I opened my mouth to seek more, he groaned and cupped the back of my head. His tongue danced with mine, provoking me to feel more than I ever had. My skin tingled with energy, and I pulled away with a gasp.

"Wait," I panted when his lips moved to my neck.

"You can't hurt us."

"But I can hurt the land, Brandle," I said, threading my fingers into his hair and tugging him away from me.

He let loose a frustrated growl.

"Don't make me call for one of the others," I said.

Brandle was silent for several heartbeats.

"It feels as if you are forever retreating from me, Kellen."

I let loose a very Eloise-like snort.

"I've kissed you, slept on you, and admitted more truths to

you than I have my own mother. I am not retreating, Brandle. You're simply a bullish lout who is refusing to allow me to set my own pace."

A bark of laughter rang out from above.

"And Eadric agrees," I said.

"We all agree, Lamb," Daemon said. "But it's not kind to say it to the lout's face when he's trying to confess his feelings for you."

"His feelings? In a dark cellar? I should hope that's not what this is," I said.

More laughter drifted from above.

"Go," Brandle said. "I will fetch what we need."

When I emerged from the cellar, the cottage was empty and the rest waited in their same positions outside.

Eadric held up his hands pleadingly. "I wanted to comply and remove my pants, Sparrow, but they said they would cuff me if I did."

I shook my head at them all and went to switch the cloth covering Liam's eye. Garron's stitches from his previous injury were bleeding lightly where he'd strained them too much. The skin around Darian's eyes was starting to darken near his nose. He truly had my pity, and I didn't scold him when he tugged on my shirt and pleaded for a hug. Eadric playfully opened his arms and asked for his due several times as well.

"Affection-starved scoundrels," I said under my breath as I prepared the midday meal. "Shouldn't you focus on what you'll do when they return?"

"*If* they return," Edmund said. "We moved them deeper into the trees, closer to the path leading back to Drisdall, and left them with a lit fire and a supply of wood to keep the beasts at bay until they stop bleeding. It will take a few days for them to return. If at all."

"Truly?" I asked.

Edmund nodded, and I surprised him by cupping his face and kissing him on the lips.

"That is welcome news," I said with a smile.

Edmund didn't grin in return. His gaze shifted from my eyes to my mouth and back again.

"He's thinking about that copper," Eadric said.

"He should be thinking about Darian's broken nose," I said.

A smile briefly tugged at Edmund's lips. "I'll prove myself a man of control. For now."

"Thank you," I said, escaping his hold. "Drink your tea. I think I'll read for a bit."

I HEARD someone by the door but didn't lift my gaze from my book.

After reading for hours, I understood how little I knew about what I could do. And how unique I was. Many of the things the book warned could tax a beginner I could do with little effort—such as checking the weather.

It was going to rain again before dusk.

I wondered what excuse they would use to remain outside.

Another novice spell, to heat water, I could cast by simply thinking of the spell rather than speaking it aloud. Again, I felt no tiredness. I even went outside to check the grass and the trees. Nothing was dead.

Why, then, had things died when I was twelve? What had I done differently?

Determined to unravel the mystery, I read and ignored all else.

However, the men of the glade weren't of the mind to be ignored for long. I knew they'd run out of patience when Liam shuffled to the door and said he couldn't see anymore, and Eadric refused to feed him his meal.

Liam truly looked terrible with his swollen eye. So, I closed the book and rose to kiss both his cheeks.

"Poor thing," I said, struggling not to laugh.

While I did feel terrible about the injuries he'd gained defending me, I knew he wasn't so hurt that he needed comfort. He'd been sent to gain my attention because he looked the worst among them.

He took my hand and led me out to the others. Brandle and Edmund were missing, but the sound of chopping behind the cottage told me where they were. Garron walked near the tree line. Eadric lounged in his strung bed. Daemon poked at the fire. Darian sat on a bench by the table, watching his twin. Likely he was unable to lie down due to his nose. The swelling looked equally as terrible as Liam's.

Liam led me to the bowl beside Darian.

The casting books had provided a glimpse into a world of which I knew very little. Yet, it was that world I needed to grasp in order to help these men break whatever curse had been cast upon them. And I realized that, although they weren't allowed to give me hints, they could still guide me to the answer. And perhaps they had been doing so already with their playful bids for attention.

So, rather than sitting on the bench, I nudged Darian to straighten his posture, then perched on his lap to face Liam.

They all stared at me as I grabbed the bowl and lifted a spoonful of soup. Liam didn't make any move to eat it.

"Is this not what you wanted?" I asked.

Darian's arms snaked around my waist, and he pulled me more firmly onto his lap.

"I most certainly wanted this," he said.

"Liam?" I asked, watching him. "Can you not see the spoon? Do you need me to bring it to your mouth?"

Though his eyelids were quite swollen, he proved he could see by darting forward and eating the bite.

"I could eat better if you were on my lap," he said after swallowing.

"Then perhaps you would like to wait until Darian is done petting me."

Daemon laughed, and Darian groaned.

"Princess, I can't tell if you're provoking me or have no idea what you say."

I turned to look at him. "Is your hand not petting my side?"

He set his forehead on my shoulder and mumbled something about pleasure and pain.

"If I'm making you uncomfortable, I'll sit on—"

"No," Darian said, tightening his hold. "Stay. Please."

I agreed and finished feeding Liam while Darian held me and rested his cheek on my shoulder.

"Does anyone need more pain tea?" I asked.

"Not yet, Lamb," Daemon said. "But Eadric wouldn't mind a bit of a snuggle next. His leg pains him."

I glanced at Eadric in his swinging bed, and he lifted his arms and wiggled his fingers to beckon me. Could allowing them these liberties truly free them of their spell, or were they simply starved for female companionship?

"If I lie with Eadric, who will start the evening meal?"

"Garron and I will cook tonight," Daemon said a moment before he called Garron over.

I went to Eadric and puzzled over how to join him on his swinging bed without injuring him. Hands clasped around my waist and lifted me. In short order, I found myself lying on top of Eadric. His arms wrapped around me to keep me in place.

"This is nice," he said. A hand slipped up under the tunic and skimmed my lower back. "You're so warm."

I opened my mouth to tell him to remove his hand, but he nuzzled my cheek and cuddled me closely in a way that felt too divine to refuse.

"How does he not get hit?" Darian grumbled.

"Shut your mouth and let him be," Garron said. "If he goes too far, Kellen will tell us."

I tilted my head to look at Eadric. His smile was full of mischief. He wiggled his eyebrows and gave an exaggerated wink before saying, "A kiss would help my leg feel better."

Understanding that he wanted to annoy his brothers, I lightly kissed his mouth.

"Ah, that was nice. More, please."

Struggling not to laugh. I kissed him again. This time lingering a bit longer.

He sighed happily when I lifted my head. "More if it pleases you."

"Greedy git," Daemon muttered.

Eadric laughed silently underneath me. I lifted myself up enough to cup his face and kissed him the way Brandle had kissed me. Eadric's tongue playfully teased mine, drawing me deeper into the kiss and distracting me from his hands until one closed over my bare breast. I tore my mouth from his and stared down at him as his fingers stroked over my nipple.

A shiver ran through me.

He smiled beautifully and kissed the tip of my nose as he withdrew his touch.

"I believe I will need your protection again tonight," he said.

My eyes rounded, and I lifted my head to look at the others. They stood around the fire, staring at us. I'd expected shock and censure in their gazes but found none.

"How?" Darian sputtered. "I would have been unmanned for attempting that."

Daemon grinned. "I would very much like to see that."

"Leave them be," Garron said. "Kellen is free to do as she pleases."

"Including unmanning Darian," Daemon said. He nudged his twin. "Go give it a try."

I shook my head at them and looked down at a grinning Eadric.

"You have no shame," I said softly.

"None," he agreed. "Can I have another kiss?"

I thought again of the curse holding them and slowly nodded.

Eadric laughed and drew me down to his lips for another long kiss. He waited until I was just as distracted to move his hand to my breast. I didn't pull away. I let him touch me, stroking his fingers over a part of me that no one else had ever touched. He teased the skin until I was making small sounds against his lips.

Eadric pulled back, kissing the corners of my mouth then my nose.

Panting for breath, I hid my face in the crook of his neck and struggled with what I was feeling. Things that Mr. Bentwell's books had hinted at—desire...need—coursed through me

Eadric's palm still covered my breast, teasing it lightly. And I didn't bat him away. I lay on top of him, enjoying the closeness and the feel of him.

"Are you angry?" he asked quietly.

"No."

"Are you afraid?"

"No...yes...I don't know."

He removed his hand and simply hugged me.

"You don't need to be afraid. I'm here. I won't ever leave you."

How did he know that was what I feared most?

I wrapped my arms around him and hugged him in return.

When I left Eloise, I'd understood the danger. If giving my life would spare hers, I was willing to do so. Yet, I was no longer sure my life would be enough. What if saving my sister meant the lives of the men in this glade too?

"Are you feeling adequately cuddled?" I asked Eadric after several moments.

"I am."

"I'm not," Daemon said.

"I'll cuddle you," Eadric called with a grin.

Daemon scoffed and turned his back on us.

"Aren't you going to help me down for your cuddle, Daemon?" I asked.

He whirled about and had me out of the swinging bed before I could blink.

"What liberties am I allowed, Lamb?" he asked, setting me down.

"What would you like?" I asked.

His gaze heated as he considered me. "I think you wouldn't speak to me if I voiced what I'd like. So I will gratefully accept whatever you wish to allow."

I stepped close to him, crowding his space, which made him grin.

"Are you saying you'll concede to whatever I wish?" I asked, running my hand down his chest.

He nodded eagerly.

"What if what I wished for involved less clothing?"

His gaze heated significantly. Then, he bent and tossed me over his shoulder in a single smooth move.

"Tell me where," he said.

"The well," I said, bubbling with laughter. "You need to bathe."

He muttered a curse as Darian plucked me off his shoulder.

"Now you know how it feels," he said to his brother.

"You *all* need to bathe," I said. "It's going to rain before dusk, and we'll need to sleep inside again."

I didn't add that it would continue to rain throughout the next day, too. I wanted to see what they would do.

"And I'll comb your hair when you're done," I added when no one moved to leave.

Darian and Daemon raced to the well. Liam and Eadric followed more sedately.

"I'll watch the food," I said to Garron.

"No need. I'll let them fight for the bucket and wait until they return."

I fetched the comb and sat in the chair near the fire to wait.

"Did it upset you? What Eadric did?" Garron asked

"No. But it should have, and I think that upsets me the most. That none of the playful demands you and your brothers put on me has truly upset me. Have I been startled? Yes. Confused or unsure? Yes. But not upset. And any fear I've felt has been out of concern for all of you.

"Reading has helped with some of that. I understand how to heat water now. I suppose I could have offered that for their baths."

A small smile tugged at Garron's mouth. "You can heat mine for me."

I nodded my agreement and watched Darian race around the house, wearing a clean set of clothes.

"Where would you like me?" he asked, stopping in front of me.

When I said I had no preference, he sat at the table, facing outward, leaving me to stand between his splayed legs. He used my nearness to tease me with a few words or a wink as he subtly petted my hip.

His frigid hair was in an exceptional tangle and took a bit of time to work through. But he didn't seem to mind.

When I finished, I cupped his face and gave him a chaste kiss on the lips, careful of his nose.

"Thank you for protecting me and for bathing."

"My turn," Daemon said, sitting beside Darian.

"Little remains to comb," I said.

Regardless, I repeated the process, withholding my amusement over how Daemon's hand skimmed from my hip to my waist. Each time his fingertips brushed bare skin, he would watch me closely. I gave nothing away, though, not even at the end when I kissed him as I had Darian.

"I will bathe daily for this," Daemon said.

"Move aside," Liam said, nudging his brother though there was plenty of space on the bench.

Daemon gave up his spot, and I took my time combing through Liam's hair. Like his brothers, he held onto my waist. However, he didn't try to steal more. When I finished, I kissed his mouth lightly, then his swollen eye, before thanking him.

Edmund took his spot, and I eyed his short, wet hair.

"You combed Daemon's," he said with a slight scowl. I reached up and ran my fingers through his wet hair. "Is it the comb you want or what comes next?"

He gripped my hips and hauled me closer until my front touched his.

"I want everything you are willing to give."

I stroked a finger between his brows, easing the tension there before I set my lips to his. He moved, nipping my bottom lip. I gasped, and he deepened the kiss. Caged by his legs and held in place by the hand on the back of my head, I braced my hands on his shoulders as his tongue stroked against mine.

Edmund demanded my attention with an aggression none of the others had. It almost felt like a test to see how much I would willingly give.

Everything. Anything to get the help I needed, and I proved it by straddling his lap.

He tore his mouth from mine and looked up at me. I kissed the corner of his mouth, which was pulled down in a frown, then the place between his brows.

"Are you finished?" I asked.

His fingers twitched on my hips.

"He is," Brandle said from beside us.

I could see the flare of anger in Edmund's gaze and wanted to scowl at Brandle as well. Instead, I ignored him as I pressed another kiss to Edmund's frowning mouth.

"Are you finished?" I asked softly.

He exhaled heavily, closed his eyes, and nodded.

"I am," he said.

I stood and looked at Brandle.

"Are you ready?" I asked.

He looked at the comb I held up and then at me.

"What are you doing, Kitten?"

"Combing their hair like they wanted."

"And the kisses?" he asked.

The disappointment in his gaze was starting to make me feel uneasy, and I glanced at the others.

"I thought…"

"You kissed them because they wanted it?"

I nodded hesitantly, wondering if I'd made a mistake.

"Didn't they?"

"They did," Eadric said. "You didn't force yourself on them, Sparrow. You're not in trouble. Tell her, Brandle."

Brandle sighed and pinched his nose.

"You're not in trouble, Kitten. We are."

CHAPTER 3

"I DON'T UNDERSTAND." MY GAZE DARTED BETWEEN BRANDLE AND Edmund. "I'm only trying to help like I promised."

Edmund cursed under his breath and stalked off behind the cottage.

"Ah, Lamb," Daemon said, shaking his head. He followed his brother.

My temper flared.

They were disappointed? Why? I was doing my best without any help from—

Cutting off those angry thoughts, I fisted my hands and fought for control.

Brandle noticed.

They all did. And their sympathetic gazes did not help ease the emotions churning inside of me.

"I think I'll go read for a while," I said.

No one moved to stop me from entering the cottage or closing the door.

"Boorish ungrateful louts," I mumbled, stomping to my chair and picking up the book I'd been reading.

Eloise didn't have time for me to guess and bumble about

blindly, which is why following their lead had seemed the wisest choice. Obviously, it was a mistake. My mind kept circling back to why they'd wanted kisses and touching and sleeping near me.

Edmund told me they would say something if I was doing something unhelpful. If kisses weren't helpful, why had they been asking for them? If not for gaining my help, were they simply amusing themselves with me? Did they truly see me as a wanton woman?

My frustration was so strong that I wanted to throw something.

The book flew out of my hands and hit the wall. I stared at it with wide eyes. I hadn't physically thrown it, yet I could feel the book. Not the weight of it in my hand but the energy of it as if I'd connected to it in some way.

Terrified, I gripped the arms of the chair and closed my eyes to focus on the well. I'd been allowing myself to feel too much without thought about the consequences. It was a miracle I hadn't accidentally drained the surrounding energy and killed something.

I focused on my breathing—the calm of each inhale and exhale—until I felt fully in control. Then, I opened my eyes and glanced at the window to gauge the time. However, the sky remained overcast.

It would rain soon. I could feel it in the air.

I frowned and realized I could feel the weather *with* the lid tightly in place on the well.

While I'd known I would never be able to return to the life I'd had because I wasn't the same person I'd once been, I'd still believed I could return home to Drisdall. Now I was no longer certain. My abilities were no longer as hidden as they once were.

"What are they doing to me?" The room gave no answer to my softly voiced question.

Standing, I stacked my chair with the others and then began setting out the bedding before the hearth. When I finished, I lit the fire and climbed the cabinet to the loft above. With a blanket wrapped around me, I lay down and forced myself to read by the weak light cast by the fire below.

The information distracted me from my frustration. Absorbed in learning, I read until I heard a knock on the door. Softly closing the book, I set it aside and waited.

"Kellen?" Brandle called.

"I told you, she's not there," Edmund said.

"The fire didn't light itself," Brandle said.

Another knock sounded.

"Kellen, close your eyes. We're coming in."

I closed them, not because I was listening to him but to ignore the meaningless act they put on. What did it matter if they grew large when in the cottage? Why couldn't I see that? Would it stop me from helping them? Edmund had said that nothing I discovered on my own could invalidate my help.

The door creaked open.

"Kellen?" Brandle called softly.

I wanted to call him an ass in return, but honestly, he wasn't the one who'd behaved like one. I had. And that was the most frustrating part of all of this. So, my self-recrimination kept me silent.

"I'll check the cellar," Liam said. "She fainted down there before."

I listened to someone's soft footfalls on the stairs with a growing sense of guilt. They were worried about me. They'd done nothing wrong. They hadn't purposely misled me. I'd done that on my own.

"She's not down here," Liam called.

"Why was the door open then?" Darian said.

"So I could climb up to the loft," I said. "The rain will start in a few minutes. Go to sleep."

Silence met my grudging response for a few moments.

"Sparrow, why are you up there?" Eadric said.

"Because I want to be alone. Please."

"All right, Princess. We're here if you need us."

I wrapped my arms around myself and blinked back the need to cry. If I needed them? Since the moment I'd crashed into their glade, I'd needed them. Their protection and their help. But they could only give one. The other I needed to earn, and I didn't know how.

The empty bedframe beside me shook against the floorboards.

"Stop talking," I said, fisting my hands and fighting for calm.

No one else spoke.

It was a long time before I fell asleep.

I woke to the sound of a steady drip and wet, cold feet. Curling into a tighter ball, I moved my feet away from the leak.

"They're trying to fix it," Liam said from below. "Do you want another blanket?"

My answer was to ball up the one I had and toss it over the edge. A few moments later, a new blanket landed on me. A second followed.

"Let me know if you need another," Liam said.

I huddled under the dry blankets and rubbed my feet together as I listened to the rain fall outside. Eventually, the drips stopped.

"That's it," Garron called.

Daemon said something I couldn't quite hear.

"She's awake. Her bedding was wet," Garron said softly.

The light from the fire increased as one of them added wood. Outside, the sky rumbled softly.

The door closed, and I listened to the soft rustle of clothes.

"Kellen?" Brandle called softly.

"The leak stopped," I said. "Go to sleep."

"What happened before dinner…we didn't mean to—"

The bed started shaking beside me.

"Go to sleep," I repeated.

"We can't. We're worried about you."

"You should be. Unless you want this cottage to shake apart, you will remain silent and give me the peace I need to calm myself," I said.

Eadric, that sweet man, was the first to succumb to sleep. His soft snores comforted me, and I eventually joined him.

When I woke, rain still fell outside, but the sky was lighter—light enough that I could see inside the cabin.

I rolled onto my back and opened the book beside me.

"There are oats on the table when you're hungry, Princess," Darian said from below.

His soft footfalls sounded across the floor, and I heard the latch rattle. As soon as the door closed behind him, I turned onto my stomach and peered over the edge of the loft.

The cottage was empty save for a bowl of steaming oats on the table near the fire. The food called to me since I'd skipped my dinner, but I descended from the loft and slipped on my boots and cloak instead of eating. Though I had no desire to face the men of the glade, I needed the privy.

Pulling my hood low, I opened the door and stepped out into the steadily falling rain. I didn't look to see where they might be but walked the path to the privy alone. When I finished, I fetched a pail of water and carried it back to the cottage.

After shedding my cloak and boots, I filled the washbowl and warmed it with a silent spell. Twice. I washed my hands and face with the steaming water and began to feel more like myself. Enough so that I sat at the table, opened the book I'd been reading, and ate the oats.

The book consumed my thoughts, for which I was grateful. I learned to light a candle before starting a more in-depth study of the energy cost of spells.

The book suggested that, to determine the energy use, I'd need to check the well before and after the cast. How did one check the energy within their well, though? It wasn't as if I could drop a rock and count the seconds.

It went on to recommend that I visualize a scale and compare the energy consumed by the different spells I previously learned —such as warming the water, checking the weather, and lighting a candle—to determine a baseline cost.

Frustrated, I looked up from the book.

"Magic and men are the same. Both are too troublesome. What point is there in attempting to understand either?"

I rose and paced across the room as I continued to read. The book warned that the next spell, cast on herbs to aid with quicker healing, might be too taxing for beginners.

Pausing, I glanced at the cellar door and thought of the herbs Henry had stored away below. The same ones that were called for in the spell.

Casting to warm water had seemed harmless enough. After all, if something went awry, only the water would be affected. But if something went wrong with the herbs, the person ingesting them could be affected.

Someone knocked on the door.

"Kellen?" Garron called. "We made some soup if you're hungry."

I opened the door, surprising him.

"How much do you know about magic?" I asked.

"A fair amount," he said. "It's something Henry had us study."

"There's a spell here about enhancing herbs for healing." I pointed to it in the book. "Is it dangerous? If I cast it wrong, could something bad happen to the person who drinks it?"

"No. Either the spell works as it's intended, or it doesn't work at all."

"Can I try?"

"Of course."

I turned away without closing the door and raced down to the cellar. Henry had all the herbs and the required beeswax candle. I bundled everything in my tunic and carried it up the ladder. The spell was a bit tedious, requiring me to boil the water using the candle wrapped with a strand of the caster's hair. Once the water boiled, I added the herbs in the correct measurements and waited for it to cool.

The resulting brew smelled unpleasant—bitter and a bit rancid. I made a face and reread the notes in the book.

"If it smells awful, it's correct," Brandle said.

I looked up from the spell and realized they were all standing in the doorway.

"Worse than awful," I said. "It will likely make a person vomit."

"Then Eadric should try it first," Daemon said. "We're owed."

Eadric grinned. "Bring me the brew, Sparrow. I'm ready to walk without a limp."

I poured a cup, watching the herbs swirl and settle to the bottom.

"You won't hurt us, Kitten," Brandle said.

Not hurt him? Was he not paying attention?

Frustration spiked along with the wish for someone to cuff him.

The book that had been resting on the table flew across the space and hit him squarely in the chest. I wasn't as stunned as previously and took a moment to feel my connection with the book and how much energy it had. It felt the same.

I quickly checked the well, but it felt securely closed off. How, then, was I doing that?

"Open your damned eyes, Brandle," I said. "I just threw a book at you and have no idea how. I am barely in control and able to do things the book I'm reading does not mention. So, yes, I *can* hurt you. Stop being a fool."

He had the grace to look down at the book he'd caught.

"I am *trying* to do as I promised and growing very frustrated in the process," I said. "I thought yielding to your requests was furthering our mutual goals. Clearly, I was wrong. Though I understand that you cannot give me the answers I need, I am losing patience.

"The five men waiting in those woods will not give up and leave. By staying here...by asking for your help, I *will* risk your well-being regardless of my intent. So, please...stop acting as if we are not in danger and have all the time in the world for me to figure this out."

"Forgive me, Kellen," he said quietly, returning the book to me.

Realizing I'd done it again—blaming them for something that I caused—I let out a heavy breath and focused on being calm.

"It is not my place to forgive but yours," I said. "Forgive me for bringing my troubles to your door. Forgive me for being so ignorant about what I am that I'm a danger to everyone around me. And forgive me for needing to use you to help me reunite with my sister."

I handed him the cup. "It should be enough for all of you."

They didn't stop me from closing the door. I returned to my seat and opened the book. I desperately needed the knowledge stored within those pages.

After I finished it, I selected another from the study, hopeful that it would contain more answers than the first.

The rain stopped. They knocked on the door to deliver meals but otherwise left me alone.

THE NEXT MORNING, I once again dressed in my own clothing. When I opened the door, Darian was standing there, grinning widely.

"Give it a tweak," he said.

"Pardon?"

"My nose. Look at it."

I did. The swelling had vanished, as had his blackened eyes.

"It worked?" I asked.

"It did. Eadric can walk without a limp. Liam can see. Brandle is still an ass, but magic can't fix everything."

Something had finally gone right. I grinned.

"What would you like to break your fast today?" he asked. "Pastries? Oats? We can do both."

"Biscuits with honey," I said.

Some of his joy faded.

"The trackers remain. It would be wise—"

"You are healed, and they are not. It would be wise to leave for supplies while you can, don't you agree?"

I'd considered our current circumstances carefully between books the day prior. Once the five men healed, the brothers would have no opportunity to leave for supplies again.

"That does make sense," Darian said.

"Go speak to the others. Take what supplies you need from the cold storage while I'm out. We should have a stew again for the evening meal."

I walked to the privy, ignoring the others by the fire. When I emerged, Eadric was waiting.

"What news did they send you to deliver?" I asked, moving to the well.

"We'll get the honey. Is there anything else?"

"Eggs…cream…whatever else you need for however long you think it will take for me to help you." I paused washing my hands. "Are you truly in danger each time you leave for supplies?"

"We are."

"Is that danger greater than running out of supplies?"

He smiled, grabbed my shoulders, and kissed my cheek.

"Worry doesn't suit you. You're prettier when you're scolding Brandle."

"I'm sure Brandle would disagree."

"He wouldn't. None of us like it when you worry. We want you to be happy."

"I wish for the same," I said. "And that will only happen once my sister is free and safe."

Eadric frowned slightly at what I'd said. Just as he didn't like me worrying, I didn't like him as anything other than his happy, playful self. Taking his hand, I smiled at him.

"Come," I said. "Let us see what they're cooking."

He didn't say anything more as we walked to the cooking fire where Brandle was stirring a smaller pot.

"We don't have honey, but we do have berries and sugar," he said without looking up. "You might want to supervise Garron's attempt at biscuits."

Instead of moving away from him, I sat beside him.

"Do you think it's unwise to leave?" I asked.

"Why do you believe these trackers won't give up like the previous one?"

I looked at the trees. "It takes half a day or more to travel from Drisdall to your glade, depending on the number of beasts between here and there. These men appeared two days after we last saw the previous tracker. That they multiplied and arrived quickly shows urgency and determination, does it not? I feel both as well. Do you believe I will give up?"

"No," he said.

"Precisely."

"Then it's wise to leave for supplies as you suggested. However, I do not trust the trackers not to attempt to take you again, regardless of their state."

"They may, but their attempt would be significantly weaker due to their injuries. If you do not leave for supplies now, do you believe we have enough supplies to last until I learn how to help you?"

I could see the doubt in his gaze.

"I would prefer you remain as well, but I fear what troubles we may face if we delay," I said.

A glint of something crept into Brandle's gaze.

Before I could decipher it, Eadric said, "She's worried we'll be in danger when we leave."

With a grin, Daemon pulled me to my feet. "Ah, Lamb. You do care!" He swirled me around in an energetic dance as the rest laughed.

Embracing his attempt to distract me from what I'd glimpsed in Brandle's gaze, I asked, "You doubted me? Even after I only threw a book at Brandle instead of all the chairs?"

They all laughed as I'd hoped. I didn't want any of them to leave believing I was angry. I wasn't.

When Daemon finished spinning me around, he stopped by the table and pulled me onto his lap.

"If this doesn't directly help me achieve our mutual goal, I respectfully ask that you stop taking liberties with my person."

"Ah, Lamb, now I have no idea what to do. If I pushed you away, that would be a hint that this is not a direct help. Or if I keep you, it would be a hint that it is. And hints in any form are not allowed."

He wrapped his arms around me and set his chin on my shoulder.

"Let me think of an option that does not give a hint," he said. "Perhaps I should kiss you and then release you so it's both and neither at the same time."

He captured my chin with one hand and kissed me soundly before setting me on my feet.

"There. No hint given," he said with a grin.

"You make me want to kick you in the shin," I said without rancor.

"Will you bestow another kiss if I'm injured?"

"Unlikely," I said. "But I can brew more tea after I request your brothers beat you."

He held up his hands in surrender. "Truce, Lamb."

I pivoted to walk away but crashed into Darian.

"He's a scoundrel, to be sure," Darian said, wrapping an arm around my shoulders. "Come sit with me, Princess. I'll vow to protect your virtue from his advances."

He spun me around and tugged me onto his lap. I arched my brow at him.

"Do I look like a loose woman to you?"

"Never."

"Then why do you continue to treat me as such after I've clearly stated my view on the liberties I've allowed?"

"Release her, Darian," Garron warned.

Darian made a face.

"Princess, you wound me with your disregard." As he spoke, he stood with me. "Can't you see you've won a place in our hearts? Can we not win a place in yours?"

"Enough, Darian," Edmund said sharply. "Leave her be."

With a wounded look, Darian let go of my hand and retreated to his strung bed.

"I'll be inside reading," I said, returning to the cottage.

THE SUN WAS SINKING low in the sky when I heard the sounds of their return.

"Kellen, come see what they've brought," Garron said from the door.

I set the book aside and stood. Stiff from the hours I'd spent reading, I stretched. Garron quietly watched me, waiting for me to join him. When I did, I wrapped my arm through his.

"I forgot to ask if Brandle removed your stitches."

"Not yet. He worries that it might be too soon even with the tea."

"Do they itch?"

"Fiercely," he admitted.

"They should be removed soon then."

The others waited around the table where they'd set everything. They'd procured more eggs, cream, sugar, honey, and a new water pitcher. Next to everything were two cloth-wrapped bundles.

"For you," Eadric said.

I opened the smaller bundle and found two books.

"More books on magic," Darian said. "They're from a reputable source."

When I reached for the second bundle, Liam stopped me.

"You can open that one later," he said.

Trusting there was a reason he didn't want me to open it, I left it alone.

"The stew should be done," I said, turning my back on the cottage to stir what Garron and Edmund had made.

Brandle joined me, setting a hand on my shoulder and stealing the ladle.

"Did you learn anything interesting today? Edmund said you didn't leave the cottage except to use the privy."

"Everything I'm learning is interesting," I said. "However, it's not enough. Nothing has helped me understand how to better control what I can do."

"You've barely begun. Give yourself time."

"Time is something I have very little to spare."

"Eadric told us what you said. That you cannot be happy until your sister is safe and free. Is she in danger, Kellen?"

I purposely did not think of Maeve when I nodded. My throat didn't constrict.

"Is she being held against her will?"

Steadily, I met Brandle's gaze and did not respond.

"I see." He glanced at the trees. "The trackers were not sent by her, were they?"

"No. She would never send such men after me. She would give her life to keep me safe. When I left, she was the only remaining protection I had in this world, and I was hers."

He nodded thoughtfully.

"If I asked who sent the trackers, would you be able to answer me?"

"No."

"Will not or cannot?" Edmund asked.

"You're on the right path. However, knowing won't change what any of us must do. Guard yourselves well. I did not simply bring trouble to your doorstep. Trouble is too simple of a term. Misery. Devastation. Those are more apt. I truly hope that the help I give you makes up for what yet may come."

Brandle's hands gripped my arms, and he leaned in to kiss my cheek.

"It will be worth it. We have no doubt of that. Please don't turn away from helping us in fear of hurting us."

He knew my mind too well.

"I don't believe I will be afforded that opportunity. If the seven of you aren't able to stop me from leaving, the trackers and the beasties surely will."

CHAPTER 4

AFTER DINNER, I RETURNED TO THE COTTAGE TO READ BY THE light of the fire. The words began to blur, and I knew I needed to rest.

I glanced at the door, wondering what rest meant now. Did they still want me to sleep near them? If so, why? Was it helpful, or wasn't it? And if it wasn't helpful to them, did I still want it?

Unsure, I set my book aside and unrolled a single stuffed mattress.

No one appeared at the door despite the noise I made. I stripped off my boots and covered myself with a blanket as I faced the open door. Would they come? Did I want them to?

My eyelids grew heavy, and I gave in to the need to sleep before I had an answer.

I woke shivering and regretted not closing the door before bed as I tucked my cold fingers under my arms. The dying coals were barely enough light to illuminate the hearth.

Torn, I debated what to do. I could leave my blankets to add more wood or ask them to join me. One required more time and effort on their part—to chop additional wood. The other might help me learn more about the spell binding them.

The decision was easy.

"The fire is out, and I'm cold. Is anyone awake to warm me?" I called softly.

The flurry of movement drew a snort from me, but the sound of numerous boots hitting the floor as they discarded them almost drowned it out.

"Ox."

"Oaf."

"Bast—"

"Who cuffed me?"

"Shut it."

"I was assured you would never fight due to me," I said over the scuffle.

"This isn't a fight, Princess," Darian said, lying in front of me. "It's a competition to see who can get to you first." He pulled me into his arms.

I pressed my cold nose against his warm neck.

"Shite!"

His head jerked as someone cuffed him.

"No cussing," Garron said from behind me.

I reached back for his arm and used it to pull him closer. The heat of his chest warmed my back, and the shivering eased slowly, helped by Darian's roving hand that drifted over my hip and up my arm. I sighed contentedly, enjoying the feeling as I debated how to gather more information about the curse binding them.

After mistaking their previous advances, I hesitated to presume anything. Yet, I also knew I couldn't question or state what I thought I knew as it could lead to a hint. Perhaps subtlety was the key.

Lightly tracing the breadth of Darian's chest, I said, "I'm glad there is more of you to warm me when you're inside."

"More of us? Did we gain a brother?" he asked with a soft laugh. I could hear the underlying uncertainty, though.

This time, I ran my hand from his shoulders to his waist.

"We both know the gain was not in the form of another brother. Goodnight, Darian. Thank you for keeping me warm."

Silence followed. They would either acknowledge what I knew or continue to pretend that they did not change size when entering the cottage. I could only choose my next step once I knew their direction.

As I waited for them to decide, I closed my eyes and enjoyed their warmth.

WHEN I WOKE NEXT, the sun was up, and I was not alone. Brandle held me from behind. I didn't know how I knew it was him; I simply did. Wrapped in his arms, I felt warm and comforted... until his lips brushed the back of my neck.

"I understand there are things you are not permitted to tell me, and though I've tried not to let it frustrate me, it has. Considering my dangerous lack of control when my emotions overwhelm me, perhaps it would be wise not to provoke me until I have a better understanding of the help you require."

"I well understand your frustration, Kellen. I've lived with it for years, waiting for the right person to appear to help us. You ask for our patience? We have none. It left us with Henry.

"If you're frustrated and wish to throw a book or a chair, then throw them. But don't give up on us, Kitten. Please. That is the only way you could truly hurt us."

"I have no intention of leaving, Brandle."

"Not leaving, Kitten. Giving up. Allow us to do as we will, and in return, react however you wish. If it's the heel of your palm to our noses or a chair thrown by magic, so be it."

He punctuated his request with another kiss on my neck.

"You make very little sense, Brandle. Was it not only yesterday that you expressed your disappointment that I yielded to your advances? And now that I've requested they stop, you're again asking me to allow them?"

As soon as I spoke the words, I understood. The trouble lay in my yielding to their desires, not the advances themselves. That he wanted me to allow the advances and to react however I would meant simply yielding wasn't what they'd wanted. And they saw refusing their advances all together as giving up.

A sound of frustration escaped me, and I took three calming breaths.

"Very well," I said. "I will do as you say. However, if you find yourself bandaging any of your brothers' bruised bollocks, the fault is not mine but yours."

He snorted a laugh behind me and nuzzled my neck.

"I will keep your wise words in mind."

"Are we going to speak of the real reason you've lingered at my side after daybreak, or should I continue to pretend I do not know?"

His arms wrapped around me and held me more firmly against his hard chest.

"Tell me what you think you know," he said softly.

"You grow larger when you are in the cottage and are smaller when you are outside. I believe you've been cursed, and that is why you need my help. I can think of no better explanation for such a cryptic letter left by Henry than that."

Brandle was quiet behind me, and I wasn't sure if it was because he couldn't say anything or due to indecision over what to say.

Turning in his arms, I faced him. His face looked different but still familiar. Still very handsome.

"Does it frighten you?" he asked softly.

"Which part? Your curse? Or the need to break it without any help when I'm completely clueless about all things magic?"

"My size. You did not have a favorable opinion of men who tower over you."

I was surprised he'd remembered that.

"Your size has never mattered, Brandle. Who you are as a person always has."

His hungry gaze swept over my face.

"I want you to kiss me, Kitten."

"And I want honeyed biscuits to break my fast. It would seem we must accept that we cannot always have what we want."

Instead of getting angry, his eyes crinkled with his wide smile.

"Garron, I believe Kellen is ready for her honeyed biscuit."

My eyes rounded, and I twisted to look at the door. Garron entered, holding a plate. I barely noticed it as I watched him shift from the size I knew to the larger version. Uncertainty pulled at his brow.

Brandle caught my chin and nudged me to face him.

"My kiss, Kitten?"

I considered him for a moment. He didn't want false affection, I realized. He wanted whatever I truly felt. What did I feel? Afraid. Afraid that it would be easy to lose my heart to him and each of his brothers. Where would that leave me?

"I have no wish to be heartbroken and alone, Brandle."

His gaze searched mine.

"And you fear that's what will happen if you kiss me?"

"You're not asking for a simple kiss. You're asking for my affection. I have lost everyone I've held dear. Do not ask me to care for you. Please."

He crushed me in a fierce hug that should have felt suffocating but didn't.

"Trust me. Trust us," he said with a raw whisper. "We will not leave you, Kellen. Ever."

"Death is the one certainty in this world, Brandle. We will all leave."

"Kitten, I—"

"Enough, Brandle," Garron said. "Let her be."

I felt Brandle's heavy exhale and the kiss he placed on the top of my head before he released me and stood in one fluid motion.

Garron crouched down beside me as Brandle left.

"Hungry, Snow?"

He offered me the plate.

"Do you know how frustrating it is to feel as if you are always making the wrong choice?" I asked.

He smiled slightly.

"A choice isn't right or wrong; it's simply a choice. It's not until you see the result that you can decide if it was right or wrong. And you're still in the middle of your choice. So stop thinking and just enjoy your biscuit."

When he started to rise, I caught his hand.

"Will you sit with me while I eat?"

I sat up on my mattress to make room for him.

"Who is staying with me today?" I asked.

"We all are."

"Do you believe the men are healed enough to try something?"

"None of us wants to take that risk," he said.

I nodded and took a bite.

"This is good. Tender. Perhaps, once I break your curse, you'll become a baker."

Garron ducked his head as a flush stained his cheeks.

"Or do you think you'll stay here?" I asked.

"We wish to return home," he said quietly. "It's a memory for Brandle but only a story told by Henry for the rest of us."

"Will you tell me about your home?" I asked.

"I would rather see it for the first time with you," Garron said.

I met his gaze, seeing the hope there.

"It's a deal then. I'll help you, and after we help my sister, I'll see your home with you."

He glanced down. "We'll need to go to Adele for the help we

need to free your sister and ensure her safety. It may take some time."

I didn't care for the way he wasn't meeting my gaze.

"How long, Garron?"

"A fortnight, perhaps."

Dismayed, I set my half-eaten biscuit on the plate.

"That long?" I asked.

"Adele is nothing like Drisdall. The people don't trust easily."

I nodded in understanding even as my heart sank. Another fourteen days before I could reach Eloise? And it would likely take me double that to figure out how to help break the spell binding these men.

Could Eloise endure that long? Maeve had deceived Eloise and me and kept us alive for a reason. I had to believe she would continue to do so. The thought didn't comfort me, though. I knew the suffering one could withstand and still live.

"Rather than think of it as time lost," Garron said as if hearing my thoughts, "Perhaps you can devote yourself to learning."

"Learning?"

He held up the book I'd been reading the night before. "If you don't understand something, ask. We may not have your ability, but Henry did, and he taught us what he knew."

I nodded and accepted the book.

Garron didn't linger in the cottage, and I watched him leave and marveled at the spell that held them. What purpose did it serve?

My gaze returned to the book I held. Could the answers to breaking their spell lie within the pages of the books Henry left behind? Brandle thought not, but couldn't a cast spell be uncast?

They left me to read in peace as I nibbled on my biscuit. However, when I rose to use the privy, Daemon hurried toward me and took my arm.

"Of course I'll escort you to ensure your safety, Lamb," he said in a normal tone before whispering, "Please invite me into the cottage with you. Any pretext will do."

Undoubtedly, he was up to no good.

"And what will you give me for this favor?" I asked.

"My currently unrequited love and devotion?"

"No thank you."

"Anything you wish, then."

"Your agreement to a future request," I said.

His gaze grew suspicious. "What request?"

"I'm not yet certain. However, I vow it will not cause harm to others."

"Very well. I agree."

With a suspicious glint in his eyes, Darian watched our return. Rather, he watched Daemon. Knowing that Daemon was likely provoking Darian in some way, I played along and threaded my arm through Daemon's.

"If no one minds, I would like to claim all of Daemon's unrequited love and devotion for the day."

Without waiting for a reply, I steered him toward the cottage with me.

"Bloody git. He bribed her," Darian grumbled.

"A deal is a deal," Garron said. "You wash the dishes."

I glanced at Daemon, who was grinning from ear to ear and already kicking off his second boot. He guided me to the bench and knelt before me.

His hand slid up my calf in his quest to remove my boot and earned him an ear tweak. He chuckled but properly adjusted his hold.

"And how would you like me to spend the day with you?" he asked.

"In silence. I wish to read."

He followed me across the room where someone had already stacked the bedrolls under the window. He removed a chair from the stack for me.

"Would you like it before the window or the fire?" he asked.

"The window, please."

I settled onto the chair and opened my book to where I'd left off.

Daemon was completely attentive. He brought me food and drink, fed the fire, and found ways to subtly provoke me into giving him attention.

He sat on the floor and rubbed my feet—which resulted in more calf touching and earned him a kick to the side. He asked to comb and rebraid my hair then claimed it was too dirty and needed washing.

The others hauled in water at his behest. I ignored them and read.

When Daemon tugged me to my feet, I paid him little mind... until he started untying my lacings.

"Unhand my clothing, Daemon."

"Keep reading, Lamb, and pay me no attention. I will have you washed, clean, and redressed before you reach the end of the book."

"You are not bathing me, Daemon."

"Not presently. You're still dressed. Come, let's remedy that."

His fingers plucked the ties loose before I could tug them from his hold.

I caught his hands as my bodice loosened.

"I've already seen you in your shift, Lamb. There's no need for feigned modesty between us."

"Feigned?" I arched a brow. But rather than lose my temper, I decided to teach him the meaning of feigned.

"You believe me to be immodest, then?" I asked, giving him my pitiful, sad look—the same one Eloise often used on Judith when caught stealing pastries.

"No. Never," Daemon said quickly, concern and a hint of panic creeping into his gaze.

I released his hands and slowly tugged at the top of my dress.

"Perhaps you're right. Perhaps I am immodest." The ties loosened enough for my dress to fall off my shoulders. It wasn't anything he hadn't seen before, yet his gaze heated.

"Did you like seeing me in my shift?" I asked softly.

His gaze swept over my face. "Yes. I liked it very much, Lamb."

"And would you like to watch me bathe?"

He swallowed hard and nodded once. I let my dress fall to the floor and closed the meager distance between us.

"Brandle wanted me to kiss him this morning. Do you want the same?"

He ducked down just like I'd hoped he would. With his focus on my mouth, he never saw me reach for the new pitcher beside him. As I stood on my toes, I lifted it over his head. My aim was true, and the cold water drenched him.

I watched it cascade down his face and drip from his nose.

Laughter echoed from outside.

He blinked at me as he slowly straightened. Several seconds passed before he began to smile.

"Does this mean I don't get a kiss?"

"No kiss and no helping me bathe. I'm quite capable on my own."

He shook his head, sending water flying. He didn't leave, though. His gaze swept over my face again. Considering. Devious.

"I need to check something," he said softly before pulling me against his damp chest and pressing his lips to mine. The kiss was sweet and too short.

When he pulled back, he watched me warily.

"Either leave on your own, or I will ask Darian to help you. I believe he would be willing."

"Very willing!" Darian yelled from outside.

Daemon smirked at me, darted in to kiss my forehead, then strode out the door, closing it behind him.

I listened to the low murmur of their conversation as I glanced at the window, then removed my shift to bathe.

The steaming water melted away my tension as I leaned my head against the tub.

Daemon and Darian both liked to play and cause trouble. Daemon did so to avoid work, and Darian did so for fun. Was that why Daemon kissed me? Was it simply a playful thing to do? What had he been checking?

"Do you need any help with your hair, Lamb?" Daemon called through the door. "Edmund is willing."

"I've entertained you enough for today, Daemon," I said. "Leave me in peace."

"Was he bothering you, Princess? Should I have Garron cuff him?"

Deciding to ignore them all, I closed my eyes and focused on the feel of the water around me. The heat of it. Its comforting embrace.

In my mind, I could see it—a glowing mass surrounding me.

The energy in the plank boards of the floor appeared next. Then, the bound clumps of grass that made up the thatching. I could feel its energy in its brightness. The water glowed vividly, the floor more mutely, and the thatching fainter yet, except for the place they patched.

And outside, seven men shone like the sun.

"Kellen, love…are you angry?" Liam asked

"No."

"Are you casting, Trouble?" Edmund asked, worry lacing his words.

My eyes snapped open, and I saw it in the air around me— energy. It moved like mist, slowly circling and curling around me.

"I…don't know. Something happened."

The door banged open behind me. With a gasp, I sank lower into the water as I glanced over my shoulder.

Edmund stormed in like an enraged bull. Garron was only a pace behind him. His eyes widened as his gaze swept the room.

"Do you see it?" I asked.

"I do," Garron said.

"What is it?"

"What is what?" Edmund asked.

"The colorful mist," I said, sweeping a wet hand to indicate the room.

The glowing particles moved as if I'd disturbed them.

Edmund's gaze stopped searching the space for danger and settled on me. I saw the moment interest replaced his concern in his gaze and crossed my arms over my chest.

"Edmund, out."

Brandle reached in through the door and pulled his brother out before Edmund could do anything more. The door closed softly.

I glanced at Garron, who was running a hand in the air, staring at the swirl of colors.

"Do you know what it is?" I asked.

He glanced at me, flushed, then focused on the room.

"Energy, but I've never seen it like this. When Henry cast the spell for the barrier around the glade, it was close to this."

Garron suddenly rushed over to me and pulled me from the water. Shocked, I didn't think to fight him when he turned me away from him and then back again.

His gaze swept over my nakedness without hesitation until it met mine. A flush exploded on his face, and he released me like a hot coal. I hurriedly sank into the water.

"Forgive me. I—" He swallowed hard and looked frantically around the room. "Henry lost twenty years of his life when he cast that spell. I feared—"

I watched Garron tuck his trembling hands into his pockets.

"I'm sorry. I didn't mean to upset you."

He let out a slow breath. "What spell did you cast?"

"I didn't cast any. I closed my eyes to relax and focused on the feel of the water. Its energy was there in my mind—bright and glowing, like what you see in the air now. Then I could feel the floor and the thatching. I could *see* it all, even with my eyes closed. I didn't know that I was casting until Edmund asked. How did he know?"

Garron tapped the amulet tucked away under his tunic. "It glowed."

I nodded slowly and rested my head against the tub again. "I could see all of you too. You glowed so brightly. If not for your protective charms, what would have happened, Garron?" His silence was answer enough. "I'm a danger to all of you."

He touched my hair lightly. I kept my eyes closed, knowing I should send him out but needing the comfort.

"Brandle doesn't lie, Snow. The only way you can hurt us is by giving up. We rushed in here because we were worried for your safety, not ours."

"Foolish," I muttered. Yet, so like my sister. "Why could you see the colors but not Edmund?"

As soon as I asked, I knew.

Sitting up, I turned to look at him. His fingers feathered against my cheeks.

"You can cast, can't you?"

CHAPTER 5

Garron looked away and started to stand. I grabbed his arm to stop him.

"Please, Garron. I'm going mad with frustration. The books speak of things I don't understand. If you do, please teach me. Please. I don't want to hurt anyone."

He looked at me, his gaze dipping to where my chest pressed against the edge of the tub.

"Will you kiss me, Snow?" he asked softly, his cheeks coloring brightly.

"A kiss freely given in exchange for your guidance?"

"Yes."

"Close your eyes, Garron."

Once I knew he couldn't see me, I rose to my knees and leaned out of the water to cup his cheeks. The stubble of his emerging beard teased my fingers, and I gave in to the need to caress it. I watched his face as I touched him. His brow moved slightly. Perhaps wonder. Perhaps nerves or anticipation.

I checked that the lid on the well was tightly closed then tried to feel what he felt. It came easily. Adoration. Desire. So much of it.

He wanted my kiss. No, he craved it.

Leaning closer, I brushed my lips lightly over his. They were soft and warm and welcoming. His parted, inviting me to deepen the kiss, allowing me to lead. My heart gave a fluttering beat. Heat pulsed around me. In me.

I tentatively stroked my tongue against his bottom lip and felt his hand settle on my hips. The heat of his touch on my bare skin warmed me from the inside.

The well gave a shudder, and I quickly pulled back.

"I can't, Garron. It's too danger—"

He opened his eyes and darted forward to cover my mouth with his.

I sank into the desire...the feel of his lips...the caress of his hands over my wet sides. When he finally pulled back, I struggled to remember why we needed to stop.

Then I opened my eyes and saw his charm glowing brightly.

"Don't," he said the second guilt claimed me. "You didn't hurt me."

"Because of the charm. Without it, I would be a monster and hurt what I hold dear. Help me, Garron. I never want to hurt anyone."

He nodded once, his gaze dipping to my lips.

I decided for him and leaned in to give him one more chaste kiss.

"Thank you, Garron," I whispered against his lips.

He nodded, and when I pulled away, I saw he'd closed his eyes.

Giving into temptation, I stole another kiss then turned my back on him and sank into the tepid water.

A moment later, I listened to him leave. Alone, I heated the water while I sat in it without any ill effects then looked for the soap to wash. It was out of reach.

Daemon.

I shook my head and debated what to do.

"Are you all right, Trouble?" Edmund asked.

"Yes. No. Daemon is an ass and left the soap out of reach. And no, I don't want anyone barging in here under the pretense of help. I've given as much as I'm willing to give today. Unless one of you is interested in feeling the heel of my hand against your nose, I suggest you all remain outside."

"Does this mean you won't join us for dinner, Kitten?"

I knew they were purposely provoking me, but knowing didn't stop my reaction. I slapped the water with an open palm in frustration. Water splashed upward then stayed where it was. Droplets the size of rain hovered in the air before my eyes.

Focusing inward, I replaced the lid on the well and pushed down everything I was feeling. The droplets fell into the water.

Movement at the window caught my eye, and I saw Eadric there. He smiled warmly at me and clapped. His enthusiasm vanquished any irritation I might have felt at being spied upon. Instead, I smiled slightly, crooked my finger, and pointed to the soap out of my reach. He nodded and disappeared.

When the door opened, I didn't turn to look. I didn't need to. I heard the grumbling of the others.

"How does he get away with everything?" Daemon muttered.

"If I looked through the window, my nose would suffer," Darian said.

"Better your nose than your bollocks," Edmund said.

"If you keep complaining, she'll think you're jealous," Garron said.

Eadric grabbed the soap and handed it to me. I shook my head and ducked under the water. When I emerged, I looked at him.

"Would you mind washing it?"

"Sparrow, I've dreamed of helping you bathe," he said happily as he sat on the floor beside the tub. He gently lathered the strands, playing with them more than washing them.

The temperature in the room dipped considerably, and I heated the water several times.

"Does it tire you to do that?' Eadric asked, noticing the increased steam rising from the water.

"No. According to what I've read, each caster's endurance is different. Some tire more quickly while others don't. I am not yet sure of my capacity, though, as the book speaks in confusing circles about a person's inherent energy level."

"Then we shouldn't unnecessarily tire you. Edmund, come tend the fire so Sparrow doesn't catch a chill."

The latch didn't rattle before I heard Edmund's footfalls on the floor.

"It would be less chilly in here if you had closed the door," I said.

"It would," Eadric said. "But then how could my brothers watch all the liberties you allow me?"

I tipped my head back to look up at Eadric. "Are you boasting to them again?"

"Absolutely." He grinned, darted in to kiss my forehead, then licked his lips. "A little soapy."

I snorted at his absurdity and didn't question when he dipped his hand into the bath water to clean the soap from my forehead. When he rinsed his hand, his fingers brushed over my nipple. I swatted his hand away, splashing him in the process. He chuckled and returned to washing my hair as I glanced at Edmund, who was focused on adding logs to the fire.

"Your brother's pet name should be Trouble, not mine," I said.

Edmund glanced at me and nodded. His gaze dipped to the water and then to his brother.

"He's knotting your hair," he said before turning back to the fire.

I reached up and indeed felt the tangle he was creating.

"It's clean enough, Eadric. Time to rinse."

"How do I do that?"

Edmund stood. "Let me."

"Then I'll wash something else," Eadric said. I watched him closely as he moved from the end of the tub to the side. As Edmund poured warm water over my hair, Eadric plucked my pruning hand from the water and used a cloth to start washing it.

"I can do that myself."

"You can," he agreed. "But then, what would I do?"

"Leave?"

"If I leave, I won't be able to help dry and dress you."

"You're not drying me, Eadric."

"Did you hear that? She didn't say no to dressing her."

I gave a choked laugh. "You're incorrigible."

He placed that hand back in the water and reached for the other. In the process, he brushed the back of his hand over my breast.

"Are you determined to slyly touch every inch of me before this bath is done?" I asked.

"No. Just your breasts. It drives them mad that I can get away with that much when they get cuffed for much less. My success in the face of their failures is good for their spirits."

"How so?"

"It keeps them humble and determined."

I tipped my head to look at Edmund. "Do you feel humbled and determined?"

"Very," he said, not meeting my gaze.

I lifted a hand to touch his cheek. His gaze met mine then dipped to the tub. Eadric's fingers gently plucked at the nipple that was now out of the water due to my position. I tried to drop my arm, but Edmund caught my hand and kept it pinned to his cheek.

"Will you kiss me, Trouble?"

"No."

"Perhaps she's tired of giving all the kisses and wants one in return," Eadric said a moment before his mouth closed over my breast.

I gasped and stared at Edmund with wide eyes.

A glow appeared under his shirt, growing stronger with each swirl of Eadric's tongue.

"Breathe, Trouble," Edmund said, leaning closer.

He brushed his lips over mine, adding to the confusing emotions storming me.

The light in the room increased with each shuddering breath and exploded to blinding levels when Eadric drew my nipple firmly into his mouth.

"Enough, Eadric and Edmund," Brandle said. "We agreed to take only what she freely gives."

Edmund drew back enough to look at me.

"Kiss me, Trouble. Please."

The sexy bow of his bottom lip beckoned me. I wanted more. More kissing. More touching.

Eadric's mouth left me.

"Did you like my kiss, Sparrow?" he asked.

I closed my eyes and tugged my hand free of Edmund's hold.

"Is my hair rinsed?" I asked instead of answering.

"It is."

"Go. Both of you."

"But I can help dry you," Eadric said.

"Go," I repeated.

I listened to their retreat and the sound of the door closing. My limbs shook as I stood and dried. My hands gradually stopped trembling as I dressed, but the feel of Eadric's mouth lingered.

It took a long while to calm.

Once my hair was dry, I worked through the knots Eadric had created and then attempted to read the next lesson in the book. The words held no meaning, though. My mind lingered on the bath and how I'd allowed two men to kiss me at the same time.

With a sigh, I set the book aside and went to the door. I opened it quietly and watched the brothers. Daemon lounged in his bed as usual, his leg hanging over the edge, idly swinging. Garron paced at the edge of the clearing. Brandle and Edmund were missing, but I heard the ax behind the cottage. Eadric was sniffing appreciatively over the cooking pot. And Liam and Darian were sparring.

Everything appeared unchanged, but I knew nothing remained the same. *I* had changed. How they saw me had changed. How and why remained a mystery that I couldn't question. I could only hope to discover the answers before I lost more of myself to this place.

I glanced at the late afternoon's long shadows and quietly slipped from the cottage.

As soon as I rounded the back, Brandle noticed me. He straightened away from the pile of wood he was stacking and watched me close myself into the privy. The continued sound of chopping gave me a false sense of safety, causing me to jump when I opened the door again and found Brandle there.

He'd set the washbowl and soap on a tall log beside the privy.

"So you can wash in peace," he said softly.

I warmed the water and washed quickly, aware he was lingering.

"Speak what's on your mind, Brandle," I said.

"I'm uncertain what to say. I'm afraid they pushed you too far. I'm afraid you'll leave."

I wiped my hands on my skirt and met his gaze. "Given the frequency in which you and your brothers test me, I can understand your concern. However, I have no desire to reassure you after each occurrence. Instead, I find myself in need of comfort and assurance.

"I stand by my vow to give whatever is needed to save my sister. Yet, I find myself doubting."

"Doubting what?"

"My purpose here and whether you and your brothers are treating me fairly...or if I am simply being used for your amusement."

"Kellen, I—"

"Truthfully, it matters little so long as you fulfill your promise. I do not hold my virtue at a higher value than my life. If I must sacrifice it, so be it. I will sacrifice whatever is necessary to secure the help I need. But I would like your assurance that you are not using me cruelly, Brandle. I have suffered enough, I should think. I've lost everyone dear to me. Must I lose myself, too?"

He pulled me into his arms, hugging me close. I set my head on his shoulder and returned the hug, needing the comfort.

"Forgive us, Kellen. I vow that we are not using you for our entertainment. Never."

I nodded against his neck but didn't release him, pretending for a few precious moments that he was Eloise. If she were here, I would have confided everything to her. My frustration regarding my magic. My fear that I was being used. The beauty and wonder of what I could do and what the men in this glade often made me feel.

"I will warn the others to stay away," he said.

"We both know that distance from each other will not help me do what I must. If it *were* an option, you wouldn't have asked me not to close myself in the cottage. Rather than warn them away, remind them I am a daughter and sister, grieving the loss of her family while struggling to understand powers that could see her forever removed from her home. I am risking everything to help you and your brothers and my sister. All I ask for in return is your consideration of the emotions I am forever struggling to contain for the safety of everyone."

His hand stroked over my hair.

"We have been so focused on reassuring you that your emotions can't hurt us, and we've forgotten that they can hurt you."

His understanding brought forth a dangerous tingling in my nose and eyes. I took a few calming breaths before continuing.

"I thought that I'd long ago stopped caring what others thought of me. However, the idea of people learning what just happened...I am not as immune to the harsh judgment of others as I believed."

"What part of what happened?" Brandle asked.

"Your brothers kissed me *at the same time*, Brandle. Do you know what type of woman allows that?"

His hand left my hair to nudge my head. I reluctantly met his gaze.

"The type of woman who we will forever protect and never betray," he said.

I studied his sincere expression and nodded. It mattered little if they would betray me or not. Without their help, I would never reach Turre.

"I see the despair and hopelessness hiding in your gaze, Kitten. We will prove ourselves to you and earn your trust, starting with Garron. His abilities are rudimentary compared to Henry's, but he will do what he can to help guide you when you're ready."

Hope ignited within my well.

"I'm ready now," I said, withdrawing from Brandle's embrace.

The corners of his eyes crinkled with his smile.

"Then go find him."

"Thank you."

I turned and found Edmund watching us from his place by the woodpile. His gaze tracked me as I retreated to the front of the house where the others watched me as well. No one spoke to me, though, or attempted to stop me on my way to Garron.

"What are you doing?" I asked as I approached.

"Watching the men in the woods," he said. "They gathered more wood. I'm not sure how. The beasts are waiting in the shadows."

"How are you watching them?" I asked.

"The same way you saw the weather. It's more like feeling than seeing."

Standing beside him, I looked out at the trees and opened myself to what was around me while keeping the lid firmly covering the well. I felt the weather first—a mist would come tomorrow with warmer temperatures—then attempted to feel the men.

"I don't feel them, only the weather."

"The weather is bigger and easier to feel. They're smaller, like the trees. Can you feel those?"

I focused on the tree in front of me and attempted to feel it.

"No."

"Can you feel me?"

I knew I could...if I opened the well a little. His concern wrapped around me an instant later. I focused on the tree and *felt* it. Its age. Its energy. It had no emotions; it simply *was*. Moving beyond it, I found more trees. Then the beasts.

Nudging the lid a bit more, I let myself feel them like the day I'd felt my father. Each beast's energy resonated differently from the one before it, like variations in shades of color rather than different colors.

Then I felt the men. Their anger. Their fear. Their determination.

"They will try again soon," I said. "Likely with the mist tomorrow morning. The one I unmanned is angry. He wants to hurt me for what I did."

"We won't let him," Garron said.

I tilted my head, staring at the trees but not focused on them. The vibrations of the men were like those of the beast. They varied slightly. But they had something with them. Something that was exactly the same yet separate.

"I feel something wrong."

I turned and focused on the brothers. Similar vibrations like the beasts. And something that was exactly the same.

Without thinking, I reached out to Garron and set my hand on his amulet hidden under his shirt. It pulsed under my palm in time with my heartbeat. I could feel the same pulse in the other amulets.

"Snow?"

"The men have charms too," I said. "I can feel them. They're like yours. Protection, perhaps?"

I frowned at what that might mean. Why would Maeve send men protected from magic to retrieve me? Did she know I could cast? But how when I hadn't even known when I'd left?

"Can casters sense one another?" I asked.

"If a caster is not masking their presence, yes," Garron said. He took my hand, gently dislodging it from his charm.

"I apologize," I said.

"We trust you, Kellen. I removed your hand to hold it because you looked worried, not because I thought you might do something."

"I *am* worried. Why do they need protection against magic?"

Understanding lit his gaze. "You fear that they know you can cast. I doubt that is the case. Not all charms are to protect against magic. Likely, theirs are to protect against the beasts. But it would be wise to teach you how to sense magic."

We stood by the trees and practiced until the light faded from the sky. By the time we turned to join the others for a late meal, I could feel the barrier that kept the beasts from the glade. It pulsed like the charms around each of the brothers' necks. The same but different. Theirs were so much stronger than the barrier and the charms with the trackers in the woods.

"The book speaks of determining the energy used to cast based on how much is depleted from one's well. How do I know how much is in my well?" I asked between the bites of stew Eadric fed me.

"I struggled with that too," Garron said. "It's a feeling, like sensing the barrier."

"I can't feel anything though."

Garron nodded. "I was the same and found it very frustrating. Henry told me to be patient. He said gauging the cost is something we learn as we cast more spells. He was right. I began to feel the cost the more I did. Once I felt the cost, I could sense what was in the well."

"Which is the opposite of what the books say," I said.

Garron grinned slightly. "Casting does test one's patience."

Eadric chuckled at the face I made and fed me another bite.

"You look like you could use a cuddle, Lamb," Daemon said. "Join me, and I'll help you forget your frustrations."

"It is your turn to wash the dishes, isn't it?" I guessed.

"No, it's Brandle's."

I gave him a suspicious look.

"I believe I'll rest inside."

"It would be better if we remain outside tonight," Garron said. "We will be more aware when the mist rolls in."

"Mist?" Brandle asked.

"Kellen said the trackers will likely attack with the mist in the morning."

The brothers all looked at me, and I shrugged lightly.

"I can feel the mist, and I can feel their intent. The one I unmanned is angry and wants to take me quickly. The one I injured is still in too much pain to move." I paused eating and looked at the trees. "I don't know if he will be able to join the others when they attack."

"If he doesn't, that would give one of us a chance to check for the charm you mentioned," Garron said.

"Alone?" I asked at the same time Edmund and Brandle said, "Charm?"

"She can feel they have something with them that's similar to our amulets."

Eadric fed me another bite then darted forward to lick my bottom lip.

"I missed a little," he said. "Tastes better on you than from the bowl."

"How does he get away with it?" Daemon muttered. "I bet he could have had her bathed and redressed before she noticed."

"I'll take that bet," Eadric said.

"No you won't," I said firmly, trying to ignore the flush creeping into my cheeks and the tingle of awareness in my breast.

He nodded solemnly to me but gave Daemon an exaggerated wink.

"Impossible, annoying men," I muttered.

CHAPTER 6

ABANDONING WHAT WAS LEFT OF MY DINNER, I CLAIMED EADRIC'S swinging bed until he attempted to join me. Then they made a game of rushing to their beds so I would need to choose who to cuddle. Brandle, the most responsible one, ignored them and gathered the dishes, leaving his bed open. I took it and closed my eyes.

The night air had a chill in it that slowly bled the heat from me. I shivered lightly and listened to the brothers' soft conversation about keeping watch as I waited for sleep to claim me. The clank of dishes and the creak of the well's handle echoed from around the side of the cottage.

When I felt a blanket cover me a while later, I opened my eyes to look at Brandle.

"It won't be enough," I said. "Can you join me without spilling us into the dirt?"

He studied me for a long moment then leaned close.

"Put your arms around my neck."

I did as he said and gasped when he lifted me out of the bed and nimbly climbed in with both of us. I lay partially on his chest with one leg over his hips and the other wedged beside him.

"Cover us, will you, Eadric?" he asked.

A blanket settled over us. Then Eadric began tucking it around me, kneading my backside briefly in the process.

"What did he do?" Brandle asked, having caught the flicker of surprise in my expression.

"Just making sure she's adequately covered," Eadric said as he sauntered to his bed.

"Kitten?" Brandle asked softly when I remained silent.

"Just hold me, Brandle, and let me sleep."

He nodded, pressed a kiss to my temple, and rubbed my back as I closed my eyes.

I woke to the low murmur of conversation.

"Do you think she would notice if we pulled Brandle from his spot and took his place?" Darian asked.

"Yes," Brandle said beneath me. "I wouldn't recommend it."

"You just don't want to lose your place," Daemon said.

"Her arm is wrapped around me. She will notice."

"What's she touching?" Eadric asked. "I like when she touches my chest. Are you touching hers? She likes it too."

Brandle's fingers lightly brushed over my breast. Without the protection of my dress, I would have shivered.

"He's not answering," Liam said. "Either he's thinking about it or doing it."

"Go back to sleep," Brandle said. "All of you."

"Can't," Garron said. "It's almost dawn. The weather is starting to change. I can feel it. The mist is coming. You should wake her."

"I know how I'd wake her," Eadric said.

"Boastful git," Edmund muttered a moment before I heard the hushed sounds of a scuffle.

I snuggled closer to Brandle, not yet ready to give up the peace I'd found sleeping next to him.

A soft sound, like a groan mixed with a growl, sounded from Brandle. The scuffling stopped.

"What did she do?" Eadric asked.

"She—"

Feeling mischievous, I brushed my lips against Brandle's throat, and he exhaled a curse. His hand returned to my chest, brushing gently over the material.

"Kitten, you need to wake up," he said.

I pushed his hand away, and instead of kissing his neck, I nipped it.

"Garron, take her," he said. "Now."

I found myself plucked off Brandle and facing Garron.

Before I could open my mouth to ask why, Brandle spun me around and kissed the side of my neck. Then he nibbled a path from my collarbone to my ear. I was breathing heavily when he pulled back to look at me.

"I welcome every bit of affection you wish to give and beg that you will return to this bed with me to continue your efforts after we deal with the men who wish you harm this morning. Tell me you agree."

Before I could do either, he kissed my neck again.

"What do you think she did to get that reaction out of him?" Liam asked.

"I don't know, but I would like to discover it for myself," Daemon said.

"As would I," Darian said.

I tried retreating from Brandle but bumped into Garron. It was enough to get Brandle's attention, though.

"Right. Sorry, Kitten. You caught me off guard."

"We should stick to our normal routine to catch them off guard as well," Garron said. "Eadric, walk her to the privy."

The mist had started to roll in. Between it and the gloom of pre-dawn darkness, it was nearly impossible to see by the time I left the privy. Eadric was there, though, and helped me wash at the basin, playing with my fingers more than cleaning them. I didn't complain, appreciating the distraction.

"All clean, Sparrow," he said softly. "Is there anything else I can wash for you?" He made a humming sound. "No, I think a bath later would be best. I can reach everything better that way."

"You are not bathing me, Eadric," I whispered.

He chuckled and took my hand, leading me through the mist.

To the east, I could just start to see a hint of light.

"It's us," Eadric said softly.

"They're moving in the trees," Garron said. "I think Kellen is right that they have protective charms. They have no fear of the beasts. They left the wounded man at the fire and are walking toward us with no light."

"I'll see if I can learn more," Eadric said.

I grabbed his arm and kissed his cheek. "Please be careful."

"If I promise to come back without a scratch, can I bathe you later?"

"You're ridiculous. Go."

"She didn't say no, did she?" I heard Darian say from somewhere nearby.

"No, she did not," I heard Edmund say with a hint of something in his tone. Satisfaction? Anticipation?

I didn't want any of them to be seriously hurt, but perhaps a slight cosh upon the head wouldn't be amiss.

A hand closed around mine.

"Come, Princess. It would be better if you were tucked away somewhere safe so you aren't accidentally caught in another brawl."

I held his arm as he led me away from the muted glow of the cooking fire, and I listened to the latch clank quietly as he opened the cottage door.

Behind us, I heard a grunt.

"They're here," Edmund called.

"Stay inside," Darian said before bolting away.

The sun was just cresting the trees, changing the mist's color in the glade from midnight blue to milky white. It obscured the fight and muffled the sounds.

I opened myself to feel what I couldn't see. The brothers shone as brightly as before, moving quickly as if dancing with less bright energy—the trackers. Beyond them, I could feel Eadric advancing through the trees.

"Where is she?" one of the men demanded. The sound of a solid punch followed.

Fluctuating between the need to flee and the need to help, I hesitated just outside the cottage. Something whispered that I'd be taken if I didn't move. It said I needed to be higher. Higher than the roof of the cottage.

"Kellen, hide!" Brandle bellowed.

Pivoting away from the open door, I ran around the back of the cottage. My feet carried me past the shrouded garden and toward the cave. The opening didn't beckon, though. It echoed a warning of danger. The craggy face of the rock around it called to me.

"Grace me with handholds and the foresight to reach them," I said under my breath a moment before I reached the sheer face.

Without hesitation, I placed the toe of my boot on the first ledge and reached for the first handholds to pull myself up. The tingle of warning drove me to climb higher quickly a moment before a loud crash echoed from the cottage. I remained focused on the next hold and the next, not turning to look. My skirts saved my legs from the rough edges of the rock as I blindly moved.

My fingers were raw and cramping when I finally broke through the mist and spotted the rocky ledge above.

Pulling myself up and over, I tumbled onto my back and

stared up at the blue sky as I caught my breath. As it slowed, I looked at my hands. Brandle would not be pleased.

Another crash, followed by a shout, drew me upright. Sitting near the ledge, I looked out over the mist-shrouded glade below, seeing nothing of the fight. So, I closed my eyes to let myself feel what was happening.

Edmund fought a man alone near the edge of the trees. He moved quickly, avoiding the man's punches and landing his own against the man's torso.

"Find her," the man bellowed.

Edmund hit him in the mouth.

A man flew out of the cottage and landed in an unmoving heap just outside the door. Liam and Daemon emerged. Liam grabbed the man's shirt and began dragging him toward the trees. Daemon leaned against the door, seemingly at ease, while Brandle, Garron, and Darian continued to fight the remaining two trackers.

A blow connected with the side of Darian's head. I felt what he was feeling. Dazed. Disorientated. Angry. The man knocked Darian down easily and ran for the cottage.

Unaware of his twin's struggle, Daemon straightened at the sound of running feet. He met the man blow for blow as Darian shook his head and slowly got to his feet.

I opened my eyes and stared at the mist. If I wanted this fight to end, I needed to remove the trackers' cover. I considered how I'd previously moved the book and suspended my bathwater. Surely, I could move mist.

A sudden searing pain clawed through Daemon, stealing my breath and his for a moment.

"Knife," he yelled.

Understanding thundered through me as Edmund's angry curse echoed in the glade.

I didn't think; I lashed out, pushing aside the mist. It filled the trees, creating a dense barrier while everything inside the glade was bathed in the light of the early morning sun.

From my perch, I watched Darian bolt for his twin as Daemon dealt the man a solid blow.

The tracker stumbled a step. Darian worked with his injured twin, driving his fists into the larger man again and again until he stumbled a second time and fell to his knees. The brothers didn't stop. They hit hard, causing the man's head to jerk back with each strike. It would take a miracle for him to string two thoughts together once he regained his feet.

"Retreat," the one fighting Edmund yelled.

Edmund didn't try to stop him as the man turned and ran into the trees. The brothers let the other two flee as well.

Brandle hurried to Daemon's side and checked his bleeding arm.

I turned my attention to the trees, checking for Liam and Eadric. They were moving together and emerged in the clearing not long after Edmund went to the well for water to clean Daemon's wound.

"Is Daemon all right?" I called.

The seven of them lifted their gazes to look up at me. Even at this distance, I could see Edmund and Brandle's fierce scowls. Likely, they were wondering how I would manage to climb down again. I wondered the same. Eloise always made climbing look effortless, but my hands hurt, and my arms were tired.

"Sparrow, remember that you eat like a bird and don't fly like one," Eadric called.

Liam elbowed him.

Darian and Garron hurried over to the base of the rock face.

"How did you get up there, Princess?" Darian called.

"I climbed."

"Will you be able to climb back down?"

"I won't know until I try."

"I'd rather you wait for one of us to climb up to get you," Garron called.

I flashed him a smile. "My bedroom was on the second floor of our home. This isn't my first time climbing down something with few handholds."

Garron shook his head and said something I couldn't hear.

"He's very worried, Princess," Darian said as I eased my legs over the edge. "If you want any freedom after this, be sure you don't fall."

"I will do my utmost," I murmured, focusing on recalling where all the footholds had been.

Garron and Darian called out their guidance whenever I struggled to locate the next ledge to place my feet.

By the time I reached the bottom, my limbs shook, and I gratefully accepted Garron's embrace. When he passed me to Darian, who pressed kisses to every inch of my face while whispering I'd scared three years from his life, I didn't mind that either.

Darian carried me to the well and sat me on the edge so that Eadric could wash my raw fingertips. Darian rubbed his temple as if his head ached, and Eadric's voice was raspy as he made sympathetic sounds about my hands. The redness around his neck indicated someone had choked him at some point. Yet, the way they were standing so I couldn't see the others meant they hadn't received the worst of it.

"How badly was Daemon hurt?" I asked, attempting to see around the pair as Eadric finished with my hands.

"The bastard cut his arm fairly deep," Darian said.

"Language," Brandle called distractedly.

"I can make the tea," I said. Darian helped me to my feet and looked at my fingers.

"Garron thought you might want to and is gathering everything you need," Darian said. "Will you be able to work with your hands like this?"

"How bad are her hands?" Brandle asked, sounding worried.

"I'll kiss you if you don't answer that," I said with an arched brow at Darian.

"Agreed." He darted in, claiming more than the chaste kiss I'd intended. His tongue danced with mine as his hands roamed over my sides.

"Me too, or I'll tell," Eadric rasped.

Darian pulled back and grinned at me with a mischievous twinkle in his eyes.

"I say let him talk." He dipped his head, intent on continuing our kiss, but I pushed his face aside. He chuckled and turned me in his arms. "Very well."

I thought he meant to release me. Instead, he passed me to Eadric, who swept me off my feet.

"I can't kiss you after kissing—"

Eadric darted in and chastely kissed my lips.

"There is a difference between not wanting to do something and being unable to do something. I can't cast. You can. Just like you can kiss me after kissing Darian. You simply didn't wish to do it. And that's okay. I can wait for my kiss." He frowned slightly. "How many minutes after kissing one of us does the next one need to wait?"

I sputtered in disbelief.

"It's okay, Sparrow. Think about it, and let me know after you're done brewing the tea. Daemon's cut is quite deep, so make sure the tea tastes awful."

He deposited me at the cottage door, kissed my cheek, and sauntered away.

"I think I have everything ready," Garron said.

Shaking my head, I turned toward the most sensible brother of the bunch and scanned the ingredients set out on the table.

"Thank you, Garron."

He gave me room to work and assisted as needed. Having performed the spell previously, everything went quicker, and I had the tea ready within an hour. I held it up to Garron, whose eye was swelling shut, but he shook his head.

"Daemon first."

"Mm. I think you should have Brandle remove your stitches before you take your sip as well."

"He already removed them. Daemon needs this tea more than I do. Go. Comfort him if you can."

I left the cottage with the drink and found a pale Daemon with blood-soaked bandages. His vacant gaze drifted over me as I lifted the cup to his lips and told him to drink it all.

Once he finished swallowing the contents, he set his forehead against my side. I ran my fingers through his short hair and looked at Brandle.

"How quickly will it start working?" I asked.

"Within an hour," he said. "I've bound his wound, but it bled fiercely. He's dizzy and too weak to stand. He wants to sleep, but I'm worried…"

"He fears I won't wake," Daemon said weakly.

I handed the cup to Darian, who was standing nearby, and took Daemon's face between my hands to look at him. His skin was cool when I brushed my lips against his cheek.

"Let's make a deal. If you stay awake while I make more tea, I'll sleep with you tonight."

His unfocused gaze swept over my face, and the corners of his mouth lifted weakly.

"I'd like that."

"Then stay awake," I said.

Taking the cup, I returned to the cottage and started on another tea. They were all sporting various injuries again, though none as grave as Daemon's. Edmund was keeping an arm tucked close to his ribs. Brandle's nose looked a bit crooked. And Liam was limping.

I tried to control my emotions as I worked but failed. My anger at Maeve and the men in the woods boiled inside of me.

How dare they hurt another person I held dear? I refused to lose anyone else to her evil.

"Are you all right?" Garron asked.

"No. I am angry, Garron. So much so that I no longer care about the fates of the men in the woods. I simply want them gone. And that compounds my anger, for is that behavior not like every other ill-intentioned person? Does my anger over their actions give me the right to lash out at them in kind?"

I closed my eyes and focused on my breathing.

"Hate and anger breed more hate and anger. Yet, how does one stop those determined to hurt others without causing harm themselves? I very much doubt politely asking them to go away will work."

"You're right. It likely wouldn't. But you're smart enough to know that taking lives is not the way to bring about peace either."

Someone snorted from the doorway, and I looked to find Edmund leaning against the cottage just outside. With his back to us, it looked like he was guarding the door while also watching over his injured brothers.

"And you believe taking lives is the answer?" I asked.

He glanced back at me. "I wouldn't hesitate to take a life if it meant protecting someone I love."

My stomach sank, and guilt consumed me.

"Do you blame me for what happened to Daemon? Because I didn't want any of them to die the last time they attacked?"

"No, Trouble. I blame them for their actions, not you." Yet, he didn't look at me when he spoke.

"Liar," I whispered before turning back to the tea.

A few moments later, he wrapped his arms around me from behind and set his chin atop my head.

"I don't blame you, Kellen," he repeated. "I'm angry. Angry Daemon was hurt. Angry I can't do anything to help. Angry that we're stuck here in the glade and not—" He took a calming breath, and I turned in his arms to cup his face.

This close, I could see the storm he was desperately trying to hide from me.

"You've gotten better," I said. "When you can't stop the storm, redirect it to something safe. Kiss me, Edmund."

Surprise lit his gaze a heartbeat before his lips crashed to mine. He released all the raw emotion he'd tried to contain and kissed me with a bruising intensity. I shouldn't have liked it—his rough handling of me—but I did. It allowed me to kiss him back in kind. Angrily. Hungrily. *Desperately.*

He groaned into my mouth and lifted me off my feet. His hand guided my leg up, hooking it around his waist. My skirts stopped my other leg, and he growled as he pushed them up my thighs.

I broke off the kiss and looked down at him. His breathing was just as ragged as mine.

"Are you less angry?" I asked.

I knew he was when, rather than speak, his gaze dipped to my mouth again.

"Do you think she'd kiss me like that if I said I was angry, too?" Darian asked from the yard.

"Doubtful," Daemon said. "But I'll try it when I'm sleeping beside her tonight."

Edmund groaned and set his forehead against mine. "Tell him to sleep with Darian."

I laughed and untangled my legs from around Edmund's waist. He reluctantly released me.

"The tea's ready," Garron said from behind me as soon as my feet touched the ground.

"I'll take it out."

CHAPTER 7

Brandle saw my raw fingers and insisted I sip the tea as well. I did so without argument. Truly, my fingers were the most minor of our injuries. Edmund had to reset Brandle's nose before he drank.

I entertained them with a few stories of the trouble Eloise and I found during our early years while we waited for the brew to work its magic. They laughed as I'd hoped. Even Daemon. His color slowly returned to normal, and Brandle eventually agreed he could nap.

Daemon attempted to coax me into joining him. I declined after seeing the coin Eadric had stolen from the tracker the others had left behind.

"He wasn't happy when I took it," Eadric said. "Cursed up a storm."

"How do we know what it's for?" I asked, looking at Garron.

He shook his head. "That is something I never mastered."

I held the coin in my hand and opened myself to the power it held. At first, it felt like the tree—energy without any intent. Then I felt a slight echo in its pulse. It wasn't a variation in vibration but an actual secondary pulse, faint but true and leading away from the coin. I followed it in my mind and found the wounded man on the other side. However, the pulse wasn't his, even though it was buried deep within him.

I stumbled, and the coin dropped from my hand.

"Snow?" Garron asked, catching me. "What's wrong?"

"I don't know. I feel dizzy."

"Check your well."

The lid was firmly in place. As soon as I nudged it aside, all seven of their amulets flared brightly. I closed the lid firmly again.

"I can't."

"What happened?" Garron asked.

"I don't know. I don't know why I feel dizzy. I don't know why your amulets flared when I removed the lid from my well. I don't know!"

Arms wrapped around me from behind.

"Breathe, Love," Liam said. "Would you like a honey biscuit?"

Since the simple offer of food made my eyes water in gratitude, I nodded. Eadric fed me a biscuit while Liam combed my hair. Edmund took Liam's place to rebraid it.

"Are you feeling better?" Garron asked when they finished.

I nodded.

"Good. Check the well again."

When I hesitated, he added, "I find it fascinating that you have a lid on your well. Mine doesn't."

"How do you stop energy from flooding it?"

"Flooding? It takes effort for me to pull energy into the well before I cast."

"Effort?" I asked absently as I focused inward.

With a nudge, I partially opened the well. Energy flooded into it. From the land. From the trees. From the water deep within the earth. I felt it run toward me like spring streams created by winter's snowmelt. It didn't only come from the immediate area but farther afield too, which explained why things in my immediate vicinity didn't wither.

I closed the lid.

"There is no effort," I said, looking at Garron. "I open the well, and energy floods me. I don't choose from where. It all comes to me."

"Which is why our charms flare," he said with a nod. "Today, let's try to focus on control and how to draw from a specific source."

"What about the coin?" I asked. "It's connected to the man who had it. And he's connected to...something dangerous." I spoke the word, knowing it was true but uncertain why. Was the coin leading to Maeve? Was it her magic I'd felt?

"I'll melt the coin and see if that takes care of the spell," Liam said.

IT DIDN'T SIMPLY TAKE me the remainder of the day to learn how to control the energy that flooded the well. It took *five* frustrating days before I successfully killed a single tree, during which time the trackers made no move to attack again.

"Well done," Garron said, beaming.

I set my hand on the decaying tree's trunk but felt no joy.

"Well done?" I echoed. "I stole the energy from a living thing until it withered and died. That's nothing to celebrate, Garron."

"You're right. That isn't. It's your control we're celebrating. If you can control the energy you draw, you can stop before killing anything. Now, feel what's around you, and choose your source."

"Again?"

"Again, until your well is bursting with energy."

I frowned and focused on my well. Even with the lid in place, I could feel the energy of the tree within it. But it had no depth.

No notable volume. Neither the energy of the tree nor the capacity of the well.

"How many trees would your well contain?" I asked.

"Not even a full tree," he admitted. "But Henry was different. Like you. This glade was filled with trees. He drained dozens but not to the point they withered since he wanted to fell the trees for the cottage. He held it all within him and used the energy to create our drinking well. The next draw, he gathered and used more energy to create the cottage. The glade started to take shape."

"How old were you?"

"Too young to remember, honestly. But Henry told the story many times."

"How many trees did it take to cast the spell for the barrier?" I asked.

"More than he could hold, which is why he needed to use some of himself."

I looked out at the trees. "I think I'm different, Garron," I said softly. "I think I could create a path of dead trees right to Turre."

"Can you feel Turre?" he asked, a hint of worry in his voice.

"I'm too afraid to try," I admitted. "I'd prefer to learn how to conceal myself from others first."

Over the last several days, while learning to control which energy I consumed, I'd also learned how to feel magic in others. I could feel Garron's ability when he allowed it. However, he knew how to hide it at will. He'd wanted me to master control before attempting to teach me anything more.

"That's wise of you to wait," Garron said.

"It's my turn," Eadric said, scooping me into his arms.

Glad for the reprieve but not showing it, I arched a brow at him.

"It's time to eat," he insisted. "You haven't had anything for hours."

"I just ate a pastry."

"This morning. It's midday now."

I glanced at the sky and realized he was right. I'd spent hours with Garron again. When I glanced at the cooking fire, I saw the others gathered there. Though they understood why I spent so much time with Garron and never complained, they were impatient for their share. It required being creative in how I gave it.

Edmund braided my hair every morning and night. Eadric fed me every meal while someone else held me. They took turns sleeping beside me at night. It never seemed like enough, though. It was a miracle they allowed me to walk on my own two feet.

Eadric deposited me on Daemon's lap. Daemon's arms wrapped around me, and I trailed my fingers over the scar the knife wound had left.

"I don't like that the trackers are lingering," I said.

"It would be nicer if they left so we could work," Daemon said. "Edmund gets irritable when he's idle for too long."

"What work aren't you doing?" I asked, twisting back to look at him.

He kissed the tip of my nose.

"We mine, Lamb."

"Mine what?"

"Fewer questions and more eating, Sparrow," Eadric said. Facing forward, I took the bite of stew and dumplings he offered as Daemon cuddled me in his lap.

Between bites, I answered their questions about what I was learning, even though I knew Garron told them everything each night. Like their brother, they seemed unbothered by the dead tree and glad for the control I now had.

The only one who seemed to share my impatience with the situation was Edmund. Though for different reasons.

He flipped Darian onto his back and stalked over to the table, his bare torso covered in sweat.

"What are they doing now?" he demanded.

"Speak nicely," Brandle warned.

DESIRE

"They are gathered around their fire. The wounded one is almost recovered enough to move without pain. They'll be ready to attack again soon. Perhaps the day after tomorrow."

"We need to strike first, Brandle," Edmund said.

"It's safer for them to come to us," Brandle said.

"For us, but not for Kellen."

"I'll be safe, Edmund. At the first sign, I'll run to the cave again and climb."

A resounding "no" came from each of them.

"My heart can't take watching you descend again," Darian said, joining us.

"You trusted my warning that they would attack with the mist. You're trusting I'm correct that they will wait another day or two. Why can't you trust that I will be safe climbing when I say I will?"

"Be reasonable, Princess," Darian said.

I snorted. "I'm the only one present who *is* being reasonable."

"Be reasonable about our fears over losing you when it's taken so long to find you," Brandle said.

His request was…understandable, but I chose not to acknowledge it.

"Why do you think it's safe to wait for them to come to you?" I asked Brandle.

"The beasts," he said simply. "We're more protected in the glade."

"As are they," Edmund said.

"What benefit is there to fighting them out there?" I asked him, truly curious. "Here, there is open space to fight and no beasts to distract you or ways to separate you from one another. They face more danger in the glade because of all of you."

"Exactly," Brandle said. "It makes sense to wait for them to come to us."

"Fine," Edmund growled. "You're next."

Brandle meaningfully glanced at me.

"Don't hurt each other," I warned.

"Not the help I was hoping for," Brandle mumbled.

"It is not my responsibility to distract your brother from his anger." I turned away from both of them to accept Eadric's next bite. He grinned at me.

"Daemon, Eadric, and Brandle," Edmund said. "All three of you at once."

Eadric sighed and gave me a pleading look.

"Impossible men," I grumbled.

I extracted myself from Daemon's lap and strode toward Edmund, ignoring his scowl. I knew it wasn't directed at me but his general state of frustration.

"Teach me something useful, Edmund," I said.

He closed the distance between us and grabbed my shoulders. I thought he would instruct me how to stand. Instead, he pulled me against his chest and captured my lips in an angry kiss.

I stomped on his toes.

He jerked back and growled his anger at me. I growled in return.

Eadric laughed.

Edmund narrowed his gaze on me.

"Stop me," he said before he tried to grab for me again.

I swatted his hand away and spun out of reach. He caught my skirt. I kicked him in the leg then took off running. It was my best defense. When I touched the energy in the well, I could run as fast as any of them.

"Not the trees," Edmund bellowed.

I veered. He'd anticipated it and caught up to me, wrapping an arm around me from behind and lifting me off my feet. Not forgetting his lessons, I used the back of my head to crack his nose.

He cursed mightily and tossed me in the air to catch me over his shoulder.

His mistake.

I bit his arse cheek hard.

He bellowed his pain but waited until Brandle was there to catch me before tossing me away.

"It stings, doesn't it?" Brandle asked with a smirk.

"Dammit, Trouble, that hurt."

"And I won't apologize for it. You wanted trouble. I gave it to you."

"That wasn't the kind of trouble I wanted, and you know it."

"I do. But you can't always have what you want, Edmund."

"Neither can you," he said angrily.

"Edmund, respect," Garron snapped.

Edmund snarled and spun away from all of us. I could see my wet bite mark on his pants.

"He won't last two more days," Brandle said.

"Let him go to the mines," Garron said.

"He can't go alone, and facing the trackers with even odds is dangerous."

"Then what do you want to do?" I asked.

"Every time he's been this angry, you're the only one who has managed to calm him."

"I believe I had the opposite effect," I said.

"Because you're frustrated as well. Please, Kitten. Two more days."

I wanted to kick Brandle in the shin. Instead, I stomped off in Edmund's wake. He was at the well, splashing water on his face. I took a spare cloth from the pile one of them had left nearby and wetted it in the bucket Edmund had drawn.

He watched me warily.

"Sit," I said.

He did, but I could see the petulance in his expression. Taking his chin in hand, I gently wiped his face then checked his nose.

"It's not broken," I said.

"I know."

"Are you angry?"

"Yes."

"At me?"

He scowled even harder at me and tugged me closer so I stood between his legs.

"Kiss me," he said.

"Kiss me—kiss me—kiss me," I said in frustration. "Do none of you have any other thoughts?"

"Do you? All you think of is casting now."

"Unfair, Edmund."

He slowly drew me into his arms. I didn't go willingly, but I didn't fight it either.

"Kiss me, Kellen. Please. Show me patience."

I sighed and tossed the cloth aside. "Close your eyes."

He did. I studied the tension in his expression then placed my first gentle kiss between his brows. The next was along his jaw. Then his eyelids. Kiss by gentle kiss, I soothed his tension and watched his anger bleed away.

When nothing remained on his face, I picked up the cloth and washed his hands.

"I never hated you," he said softly. "I resented your presence because I feared what it might mean, but I never hated you. I never will. You've done the impossible, Kellen, and claimed a piece of a heart I didn't think I had. And I'm giving it to you gladly. No regrets. It's yours. I love you, Trouble. Even when you put me in my place and bite my arse."

I stared at him, my hands frozen on his. He wasn't the first of them to mention his heart, but he was the first to say it with an absolute seriousness that I couldn't ignore. He *meant* it.

Edmund loved me.

"Breathe," he said softly. "You're safe with me. Always."

"It's not safe to love me."

"Then love me back, and we can be dangerous together."

I tugged my hands free and backed away from him. The corners of his mouth lifted in a sardonic smile.

"And where do you think you'll run to?" he asked.

"Ass," I breathed.

He laughed and let me walk away.

"Is he better?" Brandle asked when I approached the table.

"Yes."

I strode into the cottage and, with a flick of my hand, slammed the door behind me.

"Kitten?" Brandle called. "Did he do something that upset you?"

I realized what I'd done—without thought, I'd connected to the air's energy and manipulated it with my own will to close the door. Nothing I'd read had talked about it. I'd just done it.

My control frayed further.

The chair beside the hearth shook and jittered against the floorboards. The dinnerware rattled on the shelves.

I could feel Brandle on the other side of the door. His worry. His need to comfort me.

"Sing to me," I said as I sank to my knees. "Anything."

Brandle immediately began singing a lullaby I recalled my mother singing to Eloise and me when we were young. I wrapped my arms around my legs, closed my eyes, and emptied my mind.

When Brandle's song ended, Eadric started a jaunty one. Liam sang something he likely heard from traders. Garron sang something about the stars and the moon sharing the sky.

Slowly, the shaking inside the cottage stopped.

So did the singing.

I dropped my head to my knees and thought of my mother. If she were there, I would have told her that Edmund had confessed his feelings to me. I would have shared my fear that they would start fighting and I would lose the help they'd promised me.

Thoughts of my sister filled my head, and the first tear tracked a path down my cheek for the second to follow.

No one knocked on the door or tapped at the window. They left me alone as the sun set.

I fell asleep on the floor in front of the unlit hearth.

When I woke, I was curled against one of them with another one behind me. I didn't open my eyes, but I knew it was light out. How did I know? It was simply there, like feeling the distant weather.

"How long are you going to sleep, Love?" Liam asked softly. "I'm not sure how much longer the rest of them will be able to keep Edmund out."

I sat up abruptly and looked at the door as I tried to quell the panic that was threatening to rise.

"Why did hearing that he cares for you upset you, Snow?" Garron asked from behind me.

"He didn't say he cares," I said. "He said—"

My attention shifted from the door to Liam, who was watching me closely.

"That he loves you?" Garron supplied.

I slowly nodded.

"Are you afraid of his love or all love?" Liam asked.

"It isn't love that I fear," I said.

"Then explain it to us, please," Garron said. "We want to understand."

I turned to look at him.

"Does it upset you that your brother confessed his love for me?"

"Should it?"

"Don't answer a question with a question, Garron. It's rude."

Liam chuckled but quieted when I scowled at him.

"It doesn't upset us," Liam said. "We're well aware of how each of us feels about you."

"We don't keep secrets from each other," Garron reminded me.

I glanced between the pair of them. How *each* of them feels about me? Were they implying…

"You don't love me," I said.

"How do you know that?" Liam asked.

"Because you can't."

"Love is affection for another person. Mothers feel it for their children before they even meet them. Why is it impossible for us to love you after spending so long with you?" Garron asked.

Based on his argument, I had no grounds on which to refute his claim. Love was affection. Didn't I also have affection for them? Wasn't that why I was so angry when they were hurt by the trackers? Yet, I found the idea that they might all love me terrifying.

"I'm hungry," I said, standing fluidly.

"Eadric is waiting for you. After you've eaten, we can continue our lesson," Garron said.

I left the cottage and saw Brandle pacing with Edmund near the edge of the clearing.

"Sparrow!" Eadric called loudly, drawing their attention.

Edmund paused his prowl and stared at me across the distance.

I rushed to the table, stole the pastry from the plate in front of Eadric, and took hurried bites as Edmund started across the clearing.

Eadric tried taking the small, misshaped bakery from me.

"Sparrow, not like that," he said.

I turned away from him and would have left, but Darian caught me around the waist and pulled me into his lap.

"Rest while you eat, Princess," he said, kissing the side of my neck.

The force with which I shot from his lap drove my shoulder into his jaw, and his teeth clacked together. He grunted in pain and cupped his chin.

"I fink my pung iv beebing," he said.

I didn't look at him as Edmund closed the distance between us. His expression betrayed no emotion. Did anger boil behind the surface because his brother had kissed my neck?

Struggling not to let panic consume me, I stopped Edmund from coming closer. He glanced at my raised hand and then my face.

"I cannot accept your feelings, Edmund. Please understand. There is much at risk. Now is not the time for quarrels but to work together to achieve the results we all desire."

He studied me for several heartbeats.

"You're afraid," he said. "Why?"

My gaze darted to Garron, who stood by the fire, then Eadric. Behind me, Darian tugged at my skirt.

"Do you need a snuggle, Princess? I'll help ease your fears."

"Stop it."

I glanced back to tug my skirt free and step away from Darian, only to bump into Edmund. His arms wrapped around me.

"Release me," I said.

"No. Tell me why you are upset."

Maddening, provoking oxen, the lot of them.

"Because you cannot love me, Edmund!"

"Why not?"

"Because I have no wish to bear witness to you beating your brothers. Please, Edmund. There must be peace. I am not here to find a match but to find help for my sister. I cannot accept your feelings."

"She thinks you'll cuff me for this," Daemon said, pulling me from Edmund's arms and spinning me about. I opened my mouth to scold him, and he kissed me. I grabbed his hair and pulled hard.

He *laughed* as he released me.

"Don't you see, Princess?" Darian asked. "It's not Edmund we fear when we steal a kiss."

Confused, I pivoted and faced Edmund. He frowned at me.

"You gave me a sound thrashing for much less yesterday," he said. "I demand you treat us equally. If a stolen kiss is a mere hair tug—"

Eadric grabbed me, spun me around, and kissed me like Daemon had. I pushed at his shoulders. He pulled back and grinned down at me.

"I knew I was your favorite," he said. "Not a hair tugged."

"Idiot," I breathed, hoping he wouldn't incite the others' anger. Someone grabbed me again.

My temper flared, as did the amulets of every man in the clearing.

"I am not a toy to be fought over. Unhand me or suffer."

CHAPTER 8

Edmund's thumbs smoothed over my sleeves as he met my gaze.

"Release you? I would rather take another blow to my head than see you walk away from us. And we do not see you as a toy, Kellen. We only meant to prove to you that I will not react with jealousy when you are with my brothers, no matter what they do."

"I told you…we won't fight over you," Eadric said.

"We'll save our fighting for the trackers," Garron said.

Whether Garron intended for it to be a reminder or not, he was right. Any quarrel I had did not apply to those in this glade but to those waiting outside it.

I cautiously eased from Edmund's hold.

"I believe I should return to my studies."

Edmund kissed my forehead. "Run while you can, Trouble."

"I'm not running, Edmund. I'm walking away. Know the difference."

I retreated to the back of the cottage, seeking a quiet place to practice. Yet, when I arrived, I stared at the trees, lost in my thoughts.

Previously, I'd allowed their kisses because I'd thought them playful, a lark. But now I knew they were not.

Edmund had said he loved me.

Liam had implied they all did.

I'd worried their feelings would lead to conflict. However, they hadn't. They'd kissed me in front of each other and had proven they had no quarrel. Even Edmund, who lost his temper at most everything, hadn't reacted badly, only as his usual self.

What about me, though? Had they considered the turmoil I would feel? Both the emotions they were evoking and the distraction of them were something for which I had no time.

A frustrated sound escaped me. Why couldn't they focus on what was important? Their fanciful notions regarding what they felt for me were not as important as the trackers attempting to hurt them. Or as important as breaking their curse. Could they truly not see that? Could *I* not see that?

Closing my eyes, I let out a steadying breath and focused on what mattered at present. In order to break a curse, I needed to learn everything I could about casting.

I opened myself to the energy around me. The forest pulsed with it. Ignoring the trees, I fixated on the grass beginning to renew its growth with the coming of spring. The vast spread of it wasn't small enough for what I wanted, though. I needed to test my control.

Slowing my breathing, I searched for the smallest pulse of energy and found a seed fallen from a tree. Its uniqueness caught my attention. The seed's energy was insignificant compared to that of a mature tree, yet I saw it shone brighter.

"What did you find?" Garron asked quietly beside me.

"A seed. It's small, almost unnoticeable, but I think—" I touched its energy with my own, neither taking nor giving, curious what would happen. Its energy expanded, growing. As it grew, the brightness didn't fade or increase but spread out. I realized it wasn't only the energy expanding but the tree itself growing.

"It contains the same energy, regardless of its size." I opened my eyes to look at Garron. "May I have some seeds from the cellar?"

He retrieved a handful of dried peas. Their energy was much smaller than the tree's seed. I set one on the ground at my feet and focused again.

With barely a touch of my energy, the seed sprouted before our eyes. Its roots sank into the ground as its vine grew. Buds appeared. Flowers turned to pods. Leaves withered, and the pods hardened, creating more seeds.

"Did you see that?" I asked.

"I did. Are you tired? Dizzy?"

Confused, I glanced at him. "Why would I be? I only touched it with my energy. Didn't you see how it pulled energy from the ground?"

Garron frowned. "Can you do it again?"

I did and watched how the seed's energy expanded to encompass the plant until the buds formed. Then, the plant began to pull energy from the ground to place into the pods. Once the plant withered, the original energy returned to the earth, a cycle that kept a perfect balance.

"I never saw that casting is a work of balance before this," I said. "We take the energy but return it when we cast."

"Correct. And how it returns depends on the spell," Garron said.

Knowing I wasn't causing harm freed me of some of the fear I'd held onto since the first time I cast.

I connected with the air and shook the seeds free of the plant. Once they touched the soil, I touched them with my energy again and watched them grow. A tangle of vines rose, and the pods ripened before our eyes. Once I withdrew my connection, the vines stopped growing.

Perfectly ripe pods beckoned. I plucked one free and ate it.

"It tastes the same," I said.

Garron ate one as well. "Try to touch the seeds we've planted in the garden."

"All of them?"

He nodded. I closed my eyes and focused. There were many seeds in the dirt, and it was impossible for me to discern which were planted and which were blown there by nature.

I opened my eyes and watched as I touched them all with my energy. Green sprouted from the ground, covering everything. I stopped when they were all just a few inches tall.

"Well done," Garron said, taking my arm and turning me. He looked into my eyes for several seconds. "And you feel well?"

"Not a bit tired. I promise."

"Why did you stop then?"

"I thought Daemon and Darian would like a chance to weed before I went further."

Garron laughed and called for his brothers. They came running from around the cottage. Worry and anger reflected in their gazes until they saw us standing peacefully by the newly sprouted garden.

"Claim your rows. He who finishes first gets to sleep next to Kellen," Garron said.

"I didn't agree to that," I called as all seven brothers jumped the fence and started squabbling over rows.

I found more unsprouted seeds deeper in the ground in the rows with too few weeds and listened to Darian curse when they emerged larger than the others.

"Tell us when to start," Eadric called.

"Go!"

I watched weeds fly from the garden. Edmund and Brandle moved with determination. I slowed them down with more weeds. Eadric missed a good portion of his. I withered those by absorbing their energy. Liam caught me and arched a brow. I withered some of his, too.

"Lamb, where is my help?" Daemon demanded.

"Oh, my poor thing," I crooned as I gave the weeds in his row more than a nudge. They exploded from the ground, tall stalks as thick as sapling trees. A few of them were trees. I bit my lip when I saw what I'd done.

Daemon blinked at the tree trunk as thick as his forearm.

"I didn't mean for that to happen. I apologize."

They all started laughing as Daemon jumped the fence and fetched the ax. I drained the tree's energy until all that remained was soft wood that disintegrated at the first touch of the ax.

Darian and Eadric won, and I found myself cuddled between the pair inside the cottage after dusk.

"This is nice," Eadric said, nuzzling my neck.

I lightly elbowed him.

"Behave."

"But you like it when we touch you."

"I do not."

"Liar," Darian said, petting my arm, which he'd pulled across his chest. "You like it very much, which makes you skittish and contrary."

I lifted my head to scowl at him. "It does not."

"Sounds contrary to me," Eadric said.

"Continue to vex me and you will lose your place. I believe Liam finished after you did."

"I will gladly take Eadric's place," Liam said from his spot farther away.

Eadric patted my hip. "You are very agreeable, and I was wrong, Sparrow. You hate when we touch you." His hand trailed up my hip and curved around my waist. My breast was in his palm before I knew his intent. My breath left me as he gently pinched my nipple and caused it to pebble.

"Yep. Definitely an adverse response." He continued to pluck and roll the sensitive bud between his fingers as I fought to deny the sensations it created.

"You've proven your point," I rasped. "Please stop."

"Why must you refuse the truth, Princess? Do you truly believe we have ill intentions toward you?"

"What would you have me do, Darian? Allow you all to take turns with me? Use me while you wait for me to break the spell holding you? Not only will I be exiled from my home for the magic I wield, but I would also be rejected from any polite company wherever I go for being a wanton woman. Is that your level of care for me? To see me with a future where I am alone and rejected by everyone?

"No, Princess. A future where you are never alone because you have us."

I snorted.

"I am young but not as naive as you would have me be. I know men speak sweet words when they want something and cruel ones when it suits them. Do as you will." I rolled into Eadric, giving him access to my other breast.

"No, Sparrow. We want to do as you will." He nuzzled my neck, creating more heat. "Tell us what you want."

"I want you to stop plucking at my breast and go to sleep."

"How many times has he gotten away with touching her now?" Daemon asked. "Not a single cuffing."

"I question my sanity," I responded.

Darian pulled me away from Eadric's wandering hands and onto his chest. His fingers stroked over my hair.

"Sleep, Princess. I will protect your virtue."

"SHE'S STRONGER THAN SHE KNOWS."

The words penetrated my dreamless sleep and drew me

toward reality. I had my hand under Darian's shirt and my head pillowed on his chest. Eadric's arm was wrapped around my waist, and his hips were firmly anchored to my backside. His desire for me pressed against me quite noticeably.

"Is she in danger?" Brandle asked.

"I'm watching for signs but haven't seen any yet," Garron said. "I would like to take her to the mines tomorrow."

"No," Edmund said. "She said they would attack soon."

"After then," Garron said.

"You'll need another to go with you," Liam said.

"I think it's too soon," Eadric said from behind me. "She needs more time."

"I agree," Brandle said. Edmund and Darian echoed his approval.

"Tomorrow matters little when I won't survive the night," Darian whispered.

"What's she doing now?" Daemon asked.

"Now? Nothing. She settled again. But she keeps tugging at my shirt. I think the material is bothering her and she wants it off."

"Here," Eadric said a moment before he stole me away from Darian.

"You two better not wake her," Edmund said as I listened to a rustle of cloth.

"Ready," Darian said.

Eadric returned me to Darian's bare chest. I was awake enough to know I should protest and sleepy enough to rub my cheek against the warm expanse of skin. His hand captured the back of my head, cradling it. Petting it. Encouraging me to do more than nuzzle against him.

I turned my head and kissed his chest the way Eadric had kissed mine.

Darian's low groan echoed in the cottage.

No one spoke as I swirled my tongue around his nipple.

Under my palm, I felt the thundering of his heart and took pity on him. With one last flick of my tongue, I released him and rested my head against his chest.

It took a long while for his pulse to slow.

Sleep drew me closer to its welcoming embrace.

"What did she do?" I heard Daemon ask just before I succumbed.

"She kissed my chest. With her tongue."

"Lucky bastard," Edmund said.

"You cook and do dishes tomorrow," Brandle said.

His brothers all agreed. Darian did too. I fell asleep to the sound of his chuckle.

THE WARM EXPANSE of the chest beneath my cheek was Daemon's, not Darian's. I didn't know how I knew; I simply did. It rose and fell in a steady, soothing cadence. My fingers drifted over his bare skin, memorizing the feel of it as I thought of Eadric's words before I fell asleep.

I'd read countless books from Mr. Bentwell about heroes loving damsels who desperately needed their protection. It seemed perfectly acceptable for the women to accept the hero's advances—written in splendid detail—in exchange for his total devotion.

If it were only one brother, would I have already succumbed like those damsels? Without a doubt.

The problem lay in the number of them. Yet, hadn't I said I would give my life to save my sister?

When I thought of Maeve and the power she wielded, I knew one brother would never be enough to stop her. I would need them all. Why, then, was I so hesitant to give my heart to seven brothers in exchange for their help?

Daemon twitched under my wandering touch, bringing me out of my thoughts.

"Eloise is the bold one," I said. "She acts with very little thought of the consequences. I consider things thoroughly so that I'm not surprised by any outcome.

"Since arriving, I've had very little time to think, Daemon, and with each passing day, you ask me to give more when I still haven't come to terms with what I've already given.

"I'm willing to put Eloise's life before mine. Unconditionally. However, that doesn't stop my fears of what might come. The certainty of death was easier for me to accept than the uncertainty of the future I imagine after I accept the seven of you."

I lifted my head to look down at him.

"You've all kissed me then asked for more kisses. I thought it was playful at first and then a means to force me to choose between you. You've proven it wasn't either of those.

"It's plain all of you want more from me. But what then? What happens when each of you has bedded me and I am heavy with child? Will the seven of you decide who is to marry me without consulting me, as you do now? Or will I be cast aside by all? Homeless and ruined?

"I can accept any outcome that sees Eloise safe and free. But can you? Have you all considered the possibilities? Will you go mad not knowing if I'm carrying your child or Darian's?"

"Ah, Lamb, you're breaking my heart," Daemon said. He wrapped me in his embrace and comforted me in a way I desperately needed. "We will not cast you aside. Ever. That you've thought of allowing any of us the privilege of fathering a child fills me with untold hope. If that should come to pass, we would rejoice. The entire kingdom of Turre would hear our joy.

"For now, we simply want this. Talk to us. Spend time with us. If you wish to show us affection, we want *how* you do so to be your choice. Don't do things to please us. Please yourself first."

I lifted my head again to meet his gaze.

"And how will we endure the judgment of others?" I asked.

His mouth tilted at the corners.

"Judgment? You mean envy." He gestured to the length of himself. "Do you not see the glory of my body? Women would stand in line for a chance to view this. And you would have seven of us. You will be the envy of every woman in the kingdom."

I snorted. "Conceited man," I said without rancor. "And what of the men in the kingdom? Will they look kindly upon a woman who lives with seven men?"

"With your powers, they dare not look at you in any other way."

"I am not cruel, Daemon. I will not use my powers to subdue or hurt those whom I offend."

"That is why you have us. I dare any man to object, though I doubt any would for the reasons you think. They will likely see you and be jealous of our good fortune."

I snorted. "Unlikely."

He rolled us so I lay beneath him and framed my face with his hands as he supported his weight on his forearms.

"You do not see yourself as we do. You are beautiful, Kellen, and everything we've dreamed of finding."

I studied the sincerity in his gaze then lifted my head to brush my lips against his, needing to know how he truly felt. He groaned at my offering and deepened the kiss. The stroke of his tongue against mine reignited the heat that Eadric had coaxed forth the night before.

Wrapping my arms around Daemon's torso, I let myself sink into the sensation of being kissed—the feel of his lips, the touch of his fingers against my temples and hair, the weight of his hips settling against mine.

I tore my mouth from his, breathing heavily as he kissed his way down my neck. When he reached the ties of my shift, he lifted his head to look at me.

"Eadric is right," I admitted. "I like being touched. But I would like more time to accept the change my life is about to undertake. Please."

Daemon groaned and kissed me again. I felt his desire for me. The burning need to kiss me until he ran out of air. To lose himself in me. Then, I felt the truth of his devotion. He was ready to give his life to protect me.

I threaded my fingers in his short hair and kissed him until I ran out of breath. Panting, we broke apart and stared at each other.

"You are beautiful, Lamb."

"And you are too handsome for your own good, Daemon."

He gave me a cocky grin and rolled to the side, taking me with him so he could hold me in his arms.

"I'm still afraid," I admitted.

"I know. We're a patient bunch, though."

"Patient?" I laughed. "Liar."

A throat cleared, and I lifted my head to look at the open door where the other six stood. Heat flooded my cheeks, and I tried to remove my leg, which had crept around Daemon's waist. He caught my thigh and shook his head.

"You can worry about judgment from other people, but not us. It's not allowed."

I arched a brow at his commanding tone, and he shrugged.

"He's right, Kitten. With us, there is no judgment."

"We also won't ever cast you aside," Liam said.

"We may try to steal you from each other, though," Darian said. "Playfully, of course."

Daemon lifted his head to look at his brothers.

"But she has the final say."

They all nodded and looked at me expectantly.

Not yet ready for the level of hope and encouragement I saw reflected in their gazes, I changed the subject. "Is breakfast ready?"

"It is," Darian said, elbowing his way through his brothers. I watched him grow and duck to accommodate the low beams as he crossed the room.

"She's mine," Daemon said, wrapping his arms around me.

"She's hungry," Darian said. "Give her over."

Daemon kissed my chin, nose, and forehead then lifted me as if I weighed nothing. Darian plucked me away with the same ease and hugged me close.

"Hmm. You're so warm," he said. "I like it." He started walking toward the door.

"I won't stay warm in this shift. Let me get dressed first."

It was usually a task I completed alone. Darian wouldn't hear of it. While Daemon folded the blankets and rolled up the mattress, Darian helped with my lacings and took great care in straightening my skirts—a ruse to pet my legs and backside.

"End the idle wandering of your hands and feed me, or suffer," I said, swatting the straying appendages. He chuckled and finished lacing my boots.

"There you are, Princess. Adequately dressed, to my misfortune."

"Incorrigible," I muttered.

At the table outside, Brandle ladled out a portion of boiled oats and berries for me, which he handed to Eadric.

"Who is serving as my cushion?" I asked.

"Do you have a preference?" Garron asked.

I shook my head and watched him and Liam race to the bench in front of me. Liam won. I didn't simply sit on his lap; I made myself comfortable, reclining against his chest as Eadric fed me a bite at a time. When Liam's arm curled around my waist, I held it and allowed myself to like it—openly, without shame or regret.

He kissed my neck and told Eadric not to feed me too quickly.

I laughed, and it was…good.

The pair playfully fed me then relinquished me to Garron. He and I had only just begun to work on a new spell inside the cottage when a tingle of warning had me pausing.

A shout rang out in the clearing.

"Protect Kellen!"

"Stay here," Garron said. He ran out the door and slammed it closed behind him.

I glanced from the door up to the loft and to the hidden cellar. Something whispered that none of those options were safe. I wasn't safe. No matter what I chose, I would face danger.

Glass shattered behind me.

CHAPTER 9

Whirling around, I saw a tracker pull himself through the small window. The man was the same one who'd attempted to take me from the cave.

Glass crunched under his boots as he stepped down, but he paid it no mind.

"It's time to pay your debt." The way his gaze raked over me left no doubt the payment he would demand.

Fear and anger were a terrible, frightening combination. They threatened my control…and control was what kept those I cared about safe.

"Leave," I said. "I don't want to hurt you."

He laughed. "You were lucky the last time we met. You won't be this time."

He lunged forward and grabbed me by the throat with one hand and slapped me hard with the other. My ears rang.

The emotions suppressed underneath the lid of my well boiled out, and my control fractured.

Behind him, the glass shards jittered on the floor and then began to rise into the air. My gaze shifted from them to his rage-contorted face.

"Stop. Please," I rasped.

"Beg harder." He slapped me again.

I closed my eyes and tried to focus on better, happier moments. Daemon and his kiss. Eadric's innocent smile. Garron's sweet blush. Brandle's care and kindness.

It wasn't enough. The dishes started to shake on the shelves.

The tracker slammed me into a wall. When his hand fumbled to pull up my skirts, my eyes flew open. My need to strike out threatened to swallow me whole.

I gripped the arm suspending me above the floor for support.

"My name is Kellen Cartwright," I rasped. "I am the daughter of a merchant and a noblewoman."

"Do you think that will spare you? I've always wanted to fuck a noblewoman," he said.

"My name is Kellen Cartwright," I repeated, desperate to remind myself who I was. "I am the daughter of a merchant and a noblewoman."

Behind him, the glass trembled in the air.

"I am not cruel!" I screamed. "I will not kill you."

He yanked his hand from under my skirt and slapped me so hard I tasted blood.

"In what world could a girl like you kill me?"

My world, I thought, boiling with rage.

The lid moved to the side, and energy in the well exploded outward, washing the inside of the cottage in hues of violet and blue. The air crackled with the freed power, and my hair floated around me like it did when I swam with Eloise in the pond.

In front of me, the man made a strangled sound. His eyes—the only things he was able to move—darted around frantically.

Terrible, hateful anger pulsed through my veins. My throat burned from his punishing hold, and I wanted to hurt him for daring to hurt me. That need for revenge ate at me.

Refusing to give in to it, I touched his chest and pushed him back. His grip remained firm around my neck until I tugged myself free. He whimpered as he slowly floated away, adrift in the current of violet-blue dust.

The anger inside of me didn't abate. Neither did the fear. Of him. Of myself.

Energy sparked under my feet with each desperate step toward the door. I reached for the latch, seeking my salvation. But what I saw outside wasn't the help I needed.

Chaos reigned. Near the trees, Edmund, Eadric, Darian, and Daemon were fighting the other four for all their worth.

Garron, nearest to the cottage, wasn't looking at me but at Liam and Brandle near the upturned table that lay partially in the cooking fire.

Liam swayed on his feet, and Brandle caught him by the arm.

"Stay upright," Brandle said to him before spotting me.

"Kellen. The tea. Quickly."

Garron turned to look at me and then through the open cottage door behind me. I knew he saw what I'd done when his eyes widened.

As he met my gaze again, the panic and wild need to cry overwhelmed me.

"I can't stop it," I said with tears streaming down my cheeks.

He closed the distance between us and held me.

"Focus on the beat of your heart and the sound of your breathing."

Over his shoulder, I saw Brandle's gaze shift from me to Liam. The concern etching his features was…discordant.

"Just breathe, Liam," he said. "Kellen will fix this."

My first thought was that my magic had managed to harm Liam despite his charm. Then he turned slightly, leaning into Brandle's hold on his shoulders, and I saw Liam's back. Little remained of his charred shirt to hide the raw, red and black burned skin beneath.

The world dropped out from under my feet.

"Kellen," Garron called, his voice distant and barely audible over the ringing in my ears.

Darkness crept into my peripheral, and with it, I heard Eloise —not her words, simply her voice—and I welcomed the abyss.

"I DON'T KNOW, Brandle. She cast more energy than I could ever dream of casting. When Henry cast extensive spells, it took him days to recover."

"Liam doesn't have days, Garron."

The anger and urgency in Brandle's voice drew me from the comforting nothingness that held me. Thoughts swam just out of reach for a brief moment before I recalled the extent of Liam's injuries.

"I'm here," I slurred, struggling to open my eyes.

"Princess," Darian said. "Are you all right?"

"Fine." My eyes opened on the fourth try. Five of the brothers stood around me. Inside the cottage. The air was normal again.

"It disappeared when you fainted," Garron said, noting my searching gaze.

"Good. And the tracker?"

"In the cellar for now."

"I meant, is he alive?" I clarified as I took Darian's proffered hand and sat up.

"He is."

I glanced at the table and saw they already had everything prepared for the tea.

"Wait," Garron said when I attempted to stand. "Look at me, Kellen."

I met his gaze and let him search mine.

"What are you looking for?" I asked.

"Any sign that casting now might hurt you."

"I'll be fine."

"You don't know that, Sparrow," Eadric said.

Looking them over, I took in their concern and injuries. Brandle's nose looked crooked again. Garron's lip was split and swollen. Eadric had a red, puffy cheek. Darian kept his weight off one leg, and Daemon held one of his hands under his arm.

"I know that I feel better than you look. Isn't that enough? Where's Edmund? Is he with Liam?"

"He is," Brandle said. "We need you to make four cups of tea, Kitten. If you can."

"I can."

Darian helped me stand and guided me to the table. The extra consideration, while endearing, was unnecessary. Not a hint of dizziness remained.

The others left to straighten the mess outside, and Garron remained to assist me with the tea. His continued glances conveyed his lingering worry.

"I am well, Garron. I promise."

"You didn't look well. You fainted."

"I don't think it was due to what happened in here but what happened out there. I saw Liam's back."

"Ah."

"Will he be all right?"

"He will be after he drinks the tea. Is that why you asked if the tracker was alive? Did you think we would seek revenge for what he and the others did to hurt us?"

I looked up from the candle to meet Garron's gaze.

"I don't doubt your intentions, Garron. I doubt my own. You saw what was in this room. I don't know how I did that. If I hadn't walked away when I had, I think the glass would have flown at him."

Garron nodded slowly and looked down at the tea leaves he was grinding into a powder.

"It's not your intentions you doubt, Snow, but your control.

You walked away to spare him and asked about him as soon as you woke. People with evil intentions wouldn't do that."

"I would like to believe that, but I was angry, Garron. A part of me wanted to hurt him for what he was trying to do."

He paused and looked at me.

I held his gaze. "Many men believe a woman's only worth lies within the ability of her womb."

He averted his gaze and stared down at the ground tea leaves.

"I don't keep secrets from my brothers."

"Yet if you tell them what I've said, they will not allow the tracker's continued existence," I guessed. "It worries me that I find myself conflicted whether or not to protest that decision. Am I changing, Garron? I thought my control was improving, but you saw the energy born of my anger and fear. Perhaps I am growing more wicked with my abilities."

"Your fear that you are proves that you aren't. And I vow the tracker will leave this glade alive. His death will not stain your hands."

I nodded and focused on my work for several minutes. Once the candle was heating the water, I asked what I was dreading to know.

"What was that? The energy I cast?"

"I'm not certain. It wasn't like anything I've ever witnessed. But I've only seen Henry cast, and he only cast when necessary."

"And you're sure it disappeared when I fainted?"

He nodded.

"Good. If it happens again, don't allow me to hurt anyone."

"I won't."

Feeling relieved, I spent the rest of the time silently focusing on the tea. When Garron suggested I speak an additional spell over the finished brew, I opened myself to the well, willing the energy to touch the tea so Liam could heal faster.

"Is it done?" Brandle asked from the door. His hair stood up on end like he'd been running his hands through it.

"It is," I said. "Garron and I will carry them out."

"No. Eadric, get over here!" he bellowed, startling me. His gaze held mine. "Stay here with Garron."

"Why? What's wrong?"

Garron passed Brandle two cups and grabbed me when I would have followed with the one I held.

"Snow, it's better to stay in here."

Looking pale and without his usual smile, Eadric appeared in the opening and took one of the cups from me.

"Take a sip quickly, Sparrow," he said.

Garron lifted the cup to my lips when I didn't immediately move to do so. After I swallowed once, he handed both cups to Eadric, who vanished as quickly as he appeared.

I turned to Garron.

"Do not keep secrets from me, Garron. What's wrong?"

"Liam's burns are bad. He's suffering, and none of us want you to witness it. You already fainted once." He paused. "Edmund was stabbed as well."

"How badly?"

"Very."

I stared at the door and felt the dangerous combination of anger and fear again.

The dishes started to rattle.

"Snow?"

"Don't let me hurt anyone."

He spun me around and kissed me. It wasn't his typical soft and sweet kiss that melted my resolve. It was desperate and demanding. I answered in kind, tangling my fingers in his hair.

His hands smoothed down my sides and curved around to my backside. With a firm grip, he effortlessly lifted me. I pressed myself close, taking in the heat of his body and reveling in the contact.

When we finally broke apart, the dishes no longer rattled, and I didn't feel a hint of anger—though the worry for Edmund and

Liam remained. Garron held me as his breathing slowed then carefully set me down.

"Will the tea be enough?" I asked.

"Four cups should be. Edmund and Liam will drink a full cup and whatever is left of the other two."

"We can't continue like this." I glanced at the cellar door. Garron had said the tracker was down there. Where I was cursed not to utter a word against Maeve, perhaps he was not. But even if he couldn't speak of Maeve's evil intent, there were other questions to ask.

"What are you thinking?" Garron said.

"I would like to speak with the tracker."

"Brandle won't—"

"Brandle needs to remain focused on Liam and Edmund. We need to find out what the others have planned and why they attacked after five days of hesitancy."

I opened myself, feeling the weather and the forest around the cottage. In it, I felt the beasts, my father, and the remaining trackers.

"They're looking for him and will return to the clearing if they don't find him soon. That is not something we can allow."

Garron considered me for a moment before reluctantly agreeing. He went down the ladder first and lit the candle before telling me to come down.

The tracker lay on his side with his hands bound behind him to his ankles. A rag in his mouth muffled his panicked sounds when he saw me.

"Choose who you fear more—the person who sent you or me —and answer accordingly," I said.

The tracker quieted, and I saw a glint of green flash in his eyes.

"He's bespelled," Garron said. He paused. "It's deeply rooted, almost to the bones."

"I don't know what that means," I said, even as I opened

myself to sense magic. I felt it then, a tingle of awareness coming from inside the tracker–but also from the coin in his pocket.

"I'll explain later," Garron said. "Ask your questions so we can release him."

I nodded and crouched down to pluck the rag from the man's mouth.

"What are you here to do?" I asked.

"Bring you home."

"Will you be permitted to return without me?"

He didn't respond, but I glimpsed the flash of fear and desperation in his gaze. I shared the same feelings about Maeve, who had proven her ability to inflict pain without remorse. Death was not out of her reach.

"Take the coin from his pocket," I said, stepping back so Garron could approach him.

"No. Don't." The tracker started thrashing to dislodge Garron's searching hand.

Garron pinned the man down with a knee to his head. I felt no pity for the man. Garron plucked the coin free and released him.

"The coin holds magic," I said. "For what purpose?"

The tracker glared at me, saying nothing.

"Answer me or answer them. While it makes no difference to me, it will to you."

I could feel his hate for me overcome his fear.

"I heard what you said and know that you need to release me. I promise I will make you suffer. We will kill your protectors one by one until you have no one. Then, I will hold you down and take my due while you scream in pain," he said.

Garron's fist shot out, connecting with the man's mouth. The tracker grunted and spat blood.

"That's for my brothers," Garron said. He hit the man again. "That's for hurting her."

He drew back again, but I set a hand on his shoulder.

"What purpose does the coin serve?" I asked again.

The tracker chuckled low.

"You're the one with the magic. You tell me."

I could feel his fear but, under it, his inability to speak the coin's purpose.

"He has spoken all that he can," I said. "Release him."

Garron stood and pocketed the coin. "Would you like to learn a new spell?"

Curious, I nodded and watched Garron face the man.

"From your memories, I now draw our time together and everything you saw. In their place, you will keep seven small men who fiercely defend their home and a weak woman with no power of her own. Now sleep."

Garron touched the man's forehead, and I watched the tracker's eyes close.

"He won't remember what happened in this cottage," Garron said. "Removing a person's memory was the first spell Henry taught me. I practiced on Eadric so many times that I lost count. Once I mastered the spell, I vowed never to cast it on them again except when absolutely necessary to protect us. I would ask for your promise as well once you master it."

"I think it will be a long while before I'm ready to try anything like that."

"Ready or not, you need to learn. No one can know we're here. If something were to happen to me, you're the only other one who can cast."

Reluctantly, I agreed and went up the ladder first as Garron followed with the tracker unconscious over his shoulder.

"I'll toss this one into the woods then check on the others. Call out if you need anything."

I watched him walk out the door then began clearing the table. He returned as I was hanging one of the blankets over the broken window's opening.

"It's good that winter is easing its hold," he said. "Once the trackers are gone, we'll replace the glass."

"Gone? Did you not see the fear in his gaze when I asked if he would return without me? They will not leave willingly. How are Edmund and Liam? Can I see them yet?"

"We would prefer you wait for—"

Edmund bellowed and started cursing a storm. I only made it one step when Garron caught me up in his arms. Darian strode in, took one look at me, and cradled my face between his palms.

"Please, Princess. Stay here."

"Is he fighting?" I asked.

Darian glanced at Garron in question.

"She knows Edmund was hurt badly and asked that we not keep secrets from her," Garron said.

"I think the secret of your curse is enough," I said.

"Edmund was near gutted," Darian admitted. "He wanted to let the tea heal him, but it's working slower without stitches. So Brandle is placing them. Edmund isn't happy."

"Tell Edmund pain is like anger," I said. "He can't show it, not now while they're listening. He needs to hide it to keep everyone safe. The trackers weren't hurt badly enough to stay away. I can feel them now. Their search for their missing partner is the only reason they haven't returned."

Darian placed a quick kiss on my forehead and left to relay my message.

"I wish I could take his pain," I said, staring at the empty doorway.

"None of us wants you to suffer in our places," Garron said. "Ever. Once Edmund is healed, this will serve as his reminder to dodge faster."

"Pain is a cruel teacher," I said.

"It is. But it is also effective." Garron led me to a chair, sat, and coaxed me to sit on his lap.

Outside, the cursing quieted.

"Let's begin practicing the memory spell. Since you can already feel a person's intentions, I believe you will master this quickly.

"The words you speak as you gather your energy are simply to focus the intent of your cast. Open yourself to what I'm feeling. The anger that the tracker hurt you and his determination to do so again. I want you to try to erase what he wanted to do to you. What he still wants to do to you. Do you understand? Follow my anger to the reason, speak the spell, then touch my forehead and send your energy into me."

I hesitated.

"You're doing this to keep us safe, Kellen. Trust me. This is important."

Holding his gaze, I opened myself to Garron's anger. The intensity of it became my own. His anger wasn't a simple emotion but complex with branches. One for the tracker who'd purposely pushed Liam into the fire. One for the trackers who'd worked together to seriously harm Edmund. One for the tracker who'd threatened me. That branch carried more than the rest. From it, I found fear, love, and determination to protect me.

I understood then why Garron hadn't simply removed the tracker's memory but replaced it. Without that branch of anger, Garron would lose the reason behind the fear, love, and determination he would still feel.

I thought of the spell he'd spoken and considered the words that would help focus my intent.

"Of all the deeds the trackers have shown, let only those done to you and your brothers remain known. When the day comes that they are no longer a threat, you will remember what I caused you to forget." I touched his forehead lightly, sending a very small thread of energy into his mind to touch the memory attached to the emotion. The energy wrapped around it and blanketed it in a shadowy fog.

Garron blinked sleepily as I lowered my hand.

"Did it work?" I asked.

He frowned slightly. "I asked you to cast a memory spell, but I don't know why."

"Then it worked," I said.

His frown deepened for a moment, and I could feel his fear.

"The memory isn't gone," I said. "It's still there, waiting to return when the time is right."

"Promise me you'll never do this again."

"I already made a vow to you. Do you not remember?"

He nodded slowly. "Never to use it on us except to keep us safe."

"You said removing the memory would keep you safe, Garron. That is the only reason I agreed."

He hugged me close and rested his chin on the top of my head.

"They won't be happy when they learn what I asked you to do. They'll want to know why."

"I know." I patted his chest. "They will trust you had a good reason, though."

Darian appeared in the doorway again and smiled slightly when he saw us.

"I think I could use a cuddle next," he said.

I lifted my head and took in his less hitched stride as he entered the cottage.

"Would you mind if we switched?" I asked Garron.

"Not at all."

He stood and handed me over to Darian. I tilted my head back as he nuzzled my neck and sat with me.

"I like this," he said against my skin. "How much am I allowed before cuffing?"

"I promise not to cuff you if you promise not to get angry," I said.

He lifted his head to look at me. "Angry? Why would I get angry?"

"Kiss me here, and I'll tell you," I said, tapping the spot just above the neckline of my gown.

His gaze dipped to my skin then back to my eyes.

"Are you attempting to distract me?"

"If I truly wanted to distract you, I think I would need to remove my dress."

He groaned and dipped his head to kiss me where I'd asked. I ran my fingers through his hair.

"Garron asked me to learn how to remove memories. He said, if anything happened to him, I needed to ensure no one would remember you live here."

Darian lifted his head to look at Garron, who shrugged.

"What I asked and why is a little unclear," he said.

Darian looked at me again. "What memory did you take?"

CHAPTER 10

"I didn't take any memory. It's hidden, not gone. When it no longer matters, it will return." I held Darian's gaze and felt his doubt. It cut deeply.

"You don't trust me," I said.

Guilt flitted over his expression.

"I understand," I said. "I don't fully trust myself either. But I trust Garron. If he thought it was dangerous to teach me the spell, he wouldn't have. And if he thought the memory was better forgotten, then I believe him."

Darian sighed and held me close. "Brandle won't be happy. You might need to offer more than a kiss to distract him from it."

"Such as?"

"A bath should do. I would find it difficult to focus on anything you said if your hands were sliding over my skin unhindered by clothes and aided by soap." He shifted underneath me. "Bathe me instead, and I'll gladly calm Brandle's temper."

I snorted and set my head on Darian's shoulder.

"I'm less concerned about Brandle's reaction and more about Edmund's. I don't want him to lose his temper and tear his stitches."

"And you can't bathe him," Garron said in agreement. "You are wise. How do you plan to tell him?"

"I don't know. Do you have a suggestion?"

"He's Eadric's twin and has a similar fascination. We all do, truthfully."

I frowned in confusion for a moment, then flushed in understanding. Darian grinned widely.

"My smart, beautiful Princess. I look forward to seeing how you tame my brother's temper." He stood with me. "Since Brandle just finished, I believe now is the perfect time."

He carried me out the door with Garron trailing behind us.

"Let me walk, Darian, or they will misunderstand and worry that I'm unwell."

He kissed my neck again and set me down.

The others stood around the benches. Liam lay on his stomach on one and Edmund on his back on the other. Wet cloths covered Liam's back, but nothing covered Edmund's bare torso and the neat row of stitches that almost crossed his midsection.

His eyes were closed, and his breathing steady.

I went to him, kneeling near his head to kiss his cheek.

"Here. Get him to drink the rest of this," Brandle said, handing me the cup.

I took it and slipped my hand under his head. Eadric knelt on the other side and placed his hand under mine to help me.

"Drink, Edmund," I said.

He opened his mouth and drank the rest of the tea. Feeling the echo of Edmund's pain, I looked at Brandle.

"I added the leaves to take away the pain. Why isn't it working?" I asked.

"It is working," Brandle said. "His breathing isn't hitched, and he's not shaking anymore. Liam's already sleeping. They will be fine, Kitten. I promise."

"Should we move them inside?" I asked.

DESIRE

"I would prefer not to move them until they wake again."

I gently stroked Edmund's cheek and looked up at Darian.

"Why don't you go with Brandle and leave Edmund for now?" He nodded his head toward the well.

Understanding, I stood and held out my hand to Brandle. He picked up the empty water bucket and twined his fingers through mine.

"Is there a reason we need to be alone?" he asked as we rounded the corner of the cottage.

"Alone? No. Away from Liam and Edmund so we don't disturb them? Yes."

He set the bucket down next to the well and started drawing some more. He didn't say anything as he worked, and I waited until he had the clean water up before taking it from him and heating it.

"Garron asked me to do something. I did it, and Darian believes you'll be upset by it," I said, dipping a cloth into the wash bucket. I motioned for Brandle to sit on the edge of the well and moved to stand between his legs.

"No falling into the well," I warned as I began washing his face.

"Are you going to tell me what Garron asked you to do?"

"I will. Darian said you all have patience. I disagree. You're an impatient lot."

Brandle smiled widely, the corners of his eyes crinkling with it.

I stared into his eyes and lost myself. "You are so handsome."

He chuckled and reeled me closer.

"We heard what you said to Daemon this morning. Thank you for trusting us."

I tipped his chin up and wiped the cloth over his neck.

"I do trust you. But do you trust me?"

Some of his humor faded. "Why do you ask?"

"Garron said I needed to know how to remove memories to

protect everyone in the glade if something should happen to him. I successfully hid a memory of his, one he asked me to remove. Darian said you wouldn't be happy."

"And that's why we're at the well? So I wouldn't disturb Edmund and Liam with a lecture?"

I nodded.

"The wrong person accompanied me, then. Any lecture I have is for Garron, not you."

"Lecturing him won't undo what's been done. And he can't explain why he did it. The memory is gone for now."

"But you can explain," Brandle said.

"I can, but I won't. I trust Garron. If he believes it's best forgotten, then so do I. When it's no longer an issue, the memory will return as it will no longer need to be a secret." I set the cloth aside. "I don't like secrets, Brandle. They're frustrating and often cause problems when they finally are revealed."

"In that, we agree," he said. He reached up to smooth back a wisp of my hair. "I saw Garron return the tracker to the forest. Was the tracker's memory cleared?"

"Garron ensured he would only remember small men and a weak woman. Nothing of what he saw or heard in the cottage."

"Good. His memory will then match what the ones outside the cottage saw."

"We also took the tracker's coin. He wouldn't say what it was for, though."

"You both did well."

"Not well enough. Once the others find him, they will try again."

Brandle leaned in and kissed my cheek. "Until Liam and Edmund are well, I would like you to stay inside the cottage."

"And I would like to be where all of you are," I said. "It feels safer."

"All right," he agreed much too easily. He saw my suspicion and chuckled. "I would rather keep you where I can see you."

He took my hand, and we returned to the others with the warm bucket of wash water.

I bathed Liam's hands and face while he slept. Edmund roused at the first touch of the cloth to his swollen knuckles.

"I'm so sorry you were hurt," I said softly.

"Not your fault, Trouble," he slurred. "Stay close."

"I will."

He closed his eyes and held my hand as I cleaned all the minor cuts. By the time I finished, they were almost healed.

Daemon took Garron around the back with a saw, intent on creating boards to fix the table.

Darian and I stared after them.

"Did you promise Daemon something?" he asked.

"No. They both don't want Liam to see the reminder of what happened. But I think Daemon's feeling guilty that Liam was hurt so badly when he only suffered a bruise. He thinks it's because he didn't try hard enough."

Darian glanced at me in surprise.

"I'm keeping myself open to watch the trackers. That means I can feel what you're feeling."

The corner of his mouth tilted. "You don't say."

His desire wrapped around me. Inviting. Coaxing.

"You want me to sleep on you again. You liked holding me."

"That's easy to guess. Tell me something harder." He held his arms out, inviting me to delve deeper.

His desire branched out with love and fear. Love because he adored everything about me—even the way I lashed out when they pushed for too much. He feared losing me before I could grow to love them.

Them.

I searched for jealousy. I found hints of it but only with yearning, never with anger or hate.

"You like when I hit you," I said, unwilling to admit the rest. "Perhaps I'm not hitting hard enough."

He laughed and pulled me into his arms. "I would prefer your caress to a strike if I have a choice."

I reached up and trailed my fingers over his brow and along his jawline.

"Like this?" I asked with a small smile.

He made a pained sound.

"I like touching as much as I like being touched. Thank you for removing your shirt last night."

"Vixen," he said before kissing my temple. "Tell me you'll sleep on me again tonight."

My gaze searched his as I said, "I think Eadric needs me most."

I saw his disappointment even as he nodded his agreement. "Edmund scared him. He scared us all but Eadric the most."

"Agreed," Brandle said, proving he'd been listening to us. "That leaves the four of us to keep watch tonight. Help me prepare a light stew Edmund can eat when he's hungry, and then go nap, Darian. You'll take the first watch."

We worked together to boil the root vegetables and mash them into a very watery soup. Once it was ready, Darian coaxed me into helping him make his bed in the cottage.

While he unrolled the mattress, I gathered two blankets. Turning my back on him was a mistake. Once I faced him again, I saw he had his shirt off and his hand extended in invitation.

He tempted me. They all did.

"Will you sleep if I lie with you?" I asked.

"Will my answer influence your decision?"

"Yes."

"Am I allowed to lie?"

I laughed and settled in next to him, resting my head on his chest.

"Close your eyes and sleep, Darian. If you do, I promise to kiss you awake."

He rumbled his anticipation and held me close, running his

hand over my hair. Soothed by his touch, the tension from what had happened began to melt away.

"There it is," Darian said softly.

I realized my fingers were wandering lightly over his ribs and smiled against his chest. A few minutes later, his breathing evened out. I carefully eased out of his hold and studied his sleep-relaxed face. He, like his brothers, was a very handsome man.

Shaking my head, I stood and turned to leave.

Brandle leaned against the doorframe outside the cottage, watching me.

"What were you thinking just now?" he asked gently.

"How impossibly handsome you all are. What will I do with seven of you? Daemon believes I'll be the envy of every woman in Turre. His idealistic imagining of the future is a bit unrealistic.

"It's never the man who suffers due to a tryst; it's the woman. I will suffer seven times over when I accept the love each of you holds for me. Yet, I won't turn away. I will endure whatever fate may result from my choices so long as I am the only one to suffer."

"We've given you our trust. Now give us yours. We vow to protect you and keep you as our own for the rest of our lives if you allow it. You will not live a life filled with persecution and hate as you imagine. Please believe in us."

I crossed the room and studied the sincerity in his gaze.

"Very well. I will choose to believe you. But we both know achieving such a life will come at a steep price. Are you certain it is one you are willing to pay?"

"Without hesitation."

I thought of Maeve and all of the lives she'd already taken and the people she'd hurt.

"You know nothing of what you will need to face to free my sister."

"And you know nothing of what you will need to face to—"

He stopped speaking abruptly. He held my gaze steadily, and

I knew what he couldn't say. The curse that bound them wasn't an idle curse. It had been cast by someone powerful. Someone with ill intent. Someone like Maeve. Or...perhaps Maeve herself since I knew nothing of Maeve's life before she'd arrived at our home.

"I believe I have an inkling," I said. "Do you truly believe I can help you? My abilities are chaotic and unreliable."

"We don't need your abilities, Kitten. Just you."

I nodded and made to leave. He caught my hand and spun me into his arms.

"Will you kiss me, Kitten?"

"Do you know no other question? You repeat it so often that it makes me wonder if you were starved for attention as a child or are simply a lustful man. Which would you prefer me to believe?"

He grinned at me. "Whichever will earn me a kiss."

"Your answer will help me understand the type of kiss you desire." As I spoke, I leaned into him and trailed my fingers from his temple to his chin, following the line of his jaw.

"Are you teasing me, Kitten?" he asked.

"Am I allowed to?"

"Most definitely."

A small smile tugged at my lips as I shifted close enough to press a kiss to his chin and jaw.

"I like to tease, Brandle." Remembering his reaction to my last kiss, I set my hand on his chest, just over his heart, and I dipped my head and flicked my tongue against his neck. My teeth lightly followed. His hands caged my sides.

"Which do you prefer?" I whispered against his skin. "My tongue or my teeth?"

I felt the shiver that ran through me and grinned.

"A little of both, then?" I licked and nipped his neck until I found a particularly sensitive spot. He growled and grabbed the back of my head. His heated gaze met mine a moment before his lips crashed onto mine in a kiss that melted away my teasing intentions.

"Do you think she'd kiss me like that if I asked for tongue and teeth too?" I heard Daemon ask.

I broke off the kiss, panting for air, and turned my head to see Eadric, Daemon, and Garron watching us. Garron had his arms crossed, but his gaze held no censure. Only adoration. Daemon's gaze held hunger. So much hunger.

Brandle's fingers caught my chin. His gaze swept over my face when I looked at him.

"Thank you for the kiss."

"You're welcome," I said. Leaning in, I lightly brushed his lips again and whispered, "I'll choose a different place to use my tongue and teeth the next time."

I slipped out of his stunned hold and laughed my way to Daemon's side.

"I think you broke him, Lamb," Daemon said, watching Brandle over my shoulder. "What did you say to him?"

"He invited me to tease him. So I did."

Daemon's gaze shifted between Brandle and me. "I want to be teased too."

"Me too," Eadric said, opening his arms to invite a hug. I could feel his desperate need for distraction and his worry for Edmund. They were all worried, but Eadric's clung to him like a wet tunic.

Daemon's arms wrapped around me before I could oblige Eadric.

"Me first," Daemon said. "Tease me."

I lightly kissed his lips. "I don't believe you would survive, my earnestly handsome pillow." As I spoke, I dragged my hand down the front of his chest, stopping at his waist.

He made a playfully pained sound. "We will never know what I can survive until we try." He dipped his head, but I twisted out of his hold and retreated several steps.

He tried grabbing for me, but I laughingly danced out of his way. He chased me around the partially repaired table and right into Eadric's waiting arms.

Eadric's grin didn't fully reach his eyes as he kissed my face and vowed to protect me from his brother's roving hands.

"What of *your* hands?" I asked, plucking one from my backside.

"They are your shields, covering your most precious places." He palmed my breast through my dress, and I rolled my eyes at him.

"I see through your ruse, Eadric. Unhand my person." My actions contradicted my demand, though, as I arched into his hold. He needed my distraction, and I felt the moment his worry shifted toward desire.

Unerringly, he pinched my nipple through my dress. My heart skipped a beat, and I fought to keep my breathing steady.

"I could release you," he said agreeably, "but then I couldn't help you tease my brothers by making you flush so prettily." He rolled my nipple and added in a conspiratorial whisper, "It tempts them to the point of madness. Look at them."

I turned my head and saw Daemon, Brandle, and Garron watching us. I met their gazes as Eadric continued to fondle me through my dress, and I felt myself sinking. With my hand on Eadric's shoulder, I tried to anchor myself. He brushed his lips against my ear, turning me slightly so I faced the others.

"Let's show them how much you like being touched, Sparrow," he said softly.

His words wrapped around me like a weight and pulled me deeper into what I was feeling. The well pulsed, begging to be opened. I shook my head, denying the well and trying to deny what Eadric wanted me to acknowledge.

His fingers left my breast only to delve into my bodice and tease the skin directly.

"Then tell me to stop," he whispered against my ear.

The sound of my pulse in my ears muffled his heavy breaths

as he kissed my jaw. The lid on the well slipped a fraction, and drowning in the flood of desire not my own, I moaned softly. Eadric's whispered praise encouraged another moan from my lips, and I arched into his palm.

Another wave of desire swept over me. My skin tingled with it.

"I think that's enough, Eadric," Brandle said, his voice low.

My eyes snapped open, and I flushed scarlet at the realization of what I'd allowed.

The hue of Garron's face matched my own. Shame crashed over me.

"I-I'm sorry," I stammered.

Garron strode forward, plucked Eadric's hand from my dress, and hugged me.

"You humble me," he said. "Your courage. Your strength and unwavering determination. Never lose that. Not for anyone... even us. Don't ever apologize when you've done nothing deserving of regret."

He pulled back and met my gaze. "If we push too far, it's us who owe the apology. Do you understand? You only need to speak our offense, and it will be corrected." His hands shifted to my shoulders. "Now, did Eadric press too far?"

I glanced at Brandle and Daemon over Garron's shoulder.

"No, Kellen," Garron said gently. "Only you can answer this question. Did Eadric take more than you were willing to give?"

Meeting Garron's gaze, I considered what he was asking.

If I were home and the same coddled miss I'd been months ago, the answer would have assuredly been an affirmation. But the home I knew had been cruelly ripped away from me. The life I once thought I would live—one of solitude with only my sister at my side—no longer seemed possible. Not the way it once had. In my heart, I knew I would never again be content with that future. What I truly wanted was here in this glade with these men. Companionship. Adoration. Devotion.

"No, Eadric didn't take more than I was willing to give," I said. "I am embarrassed and fear censure from you, but I liked what Eadric did."

Daemon pivoted on his heel and walked away. His need to touch me as Eadric had heated him from the inside. Eadric's gratitude and need to tell his twin what I'd admitted kept me where I was instead of closing myself in the cottage.

"He's not angry, Kitten," Brandle said.

"I know," I said. "I can feel his desire."

"Let me know what you feel when he douses himself with a cold bucket of water," Brandle said with a chuckle.

"Perhaps it's time to focus on something else," Garron said.

I nodded, ready to escape from my embarrassment.

Garron and I spent the next hour in the small study, trying to solve the question of energy consumption while we also monitored the trackers. It worried Garron that I couldn't tell how much I used or how much energy was in my well.

"What if you remove the lid from the well and leave it off? Perhaps allowing it to fill will help us understand what's already in it."

"No," I said firmly. "Things will die, Garron."

He scratched his jaw, clearly frustrated that he wasn't able to better guide me.

From the main room, I heard a rustle of movement.

"Let's take a break. I made a promise to Darian," I said.

"I heard. A kiss. He'll try to negotiate for more if you make it interesting. The privy will need to be re-dug soon." Garron's smirk didn't hide his intent. They needed me to be the playful instigator to help them forget their worries. So I grinned at his suggestion.

"Oh, that's positively devious," I said before hurrying from the room.

Rather than lying next to Darian, I straddled his waist and carefully lowered myself, bracing my weight on my hands and knees. When I was in position, I leaned forward and licked his nipple before nipping it gently.

His breath left him in a rush. Knowing he was awake, I settled my weight against him.

"Princess," he murmured, running his hands down my back and gripping my hips. He arched into me and ground his hard length against my center.

My eyes went wide, and I lifted my head to meet his sleep-fogged gaze.

"I never want to wake," he said, arching against me.

The shock of our contact faded as a tingle expanded from my center. On his next arch, I rotated my hips. Intense pleasure sparked to life inside of me, and my breath caught.

He groaned and had me pinned underneath him a second later.

CHAPTER 11

DARIAN NUZZLED THE TOP OF MY HEAD, AND HIS BREATHING CAME in harsh rasps as he steadily arched his hips, rubbing his hard length against a place that sparked a need I'd read about and never fully understood. Hands gripping his shoulders, I met each thrust with a roll of my hips and tipped my head to kiss his throat, nipping and sucking the skin. His rhythm faltered at the scrape of my teeth, and one of his hands slid under my backside. He didn't fumble with my skirts which had hitched higher around my thighs but gripped my arse to change the tilt of my hips.

The new angle sparked flames that licked through my insides, burning away any inhibition. I didn't notice the lid slipping off the well, only the feel of Darian's body moving over mine and the growing pleasure he was creating. It curled inside of me, expanding. Consuming me until I could think of nothing else but more.

"Darian…please," I begged. For what, I knew not. Only that I *needed*.

Everything.

The hunger inside of me screamed its insatiability, and I

opened myself to it, accepting everything Darian was willing to give me. I consumed his desire and demanded more. He gave it, moving faster.

Sweat coated his chest. I kissed his neck, my moves matching his own until that swelling ball inside of me burst.

I shattered with a cry. Waves of pleasure pulsed through me. Darian's smooth rhythm faltered, and he let out a low, broken groan. The surges of euphoria rippling through me slowed, decreasing in intensity. Gradually, I became aware of his trembling arms and our thundering pulses as he held himself still over me.

My hands, which had fallen to my sides, rose to touch his sweat-coated sides.

"Do I owe you an apology?" I asked softly.

He gave a tortured groan and rolled us so we lay on our sides, facing each other.

"Princess, I..." He swallowed hard and brushed back the hair clinging to my face. "Did I hurt you?"

I shook my head, and with a growing smile, I asked, "Did you like my kiss?"

"Like? I loved it. When can I have another one?"

"You need to pay for this one first. Garron said a new privy needs to be dug."

Laugher rang from the study, and Darian lifted his head to look in that direction.

"Bastard," Darian said without rancor.

"Language," Garron replied, not sounding as severe as he usually did.

Darian dropped a kiss on my forehead.

"I'll haul water for a bath then start on the privy," he said. "Will you heat the water for me?"

"Yes."

He kissed me gently for several moments then helped me

stand and straightened my skirts for me. When he turned, I hugged him from behind. His hands closed over my arms, and he held me in return.

"If I had a choice, I would never leave you, Princess. Not for a moment. Not for anything."

I kissed his back and rested my forehead against him.

"Thank you," I said softly.

He chuckled. "I'm happy to repeat the experience whenever you wish. You only need to crook your little fingers." He toyed with the digits then loosened my hold to bring them to his lips, kissing each one before facing me and kissing me gently once more.

"Ask me to stay, and I will," he said.

I was exceptionally tempted, and he saw it in my gaze.

"If you ask me to stay, Garron can dig the privy," he added with an eyebrow wiggle.

We shared a smile, and he nodded when I retreated a few steps.

"I'll return to you quickly," he said. "I received the better end of the trade, Garron," he called over his shoulder as he strode out.

I hesitantly turned toward the study and found what I thought I would. Garron leaned against the doorframe, watching me.

"Check your well," he said.

Surprised by the unexpected topic, I did so.

"It feels different. I can't explain how."

"Our charms flared briefly while you were with Darian."

I flushed. "I wasn't focused. I'm sor—"

"I didn't ask to rebuke you, Snow. I was simply curious how much energy you drew and if you had a target."

My eyes went wide. "Do you think I drew from Darian?"

"No. Not that," he assured me. "We're safe. I promise. I was simply curious. Come. Let's keep working on spell theory and brew another cup of tea."

We worked together until dusk when Liam and Edmund woke. Both could sit up. Edmund wasn't happy with his soup or with Eadric feeding him, but Edmund ate with a little coaxing from me. Liam ate his portion of stew slowly, and I could feel the pain he tried to hide.

"Do you want more tea?" I asked.

"Please."

"We need to apply more salve, too," Brandle said. "Kitten, would you mind going inside and preparing the beds with Garron?"

"I can stay and help—"

"Not this time," Brandle said. "Daemon will help me distract the pair as we change their bandages."

"I have just the story to tell," Daemon said with a grin. He sat next to Liam as Garron drew me back to the cottage.

"It won't take them long, and both will want to rest again as soon as they're finished," Garron said. He removed two mattresses and set them in the alcove on the other side of the shoe bench.

"Should we move the tub to make room for them before the hearth?" I asked, glancing at the fire.

"No, Darian is almost done digging and will need that bath after we help him move the privy to the new place. And it's better to have Liam and Edmund over here. We don't want to accidentally bump into them while they're healing, which is why you're sleeping next to Eadric and not Liam and Edmund tonight."

I nodded and climbed to the loft for the extra blankets Garron said were stored in a chest. He caught everything I tossed down, and we had their beds ready by the time they shuffled into the cottage, leaning heavily on Brandle and Eadric.

Edmund paused when he saw me and looked from me to the bed.

"Garron was worried someone would hurt you in their sleep," I explained.

Edmund grumbled under his breath and made his way to his bed. Eadric helped him lay down while Brandle helped Liam. Sweat dotted Liam's brow as he eased onto his stomach. I sat by his mattress and gently ran my fingers through his hair.

"Thank you," he breathed, closing his eyes.

"Tomorrow will be better for both of them," Brandle said softly.

He left with Garron while I played with Liam's hair. His breathing evened out after a few minutes, and I looked at Edmund, who was still awake and watching me.

"Is it true?" he asked.

"Is what true?"

"How you woke Darian."

My cheeks heated. "I kissed him. He rolled us and did...things. I lost control, but Garron said I didn't hurt Darian."

Edmund closed his eyes and shook his head.

"Ah, Trouble. You're lucky they tried gutting me."

I bit my lip, feeling guilty as I toyed with Liam's hair.

"Garron said I have nothing to apologize for. That I can't hurt you and should stop worrying. So you shouldn't be angry. Please."

He opened his eyes to look at me.

"Angry? I'm not angry, Trouble. I'm impatient to be the one feeling your nails clawing my back as you find your pleasure with me."

I forgot to breathe as his hungry gaze held mine.

"Three days. Then, you let me try."

"Try?" I asked faintly.

"To make you scream like Brandle claims you did for Darian."

Face flushed and heart racing, I tore my gaze from his and looked down at Liam. I was beginning to wonder if the brothers had been cursed because they said and did the most inappropriate things.

"I'm ready for my bath," Darian said, striding into the cottage.

His gaze found me by Liam. "That looks nice. Will you wash my hair for me? My shoulders are a little sore."

Edmund mumbled something as he closed his eyes, and I motioned for Darian to be quiet.

"Ach, they would rather listen to us than dwell in silence with their pain," Darian said. He came over and helped me to my feet. "Will you warm the water for me?"

I nodded and sent my energy into the water as I crossed the room to check the temperature. I'd learned to warm it in increments so I didn't make it too hot.

When it steamed nicely, I moved to return to Liam. However, Darian caught my arms, preventing me from facing him.

"Despite the wonders we shared earlier, I doubt you're ready to view me as I was born. Close your eyes, Princess, lest I cause you to scream again."

"Braggart," Edmund grumbled. "Get your arse in the water, and she won't see anything."

Darian chuckled and leaned around me to test the water. I scrunched my eyes closed. The splashes and hissed exhale told me he had indeed stepped around me to get into the tub.

I turned away, ready to retreat.

"Princess, will you bring me the soap, please?" Darian asked.

I opened my eyes and looked down at the soap waiting on the low stool within reach of the tub.

"No." He quickly caught me by my skirt when I would have retreated.

"Won't you wash my hair?"

"Wash your own hair," Edmund growled.

"I think my brother needs a distraction, Princess. If you go to comfort him, though, I fear he'll tear his stitches. Let me help you distract him."

Darian tugged on my skirt hard enough that I lost my balance and went tumbling backward. My backside landed in hot water with a splash. He laughed at my gasp and let my weight settle on his lap.

"Are you mad?" I asked, twisting to glare at him.

"Mad for you. Bathe with me, Princess."

"Don't forget how I taught you to drive your forearm into a throat," Edmund said.

Since Darian was expecting it, I knew it wouldn't work. Driving my elbow into his gut instead, I pulled myself free of his hold. Water drained from my heavy skirts, leaving a trail in my wake as I strode toward the door.

"Where are you going?" Darian asked.

"To tattle," I said.

Edmund's chuckle followed me out.

Brandle looked up from the fire at my approach. His gaze swept over my soaked gown, and he arched a brow.

"Darian pulled me into his bath," I said.

"Judging by your expression, you did not want to join him."

"I did not." The dropping temperature and cool breeze stole the lingering heat from the bathwater. "I'm wet and cold and annoyed."

Garron approached from behind me. "I believe Darian needs a taste of his own mischief."

I looked back at him. "How?"

"You can heat water. Can you cool it?"

Pleased with the idea, I closed my eyes and opened myself to the energy around me. It came to me as naturally as breathing now. The bathwater's energy shone more brightly than that of the tub it occupied and duller than Darian's. Focusing, I connected with the energy and moved the heat from his water to my skirts.

Opening my eyes, I looked down at the steam rising around me and grinned at the sound of Darian's cursing and splashing.

Brandle and Garron chuckled.

"I believe he will take more care with the mischief he causes you in the future," Brandle said.

Garron turned me toward the cottage. "Let's go back in and get you changed. I'll hold up a blanket for you."

"Thank you."

I hadn't considered that the cold water would drive Darian from his bath and entered the cottage unprepared for a full view of his unclothed person. A small 'eep' escaped me, and I quickly whirled around to escape, only to crash into Garron.

He caught me in his arms and held me tight. "Have enough decency to cover yourself, Darian."

"I would, but I can't feel anything below my waist to safely move."

"Good," Edmund said. "Serves you right."

"You would have tried coaxing her into a bath, too," Darian said. "You're just bitter that she found her release with me first."

I covered my ears and buried my face in Garron's chest. When he started scolding, I hummed so I wouldn't hear any of it. I'd reached my limit for what I cared to deal with in a single day.

Garron lifted me and walked farther into the cottage. I waited until he released me to uncover my ears but didn't open my eyes until he told me it was safe. Like a well-mannered man, he retrieved my spare shift and a towel for me then held up a blanket so I could change.

"Do you think you can heat the water again?" he asked. "The rest of us wouldn't mind a bath."

Tugging my wet dress free, I focused on the water's energy and warmed it with ease.

"You've given me a reason to be thankful for being an invalid," Edmund said. "I hate sharing bathwater. It was never clean by the time it was my turn."

I empathized with Edmund. Eloise and I had often shared bathwater, but never after she'd fallen to her usual misfortunes.

The muddied water she left behind would have seen me dirtier than when I started.

After considering the problem, I wondered if there was a way to clean the water without changing it. If I could use my energy to move a book and find a small seed in a garden filled with seeds, could I not locate and remove impurities from the water?

Idly drying myself, I focused on the water's energy, searching for what wasn't the same. Smaller than seeds and almost invisible, the impurities took more concentration to find. But I found them and separated them from the water.

"Um…what are you doing, Princess?" Darian asked from the other side of the blanket.

"Refreshing the bath? Is something wrong?" I quickly put on my shift and peeked around the blanket. A cloud of glowing dust hovered above the water.

Garron looked from the dust to me as I nudged the impurities with my energy and sent them out the door.

"It should be clean now," I said.

Darian leaned over the water and stuck his finger in it. "Warm too." He started tugging at his pants.

Garron threw the blanket over his head. "You had your chance."

Darian tugged the blanket away and scowled at Garron.

"Hold the blanket so Kellen doesn't need to go outside dressed like that," Garron said.

Darian served as a modesty barrier while Garron got into the tub. However, Darian quit his duty the moment his brother sat. The tub, while spacious for me, didn't accommodate Garron's size well. His knees were almost to his chest, leaving only a little hollow of space—which explained why I hadn't sunk any further when Darian pulled me in. Darian's request to help wash his hair made more sense. They couldn't move with much ease.

"Here," I said, taking the bucket. "Lean forward."

I wet Garron's hair and lathered it with soap. He kept his hands over his lap as I scrubbed and rinsed.

When I finished, I sat by Liam and Edmund with my back to the tub. I thought Edmund was sleeping until I touched his hair and he opened his eyes. He caught my hand and brought it to his lips. Without a word, he closed his eyes again and simply held my hand to his chest.

"I'm done," Garron said.

"My turn next," Daemon said, walking in.

"Wait a moment." I repeated the process of removing the soap and other impurities. This time, when the cloud rose in the air, I focused on absorbing the energy. All of it. I watched it wink out of existence. I used the energy I'd absorbed to heat the water.

"It's ready," I said.

Edmund's fingers toyed with mine as Daemon undressed and got into the tub.

"Will you wash my hair, Lamb?" Daemon asked.

I glanced over my shoulder at him.

"I refilled the buckets," he said, nodding to them.

"Will you behave?"

"Yes. Darian already warned me how painful his ice bath was."

I frowned. "Painful?"

"Ah, no need to worry, Lamb. He will recover and father children someday."

Edmund chuckled, and I glanced at him in confusion. Without opening his eyes, he released my hand.

"Go help if you wish. It's not easy bathing in that tub."

I repeated the process for Daemon, then Brandle, and Eadric.

"Ah, this is nice," Eadric said with a sigh as I scrubbed his hair. "I like when you touch me." Some of his happiness faded, and he glanced at Edmund, who was finally sleeping again.

"He won't be happy if he catches you worrying," I said.

"I can't help it. Edmund never gets hurt. Not like this. He's the strong one. The fast one. He can best any of us."

"They targeted him," Brandle said. "They knew who our real fighter was and used Liam to distract us so they could get to Edmund."

"So they won't wait long to try again," Darian said.

"Agreed," Daemon said. "Do you know what they're doing, Lamb?"

I paused scrubbing and let myself feel the forest around us.

"They found their companion. They're angry. Very angry. And afraid," I said, sifting through everything. "It's the coin. They're afraid we know what they're for. They won't attack tonight. Or any time soon. They're going to watch and heal."

"Good," Brandle said. "That will give us time to heal. We'll still keep watch as we planned, though."

"I'll take the first watch," Darian said.

IT TOOK three days and another cup of tea for Liam and Edmund to fully heal. During that time, the trackers watched but didn't make any move to attack again.

I also told Edmund of the spell Garron taught me. He was predictably angry, but at Garron. However, I didn't distract him from his temper as the others tried coaxing me to do. Edmund's promise hung between us every time he looked at me, and I wasn't yet ready to repeat what had happened with Darian.

Instead, I stole Garron away to study and hone my skills until I could cleanse and reheat bathwater with barely a thought. Once I mastered that, he brought me outside to work in the garden again.

"Most casters are limited to indirect magic, which is the manipulation of energy to boost what is already there. However, I think you have the ability to cast direct magic."

I recalled the concepts from the books Mother had placed in the attic.

"You mean blood magic?" I asked, alarmed.

"No, that is not what I'm suggesting you practice. Ever. Remember, when you cast, it's using energy. Always. The energy source you use isn't what defines direct or indirect magic. It's the type of casting that defines that."

"I don't understand."

"Think of the tea you make. The spell is simply enhancing the existing healing properties of the herbs used, which are then consumed by the person who needs healing. That's an indirect cast since the magic is indirectly affecting the person consuming it. Removing dirt from the water, heating it, and growing seedlings are all indirect as the cast encourages what is already there.

"A direct cast is a spell that directly influences a person or object outside of its natural order. The barrier protecting this glade, for example. It was a direct cast and is embedded in the land.

"Focus on the perimeter of the glade and see if you can feel where it's buried."

Since I'd already felt the barrier, it was easy to detect its roots deep within the earth, along with the corruption of the Dark Forest. Curious, I sank deeper, searching. The wrongness of the corruption seemed endless until I finally reached pure earth.

"How deeply they must have cast," I said mostly to myself.

"They?"

"The casters who corrupted the forest. It's a hundred times deeper than the barrier Henry placed on the glade."

Garron nodded. "Henry said the same. When my parents still lived, Henry dedicated his life to researching a way to lift the curse. I think that's why he brought us here. He knew so much about this place. What other people feared, protected us.

"Now, let's try some direct casting, shall we?"

He opened his palm and showed me a pea seed.

"We already know that you can make this grow. Instead of using your energy to nudge it to do what's natural to it, I want you to nudge it to do something against its nature, like grow thorns."

"I don't know how to do that."

"Energy and intent, Snow. Focus your energy, and encourage it to grow but according to *your* intent, not its intent."

He set the seed on the ground.

"Begin."

CHAPTER 12

I collapsed into the chair and rubbed my head.

"Does it ache? Do you feel dizzy?"

The glare I sent Garron's way quieted him.

"Yes, my head aches. From frustration."

"I know you can do this, Kellen. You just need to focus your intent."

"I have been, Garron. It's not working. I've grown a field of useless peas with not a single thorn on them. I can't do it."

"You *can*."

His insistence crawled under my skin.

"Why are you being so stubborn?" I demanded.

"Why are you? I've seen what you can do and know you can do this too."

"Go away."

"No."

Fisting my hands, I shot to my feet. Garron flew backward toward the open door. On his way out, his head hit the threshold with a hollow thunk.

Stunned, I stared at the empty space for a moment before I

ran outside and fell to my knees beside him. His eyes were closed, and he wasn't moving, but he was breathing.

"Kitten?" Brandle asked, slowly standing from his place at the table.

"I lost my temper," I said, tears streaming down my cheeks. "I didn't mean it." My hands clutched at Garron's shirt, jostling him. "Garron, please. Open your eyes."

Brandle hurried over and checked Garron's head.

Garron groaned and opened his eyes. I threw myself on him, crying uncontrollably.

"Shh," Garron said. "It's okay. I'm okay."

"I threw you."

"You did," he said, his voice lacking its usual strength. "Help me sit up, Brandle. I think I might be sick."

Brandle eased Garron into a sitting position. I held Garron's hand and watched him breathe deeply as I silently berated myself.

"I'm so sorry, Garron."

He looked at me then gently wiped the tears from my face. "It's not like you to cry like this."

It wasn't. I checked the lid, but it was firmly in place, which only confused me further.

I didn't cry, and I didn't lose my temper. Ever. It was too dangerous. Why did I feel so out of control?

Eadric cleared his throat. "Sparrow, have you, perchance, used what I brought you?"

"Brought me?" I echoed, confused until I recalled the extra supply bundle that he'd told me to open later. So much had happened since then that I'd forgotten about it.

"No, I haven't."

"Ah," Brandle said.

"Ah?" I glanced at the rest, but they said nothing.

Garron broke the silence. "I think we should temporarily suspend your studies."

"Good," Liam said. "I've been waiting for some Kellen time." He took my hand and coaxed me to my feet. "What would you like to do? Take a bath? Have your hair brushed? Perhaps something to eat?"

"We'll haul the water," Darian said, towing Daemon with him before I could answer.

"We'll get everything ready inside," Eadric said, nudging Edmund.

"I'll brew some tea," Brandle said as he helped Garron to his feet and led him to the table.

Unsure what was happening, I followed and went to sit beside Garron. However, Liam was quick to sit first and tug me into his lap. Irritation scratched at me, and I flashed him a disapproving look.

"Thoughts of holding you again helped me endure the pain," he said. "Please allow me this."

The irritation vanished, replaced by guilt. How could I have forgotten all that he suffered to keep me safe? Edmund too.

I twisted to face Liam and apologize. He darted in, stealing a sweet kiss. The press of his lips, combined with the devotion he felt for me, melted any lingering irritation. Cupping his jaw, I kissed him in return. He groaned and deepened the kiss, teasing me with his tongue as his hands smoothed down my back and gripped my hips.

He lifted me, turning me on his lap. My knees touched the bench on each side of him as my weight settled on his hips. He groaned into my mouth, and I felt his hunger. It wrapped around me and became my own, pressing me to kiss him without reservation. To demand more.

His hands tightened on my hips, and he arched into me. The pleasure it sparked became my focus. I ground against him, chasing the sensation our movements created.

Desire flooded me. His. My own. Then Garron's.

I lifted my mouth, panting. When I would have looked at Garron, Liam caught my face between his gentle hands.

"Stay with me," he murmured before kissing me hungrily again.

His hands returned to my skirt, slipping beneath to grip my bare thighs, guiding me over his hard length.

I broke away from the kiss and tipped my head back, holding onto his shoulders as I undulated over him.

It wasn't enough. Frustration began to creep in. I needed more. More kissing. More touching. More of his hunger.

Fingers brushed the back of my neck.

"You are so beautiful, Snow. Take what you need. It's yours."

Their desire enveloped me. I sank into it, letting it fill me. Endless desire.

Garron's hands gripped my sides, steadying me. Liam's fingers tugged at my lacings, and his mouth closed over my breast through the shift as he guided me over his length again and again. The feel of his teeth on my nipple at the same time Garron nipped my neck sparked an explosion of sensual gratification.

A strangled cry ripped from my throat.

Liam continued his ministrations as waves of pleasure coursed through me and slowly faded. Languid with the residual bliss, I released his shoulders and wrapped my arms around Garron's neck behind me. He kissed his way along my jaw and claimed my lips in a sweet, tender kiss that spoke of his love.

Liam's rhythm faltered, and his grip on my hips tightened. His heavy exhale drew me from my daze, and I eased back from Garron's kiss. Garron met my gaze with a warm smile and pressed his lips to my forehead before releasing me.

I looked down at Liam as he lifted his head from my breast, his gaze hooded and full of adoration.

"Forever with you won't be long enough, Love," he said.

My pulse skipped, and a flush started to creep into my face as

I realized what I'd done. My gaze lifted to sweep the glade, but the others weren't present.

"Please tell me you don't regret that," Liam said quietly.

I looked down at him again.

"Did I go too far?" he asked. The distress in his gaze helped me set my fear aside.

I shook my head. "I'm struggling with embarrassment," I admitted. "I liked it. But should I have?"

He hugged me, and my nipple tingled at the press of his cheek. My fingers went to his hair, tangling in the strands to discreetly add to the pressure.

"Like what you like without apology, Snow," Garron said from behind me.

I looked over my shoulder at him.

"I'm sorry I hurt you."

"I know. In the future, I will be more mindful of how to demand more of you. How do you feel now?"

"Good," I admitted, flushing further. "Not angry."

"How is your well?"

"My well?"

"Our amulets glowed again just before you found your release," Garron said.

My face flushed scarlet along with his. "I would prefer not to discuss this."

He nodded and said nothing more.

"The tub is full," Eadric called from inside the cottage.

Liam stood with me and waited until my dress covered me and I was steady on my feet to hand me over to Garron, who escorted me to the cottage.

When I glanced back, I saw Liam head toward the well. Garron caught my chin and gave me a quick kiss as Brandle left the cottage with the kettle.

"I'm going to help Brandle with the tea. Relax today, Snow. We'll try again tomorrow."

He left me at the door with Eadric, who took my hand and led me to the tub.

"I see Liam was helpful," he said, touching my untied lacings. He had them loose before I knew what he intended. "Arms up, Sparrow. You can heat the water next."

He lifted the gown off me and left me standing in my shift as he shook it out.

"Do you want me to give this a wash while you wash?" he asked. "Hmm. When did we last wash anything for you?" He gave me a speculative look. "Best to do it all."

Perhaps I was overly relaxed from what happened with Liam and Garron. Perhaps I was losing what was left of my sense of modesty. Whatever the case, when Eadric tugged my shift over my head, I didn't resist or get angry. I allowed him to steal every last bit of my covering and toss it toward the door.

His gaze swept over me, and he grinned.

"A laundering for both person and clothing is due. You have a bit of something here." He touched my reddened nipple. Sensitive from Liam's ministrations, it immediately pebbled.

"My mistake. Not dirt, then. But I'm certain you'll find some in the water once you're done. In you go."

He took my hand and coaxed me into the water, which I quickly heated. It wasn't until I was sitting that I saw Edmund standing behind Eadric. He gripped the soap and a cloth in his fisted hands.

My gaze flicked between him and Eadric.

"Allow me to wet your hair first," Eadric said. "Head forward."

I obeyed without thought and closed my eyes as the warm water cascaded over my head.

"There we are," Eadric said.

Fingers tangled into my hair, rubbing the scalp firmly. I knew it was Edmund and tensed.

"Let me have a bit of that soap," Eadric said.

A moment later, a soapy palm massaged the breast Liam

hadn't kissed. My center clenched pleasantly, and I forgot my tension.

"There. Isn't that nice?" Eadric asked.

"Yes," I said.

Edmund continued rubbing the soap through my hair for several more moments as Eadric toyed with my breast, rubbing it deeply then teasing the nipple.

"Time to rinse," Eadric said. "Close your eyes."

Water cascaded over my head, and hands squeezed away the excess from my hair.

"Let me get another cloth," Eadric said. "The sooner she's clean, the sooner she can relax. Lean back, Sparrow."

When I would have glanced at Edmund, Eadric caught my chin and kissed my wet nose.

"I like this," he said. "If I could do everything for you, I would. Give me your hand."

I lifted my hand from the edge of the tub that I hadn't realized I'd been gripping. He dipped the cloth he held into the water then smoothed it over each digit. Edmund lifted my other hand, mirroring his brother's actions down to the kiss that the tip of each finger received once clean. They moved from my hand to my arms. The pressure they used melted away any hesitation, and I closed my eyes and leaned back as I let them have their way. When they moved to my chest, I sighed contentedly. Eadric took great joy in teasingly cleaning my belly button and drew a smile from me.

When he lifted a foot out of the water, I giggled at the sensation of the cloth between my toes. The feel of their hands on my calves caused a contented sigh. That vanished when they washed my thighs. Each swipe of the cloth disappeared under the water and brought them closer to that part no one had ever touched but me.

Anticipation warred with hesitation, making my heart race.

Eadric's cloth lightly skimmed over that place, and my breath caught.

"Let me get a towel and start drying your hair before you catch a chill," Eadric said, retreating.

Edmund's cloth dragged over the spot Eadric's had. My eyes snapped open, and his hungry gaze captured mine.

"I need to hear you, Trouble. Just for me. Please." The cloth brushed over me again then disappeared, and his fingers brushed over my dusting of hair.

He touched me gently, exploring. Feeling places I'd only ever touched while washing and not the way he touched me. A small gasp escaped when he parted me and found that place that brought so much pleasure.

"Keep your eyes open, Trouble. I want to see everything."

I snapped my eyes open, not realizing I'd closed them.

"Good girl." His finger circled that spot until I was moving my hips under the water. Then he gently plucked at it.

"Eyes, Kellen. Open them."

I opened them once more but couldn't seem to focus on anything other than the building tension in my center.

"Please," I murmured.

"Not her mouth. I want to watch her," he said a moment before Eadric's fingers tangled in my hair. He tilted my head and kissed his way along my neck while his other hand found my nipple.

My whimpers filled the cottage. I could feel Edmund's desire. Its intensity glowed brightly for me. Only me.

"Yes, that's it," Edmund said as my hips lifted to demand more.

The tip of his finger brushed my opening. "This is where you want me, isn't it?" He teased that place while his thumb continued to circle higher. He dipped his fingertip farther in, and I shattered with a scream.

Edmund's mouth closed over mine, stealing the sound and my air as he kissed me with a savage need. Pulse by pulse, my release ripped through me, gripping the end of his finger. He tore his mouth from mine and caught my chin.

"Look at me, Trouble."

I fought to open my eyes.

The pressure between my legs increased as he slowly inserted more of his finger. I liked the feeling until the unexpected stab of pain. The lingering pleasure vanished, and I grabbed his arm, stopping him, though I knew it was already too late. He'd claimed what I'd dreamed of giving to him and his brothers.

"Breathe, Sparrow," Eadric said. "The pain is already fading, isn't it?"

I turned my head and saw him kneeling beside the tub. He held a towel and the end of my hair.

"Trust us. We're trying not to hurt you," he said. "Would you like a kiss?"

I nodded and tipped my head to welcome his gentle kiss. While his lips were on mine, Edmund moved the finger inside of me. It didn't send another stab of pain through me, but it didn't feel as nice as it had before, either.

When he withdrew, I sagged in relief.

Eadric drew back and smiled at me. "Better?" he asked.

"Yes." I glanced at Edmund with a frown. "That hurt."

Then I saw his finger coated with blood.

My eyes went wide, and I shot to my feet. Pink water ran from between my legs.

"Breathe, Sparrow. You're not hurt. I think it's your monthlies. The bundle I brought has everything you need. The tea Brandle brewed will help with any discomfort."

Embarrassment consumed me. I grabbed the towel from Eadric and pressed it to my front, hiding what I could of my nakedness.

"Leave. Please." I barely managed to speak the strangled words.

Edmund stood slowly. I could feel his gaze on me but refused to look at him.

"Please," I begged.

"You're beautiful, Sparrow. It's not easy to leave you, especially when we know we've upset you. Perhaps if we knew that you still held us in a kind regard..."

I closed my eyes. "Thank you for helping me with my bath. It was very nice. Please leave so I can make peace with my embarrassment. I will join you when I'm finished."

Lips brushed mine. Edmund's.

"Liam is right," he whispered as he set his forehead to mine. "Forever wouldn't be long enough with you."

They left, and I sank to my knees in the water. I cleaned it with a thought then washed again. The blood returned when I stood once more, and I knew what Eadric had said was true.

My monthlies. Had it truly been so long since I'd arrived?

I opened the bundle and found what I needed—the cloths and the ties to hold them in place around my hips. After I'd secured them, I dressed in a clean gown and looked at the door while toying with the comb in my hand.

Leaving Eloise had been the hardest thing I'd ever done in my life. But living in the glade with these men might soon surpass that torment. I pressed the back of my free hand to my hot cheek and took a calming breath.

The cool mask of indifference that I'd used for so long easily slipped into place, and I strode for the door only to stop at the last moment. Edmund's demand to look at him so he could see what I was feeling rose to mind. He wouldn't want my indifference. Not now. Not after what he'd—

I looked down at the comb I held, knowing that they wouldn't allow me to hide in the cottage for much longer. Then berated myself for my foolishness. If I couldn't overcome embarrassment and face the seven men who I knew cared for me–and who I cared for in return–what hope did I have of facing Maeve?

"I liked it, and I have nothing to apologize for," I said softly to myself. And Eadric had been knowledgeable enough about monthlies to purchase what I needed. Why should I feel embarrassed about anything that had transpired when neither man had seemed affronted while bathing me?

After another calming breath, I opened the door and strode into the yard.

"I need a hug and someone to brush my hair," I said.

Daemon dashed for me, catching me up in his arms and spinning me around as he held me tight. I clutched the comb and his shoulders.

"Ease up, you fool," Darian said. "She'll vomit if you continue."

Daemon stopped and carried me with his arms around my waist to the table where he settled me sideways on his lap so Darian could work the comb through my hair.

"Hand over the tea, Brandle," Daemon said.

Coddled in Daemon's arms, I sipped the tea Brandle had brewed and tried to relax as Darian freed the tangles from my strands.

"How are you feeling?" Daemon asked. "Does anything hurt?"

I shook my head.

"Good. Good." He hugged me a little closer and kissed my temple. "I'm glad Edmund didn't go too far. He's not easy to cuff."

I flushed at what Daemon was inferring but didn't duck my head. Instead, I looked at Edmund.

"My mother warned me that losing my maidenhead would be painful." My face heated further. "It hurt less than I'd anticipated. Thank you for showing me the pleasure that could be found with a man before the pain."

His lips twitched as he studied me. "If I'd taken it the usual way, it would have been more painful. I wanted to spare you that."

"Thank you."

"I don't believe I've ever heard a maid thank a man for taking her maidenhead before," Eadric said.

"You'll likely never hear it again," Darian said. He combed my hair away from my neck and kissed the exposed skin. "You're too sweet for the likes of us, Princess."

"Shut your mouth," Daemon said with a glare at his twin. "She's perfect for us."

I shook my head at them, not enough to dislodge Darian's roaming lips, though.

"Are you hungry?" Garron asked.

"A little," I admitted.

That sent them into a flurry of activity. I watched them mill some flour to make me honeyed biscuits and found myself handed over to Brandle, who acted as my cushion while Eadric fed me. Then, Edmund braided my hair.

They were attentive, amusing, and, most importantly, thoroughly distracting. I fell asleep between Brandle and Darian and woke on Brandle's bare chest.

"Good morning," he said. "We have a bath ready for you."

I nodded but didn't move to get off of him.

"Will it always be like this?" I asked. "Sharing me. Taking turns caring for me."

"Would you rather only spend time with us individually?" he asked.

I thought about it and shook my head. "No. I see how each of you yearns for my attention. If I only focused on one of you at a time, the others would feel left out."

"I asked what you preferred," Brandle said.

Lifting my head, I met his gaze. "I like everyone's attention."

"I sense hesitation."

"What I did with Garron and Liam didn't feel wrong. If felt... right. As did my time with Eadric and Edmund."

Brandled studied me, then said, "Pairs are good, but the idea of more overwhelms you."

I nodded.

"We already guessed as much," he said. "We can respect your privacy, Kitten. You choose who to keep in your company."

I arched a brow at him, and he chuckled.

"We will always vie for you, Kitten. The final choice is yours."

Content, I rested my cheek on his chest once more.

"Is anyone disappointed that Edmund took my maidenhead yesterday?" I asked.

"Just when I believe there is nothing you can do to surprise me, you show me how wrong I am." He smoothed his hand over my hair. "Disappointed? No. Relieved. Happy. Filled with anticipation."

I lifted my head again and rested my chin on his chest.

"Why relieved?" I asked, choosing not to address the other emotions.

"None of us wanted to be the one to hurt you, Kitten. It breaks our hearts to see you suffer even the smallest amount."

"But not Edmund."

"Edmund is braver than the rest of us. He knew a little pain now would spare you suffering later. Are you truly okay? No lingering pain?"

"I haven't moved yet, Brandle. Don't be impatient."

He chuckled and smoothed a hand down my back the way I liked.

"And how are you feeling otherwise?"

I knew he meant my mood, and I felt guilty for having lost control the day before.

"Is Garron okay?" I asked.

"He is," he said. "A small lump on the back of his head. Something Edmund's given him before to no lasting effect."

"I want to try again."

"Throwing him?" Brandle asked with a laugh. "Darian and Daemon will approve."

"Of course not. I meant the spell we were working on. Will he be willing?"

"I think that's a question you should ask him. Are you ready for your bath?"

I rolled off Brandle in answer and stood. The light cramping in my middle had me wrinkling my nose. Eloise's monthlies passed without fanfare. Mine, while more agreeable than most, liked to make itself known.

After Brandle put on his shirt, he wrapped me in my cloak and carried me to the privy. When he returned me to the cottage, Darian and Daemon were already waiting inside.

Both bowed deeply to me.

"We will be serving as your attendants today, m'lady," Daemon said.

He whisked me away from Brandle and stripped me of my shift before I could blink. I swatted his hand when he tried to untie the strings.

"No attendants," I said.

Darian—the deviant man—untied the strings from behind me and kissed my shoulder.

"Darian, you can't simply—"

He swept me up and placed me in the cold water. I sputtered at the chill engulfing me.

"Heat it quickly, Princess," he said.

I bared my teeth at him even as steam rose around me.

"She looks upset," he said to his brother. "It's our duty to bring a smile to her lips."

"No, it isn't," I said, stealing the cloth from him and wetting it. "I can wash myself, thank you very much."

Daemon knelt beside the tub and gave me a pleading look.

"We have been waiting for you for as long as any of us can remember, Lamb—the woman who will set us free. We've dreamed of the day that we would be able to care for you. Please don't take this from us."

His pleas softened my resistance. "Daemon, be reasonable. I have my monthlies. Let me wash in peace."

"Exactly so! Do you think we haven't prepared for this? Allow us to prove we know how to care for you at all times."

"And we'll bring you the peace you need so you can calmly study with Garron," Darian added.

When I looked at him, his shirt was off and he held another washing cloth.

"Shall I start with your feet?"

CHAPTER 13

I DIDN'T TRUST THE LOOK IN DARIAN'S EYES WHEN HE REACHED into the water and lifted my foot out.

"Look at these toes, Daemon," he said, washing them. "They're so adorable that I could eat them up."

He kissed my big toe then shocked me by running his tongue along the side of it. My center clenched around nothing and cramped slightly. I jerked my foot free in response, but he recaptured it quickly and continued washing.

"It was just a little taste, Princess," he said. "Not even the nibble I wanted."

Daemon lifted my hand. "I find her teasing little fingers tempting, myself, brother."

He nipped the pad of one. Instead of trying to take it back, I splashed him with my free hand.

"Ah, you wish my shirt off as well, I see."

I opened my mouth to correct his assumption, but my words turned into a gasp at the feel of Darian's mouth closing over my toe. He hummed as his tongue swirled around it.

"There," Daemon said, pressing my hand to his suddenly bare chest. "Is this better, Lamb?"

The pair of them were assaulting my senses, leaving me no time to react—only to feel.

"Hmm," Darian said, releasing my toe. "I think I need to taste her ankle."

He washed and kissed his way down my leg while Daemon washed and kissed his way up my arm. When Daemon's cloth swiped over my breast, I closed my eyes and gave myself over to their playful care.

"Sweet Princess," Darian said softly. He kissed my knee and ran his hand up my thigh as Daemon's tongue swirled around my nipple.

As Daemon sucked the tender peak into his mouth, his brother's fingers parted my folds. My hips moved to welcome his circling touch around the place they all seemed to know enjoyed their petting the most.

Their desire for me grew, feeding the pleasure I found in each kiss, lick, and stroke. When Darian's hand nudged my legs wider, I let them fall open for him. He mumbled something about tasting that I couldn't hear over the sound of my pulse pounding in my ears.

Daemon's mouth left my chest with a pop. "Patience, brother, lest you find yourself flying around the room."

I sank my fingers into Daemon's hair and drew him back to my chest. He chuckled as he obliged.

Darian's circling fingers dipped lower to my opening, and I tensed. Darian made a frustrated sound and returned to the little nub he'd abandoned to pluck it. Bolts of pleasure shot through me, building pressure.

"Daemon," I murmured, tugging at his hair. He lifted his mouth and welcomed my hungry kiss.

Darian's plucking continued at the same time I felt another finger tease my opening. His excitement fed mine, and I broke apart as he slowly slid the digit into my spasming center. Daemon swallowed my cry and held me as wave after wave of pleasure washed through me.

When I stopped twitching, he kissed me sweetly and pulled back to brush my hair from my face.

"There," Daemon said. "Do you feel more relaxed?"

As he spoke, Darian unhurriedly worked his finger farther into me. Once he reached the hilt, he withdrew it and did it again, setting off another round of minor spasms that felt quite pleasant. So I nodded.

Daemon continued to pat my hair, supporting me with his arm and kissing my nose and cheeks as Darian took his time stroking me from the inside.

"Princess, the water's growing cold," Daemon said softly.

It roused me enough to realize they would keep me in the bath all day if I allowed it. With a sigh, I lifted my head and kissed Daemon's cheek.

"Thank you for bathing me. It was quite enjoyable." I looked at Darian. "Will you remove your finger, or will I be forced to walk with you crouched under my skirts?"

He threw his head back and laughed. His finger slid free and petted my folds before withdrawing completely.

"Under your skirts is where I long to be," he said. "But I will wait for a more convenient time. I believe Garron is waiting for you outside. We'll leave you to finish alone...unless you wish for more help."

I shook my head. "Go. I will be out soon."

Since I hadn't washed my hair, it took less time for me to finish and dress. I glanced at the water in the tub. They'd hauled the water from the well for me twice in two days now. Other than brewing their healing tea, I did very little to assist in their daily tasks.

Not wanting to add to their burdens, I focused on the water, feeling its energy. The impurities were easy to find now. Rather than lifting them, I absorbed their energy—all of it—until they disappeared completely. Then, I did the same with the water. The new energy settled into my well, melding with what was already there—not increasing it, simply merging with it.

Satisfied with my efforts to help, I joined Garron outside.

"Would you like to try again?" he asked. "I promise to follow your lead and not push for more than you're willing to attempt."

"No, Garron, I need you to push. I apologize for yesterday and promise not to lose my temper again. Are you well?"

"I'm well. I promise."

With a small smile, he took my hand to lead me to the garden where I spent another frustrating hour attempting to grow a thorn on a pea plant.

"It would be easier to grow a pea on a bramble at this point," I said, crossing my arms in irritation.

"Then let's try that," Garron said. "I'll be right back."

He disappeared around the cottage and returned several minutes later with a piece of thorn-covered bramble, which he poked into the ground at my feet.

With barely a brush of my energy, I rooted it and watched it grow. I allowed its trunk to thicken but suppressed any offshoots, holding the energy back. The plant was brimming with the need to use the excess energy it stored.

I focused on the pea plant beside it, feeling the energy of the bloom. Clearing my mind of everything else but that pea bloom, I touched the bramble with my energy once more and whispered to it in my mind.

Be more than you are. Be what I need.

I watched a small bud burst out from the thick stem of the bramble. Then another and another. They bloomed and grew into pods in seconds. I didn't stop there. I turned to the pea plant and touched it with the same intent—to make it more than what it was. To make it what I needed.

Thin thorns erupted from the vines.

Smiling, I looked at Garron. Awe reflected in his gaze as he looked at the plants.

"You truly are incredible, Snow," he said. "Well done."

"Thank you."

We didn't stop at pea pods on bramble or thorns on the pea plants. He pressed me to try more, watching me closely for any signs of fatigue.

By dusk, I could change a rock to soil and soil to water.

I yawned continuously as Eadric fed me and leaned into Brandle's comforting hold.

Liam walked me to the privy and playfully washed my hands for me, claiming I was too tired for such work. I didn't contradict him. The day's effort had seemed to drain me. Yet, when I checked the well, the energy within seemed the same.

"Come, Love. Let's put you to bed."

After guiding me to the cottage, he helped me undress then handed me to Edmund, who rebraided my hair and kissed my forehead.

"Sleep soundly, Trouble. You've earned it."

Nodding, I lay down on the mattress and listened to them clean up our dinner. I never felt who settled in next to me.

I woke on Liam's chest with his hand gently stroking my hair. Outside, I heard the low murmur of conversation.

Rather than opening my eyes, I opened my senses. Dawn had passed several hours ago. Another spring storm was on its way. The trackers were oddly subdued, with no immediate intent to attack.

Eadric was still hungry. Edmund was bored and annoyed. Garron was worried he'd pushed me too far. Daemon slept, and Darian was thinking of tipping him out of his bed. Liam wanted me to continue moving my fingers against his skin. And Brandle was worried about…so much.

I turned my head to kiss Liam's bare chest.

"Thank you for holding me. I slept well."

"It was my pleasure." He kissed my temple. "We have another bath waiting for you."

I nodded and stroked my fingers over his side like he'd wanted before easing away with a stretch.

"Are you feeling well?" he asked, watching me.

"I have some light pains, which are normal with my month-lies," I said. "Those will pass, though."

"Nothing else?"

"Should there be?" I asked, sitting up. He moved with me, and I gazed at the expanse of his exposed chest.

He chuckled and shook his head. "No. We're just worried that you pushed yourself too far yesterday."

"Unless you see my hair greying, I don't believe I did."

I kissed his cheek then stood and retrieved my cloak.

"Brandle," I called. "Would you be willing to carry me?"

He appeared at the door several moments later. I smiled and moved so he could pick me up without entering the cottage.

"Do you think they would find this odd if they were watching?" I asked as he moved.

"What do you mean?"

"That you're able to easily carry a woman several inches taller than you?"

"They've fought with us several times and know not to underestimate our strength."

The worry he wore like a cloak grew heavier.

"Will you help me bathe when I'm finished?" I asked.

His gaze met mine, and I felt his surprise and relief.

"I will."

The fire was burning brightly in the hearth when we returned, and he closed the door behind us.

"Will you tell me what's worrying you?" I asked as I freed my shift's tie.

He helped me lift it over my head and turned me. His fingers swept through my hair, twisting it up into a coil, which he secured with a smooth stick.

"Please, Brandle," I said when he remained silent.

He plucked the tie holding my bleeding cloths in place, and I fought not to flush as he removed them.

"Some things, I cannot tell you," he said, clasping my hand and helping me into the water. "And some things, I chose not to share out of fear. You're helping us, Kellen, and I don't want to do anything that will cause you to run."

"I won't run, Brandle," I said as I leaned back against the tub.

His gaze searched mine; then he took the cloth, wetting it and soaping it.

"I would like you to treat me as you do your brothers." He froze and looked at me in panic. I laughed. "Only in the regard that you don't keep secrets from me. If your curse isn't preventing you from speaking it, speak the truth as I have been doing. Even when it's uncomfortable. Please."

He sighed and took my hand, washing it first and working his way up my arm.

"I'm worried that the spells you're casting will attract attention we cannot afford to attract. I'm worried that it's taking so long to break the spell, not for our sake but your sister's. I know you fear for her safety. I'm worried we won't be able to keep my promise of protection. I'm worried that, once the curse is broken, it won't be enough. I'm worried—"

I leaned forward suddenly and kissed him. He didn't try to take control, but he didn't turn away either. He allowed me to kiss him sweetly as long as I wanted, and I felt his satisfaction that I was doing so.

Slowly withdrawing, I studied him.

"Those concerns are not your burden alone, Brandle. Trust your brothers—trust me—to carry those concerns with you.

"When I agreed to help you, I did so because I believed you

were the best option to help my sister. I knew that it would take time to break your curse, and I am using that time to my advantage by learning more about casting, which I hope will help us achieve that goal. So, while I do appreciate your concern for my sister, know that it is a useless concern. It will take as long as it takes, and we are doing everything we can while we wait.

"Now, regarding my spell work attracting attention... according to Garron, Henry cast the spell for the barrier at a great cost. Yet, you weren't discovered. The spells I've cast seem to have very little cost. However, it is wise to practice caution. Garron mentioned methods casters use to cloak themselves. I'll work on mastering that next. Hiding what I can do will protect me, and mastering what I can do will protect all of you.

"And as for your promise of protection, when you vowed to keep me safe, we both understood you were not promising an outcome but your intent...just like the spells I cast. Do your best, and I will do mine, Brandle. That is all we can ask of one another.

"Regarding whether breaking your curse will be enough... I may not understand the problems you face, but your brothers do. Spend time with them. Think of all the possible outcomes, and create plans." I feathered my fingers over his cheek.

"Worrying solves nothing. Stop worrying, and start planning, Brandle."

He darted forward and kissed me hungrily. I could feel his desire, but it was as strong as his devotion and adoration. When he pulled back, I was lightheaded. It took a moment to realize he was washing me and not using it as a means to draw pleasure for me.

The corners of his mouth lifted in a charming smile when I frowned at him.

"I doubt my control to stop once I start, Kitten."

My heart skipped a beat at his meaning.

"And when you look at me like that, you test my restraint. Whatever lingering concerns you have about being with us, resolve them. Once you do, I am yours for the rest of my life. Do you understand?"

I studied him.

"And if I'm unable to resolve them?" I asked.

"I will need a frigid bath like the one you gave Darian. He said it cooled his desire for hours."

I laughed and sank deeper into the tub as Brandle idly washed my neck.

"I will do as you ask."

WITH MY SENSES OPEN, I stood at the edge of the clearing. After a week of practice, I'd finally braved casting my senses far afield.

"I can feel one," I said to Garron. One caster among thousands of people living at the edge of Turre.

"Is your lid firmly on your well?" he asked.

"It is."

"Good. Have they cloaked their energy?"

"No."

"I think we are right then," he said.

I brought myself back to the clearing and looked at Garron.

"Have I truly been cloaking myself since that day in the woods?" I asked, still struggling to believe the lid I had on my well was my protection.

"It's the only explanation that makes sense," Garron said. "When you first arrived, I couldn't sense you. It wasn't until you lost control that we knew."

"When I lose control, the lid moves off the well to some degree," I said with a nod. "When I cast, I only lift it a little, so energy doesn't flood in." I thought back to when my abilities first appeared. The panic of seeing everything dying at my feet and how naturally I'd closed that part of myself off. Without understanding, I'd not only protected those around me but myself as well.

"Is the lid why I can't sense how much energy is in the well?" I asked.

Garron considered the question. "Even when cloaked, I sense the energy within my well. However, I don't believe comparing yourself to me is an accurate assessment of what is possible. I don't have the same level of control or talent you do. I would be able to sense an uncloaked caster near or in our glade, but not farther afield as you can."

"I find it frustrating to have so many unanswered questions."

"I understand. Truly. For now, let's continue our test. Locate the caster again."

After I said I found them, he had me cast a simple spell to see if the caster would cloak themselves.

"Nothing changed," I said, closing myself off again. "Why would the caster cloak themselves even if they did sense me all the way out here? Casting is allowed in Turre, isn't it?"

"It is. However, casters in Turre cloak themselves if they sense another caster's attention on them."

"Why?"

"The queen," he said. "Her need for power is absolute. She would never allow another caster of significance to exist in her domain. And the abilities she deems significant vary. To protect themselves, most casters hide."

"Which is why I would have never been able to hire the caster I needed," I said, understanding.

"Precisely."

"Then how will I manage once I break the curse?" I asked.

"That is a question for another day," he said. "I believe my brothers are seconds away from tossing me into the well for consuming so much of your time."

I glanced over my shoulder at the others lingering around the cooking fire. Edmund caught my gaze and took a step in my direction. A word from Brandle, which I couldn't hear, stopped him. Edmund pivoted and stalked off toward the clearing. Eadric jogged after him. I'd warned Edmund the day prior that he would lose his next chance to sleep beside me if he injured his brothers. Though Edmund's feelings were the most visible, he wasn't the only one struggling.

"I can feel their frustration and impatience," I said. "Why did everyone stop touching me, then?" It had been days since any of them had helped me with my morning bath or even petted me while sleeping.

Facing Garron, I watched him lift a hand in the air, even as his face flushed red. I swatted his hand down.

"Don't call Brandle over here. I want an answer from *you*, Garron."

"You stopped bleeding."

"And?"

A deeper hue consumed his face.

"They...we..."

"Until I'm ready to have sex, no one will touch me again? Is that it?" I guessed.

He nodded, and I crossed my arms.

"No."

He frowned a little, and some of the heat eased from his face.

"No?"

"Correct. I do not accept that sex must be a condition to receive your affection."

He shot a panicked look at Brandle. I grabbed his chin and forced his attention back to me.

"Garron, I've been told to do as I've pleased, and I have. I've embraced all of the touching and petting and affection given to me and pushed aside my embarrassment and guilt. Changing the rules now feels like you're all changing your minds."

"Snow, that's not—"

I covered his mouth with a hand.

"I love the names each of you have given me, but I need to know that you no longer believe my presence is as fleeting as winter, Garron. That you continue to call me that at the same time you've all withdrawn from me leads me to doubt. Everything."

Arms circled me from behind. Brandle. He kissed the back of my neck and cupped a breast.

"Forgive us, Kitten. We didn't consider you might misunderstand our actions. We are not withholding our affection to force sex upon you. We are keeping our distance because your welcoming presence tempts us to the brink of control. I have no wish to pull Edmund off of you for going too far or to see you throw Edmund to protect yourself and weep in regret as you did with Garron.

"We want you, Kitten, with a desperation that is maddening. The more you accept, the more impatient we've become for your surrender. We wish for that above all else—but given freely. Willingly. In your own time. Do you understand?"

"If I can control my urge to fling the lot of you across this clearing, each of you can find the control not to force yourselves upon my person. Do better, Brandle. All of you."

He kissed the back of my neck.

"We will."

After, I sat on Liam's lap while Eadric fed me dinner and purposely selected Eadric and Edmund to sleep beside me. I could feel Edmund's barely contained aggression and lust as his hands wandered over my person. It called to me, feeding my need to be touched. Since introducing me to the pleasure they could bring, their desire for me had grown. And mine for them. But sexual desire wasn't what I wanted from them just then.

So when Edmund's hand dipped to the hemline of my shift, I caught it in mine and shook my head.

"Hold me, and let me hold you. Please," I said softly. "Show me that you love me, and let me love you in return."

His aggression faded, and devotion replaced it as he wrapped his arms around me and held me close. Eadric moved closer behind me, stroking my back and hip, soothing me to sleep.

When I woke, I rested on Edmund with my hand petting his chest.

"I love the pleasure you've shown me, Edmund, but it isn't enough. I need more. Kind words. Gentle touches. Understanding. Comfort. All of that together is love. A relationship with only pleasure isn't truly a relationship at all." I lifted my head to meet his gaze. "When you said you loved me…when Liam admitted you all feel the same…I thought you wanted a relationship. If I've misunderstood—"

"You haven't. Brandle shared what you said to him. I was wrong, and I'll do better. I promise."

Resting my chin on his chest, I smiled at him as I circled my finger around his nipple.

"Eadric didn't lie. I do like being touched and like touching in return. I don't want the pleasure you've shown me to disappear, but I need to know I mean more to you than that."

"You mean more than I ever thought possible, Trouble. Whatever you need, I'll give it. Without reservation or hesitation. I'll be your shield and your strength."

"And my pillow?"

"Always."

CHAPTER 14

GARRON WATCHED A BARRIER OF BRAMBLE ERUPT IN FRONT OF US, taller than the cottage and so dense that not a speck of the setting sun's light shone through.

"Your powers are growing," he said.

"If that were true, wouldn't I feel some kind of change in the well?"

"Perhaps. Perhaps not."

"Casting is vastly provoking," I muttered.

He heard and chuckled. I focused on the bramble barrier and reversed the growth to return it to the individual sticks I'd poked into the ground. Before the barrier finished shrinking, I felt a tingle of warning so strong it stole my breath.

Opening myself, I stretched my senses, searching, and found the trackers. I felt magic coming from a puddle near them. After days of nothing but idly watching us, I felt their intent change.

"They're going to attack again. Soon. Just after dark."

Garron's hand settled on my shoulder.

"You have nothing to fear. We've beaten them back twice already."

"At a cost each time." I lifted my skirts and jogged to the

cottage. "Garron, start the tea. Eadric and Edmund, gather bramble branches. Daemon, go to the cellar and find a bag of peas."

"Kitten, what's wrong?" Brandle asked.

"She said they'll attack again," Garron said.

"It's nothing to worry about—"

"Whatever magic I sensed a moment ago has hardened their resolve. They *will not* fail again. What means will they use to ensure that if they were willing to burn Liam and eviscerate Edmund previously? I would prefer we not underestimate them."

"All right. What do you have in mind?"

"They've chosen not to fight fair. I see no reason to do so either."

While Garron and I brewed the healing tea as a precaution, Eadric, Edmund, Liam, and Brandle scattered pieces of bramble around the glade's perimeter, and Daemon and Darian placed the pea seeds around the cottage and fire.

"You said you sensed magic. Was it from the coins they hold?" Garron asked as we worked.

"No. It came from a nearby puddle...not from it but through it."

"Through it?"

"Like the coins. I can feel the magic in them and how they connect to the trackers and through the trackers to someone in Drisdall."

"Is it the same person?"

"Yes." I stared down at the tea leaves, struggling to maintain calm.

What did it mean that Maeve was communicating with the trackers now? Had something happened to Eloise? Was she in danger, or was my twin acting out, forcing Maeve to need my presence to control her?

Returning with the trackers, willing or otherwise, would not protect my sister.

"Everything is ready," Brandle said from the door. "I've also put out the cooking fire. Do you know when they intend to attack?"

"Once the light fades."

"I know you feel safer when you're near us, but I would prefer you somewhere out of reach."

"Not the cliff," Darian said, appearing beside him.

"I will go to the roof at dusk then and help as I am able."

Brandle considered my dark dress and nodded. "Lie low and you should remain hidden."

At the appointed time, I left Garron to store the tea in the cellar and asked Edmund to boost me to the roof. He kissed my forehead and told me to stay until he fetched me. Then he took the ladder away to stow by the garden fence.

The seven of them returned to their normal places, lounging in their swinging beds and idling around the table to converse as the moon rose higher and the remaining daylight faded from the sky.

Crouched low against the thatching, I followed the trackers' movements in my mind as they quietly approached. I could feel their concern that the fire wasn't lit. They'd hoped to use it like last time to distract and disable so they could work as a group to kill one brother at a time. They were determined to take me at all costs.

However, my determination to protect the men of this glade was stronger.

Once they entered the glade, I touched my energy to the hidden bramble, silently growing it in their wake and cutting off their chance to escape.

Edmund started arguing with Daemon and flipped him out of his bed. Daemon came up swinging. The ruse worked to distract the trackers from the wall encircling the glade as they drew closer to their quarry.

The first tracker moved past a patch of pea seeds. I waited as, one by one, they moved forward, unaware of the danger. When the final tracker stepped over the patch, I touched the peas with my intent. Strong thick vines silently erupted from the ground and ensnared his legs, twining upward toward his torso. His muffled grunt of shock had his group spinning back toward him.

The brothers used the distraction to run toward the trackers.

Unaware, the trackers withdrew their blades. Metal glinted in the moonlight, and I felt their rage-filled intent to gut whoever had their companion.

Reminded of what they'd done to Edmund, my fear rose sharply.

No, never again.

I stood, feeling the anger churning in my well.

"Obey me," I whispered to the vines. "Protect what is mine."

The vines slithered over the ground, moving faster than Edmund could run, and wound around the trackers' feet, snaking their way up their legs and torsos. Unable to flee, the trackers hacked at the plants. The vines grew thicker and stronger without needing to be coaxed.

"Your parlor tricks are useless," one of the trackers snarled. "Give us the girl."

My intent changed, and the vines snared their hands. Immobile, they could do nothing as offshoots plucked their blades from their grips and brandished them before their faces.

Edmund stopped short at the sight.

His surprise wasn't shared by the tracker I'd unmanned. That one laughed.

"Are blade-wielding plants meant to strike fear in us? We cannot be harmed by anything made of magic. Release us and take your beatings like men."

"Take their coins," I called.

Garron began searching the tracker nearest him, patting his clothes.

"Eh! Remove your bloody hands or lose them."

Garron dug into the man's coat and removed a coin. Angry curses rang out in the glade as the rest also lost theirs. The vines held strong against their struggles.

Edmund left the group and jogged back to where I waited. He silently helped me down and walked beside me as we joined the rest.

"Your mother awaits your return," one of the trackers said when he saw me.

"She is not my mother."

"And your sister? Is she no kin of yours either?"

With a touch of my will, the vines covered all of their mouths.

"You have no reason to speak of my kin. We will keep your coins and set you free. You fought fiercely, wounding several of the glade's inhabitants, but your coins were lost in the process. You can choose to leave the forest or allow the oath that binds you to keep you here until the beasts eventually take you all."

Connected to them through the vines, I removed their memories and replaced them with the new one without touching them.

"Now sleep."

I faced Brandle. "They are men filled will ill-intent and no remorse. If the opportunity presents itself, they will kill all of you and return me to Drisdall. Yet, knowing this does not change our need to spare them. We cannot become the monsters we are fighting to free ourselves from."

"We agree," he said.

I glanced at Edmund and watched him nod.

"We'll return them to their place and leave them with enough wood to see them through to dawn. After that, their fates are their own," he said.

Nodding, I withdrew my energy from the vines and watched the men crumple to the ground.

Edmund grabbed a pair by their collars and started dragging them toward the trees. Eadric took two more and winked at me. Liam followed with the final tracker.

I trailed behind them, stopping at the edge of the glade.

"Father?" I called once they'd disappeared.

A set of red eyes moved from deeper within the trees, approaching. He stopped short of the moonlight that shone on the ground several feet from the trees.

"Eloise and I yet need your protection. Please hold onto what remains of your humanity and avoid the trackers."

"Love," he growled.

"I love you too, Father."

He grunted and retreated into the shadows.

Garron came to stand beside me and wrapped an arm around my waist. I met his concerned gaze.

"I feel well," I said automatically. "No depletion of note."

He sighed and leaned his head on my shoulder.

"I fear you will attempt to cast a spell beyond your abilities. Be wary of your limits, Kellen, or you truly will leave us like snow."

I kissed the top of his head and watched the forest for the others' return. Edmund's knuckles were raw and split when he joined us. I didn't question why; I simply told him to fetch the tea.

THE FIRST TRACKER died the following morning. Aware of their intent, I had kept myself open to their presence. He disappeared abruptly, surrounded by the beasts.

"You paled," Eadric said.

I leaned into Brandle's warmth and closed my eyes.

"The beasts claimed a tracker's life."

Brandle stroked my arm as he said, "They made their choice by not leaving with the dawn. Their fates are their own."

I nodded and forced myself to take the next bite of oats that Eadric offered.

By dinner, another tracker lost his life. I could feel the fear growing in the remaining three.

"It's plain that the coins protected them from the beasts," Garron said. "It's unfortunate we melted them."

"Nothing good would have come from keeping those coins," I said.

That night, I settled between Daemon and Darian. As I closed my eyes, something whispered that danger would come to our door again soon.

I slept fitfully and checked the trackers often. Shortly after dawn, only one tracker remained.

My restlessness grew with each passing minute until I felt it— magic from a pool of water near the tracker. A tingle of warning, unlike anything I'd ever felt, washed over me, making the hair on the back of my neck stand on end.

Danger.

Death.

Fear flooded me, and I reached for the bramble. It burst from the ground, creating a dense, impenetrable barrier.

"Kellen? Love?" Liam said from beside me. "What is it?"

I opened my mouth, but my throat tightened, trapping the words I desperately wanted to speak.

She's coming.

"Kellen?" Brandle said, clasping my chin.

His warm gaze held mine as I struggled with what Maeve's arrival would mean. The charms would keep them safe, wouldn't they? I thought of all the times I'd lost control and hadn't hurt them. But Maeve wasn't me. She understood how to cast. I'd seen what she could do, and the tracker was right that my abilities were parlor tricks in comparison.

"Kellen. Kitten. What's wrong?"

"I'm afraid," I said.

"You're not alone. We're here," he said.

His fierce embrace didn't make me feel safer, only more desperate. I couldn't let them face Maeve. Not yet. I could protect them against the trackers, but in my heart, I knew they would not be safe from her when she arrived.

I wrapped my arms around Brandle in return and held him for several long minutes. When I pulled back, I smiled reassuringly enough that he released me.

"The remaining tracker won't last much longer, and with each passing day, I fear more for my sister. Can we begin to prepare to travel to Turre while I work to break your curse?"

Brandle's gaze shifted from me to his brothers.

"Waiting may be the problem," Daemon said. "Worry is a distraction."

I frowned, uncertain of what he meant, even as Darian and Liam nodded their agreement. Did they believe my worry for Eloise was distracting me from breaking their curse?

"I believe it would benefit us all to start making arrangements," Brandle said.

"Agreed," Eadric said. "We should attend to the mines first since it will take several days."

The rest echoed their agreement.

"All right," Brandle said. "With one tracker remaining, four can go to the mines, and three shall stay. Kellen isn't left alone for any reason."

They decided amongst themselves that Edmund, Liam, and Daemon would stay with me while the others went to the mines.

I kissed them farewell and did my best to hide my fears as that tingle of warning continued to grow. Brandle saw through me, though. He kissed my forehead and promised they would work hard to do what was needed quickly.

"We will return at dusk."

WHAT HAD BEGUN as a whisper grew to a roar. The warning refused to be ignored.

Maeve was coming.

Fighting the urge to stretch my senses toward Drisdall, I focused on preparing a stew for the evening meal and checked on the tracker. He was surrounded by beasts and wouldn't likely live to see the light of a new day.

Daemon stayed beside me, helping with whatever I needed while Edmund sparred with Liam.

"You seem distracted, Lamb," Daemon said, watching me.

"I am. I'm wondering what's happening back home. Something feels wrong, and it has me on edge."

He caught my skirt and drew me back to his lap to comfort me with some cuddles.

"Will you tell me more about your sister?" he asked.

"Eloise is the sun to my moon," I said. "Golden hair and golden skin with a welcoming personality. On the surface. Cross her and she will lob a rock at your head with practiced accuracy. Yet, for all her fierceness, she is like me. A defenseless young woman."

Daemon snorted. "It would be amiss to consider you defenseless, Lamb. Do you not see the barrier surrounding this glade?"

I twisted to scowl at him. "The tracker from a kingdom without magic called what I can do a parlor trick, Daemon. What do you think that means? He knows there are far more powerful casters than me out there. So, yes, against those who seek to harm me, I remain a defenseless young woman."

Enlightenment glinted in his gaze.

"The mother who is not a mother is a strong caster," he said.

I said nothing as my heart thundered in my tight chest.

"Breathe, Lamb. Our vow to protect you remains unchanged."

His words affirmed my worst fear—they would stand with me, even if it meant their quick deaths.

Near dusk, the forest shivered. I had no explanation for the feeling other than it knew something dangerous had entered its expanse.

I checked the lid on my well, willing it to remain sealed at all costs.

Perhaps, if I remained hidden, she wouldn't find us.

The others returned, laughing and animated by their achievements. While they washed, I served the stew and gently expanded my senses. The weather would hold and continue to warm—a cloak wouldn't be needed during the day any longer unless it rained. The beasts were restless and had surrounded the tracker, waiting for his meager fire to give out. However, the tracker didn't fear them. His calm had grown with each passing hour, which didn't bode well for us.

I considered leaving the bramble barrier around the glade but worried she would sense my touch in the obstruction, so I withdrew my intent and watched it wither. No one commented on its absence as we retired for the evening.

As I lay between Brandle and Garron, I silently begged my mother to stay Maeve's hand until after they left the next day.

Restless, I slept little and checked the tracker often.

Before dawn, I felt his change: excitement, adoration, and lust, which grew even as his life's energy faded to nothing.

"Are you cold?" Brandle asked, feeling my tremble.

"Afraid," I said truthfully. He would know it regardless. "I know you worked hard yesterday. Can you leave at first light today? I made biscuits you can take with you."

He petted my hair and agreed. "Wake the others."

I watched him stand and pull his shirt on then I turned to kiss Garron's chest. His hand moved on my hip as he woke with a soft grunt.

"Good morning, Snow," he said softly.

"Good morning. Brandle agreed to leave for the mines at first light. He told me to wake everyone."

A sleepy smile tugged at Garron's lips. "Wise of him."

He kissed my forehead then slipped from bed to allow me to wake Eadric next. I could feel he was pretending and knew he likely planned something indecent. Impatience tugged at me, but I pushed it back. Worried or not, if I acted too out of character, they would not leave quickly.

So I woke him with a light kiss on his cheek and found myself pinned underneath him, my legs wrapped around his waist and held in place.

"I have a better idea to wake the rest."

He arched into me, sending a spark of unneeded pleasure through me.

"Eadric, Brandle is—"

Eadric sat up suddenly, keeping my legs around his waist as he lifted me. Then he dipped his head and sucked my nipple into his mouth through the thin material of my shift. A small sound escaped me at the feeling, and I threaded my fingers through his hair to keep him there. His hands encouraged me to move my hips, grinding me against his hard length and feeding the growing pleasure.

Lips brushed the side of my neck as Edmund's hands stroked my sides. They caught on my hem and slowly drew my shift up. Eadric broke away briefly, allowing his twin to remove what kept him from directly kissing my skin. I shivered when he shifted his attention to the other breast and kneaded my bare backside.

Tipping my head back, I allowed Eadric more access and sighed in pleasure. Eadric lifted my hips off his hard length, and a second later, I felt Edmund's fingers brushing through my folds from behind. They worked together to shatter my composure quickly.

Panting and relaxed, I dropped my head to Eadric's shoulder

and shivered as Edmund slowly inserted a finger into my spasming opening.

"Have we appropriately repaid you for waking us so prettily?" Edmund asked, dropping a kiss on my shoulder.

I nodded as he carefully stroked his finger in and out of me.

Eadric's hand left my hip to explore my folds with his brother.

"You're taking his finger so much better, Sparrow," Eadric said, kissing my temple. His finger joined his brother's slowly pushing into me. I tensed. Edmund bit my shoulder lightly, and I spasmed around his finger as he withdrew. When he inserted it again, it was with Eadric's. The burn, as I struggled to accommodate the intrusion, drew a whimper from me.

Eadric's thumb circled my nub. "Better?" he asked.

"I would feel better with no fingers," I said.

Eadric chuckled. "Perhaps, but then our cocks would likely hurt when you're finally ready for more."

"Language," Garron said weakly. I lifted my head and saw he stood in the doorway with his back to us. Only Eadric and Edmund remained in the cottage. I kissed Eadric's neck in gratitude for their thoughtfulness then carefully moved against their fingers.

"Good," Eadric crooned. "Just like that. Accept as much as you can. Relax, and it will be easier."

As my heartbeat slowly settled, they worked their fingers in and out of me until they moved without any resistance. Wet squelches sounded in the cottage as they stopped working together and moved in opposite directions.

"It's time," Brandle called.

"Edmund looks like he would rather cut off his own—"

"Shut up, Eadric," Edmund snapped, withdrawing his finger.

Eadric gave me a playful kiss and stood, carefully setting me on my feet.

"I'll stay with you today. Let's dress you."

Dressing me involved kissing as much of me as possible and

more fondling until I batted his hand away. When he walked me to the privy, the others were waiting by the garden. I kissed Edmund, Garron, Liam, and Daemon goodbye and went to the table to join Brandle and Darian.

Darian pulled me into his lap and nuzzled my neck as Eadric offered me a bite of biscuit.

"The sounds you make when you find your release will be the death of me," Darian said.

"She took two fingers today," Eadric said proudly as I flushed scarlet.

"Please refrain from sharing the details of our time together in front of me," I said.

Eadric nodded and fed me another bite. "I apologize, Sparrow. I forgot myself in my excitement. You did so well."

I closed my eyes as I chewed and felt something to the south. Barely a caress on my consciousness, the small space of nothingness would have been easy to overlook. Yet, once I perceived it, I couldn't pretend it didn't exist.

We were being watched.

Maeve had found us.

Panic bubbled in the well, but I gave it no chance to escape. I needed to find a means to send them away. Brandle wouldn't agree to leaving me alone, though. Perhaps, if I—

A rumble vibrated under our feet. Rock grated and groaned behind the cottage.

"No," Brandle yelled.

Dropping his bowl, he went running toward the sound. Eadric's eyes went wide, and he raced after his brother.

Without willing it to happen, I sensed Daemon, Edmund, Liam, and Garron. Unhurt but aware of the danger they faced, they hurried to the nearest supports in the mine. They knew their brothers would come for them.

I stood so Darian could follow. But he didn't. He grabbed my arm and started pulling me with him.

Knowing I needed to stay, I balked.

"Wait, Darian. They'll be injured. Let me go to the cottage to gather supplies.

He looked at me, his eyes wild, and I caught his face between my palms.

"Breathe. Focus. Save your brothers, and don't forget my sister needs you."

"We won't, Princess. Thank you."

He kissed me quickly, and I released him.

After he disappeared around the side of the cottage, I turned and found Maeve standing behind me. Although only a little over a month had passed, she looked nothing like the vibrant woman I'd known. Barefoot, hem covered in dirt, and twigs stuck in her long grey hair, she'd aged several decades.

"'Ello, dearie," she crooned with a kind smile that showed missing teeth. "If not for the noise, I would have missed this haven."

"I doubt that, Maeve," I said.

Slowly, she straightened from her stooped stance.

"Your eyes gave you away," I said. "While the rest of you has changed, those have not. Have you come to take me home since the men you sent failed so abysmally?"

Through Eloise, I'd learned the danger of provoking Maeve. Yet, I dared not pass idle time with false pleasantries when any of the brothers could return abruptly.

She considered me for a long moment.

"No, I don't believe it wise to return you to your sister. It is best to keep you here. You have much to learn."

"Oh?"

"Your cool regard spared you in the past. We will see if it continues to serve you well in the future." She plucked the best apple from the basket she held and offered it to me. "Eat the apple and spare your sister. Refuse it and I will unleash such horror onto Eloise that she will forget her own name. The choice is yours."

Without hesitation, I took the apple and bit into it.

Maeve's wicked grin grew as I swallowed the bite.

"Sleep well, Kellen," she said.

The spell coursed through me, settling into my bones. Everything went dark, and I collapsed to the ground, still very aware.

Fingers brushed the hair back from my face.

"You are truly a beauty. If you ever wake, no man of worth will ever want you. This, my sweet daughter, will be your greatest fall."

CHAPTER 15

I LISTENED TO THE SWISH OF MAEVE'S SKIRTS FADE AS SHE retreated. After several moments, I cautiously opened my senses. Her energy entered the forest and continued to move away from the glade. I wanted to weep with relief that she'd left before anyone else returned...until I remembered how she'd distracted my protectors.

An ache filled my chest as I focused on the cave where Darian, Brandle, and Eadric worked to remove the rocks that blocked the opening. Inside, Daemon, Edmund, Liam, and Garron struggled to do the same. I felt their fear, and it fed my own.

It would take little effort for me to move the rocks, but would Maeve sense if I cast now? She was still so close, and I couldn't risk her returning.

With little else to do, I focused on the spell she'd cast on me. I felt where it had settled. Sticky like sap, it coated me from the inside and made it impossible to move. The paralysis felt familiar. Had the previous times also been due to Maeve?

A span of time later, a shock of rage, not my own, screamed through me. It came from the spell. I checked Maeve's progress and saw beasts running in her direction. Not Father, though. He was close to the clearing, watching me from the shadows. Had he seen Maeve?

Once the nearby beasts had fled, he howled long and low.

Father, quiet! I thought frantically. *If she returns, we could all die.*

The howl continued, and I felt Darian's attention shift away from the rocks.

"Kellen?" he called.

His concern grew and became my own as he rounded the corner of the cottage.

"Princess?" He knelt beside me and carefully lifted me into his arms.

Father stopped howling, and I felt hope in knowing that he had purposely called their attention to help me.

Don't give up, Father, I thought, even as I struggled to respond to Darian's gentle touch in some way.

"Come now, Princess. Now is not the time to fall into a faint. Open your eyes for me."

Every attempt to do so failed.

He set me on the table, and his fingers stroked over my face, coaxing me to respond. I could feel his worry growing.

"It's never lasted this long before," he said softly.

His need to call out for Brandle and Eadric warred with his need for them to free Edmund, Daemon, Garron, and Liam. The six of them strained against the larger boulders, working together to move rocks as Darian stayed with me. I checked Maeve's progress continually, but she didn't move far, surrounded as she was.

Eventually, they cleared a small opening at the top of the entrance. Their relief echoed my own.

"Please wake up, Princess," he said, unaware of his brothers as they climbed out of the cave.

I knew the moment they saw me on the table. Their low murmur of conversation ceased. The worry that had just left them came rushing back.

"What happened?" Brandle asked.

"I found her lying on the ground by the apple," he said.

The apple. I'd forgotten about it.

I fought against the spell, desperate to warn them not to touch the apple, but my body wasn't my own. It refused to respond to my will.

"It isn't an apple from the cellar," Garron said. "It's fresh and…" I heard the apple hit the ground. "It's been touched by magic. Where did it come from?"

"It was here when I found her. I think the howl was her father. Try talking to him."

Daemon's energy moved off toward the tree line and returned moments later.

"His exact words before leaving were: woman and dangerous."

Their fear grew until it squeezed in on me, creating a panic that made my heart race. I tried to close myself off from what they felt, but it didn't work. Everything they felt became my own. Their fear, anger, hopelessness, and desperate need to protect.

"What did the Foul Queen do to her?" Edmund asked, his voice shaking with rage.

"Kellen's breathing," Darian said. "Maybe she's just resting."

"And you call me simple?" Eadric said with a snort. "The spelled apple has a bite out of it, and our little sparrow isn't waking. She's been cursed."

"In order to create a curse, it must have an end," Garron said. "We'll find the end to this one."

"How? The Foul Queen *knew* we were close. The cost of breaking this spell will be high," Brandle said.

"For us or for our lamb?" Daemon asked.

Liam reached under my skirt to touch my ankle.

"She's chilled. We should move her inside."

Darian lifted me again, and from the safety of his embrace, I listened to them speak as they made a bed for me in the cottage and started the fire.

"The spell is obviously meant to stop us," Brandle said. "That means we were close."

"But why not kill her if we were close?" Edmund asked.

No one answered. Even I could not understand why Maeve chose to cast another spell when I already couldn't speak of her ill deeds. Edmund was right. If I had been close to gaining the help I needed, why spare me? Not that I felt spared.

Darian carefully set me on the mattress and kissed my forehead.

A tingle of energy swept through me, and for a moment, I felt my eyelids move. But the sensation disappeared when he retreated.

"If we were close, we should continue as we were," Liam said.

The heat from the fire warmed me as they took turns washing and discussing what to do about the mine. Garron was certain it was safe to return to it and didn't understand how the collapse happened in the first place.

"We have enough from yesterday for another delivery," Liam said. "It's not safe to leave Kellen, though. Look what happened when our backs were turned."

"They were more than turned," Brandle said, frustration lacing his words.

Their emotions fed the storm growing inside my well.

"It's no longer safe to remain here if she knows where we are," Edmund said.

I could feel the edge of his temper bubbling beneath the surface. His fingers traced over my face, and his lips brushed my brow. A tingle of energy washed through me. I grabbed onto it, but too late. It disappeared with his retreat.

Frustration—my own—surged, demanding to be answered.

I opened my senses, checking for Maeve again. Hundreds of beasts continued to hamper her progress. I felt no remorse for my fervent hope that they'd kill her before she reached the edge of the forest. Yet, I couldn't risk attempting to free myself while she remained close.

"Lamb," Daemon said. "Please open those beautiful eyes of yours."

This time, when his hand slipped under my skirt to stroke my leg, I was ready for the tingle of energy. Seizing it, I tried to open my eyes.

"Did you see that?" Daemon said. "Her lashes moved."

"Kitten?" Brandle called. His hand cupped my face.

I latched onto his energy and added it to the rest. My eyelids weakly obeyed my will; however, rather than opening, they fluttered twice before stilling.

"They moved," Eadric said. "I think she's awake. Remember? She said she could hear us the last time this happened."

"The last time, our amulets glowed when we touched her. This is a different spell," Garron said.

"Can you hear us, Kitten?" Brandle asked. His fingers trailed over my brow as Daemon massaged my foot.

I fought to open my eyes again, but the energy wasn't enough. I needed more and sought to pull a small amount from the area around me. Certainly, Maeve wouldn't sense something so minute. Yet, when I tried to draw from the floor, the earth, or even the air around us, I couldn't touch it.

Trapped inside myself, I screamed my anger.

The plates on the shelves rattled.

"She *is* awake," Eadric said.

Brandle's lips brushed my cheek. "We won't leave you, Kitten. Not this time." His mouth settled on mine, and I felt his need to protect me...to avenge me...to never let me go. I wished more than anything I could do the same for him.

The need to lift my hands, run my fingers through his hair, and kiss him in return consumed me.

"Her fingers moved," Garron said.

I could feel him kneel beside me as Brandle lifted his head.

Garron held my hand. "You're stronger than you know, Snow. Fight the spell she cast on you. You can break it and free yourself. I know you can."

"Break it, then break the one holding us," Darian said.

"Together, we'll free your sister," Eadric added.

Focusing inward on the sticky layer of the spell she'd cast, I tried to imagine myself physically lifting it. However, my arms slid through it, finding no purchase regardless of how I tried. The shelves rattled more earnestly as I fought against the spell.

Daemon took my other hand. His love and desire sparked more energy, which crawled beneath my skin. The four points of contact forced a response from me, but not one I intended.

Instead of my eyes obeying my will, a small pained sound escaped me.

"Kitten?" Brandle said. "Are you hurt?"

I tried to answer as their hands ran over my limbs, but nothing worked as the energy they fed me continued to build just beneath the surface of my skin.

"Help me," Brandle said. His fingers plucked at my lacings.

Garron gently lifted me, leaning me against his chest as they freed my arms then slowly worked the dress down my hips. Their handling of me felt so right—a comforting reminder that I wasn't alone and that they cared.

"No cuts or marks," Brandle said, running his hands over my arms.

Daemon's hands smoothed up one leg while Darian checked the other.

Another involuntary moan escaped me.

"No cuts or marks here, either," Daemon said.

"Get some water," Brandle said.

A cup pressed to my lips a second later, but the water only dribbled down the front of my shift.

Their frustration grew. Edmund, Eadric, and Liam left. The low murmur of their conversation was marked with the sounds of their scuffles. Did they not know they would break my heart if they hurt each other because I wasn't there to stop them?

A chair clattered to the floor.

"She's upset," Garron said.

"She's been twice cursed, Garron," Darian said. "I believe she's more than upset."

"My poor Lamb," Daemon said. His hand traced up my leg, hooking around my knee to play with the sensitive skin behind it.

A spark ignited in the spell. Heat burned through me. My eyes snapped open, and I met Brandle's shocked gaze.

"Kitten, are you all right?"

Daemon removed his hand, withdrawing the energy that had animated me. My eyes closed.

Unable to clench my hands in frustration, the emotion set the objects in the cottage rattling.

"Shh, my little Lamb. We're here," Daemon said, his hand returning to my leg. The spark the contact ignited wasn't as strong as before, and my eyelids only fluttered.

"We're here. We're not going anywhere," Brandle said. He kissed my brow.

I could feel the surge of energy. Four points of contact: one kissing, three simply touching. Yet, previously, it had been Daemon's touch that had enabled me to open my eyes. What did it mean that I could feel their energy when they were protected from me by their amulets?

Worried, I tried to close myself off from it. I didn't know how, though. The lid on my well was still firmly in place.

Rather than panic, I focused on my breathing until everything in the cottage stopped moving. Through it all, they continued to touch me in small, comforting ways.

"Dinner is almost done," Liam said. "Any change?"

Dinner? Had so much time passed already?

"Nothing yet," Brandle said. His hand left my hair as he stood.

"Edmund's right. Whether Kellen wakes or not, it won't be safe to remain here for long. I'll help the others clear the opening so we can leave as soon as possible."

I listened to his retreating footfalls and wondered what they planned to do next. Even if I could speak, though, I wouldn't ask, fearing that any answer they might provide would risk my ability to break their spell. Yet, I couldn't close my ears as Garron held me and I listened to his conversation with Darian and Daemon.

"How did the Foul Queen find her?" Daemon asked. "Was it the casting?"

"I don't know," Garron said. "It seems most likely, though I find it hard to believe. We tested Kellen's range. The queen shouldn't have been able to sense her. But what other reason could there be other than she's known where we were all along?"

"Which is unlikely," Darian said. "If she knew where we were, the glade would have been empty when Kellen arrived."

"I agree," Garron said. He kissed my brow and rose. "I'll check the barrier and attempt to speak with Kellen's father again."

"We'll stay with her," Darian said. "Our eyes won't stray for a moment."

Garron's steps retreated. Darian's hand smoothed over my leg.

"I know you can hear us, Princess," he said. "Can you make the dishes rattle when you will it?"

I thought about it for a moment and freed some of my frustration. The dishes rattled. I immediately calmed my mind, which quieted the dishes, and felt Darian and Daemon's pride.

"Well done, Lamb," Daemon said.

"We have questions. Rattle the dishes if the answer is yes," Darian said. "Are you hurt?"

He waited a few moments then let out a relieved sigh. "Good. Very good. Do you know how to break this spell?"

I couldn't say for certain that I did, so I kept the dishes silent as I checked on Maeve's progress once more. She remained too close yet. Until she was a safe distance away, I couldn't attempt to break the spell.

Darian patted my thigh over my shift.

"It's all right. We'll figure it out together," he said.

Daemon reclined beside me and pulled me into his arms.

"We should sleep while we can," he said. "Brandle will want us to keep watch tonight."

I lay there and listened to his breathing slow as I monitored the others. They milled around the yard, and I could feel what they were doing. Cooking. Washing the dishes. Garron was even checking the barrier.

I could feel the sun's energy fading. Edmund, Eadric, and Liam drifted in a short time later.

"Brandle and Garron will take the first watch," Edmund said.

They settled in. The temperature dropped. Darian sighed and rolled toward me. His fingers brushed over my face.

"She feels cold," he said softly.

"I'll get a blanket," Eadric said.

Once I was covered and warm, I felt the tug of sleep. After checking Maeve one last time, I gave in to it.

"EDMUND, WAKE UP."

DARIAN'S WHISPERED words penetrated my sleep.

"Is it my turn?" Edmund asked groggily.

"Yes. Keep her warm for me."

"I'll keep her warm for me," he said, sounding more awake.

Darian moved away, and Edmund took his spot, sliding an arm under me so he could steal me from Daemon's loose embrace. Daemon grumbled and burrowed closer, not waking.

"You smell so good, Trouble," Edmund said in my ear. "If you're awake, can you make the dishes rattle for me?"

I rattled the cup on the table and checked Maeve's progress. She was outside of the forest now, and the sun was close to rising.

Edmund's lips caressed the back of my neck, snapping my focus back to him as my eyes opened. A breathy moan escaped me. He withdrew, and my eyes closed. Yet I could feel him shifting his weight to look at me. After several beats of silence, he dipped his head and captured the shell of my ear gently between his teeth.

The energy didn't simply tingle under my skin this time. It heated my skin, pebbling my nipples and creating an ache between my legs as my eyes opened and another sound escaped me. I recalled the previous times Edmund had touched me in the bath and the pleasure he'd shown me. Though I'd liked it, I hadn't responded like this.

Need churned beneath the surface.

The contact ended too quickly, though, as he lifted his head again.

"I saw that, Trouble. Shake the house if I go too far, okay?"

He reached over me and nudged Daemon awake as he kissed my neck again. The fire spread under my skin, heating me. My exhale was filled with longing I truly felt this time. Edmund's desire echoed my own.

"Lamb, finally," Daemon said softly.

"She's still cursed," Edmund said against my skin. "Kiss her."

My heart stuttered in my chest, and the tingle of need spread, but my eyes remained shut.

"Are we trying to make her mad enough to throw us like she did with Garron?" Daemon asked.

"No. She opened her eyes when I kissed her ear."

"They're not open now."

M . J .   H A A G

"I know. That's why I'm asking for your help. Kiss her and watch her eyes."

A moment later, I felt Daemon's mouth close over my nipple. A sound escaped me, and my eyes opened. Edmund met my gaze.

"Don't stop, Daemon," Edmund said, his hand gliding down my leg to the edge of my shift.

I could move my eyes, but nothing else.

His fingers glided up my thigh, teasing the sensitive flesh and quickening my breath. Daemon's hand closed over my other breast, adding to my building need.

"Can you speak, Trouble?" Edmund asked.

My tongue wet my lips. His gaze dipped to my mouth.

"Rattle the cup if you want me to continue," he said softly.

The cup fell off the shelf, and he chuckled.

"Focus on the spell. Find a way to break it. We'll help keep you here," he said.

His hand tugged my shift up over my hips, baring me to his touch beneath the blanket. Daemon caught the hem and tugged it up further so his tongue moved over my bare nipple. I arched into his mouth.

Daemon groaned and caught my tender peak between his teeth.

A moan escaped me, and I felt the desire of the others increase, proving they were awake and listening.

Edmund's fingers found my folds, and I gripped his forearm.

"Can you speak yet?" he asked.

"Edmund," I managed on an exhale.

"Lamb," Daemon whispered, replacing his mouth with his hand. "We need you. Please."

I understood what he wanted. He wasn't asking for my body but completely committing myself to doing whatever was necessary to free myself, them, and my sister.

"Yes," I breathed.

He groaned again and tugged me from Edmund's hold so I lay

on my back. My eyes closed at the loss of contact, but I knew they wouldn't stop what they'd begun when the blanket covering me vanished.

"Not everything, Edmund," Brandle said softly. "Not when she's unable to tell you to stop."

"Not everything," Edmund agreed.

"Just a taste," Daemon said before suckling my other breast.

Edmund groaned this time, and I felt him move beside me. His hands caressed down my legs.

"Throw the cup at me if you want me to stop," he said before hooking his hands behind my knees and lifting them. I didn't know what he intended until he spread them wide to the sides. I could feel my folds part for his view and struggled with shame and embarrassment for only a moment until I felt his fingers gently caressing my opening.

"So wet already."

He circled the center of my pleasure with a fingertip, and my eyes opened.

"Brace yourself, Trouble."

I watched him lean down and kiss me right on that sensitive bundle of nerves. My hips jerked.

"Edmund," I rasped.

"Break the spell," he said as he opened his mouth and began kissing that nub the same way that Daemon did my nipple.

The intensity of the pleasure was too much.

Planting my foot on his shoulder, I pushed him away and instantly returned to the spell's cocoon. Edmund tumbled to his side and grunted while Daemon laughed around my breast. Had I had use of my hands, I would have cuffed him.

"You're lucky she used her foot and not magic," Brandle said softly. "Do better or move aside."

Edmund mumbled something under his breath and settled between my legs again. I paid him little mind, though. Brandle's words had struck a chord.

Why hadn't I reacted with magic?

I focused on my well as Edmund kissed my inner thigh and Daemon kissed my neck. Energy tingled through me, and I could feel it gathering within my well, but I couldn't move the lid to connect with it. The lid was firmly closed, weighted down by the spell that bound me in place.

Fear built behind that barrier, screaming for release. I was so lost in it that I wouldn't have noticed when Edmund's attention shifted from my thighs to my folds if not for the influx of energy.

My eyes snapped open. Instead of focusing on the stimulation, I turned my attention to Maeve's binding spell. It had lifted so minutely that it hardly rose at all, but that tiny space was why I could open my eyes. I attempted to nudge the lid from my well, but it didn't move. The spell weighed too much. It needed to be higher in order to reach my well. How?

Understanding filled me. The spell lifted with their touch... their sensual touch. And the more they touched me, the more the spell reacted.

I recalled Maeve's words.

"If you ever wake, no man of worth will ever want you. This, my sweet daughter, will be your greatest fall."

In the darkness of my mind, I understood what Maeve had done and what her words had meant. I alone could not break the curse. Only the seven men with me could.

Edmund's tongue swept along my seam, and the spell lightened a bit more. Enough that my fingers twitched.

Maeve thought these men would be my ruin? If I could have laughed, I would have.

They would be my salvation. One I was ready to fully embrace.

CHAPTER 16

"HER FINGERS JUST MOVED," DAEMON MURMURED AGAINST MY skin.

A log in the fire fell, illuminating the thatching above as Edmund's fingers threaded through mine. I welcomed his touch and silently demanded more as his exhale teased my exposed center.

"If I make a mistake again, kick me...send me flying...do whatever you wish," he said. "When you need me to stop, make the cup rattle again. Now, let us see if we can help you do more than moan and open your eyes."

I wanted to hug Edmund for realizing what I had—that their touch was the key to lifting the spell. Instead, I focused on the feel of his fingers gripping my thighs and Daemon's mouth on my breast.

The discipline I'd gained through the endless hours of casting under Garron's guidance vanished the moment Edmund's tongue slicked through my folds. Pleasure coursed through me more intensely than ever before, and with it, that tingle of energy under my skin grew. That same energy made it easier for me to feel his desire, which fed my own.

I moaned. Edmund chuckled. The vibrations unmade me. Had my hands been free to move, I would have tangled them in his short hair and demanded more. More licking. More vibrations. More touching.

Daemon's desire grew as he released my breast and leaned over to meet my gaze as his brother lapped at me.

"I missed the sight of your beautiful blue eyes, Lamb. Keep them open for me, all right?" He tenderly kissed my lips as his fingers trailed over my breasts.

The energy from their combined attention sizzled through me, but it wasn't enough. Thankfully, Edmund had more to give. His hunger increased as his tongue swirled around the source of my pleasure.

His fingers trailed up my thigh toward where he kissed me. A fingertip breached my opening. Teasing. Testing. He groaned and pressed deeper in one long slide.

The slow penetration pulled another moan from me and the weight of the spell lifted fractionally. Yet the lid covering my well remained firmly in place.

Although Maeve's spell had layered over the source of my energy, it hadn't blocked my ability to sense energy. I could still feel it around me; I simply couldn't directly use it. How, then, could I break this spell?

Edmund distracted me from my thoughts by turning his finger and touching a place inside of me that intensified my growing pleasure. His strokes grew more demanding as his tongue swirled in an increasingly tighter circle around my nub.

The spell rippled inside of me. Small sounds not of my own making emitted from my lips.

Daemon groaned, switching his mouth and hands between my breasts and my neck. Edmund shifted slightly between my legs and withdrew his finger to add a second. The stretch and his hunger fed my desire.

Breath by breath, I climbed higher until I tumbled over the edge with a low moan.

I felt something shift inside of me.

The spell.

I'd forgotten.

Panting, I focused on it instead of the way Edmund kissed my inner thigh as he continued to stroke my insides with two fingers.

The spell was lighter. Much lighter.

"Don't stop," I rasped.

Daemon lifted his head to look at me.

"Are you back, Lamb?"

I wasn't. With the loss of contact, the little energy I'd gained dissipated quickly, and my eyes closed of their own accord.

"She said not to stop, you idiot," Liam said.

Daemon returned his mouth to my chest. Though it still felt nice, it didn't evoke the same tingle of energy as before. Neither did Edmund's touch. They tried to coax a response from me for several more minutes to no avail.

"Perhaps she needs rest," Daemon said. "And a wash."

Edmund gently cleaned me then held me in his arms. My frustration grew with theirs.

"Let us try," Liam said.

Liam and Garron switched places with Edmund and Daemon.

At Liam's first kiss to the top of my breast, energy sizzled through me, and my eyes opened.

He saw but didn't stop, the smart man. As he kissed his way across my chest, Garron kissed the sole of my foot.

A giggle escaped me, and I felt Garron smile against my skin.

"Looks like switching was the right thing to do," Daemon said softly.

His longing caressed me, feeding the energy Liam and Garron were creating.

"She'll be more sensitive now," Edmund said. His hunger for me rose.

My breathing hitched, and my need climbed.

Liam kissed his way to my lips, and by the time he reached them, I returned his kiss without restriction. He moaned into my mouth just as Garron's mouth found the sensitive skin behind my knee. The dual sensations pulled me into the web of desire woven in the air around me.

I welcomed it all and gathered it inside of me as Garron stroked my other leg. Kiss by kiss, they renewed my need for them. Edmund was right, though. Everything was sensitive, so the pair wisely moved with more care. Rather than play with my breasts, Liam focused on my face, neck, and ears. And rather than torment that swollen bump between my legs with his tongue, Garron dipped that hot, wet appendage into my opening.

A raspy moan escaped me. The men continued their efforts until they brought me the same pleasure as Edmund and Daemon had.

During the peak of my release, I managed to speak the truth.

"Pleasure weakens the spell."

As my release ebbed, so did my ability to move and speak. But it didn't matter. They'd heard and understood.

"Rest, Love," Liam said as Garron washed me. "You've done so well."

Partially draped over Liam's bare chest, I slept until dawn when they changed positions again.

Brandle's chest pressed against my back as he held me in his arms while Eadric lightly kissed my face to wake me. I could feel their love and yearning for me. Their worry too. Especially Brandle's. It called to me too. I wanted to soothe him and tell him that I was well and knew they weren't using me.

That I trusted them completely.

"Are you ready to break the spell, Sparrow?" Eadric asked.

Trapped in my own body, I had no way to respond. That didn't stop Eadric from kissing his way down my neck.

"Your skin is so soft, Sparrow. I could kiss it all day," he said between teasing pecks. "Garron and Edmund said you taste even better between your thighs. Should I have a taste before Brandle takes over?"

My center clenched around nothing at his suggestion. Their desire fed mine, and I felt the now familiar tingle under my skin.

"I'll take the silent tableware as your agreement," Eadric said.

Brandle's hands stroked down my arms, and he shifted back a bit so I lay angled against him. Eadric lifted my top leg and hooked it back over Brandle's legs. Then his fingers brushed over what the position had revealed to his hungry gaze.

"You are so pretty here." Eadric placed a gentle kiss on my folds, which ignited the tingle of energy crackling through me. "You smell nice too. Should I taste you?"

Brandle's fingers came around to toy with my breasts. He kept his touch light as Eadric's tongue darted out to tease me. Bit by bit, I forgot about the spell that held me and only thought of the pleasure Eadric could give me. When his tongue delved into my core repeatedly, I moaned.

"My sweet Sparrow," Eadric murmured between lapping. "Are you ready for more?"

Brandle moved out from behind me. His touch never left me; only the heat of his chest did. A moment later, his mouth closed over my right breast.

With my eyes now open, I watched him reach down and tug at his pants.

Understanding coursed through me.

Brandle meant to bed me. Here. Now. With Eadric present. My pulse thundered. Fear mixed with desire. And when two of Eadric's fingers replaced his tongue, I moaned at the slow, deep intrusion.

"She's wet. Would it be better to let her find her release first?" Eadric asked.

As he spoke, he curled his fingers upward within me, touching the same place his twin had the day before, building my need for what would come next.

"No," Brandle said around my flesh.

I scowled. If I would have had use of my hands, I would have tugged his hair.

Eadric didn't give me time to dwell, though, as his fingers unerringly stroked over that place again and again.

As Brandle kicked away his pants, his teeth lightly scraped my breast. I shivered in response and clenched around Eadric's fingers. Their desire for me climbed.

Eadric kissed his way up my torso to claim my other breast as Brandle's hand replaced his mouth so he could adjust his position. I felt him kneeling between my legs. Eadric's fingers were still buried deep inside of me. Moving. Coaxing.

"Kitten, you know what will happen next, don't you?" Brandle asked, meeting my gaze over his brother's head.

I managed a faint nod.

"Edmund did his best to prepare you for this when he first started touching you here." Brandle's fingers trailed over my hip and traced over my folds as Eadric's continued to stroke that magical place. "We've discussed the spell. You said pleasure lifts it, but you stop responding once you find your release on our mouths or fingers. I think more is needed to break the spell."

Brandle's fingers circled my sensitive bud; then one slid in with his brother's in a single slow thrust that would have curled my toes if I'd been able to do so.

"Once we do this, Kellen, we won't let you go. You'll be ours, do you understand? All of us. Together. Always. Once we remove this spell, we will go to Turre to rally the help we need to free your sister. After she is freed, you will not return to her. You will return to us. If you do not agree to this, stop me now by any means necessary."

Eadric removed his fingers on the next withdrawal so only Brandle stroked me from the inside. The way they were working together to touch me was making it more difficult to focus on his words, but it mattered little. I already belonged to them, and they belonged to me. I had no intention of letting them go either.

After several moments passed without the dishes rattling, Brandle nodded before briefly leaning in to kiss me. His lips touched mine lightly.

"Are you ready to distract her?" Brandle asked.

Eadric's teeth briefly closed on my nipple.

I groaned loudly.

"Good. Like that then," Brandle said, withdrawing his touch and replacing it with something much broader that he moved through my slick folds.

The wet head nestled into the dip of my entrance. His need to feel me accept his hard length as I had his fingers consumed him. His desire became my desire.

A wanton sound escaped my lips. Brandle cursed under his breath and slowly pressed forward, trying to force my small opening to accept his girth. My tender flesh seemed to give very little, though, until Eadric bit my nipple lightly again.

I clenched around Brandle's head. He grunted and stilled. When my core relaxed once more, he eased in another inch.

"Kitten, this isn't the way I imagined my first time with you. Please. Please give me something. Show me I'm not hurting you or taking what you are unwilling to give. Show me that you like this."

His fear and hunger wrapped around me.

Eadric took my hand and pressed it against his cheek as he switched to my other breast.

I moaned, and my fingers twitched against Eadric's skin.

"It's working," he said around my breast before nipping my nipple.

I clenched down on Brandle again. He pressed forward another inch then stilled. Sweat dotted his brow as he searched my gaze.

"More," I whispered.

He swore under his breath and pushed forward again. The intrusion stretched and burned as I struggled to accommodate him. The pleasure started to fade, but the energy buzzing under my skin didn't, proving that this truly was the intent of the spell.

Maeve had thought to ruin me.

A smile curved my lips.

The energy pooling beneath my skin tripled.

"Kitten, you steal my breath and test my control." Brandle closed his eyes with a pained expression.

"Then lose it," I rasped.

Another curse slipped from his lips, and with a growl, he thrust home.

I gasped at the shock of the invasion...and at the movement of the spell. It rippled strongly within me as if, by burying himself to the hilt, he'd hit it. So I threw all my will at the lid, demanding it lift and free what was mine to control.

And it listened!

The lid lifted, and I connected with the energy within myself.

The moment I did, I also connected with energy in everything around me. The air. The earth. The fire and wood. It ignited what was inside of me as it flooded toward my well.

Above me, Brandle's amulet exploded with a blinding light.

"That's it, Kitten," he murmured as he closed his eyes. "Break free. Come back to us."

He slowly withdrew and advanced.

The discomfort of his invasion remained as the spell tried to settle over my well again. However, with the lid nudged aside, it didn't have the power to do so. I held it where it was and used the energy to start peeling it back in time with Brandle's careful thrusts.

Within the depths of the spell, I felt its intent.

Seven layers. One for each of the men. The first one dissolved on its own as Brandle continued to move within me, and I knew the others would also disappear once each of the brothers bedded me.

But I refused to allow Maeve's spell to dictate the path our lives took.

Using my magic, I sent my intent into her spell. I would bed each brother–but in my own time and in my own way. The spell would not control me.

Never again would I allow another spell to control me.

The spell broke apart inside of me and flew outward in millions of glowing sparks that only I could see. In the absence of its weight, the light from Eadric and Brandle's amulets faded away.

Brandle paused and cautiously opened his eyes.

I smiled at him and tugged gently at Eadric's hair until he lifted his head too.

"Sparrow?" he asked, looking at me.

"Yes," I said, fighting not to flush. "I am very much myself again."

He gave me a resounding kiss on my mouth and grinned widely. All the while, I felt every inch of his brother buried deeply within me. I clenched around Brandle involuntarily and looked up at him.

"Did I hurt you?" he asked.

"Any discomfort I felt is not your fault but hers for casting such a spell." I lifted my hand and touched his cheek. "Did I hurt you? By asking this of you?"

He groaned and leaned in to kiss me. It was tender and

demanding at the same time. Filled with need, desire, and questions.

When he pulled away, I was breathless. Holding my gaze, he withdrew and reseated himself.

"You didn't hurt me, Kitten. I've been dreaming of this since the moment our glade echoed with your laughter. Tell me you want this too."

"I want this."

He braced himself on his arms again and began moving within me in a steady rhythm. The discomfort faded, and in its place, I felt a pleasant fullness.

"Help her, Eadric," he said, holding my gaze.

Eadric's mouth dipped to my chest, and he teased my nipple until it pebbled, then nipped it so I clenched around Brandle.

"Again," Brandle gritted.

Eadric reached between us, and his finger found my nub.

I groaned as he circled it, and my eyes started to close…of my own accord this time.

"I want to see you, Kitten. Keep those eyes open."

Brandle's thrusts increased as my pleasure climbed until I cried out with my release. His rhythm faltered soon after, and he groaned. I felt his hard length twitch within me and the hot wash of his seed. When it stopped, he nudged Eadric aside and gathered me into his arms.

"It's done," I said, breathing heavily. "I won't let you go now, Brandle."

He chuckled in my ear and kissed my temple.

"Can you hear thoughts now, too?" he asked.

"No." Yet, I could feel what he felt. Love. The need to protect me and hold me close. Forever.

And it was echoed six more times.

Turning my head, I looked at Eadric, who was kneeling beside us and grinning widely.

"I won't let you go either, Eadric. You'll need to share me with your brothers until the day I die."

"Gladly," he said.

"Um, is the sharing going to start soon?" Darian asked from the doorway.

I met his gaze and smiled at him and the others gathered behind him.

"Perhaps. We will decide how and when. Just the eight of us. No one else."

"Of course, just us," Daemon said with a snort. "Do you think we want to start a harem, Lamb?"

"We *are* the harem," Liam said, standing on his toes to grin at me over his brothers' shoulders.

"You are not a harem. You are simply mine, and I am yours." I looked up at Brandle. "I love my sister and will do anything to free you. Anything but give any of you up. You mean too much to me to leave."

Brandle and Eadric's amulets flickered oddly. When I glanced at the others to see if theirs had done the same, my mouth dropped open in surprise. They still stood outside of the cottage but were no longer their smaller versions.

Daemon shouted in elation and hugged Liam.

Edmund's expression reflected shock as he ducked to see inside. Our gazes met, and I felt his surge of desire.

Brandle kissed my temple, then my mouth, and fully reclaimed my attention when he stirred inside of me.

He broke off the kiss and looked down at me. Joy lit his gaze.

"We love you, too, Kellen. Without reservation or hesitation."

My heart stuttered with hope and fear.

Love? Love was dangerous. Love meant being hurt when you lost it.

Yet, I could no longer deny that was what I felt for each one of them. I loved them. Completely. Without hesitation.

And I feared what that would mean for my heart in the days to come.

I will not lose another person I hold dear.

THANK YOU FOR READING DESIRE, Book 2 of the Tales of Snow. The trilogy concludes in Degradation, Book 3. I hope you're ready for what comes next!

DEGRADATION

CHAPTER 1

ALONE, I LEANED BACK IN THE TUB AND WATCHED THE STEAM CURL up from the water. My limbs ached, but I knew the bath would help.

Outside, near the cooking fire, the others conversed quietly and prepared breakfast. Liam asked a question loud enough for me to hear.

"Do you think she's angry?"

He was sweet to feel concerned, but surely he didn't believe I would hold any of them to blame for what happened. If anything, they should be angry with me. Because of my presence, Maeve had appeared and had caused the cave-in that could have cost them their lives.

No, I found no fault in their actions to free me from the curse that Maeve had cast. And though I didn't regret how we'd broken the curse, I regretted that I hadn't been able to speak freely, which caused them all to doubt their contributions. Even now, I could feel Brandle's lingering guilt as he fetched another pail of water from the well.

"How long must we leave our Lamb alone?"

I opened my mouth to tell Daemon I didn't want to be left alone when Brandle entered with the rinse water.

Tipping my head back, I looked up at him.

"I'm not angry, and I don't want to be left alone."

He smiled, kissed my brow, and sat on the stool beside the tub.

"Then I won't leave you alone."

He unwound my braid and worked the tangles out of it in silence. His expression remained troubled, like his thoughts. I caught his chin with my wet fingers to draw his gaze.

"I don't want to be treated any differently than before, Brandle," I said softly. "I'm neither damaged nor fragile. So please release the guilt you feel, or I will be burdened to feel the same."

"How so?"

"Without me, Maeve would have had no reason to appear in your glade." I dropped my hand. "She caused the cave-in so she could speak with me alone. Will you choose to hold her to blame, or will you blame my presence here?"

"I hold her to blame. Never you."

"And I do the same. I don't regret what we shared, Brandle, only that she forced your hand."

He nodded, and I felt his guilt lift as he wet my hair and soaped it.

"Why do you call her Maeve?" he asked.

"It's the only name she gave us. Why did Edmund call her the Foul Queen?"

Brandle was quiet for a long moment. "I'm uncertain how to answer your question until you answer a few of mine. Has the spell binding you to silence broken? Are you able to speak of what happened to you? Is Maeve the caster who cursed you?"

I tilted my head to study him.

"She is. This time and before I ran from home."

"Will you tell me everything?" He nudged me to lean back so he could scrub my hair.

Closing my eyes as he worked, I thought back to how everything started.

"I already told you that my father was a merchant. He loved my mother dearly, and though he left us often to travel and trade, she was never far from his thoughts. He would often send trinkets home for her. Eloise and I, as well. Ribbons and such things.

"When a beautiful necklace arrived, we thought it was from Father and put it on Mother. We saw a flash of green in her eyes but didn't understand its significance until much later.

"Knowing what I do now, I believe the necklace was bespelled to consume the wearer's energy. It was likely meant to do so over time. However, Mother had so little that she died immediately.

"She had only been gone a few days when Father arrived. He didn't act like the loving man I knew. I thought it was due to grief, though, since he only stayed long enough to see Mother buried before saying he was off to trade. However, when Maeve appeared several days later, Eloise and I began to suspect something more.

"Maeve claimed to be a distant relative of our mother's and said that Father had arranged for her to care for us in his absence. My intuition had whispered something was wrong, but I'd ignored it. I know now I shouldn't have."

Brandle's fingers smooth through my hair, soothing away the sting of my regret.

"Our life at home quickly and drastically changed with Maeve's presence. Our help, who were more like family, as they had been with us our entire lives, disappeared one after the other. We found them much later, dead, with signs magic had been used.

"Maeve left our estate on the pretext of speaking with the guards about the ill luck of our household, but the Guard never appeared to investigate. Instead, Maeve sent out our one remaining staff member to acquire new help. He returned with women from a whorehouse. Something he wouldn't have done in the past.

"Eloise and I didn't judge them for their occupation, but Maeve did. Looking back, I think her objection was a ruse.

"It wasn't long after that we saw Maeve wearing and using the necklace that killed our mother. We had nowhere to turn. No Mother. No Father. No staff who could help us. Knowing that Eloise and I had discovered her wickedness, Maeve bound us to silence and used us to control each other. If I did not listen, Eloise paid the price.

"When I left, my sister was naked and bound with a chain to the hearth. Maeve had beaten her for her defiance days earlier. Eloise had begged me to leave. She believed Maeve had a purpose to keep us alive, and Eloise didn't trust that she would need both of us."

"I'm sorry, Kellen."

"You have nothing to be sorry for. I left to save myself and my sister, and I believe Eloise was right and that it still holds true since Maeve merely cursed me and did not kill me. But I don't know why." I sighed and opened my eyes to stare at the thatching. "Why did she come to our home? Why did she kill our mother, who was the kindest, most gentle woman I knew? Why is Maeve trying to control us?"

"I wish we could have met you before you lost your mother. I would have liked to meet her. Though, perhaps she would not have agreed to our current circumstance." He finished wringing my hair and took a soapy cloth to my arm.

"Perhaps," I said absently, thinking of the woman I knew. "Perhaps not. She was a person who believed in helping others. I don't believe she would condemn me for helping you. And loving and caring for another person is never wrong if it doesn't bring harm to anyone."

He kissed my fingertips and began washing my other arm.

"Did any of that help you decide if Maeve is the Foul Queen?" I asked again.

"I don't believe she is."

"Who is the Foul Queen then? Is she the one who cursed you?"

"The Foul Queen is what my brothers and I call the queen of Turre. She calls herself the Fair Queen but is neither fair in face nor grace. And, yes, she is the one who cursed us."

"Why?"

He kissed the fingertips of my other hand and then began washing my shoulders and chest.

"Like you and your twin, the seven of us were bound to silence. You broke that silence along with the curse that changed our appearances. Yet, even with it gone, I beg you allow us more time to share our story. Though we've promised no more secrets, the thought of revealing everything terrifies us.

"We just won you for our own, Kitten. We don't want to lose you."

I understood his fear well enough. Hadn't I feared his reaction once he learned what I'd run from? What we still needed to face? And if he thought that Maeve might be his Foul Queen, that meant he also had his own "Maeve" he needed to face.

"Very well. Unlike the men in this clearing, I possess patience," I said with a hint of a smile.

Brandle grinned widely at me, which lit his eyes and melted my heart.

"Would it upset you to explain how I broke the curse?" I asked.

"That I can gladly do. By loving us. All of us. Unconditionally and equally."

Something so simple yet so complex. In all the kingdoms, there wouldn't be many women willing to commit themselves to seven men as I had. If not to spare Eloise, I might never have considered doing so either. Yet, looking at the tenderness in

Brandle's gaze, I knew I would make no other choice if given the chance.

"Brandle, you're needed outside," Edmund said.

He glanced away from me, and whatever he saw on Edmund's face erased his annoyance. After swiftly kissing me, he rose. I twisted in the water to watch his retreat and look at Edmund. His gaze swept over me, and I felt his desire and fear. With a last look, he followed his brother out of sight.

Frowning, I reached for the nearby towel.

"Brandle said he wasn't able to wash everything," Liam said.

I looked up as he and Darian ducked through the doorway.

"Princess, you cannot go about your day in less than pristine condition." Darian plucked the towel from my grasp with a mischievously innocent look. "People will believe we don't care for you well enough, and then there will be men lining up, asking for a place in your harem."

I splashed water at him.

He laughed and reached into the water to pluck my foot free. I remembered the last time he'd washed me and opened my mouth to question his intent. However, what they currently felt stopped me.

Their worry, which they'd carried since Brandle helped break the spell, had changed. Their fear that I would leave them had grown immeasurably while I'd spoken with Brandle. They feared what Eloise might be enduring. They feared I would question the same and leave.

My focus shifted from Darian's smiling face to Liam's.

"Tell me," I said. "Why do you fear for Eloise?"

Liam's shock rippled through him unchecked. Darian's was quicker to fade.

"You read us better than Brandle does."

"I feel you more acutely than I did before. Not your thoughts; simply what you're feeling. It's hard to explain. But I do know it's Eloise you fear for. Why?"

"We found the remaining tracker in the woods," Liam said. Something in his tone gave away what they'd found, and I patted his hand.

"I felt him die before her arrival. I know what Maeve does. She drains them and leaves husks behind. With me here, I don't believe she'll do that to Eloise. I think she needs my sister and me alive."

"You knew?" Liam asked.

"I did. If I'd warned you, you would have stayed at my side and likely met the same fate as the tracker."

Darian slid the cloth along my calf. "Unlikely, Princess. The charms we wear are not decoration. The strongest caster's spell cannot touch us."

"So long as you're wearing them," I said. "She is devious, Darian. She caused the cave-in. Wearing your amulet wouldn't have saved you from being crushed. You put too much faith in the protection you wear. Use your head."

He lifted my foot and lightly bit my toe. My core clenched, which created an unpleasant ache.

"Stop that. Wash me quickly so I can dress, or leave me to wash myself."

His grin returned, and he nodded to Liam. I was thoroughly scrubbed clean in less time than it took for the water to cool and dressed without too much petting. Unsure whether to feel disappointed or worried, I pushed aside both emotions and followed the pair out to the yard.

My intent to join the others and reassure them disappeared when I felt Father's presence to the east where the early morning shadows were still the longest. Liam and Darian stayed close and didn't question why I strode toward the trees, but I could feel their tension when I stopped at the edge of the barrier.

"Father, are you well?" I asked.

He appeared in the shadows, his clothes looking more ragged than before.

He growled several words that I couldn't understand. But I could feel his fear that the human he once was was fading.

"Father, do you trust me?" I asked.

He bowed his head toward me, and I moved to enter the woods.

Darian caught my arm. "Princess, it's too—"

I met and held his gaze. "I am not the same person I was a day ago, Darian. Trust me. Please."

"It's not you we mistrust, Love. The father you once loved is waning."

"I know. That's why I need to give him what little help I can. I need him, Liam. Everything Eloise has suffered will be for nothing without him."

"Brandle is going to kill us if your father doesn't first," Darian muttered.

He stepped into the shadows in front of me, leading the way to my father. When we reached him, I saw his lips were pulled back in a silent snarl as his gaze flicked between the two men standing in front of me.

As I had with Garron, I touched my well and sent my energy into Father, searching his mind for the memories he held most dear. Rather than replacing memories with false ones, I meant to bind him to his memories as a man. With my intent set, I spoke the words.

"Father, in the days to come, the happiest moments in your life will shine in your mind brighter than the sun. Those memories will keep the shadows at bay, binding you to your purpose and reminding you why you must stay."

Leaning forward between Darian and Liam, I touched a finger to my father's brow.

A small spark flared under my fingertip. Father howled in pain but didn't pull away as the acrid smell of burned fur filled our noses.

"Remember, Father," I said softly. "Embrace the joy of what

you once had and the pain of what you've lost. Eloise and I love you and need you to return to us."

When I removed my hand, he dropped his head forward. His heavy panting gave away the anguish that radiated from him and curled around me.

"Forgive me," he rasped, speaking clearer yet still garbled by his elongated snout.

"I find no fault in you, Father. There is nothing to forgive. Maeve is not one to stand against and survive."

He grunted. "I will not fail you again."

"You've never failed us, Father."

"Sir, you've held out against the curse longer than most men," Darian said.

"And each time danger approached, you warned Kellen," Liam added.

Father glanced at the pair. "Protect her with your lives."

"We will," Darian said.

Behind Father, I felt other beasts slowly creeping forward, and I knew we needed to retreat to the glade.

"I love you, Father. Go. I will call if I need you."

Without waiting for his answer, I turned and passed through the barrier so he would not need to fight to protect me.

When we emerged, the others were already in the yard. As Darian predicted, Brandle was not happy to see me leaving the forest.

"No lectures, Brandle," I said. "I went accompanied and barely within the trees to help my father. Did you bury the tracker?"

He glanced at Darian and Liam.

"She already knew," Darian said.

"She felt him die when the Foul Queen arrived," Liam said.

"Maeve," I corrected. "I believe two separate casters are plaguing us. Maeve likes to leave a trail of dried-out husks in her wake. What is the Foul Queen's specialty, other than cursing brothers?"

"She kills small children," Eadric said.

Edmund moved to cuff him.

Without conscious thought, I stayed his hand. All their amulets flared blindingly, and Edmund's eyes rounded as he stared at his hand, frozen a breadth from his brother's head.

"Please don't cuff each other for speaking the truth," I said.

"How?" Edmund asked, looking at Brandle. "This shouldn't be possible."

"You can still move your hand away, Edmund, simply not forward," I said and watched him pull it back quickly. "You can thank Garron's lesson on direct and indirect casting and Maeve's visit. She proved the difference between casting directly on a person and casting on the environment around the person to indirectly affect them. I blocked your hand with a cushion of air between Eadric's head and your hand. That's all."

"And our amulets?" Brandle asked. The question held no accusation, only curiosity.

"I'm not certain," I said. "To protect Eadric, I instinctively reacted to Edmund's action."

Darian hit the back of Daemon's head, which earned him a scowl from several of his brothers.

"I thought we wanted her to try again to determine the cause," he said with a shrug.

"At times, you act no better than urchins," I said. "Perhaps, rather than focusing on my erratic control, we should now move forward with our plans to travel to Turre."

Each one of them glanced at Brandle.

"Fear the moment I do figure out how to cast directly on your persons as I will be the one doing the cuffing. You are a frustrating lot. Did we not have an agreement? I help you break the spell holding you—which I have—and you help me gain the resources we need to free my sister."

"We haven't forgotten," Brandle said. "However, the cave-in will cause another delay as we need to finish the mining before we can leave for Turre. Also, once we reach Turre, it will take time to acquire what we need as we will need to work quietly and in secrecy to avoid the Foul Queen's attention."

Though I understood why we could not immediately rush to free my sister, I struggled to understand why the mines needed to be addressed before leaving for Turre, and my frustration climbed.

Brandle closed the distance between us and took my hands in his.

"We need the gems in the mines," he said.

"With them, we could purchase the silence of all of Adele," Edmund added.

"Henry made us promise never to go to Adele empty-handed," Eadric said.

I sighed in defeat and tugged my hands from Brandle's.

"As you will it."

When I would have walked away, Garron caught my sleeve.

"I think you can help us," he said. "Especially now."

"Garron," Brandle said with warning.

"Anything that will get us to Turre faster," I said quickly.

"Princess gets to go to the mines with us?" Darian asked with barely contained excitement.

"Do you not remember what happened the last time we were in there?" Edmund asked.

"It will be fine," Darian said. "Magic caused the last one."

I snorted. "And you do not know what damage it's caused to your tunnels." I glanced at Brandle. "How Henry kept you all alive is beyond my understanding."

Humor lit Brandle's gaze. "Some days proved more difficult than others. Considering your abilities, we would fare better with you than without, but once you're rested."

"I'm rested," I said firmly. "Liam, fetch me your clothes. Eadric, feed me my breakfast. It's time I see these mysterious mines of yours."

No one contradicted me, but I could feel their reservations. They were worried I would doubt their intentions once I saw whatever was in the mine.

Cuddled and petted on Daemon's lap, I wondered what could cause them almost as much fear as finding a dried-out body in the woods.

CHAPTER 2

My impatience boiled just beneath the surface as we waited outside the mines for Garron to search for any fissures that might make it too dangerous to enter. Eadric plucked at my fingers, drawing my attention from the cave opening.

"Can you feel them, too?" he asked.

"I wouldn't know what I'm looking for," I said.

"Cracks in the rocks."

"I know that, but the cave is full of them," I said. "Small ones that only go a few inches. Large ones that bisect sections of different types of rock. Even the ones in the rock face that gave me handholds and footholds." I tipped my head to look at the cliff, searching for the holds I used. They didn't appear as deep or as frequent as I remembered.

"New ones will be cleaner, fresh breaks. Those are the ones Garron looks for. The old ones that are filled with dirt or traces of moisture he ignores."

Understanding, I opened myself to the first hold on the rock face and easily saw its age. The second one wasn't old, though. It was a clean break without sand or any other deposits and only a scant foot into the rock. I followed the holds up the face, finding a mix of new and old. Some of the new ones made no sense. Breaks without pressure behind them.

In my desperation to escape, had I made those new holds without consciously casting?

"Edmund...Eadric," Garron said, appearing in the opening. "We need to add a few more supports near the opening." His gaze found mine. "It will take us a few hours. Perhaps you'd like to read inside the cottage until we're finished?"

"I've spent as much time idle as I would care to," I said. "Show me what needs support."

I strode forward, but Edmund blocked my path. Tipping my head back, I narrowed my gaze in warning.

"What would take you hours, I can complete within minutes, Edmund. My patience has been tested enough recently; wouldn't you agree?"

"It has," he said. "Yet, I am begging for more of it. Garron agrees you are a powerful caster, and we've seen your strength with our own eyes. We don't doubt you are capable of achieving what few ever will. However, you've admitted that your abilities are erratic, and the mines are dangerous, Trouble. Why do you think we always leave two or three of us behind? It's so someone is on the outside to help dig us free. It takes experience and caution to shore up the mines after a cave-in. Please. Please don't go in there."

Held by his imploring gaze, I extended my hand.

"A twig, please," I said.

Confusion flitted over his expression. Where he wanted to question my request, Eadric did not. He picked a small twig off the ground and placed it in my palm.

"Thank you, Eadric." I stepped around Edmund and stuck the twig into the ground near the side of the cave opening.

With a light touch of my energy, I sent its growth into the cave. Sturdy lengths grew and wove together to form a thick ceiling that, bound by my will, would hold the weight of the stone and protect the people within.

I didn't stop coaxing it until it reached the first split in the passage.

"Garron, can you check if that's enough?" I asked.

A subtle wave of dizziness washed over me as he walked into the cave. I immediately checked my well but didn't notice anything different. Yet, the dizziness persisted.

Frowning, I leaned into Edmund, who was the closest. His arm wrapped around my shoulders without hesitation.

"Trouble?"

"I'm fine. It feels like I stood up too quickly. I checked my well, and it's not due to casting. Everything feels the same."

Edmund swept me up into his arms.

"If you take one step toward that cottage, I'm going to show you real trouble," I said, scowling at him.

He frowned at me, and I could feel he was debating it.

"Everything looks good," Garron said, appearing in the cave opening. "The limbs are thick—what's wrong?"

"Your brother is weighing the wisdom of confining me to the cottage against my will. I tore through the thatching without my power. Imagine what I will do with it," I said.

"Edmund, put her down. She's neither broken nor fragile," Brandle said, using my own words.

"And when she faints and falls on the rough floor? Will you be so calm then?" Edmund demanded.

The pair locked gazes until I covered Edmund's eyes and lifted myself enough to nip his neck. He grunted, and his hold on me tightened.

"The passage is too narrow to carry me, Edmund. Let me walk, and hold my hand. I promise to warn you if I'm feeling faint so I don't fall."

Eadric plucked me from his brother's hold, kissed me soundly, and set me on my feet.

"You'll need another bath when we're done in there. He might be more cooperative if you agree he can help with that."

I arched a brow at Edmund. "Or would you prefer I bathe you?"

He grabbed my hand and motioned for Garron to lead the way, his protestation gone. The others chuckled, and I grinned.

The weak light cast by Garron's lantern did little to illuminate the tunnel as we moved away from the opening, and I was grateful for Edmund's steadying hand over the uneven rocky floor. For a time, our footfalls echoed in the confines of the tunnel. Then, I felt when we came to the first fork.

Garron took the branch to the right. Three more tunnels branched off along our route, and our path tilted, taking us deeper into the earth until, suddenly, we turned a corner, and I saw light ahead.

"Is there another opening?" I asked.

"Yes, but it's not one we can access," Edmund said.

We entered a wide cavern encircled by tiered levels and ladders. A crack at the very top of the cave let in enough light to reflect off a multitude of gems embedded in the stone walls. The number astounded me.

The wealth in this cave was more than any person would dream of seeing in their lifetime—enough to feed a kingdom for a season. Or enough to buy the silence of its inhabitants. That these men were willing to use this wealth to help free Eloise humbled me.

My sweeping gaze stopped on the seven small chests that sat in the center of the space, under the light. Six were closed. The open one was partially filled with different colored gems that glinted prettily.

"What do you need to do?" I asked.

Their silence drew my attention from the cave to them. I looked down at myself, curious why they were staring, but all my clothes were in place.

"You barely glanced at the gems," Darian said. "I thought women fawned over pretty jewels."

"I have never fawned in my life and don't plan to start."

"That's a bit disappointing," Daemon said. "I'd hoped you would fawn over us in the future."

"You already lack in humility," I said, hiding my amusement. "I will not add to the problem. Now, what should we do?"

"Maybe she just needs to get a better look," Darian said to Daemon. They both jogged over to the chests and flipped back the lids. Four of the small chests were filled with jewels of varying sizes. Two chests were still empty.

"We need to fill the chests before we leave," Brandle said when I glanced at him questioningly.

"How long have you been filling them?" I asked.

"For years."

"But we've had to use some of what we've mined several times when the need arose," Liam added quickly.

"How long does it take to fill a chest?" I asked.

They all looked at Brandle again.

"We're hoping it will be faster with your help."

"How long?"

"A year."

The conversation I'd overheard when they thought me sleeping several nights ago made sense now. After witnessing my impatience at each day's delay, they'd feared my reaction to hearing a year. And rightly so.

My laughter echoed throughout the cave, and a low, ominous rumble followed.

"And you thought the dried remains of the tracker's body would be what sent me running to my sister without your questionable help?"

The tunnel behind me rumbled again, and it wasn't due to the volume of my voice. I was angry—very angry—at the half-truths and weighted promises they'd given.

"With your help, I think we can fill the rest of the partially filled chest yet today," Garron said calmly.

I could feel Garron and Eadric's certainty that I would help them, which both humbled me and calmed my temper.

"Eadric, show her how we've been removing them," Garron said.

Eadric picked up a small pick axe and began chipping away at the rock around the gem. After several minutes, he pried the gem free; however, it still had some rock stuck to it. So he then had to use the pick axe to gently remove bits at a time until only the gem remained.

"We knew that one was close to coming out," Garron said. "You can see the others we've found in this layer. They won't be enough to fill the chest, though. We'll need to work deeper to find more.

"I've tried casting to remove them," Garron said, "but the cost of the spell is high, and I'm not able to pull from the earth like Henry could."

I opened myself to the energy around us. The gems glowed more brightly than the stone, and I could see the multitude of the gems still buried in the mine, waiting to be discovered.

"And after I help free enough gems to fill the remaining chests, what else will delay us from leaving?" I asked.

"Nothing, Kitten. I vow it."

I connected with the energy in my well and sought out the first gem.

My time with Garron taught me the importance of casting with balance. I could turn a twig into a thorn-covered barrier, put thorns on a pea vine, and separate the dirt from the bathwater. But more than that, I could absorb all the energy in something until it no longer existed.

They watched as the stone around the gem slowly vanished, and a perfect ruby the size of my pinky nail fell to the ground.

Daemon's giddy reaction didn't worry me that I was being

used. I could feel they weren't interested in accumulating wealth for themselves. He was simply happy that I could remove the gem quickly because he knew it would make me happy. He had no attachment whatsoever to the gem itself.

Content that I knew what to do, I sent my will out into the cave. I found each gem on the surface and connected to the surrounding stone.

Gems fell to the floor as the entrapping stone disappeared all at once. The energy I used to cast felt the same as the energy I gained from absorbing the surrounding stone. Yet, I experienced another wave of dizziness.

Smiling to hide my concern, I waved at the gems.

"I removed them; you pick them up."

Eadric lifted me and twirled me around before setting me on my feet so he could climb a nearby ladder to pick up the gems I'd removed on the tiers above. I waited until they'd all moved away to catch Garron's attention.

"The dizziness returned the same as the last time I cast," I said softly. "I was careful to check the well before I cast and after. It feels as if I've neither gained nor lost energy. I'm certain it's not a depletion, Garron, but it is something. Does her spell linger?"

Garron considered me and slowly shook his head.

"If it does, I cannot detect it. Once a spell's criteria are met, it should resolve itself completely."

I thought of what I'd done to bend the spell's intent to my own.

"And if they aren't met?"

"The spell wouldn't be broken. How did you break the spell? Did you deduce the conditions?"

I could feel the curiosity of the others and knew they were listening.

"Yes. When Maeve arrived, she said it wouldn't be wise to reunite me with Eloise. That it would be better to keep me here because I had much to learn. She said my cool regard spared me in the past but hinted that it wouldn't in the future. Then she told me to eat the apple to save my sister.

"I could feel the spell take root when I swallowed and, not long after, fell into a faint similar to the others I've experienced.

"She told me to sleep well, called me a true beauty, and said that if I ever woke, no man of worth would ever want me. I didn't understand then, not even when she said it would be my greatest fall.

"I couldn't move or speak, just like before. Yet, unlike those previous faints, when more than one of you touched me, I felt a surge of energy different from what I was used to.

"The weight of her spell had covered the lid of my well, preventing me from connecting with my own energy. But when I found pleasure, your energies combined were enough that I could speak. It always ended too quickly to do more, though.

"That's when I understood what she meant about no man wanting me and what I needed to do. She meant for me to bed each one of you to break the spell. But when I found my release with Brandle, it was enough to lift her spell and connect with my well. The moment I touched my own source of power, I changed the spell, forcing it to bend to my will.

"I would meet the terms of the spell, but when I chose, not when Maeve willed it."

He nodded thoughtfully. "Perhaps then, you are not free of it. I simply can not sense it."

I searched inside myself for a hint of the spell lingering and shook my head.

"Nothing of her touch remains within me."

He pulled me into his arms and hugged me close.

"Take extra care when casting. We have no wish to lose you, Kellen. Not for all the gems and kingdoms in the world." He pulled back and held my gaze. "Though you are willing to give your life for your sister's, we do not agree. Your life carries the weight of—"

"She understands her life is tied to ours, Garron," Brandle said. "Now let her be and help us pick up these gems."

Garron kissed my forehead and went to collect what I'd freed. While they worked, I sat on one of the closed chests and watched them work.

They taunted and jested one another. Playful cuffing and easy laughter rang out in the cavern in bursts. Smiling, I listened to them until Daemon wrapped his arms around me from behind. He nuzzled my neck and trailed kisses along my skin.

"Knave," I said lightly. "Do you think your brothers do not know you seek to use me to shirk your share of work?"

Daemon chuckled against my skin. "Oh, they know. But they're also entertained by your reactions and won't stop me."

Tangling my hand in his hair, I plucked him away from my neck and twisted to mock-scowl at him. His unrepentant grin didn't diminish.

"Don't you want to know if the spell is truly lifted?" he asked, proving he'd been listening.

"And how will you help determine that?"

"Release me, and I'll show you."

Knowing well that the glint in his gaze was pure mischief, I released him. He lifted me, sitting me across his lap. Then, his mouth covered mine, and he kissed me hungrily, weaving another type of spell around me. I held his shoulders and met his desire with my own.

When his hand slid under my tunic and palmed my bare breast underneath, I groaned. He pulled back and lifted the material to expose my chest.

"Cast now, Lamb." His mouth closed over my nipple, and I struggled to think beyond the sensations he was evoking. The desire from each man in the cave beckoned me, and I arched under Daemon's touch.

With barely a conscious thought, I connected with my well of energy. Their amulets flared brightly around the cavern, but I ignored them and focused on where the gems lay hidden under the layers of stone. Rather than remove the stone, I changed it to sand, enabling the gems to move through the material then hardened it again once I freed the gems.

Daemon switched to my other breast, and I sighed in contentment and ran my fingers through his hair.

"Since he's had all the fun, we should leave the work to him as well," Darian said.

I tipped my head to look at him as his brother's mouth continued to caress me.

"He isn't the only one enjoying this. I can feel how much you enjoy watching."

Eadric laughed, and Darian grinned.

"You are a beautiful sight," he said. "Mining isn't as grueling a task with you here."

"That's because you're staring and not working," Edmund said with a scowl.

Though he was annoyed with Darian for gawking, he was more annoyed with Daemon for doing what he wanted to do. They all wished they were in Daemon's place.

"Any dizziness, Kitten?" Brandle asked.

"Breathlessness and aching for more where I'm not yet ready to be touched again, but no dizziness."

Daemon groaned and dropped his forehead to my sternum.

Darian laughed. "Someone's going to need an ice bath."

I lifted Daemon's head and kissed him sweetly.

"Thank you for your help."

"I will help you with anything, Lamb. Always. Especially if it involves sleeping next to you tonight."

He helped me to my feet and straightened my tunic. With one last kiss that involved lifting me and wrapping my legs around his waist, he left me to recline against the gem chest again.

Boredom and the low lighting made it impossible to stay awake as they worked. A cave floor wasn't the most comfortable place to rest, which was likely why I woke on Eadric's chest a while later.

"How did you win this privilege?" I asked.

"Because they knew I would be able to move you without you noticing," he said with a grin.

I laughed with him and rested my head on his shoulder as he smoothed a hand over my back. It was relaxing and nice, and I was close to falling asleep again when he spoke.

"If you think the spell lingers, would it be wiser to bed us before we leave for Turre?"

A snort escaped me. "Bed *you*? I believe I'm the one being bedded."

"A mutual bedding then."

I relaxed into him and considered his suggestion.

"I neither want to delay our departure nor want to feel as if the time I spend with each of you is forced due to a spell. The dizziness I felt wasn't severe and hasn't led to any problems. It's no more than I feel when I stand after reading for too long and forgetting to eat."

"Hmm. I don't want the time you spend with us to feel forced, either. Then, it seems we'll need to start packing when we return. The gems you uncovered were enough to fill the remaining chests."

I sat up to look at the chests, but they were gone—along with Edmund, Daemon, Darian, and Brandle.

"We didn't want to wake you," Garron said.

"You looked peaceful," Liam added as Eadric stood and helped me to my feet.

"Are you still tired?" Garron asked.

"Not at all." Any lingering tiredness had vanished with the anticipation of finally leaving.

Garron once again led the way with the lamp, and Eadric held my hand as Liam followed us.

When we emerged, the sun sat low on the horizon, and

Brandle was filling a pail at the well.

"There's a bath waiting for you inside," he said.

I felt Eadric's humor and Garron's concern. I patted Garron's chest.

"Don't forget…I know how to remove the heat from water." As I spoke, I heated the pails Brandle had ready for the trio. "Edmund knows to behave."

As I strode away, I heard Liam ask, "How did she know Edmund was waiting for her?"

"She said she can feel us," Brandle said.

"We'll need to be more careful," Garron said softly.

"Exactly," Brandle said. "Guard your feelings about returning to Turre well."

Returning to their home after such a long exile was certain to be hard on them. Especially to a dangerous place like Turre. Did they think I would be unsympathetic to their concerns, or did they believe they were protecting me by keeping their fears to themselves?

CHAPTER 3

ENTERING THE COTTAGE, I SAW EDMUND RECLINING IN THE TUB. No steam rose from the water, which I quickly corrected. He sighed in appreciation and watched my approach.

"I've been looking forward to this," he said.

"I imagine so. It must be difficult to wash your own back."

He didn't laugh like any of the rest would have. His hungry gaze swept over my face, and I felt his desire for me grow.

I picked up a cloth, dipped it into the water, and used the soap to create a lather.

"I'm willing to wash every inch of you, Edmund. Slowly and thoroughly. But it won't end as you wish."

His brows rose. I felt his worry…and guilt.

"The care you took to prepare me helped, but I still need more time. I feel a bit bruised inside, and though I love each touch and kiss from all of you, I am not ready for it to go further than that."

He considered me.

"I promise not to do anything without permission."

Yet, I could feel his confidence that he would bed me before sunset. His desire thickened around me, and my heart fluttered at the thought of denying him what he wanted just for the simple sake of my need to challenge him. I enjoyed baiting Edmund very much.

"Then I will take you at your word."

He leaned back in the tub as I dragged the soapy cloth over his muscled forearm. His relaxed fingers moved with ease as I washed each digit. But his ease was only a ruse. I could feel his growing tension, his need for me to touch more of him.

Fully embracing the dangerous game I played, I dipped the cloth into the tub and soaped it again.

He watched me as I washed his arms, then his shoulders and chest. An angry, desperate edge honed his need for me and wrapped around me, coaxing my desire for him, making it difficult to breathe normally as he extended a leg for me. He gripped the edge of the tub as I dragged the cloth over his inner thigh and hissed out a breath when I accidentally went too far.

His hunger for me became my own. It fed my need to touch him until it matched his need to be touched.

A part of me knew I was feeling more than I should…that there was a reason I hadn't wanted to go further with him. But another part refused to walk away from his need for me.

Holding his gaze, I set the cloth aside and reached into the water once more.

His pained groan filled the room as my hand closed around him.

Without warning, he stood fluidly, taking me with him. His mouth was on mine as he pressed me to his wet chest. I met his ravenous kiss and scraped my nails over his back as he stalked across the room and lowered me to a waiting mattress.

His mouth didn't leave mine as he tugged the ties of my pants loose and slipped his hand inside. He stroked my wet folds and circled my nub until I tore my mouth from his to gasp for air.

Then he removed his hand, and I watched him lick his finger.

My heart stuttered in equal parts mortification and fascination.

"I want to taste you, Trouble. Tell me you want the same."

My skin felt too hot. Too tight. I needed more of Edmund, but I also remembered why I should fear it. He saw my hesitation.

"I gave my word," he said. "Only what you permit."

Holding his gaze, I slowly nodded.

He removed my clothes in seconds. Laying bare underneath him, I watched him dip his head and kiss a trail down my neck and torso. At the V of my legs, he inhaled deeply and made a growling sound.

"Open for me," he said, not attempting to move my limbs.

The last time he'd tasted me, I'd been unable to move and dependent on their attention to break the spell. I felt his desperate need for me to participate, to show him how much I wanted him to touch me.

Pulse thundering, I slowly parted my legs.

"More," he rasped, his gaze fixated on what he wanted to taste. He didn't stop prompting me for more until I could go no further.

"You are lovely, Trouble. I will never tire of looking at you." The flat of his tongue swept over me, and I sighed my approval. "Or tasting you."

The second stroke had my eyes rolling back in my head.

"I want your hands on my head," he said as he swirled his tongue around me. "Show me what you want."

He teased me, avoiding where I wanted him to focus until I forced him there. I was close to finding my release when he suddenly rolled us. His hands on my torso lifted me so I didn't fall as I straddled his face.

The disconcerting position brought me back from the edge.

"Edmund, I don't—"

"You have more control this way, Trouble. Take what you need." His tongue flicked over my nub then trailed lower to my opening, which he'd been avoiding. The tip of his nose brushed alongside that sensitive bundle of nerves as he tongued my entrance, never quite breaching it.

My desperation to feel him there slowly consumed me until I could think of little else.

"Edmund. Please."

"Please what?"

"I need you in me."

He lifted me and settled me over his hips.

"Then take me."

His hand captured the back of my head, and he drew me down for a kiss. I tasted myself. It felt wrong and right at the same time as he coaxed me to settle my weight along his hard length. I rocked against him several times, letting the pleasure grow before bracing my palms on his chest and lifting myself.

"Help me."

He reached between us and positioned himself at my opening.

"You decide the pace, Trouble. Bed me as you wish."

His words teased my need for him. Desperate to feel him fill me, I slowly sank down. He stretched me, but not unpleasantly so. His intrusion eased the ache instead of adding to it, and I sighed in satiation. When I couldn't sink any further, he lifted me and let me slide down onto him again. And again. Until our hips met.

His hands stroked over my sides and fondled my breasts, tweaking my nipples until any lingering ache eased.

"Are you ready for more, Trouble?"

I nodded, and he growled as he rolled us again. Underneath him, I lost myself to his slow and steady rhythm as my pleasure climbed and then shattered. Outside, a few curses echoed my low wail. Then Edmund drove deep inside of me and stilled. His release bathed my insides and triggered secondary spasms of pleasure.

Rolling to the side but not withdrawing, he held me as our

breathing returned to normal. I felt his spent member slowly leave me and the wash of his release on my thigh.

"I could spend every day for the rest of my life with you just like this," he said, brushing the hair from my sweaty brow and kissing it.

"I would never walk again," I said.

He chuckled and pulled me close.

"You wouldn't need to. I would carry you everywhere. Like this." He rolled so I was on top of him and rose with me in his arms.

I grinned as he walked toward the tub.

"Do you want to change the bathwater?" he asked.

"It's already clean and heated."

He glanced at it, grunted, and then lowered me into the tub. The hot water soothed the soreness between my legs, and I leaned my head back to relax. Edmund used the cloth to wash all of me and then his fingers to slowly probe my channel.

"Any discomfort?" he asked softly.

"None. It feels quite nice, actually."

"Then I'll continue until you tell me to stop."

I didn't push his hand away until I found my release a second time. Too languid to care about the cooling water, I let Edmund lift me out and dry me with Eadric's help, which involved more pleasant fondling and kisses.

"It looks like I will need to feed you tonight," Eadric said.

"You always feed her," Daemon said.

"Ah, but this time, I might have to open her mouth for her."

He sounded giddy at the prospect. Uncaring why, I let him do as he pleased. And it did please him. I felt his fascination with my mouth grow with each bite of stew he fed me.

When I finished, Liam swept me away to tuck me into bed and held me from behind.

I fell asleep before seeing who I would use as a pillow.

I DREAMT OF SEX. Not involving myself or any of my men but with people I didn't recognize. Young and old, the couples writhed against each other. Their sexual need fed my own. I ached to be touched and scanned the people for the ones whom I wanted to touch me. But I couldn't find them. They were gone.

A tightness squeezed my chest. Where were they? My very bones ached with my need for them. With them, I could be free. Free to do what I wished...feel what I wished.

Then someone touched me. A tongue stroked through my folds, and I looked down at Garron's head.

Joy filled me, and I rocked against his tongue, seeking the pleasure I knew would bring relief to this heaviness blanketing me from the inside.

You need the others, something whispered.

I woke partially on my side and partially leaning back on Liam's chest. Eadric's face was buried between my splayed legs as he licked and sucked with abandon. He slipped a finger inside of me and tipped his head to meet my gaze as I moaned.

"Good morning, Sparrow. Are you hungry?"

Already breathing heavily, I shook my head.

"Maybe you're just not hungry yet," he said, adding a second finger.

My lips parted, and he winked at me. I knew what that meant. He was going to do something to test his brothers. I wanted that. Desperately.

"Or maybe you just need to taste something delicious. Like this." He dipped his head and licked me again. Then he withdrew his fingers and offered them to me. "Let me feed you, Sparrow."

He nudged my mouth open and slipped his wet fingers inside. Several soft curses erupted within the fire-lit cottage, and I felt their desire surge. It fed my own as I tasted myself on his fingers.

"Look at how perfect you are," Eadric said. "If you lick them clean, I'll feed you more."

I didn't need to look at Edmund to know he was fisting himself. I could feel it—his burning desire with that hard, controlling edge. He wanted to push Eadric out of the way and feed me something else. He wanted me to take his length into my mouth. So did Brandle. So did they all.

Stunned, I stopped sucking Eadric's fingers. The ache for them didn't dissipate with my shock, though.

"Would you like something more?" he asked. He shifted his position, sprawling out so his legs were near my head.

Eadric wasn't wearing anything.

My eyes rounded as I stared at his hard length near my face. He chuckled then lifted my leg over his head and buried his face between them, licking me hungrily.

The sounds he made fed the hunger that had woken me.

I gently wrapped my hand around his shaft. He groaned and thrust his tongue into my channel. A moan escaped me, and I licked my lips. The air in the cottage grew heavy with their collective need for me to taste Eadric as he tasted me.

Liam's hand found one of my breasts and started kneading it as I leaned toward his brother and licked the head of his shaft.

Eadric gripped my hips and rolled us so I straddled his face like I had Edmund's. While he feasted, I slowly licked every inch of his length and ground down on his tongue. The pleasure I needed remained beyond my reach. I hungered for Eadric. I hungered for all of him.

When he pulled away, I whimpered against his length.

"I know, Sparrow," he said soothingly. "You're hungry and need more."

He turned me so I straddled his hips. "Just like last time. Take it all."

With a low moan, I slowly sank onto his length and rocked against him as his hands guided me. He stretched me as Edmund had, but it felt so good. Gripping his shoulders, I sank deep, seeking the release I knew he could give me.

When he sat up and suckled my chest, I clenched around him and shattered. His release flooded me as I pulsed around him.

"To be clear, I did not feel forced to bed you. I could think of little else when I woke up to your fingers teasing my skin," Eadric said against my temple. "I didn't press for more than you were willing to give, did I?"

"No," I said, forgetting in my blissful daze what we'd done. When I did remember, I burrowed more firmly against his chest.

Laughing, he tipped my face up to his and kissed every inch of it.

"Thank you for allowing me another first. Now, into the bath you go. Darian won't forgive me if we're late for their coddled eggs and tartlets with biscuits and cream."

My gaze darted to the side, and I saw we were alone.

"If you ever change your mind, they would be willing to stay," Eadric said, kissing my brow. "Watching one of us taste you is almost as good as tasting you."

I shook my head at the mischievous grin he gave me and tried to pull away.

"Wait. Give me another moment. I like feeling this connected with you."

His hands wandered over my bare back, reeling me in again until I rested my head on his shoulder. I liked the closeness of being connected too. And I realized that, while the feel of him inside of me was the center of our connection, it wasn't our only link.

I could feel his energy, too, surrounding me, like it was trying to find a way in.

"Eadric, could I try something?" I asked.

"Anything."

I closed my eyes and focused on the energy around me. Each bit—the floor, the earth behind it, the air, the mattress, our blanket—glowed to varying degrees. Eadric glowed the brightest. His energy radiated from inside of him, which I imagined was his well. The energy I thought I felt, though, I couldn't see.

Curious, I nudged the lid off my well while watching. Even behind my closed eyes, I could see the flare of light from Eadric's amulet. Its light blinded me from seeing the glow of his well.

I closed myself off and opened my eyes.

"What did you do?" he asked.

"I just looked. I'm not sure what for, but it felt—feels—like there's something there."

"There? Where?"

"Around me from you. I thought it was energy, but it's not. Not really."

"How can you tell?"

"When I opened myself to it, it didn't flood me."

"Hmm. Would you like to look again while I distract you like Daemon did in the caves?"

I snorted and kissed the tip of his nose.

"I can feel their growing impatience. You've tested them enough for one day, I should think."

He sighed with mock woe. "I will leave you to bathe in peace then. Unless you require my assistance?"

I shook my head and smiled as he stood with me and carried me to the waiting water.

"Wash quickly, or you will have company."

Heeding his warning, I finished with haste and donned the gown they'd purchased for me before any of them could intrude. Filled with anticipation and concern, I opened the door and looked out into the yard.

Edmund was covering the fire with dirt, something I'd never seen them do. Supplies and packs waited in a pile beside a table filled with plates of food.

"Come eat, Sparrow," Eadric said, holding out his hand for

me. His hair was wet, likely from a recent washing at the well, and my cheeks flushed as I recalled why he'd needed to wash.

Darian swept me into his arms while I was distracted and carried me over to the table. He didn't place me on his lap, though. He seated me on the bench between him and Eadric. Everyone else took a seat, too, and I eyed the incredible amount of food they'd made.

"We made what would spoil and moved the rest of it into the trees for your father," Brandle said. "I expect we won't be returning here for some time."

I nodded and filled my plate. Though Eadric was more than willing to feed me, he focused on his own food while I quickly ate mine.

Garron was the first to finish and took his plate to the well. I helped him wash while the others completed the preparations to depart.

"It must be hard leaving your home," I said, feeling Garron's sadness and worry.

"While it's the only home I've known, I know it's not my true home," he said.

"Do you have any family left in Turre?" I asked.

"No. We are the last of our family," he said.

I felt his surge of fear. It had layers. Fear for his brothers and what they would face in Turre. Fear that I would run. Fear that I would hate them for withholding the truth. Fear that—

"Snow?"

Realizing I was staring at him, I focused on the plate I held as my thoughts raced.

They weren't telling me something. Why? I considered asking then decided against it after recalling Brandle's caution from the evening before. Knowing that I could feel what they felt had to be intrusive to them. Yet, they had never once admonished me for unintentionally delving into their feelings. That did not mean I should do so without consideration for their need for privacy. So, while I couldn't help sensing their feelings, I *could* choose to ignore them.

"Kellen?" Garron said when I didn't answer.

"I apologize. I'm feeling a bit disconcerted. For my sister's sake, I'm happy to leave. However, I worry about what we might face in the days to come. I don't want anything to happen to any of you."

He dried his hands on his pants and pulled me into a comforting hug.

"We know to be cautious and how to not draw attention. Trust us. Please."

"I do, Garron. Completely."

He brushed my temple with a kiss and then sent me to help the others.

Once we were all in the yard and double-checking the weight of our packs, Brandle closed the cottage door for the final time. Edmund and Eadric stood behind him, each placing a hand on his shoulder. Daemon and Darian placed their hands on the twins before them. Then Garron and Liam.

The love they felt for one another filled my heart and touched something deeper within me. The need to protect them as I did Eloise rose swiftly and fiercely. They feared what they would find in Turre. They feared I would leave them. However, that was now as impossible for me as it would be to abandon Eloise. It would never happen.

But how could I prove that?

Watching them and seeing their bond, I knew of only one way.

I sent my love to them, visualizing it as a barrier around them like the one surrounding the glade. So long as I lived, nothing born of man or magic would ever harm them. I sent my intent outward into the air, and the glade exploded in a vibrant kaleidoscope of multi-colored particles. They floated toward the men I held so dear, condensing and swirling.

Garron glanced up then back at me.

"Snow?"

"I love you. All of you."

They turned toward me, and any confusion on their faces was quickly changed to surprise.

"Is the air glowing?" Eadric asked.

"You can see it?" Garron asked.

They all nodded.

"What is it?" Brandle asked.

"It's Kellen," Garron said, watching me.

"It's not me but my love for you. Welcome it, and it will bind us together." I felt Edmund and Brandle's worry. "It means I won't run from you. No matter what secret you're still hiding, I won't run."

"Then I welcome it," Eadric said, opening his arms wide. The colorful dust settled on his skin and disappeared.

"His amulet didn't flare," Edmund said.

"Because I didn't directly cast on him. It's an indirect cast like the healing tea. You can accept it or not as you choose. And if you choose to accept it, there are no conditions you must meet for this spell. It binds me to you, not the other way around."

"I wouldn't mind being bound by you," Darian said with a smirk. Eadric cuffed him for a change, which made me smile.

"Shall we go?" I turned my back on them so they could choose as they wished without any guilt. However, when I went to pick up my sling bag, Brandle's hand closed over mine.

"I packed it for you before you woke."

I tipped my head back to smile at him.

"Thank you."

"I found the letter from the king of Drisdall."

"And you wish to know how I came to have such a letter in my possession?"

"Why didn't you go to the king to save your sister? With that letter, he would have helped you."

"Maeve didn't use her amulet like you do yours. She invited men into our home for dinners— noblemen or men of significant standing in the kingdom. Men who likely had the king's ear in one form or another.

"With barely a word, she had them under her spell. Yet, for all appearances, she was an upright, moral woman of standing.

"We had no proof of her wrongdoings, Brandle. And I feared that approaching the king was exactly what she wanted. But not us. Her.

"In the days prior to my departure, she searched all my father's documentation and used tidying as an excuse to do the same in the attic. By chance, I found the letter and some correspondence between my mother and a caster named Elspeth—a name my mother never mentioned to us.

"Though you have questions, I doubt they compare in number to the questions I have. Why was a letter from the king and several from a caster in our attic? What did my mother have to do with a caster in a kingdom that forbids magic? And what was Maeve searching for? If it truly was this letter, then why did she want it? What ill intentions does she have planned for Drisdall and its people? And how do Eloise and I play into those plans? For, without a doubt, we do. Why else keep us alive when Maeve killed or sent away everyone else?

"I didn't intentionally keep the letter from you. I have it in safekeeping, fearing Maeve's intent."

"Thank you for explaining." He placed the sling over my shoulders. "Let me know if this becomes too heavy."

CHAPTER 4

Sweat coated my back, and my thighs cramped due to the fast pace they set, but I neither slowed nor complained. Around us, twigs broke, and brush rustled, signs of the beasts' presence around us. They remained just outside the circle of weak light cast by the stone that Garron carried. He had explained that they couldn't use the one I'd arrived with—casters in Adele would have felt the strength of its power as we approached Turre.

The weaker stone Garron had made worked well enough. The few beasts who drew too close due to my presence quickly learned that the spears Edmund and Eadric carried weren't for show.

We did not stop to eat or drink until we reached a very small sunlit clearing.

"This is one of the pockets of light Henry made," Garron said as Daemon passed me a water bladder. "We've kept it clear by hand so no one would suspect magic."

I looked from the rotted stumps at the edge of the trees to the packed ground beneath our feet and wondered at the time they'd spent keeping this clear.

"Why maintain this clearing? Isn't it a clue that someone inhabits this forest?"

"It is, but it's far enough away from our glade not to call attention to us and far enough from Turre that others are unlikely to discover it."

"You said it was one of the clearings Henry made. Are there more?"

"There are. We visit them once each fall to clear them."

"When we travel to Turre, we always take different routes. These clearings provide us with a space to eat and rest briefly before continuing."

He passed me a biscuit and produced a small crock of the jam I'd previously made with some of their dried berries and sugar. I sat on Garron's pack and ate while the others stood and consumed theirs. They gave me a moment of false privacy to relieve myself and didn't comment on my flushed cheeks when I turned my back on them so they could do the same.

Our time resting was as brief as they said it would be, but I didn't mind when we set out only a short while later. The sooner we arrived, the sooner we could begin finding the help we needed.

While we walked, I kept the lid on my well firmly in place and stretched my senses to search for other casters. If any were nearby, they hid themselves from my presence like I hid from theirs.

The shadows grew darker with the sun's slow descent, and the number of beasts following us increased.

"Can other casters sense the approach of beasts like I can?" I asked.

"Not many can sense as far afield as you can," Garron said. "But we're careful to emerge from the forest in areas that are not populated for just that reason."

"Which means more walking once we're out of these trees," Daemon said morosely.

"Does that mean the Lamb's shepherd has no stamina?" Darian asked with a grin.

Daemon went to cuff him, but Brandle's warning glance stopped their antics.

Walking required more care the farther we progressed as larger rocks hid beneath last fall's leaves. My empty stomach growled loudly well before the trees began to thin and the shadows lightened considerably.

Brandle paused and turned to look behind us.

"We'll protect her with our lives from here, sir. I vow you will see your daughter again."

My father moved from the darker shadows, his glowing red gaze sweeping over my companions. When it settled on me, I could feel his profound heartache. Partly due to his inability to accompany me but mostly from the spell I'd cast. His memories would haunt him until the conditions of the spell were met.

"Wait for me near the glade. I will return to you as soon as I am able."

He nodded once and retreated into the Dark Forest once more.

"How long will your spell hold?" Garron asked.

"Until Eloise is freed," I said.

Eadric set his chest down and wrapped his arm around my shoulders.

"Our time here will not be idle, Sparrow."

I patted his side. "Aren't we idle now? Pick up your kingly ransom." He chuckled, and as he picked up his chest of gems, I glanced at Brandle. "Where do we go now?"

It took another hour through the thinning trees to reach a boulder-strewn field and a barely discernible path that Brandle said would lead to Adele. When he glanced back at me, the sight of my skeptical gaze brought a smile to his lips.

"Appearing on a more well-traveled route would have drawn attention."

"Right now, she's questioning if you know the difference between a road and a cattle path," Liam said with a smirk that I couldn't help but match.

Brandle's eyes crinkled at the corners as he nodded his agreement.

"It is indeed little more than a cattle path. But rest assured, we'll find what we need along the way."

"Good. I'm ready to put this in a wagon. My hands are numb," Daemon said.

"Do you see any wagons?" Edmund asked.

Daemon groaned and gave me a pleading look.

"Aren't your legs tired, Lamb?"

"Are you offering to carry me?"

He instantly perked up. "Yes. All the way to Adele."

I snorted and followed Garron and Brandle along the path. Edmund kept pace beside me. I glanced at the chest he carried and the pack strapped to his back.

"Is it wise for you to carry that in the open? Why not in your pack like the coins Brandle placed in my sling?"

"Coins?" Eadric asked from behind me. "What coins?"

I could feel his humor along with the others and knew he was jesting. They were all aware of the coins I carried.

"My meager possessions do not weigh enough to tug at my shoulder like this. Did you think I wouldn't notice?"

Each of them immediately offered to carry my bag for me. I waved away their concern.

"I want an explanation for openly displaying one source of wealth while hiding another."

"We're unlikely to encounter anyone until we reach our first destination," Edmund said. "It's easier to carry them than leave other supplies behind to make room in our packs."

"And the coin? Why am I carrying that?"

"So you can purchase whatever you wish whenever you wish it, Princess," Darian said from behind me.

"Shall I purchase that stone? Or perhaps this blade of grass?"

They laughed as I'd intended, and we continued along the rocky path that slowly meandered up the hill. At the top, I had a view of the rocky hills dotted with very little growth that surrounded us. Our current path led to another steeper hill occupied by a small flock of sheep. A very faint curl of smoke rose behind that hill.

"Is that where we're headed?" I asked.

"It is," Brandle said. "The farm belongs to Henry's brother and his wife. It's very remote, and they don't receive guests often. So our sudden appearance might startle them."

"Liam's appearance might," Daemon said, "but Sarah is going to fawn over mine. Don't worry, Lamb. I only have eyes for you."

Shaking my head at them, I focused on the path and not falling on the slopes. The crest of the final hill gave a perfect view of the tranquil valley below. A small cottage nestled in a meadow not far from the shores of a small lake. Chickens meandered in the muddy yard, and a goose squawked warning at the sight of us, drawing a curious cow from the opening of another small building.

"Hello to the mistress of the cottage," Brandle called as we descended the path.

A woman cried out from within the cottage, and a man appeared behind the cow, using his shoulder to push it aside.

When the man saw our group, he fell to his knees amidst the chickens and lifted his hands high.

"Thank you! Thank you!" he cried.

The woman ran out of the cottage and stopped at the sight of her husband before her gaze found us. She began weeping in earnest and ran to her husband. Had I not been able to feel their joy and love, I would have worried.

"Brandle, hurry and go to them before she dirties her skirt by joining her husband," I said.

He jogged the rest of the way and set his chest in the mud to help the man to his feet. The pair embraced Brandle. The woman, presumably the "Sarah" Daemon had mentioned, gripped him hard as the man patted Brandle's back with solid thumps.

Brandle's concern wrapped around me, and I knew he was speaking to them when Sarah abruptly quieted, but I couldn't hear his words.

"They've known you long then?" I asked.

"They have," Edmund said. "Since before we were cursed."

When Brandle stopped speaking, Sarah nodded and released him. She wiped her face dry and smiled welcomingly at us.

"This is a day I always hoped I would see," she said. "Welcome. Come inside. We don't have much, but what we have is yours."

She led the way into her cozy cottage. Like the one in our glade, it had a private room to the side, a kitchen, and space enough for sitting at their impressive table that held several loaves of bread. Edmund set his chest on the floor near the door, and the others quickly did the same before scrambling to take a seat at one of the two benches at the table. There wasn't an inch to spare between them.

Edmund caught my skirt between his fingers and tugged me into his lap. I elbowed him and tried to stand, but the arm he wrapped around my waist kept me firmly in place.

Flushing, I glanced at Sarah.

"You've arrived on a good day," she said, not looking at us as she stirred whatever she had in the pot over the fire. "Break those loaves up. There's butter too, Liam, in the cold storage."

He got up and went to the shelf behind the ladder.

"Release me," I whispered to Edmund.

"Not a chance."

He kissed my neck. My panicked gaze flew to Sarah's turned back, and I elbowed him again. He lightly bit me, and I struggled to contain the tingle of awareness that swept through me.

"Breathe, Kitten," Brandle said with a grin.

"How can she when Edmund won't leave her be?" Sarah said

without looking at us. "It's a wonder she ever agreed to stay with you lot if these are the manners you've shown her. Henry taught you better."

Brandle winked at me. "It was our persistent charm that won her over."

I snorted.

"You're obviously not cuddling her right, Edmund," Daemon said. "Give her over."

Edmund passed me left, and I had to defend my person from Daemon's roving hands.

"Daemon, I will send you flying out the door if you don't behave," I said.

"My turn," Darian said. "I know what she likes."

The dratted man plucked me from his brother's lap and kissed me soundly. In front of Sarah! And rather than stomping on his foot as I should have, I grabbed his shoulders and *let him*.

My lapse in judgment was brief, though, and I shot out of his lap. Liam caught me with one arm and steadied the crock of butter he held in his other hand.

"Breathe, Love," he said with a kiss to the side of my head. "The more you attempt to act as if you're not with us, the more they'll try to prove that you are."

"And when did you become so wise?" Sarah asked.

"The moment our precious Kellen attempted to unman Edmund for his behavior."

"That would be a defining moment of awakening, to be sure," the man said, entering the cottage.

Sarah laughed lightly and handed me a bowl of stew.

"It sounds like you've proven you're right for this lot. Now, don't be afraid to let the kingdom know it."

I nodded uncertainly and let Liam lead me back to his place where I sat on his lap and allowed Eadric to feed me while Brandle officially introduced me to Andrew and Sarah.

The couple entertained me with stories of the brothers' antics over the years since they had heard them from Henry whenever he came for supplies. The simple meal passed with laughter and my growing understanding of how loved the brothers were by the couple.

"What do you plan to do now that the spell is broken?" Andrew asked as Sarah cleared away the meal.

"Return to the home that was taken from us," Brandle said.

Andrew nodded slowly, looking thoughtful. I could feel his worry and his sadness, though.

"Will you stay here tonight?" Sarah asked.

All of them looked at me.

"The decision is not mine to make since I know not how far we are from Adele or what accommodations we might find between here and there."

"We'll stay," Liam said, hugging me from behind.

"Then the cottage is yours. Sarah and I will take the loft with the livestock," Andrew said.

When I would have protested, Liam gave my arm a quiet squeeze.

"Thank you for your kindness," Brandle said. "We won't forget it."

Left alone in their home, I twisted to look at Liam. "Why didn't you want me to say something? We should take the loft."

"No, we shouldn't." He kissed the tip of my nose. "You should take their bed and choose who you wish to sleep with you tonight."

I sputtered. "If you think for even a moment that any of you will bed me in this home, you are very mistaken."

"We only mean to sleep, Kitten," Brandle said.

"Though we could easily be convinced otherwise," Darian said.

Edmund cuffed the back of his head lightly, but I could feel his amusement.

"And can I not find sleep in the loft with the livestock?" I asked.

"Doubtful," Edmund said. "The straw is itchy and not something you're used to."

"Come," Eadric said, plucking me off Liam's lap. "It's best to sleep quickly. Andrew will wake us before dawn to load the wagon."

"We'll take a wagon to Adele?" I asked, curious.

"We will, but you'll likely wish to walk. The roads are not smooth, and your buttocks will ache within minutes." Eadric reached around to knead the aforementioned seat, and I batted his hands away.

"I believe I'll sleep with Liam and Garron tonight since the rest of you find too much joy in accosting me."

A CHILL WIND swept over the lake and tugged at my cloak as I stood in the yard surrounded by my men. They forked hay into the back of the wagon and debated if it was enough to see me comfortably to our destination.

"Please stop making it sound as if I am weak or fragile," I said. "I am neither."

"It is our egos that are both, Lamb," Daemon said. "Grant us this small favor, and allow us our concern for your comfort."

"Your concern is delaying us," I said. "I did not wake three hours before dawn to witness this spectacle."

Eadric chuckled and hugged me from behind.

"Patience, Sparrow. Sarah won't let us leave without feeding us first."

"Then I should go inside and help her."

Eadric held firm when I tried escaping his embrace.

"But then you'll miss why this wagon took months to make," Darian said.

He ran inside and returned with one of the gem-filled chests. I watched Andrew push in a section of wood on the side of the wagon and turn it. A panel fell open to the right, exposing that the wagon had a hidden compartment just tall enough to fit the chests or a slim person.

One by one, they wedged the chests into the space.

"A king's ransom," Andrew said as he resealed the compartment and winked at me.

Sarah called out that the food was ready, and we returned to the cottage to eat the boiled oats with honey. Eadric giddily took his seat across from me and radiated extra joy in feeding me. When I said I was finished, he ate the rest of my bowl and his own.

Sarah surprised me by pulling each of them down into a motherly embrace and kissing their brows. Seeing them bask in her affection melted my heart, but it also created a sad ache for the childhoods they'd endured because of their curse.

I knew they'd been in the glade with Henry after their parents died, and I knew a caster had cursed them, but I didn't know anything more about them. Why had their parents died? Why had Henry hidden them away? Was it due to the queen's need to kill small children as Eadric had said? But if so, why hadn't Henry married and raised these men as his own to allow them happy childhoods?

Though I had so many questions I wished to ask, I understood Brandle's fear of sharing too much at once. Hadn't I felt the same?

Despite my willingness to allow them to tell me their history in their own time, my curiosity grew as I watched them work with Andrew to prepare for our journey. They laughed with ease and patted the older man's back companionably, completely different from the guarded men I'd first met when entering their glade.

Edmund and Eadric held the torches aloft as Andrew hitched a sturdy ox to the wagon. The rest stacked their packs at the front of the wagon just behind the seat.

"It's time," Brandle said.

Garron lifted me into the wagon's bed and settled in beside me. Sarah waved at us as Brandle took the spot next to Andrew, and Daemon lounged on the other side of me. With the torch-bearers leading the way and Darian and Liam trailing behind the wagon, I waved farewell to Sarah.

"They won't disappoint you, Kellen," she called. "They are good men of their word."

I nodded and looked up at Garron.

"Rest," he said. "It's a long journey."

Secured between him and Daemon, I closed my eyes and slept until the sun rose. Once the torches were no longer needed, Edmund and Eadric switched places with Daemon and Garron, using themselves to steady me on the rough road.

Close to midday, we reached another farm. Vines covered the decaying buildings, and waist-high grass moved in the breeze in the central yard.

"The water's still good here," Andrew said, directing the ox to the well, which looked like it was the only thing not being over-taken by nature.

"Why was the farm abandoned?" I asked as Edmund helped me down to stretch my legs.

"The family here disappeared," Andrew said. "The wife was a strong caster. She made the best honey cakes."

I could feel his profound sadness and anger as he turned away to water the ox. All of their emotions echoed Andrew's.

"It was the queen then?" I asked.

"It was," Andrew said.

CHAPTER 5

WHEN I SPOTTED AN INN POSITIONED AT THE CROSSROADS AHEAD, I also glimpsed the white spires of Adele's castle over the distant hills. A subtle tingle of warning crept along the back of my neck, whispering that danger waited in Adele. But I'd already known that.

"How long until we reach Adele?" I asked.

"Tomorrow," Brandle said, toying with my braid.

"Will Sarah be okay by herself until you return?"

"Yes. She's used to me making these trips," Andrew said.

I glanced at Brandle. "How often do you do this?"

"We've never accompanied Andrew before," he said.

I could feel his thoughts. What we were doing now wasn't safe. They weren't safe. But his resolve was unshakable, and his purpose wasn't only to help me free Eloise. He was determined to reclaim the life that had been taken from him and his brothers.

"Can you share with me the risks? I have no wish to make a mistake that brings ruin to us all."

"We mustn't draw attention to ourselves," he said.

"How do you plan to achieve that? Your face will draw attention, no matter where you go, Brandle. And seven handsome men fawning over one woman will assuredly draw curious stares."

"Am I fawning?" he asked with a playful smile.

"Most assuredly."

He chuckled and released my braid.

"We vow to use discretion in public settings," he said. "And though you may see a handsome face, most others will see our worn, poor clothes and pay us little mind."

I wished he were wrong, but he wasn't. So many measured a person based on the wealth the person possessed.

Brandle eased away from me and leaned against the side of the wagon, as did Darian. Sitting alone, I turned in my seat to look at the inn.

"It's best if you keep your eyes down, Princess," Darian said.

"Why?"

"You will draw in suitors like flies to honey, and we will draw unwanted attention when we're forced to send them off in droves."

I rolled my eyes at him, demurely tucked my chin, and waited for the wagon to pull into the yard.

Andrew hopped down from the seat and spoke to the lad at the stable while Darian helped me down and quietly told me to stay near the wagon.

Peering up from under my lashes, I watched Andrew count out a few coppers, which he handed over to the boy; then he motioned for me.

"Move faster, girl," he said, sounding gruff. "I want dinner before it grows cold." He looked at Brandle and Darian. "Water and unhitch the ox right this time."

"Yes, sir," Brandle said, striding away.

I withheld my snort at their act and hurried to Andrew's side with the rest.

We ate a simple stew the inn provided and then went to the barn for the night. I slept in the back of the wagon with Andrew while the others found less desirable locations in the loft or stood guard.

It felt as though I'd barely slept when the gentle rocking of the wagon woke me. The flicker of the nearby torches was the only light in the otherwise dark night.

"How long have we been traveling?" I asked as I sat up.

Eadric, who was walking beside the wagon, said, "About an hour, I think."

"Why didn't you wake me?"

"No need to," Liam said from the other side. When I looked his way, he handed me a biscuit. "If it wouldn't draw attention, half of us would be in the wagon with you."

I took a bite of my biscuit and looked beyond Garron and Daemon to search the horizon for any hint of Adele.

"How much longer until we arrive?" I asked.

"The city lies beyond the next rise," Brandle said.

I looked at him, Edmund, and Darian, who walked behind the wagon.

"Wouldn't I draw less attention if I'm on the bench beside Andrew when we arrive?"

Brandle nodded, and Liam held out his hand to help me move into place. The bench was harder than the hay-filled bed.

Within moments, I was internally wincing and recalling the last wagon I'd ridden with Hugh and Eloise. The road to Drisdall had been smooth then, but our lives had already been turbulent.

Please be well, sister, I thought.

Cresting the hill, I saw Adele laid out before us. A stone wall surrounded the city. Oil lamps burned brightly in the pre-dawn darkness, illuminating the slumbering streets and making it easy to see the curls of smoke rising from the occasional home.

It seemed peaceful enough. Yet, that subtle tingle of warning buzzed along my skin as I took in the sight. It whispered that Adele wasn't what it seemed. But was anything what it seemed? Rarely. Regardless, I knew we had no other choice but to enter.

The road on which we traveled met with a more established one at the bottom of the hill. Another wagon rumbled along it, heading for a city gate guarded by at least ten armored men.

"I didn't know Adele had a defensive wall," I said. "Is it left-over from a bygone time, or have there been attacks?"

"It's new," Andrew said, "and best not discussed in the open."

"I understand."

As our wagon slowly rumbled down the hill, assisted by Andrew's braking, the other wagon reached the gates. I watched the guards search it thoroughly and speak with the driver. We were still too far away to hear what was being said. When the guard stepped back, the wagon pulled through the gates without an issue.

Garron reached out to pat the ox with his free hand and glanced back at me. He dipped his head and cast his eyes down meaningfully.

"Stubborn," I muttered. "It won't be me that calls attention but them."

Andrew chuckled, proving he'd heard me.

As we approached, I lowered my head and gaze to appear less noteworthy. Then, I opened myself to feel what the guards were feeling. They were tired and ready for the next watch to relieve them. One of them resented the queen and her order to guard the gate.

From under my lashes, I looked for that guard. His nearly white beard bespoke his age.

The older guard stepped out from the rest and lifted his hand as we approached.

"Halt. State your business in Adele and the duration of your stay."

Garron and Daemon stopped walking quicker than the ox. Andrew drew back on the reins and cursed at the poor creature until it listened.

"We're here to find a new ram for my sheep and my daughter."

A few of the guards laughed, but that laughter died as they noted how many men were with us. I could feel the older guard's suspicion growing.

"Seven extra men to help? Are they brothers?"

"Brothers and cousins. Three are mine, and four are my sister's sons. Need the help to watch the girl and the ram," Andrew said. "Heard Adele isn't safe for either."

Their suspicion turned to humor again, except for the head guard.

"And the duration of your stay?"

"If the market is as well attended as I've heard, a day or two at most, I hope."

Feeling the old guard's attention shift to me, I picked that moment to lift my head just briefly enough to meet his gaze. Though I knew a beautiful appearance wasn't the sum of my worth, it still held value, and I used it to my advantage when necessary. Softening my expression, I presented myself as a beautiful, shy young miss with a single glance.

The guard's suspicions faded instantly.

"The market is well-attended, and you are right about needing the extra help. Watch over what's yours carefully. The Guard won't help find what you misplace."

"I understand," Andrew said.

The old guard stepped back and waved for us to enter the city.

As we passed through the gate, I saw another man seated at a desk in the alcove. He studied us as we passed and made notes on a piece of parchment.

I waited until we were a suitable distance away before asking, "What happens if we don't find the ram and my future husband in the allotted time?"

"No need to feel pressured. You heard the guard. They won't come looking for us if finding you a husband takes longer. That doesn't mean you can tarry, though. Watch and listen carefully so you can make a wise choice. The rest of your life depends on this."

"Father," Garron said in soft warning.

Andrew grunted acknowledgment and continued along the road.

The sun kissed the horizon by the time we stopped before a stable on the outskirts of Adele. Though that tingle of warning persisted, my intuition said it was no more dangerous than any other place we'd passed despite the pervading smell of dung and mold.

Brandle strode toward the wagon and helped me down.

"I'm sorry these are the only accommodations we can offer," he said softly.

"You have no reason to be. Life isn't meant to be lived without hardships. Overcoming difficulties defines us. Life is the whetstone, and we're the dull blades."

"Some of us are duller than others," Edmund said, walking around us. He swatted Daemon's hands away from the harness and showed him how it was done.

Brandle tweaked my chin lightly to regain my attention.

"Don't go anywhere alone. Always have one of us with you. Understood?"

I nodded and accepted his proffered arm.

He guided me to the run-down inn next to the moldering stable.

When we entered, a woman dressed in a worn gown and well-mended, clean apron looked up from the vegetables she was chopping. A hint of fresh bread and savory stew drifted from the scrubbed hearth, making the inn feel less unfit for habitation.

"Stabling or hungry?" she asked.

"Both," Brandle said. "And we'll need whatever rooms you have for two nights."

Her brows lifted. "Two nights?"

He nodded. "Nine bowls of stew, please. With bread. And honey, if you have it."

She scurried to gather the required bowls as Brandle led me to one of the public tables. Eadric, Darian, Daemon, and Liam carried our packs in.

"The stew smells delicious, Mistress," Eadric said with a charming smile.

"Aren't you sweet." She slid the bowl with a larger portion in front of him.

I could feel Darian's amusement.

The woman promised to have the rooms ready before we finished our stew and hurried up the stairs.

"Did she say how many rooms?" Andrew asked.

"No," I said.

He grunted and started eating.

I didn't think the number of rooms would matter. They wouldn't let me sleep alone even if the inn had twelve rooms.

"The bedding is clean, and the rooms are being aired," the woman said as she descended the stairs.

"How many rooms?" Andrew asked.

"Four."

While Andrew settled the bill with the inn's mistress, I followed Garron and Darian to the rooms. Each barely had enough space for a bed and a washbasin. They put my bag in the one at the end of the hallway under the eaves.

"Girl!" Andrew called from below.

"Did he forget my name?" I whispered to Garron.

He shook his head. "It's better not to use it."

"Ah."

I hurried down the stairs and looked at Andrew.

"I'm taking your cousins to the sheep market. Stay with your brothers."

Since I wasn't sure which of them was supposed to be my direct kin, I kept my gaze on Andrew as I nodded.

He motioned for Brandle, Daemon, Darian, and Liam to follow him and left me with Edmund, Eadric, and Garron.

"Mistress, do you have a deck of cards?" Eadric asked.

THE OTHERS DIDN'T RETURN until well past midday.

"Good news," Andrew said, walking in. "We found a ram."

I looked through the open door and saw Brandle leading the animal to the stable. Questions churned in my mind. They hadn't truly gone to the market for a ram, had they? I'd thought it'd been a ploy.

Garron nudged my leg under the table, and I returned my gaze to my cards.

"The seller mentioned a new breed I'm interested in. He sent his son home for it. It will take him a few days to reach their farm."

I could feel the mistress's joy just as I could feel Andrew's need to find a reason to end our stay at this inn.

"And a husband for me?" I asked.

"That might take more time." He glanced at the brothers. "You're all of an age to look for a wife as well. I doubt many of them will wish to remain in the country to sheep farm with our family. There may be more opportunities for you here. My sister always hated that she couldn't return to Adele."

"Opportunities?" Eadric asked. He sounded confused, but I knew he wasn't.

"The farmer mentioned there are many homes for sale," Andrew said. "Go. All of you. Explore Adele. Find a home that will attract a bride and a way to support one."

"Yes, sir," Eadric said, setting his cards aside and rising.

The seven of them left quickly. I glanced at Andrew, but

rather than gain any clues regarding their purpose, I watched him signal to the innkeeper that he'd like a bowl of stew.

"After you're finished, can we go to the market?" I asked.

Andrew paused with a spoon partway to his mouth. "It's safer to wait until your brothers and cousins return."

"You've sent them out to look for homes and wives. I doubt they'll return before dark."

He grunted his acknowledgment but didn't agree to go to the market with me. I could feel his resistance to it and glanced at the innkeeper. She was busy kneading more bread.

Having nothing better to do, I joined her and offered my hands in exchange for news regarding Adele.

"I've lived outside of it my whole life and am nervous about living here," I said. "I've heard rumors, and my kin won't let me out of their sight. Is it truly not safe here?"

She slowly straightened and searched my gaze. Whatever she saw or didn't see there assured her that my question was sincere. She glanced meaningfully toward Andrew and toward the door. I understood her intent. She didn't wish to speak of anything in front of him.

"I'm wondering if Father's ox is safe in the stable when it's unattended."

"It's always safer to watch over what you need to protect, girl," Andrew said, proving he was listening to us as he ate.

When he finished, he didn't move to check the livestock but slouched in the chair, folded his hands over his waist, and closed his eyes. That he felt I needed more protection than the livestock worried me. Was it truly that dangerous here? Why had he let the rest leave alone then? While I knew they weren't alone but had each other, it still concerned me that he'd allowed them—strangers to this dangerous town—to leave with no experienced guide.

"Go practice your letters and numbers," Andrew said

suddenly. "Garron packed your books. It might help you find what we came here for."

The innkeeper patted my hand consolingly and waved me away. I wiped my hands and went upstairs with the key to my room. They'd moved all their packs there, so it wasn't troublesome to look through them all.

I found books, and as I suspected, they weren't the primers Andrew had hinted they were. Garron had packed the spell books I hadn't yet read. Since the window above the bed provided adequate light, I made myself comfortable and opened the first book.

It was easy to lose track of time as I learned more about what a caster could do. The complexity of some of the spells astounded me, and I wondered how the first caster had discovered them. It had to have taken time and endless experimentation. One of the spells did more than explain the steps to cast; it explained why a caster needed to do them.

For the healing tea spell, the caster's hair helped to imbue the tea with the caster's energy and intent. I frowned and thought of how I'd touched my energy to the tea outside of the piece of hair the second time I'd brewed it. Did that mean that the hair wasn't necessary?

It also said that the candle was used to set the pace of the healing. The smaller the candle, the slower the boil, and the slower the spell would take hold. It then cautioned that using a fire to boil the water was too quick for many injuries, and the rapid healing could cause bones to set incorrectly or the skin to grow over stitches.

Intrigued by my newfound understanding, I didn't notice the weaker afternoon light until I stretched the ache from my spine. Seeing it was close to dinner time brought out my restlessness again.

If they'd returned, they would have called for me. What were they still doing?

After only a moment of hesitation, I cautiously opened myself to the energy around me. It was different than lifting the lid off my well or connecting to my energy. Opening myself to what was around me felt more like quieting my mind to listen to the sounds of the forest when I was alone.

I sensed Andrew and the innkeeper below, the sheep and the ox in the stable, the boy hiding in the hay, and the people in the nearby houses. Then, I stretched myself farther and farther until I saw all of Adele's people.

It was easy enough to see the casters. They glowed brighter than those without the ability to sense energy. The unhindered folk were dimmer and the animals dimmer still.

After spending so much time with the seven brothers, I'd thought I would be able to tell them apart from everyone else, but I couldn't. In order to do that, I knew I would need to do more than simply open my senses. I would need to touch my well. However, I wasn't certain I could do so without being detected by other casters.

I looked from the book resting on the bed to the door.

Andrew would stop me if I told him what I meant to do. As would the others.

My gaze drifted to the window. Brandle and the others would never let me out of their sights again if I left without word. Yet, I refused to remain safely tucked away while they went about their business.

Uncertain how much time I had before they returned, I quickly stripped from my gown and dressed in Liam's ill-fitted clothing. Even with my hair tucked in an old cap, I knew my face would draw attention. So I touched my fingers to the room's charred candlewick and filled in my sideburns and dirtied under my nose.

Satisfied, I opened the window and looked out. The building's derelict exterior benefited me. I easily found footholds in the missing chinking between logs and climbed down into the side yard between the inn and its vacant neighbor.

Sensing the energy of the people around me made it easier to avoid notice. The boy hidden in the hay never saw me as I silently crept around the back of the building and cut through the yard of the business behind it.

I made my way along Adele's outskirts until I found two casters living near one another. My hope was that, if they sensed me, they would think it was the other caster.

As I strolled by, I nudged the lid on my well and touched the energy within while keeping my senses open. Neither caster hid themself. In increments, I removed the lid from my well, and it wasn't until it was almost halfway off that the energy from both casters immediately disappeared. I promptly hid my energy and continued on my way.

People filled the main streets. With their heads down, they minded their own business as they moved about. I could feel their tension and fear, which increased each time an armored group of guards patrolled the street they walked.

Following the locals' example and listening to the warning that continually tingled along my skin, I avoided the guards as well.

It took almost an hour to reach another set of casters living close together. Both homes had signs advertising their services and a large flat stone in front of their door to keep visitors from tracking in mud. I knocked on the door of the caster whose stone was more worn smooth.

A woman not much older than me opened the door. Her gaze swept over me from head to boots then back to my face.

"You look like trouble. What do you want?"

"A spell."

"Obviously. What kind?"

"Might we speak inside, please?"

She glanced up and down the street then stepped back to let me in.

CHAPTER 6

"If you want a spell that will change you into the man you're pretending to be, I can't help you. Transfiguration spells, even the temporary ones, are beyond my ability."

"You know I'm a woman?"

"I have eyes. And no man ever says please."

"I'll keep that in mind," I said, looking around her shop at the herbs and amulets. I recognized very little.

"What do you want then?" she asked impatiently.

"My father brought me to Adele to wed me off," I said, keeping with Andrew's story. "I would like to prevent that."

"Keep dressing as you are, and it should do the trick."

"We both know there are men who either won't care or will feel that a good beating will help me remember the proper attire for a woman."

She sighed and turned away from me. "My first husband was like that." She picked up a stone from one of the shelves.

"First? How many times have you been married?"

"Three."

I knew I shouldn't ask, but I couldn't help myself.

"How old are you?"

494

"Twenty-three. I married the first one at fourteen. He had a pretty face, and I thought I was in love...until he started hitting me for not sweeping the floor the way he liked."

"What happened to him?" I asked.

She shrugged and set the stone and herbs she'd collected on her work table.

"He disappeared like men often do around here."

She felt no distress over that statement, and I didn't ask what happened with her last two husbands as she began mixing herbs together. She added water to the pot and set it on the holder above a candle that she lit. I recognized her hair wrapped around it.

"What spell are you casting?" I asked as she began to murmur.

She shushed me and continued.

Knowing I could erase her memory if she discovered what I was doing, I touched my energy to hers and felt for her intent. She was casting a spell for bad luck in marriage. It was the same spell she'd cast on herself when her first husband started hitting her.

I felt her pain and sorrow. Its weight pulled at me, and I found myself searching her memories to discover why. Adogen, the caster before me, had lost so many children due to the men she'd wed. Beaten out of her body before she could love them or sold once they'd arrived. And the root of it was the spell she'd buried deep in her bones due to that first man.

She scooped out a portion of the tea with a small wooden ladle and held it out to me.

"Drink it," she said.

I looked at the steaming liquid and sensed the spell within.

"What will it do to me?"

"It will ensure you don't have to live your life with a man who doesn't love you."

I nodded and took the ladle from her.

Remembering how the last spell had taken root, I partially

opened my well and drank. Instead of settling into my bones, my well absorbed its energy and robbed it of its intent.

"There. It is done. That'll be seven copper," Adogen said.

I dug into the coin purse I'd hidden on my person. When I set the coins in her palm, I touched the spell binding her with *my* intent.

"This blessing is old and passed from generation to generation, or so I am told. When you wish to find a love who will cherish you above all others, find a man supporting his mother. His heart will know how to give gentle care, and with him, a fruitful life you will bear."

The spell lifted from her bones and entered my well.

"Guard yourself well, my friend. I hope you never again have to marry a man who doesn't love you."

She frowned at me. "You're an odd one."

I smiled. "Since I am wearing a soot mustache, I can understand your opinion of me."

She chuckled and pocketed the coin. She felt lighter. Happier.

But most importantly, she hadn't sensed I'd cast on her.

"Thank you for the spell," I said, heading for the door.

"Wait," she called before I reached it. "You're not from here, are you? Turre, I mean."

"I'm not."

"A word of advice then," she said. "Go back to wherever it is you came from. It's not safe here."

"You're not the first person to say that. But no one will tell me why."

"Because this is a land where the strong devour the weak. Where parents sell their own children to survive. And no one does anything to make it better."

"And if someone tried?"

"They would quickly find themselves in the royal dungeon."

I nodded my understanding and left without another word.

Outside, the sun sat low on the horizon. Long shadows

covered the roads as I made my way back to the inn. The number of guards patrolling grew, and I was forced to take several wrong turns to pass undetected.

Just before the sun set, I felt Edmund prowling down the center of a busy market street. Anger radiated from him, and people scurried out of his way. He ducked inside a dress shop, and I felt his anger grow along with his fear.

He was looking for me.

I slipped into a nearby alley and picked up a stone smaller than a pea. He didn't leave me to wait long. When he passed the alley's opening, I flicked the stone at him, helping it stay true with some air, and it hit his arm.

The way he stopped dead sent a thrill through me, and some inner demon made me smile when he slowly turned his head to look at me. I felt his relief, along with the need to toss me over his knee and thrash my backside until I couldn't sit comfortably.

I beckoned him to join me with a crook of my finger.

"You left," he said lowly when he reached me.

"I did. But in a way that did not call attention to me. Unlike you, Edmund. The way you just stalked down the street drew every eye. Be upset with me, but do not show it. Not here. Not now."

His hand captured the back of my head, and his mouth was on mine before I even sensed his intent. He kissed me with hunger, anger, and desperation. As much as I wished to lose myself in his kiss, I knew neither of us could afford that. So, I stomped on his toe.

He pulled back with a growl and glared at me.

"By all appearances, you're kissing another man in an alley. Stop this madness, or I will make you," I hissed.

He let out a long breath and released me. After ensuring my hair was properly tucked up into my cap, I turned away from him and started down the narrow alley.

"Where are you going?" he asked, following.

"Back. I imagine you're not the only one upset."

He said nothing else as we weaved our way to the inn's road. When we reached it, I motioned for him to continue.

"Not without you."

"And how will it look to everyone paying attention if I return dressed as this?" He opened his mouth to answer, but I cut him off. "Take a leisurely stroll down this road; then check the stable. There's a boy hiding in the hay who might like a bite to eat. While you're busy, I will find a way to reappear as if I've been there the whole time."

His anger boiled again. "Your departure will be discussed when you return."

"Of that, I have no doubt."

He pivoted away from me and took one angry stride before visibly relaxing and slowing down. Satisfied he was listening, I continued to the neighboring street and cut through the side yards of the vacant homes to reach the inn.

Despite the darkness, climbing up to my open window was easier than the descent. However, my arrival did not go as unnoticed as my departure.

Liam sat on the bed. Anger radiated from him as well—which upset me a great deal. The few times I'd seen him angry had been because of the trackers. This time, as he watched me pull myself through the narrow window, his anger was directed at me.

"Is your anger out of fear, or did I unwittingly do something that will cause harm to you or your brothers?" I asked once I was on my feet.

"I'm not yet certain."

"Does the innkeeper know I'm missing?"

"She does. It was hard to keep quiet about it when we searched every inch of this place."

"Did she tell anyone else?"

Suspicion crept into his gaze.

"Why?"

"I need to know what tale to weave since we can't very well tell her I snuck out dressed as a man, can we?" He watched me wash my face and frowned when I motioned for him to turn around.

"I won't escape out the window, Liam. I simply wish to change before the others return."

He stood and presented me with his back. I quickly shed his clothes and slipped into my own.

"Edmund was out looking for me," I said as I laced my gown. "When did you return?"

"An hour before dusk."

"That is unfortunate. I'm finished dressing."

He turned around.

"Why unfortunate? Because you were discovered?"

"Of course."

He tipped back his head and closed his eyes. "You're going to drive us mad. I can see that already. Brandle will find a stone home and lock you in a room with no windows and no thatching.

I withheld my sigh and fought not to give in to my frustration. Even my mother, who loved Eloise and me very dearly, had never sought to restrict us. She'd guided us to make better choices, certainly, but she'd never kept us from doing as we wished. And that was what it felt like the men in my life were trying to do. I knew that wasn't truly the case—they had no wish to confine me but only to keep me safe—however, in their minds, confinement meant safety, not a loss of freedom.

Rather than address that, I said, "Shall we wait for the others downstairs?"

Edmund was just entering the common area as I reached the landing at the top. I sensed the innkeeper at her work table.

"Did you find her?" she asked Edmund, not seeing me or Liam.

Edmund glanced at me, and I quickly shook my head.

"I checked the dress shops you mentioned, but none of them had seen her."

"Perhaps your brothers will have better luck. Dinner will be ready shortly. She was very curious about Adele."

Edmund sat next to Andrew, who also hadn't yet noticed me.

If I simply descended the stairs, I doubted the innkeeper would believe any tale I might tell about slipping past her unnoticed twice. While I knew I could remove her memory of me coming down the stairs and replace it with something believable, I also knew none of the brothers would like that. So I decided to try something else. If I could move air and absorb the energy from water until it disappeared, could I not do the reverse?

I drew energy from my well, willing it to form water in the air. Mist gathered at my feet, and I quickly withdrew my energy. Filling the inn with fog was hardly an inconspicuous entrance. How else could I hide myself from her sight?

With a glance at the lit hearth, the candles casting light in the room, and the open door, an idea formed. Smiling, I created a wind that swept through the room. It extinguished the candles and made the fire sputter and spark dangerously.

Smoke roiled from the hearth, filling the room.

The innkeeper ran to stomp out the sparks that landed on the wood floors. Edmund rushed to help her. With their backs to us, I pulled Liam down the stairs with me and then pushed him toward the others as I slipped out the back door.

"That's never happened before," I heard the innkeeper say.

"Let's hope it never happens again," Liam said.

Coughing lightly, I walked in through the back door and waved a hand in front of me.

"Why is it so smokey?" I asked.

The innkeeper's gaze went from me to Andrew as he stood suddenly.

"Do you have any idea how much you've upset your... kin? Me?"

"Were you looking for me?" I asked, mustering every ounce of innocence I possessed, which was a good deal since Eloise and I had practiced often.

"Where have you been?" Andrew demanded.

"I went for a stroll in the market. The folk here aren't friendly, but I did find a caster who was quite helpful."

"A caster?" Edmund asked. His anger hadn't lessened with my return. "What business do you have with a caster?"

"My own, I should think."

Garron and Darian chose that moment to enter. I could feel their relief at the sight of me.

"Trouble, you have three seconds to give me a better answer," Edmund said.

"Answer for what?" Darian asked.

"Why she went to a caster," Liam said.

They all looked at me. I gave my most innocent smile. "For my bleeding pains, of course."

"Oh, you poor thing," the innkeeper said. "You should have come to me first. I have some tea I can brew for you."

With her in the kitchen and distracted, Edmund took a menacing step toward me.

"I will not be bullied, Edmund," I said with soft warning.

"And I will have the real answer."

Brandle and Eadric entered. Their emotions ran from joy—Eadric—to relief and anger—Brandle. Eadric hurried toward me and swept me up in a hug.

"We were so worried about you, Sparrow."

I hugged him tightly in return and, aware of our audience, withdrew from his comforting embrace.

"I'm sorry to have caused you concern. But I'm well. I promise."

The innkeeper harrumphed. "Your menfolk won't learn to care for you if you don't speak plainly about what ails you, child. Whether they want to hear it or not."

Brandle cocked his head and studied me. His curiosity and worry wrapped around me.

"Are you unwell?" he asked.

"In the head," Edmund muttered.

"She went to see a caster," Liam said. "For her monthlies."

No one missed the disbelieving intonation he used while speaking the last part—including the innkeeper, who shook her head and muttered under her breath about thick-headed men and questioned what the world had come to that there was no consideration left.

"What's done is done," I said.

Daemon walked in. His gaze locked with mine, reflecting the hurt and betrayal I felt from him.

"You've returned," he said.

"What's wrong?" I asked.

"Did you truly not want to wed?"

"What?" I was so shocked that I wasn't sure I'd heard correctly.

"I was asking around for you. The caster you saw said you'd been there and spoke of your wish never to marry. The spell she gave you will ensure no marriage will last."

I could feel the innkeeper looking at me in disbelief, and I wanted to cuff the lot of them for even attempting to have a conversation with me in front of her. What did they think I could truly say? That I remained true to them? All seven of them? My supposed kin? That would certainly draw attention.

"Have you nothing to say?" Brandle asked softly.

"I do. Look at yourselves, and you'll know the answer. Now, if you're done treating me like a child, I believe I'll retire for the evening."

I turned on my heel and climbed the stairs with a level of refinement I hoped would convey my annoyance. Were they purposely being unreasonable? Did they truly not understand I could say nothing in my defense in front of the innkeeper?

Brandle's hand stopped the door from closing.

Facing him, I waited for him to speak. The silence grew, as did his anger.

"Do you truly have nothing to say for yourself?" he asked.

"I believe, in your current mood, any words I utter would be wasted."

"Try," he said. His imploring gaze loosened my tongue.

"Do you truly believe I would let another cast a spell on me?" I asked quietly. "I am not so foolish, Brandle."

"Yet you climbed out a window, dressed as a man, in a place we've repeatedly warned you is dangerous."

"Running through the Dark Forest was dangerous, too. Yet, if I hadn't risked it, I would not be standing before you now."

He pinched the bridge of his nose. I could feel the storm of his raw emotions abrading him from the inside, and I captured his face between my palms.

"What is it that truly troubles you, Brandle?"

His turbulent gaze held mine.

"We thought we'd lost you."

"You will never lose me. I'm steadfast and too resilient to fall."

I kissed him lightly on the lips. He made a pained sound and tried pulling me closer. I slipped from his grasp and shook my head at him.

"You lecture about caution in one breath then do risky things in the next. Edmund looked more fierce than any armored guards I saw today when he strode down the street looking for me."

"Did the guards take note of you?" Brandle asked, gripping my arms firmly.

"Of course not. I did nothing to stand out."

He sighed heavily. "Will you tell me the real reason you went to the caster?"

"To test how well hidden I am from other casters."

Understanding lit his gaze, along with immeasurable fear. "You cast? Here? In Adele?"

"Breathe, Brandle. I didn't openly cast. Only small manipulations. I promise. What I was testing was the effectiveness of my hiding."

"This lid on your well," Brandle said, understanding.

"Yes. In order to cast, I need to touch the energy within my well. I needed to know if I could lift that lid without being detected so I could cast if needed. And I can."

"Don't do it again. Promise me. There are casters in Adele with more power than you can imagine. If they even catch a hint of your ability, you would be in danger, Kellen. Promise me you won't do it again."

"I promise not to take unnecessary risks. Now tell me what you did today. Did you find any help?"

He glanced at the open window before saying, "It'll take time, Kitten. Please be patient."

"I am, Brandle, which is why I'm willing to wait for you to share what you've truly been doing with your time."

"We've found a home. It's run down like this one but large enough for the eight of us. We can move there tomorrow."

"What about—"

"Uncle will return home."

I heard a creak in the hallway and cursed myself for not paying more attention.

A moment later, the innkeeper knocked on the door Brandle had closed when he'd started kissing me.

"I have your tea, dear."

Brandle opened the door and bade the woman to enter.

"Don't leave without an escort again, or Edmund truly will take you over his knee out of fear for your safety. You know how unhappy that will make the rest of us."

I nodded and watched him leave.

"They're a protective lot, aren't they? Not very understanding, though." She motioned for me to sit on the bed then joined me as I sipped the tea. "It's normal for a girl not to want to leave the home she knows to marry a man she doesn't. But by using a caster to ruin your marriage before it's even formed, aren't you removing any possible chance for your future happiness? Not all men are bad. Look at your kin and how much they care about you. Even the gruff one who wants to swat your backside only does so out of love and fear for your safety."

I nodded, and she patted my hand.

"Any spell done can be undone. Take one of your men with you tomorrow and have the caster remove it. All right?"

"I will."

CHAPTER 7

Surrounded by the brothers, I looked at the place they'd found to be our home for the duration of our stay in Adele. The house looked no better than the inn. Chinking was missing between the boards. One of the upper windows was broken. And the front door hung askew.

"Did you purchase it outright or rent it?" I asked.

"We've rented it for a month, but we can repair whatever we wish," Darian said.

"How generous of the landlord," I said.

"It's a widow with an infant," Eadric said. "She would have sold the house if anyone were interested in it. It belonged to her deceased husband's parents, who died almost eighteen years ago."

Guilt wrapped around me, as it should. A restless night alone in a strange bed had left me with little rest, and the warning prickling under my skin was wearing on my nerves.

"I apologize," I said. "I was being petty without considering another's circumstance."

"Which isn't like you, Snow. What's wrong?"

"Is there no other way to help Eloise than here?" I asked.

I felt Brandle's concern grow. "Why? What is it?"

"A persistent whisper of danger. I felt it the moment I saw the white towers, which led me to believe it was grave to feel it from such a distance. Yet, the feeling hasn't grown strong enough for that."

Brandle shared a look with Edmund. I could feel their secret in that glance. Whatever it was, they still feared me learning of it. Was their secret tied to why I was feeling this warning?

"Are you lying to me?"

Brandle's hurt and disbelief were real.

"Never. At least, not intentionally. What do you believe I'm lying about?"

"That we're truly here to gain help for my sister."

He took my hands in his and leaned down so our eyes were on equal ground.

"As we are now, we are powerless to stand against the person holding your sister. We are here to gain help."

I let out a slow breath and nodded.

"Come inside," he said. "You'll feel better once we're settled."

He led me to the door, which Darian hurried to shoulder open.

"Liam and I will work on this," he said as I passed.

I walked into the main living area of the home. To my right, a broken table sat in the middle of the neglected kitchen. Dust swirled in the sunlight streaming through the dirty window. My gaze swept through that room and the one to the left. No other furniture remained in the lower portion of the home, but I could see where there'd been a lounge and rug near the base of the stairs and how there would be plenty of room for all of us.

"I'll start sorting the kitchen," Eadric said, moving around me.

Garron joined him, and Brandle took my hand to lead the way to the second floor. The stairs creaked ominously under his weight.

"They've already held me," he said with a grin at my worried glance.

We reached the top without falling through, and he showed me the four small bedrooms above the main living area.

"You can take this one," he said, opening the door to a room with a broken windowpane. "The chimney will keep it warmer."

I glanced back at him. "I'll be sleeping alone?"

"Not if we have a choice," Edmund said, entering behind us. "Daemon and I will replace the glass."

He started disassembling the window, and I left the room to look at the others. No beds. No furnishings of any kind. Likely, the owner had sold off what she could to support herself.

"Are the nearby homes occupied?" I asked.

"No. Only the ones at the entrance to the street. An old cobbler and woodcutter."

"We can finally buy the wood we burn!" Daemon called with joy from my room.

I could feel Edmund's growing irritation and hurried back to stop a cuffing.

"Think, Daemon," I said as I entered the room. "How will it look if we buy wood when none of us are employed? Based on the weight of my bag, I would guess half the coins we possessed were used to rent this home. Garron said it would take a fortnight or more to obtain the help we need. Endless days in which we will need to feed ourselves. We'll need our existing coin for that, assuming we'll use other means to compensate for the help we acquire."

Daemon's playful expression turned contrite. "I apologize, Lamb. I promise I won't waste any coin on things we can do ourselves. My words were merely meant to annoy Edmund."

"They worked," Edmund said, freeing the glass. "While we're out to find a replacement for this, what else should we purchase?"

"A bed," Brandle said.

"Don't be ridiculous," I said. "Get the rope we'll need to make one ourselves and stop at the woodcutters for the timbers, or simply buy the bedding so we can sleep on the floor."

Brandle spun me about to face him. "We didn't bring you here so you would live like a com—"

"Brandle!" Garron called from downstairs. "Have Edmund purchase a hammer along with the bedding."

I SCOURED the hearthstone with the ragged remains of the bristled brush we'd found. The water ran black with years of soot.

"Here, let me do that," Eadric said, plucking the brush from my hands.

"I can clean a hearth, Eadric."

"So can I."

Garron drew me to my feet and wiped my hands with his tunic.

"We know you can clean," he said. "But there are other things you can do better that we can't."

Darian chortled from the other room.

"Braying ass," Liam said under his breath.

"Casting," Garron said forcefully.

"Brandle said it was dangerous to cast here. He made me promise never to do it again," I said.

"I agree with him and am not asking you to break your promise. I—we—would like you to meet someone. Perhaps you'd like to change?"

I looked down at my torn mourning gown, which I'd deemed the best choice for the aggressive cleaning we'd needed to complete on the home.

"When are we expected?"

"Midday."

"And you tell me now?"

"I apologize. I didn't think you would clean the hearth."

Eadric chuckled. "Nothing is above or beneath our Sparrow. She soars as she wills."

"I'll wash and be ready shortly," I said.

Darian stepped aside for me to climb the freshly cleaned stairs. The air in the house already smelled fresher from all the open windows. Dust still danced in the light, but I knew that would go away with time and more effort.

In my room, a chipped washbowl waited for me. The water was cold from the well, and I heated it without thinking then silently berated myself. Surely, I hadn't grown so accustomed to using my powers that it had already become a habit, had I?

After washing and changing into my blue gown, I descended the stairs with the still-warm water and handed it to Darian.

"I didn't intentionally cast," I said when he felt the bowl.

He nodded, but I felt his concern. Garron's grew from behind me as well.

"And your well?" Garron asked. "Did you open it?"

"Not fully. It always remains just a touch open now. Nothing that other casters detected. I promise."

"Good." He offered me his arm.

"We'll return in time for dinner," he said to Darian.

"Oh sure. Have fun cleaning, lads," Darian grumbled.

Eadric winked at me. He already had soot on his brow.

"Who am I to meet?" I asked as Garron and I left the house.

"A friend," he said absently.

I followed his gaze to watch the patrol passing the end of our street. One of the guards turned his head and caught me looking. I demurely lowered my gaze and felt his curiosity shift from me to Garron.

Peeking up at Garron, I asked, "What if the suitor Father approves of is cruel? Or ugly? I don't want to marry an ugly man, brother."

Garron patted my hand. "Would you rather have a handsome, cruel husband or an ugly, kind one?"

The guard's curiosity returned to me as I quickly scowled in Garron's direction and tried to remove my hand from his arm. He caught it and held firm.

"Save your tantrums for your future husband, sister."

The patrol continued out of sight, and we turned to walk in the opposite direction.

"Do we wish to arrive discreetly?" I asked.

"We do," he said.

After that, I watched for groups of energy arranged in a precise formation like a patrol and warned Garron along our route. Since I hadn't any notion where we were going, I couldn't be sure we were wandering, but it felt like it.

"We need to turn onto the next street. Is it clear?" he asked quietly.

"Clear of a patrol," I said.

As soon as we stepped onto the street, a tingle of warning swept through me, and I tugged on Garron's arm.

"Something's amiss," I said.

"What is?"

"I'm not certain. I felt something."

He nodded. "Look at the third home. That's our destination."

The energy within the home seemed normal yet not. It felt like the void that Maeve had created but with energy over it to disguise its presence.

"It's dangerous," I said.

"Not for us. I promise."

Withholding the shiver that wanted to sweep through me, I waited beside Garron as he knocked on the door. It swung open forcefully, but no one was there.

"Enter," a voice barked from within.

Garron held my hand as he entered first. The door slammed closed behind us, startling me. My gaze swept the cramped room; yet, other than a filthy narrow bed, an unlit hearth, and random herbs hung by the rafters, I saw no one.

"Is she the one?" the voice demanded.

"She is," Garron said.

The voice made a dissatisfied sound. "There's nothing there."

"Garron, I would like an explanation," I said.

"This is Pogwid, a very powerful caster. I would like her to teach you."

"There's nothing to teach," Pogwid said.

With my gaze sweeping the room, I let myself feel instead of see. The energy was consistent, but the heat wasn't. I glanced at the unlit hearth. The room should be cool. Why was it warm?

I released my hold on Garron's arm and connected to the energy within my well. The room shimmered before my eyes and became cleaner. The bed was a lounge covered with a simple quilt, and the fire in the hearth crackled merrily. Some of the herbs hung from the rafters were for healing, and some, I'd never seen before. Shelves of items lined the walls. And on the opposite side of the room, an older woman stood in a doorway that hadn't been visible before.

"Not a transfiguration but an altered perception, then," I acknowledged. "How does the spell influence one's perception when it was cast on the home rather than people who enter it?" Because I would have known if she'd tried casting on me.

She smiled slowly as I looked at her.

A log from beside the fire rose in the air and flew straight at Garron.

I didn't think; I reacted. The log stopped midair, suspended motionless inches from Garron's head.

Struggling to maintain my hold on my anger, I absorbed everything that the log was, grateful I hadn't unleashed my anger as I had at the cottage.

"And now I see why you brought her to me," the woman said.

Understanding it had been a test, I took a calming breath before speaking.

"Respectfully, I have no interest in learning whatever you have to teach."

The woman chuckled and motioned for us to join her as she retreated to her back workroom.

"You might not have interest, but you need it, girl."

"Please, Kellen," Garron said.

"If I hadn't stopped her, she would have hurt you."

"Bah. I simply forced you to reveal what Garron claimed you were hiding. He's right. You're strong. And dangerous."

Garron gave me an apologetic look.

"We know you won't harm us, but your control poses a different kind of danger."

"You're worried that I'll expose you."

He nodded.

Containing a sigh, I entered her workroom and looked around at the unfamiliar objects.

"Let's start with what you know," the woman said. "Can you light a candle with a thought?" She motioned to a shelf filled with many candles.

I lit them all then put them out.

"And sensing the weather is easy?" she asked, unimpressed.

"It is. Today will be warm with a light breeze."

"And you can remove memories?"

"I believe I can." I glanced at Garron. "My only attempt was to hide a memory rather than remove and replace it."

He smiled. "And it worked. I recalled what you'd helped me forget the moment the last tracker died. I told the others while you were bespelled. It's no longer a secret but one of the many reasons we were worried when you disappeared."

"Ah."

"What else can you do?" the woman asked.

I spent an hour reviewing everything I'd learned under Garron's guidance. Heating water, making something disappear by absorbing all of its energy, and transforming objects—something I hadn't truly done outside of the briar barrier—didn't impress Pogwid at all. What did was my lack of exhaustion.

"No dizziness?" she asked while making me turn in a slow circle so she could inspect me.

"None."

"And your energy? Does it feel depleted?"

"No."

"Hmm." She sat in a chair and considered me.

"I want you to touch my well," she said.

"I don't understand."

"You can see the energy I possess, yes? Connect with it. Feel it."

Uneasy, I glanced at Garron.

"Don't look to him for guidance, girl. Look at me. I'm telling you to touch my well."

I shot an irritated glare at the grating woman and lashed out with my energy, touching it to hers. Her thoughts exploded in my head, and I realized I wasn't simply touching her. She was using the connection to explore me. Not only my well but also my thoughts. All of them.

My promise never to again allow another's will to impose mine swept through me, pushing away her touch as if blowing a leaf in the wind. I didn't retreat from her, though. I pushed forward, exploring her well as her grip tightened on her chair. It was vast or had once been vast. It had cracks in it now, preventing her from storing the energy she'd once held. I could feel the attempts that had been made to patch it. Why? Who was she?

For a second, I hesitated.

"Do it," the woman said. "Look and see for yourself."

So I delved into her thoughts, and I saw things I wished never to see. A mountain of slain children. The execution of hundreds of people. A rebellion. A beautiful woman of vast power was at the center of it all. I felt Pogwid's hate and fear toward that woman. But none of that explained the cracks in the well.

Sinking deeper and deeper still, I found Pogwid as a young woman standing at the edge of the Dark Forest. She was screaming someone's name. A beast stepped forward. He had intelligent eyes.

"I will not lose you," she said. Then she cast her energy into the man, attempting to lift the spell binding him. It was deep. Deeper than his bones. It was in the center of his being—his energy.

I felt her well fracturing even as she persisted through their combined screams of anguish until she lost consciousness.

When she regained it. It was nightfall. He was there, still a beast, pacing the confines of the forest. When she sat up, he paused and looked at her. Before her eyes, his form shimmered, and he became a handsome young man.

"Don't return," he said. "I will never again be the man I was."

His form shimmered once more, returning him to his beast form, and he walked away. Pogwid sat at the edge of the forest, crying, for a long while. She'd given everything she'd had to save him, and it hadn't been enough. Her hate for the curse and the Dark Forest became an obsession in that moment.

I withdrew from her, not daring to look further.

"Forgive my intrusion," I said. "I shouldn't have looked."

"And why not? You have the power to do so."

"Having power does not give one the right to use it against someone else," I said.

She nodded and looked at Garron.

"When I touched her, I felt nothing dark. Only determination to save what remains of her family." Her gaze found mine. "You were wise to bind your father to his memories rather than try to remove the curse. You're not strong enough for that. I doubt anyone would be."

I refused to believe that but didn't say so.

"How do I stop a caster from looking into me while I look into them?" I asked.

She smiled.

"Just as you did to me. I only got that much because I surprised you. When you touch another caster's energy, know that they can touch yours in return, and don't allow it.

"Come. Try touching my energy again, and know that I will look to see how many of the brothers you've bedded."

Pushing down my mortification, I touched her well once more. This time, I was ready and brushed her energy away from mine. Then, I focused my intent on a single question. How did she know Garron? What was she to the seven brothers?

I felt the branch of that memory—the day the beautiful woman rose to power. I followed it, seeing scared people, listening to a voice read about wrongdoings, and seeing a regal couple being led up a scaffolding.

Distantly, I heard her tell Garron to end it.

A second later, his lips were on mine, and he was kissing me hungrily.

As open as I was, I couldn't close myself off to his desire for me and the sensations it stirred. The hunger for more consumed me. It crawled under my skin, a need that wouldn't be silenced. I threaded my fingers in his hair and kissed him back with equal thirst. I drank in his desire, letting it fill me and feed my own.

"That's interesting," Pogwid said.

Shocked I'd forgotten our audience, I pulled back with a gasp and stared at Garron. His hand cupped the back of my head, comforting me and giving me an anchor as I struggled to collect myself. He struggled as well, based on the way he set his forehead to mine and closed his eyes.

"I didn't know it was possible to take energy like that," Pogwid said.

Flushing scarlet, I backed away from Garron and looked at the women.

"I can't take his energy," I said. "He's safe."

She chortled. "You don't even know? His desire, girl. You were consuming it. I never thought of emotions as energy we could take. I'll need to try that. Not desire, of course. That's beyond me now. But I have a knack for making people angry. Come back tomorrow."

Confused and dismissed, I closed myself off and followed Garron out of her workroom. The outer room appeared as it had before I'd opened myself. Filthy and unkempt. Unwelcoming to any guest.

As we left the caster's home, I had more questions than answers and looked at Garron.

"I'm not certain I like her," I said.

He laughed lightly.

"Henry felt the same about his mentor. But he vowed I could trust her with our lives, so I do."

I nodded, and in necessary silence, we returned to our house before dinner as promised.

The door hung straight and opened easily. Embers glowed in the clean hearth, and a new pot hung over them. The tempting smells of rabbit stew filled the air.

Eadric, who was in the kitchen, looked up from setting the table and stepped back.

"What do you think?" he asked.

They'd procured enough tableware for the eight of us and seven logs for stools, which surrounded the repaired table in the now clean kitchen. A kettle and two pitchers waited on the counter.

"Milk," Eadric said, catching my glance. "Brandle had it delivered."

"He also arranged for us to work," Daemon said, coming down the stairs. "Darian and I are to help the woodcutter tomorrow." His expression turned pleading. "Will you comfort us tonight?"

M.J. HAAG

I snorted. "Work is better than being idle."

"But we'll miss you."

"And I'll welcome you home enthusiastically when you return."

A smile lit his face.

"That will make our labors worthwhile."

The others came downstairs at the sound of our conversation.

"How did it go?" Brandle asked.

"Well," Garron said at the same time I said, "Awful."

"What was awful?" Liam asked.

"That woman is rude and very provoking."

Daemon had the audacity to grin while Garron led me to Darian, who tugged me onto his lap so Eadric could feed me. I melted into his hold and wrapped his arm around my middle.

I could feel his desire for me as he briefly kissed my neck, and I wondered again about Pogwid's unexpected comment about absorbing Garron's desire.

Had I truly done that? It had felt like a simple kiss.

Well, not simple. Nothing about these brothers was simple, I thought as Darian's thumb brushed the underside of my breast.

CHAPTER 8

Eadric fed me the last bite of stew, and Daemon stole me from Darian's lap.

"Come see what we've done in your room," he said. "I think you'll like it."

I thanked Eadric and Darian for feeding me and allowed Daemon to lead me up the stairs. In my room, I found a roughly made bed big enough for three to sleep comfortably. The mattress was thinner than those in the glade, but I didn't mind.

A washbasin waited beside the bed, and near the chimney sat a small copper tub.

"We can heat water downstairs and bring it up here," Daemon said.

I tipped my head to look back at him as he wrapped his arms around me from behind.

"You wouldn't mind the work?"

"To see you naked? Never."

Darian laughed behind us. "Would you like a bath now?"

I turned in Daemon's arms and looked up at him. Then, I leaned to the side and glanced at Darian. I could feel their desire. It teased me…called to me in a way that made me want to agree to a bath. But

Pogwid's comment about consuming Garron's desire left me questioning why I felt what I did toward these men. Was it because I'd committed myself to them fully or because, after a long afternoon of casting, I needed their desire to replenish what I'd used casting?

"What's wrong, Lamb?" Daemon asked.

"That woman said something I'm not sure I care for."

"Tell us," Darian said.

"I was exploring her memories—with her permission—and she told Garron to stop me. His way to interrupt was to kiss me. When I'm touching my well like that, everything you feel for me is more potent. It feeds what I feel."

"I like the sound of that," Darian said with a grin.

"It might not be as simple as influencing what I feel, though. Pogwid said she didn't know emotions were energy that we could take and that I'd been consuming Garron's desire for me."

"Would you like some of mine?" Daemon asked.

He dipped his head to kiss me, but I turned away.

"Why did consuming Garron's desire upset you, Princess?" Darian asked.

"I didn't know I was taking it. What if what I feel for all of you is—"

Daemon captured my chin, and his mouth covered mine, swallowing the rest of my fears as he kissed me slowly. Sweetly. I felt his desire, but more than that, I felt his love for me. His concern. When he pulled back, he kissed my forehead, my nose, then my chin.

"Never doubt what we feel for you. It's real. It's not because of some spell. You are witty, exciting, challenging, and sweet."

"So sweet," Darian said, kissing the back of my neck. "The looks you give can stop my heart and melt my insides. It's you, Princess—just you—that is enthralling, not your magic."

"And we know what you feel for us is love. If it weren't, the spell would have never broken."

Daemon's words soothed a very concerned part of me. When he kissed me again, I answered the kiss, meeting his tongue with my own. Darian's fingers plucked at my lacings and slowly freed me of my dress and shift so he could trail kisses over my shoulders and down my back.

Their desire wrapped around me, tingling under my skin. This time, I felt the subtle way I consumed it. It wasn't that I pulled it in; it melted into me.

Darian kissed the sway of my spine and nudged my legs apart. When his fingers parted my folds, I groaned into Daemon's mouth.

Daemon's lips left mine, and I panted as he kissed my neck and palmed my breast.

"The bed," he said against my skin.

I nodded and found myself swept up into his arms. Darian swore as I was taken away from him, and I turned my head to watch him lick his fingers. It ignited me from the inside, and my hunger for them consumed me. I needed them. Their desire. I needed them mindless with it.

Daemon lay me on the bed, and I threaded my fingers in his hair as he leaned over me to bring his mouth to mine. The hunger with which I kissed him drew another groan from his lips and he palmed one of my breasts.

Darian's hand closed over my knee, guiding it to the side. I tore my mouth from Daemon's, and meeting his gaze, I said, "Taste me as it pleases you, Darian."

They both swore under their breaths, and Daemon's mouth closed over mine at the same time his brother's tongue laved my folds. I took what they gave. Each moan and caress. Their desire filled me. Fed me. Inflamed me.

I shattered at the feel of Darian's tongue delving deep inside of me, and Daemon swallowed my scream. The sensation was still rippling through me when Darian's mouth left my skin and he joined us on the bed. Daemon rolled me toward him as his brother held me from behind.

"Tell me if this is too much," Darian said, lifting my leg back over his and slowly entering me from behind.

I groaned at the sensation and opened my eyes to look at Daemon.

Naked, he stood beside the bed, watching his brother slowly thrust into me. My gaze dipped to his hard length, and I felt myself flush. He held out a hand. I slipped mine into his and let him draw my top half away from Darian and closer to the edge of the bed.

Darian groaned and thrust deeper with the new angle, his fingers gripping my hips tightly.

"Do you like it?" Daemon asked.

"Yes," I breathed.

"Do you need more?"

"Yes."

I tugged him toward me, my gaze locked on his hard length. Their desire tripled, filling the room. I couldn't draw a breath without tasting it. And when my mouth closed over Daemon, I feasted. The taste of him on my tongue seemed to unleash something within me. It hungered in a way that should have terrified me. Yet, with Daemon gently caressing my cheek and holding my braid, it didn't.

Finding my release for the second time, I shattered around Darian, and Daemon withdrew from my mouth despite my weak protest. A moment later, I felt Darian's release. He groaned and kissed my neck.

"You are everything to us, Princess."

I felt him withdraw while the hunger still clawed at me. I struggled to push it back, but it wouldn't listen. It needed. I needed.

I looked at Daemon, letting my gaze convey what I couldn't say aloud.

"Do you need more, Lamb?" he asked.

I nodded. He fetched a cloth from the washbasin and gently cleaned me. The rough texture of the cloth over my sensitive skin sent shivers through me.

"There," he said, tossing it aside. "Tell me what you want."

My flush deepened. I wanted more of what Darian had done. It had felt so good to be bedded from behind.

He saw my flush and grinned. "Will you tell me if I do something you don't like?"

I nodded and squeaked when he suddenly flipped me onto my stomach.

"Be a Lamb and get to your knees."

On my hands and knees, I glanced at Darian beside me. He grinned lazily and reached out to trail a finger over my breast as Daemon knelt behind me.

"I hope we tied these ropes well," Daemon said a second before he entered me. We both moaned at the sensation, and I felt my center clench around him.

He grunted and withdrew only to thrust in once more. The snap of his hips was fast and forceful, and his length surged deep within me. I cried out at the pleasure and gripped the bedding.

"She liked it," Darian said softly.

"I could tell," Daemon said roughly, withdrawing and snapping forward once more.

After that, he set a grueling pace. I gasped and panted as the pleasure danced just out of my reach until Darian's hand shifted from my breast to that little bud in my folds. He circled it twice then gently plucked at it.

I came apart with a scream that echoed in the room and would have collapsed into the mattress if not for Daemon's firm grip on my hips. His rhythm faltered after a few more thrusts, and I felt his pulsing release wash my insides.

He pulled me upright against his chest and kissed my cheek and neck.

"Beautiful," Darian said, watching me. "Simply beautiful."

Smiling weakly, I closed my eyes and leaned into Daemon, who guided us to the mattress.

Sleep tugged at me as they trailed their hands over my skin, soothing me. I felt their love—and the love of the other brothers in the house.

"Think the neighbors heard her?" Daemon asked softly.

"Wipe that smirk from your face. You can bet that Edmund's already planning how to make her scream louder. How are we going to explain what's happening here if they do hear?"

"We'll need to find a way to keep her quiet when it's his turn again."

I shivered at how they might keep me quiet and at the thought that they were taking turns. Though I knew they meant spending intimate time with me, I thought of how Daemon had taken me immediately after his brother. He hadn't been repulsed. No, he'd been eager. Very eager.

Wrapping my arms around his torso, I cuddled his chest and fell asleep to the feel of Darian gently washing me.

"How much longer do you think she will sleep?" Garron asked softly.

"Go away," Daemon mumbled.

"I'm worried."

Darian sighed behind me and kissed my bare shoulder, reminding me I hadn't bothered dressing before falling asleep.

Any embarrassment I would have felt was impossible with their ever-present desire teasing me.

"Are you worried we exhausted her or that her casting did?" Daemon asked from beneath me.

"Both, but mostly the casting."

"Or perhaps I'm simply too lazy to leave this warm nest," I said, lifting my hand to tweak Daemon's nipple. He jolted underneath me, and I grinned before opening my eyes.

Garron was in the doorway with Edmund behind him.

"They're going to be late for work," Edmund said. Everything about him radiated annoyance, but I knew better. I could feel what he was feeling. Lust, pure and simple.

"Have you decided how you'll make me scream louder?" I asked, smirking at him.

"Trouble," he said softly. I knew he wasn't saying my pet name but acknowledging what I was doing.

I grinned unrepentantly and rolled off of Daemon.

"Out of bed, both of you," I said. "I won't be responsible for your tardiness."

They made sounds of protest but collected their discarded clothes and left the room. Edmund left with them. Garron lingered.

"Speak your mind, Garron," I said as I motioned for him to turn around.

With his back to me, he said, "You fell asleep before the sun set and woke after it rose. That's not like you."

I left the bed, quickly slipped into my shift, and shook out my dress.

"You ask for answers I don't have, Garron. I slept because I was tired. Whether due to your brothers or the casting, I cannot say. What I can say is that I feel fine now. However, I know that does not put your mind at ease, and I'm sorry for that. Would you like to help me finish dressing? You can look for signs of fatigue."

While I was serious, I could feel his hurt that I might be teasing him for his concern.

I crossed to the doorway and wrapped my arms around him from behind.

"Thank you for caring about me enough to worry. I have no

one else in the world to care for me now except for the seven of you."

"And Eloise," he said.

"Yes, and my sister. But I know I won't be spending the rest of my life with her, now, will I?"

He pried my arms loose and turned to hug me close.

"No, you'll spend it with us. Are you truly well?"

"I truly feel well," I said. "Irritated and frustrated, but not tired." I tipped my head to look up at him. "I've been taking your desire for me without realizing it. It's frustrating to be so uneducated in a skill that could potentially hurt those I love. Why hadn't your amulets stopped me? Pogwid's surprise at what I can do is unsettling, considering her experience and abilities.

"Am I so odd? It's upsetting to be different. It feels as if I will go my entire life set apart from others, never truly belonging."

He kissed my forehead. "You belong. Here. With us. Always. What you can or cannot do won't ever change that."

"Until the neighbors hear me having my way with all of you."

He flushed and looked away as he cleared his throat.

"I dare any of them to speak against us," Edmund said from the hallway. "Dress quickly, or you won't leave the house today. Breakfast is waiting."

His footfalls retreated, and Garron gave me a sheepish smile.

Once he finished lacing my gown, he led me downstairs where Eadric and Edmund waited for me with a breakfast of boiled oats.

"Where are Brandle and Liam?" I asked.

"Errands," Edmund said as he drew me to sit on his lap. Eadric fed me as Edmund gently fondled my person. I didn't mind either.

"What will the two of you do today?" I asked after I ate my last bite.

"We're to go to the sheep market to shear for coin," Eadric

said. "We've helped Andrew with it before, so someone should be willing to pay us. We will see you at dinner."

The pair kissed me goodbye and sent me off with Garron.

I set my hand on his arm and walked away from the house. Although he'd been concerned that I'd slept so long, we were still leaving much earlier than the prior day. No patrol crossed our paths as I carefully navigated us around them.

When we turned onto Pogwid's lane, I felt the same tingle of warning as the day prior. Rather than dismiss it, I tried to explore it. The sensation radiated from her home—a dark warning to turn away. Yet, it didn't grow stronger when I knocked on her door as a typical warning would.

As the door unlatched, I opened myself to the energy around me and searched for a spell I knew had to be present. It wasn't in the home but in the ground along the entire street. As I would expect from a caster of her knowledge, it was well hidden within the soil and not directly tied to her home.

She was hiding.

"Are you going to stand out there all day?" she called.

I entered and saw through her spell right away.

She cocked her head at me.

"Something's changed," she said.

"Yes. My understanding. Why are you hiding yourself here?"

She made an annoyed sound. "Because I'm not yet ready to meet my end, of course. And I doubt the change I sense is your understanding, but you can amuse me with what you think you've gained. Come now. Tell me."

"I now understand how different I am from most casters. You're experienced enough that you mentored Henry. I've read his vast collection of notes. Energy is in everything in a finite amount. It was stressed several times. I've experienced it when I consume the energy from an object until the point it disappears. Yet, my ability to take energy from emotions surprised you. That means it's not common. It's also very powerful since emotions are *not* finite. The life tied to the person is, but not the emotions. They ebb and flow, depending on the circumstance, but never truly end.

"What does it mean that I unknowingly consumed them? What does it mean that I cannot sense the capacity of my well when I could yours? How did I instinctively know to hide myself? And why do I never need to pull energy into me? Why does it flood me if I am not closed off?"

She nodded slowly.

"When we discover the answer to one thing, it always creates more questions, does it not?"

"That is not an answer."

"You seem upset with the questions you have. I didn't want to add to them."

"Has anyone ever told you that you are exasperating?"

She laughed loudly and rocked back into her chair to stand.

"Henry often said that to me. But the more irritating I was, the more determined he was to learn more than me."

"And did he?"

"He was my equal when he died. That will not hold true for you and me, though."

"Why not?"

"You already surpass me, child. As you've guessed, your capacity for casting exceeds mine. By how much, I cannot say. Now, are you ready to learn?"

I nodded.

Garron took a seat and patiently listened to the knowledge Pogwid imparted. I transfigured objects with increasing ease and learned to what limit I could perform a direct cast without detection. Then she taught me how to ward our house.

"Think of it as putting a lid on a pot. What is inside will be unknown to everyone from the outside. But some of the magic can seep out if you're not careful."

Then, Pogwid surprised me by asking me to cast a memory spell on her.

"Why?"

"Some things are best forgotten. If I'm taken by a patrol for questioning, I want any memory of you to vanish. Do you understand?"

I slowly nodded. While I understood her request, I didn't understand why it was necessary. She saw my hesitation and motioned for me to sit.

"They've told you little about the queen, haven't they?"

"Just what they call her and that she was responsible for their curse." I chose not to mention the bit about her killing small children.

Pogwid nodded. "They were very young when they were cursed. Henry brought them here, hoping that I could lift it, but I knew, at their ages, they wouldn't be able to withstand the pain. Liam was still a suckling babe." She shook her head. "They are not the only ones whose lives have been ruined by the queen. So many have lost their lives for one simple reason. The queen fears being overthrown as the previous King and Queen were—may their energy find peace. Any caster who comes close to matching her power is a threat and will quickly die."

"That's why you're hidden while other casters are not? So she doesn't kill you as well?"

"It is."

The pieces settled in my mind. Pogwid was powerful enough to be a threat to the queen, and my well had more capacity than Pogwid's. A spell to forget me wasn't to keep *Pogwid* safe but me.

"Am I more powerful than the queen?"

She glanced at Garron then sighed and shook her head. "Power isn't ability."

"Knowledge is power," I said, understanding. Pogwid had the knowledge, but with her cracked well, she would never be able to face the queen, who liked to kill small children.

She nodded. "And you are woefully uneducated."

"Then educate me."

She chuckled and shook her head. "I think we've covered enough today. Cast your spell to ensure I forget you if I'm ever questioned; then go home and cast your protection spell there."

She crossed the room and stood before me.

Rather than speaking the words aloud to clarify my intent, I touched my energy to hers and said them in my mind.

For the people she lost, let her light continue to shine. Mend her well with the energy I confine. Let her continue with grace and gratitude, to protect those who need protection and keep her from the queen's detection. If she's taken at the queen's behest, she will lose all memory of me at my request.

I sent my energy into her well as I clasped both her hands. Her eyes went wide, and her mouth opened in a silent scream. Her pain reverberated through me, but I held tight, focused on mending what her desperation had destroyed.

Crack by crack, I used my energy to repair the well from the bottom. Like distant war drums, my pulse pounded in my ears, growing louder as I worked upward.

"Kellen!"

Garron's hands gripped mine, trying to tear them from Pogwid's. My magic held firm.

Light flickered just beyond my peripheral as I reached midway. My lungs grew tight. Each breath hurt. But I refused to quit when the energy in my well remained unchanged.

A glint of blue sparked in Pogwid's brown gaze, and I flew backward.

Darkness closed around me before I hit the wall.

CHAPTER 9

"Do not raise your voice at me for saving that girl from her own folly, you royal pain in my arse." Pogwid's tone matched the anger she felt, but it also masked her fear and guilt toward me.

I struggled to open my eyes. Everything hurt. Especially the back of my head—and I groaned softly.

"She's awake," Garron said.

"Good. Get her to drink the tea. All of it." Something crashed. "Did you have to choose a simpleton with no sense of self-preservation?"

A cup pressed to my lips. At the same time, Garron slipped an arm behind me to help me sit. The move, along with the horrible scent of tea, made my stomach roil.

I gagged.

"Drink, girl!" Pogwid barked.

"Yell at her one more time, and I will forget how much you meant to Henry," Brandle said lowly.

"Stop yelling," I rasped as I gripped Garron's wrist and gulped the vile healing tea.

I felt the spell take hold and breathed a sigh of relief as my stomach settled despite the awful taste. It spread outward, easing the aches in my joints and finally removing the dull throbbing in my head.

Letting out a relieved sigh, I opened my eyes.

"I am not a simpleton. I took a calculated risk, Pogwid. And you shouldn't yell at Pogwid, Brandle. She now has the ability to turn you into a toad if she wishes. I refuse to kiss you if you're a toad."

Brandle fell to his knees beside me and wrapped his hands around mine.

"You promised," he said. "You swore you wouldn't cast."

I blinked at him, at a loss since I had, in fact, made that promise.

"Pogwid asked me to cast. I thought it was okay." Never mind the countless spells I cast before that while learning. I wasn't about to bring those to his attention as well.

"She asked you to remove her memory of you. To protect you."

"Yes, well, casting is casting, isn't it?"

Brandle released me and rubbed his hands over his face. I could feel him gearing up for a lecture and looked at Pogwid.

"I think I would prefer him as a toad, actually."

Her angry glare conveyed her unamused stance.

Sighing, I looked at Brandle. "What am I?"

His anger and fear faded a bit as he looked at me.

"You're ours."

"And what else?"

"I don't understand."

"I'm a danger, Brandle. To all of you because of all the things I don't yet know. My limits. My capacity. My potential. How to stay hidden. How to help. But Pogwid knows all those things about herself. She just lacked the power. I fixed that to protect us all, even myself, despite knowing my efforts could cause everyone's disapproval and another stern lecture from one of the men who loves me unconditionally."

With a shaky exhale, he took my hands again and kissed the backs of them. He was thinking dangerous thoughts that would end with both of us angry if he acted upon them.

I looked at Pogwid. "If I allow you to touch my well, do you promise not to look into my thoughts and only check my well for damage to reassure the men who will otherwise try to lock me away for the rest of my life?"

Pogwid stared at me for a moment then nodded. I felt her energy touch me, and I lifted the lid on my well—not all the way, just to the point where I would not yet be detected. Her eyes went wide, and her gaze searched mine for a moment before I felt her withdraw.

"And have I damaged myself?"

"You should have. I don't understand why you didn't when I could see your strain. Something other than your own limitations was preventing you from completing the spell."

"What did you feel?" Garron asked. "How deep is her well?"

She turned away without answering and dug around on one of her shelves for a stone. It was as large as Edmund's fist and glinted with green and gold veins.

"Do you know what this is?" she asked.

I shook my head.

"A casting stone," Garron said.

"Yes. One of the largest and oldest stones I know of. It can hold enough power to complete the spell from start to finish that your girl attempted to cast. Her well is equal to a dozen of these. Maybe two dozen. I don't know. I feared looking deeper and becoming lost."

I struggled to believe what she'd said as she approached the bed.

"Did you also cast the spell I told you to cast?" she asked.

"Yes. You won't remember me if you're taken."

"Good. Now cast it on them. Each one of them."

Brandle closed his eyes, and I could feel his despair at the thought of forgetting me forever. While forgetting me would keep me safe, it wouldn't save them once they were taken. I could feel his certainty in that and tugged my hands from his.

"What good is the secret of my existence if they're taken from me?" I asked. "I thought removing any memory of me was to protect us all."

"It is, Kitten," Brandle said. "If any of us are taken, we cannot reveal the one who broke our curse. The queen would hunt you because, without you, we would return to what we were. But if the queen learns what you truly are, she won't kill you. She'll consume your power and use it to do the one thing she isn't yet strong enough to do."

"What does she want to do?"

"Live forever," he said.

"She's taken so many already," Pogwid said. "The power she steals extends her life a little. She's been experimenting. Impregnating—"

"Enough," Brandle said.

Pogwid sighed and returned the stone to its shelf. "She's powerful and corrupt without any sense of wrong. Nothing is beyond her. To protect everyone from that evil, no one can know of your potential. Do you understand?"

With a heavy heart, I nodded.

"Good. Then cast the spell."

"No," Brandle said. "You do it, Pogwid. You said she fixed most of your energy source. Test what you can do."

"Your stubbornness isn't an attribute to cultivate," Pogwid grumbled.

"It's not stubbornness," I said. "It's fear. If you lost everything you hold dear and by some small chance find something to hold dear again, wouldn't you fear losing it above all else? He's keeping a secret from me and fears I will see it when I search his mind for memories of me."

Brandle's guilt swelled, and I cupped his cheek.

"I understand," I said. "Better than you know. At some point, though, you will need to trust that I will not run from you, Brandle, or it will be your distrust that destroys what you're desperate to hold onto."

He closed his eyes and kissed my palm then stood and went to Pogwid.

"Can you make it temporary?" I asked.

"I'm not certain that will work," Pogwid said. "It's best to make it permanent."

I watched her take his hand and cast the spell that would remove me from his mind if he were taken. Then she did the same with Garron.

"Remember to cast the spell of concealment around your home," Pogwid said as we left her workroom.

"I will. Am I welcome back tomorrow?"

"Of course."

The three of us left in silence. Both Garron and Brandle were lost in their thoughts as I guided us around patrols. Despite their distraction, they remained close and watchful when I stopped at the busy market to purchase a few more essentials for our home.

By the time we returned, so too had Edmund and Eadric. Dinner simmered in the kitchen, and a fire was lit in the back-yard to heat bathwater since they smelled like sheep.

"Didn't expect to see you with them," Eadric said when he saw Brandle.

"I went to check on Kellen's progress and am glad I did."

"What's done is done, Brandle," I said. "Just as you continue to do what you think is best for the people you love, so too will I. As a trusted friend and ally, isn't Pogwid's strength your strength?"

"I'm not angry that you healed her. I'm upset that you risked yourself to do so. Without you, all the strength in the kingdom wouldn't matter."

"There is no life without risk, Brandle. Don't let the fear of what might be stop you from enjoying what is right in front of you. Don't hold back. Live."

"Does this mean you'll ignore your promise?" Brandle asked, watching me from the door.

"Yes and no," I said. "Pogwid showed me how to create a safe place to cast like her home."

Turning toward the entry, I touched the energy in the ground around our home and that of our neighbors.

"Know my intent and bend to my will, from this home let the energy be still. Regardless of the sounds or spells that may spark from within, from without, let no one detect any cast or din."

Subtly and slowly, I created the barrier around our house and layered it with false energy a caster would expect to sense in a home.

"Now, any spell cast within this home can't be detected from outside," I said.

Eadric whooped loudly, startling me.

"That means hot water without the boiling, right?"

Grinning, I nodded.

"I trust Pogwid and her skills," Brandle said. "But we've been gone a long time and are unsure of the queen's strength. Cast with caution, Kitten, for all our sakes."

"I will."

"Come here, Eadric," Garron said. "I need to cast a memory spell."

Eadric backed away from his brother.

"Why? What are you taking?"

Edmund came down the stairs just then.

"All the memories of the one who freed us from our spell should we ever find ourselves being questioned," Brandle said.

"Oh." Eadric went to Garron but looked at me. "Even if I forget you, I will recognize you as the woman I will love forever the next time we meet. I promise."

Garron spoke a simple spell and touched his brother's forehead. Once it was done, Eadric came to me, and I kissed him sweetly for his promise never to forget.

Edmund went to Garron without a word as Eadric led me upstairs to my room.

"Can you make that bigger?" Eadric asked, pointing at the tub.

I laughed and focused my energy on making the copper tub large enough to comfortably fit Edmund, the largest of them. Then, I filled it with hot water.

"I swear I love your body and mind more than I love your abilities," Eadric said as he quickly stripped, "But I do like your abilities a lot."

I watched him sink into the water with a sigh and lean back into the tub. Taking a cloth from the nearby stack, I dipped it in the water and used it to wet his hair.

"Did you earn the coin you'd hoped?" I asked.

"Enough not to raise suspicion if we need to purchase more supplies from the market. This feels so good, Sparrow."

I saw he'd closed his eyes.

"Was sheep shearing difficult?"

"No. Being away from you was the only difficulty we faced today." He opened one eye and grinned mischievously. "I often found Edmund staring off into the distance. He's likely trying to plot how to bed you again before Garron and Liam do."

"You have no tact," Garron said from behind me.

Laughing, I handed Eadric the cloth and stood.

"He doesn't," I agreed. "But I rather like his blunt honesty. It makes up for Brandle's secrecy."

"Does it upset you?" Garron asked.

"Not enough to leave, but it does hurt that he doesn't trust me to stay. Is whatever he's holding back truly so terrible? Does he sacrifice small animals while I sleep?"

"No," Garron said, looking horrified. "No. Nothing of the like."

"Well then, I see no reason for him to worry."

"I disagree," Garron said. "We all still have cause to worry."

"Why?"

He considered me for a long moment, and I could feel that he was weighing his words.

"If I would take you to market and openly show you non-familial affection, would you allow it?"

I couldn't help but hesitate, for if Garron showed me that kind of affection publicly, then I would need to take extra care with the others or—

"That's what he fears? That I will leave if it becomes known that I am with all of you."

Garron nodded, and Eadric tugged on my skirt to gain my attention.

"We know you still feel a measure of shame," he said. "We love you and don't want to hide our devotion to you from the rest of the world for our entire lives. We want to wed you in grand splendor without shame."

My hands trembled at the thought. I felt a good deal of terror but also a measure of yearning.

"I want that, too," I said. "But that is not the world in which we live. I doubt very much that the seven of you would be condemned harshly, but I could find myself beaten and driven from Adele."

"Never," Edmund growled from the doorway. "We would never allow it so long as we lived."

"What exactly are you asking of me?" My gaze met each of theirs. "Right now, what do you want me to do?"

"That's easy," Eadric said. "Love us openly within our own home."

"Haven't I been?"

"You wouldn't leave the bed until Daemon and Darian did first; then you made Garron turn around so you could dress this morning," Edmund said.

"Gossiping fishwives," I grumbled under my breath before

saying, "And what would you have liked me to do? Parade myself naked through the house?"

"Is that an option?" Eadric said. "I would very much like that."

"Less shame," Garron said. "We simply wish for you to feel less shame when you're with us."

"Modesty isn't shame," I said primly.

"Isn't it?" Edmund asked.

I thought about it and slowly frowned. Perhaps my modesty was rooted in fear of being shamed by others. Yet, hadn't I allowed them to bed me with another present more than once? That certainly wasn't modest.

Eadric plucked at my skirt again.

"If you'd like to practice, you can remove your dress and help bathe me."

I snorted and tugged my skirt free. "You're incorrigible. I know where bathing you naked will lead."

"Perhaps you would like to taste me again while Garron takes you from behind as Daemon did," he said.

My face flushed scarlet.

"Do I smell dinner burning?" I managed to ask. "I should check."

Edmund stepped aside, allowing me to flee from the room. I couldn't outpace my imagination, though. The scene Eadric had painted made my heart race and hunger fill me. I *wanted* to taste him while his brother brought me pleasure.

Was I truly so wanton?

"Kitten? Are you all right?" Brandle asked.

I realized I was standing in the middle of the kitchen without moving and shook myself.

"Eadric is trying to help me feel less shame," I managed.

"How so?"

"By suggesting things my mind is telling me I should find inappropriate while also finding them intriguing."

"We are at your beck and call, Sparrow," Eadric yelled from

upstairs, proving how little privacy there was in our home. "Whenever you wish, Garron and I can be ready."

Brandle saw my tortured expression and hugged me.

"Talk to me, Kitten. What is going through your mind?"

"Last night with Darian and Daemon was lovely. But did I cheapen the experience by sharing it with both of them? Shouldn't our time together be alone? Private?"

"Your time with us can be whatever you wish it to be," he said. "If you're worried that either Darian or Daemon feels slighted, I promise it's the opposite. By not sending one of them away, they were both able to spend more time with you. Watching you find your pleasure, or even simply hearing it, brings us immense joy."

I tucked my head against his chest and struggled against the embarrassment and shame I wanted to feel.

"I'm glad Eadric and Garron said something to me," I said. "Understanding why you fear I'd leave has opened my eyes. However, I still hold firm, Brandle. Even through embarrassment and shame, I will not leave your side as long as you continue to stand with me."

He kissed the top of my head.

"I love you, Kellen. You're the bravest woman I ever met, and I refuse to let you go. Ever. If you do run, know that we will follow you and find you. There is no escaping us."

Tipping my head back, I silently pleaded for his kiss. He gave it tenderly at first, then with growing desire.

"Dinner truly will burn if you continue," Eadric said, coming down the stairs.

Brandle withdrew and turned me toward Eadric.

"Edmund would like some fresh bathwater," he said. "I'll stir dinner."

I made my way upstairs and found Edmund alone in my bedroom. His shirt was on the floor beside the tub, and the ties of his pants were loose around his waist. Ignoring the indecent outline of his hard length, I focused on purifying and heating the water.

"Done," I said.

When I would have left, he caught me in his arms.

"Stay," he breathed, nuzzling my neck. "Eadric was right. I could think of little else today but you. Please stay."

He stepped back and loosened my lacings. I saw the challenge in his gaze. He expected me to reject him, likely due to our previous discussion. But the truth was that I was hungry for him. For all of them. I simply didn't know if it was true lust or the need to consume their desire to recover what energy I'd lost from healing Pogwid.

"You were right. I do still fear the judgment of others. But I also still fear my reasons for being with you, Edmund. I need what we do together to only be about loving one another."

"You doubt us?" he asked. I could feel his growing anger and shook my head.

"No, Edmund. Not any of you. I doubt myself. When I'm with you, I feel your desire. It feeds my own, and I crave it so much that all thoughts of shame vanish completely. What I did with Daemon and Darian? I fear it wasn't out of love but out of hunger for the desire I consumed from them."

I could feel his confusion.

"She consumes the energy from the emotions we feel," Garron said, entering the room. "It's not the same as life energy. Pogwid tried the same, and she couldn't do it. It's something unique to our Snow."

Edmund shrugged. "I see no problem with how you replenish yourself. In fact, I think I like it more than any other method. It hurts nothing, and we already know you love us. If you're hungry, isn't it our obligation to provide for you?"

Garron's fingers finished loosening my lacings. "Whether you hunger for food or energy, it makes no difference to us. You have a need, and we want to meet it."

"Please allow us to meet it," Edmund said.

Growing more breathless by the second, I nodded.

He kissed me soundly then turned me in his arms so I faced Garron.

"Keep her entertained while I bathe quickly," he said.

Garron's face flushed. His hesitant, bashful nod soothed my nerves. Taking the lead, I looped my arms around his shoulders and stood on my toes.

"Kiss me, Garron," I whispered against his lips.

His desire for me exploded a moment before his mouth claimed mine in a ravenous kiss that curled my toes. His hands smoothed down my sides and gripped my backside as he lifted me off my feet. The few steps it took to reach the bed were too many, and I made a sound of protest when he broke away from the kiss to strip me from my gown.

My protests died when he hungrily trailed kisses down my neck to my breasts. I threaded my fingers in his hair and met Edmund's gaze over his head. Edmund's desire equaled his brother's even without touching me, proving Brandle's words.

He washed unhurriedly as Garron moved to my other breast then trailed lower. I didn't need any further encouragement to lie back and open myself to Garron's affection. The first touch of his tongue drew my hips from the bed. I closed my eyes and allowed myself to simply feel.

Pleasure pooled in my middle, growing as it gathered. When Garron's fingers slipped inside of me, I groaned and gripped his head.

"Show us you love us," Edmund said. "Scream your joy without shame."

I did. My cry of pleasure echoed off my bedroom walls. Garron's mouth and fingers left me as I still spasmed, only to be replaced by his girth a moment later. We both groaned at his slow entry. He filled me completely and stretched me to the brink.

Breathing deeply, I shifted my hips, trying to adjust as he withdrew. His desire wrapped around me, blending with Edmund's lust. Further away, I felt Eadric and Brandle's needs too.

Hungry for it all, I called it to me.

Garron's pace increased, and I felt the pleasure building again. His hand covered one of my breasts, kneading it, adding to the sensations. When he rolled the nipple between his fingers, I broke apart a second time, and he quickly followed.

I consumed their desire as I slowly calmed. The flood of it seemed endless.

Panting, Garron set his forehead to mine then peppered my face with tender kisses.

"Everything I am is yours," he said. "Without question, I belong to you. Do you understand, Snow? For you, I will be anything you need."

He kissed me gently and withdrew. A cloth replaced him, cleaning me as his loving gaze held mine. In a moment when I would have felt embarrassed, I disallowed it.

"And I'm yours," I said softly. "However you need me."

With one last kiss, he stood. But rather than leave, he gathered me in his arms and settled on the bed with me partially cuddled on his chest. Despite my continued consumption of their collective desire, I felt the love we shared, too.

Edmund's breath on my backside startled me, and I glanced over my shoulder as he nipped my rounded flesh.

"Up on your knees for me, Trouble," he said. "It's my turn to make you scream."

Despite having found my release twice and feeling tired, my heart skipped a beat at what he was asking of me.

CHAPTER 10

GARRON BRUSHED THE LOOSE HAIR OFF MY FACE AS EDMUND lifted my hips. With my hands on Garron's chest, I braced myself on my knees. Edmund's palm stroked over my backside and then he slowly slid a finger into my wetness. Heat flooded my face as I stared at Garron. He smiled slightly, and I felt his abated desire grow again.

"Are you still hungry?" he asked.

I nodded jerkily, and he leaned up to kiss me.

"Then take what you need."

I opened myself to them and felt their need for me to lose myself completely. Giving myself over to them, I did just that. Darian and Daemon arrived home in time to hear my final release, and I consumed their desire as I collapsed on Garron.

"You are so beautiful," he said in soft praise as Edmund gently cleaned me with a cloth. "I can understand Edmund's impatience to have you again, but I caution you to set some boundaries, or you will never leave your bed."

Edmund hummed his agreement. "On your back. On your knees. Riding one of us."

Their desire swelled at his descriptions, and I welcomed the endless lust.

"At some point, our poor Sparrow is going to need real food," Eadric said from the doorway.

"Too tired to walk," I said against Garron's chest. "Carry me."

Eadric made a giddy sound, and I found myself swept off of Garron and into Eadric's arms.

"I've always wanted to feed you like this," he said. "Who will be your chair, I wonder."

"Liam," I said, knowing he hadn't yet returned.

Eadric cuddled me in his place until some of the feeling returned to my limbs, and I was able to lift my head. The sun was close to setting outside.

"I'll need to dress soon," I said.

"Why?" Daemon asked, sounding affronted.

"Any passerby will be able to see me once the house is lit from inside."

"Then make some curtains," Eadric said simply.

"I would much rather have curtains than see you clothed," Darian said in agreement. "Ah, and there's the brother we need to see. Brandle told us you have a spell for us. Let's have it then."

Ignoring their lightheartedness over what I still considered a serious matter, I looked at Brandle.

"Where is Liam? Should he be this late?"

"He should be home soon."

"From where?" I pressed.

"He's meeting with some potential friends."

"Potential? You left him alone with people whose loyalty you are not certain about?" I tried to sit up, but Eadric's hold kept me firmly planted against his chest as his palm stroked down my spine to circle one hip slowly.

"He's safe, Kitten. I wouldn't leave him if I weren't certain of that. He's with friends."

"You just said 'potential' friends."

"Yes. He's meeting potential new friends with established friends."

Finding his circular talk annoying, I touched my energy to his tunic. It fell off his torso, splitting into sections and expanding into curtains.

Brandle looked down at the heap of material at his feet then grinned at me.

"You only need to speak your wish whenever you want me to undress."

"And my wish to stitch your mouth closed? Can I speak that too?"

His eyes twinkled with his mirth, but he wisely remained silent.

"I would like to get dressed now," I said, once again attempting to straighten away from Eadric.

"Are you certain you don't wish to greet Liam thusly after the long, tiring day he's had attempting to acquire the help we need to free your sister?"

I stilled and turned to meet Eadric's gaze.

"Are you attempting to manipulate me with guilt?"

"Yes, but not for my benefit. That would be beneath me."

The man was positively exasperating but too cute to stay angry at. So I kissed him.

"How?" Darian said. "At the very least, that should have been a cuffing."

"Next time she's angry, I vote we send Eadric to calm her. He's too gifted not to use."

The rest of them chuckled, and I lightly pinched Eadric's side as I ended the kiss.

"Spare me, Sparrow. I beg you. I only meant to surprise the youngest of us."

The door opened a moment later, and we all turned to look at Liam. He paused in the doorway, his brows lifting to his hairline as he took in the sight of me and quickly closed the door.

His desire added to the heady mix already in the room.

"This is a pleasant sight," he said.

"Come take your seat. Our Sparrow is hungry, and you are her cushion tonight."

Eadric passed me to Liam, and while I settled on his lap, the others worked together to hang the curtains. Liam's hands petted me throughout the meal, and though I could feel his wish to bed me, the day's activities were demanding their due. I yawned continuously, barely finishing my meal before closing my eyes.

Liam kissed my temple.

"Put her to bed; then eat," Brandle said. "You can join her again when you're finished."

"You can take the other place beside her, Brandle," Garron said.

I drifted off to their collective agreement.

"SHE'S RIGHT. Your fear of losing her shows you don't trust her to stay. You don't trust her love for us is real," Liam said softly. "But the spell proves it is. We should tell her before this goes any further."

"And if she refuses?" Brandle asked.

"Has she refused anything we've asked of her, you idiot? No. For the love of everything in this kingdom, Brandle, she was sitting on Eadric's lap, naked, in the middle of our kitchen. How much more do you need to believe her?"

"No arguing in my bed," I said sleepily.

"Sorry, Love," Liam said, petting my bare arm as he pressed a kiss to my temple. "Go back to sleep."

I gladly did so.

When I next woke, the sun had yet to rise, and I was alone in bed with Liam.

"Good morning," he said when I opened my eyes.

"Good morning. Did the pair of you continue arguing?'"

"We weren't arguing, Love. I was attempting to persuade him to see what a stubborn ass he can be."

I laughed lightly and enjoyed the feel of Liam's fingers running through my unfettered hair.

"Are you recovered from yesterday's casting?" he asked when I remained silent.

"I believe so. Why? Is there another spell I should cast?"

"No." His yearning teased my senses, awakening the hunger in my well.

"They said not to feel shame. That you all love me unconditionally, and if I'm hungry, I should appease it regardless of where the hunger stems from. And I'm trying to settle in my mind that I shouldn't hold myself to the same standards of other maidens my age—though I'm not a maiden anymore, am I?" I exhaled heavily and drew closer to him, needing comfort from the unrest in my mind. "I'm trying, but it's not easy to set free that part of myself I'd hidden for so long. A part that my kingdom would have shunned. Add loving the seven of you into the mix, and I'm not sure how to free myself to be who I am."

"Ah, Love," he said, holding me tight. It was then I felt his bare chest against mine. Skin to skin from head to toe. While his heart was filled with compassion and the need to comfort me, mine turned to hunger, the damned wanton thing.

"Don't let the others rush you," he said. "Move forward at your own pace."

My current pace felt too slow in the face of my hunger. Setting my hands on his chest, I pushed him onto his back and straddled his hips. The blanket slid down my torso as I straightened, and I felt the storm of his emotions. The love and the need.

"The pace changed," I said. "I'm hungry."

His pupils dilated, and he gave me what I needed with a single heated look. Closing my eyes, I let it in and moved against his desire for me. His hands gripped my hips, guiding me so my folds parted. I shivered at the contact and continued my slide over him.

He sat up and wrapped his arms around me, increasing our contact as he lifted me to position himself. Sinking onto his hard length drew a low moan from me. He didn't rush me to move. Instead, he let me set a slow pace that fed his desire for me.

Unhurriedly, I consumed what he felt as the pleasure inside of me grew.

"Please, Love," he said, kissing my neck. "Tell me what you need."

"More," I breathed.

He shifted his weight, folding his legs underneath him.

"Lean back," he said, gripping my hips with one hand and pressing at my chest with the other so I lay back. He half knelt between my legs, keeping my hips elevated as he continued his slow thrust. It was a position I'd seen in the book in Henry's study. And in this position, Liam hit a spot in me that sent shivers racing down my spine with each stroke. He picked up his speed until the sound of skin slapping skin filled the room.

The others heard us. Their lust charged the air and flooded into me. I couldn't think or speak. I could only feel. Their need. The sensual pleasure growing inside of me, climbing higher with each of Liam's thrusts rubbing me from the inside, coaxing me to let go…to feel…to be free.

The maelstrom inside of me clamored to be unshackled.

Liam reached between us and flicked his thumb over that sensitive nub. My mouth opened with a silent scream, and I arched at the explosion he set off inside of me.

Pleasure rippled out from my core with an intensity that flung the lid clean off my well. The air around us exploded with color as I spasmed around him.

"Don't stop," he gritted out, keeping his rhythm steady. "Take what you need."

I had no control to take. Liam was my master, and I accepted what he gave me. Even when I started shaking from the duration of the release and the growing sensitivity, I didn't ask him to stop. I simply accepted what he gave. The second release started before the first fully finished. And this time, I was not silent.

My tortured wail shook the room, and dust rained down on us from the ceiling.

Deep inside of me, I felt the spell I'd remade lift. The vow to never again be controlled by another settled deeper, and I reveled in the freedom by undulating against Liam.

He cried out and stilled. His spend flooded me, and he collapsed forward. Breathing heavily, he braced himself on his arms and stared down at me as the room continued to shake and dance with colored particles.

"I checked outside," Garron called. "The spell's holding. Inside is a different story."

His words and the slow, smug grin that tugged at Liam's lips were the reminders I needed to calm the storm within me and recap my well. It wasn't easy, but I managed.

The shaking stopped, and the colors faded.

"It's a good thing you spelled the house," he said. "I think they would have heard that one in Drisdall."

"Amusing," I said dryly. "Are you going to help me bathe now that you've had your way with me?"

"Gladly."

With a thought, I filled the tub with hot water and held on as he carried me to it. We both sighed as he sank into the steamy depths and cradled me in his lap.

"This is nice," I said.

"It is. Are you still worried about Brandle?"

"I am," I said. "You were right last night. I don't know what else to do to assure him I won't leave." I played with Liam's fingers. "Edmund's initial anger misled me to believe he would be the difficult one among you."

Liam chuckled and kissed my shoulder.

"As the oldest, Brandle feels more responsibility toward us. He's hesitant to make a decision that might cost us all that we've gained. His need to protect us is the heavy burden of being the firstborn."

"That's horse shite," I said.

Darian's bark of laughter from their shared room was cut short, and I heard the sound of scuffling.

"Does she get cuffed for cursing?" Eadric asked. I knew someone cuffed him for the remark and shook my head.

"Rather than fighting, start some biscuits," I called.

Eadric stopped at the door and peered in at us. "Do you want honey with them or jam?"

"Leave them be, dolt," Edmund said, pulling him away.

"Why? You didn't leave her alone with Garron?"

The pair made a racket as Edmund chased Eadric down the stairs, which groaned ominously. I touched the wood planks with my energy, strengthening them.

Daemon and Darian both stopped to look in.

"You look right comfortable, Lamb," Daemon said.

"Need any help washing anything, Princess?" Darian asked.

"Only your brother, if you'd care to join."

Darian threw his head back and laughed.

"Well played," Daemon said. "I believe we'll leave Liam to your tender care. Although Brandle might be willing. He has experience cleaning Liam's bollocks."

"Daemon!" Garron yelled from below. "Liam was an infant, Snow."

"I gathered," I called back.

"Stop causing trouble, and go help your brothers," I said to Daemon and Darian.

They left us alone to finish washing in peace. We didn't tarry, though. I knew they needed to be about their day and didn't want them to leave before I had my say.

Dressing quickly, I went downstairs with Liam a few steps behind me. Garron and Brandle were putting the biscuits on a flat cooking stone above the coals.

"Are we a family?" I asked.

They all stopped what they were doing to set the table.

"We are," Brandle said firmly.

"And, in this family, do we all have an equal voice, or does one voice carry more weight than the others?" I asked.

They glanced at each other.

"We're equals," Edmund said.

"Good. And when we don't all agree, how do we resolve it?"

"A vote," Eadric said. "Majority rules."

"Excellent. Then Daemon and I vote that we end any remaining secrets today."

"I do?" Daemon asked.

"Recall your promise to agree to a future request when I let you avoid your labors in the glade? I'm collecting."

Understanding lit his gaze, and he nodded. "I agree and vote we tell our Lamb everything."

"I agree as well," Liam said.

Garron's vacant gaze remained locked on the floor, and I could feel his hesitation. I went to him and wrapped my arms around his waist.

"I've tried holding myself back from you and your brothers out of fear of hurting all of you. Slowly, you showed me that I had nothing to fear. That it was safe to love you. That you wouldn't leave me. Now, you're the ones holding a part of yourself back. I want everything–like you promised."

He nodded. "I agree."

Turning, I looked at the rest. Darian was sober as he met my gaze. Brandle and Edmund shared an equal amount of fear. Eadric had calm determination and waited until I looked at him to crook his finger.

I went to him without hesitation.

"Secrets, once told, cannot be untold. Are you sure you're ready?" he asked.

"Brandle's fear is a shackle. The only way to free him is to face the truth."

Eadric kissed my forehead and turned me toward Brandle.

"I agree," Eadric said. "That's five to three. Majority rules."

Brandle's fear spiked, and Edmund set his hand on his brother's shoulder. Darian placed his on Brandle's other shoulder. Brandle exhaled heavily and nodded.

"So be it. Sit, Kellen, and I'll tell you our tale." Rather than sitting, I took his hand and led him to the table. Understanding, he sat and opened his arms for me. I settled into his lap and wrapped his arms around my waist.

Daemon and Darian sat on either side of us. Liam and Garron sat behind us on the other side of the table while we faced Eadric and Edmund, who leaned against the staircase.

"I'm ready," I said.

"It starts with the fall of Turre. Some of what happened likely reached Drisdall since the path through the Dark Forest was still open then."

"Yes, a caster killed the royal family and took over the kingdom."

"The Foul Queen did that and more."

Edmund fisted his hands. Eadric remained solemn and silent as we listened to Brandle continue.

"Before her arrival, Turre was a peaceful kingdom boasting relative prosperity. Relative because there are always those who go hungry in the shadows. The King and Queen did as they thought any caring rulers should do and handed out provisions to those in need.

"Some who received their help were grateful. The provisions fed their children and kept them warm through the lean winters. A small number saw it as a vulgar display of the kingdom's disproportionate wealth. A seed of resentment sprouted and grew, gaining the attention of a caster who believed as they did— that the royal family had everything she wanted. Wealth. Recognition. Power.

"It wasn't long after the news of another royal birth spread throughout the land that rumors reached the King and Queen. Rumors of children disappearing from their beds in the middle of the night. Patrols were doubled. Frightened parents acquired charms to prevent entry into their homes and amulets like the ones we wear to prevent spells that might lure the children from their homes.

"And the division grew between those who had the means to protect their children and those who did not. However, within a fortnight, even protected children began to disappear. The King and Queen hired every caster in the kingdom and sent them out in pairs with the patrols to find the person responsible.

"But the caster was smart. She hid in plain sight as one of the casters helping the kingdom. It was her patrol that spotted the carrion birds circling near the rocky foothills to the south. The uninhabitable fields only fit for sheep during the rainy season were seldom visited by man."

"South?" I asked, knowing it had been the direction from which we'd arrived.

Brandle paused and nodded.

"Very near where Andrew and Sarah settled.

"After we'd grown, Henry did not spare us the details of what they found there. He needed us to understand the true wickedness of the Foul Queen. Over one hundred children under the age of four, Kellen, all missing their hearts."

My chest tightened with the emotions I struggled to keep at bay.

"How could anyone be so cruel?" I said, my voice tight.

"Because she doesn't love," Eadric said simply. "Anything."

"What happened next?" I asked.

"She helped cast a spell to capture the caster responsible for the deaths of those children," Brandle said. "Then she and the patrol waited nearby. At dusk, a bright light signaled a caster's capture. They arrested the woman and brought her before the King and Queen with many other casters in attendance.

"The woman screamed her hate at the King and Queen and blamed her actions on the growing rift in the kingdom. She said that only when the current ruling family toppled from the throne would the kingdom once again find peace.

"Due to her confession, she was publicly executed. The parents who'd lost their children found the execution just. However, they still blamed the crown for what had occurred.

"Unaware of the ruse, the crown rewarded the caster truly responsible and her partner for capturing the false caster."

"The caster responsible accepted her payment of two hundred gold coins and left the castle to give a coin to each of the parents of the taken children. She acted sympathetic but subtly fanned the unrest by stating that the two gold coins awarded to her for each life lost should have been given to the parents instead of her.

"People started leaving Adele for the more remote towns in the kingdom, believing it would be safer. In the chaos, no one noticed the dwindling number of casters. Or if they did, they believed they were leaving as well. It wasn't until Henry sought out his mentor, Pogwid, who had noted a caster of considerable ability was missing, that he began to suspect our kingdom was still in dire trouble.

"The royal family was well-protected by charms made by several casters. Strong charms that would deflect any spell. But it hadn't been a spell that had killed those children. It had been a caster's knife. And when dealing with a blood caster, nothing is certain. So, he pleaded with the King and Queen to go into seclusion.

"They refused to leave their people, believing the kingdom would fall without their presence. However, they agreed to send their children away. They were saying their farewells in the privacy of their chambers when guards burst in.

"The King and Queen didn't react at first, thinking they were there to protect them. Even when the caster they'd rewarded walked in, they still believed they were safe.

"But when the caster said, 'Bring them to the courtyard so their people can see them tried for their crimes,' they understood they'd gravely misplaced their trust."

CHAPTER 11

BRANDLE'S PAIN FILLED THE ROOM AND BECAME MY OWN AS HE continued.

"By the time we arrived, a crowd had already gathered in the courtyard—proof that it had been planned in advance. Even a platform waited, ready for the King and Queen to be marched onto it like common criminals.

"The caster listed off the royal family's supposed crimes, stating they had failed their people...that the deaths of those one hundred children were due to the crown's negligence...that the wealth in the land hadn't been evenly distributed. She said in order for the kingdom to prosper, the King and Queen needed to die. However, she didn't believe in harming children."

Brandle gave a dry laugh.

"She ordered the royal descendants' amulets removed to cast a spell of protection on them, stating it was so none would hurt the innocent in retaliation for what the parents had caused.

"I can still hear her voice. 'You and your brothers will remain small men in a large world for the rest of your lives, so you understand what it feels like to be looked down upon. You will have no privilege, and no one will ever love you.'"

My heart thudded painfully as I understood that the tale he was telling wasn't the fall of the Kingdom of Turre; it was the fall of his parents, of his family, and of their rule.

"She made a show of giving us our amulets back before ordering the King and Queen to pay for their crimes. Though he was only an infant, I held Liam to my chest so he wouldn't see and bade Edmund to cover Eadric's eyes. Henry turned Darian and Daemon away while holding Garron then covered my eyes so we wouldn't see our parents hanging in the courtyard to the cheers of their subjects.

"As they died, the caster swore to be a Fair Queen. She vowed to rule justly. No one contested her. Not the court officials who'd been loyal to our parents for decades, nor the people the King and Queen had devoted their lives to protect.

"The crowds *cheered*. And in the chaos, Henry slipped away with us. He was wise to do so. Wiser still to not attempt to hide us in town after bidding farewell to Pogwid, even though, as children, we wouldn't have been recognizable.

"He led us into the Dark Forest and worked tirelessly to create a safe place for us. And there, we waited for the one who would love us and break our curse so we could return and reclaim what is ours."

Stunned, I sat in silence.

Royal descendants.

I loved the damned Princes of Turre.

My thoughts spun. I remembered the way Andrew fell to his knees and Sarah's weeping. The secrecy of the gems—enough to ransom a kingdom.

Liam is meeting with potential friends.

The building began to shake, and the air vibrated with colorful energy.

"What part has you upset, Sparrow? That our parents were taken from us? That we still carry hate for the vile woman responsible? Or that we hid who we are from you?"

Brandle grunted in pain, and his arms slowly opened against his will.

Free from his hold, I stood, shaking in my anger.

Eadric watched me, the only one of them who wasn't feeling fear or desperation.

"You used me," I whispered. "This is why we had to return? To regain your kingdom? What of my sister, Eadric?"

"Ah, Lamb," Daemon said. His sorrow and regret swirled around me. It provoked the emotions already boiling out of my well, and the air sparkled brighter.

"We have no desire to rule this kingdom," Eadric said. "Our only desire is to remove the caster who killed so many, including our parents and Sarah and Andrew's small children. Once we do, we can free the strong casters who are in hiding, like Pogwid, and return with you to Drisdall to free your sister. However, in order to remove the queen, we need to find those hidden casters. It's a time-consuming dilemma."

His sincerity rang true with each word.

"But Brandle just said—"

"I said what we've been taught," Brandle said, his arms still open wide. "Henry gave his life to keep us safe so we might one day reclaim the throne. But if we must choose between the throne and you, Kellen, we choose you."

I recalled all the times he'd said something similar. Trembling, I tried to breathe through the chaotic storm roiling inside of me and replace the lid. What I felt refused to be quelled, though.

"Will you allow me to help?" Eadric said.

I nodded and watched him close the distance between us. His kiss was the light in the darkness that I needed. It soothed the rawness inside of me, and his love for me allowed me to cover my unruly well. Slowly, those boiling emotions calmed.

When Eadric pulled away to tenderly kiss the tip of my nose, the air was once again lifeless, as it was meant to be.

"Does this mean you've forgiven us?" he asked.

"You didn't betray my trust. So there's nothing to forgive," I said.

Yet I did feel disappointment and unease. My own. They'd resisted telling me who they were because they'd feared I would run once I knew. And they were right. In what world could one woman marry the seven princes of Turre?

"Is that what you've been doing these last few days, then?" I asked, trying to distract myself. "Finding casters in hiding? Potential friends?"

"Yes and no," Brandle said. "Finding them isn't so simple. First, we needed to meet friends of the old crown that Andrew knew. And their acquaintances. And theirs. Slowly, we are building a network of contacts and gaining more information with each introduction.

"Those meetings are how we located Pogwid. We'd hoped that she would know of others, but the spell she asked you to cast on her was also cast by all the other powerful casters she knew," Brandle said.

I sighed, feeling decidedly defeated.

"Can one thing in my life just come easily?"

Darian's humor exploded around me as he discreetly covered his mouth and coughed.

"You are not as funny as you think," I said, stalking toward the door.

"Where are you going?" Brandle asked. His need to stop me warred with his need to trust me.

"Pogwid's."

"What about a biscuit?" Garron asked.

"I'll grab something in the market."

"You can't go alone," Edmund said. Before I could argue, he added, "None of us should. You were right that it was dangerous for Brandle to leave Liam yesterday. All in agreement?"

The dratted men all voted in favor.

"Who had nothing else already planned for the day?" I asked.

In answer, Garron hurriedly joined me.

We left without speaking, and I tried to convey an outward appearance of a calm maiden as we made our way to Pogwid's. The ever-present tingle of warning increased with each step, and I took more care to watch for patrols and avoid them.

Like the day before, Pogwid greeted me with, "Something is different."

"Yes. I've learned the truth of just how much of a royal pain in the arse they all are," I said, sitting heavily in the chair Pogwid favored.

The older woman arched a brow at me then cast a speculative look at Garron.

"She knows who we are but is more unhappy with the delay we are experiencing than our identities."

I didn't contradict him.

"Is there no other way to contact casters like you?" I asked.

"None," she said. "If there had been, we would have all been discovered before now."

"And even with what I healed yesterday, you are not enough to face the queen?" I asked.

Pogwid laughed, but not unkindly. "That you see me in such a light is humbling, child, but even if there were ten of me, we would not be strong enough. Perhaps when she first ascended, but maybe not even then. Remember the stone I showed you?" She waved at it on the shelf behind her. "The queen has many of them on her person. In the crown she wears, adorning her ears and fingers, on a chain around her neck and even her wrists and ankles. She has more power than you can fathom.

"How many casters will we need to dethrone her?"

"All of them."

My frustration erupted with enough intensity that the lid flew off my well. The air exploded with color as the cottage rumbled.

Pogwid paled as Garron set his hand on my shoulder. His

concern and love were enough for me to regain control and close the well once more.

"What did you do?" she whispered, sounding horrified.

"I apologize. I lost control for a moment."

"Lost control? Foolish child! When you first came here and stopped me from coshing Garron with a log, that was losing control. This was more than that. You lit a signal fire. You need to leave. Now."

"Leave? Why? Doesn't the spell prevent what's cast inside from being seen from without?"

Pogwid got to her feet and grabbed the large casting stone.

"The spell is a lid that can keep *most* of what's cast inside. Not everything. Like the lid to your well. Sometimes, the magic cast is stronger than the spell holding it."

She forcefully threw the stone to the ground, shattering it.

Garron swore under his breath—something so out of character that I turned to stare at him.

"The same happened earlier at our home," he said.

Pogwid used air to force me to my feet as she broke something else on her shelves.

"Take her. Find the others, and do not return here or home. When they come for me, I will accept the blame." Her gaze locked with mine. "My life for yours, Princess. Your sister isn't the only person who needs to be freed. Help your men free the people of Turre."

Her words filled me with denial. Not that I refused to help but due to her willingness to sacrifice herself for my mistakes.

Garron grabbed my hand and started pulling me from the workroom before I could voice anything.

He paused at the door and looked back at Pogwid.

"Forgive us."

"No," I said, tugging at his hold. "We can't—"

"As I swore to Henry, my life for yours. Do not let the queen win," Pogwid said.

The door opened, and Garron pulled me out onto the street without letting me say more. My hands started to tremble.

"Stay in control, Kellen, or we will die."

I breathed through my nose and tried to find that calm mask of indifference I'd worn so often in the past. It felt wrong. Ill-fitted. My emotions fought against being contained. I wanted to rage, to lash out...to love.

Garron turned us away from the path home.

"Get us away from here, Snow," he said. "No patrols or all is lost."

Understanding the gravity of what I'd done, I tried harder to lock everything away. Outwardly calm, I took his arm, smiled beatifically, and walked away from Pogwid's as if I didn't have a care in the world. As I did, I cast one more spell.

Pogwid's power belongs to her alone, and for any who try to take it, let them atone with boils and blisters to disfigure and cause waste.

I sent my energy through Pogwid's barrier and touched hers. She fought it, but my will was stronger, and I felt it settle into her. I filled her well as much as it allowed then withdrew.

Opening my senses, I watched the patrols far and wide.

"They already fill the street of our home," I said. "Others are leaving the castle and coming this way. Casters are with them."

"We will go to Edmund and Eadric first," Garron said.

It took more than an hour to reach the market and longer still to locate Eadric. His face was caked with muck and his hair disheveled. He smiled idiotically at the man speaking to him but was filled with fear and desperation.

"Something happened," I whispered to Garron.

"Brother," Garron called with a wave. "Our sister found a match."

Eadric's grin broadened, and he spoke quickly to the man before hurrying to us.

His embrace was filled with relief and hopelessness.

"What is it?" I asked quietly as he held me.

"No," Garron said. "Not here."

Eadric nodded, released me, and playfully took my hand, his empty smile back in place.

"Come, sister," he said joyfully.

He led the three of us toward the market entrance just as a heavily manned patrol arrived.

"Will you have enough to buy me a new dress if Father does not?" I asked, looking hopeful between Eadric and Garron.

"It would be wiser to save the coin to buy food, you nit," Garron said, shaking his head.

I tugged on Eadric's arm. "Please?" I begged.

Eadric's humor-filled gaze shifted from me to his brother.

"You know Mother will box our ears if we let her only daughter wed without a new gown." He pretended to notice the guards at the last moment then quickly pulled me back and bowed his head.

Garron and I, along with the majority of the crowd in the market, did the same.

The patrol passed us with only a cursory glance.

Eadric hurried us out of the market, and I once again used my senses to avoid the patrol as he led us away.

"Not home," Garron said when we should have taken a road to the left.

"Why?" Eadric asked.

"A patrol lingers there," I said softly.

"We need to find Brandle and Liam."

Eadric's already pale complexion paled further, but he nodded and turned to face the white spires towering above the nearby rooftops.

Street by street, they grew more looming until we reached a well-appointed home with a manicured courtyard and pristine carriage house. He led us around the back and knocked on the servant's door.

"I wish to speak to the little master of the house," he said.

The servant took in Eadric's appearance and sniffed disdainfully before glancing at me. The smell emanating from Eadric finally registered, and I understood why the older woman was pulling a long face when she stared at my shoulder. He'd mucked me. Yet, she stepped aside to allow us entry.

"Please wait here," she said.

Once we were alone, Eadric let out a shaky breath and looked at Garron.

"A patrol took Edmund."

Garron staggered as if someone had struck him. Guilt threatened to consume me, but aware of the danger, I pushed it down. I would not let another of them be taken because of me.

"When I saw them grab him, I covered myself in shite so they wouldn't notice me."

The guilt I couldn't feel, Eadric did.

"Forgive me. If I hadn't—" Footfalls silenced me.

I looked toward the door through which the servant had disappeared, and an older, exceptionally attired man appeared. His fear and guilt felt different from Eadric's. Sadness and regret blanketed him instead of desperation.

"Your majesties," he said, bowing deeply to Garron and Eadric. "Your brother awaits you in the drawing room." He motioned toward the door, and Garron led the way. I found it odd that Eadric and I followed with the man trailing behind.

When we entered an extravagantly decorated drawing room, I saw Liam pacing before an unlit hearth. He stopped short at the sight of us and flushed. Like his brothers, he was flooded with worry and fear. His knowing gaze took in Eadric's state, but he didn't say anything until the well-dressed man closed the doors behind us.

"What happened?" Liam asked.

"The guard took Edmund for his pretty face," Eadric said.

Liam swore under his breath and faced his brothers. "Brandle went to meet a new acquaintance and never arrived."

"Where are Daemon and Darian?" I asked.

"They went to the woodcutters," Garron said.

"We need to warn them not to return home," I said.

"Why?" Liam asked.

"What happened this morning—"

A knock interrupted me, and I paused to look back at the door as it opened.

"Forgive the intrusion," the well-dressed man said. "I thought you would like to wash."

He waved servants in with several washbasins and cloths. They retreated just as quickly.

"Thank you, Philip," Liam said. "We will require your assistance again in a moment."

"I will wait in the hall for your summons."

The man withdrew once more, and Eadric went to the washbasins.

"What about this morning?" he asked as he wiped away the sheep dung from his brow.

"Pogwid said that when I lost control, it was like I lit a signal fire for the queen," I said, struggling to keep what I felt within my well.

"We cannot return home," Garron said. "Kellen saw that guards have already arrived."

"Can you see if they've taken Daemon and Darian?" Liam asked.

"There are too many people in one place for me to differentiate between..." Yet, as I spoke and looked, I saw that wasn't true. Patrols now waited in the empty homes along our road. Two people stood just inside the cobbler's home, and one waited in the backroom. Likely the cobbler himself. In the woodcutter's home, two people waited just inside the door. No others.

Rather than presume the worst, I hoped for the best.

"Where do woodcutters go to work?" I asked.

"Daemon and Darian convinced him to go to the edge of the Dark Forest yesterday. They may have returned there today."

I stretched my sense further afield and found three people at the edge of the forest. Two had a vibration that resonated with the energy within my well. My relief was profound.

"They are away from Adele, near the edge of the forest," I said.

"I will go warn them," Eadric said.

"No. I will go," Garron said. "The woodcutter will want to return to his home, and it's better if he doesn't remember the men he briefly employed."

Garron gripped my arms and kissed my forehead.

"This isn't your fault, Snow. It's the queen's. Casting isn't evil. It's the intentions of the caster that determine how it's used. This morning's magic was pure joy, and you were not wrong for feeling it. Do you understand?"

"I do. However, my guilt remains. Edmund, Brandle, and Pogwid shouldn't need to face the consequences of my actions."

"They aren't," Eadric said. "The queen took Edmund for breeding, and Brandle was likely betrayed by a supporter."

"What?"

"I will leave it to them to explain," Garron said. "I know where to look if you are not here when I return with Daemon and Darian."

"Watch for the goat," Liam said.

Garron nodded, kissed me swiftly, then left the room.

"Goat?" I echoed.

The man entered in Garron's wake.

"Have we been compromised?"

"Not yet. I kindly ask your assistance in finding a gown of modest means for the Princess and a clean tunic for my brother, Philip."

The man left again, and once the doors were closed, Liam resumed his pacing.

"I need help understanding the pieces that have been kept

from me," I said. "Why should Garron watch for a goat, and why do you believe Brandle was betrayed? I thought he was certain of the acquaintances you've been meeting."

"Goats are used to keep the lawns in an estate properly trimmed and are not an uncommon sight. If a black goat is ever grazing here, it means it's not safe to return. As for our trust in our acquaintances, we've been careful, meeting only trusted friends of trusted supporters. We've thoroughly questioned the trust of each one before accepting a meeting."

He tugged at his earlobe in vexation. "We can't move forward until we know who betrayed us. Yet, neither can we afford to sit idle."

"Then how do we find who betrayed us?" Eadric asked.

"We ask," I said.

"Ask?" Liam echoed. "Do you think they will simply tell us?"

"You? No. Me? I believe I can seek the truth the same way Garron taught me to remove memories. Rather than remove them, I will expose them. I believe we should start with the newest acquaintance Brandle was supposed to meet."

"Love, it's too dangerous."

"And apparently, so am I," I said. "Should I remain idle and wait to lose you one by one? I think not. Either you go with me, or I go alone. But I will go, Liam. You have five minutes to decide."

"When we find Brandle, he's going to kill us himself," Eadric said.

CHAPTER 12

I sat in the carriage across from the new acquaintance Brandle had intended to meet and watched the well-dressed woman struggle to keep her panic at bay.

"Breathe, Mrs. Wimbles," I said softly. "All will be well."

She nodded and took several calming breaths in vain. I touched her energy and willed her to remain calm regardless of what might happen during our visit. She relaxed visibly.

"Thank you, dear."

Liam's annoyance surged from his perch by the door. Neither he nor Eadric liked that I was alone with Mrs. Wimbles. However, I'd convinced them it was more discreet for me to arrive with her for a social call than it was for the four of us to demand an audience with the last "acquaintance" introduced to the heirs.

"Do you think Ascott will see us?" she asked.

"I do," I said.

I'd already touched my will to Mrs. Wimbles and determined that she truly supported the rightful heirs taking the throne. She was willing to do anything to get rid of the Foul Queen since she'd lost her husband to the woman's wrath when he refused to surrender their grown son for breeding.

Learning what that meant had almost been my undoing.

The queen wasn't using men and women to breed the children that she was sacrificing to prolong her life. No, she was taking men, fair of face and physique, to breed with herself. Rumors were that she cast spells during the act, hoping to create a powerful child—one who would reverse the aging the queen had already sustained. The spells involved blood magic, and the men never survived.

My thoughts briefly turned to Edmund before I forced them to the task at hand as the carriage slowed.

"We've arrived," Liam said through the door.

"Thank you...Liam," Mrs. Wimbles said.

I could feel how uncomfortable it made her feel to address him so informally.

He opened the door and helped us down then ran ahead to knock on the door. The butler who answered only looked at Mrs. Wimbles and me. I smiled beatifically under his regard.

"Please tell Mr. Ascott that Mrs. Wimbles has come to call with a guest."

The butler showed us to a sitting room while Liam returned to the carriage. Neither he nor Eadric had liked this part of my plan, but I saw no other way. If they openly arrived at the traitor's door, either we would be turned away, or all of us would be caught. As long as I remained hidden, I was safe. As far as Mrs. Wimbles knew, I was a simple caster helping the heirs attempt to find their missing brother.

A distinguished man with a greying beard and welcoming smile strode into the sitting room.

"Ladies, welcome to my home. To what honor do I owe your visit?" he asked.

"I wanted to introduce you to my new acquaintance, Miss Cartwright," Mrs. Wimbles said. I rose and curtseyed gracefully.

"Miss Cartwright, allow me to introduce Mr. Ascott, an old friend of my husband's."

The man smiled and bent low over my hand.

At the moment of our contact, I touched his mind and searched for any hint of betrayal. Like Mrs. Wimbles, he devoutly wished for the heirs to overthrow the queen. He feared that she would discover the son he'd hidden away in a distant corner of the kingdom. The lad was a few years older than me, and the elder Ascott thought that, with my gentle bearing, I'd make a fine wife for his son.

I smiled in return and allowed him to guide me back to my seat.

"From where do you hail, Miss Cartwright? I thought I'd met all the fair maidens in Adele."

A servant entered the drawing room while carrying a tea tray set for three.

"My father and brothers hid me away in a far corner of the kingdom when I was born. They told me I was a beauty from my first breath and feared a hectic life chasing away suitors."

Mr. Ascott chuckled as I'd hoped. "Since you are here, I deduce their plan did not work?"

"It did not. The quality of the suitors they needed to chase away had simply decreased. So here I am, where my father believes I will find a suitable match."

I reached out to accept my tea directly from the servant, and our fingers touched. I felt her hate for the rich and her despair for the child taken from her. Her yearning and desperation boiled over, and she wondered if the guard would also be interested in news of a maiden from the countryside.

In her mind, I saw her last conversation with the guard. She'd gone to them to share the appearance of a handsome young man at her employer's home. She'd been certain the news would interest the queen and win her favor.

"Sleep," I said.

The woman partially fell onto the table. My teacup rattled, but I steadied it and met Mr. Ascott's shocked gaze.

"Your servant went to the guard and reported that you met with a handsome young man from the countryside. She overheard your arrangement for him to meet with Mrs. Wimbles today and conveyed his expected arrival."

"His highness never arrived," Mrs. Wimbles said calmly.

Mr. Ascott's gaze shifted between the two of us. "Who are you truly?" he asked me.

"A friend of the princes. They asked me to help find their brother."

He looked down at the maid, and I felt his contempt.

"Her child was taken," I said. "She was desperate and did not know who she had reported to the guard. She only hoped to gain favor and ask for the return of her child."

His shoulders slumped.

"It is a story told again and again in Adele—children taken in the night, never to be seen again. Her hope to see her child again is a foolish one."

Setting the tea aside, I touched the woman's hand again and searched her mind more deeply.

"The child was taken a year ago. Her husband killed himself. Her mind broke in her grief. She sought employment here, hoping to find a way to regain her child even though a part of her knew that wasn't possible." I removed the memory of our visit and soothed the edge of her grief with happier thoughts of the people she'd lost.

"Please take pity on her when she wakes," I said, withdrawing. "The fault is not hers but the queen's."

He nodded and rose when I did. Mrs. Wimbles did the same.

"The purpose of our visit was solely to look for a clue as to where Brandle might have gone. If he was taken by the guard as a potential breeding partner for the queen, where would he be kept?" I asked Mr. Ascott.

"In the castle. She keeps the young men close to her. They're fed well and cared for until she needs them."

My skin grew hot and tingled dangerously. "It's time for us to take our leave. Thank you for your time."

"I hope to meet you again, Miss Cartwright." He wondered if I would be willing to retire to the countryside with his son.

Retiring to the forest with my companions sounded like a dream, and I shamefully found myself wishing we had never left.

Forgive me, Eloise, I thought as I nodded my farewell and left the house.

Liam helped us into the carriage and didn't ask questions when Mrs. Wimbles said to return to her home. When we arrived, she gathered all five of her servants and introduced me openly as a caster who would test their loyalty as Liam and Eadric stood to the side, dressed as one of her staff.

When I touched the arm of the last person and detected nothing, I nodded to her.

"Your home is safe."

She hugged each one of her servants and asked the head of the household to give each of them an extra gold.

"Speak of nothing you see or hear here," she said.

I thought of Maeve's spell that had bound me to silence and felt torn. Casting the same on these servants would ensure our safety. Yet, I also knew the pain of such a spell. But did it need to be painful? Had it been so because we'd been unwilling or because Maeve wished it? Intuition told me it was the latter.

"Wait," I called when they would have left. "May I cast a spell to ensure your silence? It won't cause you harm. If you attempt to speak to anyone outside of this home regarding the visitors who have called in recent days or in the days to come, you will simply lose your train of thought. It's for your safety as well as Mrs. Wimbles." They agreed, and after briefly wishing Garron was there to guide me, I touched my energy to theirs and focused my intent.

"There. It's done," I said.

I turned toward Eadric and Liam, who had remained quiet observers.

"Brandle was taken by the queen's guard, not for who he is but for his pretty face."

Eadric swore colorfully. Although Mrs. Wimbles didn't look shocked by his profanity, she felt it.

"Anger and fear are emotions we all endure," I said to her. "Even royalty. It would be wise for us to return. Before we do so, may I also cast the spell upon you?"

She readily agreed, and I took more care when casting on her, adding a forget spell regarding the brothers' identities.

"Thank you for your help and support," I said.

We left her home and returned to the previous residence where I was prepared to repeat the process.

"Pogwid already ensured everyone here would never speak of their highness' existences or yours should you ever join them," Philip said.

"What do we do next?" Eadric asked, looking between me and Liam.

I opened myself to the energy of the people in and around Adele. Near the edge of the forest, Garron had almost joined his brothers, and the guards near our home still waited patiently for our return.

Previously, I'd never looked at the castle, fearing attracting the queen's attention, and I hesitated to do so this time, especially after what transpired earlier. I closed myself off again and looked at Liam and Eadric.

"Garron is close to reaching Darian and Daemon. They likely won't return until dark," I said.

"If Brandle and Edmund are in the castle, there is little we can do for them except carry on with our plan," Liam said.

The search for casters, though, likely would take more time than either brother had.

Frustration threatened to overwhelm me, and I felt the tingle that forewarned an impending loss of control. I turned to Eadric, who stood beside me and, uncaring of our audience, pulled him down for a kiss.

His hunger met mine willingly, and his desire blanketed me, soothing away the frustration and helping me remember something more than fear for Brandle and Edmund. I wasn't alone. And the men of the glade would never forsake one another no matter the difficulties.

Eadric eased back with a gentle kiss and searched my gaze.

"Speak what you need, and it is yours," he said softly.

"You already gave it. I was dangerously close to allowing my frustration to rule me. It wasn't Mr. Ascott who betrayed Brandle's presence but a maid desperate for her child. I do not fault her, but the damn Foul Queen. It's the queen who has turned neighbor against neighbor. The queen who forced the casters into hiding. And the queen who is taking the kingdom's strong men. She is a blight that must be removed."

Liam's arms circled me from behind, calming the agitation that had grown.

"I think it would be wise to throw a dinner party," he said. "With you in attendance, perhaps they would be persuaded to move sooner against the queen."

"Or, at the very least, be willing to introduce our Sparrow to their casters."

"They have casters?" I asked.

"Most of the noble family do, Princess," Philip said, reminding me of his presence. "We openly employ the weaker ones and keep the stronger ones in secret. The noble families protect and support them, and the casters protect and support us."

I leaned back into Liam's arms to contain my burst of irritation.

"We've been here four days. How many noble families has Brandle met with? Why has only Pogwid come forward?"

Philip lowered his gaze and bowed slightly.

"Forgive me. I have been making discreet inquiries to meet with the other families, fearing I might draw the queen's attention."

Before I could assure Philip I did not hold him responsible, Liam spoke.

"Our time for moving cautiously is at an end. Arrange a dinner for tonight for the nobles we've already met. Beginning tomorrow, we will host small luncheons and dinners to introduce your recently returned niece—" he ran his hands over my arms "—from the countryside. We won't stop until each noble family has been contacted."

"Some families are loyal to the queen," Philip said nervously.

"I don't think they are truly loyal," Eadric said. "She isn't the type of person to foster close relationships or loyalty. Most likely, she controls them in some way."

I thought of how Maeve had controlled Eloise and me and agreed with Eadric.

"But we will heed your counsel, Philip," Liam said. "Though we cannot postpone meeting them all, I vow not to speak of anything significant until we're certain of their true intent."

"How can you be certain of their intent?" Philip asked.

"*They* cannot," I said, stepping out from between the brothers. "However, I can."

I could feel Philip's concern. It stemmed from doubt. He didn't doubt I was a caster; he doubted my experience dealing with his peers who might be more adept at hiding their intentions. He also feared I was no match for the queen and that the heirs to the throne would lose their only chance to reclaim their birthright because I wasn't strong enough.

His concerns were quite valid, so I didn't attempt to persuade him out of any of them. I simply waited for his decision. After a moment, he bowed his head.

"I will send out the invitations immediately," he said.

Eadric waited until Philip closed the door behind him and pulled me back into his arms.

"I don't like that we need you to attend these meetings," he said. "Brandle was trying to keep you from them."

"Why?" I asked, hugging Eadric in return.

"I think Brandle's disappearance proves how dangerous they are," Liam said.

I eased out of Eadric's arms and faced Liam. His soft brown gaze swept over my face as I placed my hands on my hips.

"Staying in my home was dangerous. Running through the Dark Forest was dangerous. Scaling the cliff was dangerous. Yet, I've survived it all." He took my hands and brought them to his lips.

"Which is why we want to protect you. You've suffered enough."

I exhaled heavily. "Life is filled with dangers, Liam, and I am not interested in being sheltered from them. Let me live beside you, not in your shadow or locked away in some room for my safety. That's not living."

He kissed my forehead. "I would like to see Brandle deny you when you state it like that."

A laugh escaped me. "He and Edmund can be equally stubborn when it comes to my safety."

"Garron too," Eadric said.

Someone lightly knocked on the door.

"Enter," Liam called.

The moment the door opened, I felt the woman's judgment. Philip hadn't felt anything notable when I'd kissed Eadric and Liam; however, the maid entering had strong thoughts about my impropriety for allowing Liam to stand so close to me.

Liam didn't stop me from stepping away from him and remained quiet as I walked to the woman and took the tray from her.

"Not everything is what it seems," I said. "I've done far more to be deemed improper than to embrace a man."

Goading another to force them to reveal their deeper thoughts was something I considered Eloise's specialty. However, I wasn't without skills of my own, and they proved themselves when the maid's expression reflected her shock.

Her chaotic thoughts imagined what indecencies I'd allowed Liam—only Liam, though. Her affront almost hid her yearning. She knew who these men were and wished she'd been able to catch the youngest's gaze since status didn't seem to bother him.

She thought me a maid.

Humor lit within me as I recalled how the men in the glade had first reacted to me as well.

Then her thoughts turned to catching Eadric's eye since Liam was obviously taken.

The whole while, she still looked properly aghast.

"What is your name?" I asked her.

"Margret," she said.

"A beautiful name. It was my mother's." I looked at Eadric and lifted the tray toward him. He immediately fetched it from me. Margret's thoughts churned. She questioned why a prince of the kingdom—even a dethroned one—would answer to my beckoning.

"She was a very open and understanding woman. I hope you're the same."

"Miss?" she said, clearly confused.

"I am not a simple maid. Nor am I simply a caster."

She began to fear she offended me.

"You did not offend me. I'm merely telling you that I am more than either of those things. I am the woman who will do anything to help the princes regain their throne. Even love all of them if that is what they ask of me."

"We do," Eadric said.

"In return for giving everything I am to help them free this kingdom from the queen, I ask that you do not judge me harshly for the choices I've had to make along the way or for the happiness I've found despite the hardships I've suffered."

Her chaotic thoughts slowed as she grasped what I was saying, and she took my hand, her grip firm.

"Forgive me," she said. "I was wrong to think ill of you."

"Ill?" Liam echoed softly behind me.

"You will not be the last to think of me so. I do ask that you remind others of all that the princes and I have given in return. I've lost my mother. My father. Perhaps even my sister. But I am committed to staying and helping however I can until the queen no longer sits on the throne."

The woman nodded, and I felt her embarrassment and wish to leave. Her shame for thinking ill of me was just a bit heavier than her thoughts of me loving *all* of the princes.

After she left, Eadric led me to the lounge where I sat in Liam's lap while Eadric fed me bites of a sweet biscuit Margret had delivered. I could feel the weight of their concern.

"Are you upset?" Liam asked finally.

"About Margret's thoughts of me? No. About everything else? Yes."

"Even the biscuit?" Eadric asked cheekily.

"Not the biscuit either. It's one of the fluffiest I've had in a long while." With a pang, I thought of Judith and the sweets she used to make in our kitchen.

"I am well-rested yet so very tired," I said. "Although I don't regret meeting all of you, I miss my old life—the simplicity of it."

Their worry climbed, and I patted Liam's arm. "None of that, now, or I'll stop sharing my thoughts. I only meant that I am prepared to face whatever I must for all of this to end, and I look forward to the day I can spend hours lost in a book, learning about spells and casting, with only the interruption requests for affection from the needy men in my life."

Liam hummed his agreement and kissed the back of my neck.

The door of the sitting room burst open without warning, startling me. Eadric was on his feet in front of me before I could see who it was. I could feel Philip's tumultuous thoughts and his fear, though.

"Apologies, Your Highness," he said in a rush. "I received word of a public hanging. All nobles are to attend."

My heart shattered at one very clear thought, and I stood.

"Pogwid," I said.

Philip nodded.

Intuition told me I needed to go despite the increasing tingle of warning. Why though?

My mind raced. The spell I'd placed on her would ensure she wouldn't be able to speak my name and should protect her power, but what of her life? I couldn't—no, I refused—to hide and allow the queen to take Pogwid's life. While I knew I lacked the knowledge to face the queen, Pogwid did. Perhaps if I were there, I could lend her more of my energy.

"As your niece, it is right that I should go with you."

"No," Liam and Eadric said at the same time.

I turned and set my hand on both of their chests, just over their hearts.

"Forgive me. I am not a woman you can push into a corner. Cherish me, but never again attempt to cage me."

Eadric groaned. "It was one time."

I grinned slightly. "One time too many."

"If you insist, then we will accompany you," Liam said.

"It's too dangerous, Your Highness," Philip said.

"I won't dissuade you," I said. "However, it would be wise for one of you to remain to prevent Garron, Darian, and Daemon from rushing into a potentially dangerous situation when they return and find us absent."

Liam closed his eyes.

I could feel his frustration, so I stood on my toes to kiss his chin. He caught me up in his arms and kissed me soundly, pouring all his fear and need into it. When he finally released me, I was breathless and thoroughly distracted by his desire for me.

"Eadric, you should remain," Liam said. "If the queen and her people took Edmund for his pretty face, yours will surely attract their attention."

"As will yours," I said. "Your servant clothing does little to detract from your handsome face."

"He can remain with the carriage," Philip said. "Nearby but easily overlooked. We must hurry."

CHAPTER 13

The sun sat low behind the palace's towering white spires as I stood in the courtyard amidst the throng of nobles. An occasional murmur whispered through the silence but nothing more. Their collective fear and anger grew thicker around me, adding to the increasing tingle of danger.

Ahead, the loop of a single rope swayed on the gallows.

The queen, her representatives, and Pogwid had yet to appear. However, no one voiced a complaint. We simply waited.

Beside me, Philip conveyed the picture of calm nobility, despite the concern he'd expressed on the way here about the required attendance of the nobles. Usually, such a thing was done to set an example, but he wasn't certain what example was being set. Did the queen know that a noble had been hiding Pogwid under her nose? Was she sending a message to nobles to turn their casters in? Or had she learned the royal heirs had returned?

To our right, a door set in the courtyard's white stone wall opened. A procession of people filed out. Pogwid walked in their midst. Hands and feet bound, she moved with her head high and a good deal of defiance in her expression.

It wasn't until she reached the gallows and stood above us that

I saw the blood staining her dress and the wraps on her hands. My gut clenched in horror at what they'd done.

They'd taken her fingers. Or at least some of them.

The ever-present tingle of warning, which I'd grown accustomed to over the last few days, exploded within me.

A figure swathed in an embroidered red veil regally joined a man on the platform behind Pogwid. I could feel her—a pulse of energy that demanded an answer—her anger, her hate.

I checked the lid on my well. It was as close to closed as I dared.

"People of Turre," the man called out. "Caster Pogwid stands before you, accused of treason against the crown."

"HA!" Pogwid barked.

A garbled string of sounds spilled from her mouth, and I realized they'd taken her tongue. Mere hours had passed since I saw Henry's mentor. How had they done so much to her in such a span of time? Fear started to boil under the lid as I thought of Edmund and Brandle...taken for their handsome faces. Would they fare differently than Pogwid?

I looked at the woman who'd helped me and swallowed hard.

Me. I'd caused this.

My gaze shifted to the queen. My hand trembled against Philip's arm.

No. Not me. The queen.

I could feel her regard sweeping the crowd, searching. She suspected...something. It was buried deep. To find it, I would need to touch my power to hers.

Too dangerous.

Yet, my fear for Brandle and Edmund had me considering it. If she'd handled Pogwid to this extent simply for being a strong caster, what would she do if she thought Brandle and Edmund were the princes?

Philip's hand closed over mine and patted it lightly.

He was terrified that I would do something to give us away.

He didn't fear his death but mine. Brandle had impressed my importance upon the man.

"The sentence for treason is death by hanging. Save yourself, caster Pogwid, and beg our Queen for mercy. She is Fair."

Pogwid barked another laugh and tried to say more. The queen's rage grew. Pogwid was purposely provoking her. Why? What did she hope to gain? A quicker death?

With barely a thought, I coaxed a sudden breeze that swept up the queen's person, intent on distracting her so I could touch my power to Pogwid's. However, the moment the veil lifted enough to see the queen's face, I understood.

The queen had attempted to take Pogwid's power, and the spell I'd cast on Pogwid had worked. Boils and blisters covered the queen's face.

The queen flattened the veil against her face, but the damage had been done. She knew the crowd had seen. Her rage boiled over, and her power burst out like a whip. It demanded subjugation. Philip's legs began to buckle along with everyone else in attendance, and I quickly fell to my knees beside him as if also under the queen's control.

"Wretches! Knaves!"

Pogwid's mad laughter redirected the queen's ire from the crowd to her.

"I have given you more lenience than you deserve," the queen said.

Lenience? She'd cut away pieces of Pogwid because she'd been unable to take her power. My anger boiled brightly, and I focused on the queen. Power pulsed around her but not from within her. Casting stones. She wore them all over her body. Stones to hold power that wasn't her own.

The larger the stone, the more power it held.

I opened my senses to the stones, feeling them like I felt the fear in the people around me. Three of the larger ones were imperfect. Fissures ran through them, large enough for an accumulation of water.

It gathered in the small space, and I thought of the deep chill of winter.

Vividly colored sparks burst out from her wrist and neck, and likely her thigh, though that one was hidden by her dress. The multicolored dust floated around the queen, whose disbelief robbed her of her rage for a moment.

Yet, that was all it took.

Pogwid breathed deeply, and I watched the dust flying toward her.

The queen's hand whipped out, but it was too late.

The power sank into Pogwid.

I touched my energy to Pogwid's and felt her brief resistance before she recognized my power. The spell I'd cast had worked. She didn't remember me, but at the familiarity of my touch, she understood what had happened—that I was the reason she couldn't remember and that it was important for her to protect me and the kingdom. So, she let me see what she had since our last parting as the ropes fell away from her hands, and she healed her own tongue.

"Hear the truth," Pogwid yelled.

"No!" The queen howled. "You used it! You used it all."

"You desire power above all else, and I will gladly destroy all that I am to stop you from taking even a small measure of my power," Pogwid said as I was still connected.

She nimbly stepped onto the stool in front of her and threaded her head through the loop.

"For the kingdom!" she yelled.

I felt her farewell and her plea not to intercede as she stepped off. In her heart, she knew I wasn't yet ready to face the queen. If I had been, we would have already faced the queen together.

Gripping Philip's arm, I willed myself not to *feel*—to keep everything contained—as Pogwid's energy winked out in an instant.

She was gone. The most powerful caster I knew was gone. Our hope to fight the queen and free Edmund and Brandle...

My need for Liam clawed at me. My anchor. My safety.

The queen visibly calmed and smoothed her hands down her skirt. She didn't feel calm, though. She wanted to make someone bleed. However, the person she wished to vent her ire on was dead.

Needlessly... Uselessly... While I watched and did nothing.

The hold on my thin control began to fracture.

"Let this be a message to all my people. Defy me and die," the queen said.

She swept off the gallows, turning her back on Pogwid, who swung like a pendulum in the light breeze as if the loss of her life didn't matter.

Inside of me, a long, thin line of sorrow split through the wall of my well.

The earth beneath us trembled just before the queen retreated within the white stone of the castle.

The strain to keep myself together continued even as the tingle under my skin eased. I couldn't lose control. Not here. Not amidst so many who would be injured.

I needed Liam. Desperately.

"Come," Philip said, helping me to my feet. "You look unwell."

I couldn't respond but did hear several people call his name. He ignored them all as he led me out of the courtyard and to the waiting carriage.

The moment Liam's hand closed around mine to assist me into the carriage, I knew I wouldn't last much longer.

"I need you," I said softly.

He nodded once and looked at Philip.

"Quickly," Liam said.

Philip joined me in the carriage and thumped on the roof.

The carriage jolted, and I leaned heavily into my seat. I fisted my hands and attempted to focus on the sound of the wheels rattling over the cobblestone or how my teeth chattered together because of the rough jostling. But it didn't work. Another fracture reverberated through me.

I flew forward as the carriage came to an abrupt stop, and I would have fallen to the floor if not for Philip's quick reflexes.

The door opened, and Liam climbed in, lifting me onto his lap.

Philip hit the roof again as Liam buried his fingers in my hair and pressed his forehead to mine.

"Tell me what you need," he said.

"Kiss me."

He did. Tenderly. Sweetly. His love and devotion wrapped around me, soothing some of my anguish. His desire filled me, becoming my own. I gratefully took what he offered and let it anchor and calm the storm within me.

When he pulled away, tears ran down my cheeks.

"Forgive me, my love," he said.

"For what?"

"For not trying to lock you in a room."

I made a pained sound and kissed him more deeply, loving that he understood me so well to see my regret but not berate me for my choices.

When we broke apart the second time, he pressed me to his chest and simply held me as my racing pulse calmed. The remaining distance to Philip's home passed in silence.

When we arrived, the driver jumped down to open the carriage door and didn't register even a moment of shock when Liam swept me into his arms and strode toward the front door. The butler opened it before we reached it.

"Take her to the sitting room," Philip called from behind us. "I'll have the cook brew some medicinal tea."

The sitting room wasn't as empty as we'd left it.

Darian shot to his feet when Liam entered with me in his arms.

"What's wrong? Is she hurt?" he demanded.

Daemon was a second behind his brother in reaching for me.

"She is not hurt," I said, answering for myself. "She is very angry."

Liam surrendered me to Darian, who settled onto the lounge with me on his lap. Daemon picked up my feet and removed my shoes. I exhaled heavily, focusing on their love rather than the hate that still bubbled inside of me.

"When I left Pogwid this morning, I cast a spell to protect her should the queen attempt to take her powers. It worked. The purpose of the public hanging was to find the caster and anyone else who'd helped Pogwid evade the queen's reach.

"The queen took Pogwid's fingers one by one to make her speak. Then she took Pogwid's tongue because that bold, abrasive woman dared speak of nothing but the vile crimes the queen had committed. In an attempt to find Pogwid's supporters, the queen left Pogwid's eyes so she would look to those who helped her before the moment of her death."

"Thus, the public hanging," Liam said.

I nodded and felt more tears rain down my cheeks.

"I wanted to help her, but she said I couldn't. That the queen was too powerful and that I would risk all of you to do so."

"She said that?" Liam said.

"Not aloud. When I was connected with her."

"My poor Lamb," Daemon said, rubbing my feet soothingly.

"Did the queen know you connected with her?" Garron asked.

"No. She was too focused on the three of her casting stones that had shattered and how Pogwid and taken their power to heal her tongue so she could speak. It was a warning to other casters to choose death rather than allow the queen to take their power."

Liam paused his pacing before the hearth when Philip entered with a tray.

"Have you received responses for tonight?" Liam asked.

"I have. Everyone will attend."

"Even after what happened?" I asked.

"Because of what happened," Philip said. "The queen has never lost control like that before. The state of her face, which she has always shown, proved she is not infallible. As did the way Pogwid shattered her casting stones."

I didn't correct him.

"What of the woodcutter?" I asked Garron. "Did he return home?"

"He did. But with no memory of us. There was nothing I could do for the cobbler, who likely saw us leaving as well."

I opened my senses and felt the people still waiting for us at our home. The cobbler was no longer in the back room, and I doubted that the people standing near the door were him.

"I believe he's already been taken," I said. My gaze went to Darian and Daemon. "I'm sorry I lost control this morning."

Darian shook his head. "Your loss of control this morning isn't a problem. You didn't hurt anyone. The queen did."

The others nodded.

"We'll find a way to get Edmund and Brandle back," Daemon said.

Yet, I felt his doubt. His brothers nurtured the same seed of disbelief, though they tried to hide it.

"How many nobles are attending tonight?" I asked.

"Twelve," Philip said. "I've prepared the invitations for tomorrow as well if your highnesses would care to review them."

Garron shook his head. "The names won't indicate the loyalty of the noble. Only the person will do that. Invite as you see fit."

"Very good, Your Highness," Philip said. "Guests should arrive within the hour."

I looked at the darkening window and felt a stirring of trepidation that had nothing to do with the now calmer tingle of warning under my skin.

"Can we agree that I will only be introduced as Philip's niece during these meetings?" I asked, briefly meeting the gazes of each of my five men. "I feel no shame in my relationship with all of you. However, others may not feel the same, and I have no wish to distract those in attendance from what is most urgent.

"The queen will not sit idly now that she knows someone with power, whether with magic or influence, has helped Pogwid evade her grasp. She will expend more of her power to search for Pogwid's supporters in the coming days. We need to meet with the other casters quickly for the sake of the people and Edmund and Brandle."

Liam slowly nodded. "Although I have no wish to hide what you mean to us, I believe you're right."

I turned toward Philip. "People are often caught in the web of their own lies. The less we say about me, the better. Your niece with a modest aptitude for casting should suffice."

"Yes, Princess," he said. "If you would care to change, I can show you to your room."

"No need for that," Darian said, standing with me in his arms. "We'll show her."

Philip nodded in agreement and retreated as Darian took several steps toward the door.

"Please allow me to use my own feet," I said.

"Aw, Lamb. You already stole our hearts. Must you steal our joy too?"

I looked over Darian's shoulder at Daemon and rolled my eyes at him.

"If I concede to your every wish, I would never leave my room."

He laughed. Darian eased me to my feet but didn't surrender his hold. He looped my hand around his arm and escorted me in a proper fashion.

Philip's home was larger than anything I'd ever visited. It boasted twelve guest rooms in a separate wing from the main house. The grandeur spoke of a familial wealth with which I wasn't familiar, and I briefly wondered if my mother had lived in such a home and why she'd left it.

Mother had rarely spoken of her family, only answering questions when directly asked. I only knew the name of my grandparents and my aunt from my father, divulged after I'd vowed never to tell Eloise, who we'd both known would approach the pair more so out of curiosity than desire to establish a relationship.

"You're quiet," Garron said.

I realized we were standing in the center of a large bedroom. A dress waited, neatly laid out on the bed. Margret stood off to the side, her head bowed.

"Distracted by thoughts of my family," I said.

"Are you worried for Eloise?"

"Always, but it was thoughts of my mother. I wondered if, as a noblewoman, she would have been more at ease here than I am."

Margret's head lifted briefly in shock. "If you would prefer a different—"

"The room and dress are beautiful," I said. "Please extend my appreciation to Philip. I simply miss my home."

Understanding lit her gaze as she nodded and retreated from the room, leaving me alone with Garron, Darian, and Daemon.

"Where are Eadric and Liam?" I asked.

"Speaking with Philip. They wished to ask more questions about the hanging without upsetting you."

I frowned. Daemon reached out and tapped the bridge of my nose.

"You are not fragile, we know. But your tears break our hearts. We would prefer not to cause more of them."

"But when I'm crying, someone can cuddle me. Isn't that a fair trade?"

Darian laughed. "She makes a point."

"More importantly, I don't like being excluded, and I know more than Philip. He only saw with his eyes. I didn't. The warning I've felt growing under my skin is related to the queen. I felt it the moment she appeared. I also felt her power. It pulsed around her, but not from within her. At least, nothing significant did. Her power is in the casting crystals she has, which is why I shattered three of them."

"You what?" Garron asked.

I knew it wasn't truly a question but an utterance due to shock.

"I was barely in control, Garron. In my mind, doing nothing wasn't an option. The queen couldn't touch Pogwid's power. Neither could Pogwid. Breaking the stones gave Pogwid the power she needed to speak out and make her choice clear." I fisted my hands in my skirts so they wouldn't see how angry I still felt. "Death was better than surrendering even an ounce of her power to the queen, and I understand why. The queen carries so much already. The three casting stones I broke are merely a drop in the power she possesses."

Darian and Daemon exchanged troubled glances.

"It would be wise not to speak of that to the casters we meet," Garron said.

I scoffed. "Wise? No, it would be a mistake to hide it."

"Kellen, they—"

"Won't join us if they know the true risk?" I finished. "Then we tell them the risk of remaining hidden. The queen *knows*, Garron. She knows someone powerful is out there because of today. Pogwid's willingness to sacrifice herself only proved to the queen that powerful adversaries are lurking, waiting for a moment of her weakness. What do you think she will do as a power-hungry ruler who fears being overthrown?"

Garron tiredly rubbed his brow.

"We will impress upon them all the reality of their situation," I said firmly. "Secrets never unite people."

"Yet you're being introduced as Philip's niece," Daemon said.

It annoyed me that he was right. "Then we reveal the truth as soon as possible, so long as it doesn't distract from our goals."

"Claiming you as our own *is* our goal," Darian said.

"Yes, yes," I said impatiently. "Once our other goals are met."

I felt the surge of their collective fear and wanted to stomp my foot. Instead, I turned toward Darian.

"Help me undress."

He deftly disrobed me within moments and trailed his fingers over my bare shoulders.

"Your shift appears dirty, too," he said, his voice soft.

I understood their need to distract themselves from the mess I'd made of their return. They didn't blame me, and I knew blaming myself would change nothing. So, instead, I gave myself over to what they needed.

Me.

"I believe you're correct," I said.

Daemon swept the shift over my head from behind me. His lips pressed against the back of my neck as Darian dropped to his knees in front of me. The tender way he kissed me below the navel brought a pang to my chest.

Reaching back, I tangled my fingers in the hair at the nape of Daemon's neck while also running my fingers through Darian's hair as his sweet kisses trailed lower. Darian's hand teased the skin behind my knees a moment before he gripped one and lifted it over his shoulder.

My head lolled to the side, giving Daemon access as he nibbled my skin. Their desire wove a spell of its own on me. I forgot everything and simply felt them. Their need for me. To love me. To care for me. To hold me and make me their own.

Darian's tongue toyed with me until I shook.

"The bed," he said against me.

CHAPTER 14

I GROANED AT THE VIBRATION OF HIS WORDS AND BARELY NOTICED Daemon's arms wrapping around me until he plucked me away from Darian's kiss. A whine escaped me, and Daemon chuckled.

"This will be better, Lamb," he said, nipping my neck and distracting me. "I promise."

He lifted me high and set me on my knees on the bed. When I would have turned to look back at him, his hand pressed between my shoulders. Giving into his urging, I braced my weight on my hands and knees. The bed dipped as Darian joined me, naked.

I needed no further coaxing when he lay opposite me and took hold of my knee. Straddling him, I sank onto his mouth and kissed his stomach as he kissed me more intimately. Daeman's hand smoothed over my buttocks. His desire sparked higher each time I rotated my hips against Darian's tongue. I increased my pace, gripping the sheets and leaning my forehead against Darian's abdomen.

The slow insertion of Daemon's fingers added to the building pleasure. The sounds I made softly rang out in the room. Daemon gently bit my shoulder blade and curled his fingers as he partially withdrew them. My world broke apart as I came with a scream.

Shuddering and gasping, I held onto Darian, and I floated back to reality.

Daemon lifted me, allowing Darian to shift on the bed so I no longer straddled him. When my knees touched the bedding once more, I felt his hard length prod my pulsing core. My eyes closed, and I groaned at the penetration.

Darian watched me with hooded eyes. His thoughts were turning more chaotic, and I knew what he desperately wanted. I reached for his hard length and kissed the end as his brother slowly thrust into me.

Daemon and Darian's desire bled into me, flooding into the well that seemingly had no end to its capacity. Yet, their desire was nothing compared to their silent brother's.

Without taking my mouth from Darian, I lifted my gaze to Garron who was leaning against the bedpost, watching with a yearning I'd never witnessed before.

When he caught my gaze, he started to turn away.

"Stay," I murmured.

Their desire and adoration surged at that answer.

Smiling, I went back to kissing Darian as he'd kissed me. His fingers tangled in my hair.

Daemon's hands stroked my hips as he found a steady rhythm that hit the same spot he'd touched earlier. The pleasure climbed more quickly the second time.

I needed them. I needed them all.

From somewhere else in the estate, I felt Liam and Eadric. Their desire for me. I took it and begged for more.

"Stop!" Garron said.

Daemon abruptly withdrew from me, and I lifted my head from Darian in confusion.

"I felt you," Garron said. "You connected with me just like you did this morning right before the air changed."

I blinked at him, attempting to focus on what he was saying. It wasn't easy. Need clawed through me. I hungered. For them. For their desire.

"The queen will find us and kill us, Snow," Garron said, holding my gaze.

It broke through the fog in my mind, and I shook myself free from the remains. Carefully, I sat on the bed and brought my knees to my chest, not because I was hurt but to focus on what was happening within me.

I could feel them—all seven of my men. And if what Garron said held true for them all, they could feel me, too. Yet, my lid was firmly covering my well. Their desire continued to flood it through the lid.

Stunned disbelief coursed through me.

Never once had I considered the lid anything other than solid. But as I focused, I realized that when energy existed within me, it had no form—my mind created the form. The same held true of the well. No physical container existed; it was simply an invention of my mind to explain what I felt and what I could do.

"Lamb? You just paled," Daemon said, instantly beside me.

Darian's hands ran over my back. "It's not your fault, Princess."

I realized they thought I was upset that I'd almost lost control. But had I almost? Or was it something else?

Unable to explore further out of fear of gaining the queen's attention, I closed myself off from all of them.

"I wasn't reproaching myself," I said. "I was trying to determine what was happening inside of me. It's...confusing."

"Though it pains me to say this—and I mean that quite literally—we should stop here," Darian said.

Their collective disappointment and regret made me laugh. "Dinner guests will arrive soon, and I'm not the only person who needs to dress."

The pair kissed my cheeks then left the room.

I held out my hand to Garron, who helped me stand.

"Thank you," I said.

"There will come a day when you will not need to worry about losing yourself in loving us. I promise."

I kissed his cheek and lifted my arms so he could slip the clean shift over my head. Garron's skills paralleled those of any practiced handmaiden and brought a happy smile to my lips as he brushed through my long hair.

"The best I can manage is a braid. Would you like me to summon someone?"

I shook my head and, keeping my lid firmly in place, attempted to connect with the energy in my well. No resistance existed, and I realized that I'd been unconsciously connecting with the energy within me every time I had opened my senses.

Energy had no form. Intent formed it. My intent had broken Maeve's spell. My own misunderstanding had prevented me from breaking it without Brandle's aid.

Foolish girl, I thought, echoing Pogwid's voice.

With little effort, I used the wind to twist my hair into thin braids and a fashionable coif.

"Could you sense me?" I asked.

"No, but I'm not the queen," Garron said. "This home isn't protected like ours had been. And don't even think about attempting to protect this place. It's too large."

"You doubt I'll be able to do so without being detected or that I lack the power to do so?" I asked without censure.

"Both, actually. We've run from her enough, Snow. I don't want to run again."

"Then we won't," I said. "We'll find the help we need and stand and face her. I vow it."

He kissed my brow and escorted me to the sitting room where Eadric waited with Liam and Philip. All three wore coats cut from a rich cloth with stitching so fine I couldn't see it.

I smiled at them when Eadric gave a low whistle. He crossed the space between us and strolled around me.

"Do I pass your inspection?" I asked.

"Most assuredly," he said, bringing my hand to his lips.

The first guest arrived shortly after the others joined us in the sitting room. As we'd agreed, Philip introduced me as his relative. Instead of a niece, I was a distant one from the country. He kept it vague, and no one asked for more information.

Most exuded eagerness and welcome. Maeve had taught me not to trust what people showed on the outside. So, each time I touched someone in greeting, I connected with my well and touched their minds. I searched for fear or anger, trying my best to maintain their privacy while also ensuring our safety.

Many feared the queen and what would happen to Adele if her reign continued for much longer. They feared losing their lives attempting to free themselves but also feared losing them if they did nothing. The impending doom, regardless of their chosen path, created a volatility that worked in our favor.

"May I have your attention," I called. The room quieted, and I lifted my glass. "To Pogwid. May she forever be known for the extraordinary gifts she possessed and the light she brought into this world rather than the sacrifice she made to leave it. Death to the Foul Queen."

A subtle ripple of shock ran through the room before a nobleman lifted his glass high.

"To Pogwid. And Death to the Foul Queen."

The room echoed with similar sentiments, and they drank their watered wine.

"Thank you for answering our call in the wake of Pogwid's capture," Liam said. "We can no longer wait to move forward with our plans. The queen understands that Pogwid could not have remained hidden within the castle's shadow for so long without aid. She will seek out and imprison every person involved. And where one noble can hide a powerful caster, she will look to the others suspecting the same."

"What do you need of us?" one of the noblemen asked.

"We need to meet with the remaining casters in this kingdom who have the strongest abilities," Liam answered. "We need to unite and fight the queen."

I COLLAPSED into the chair and lifted my foot. Darian knelt, plucked off my shoe, and rubbed my pinched toes.

"Two days," I said angrily. "We've met countless nobles, yet not a single caster. What are they waiting for?"

"Perhaps a sign that they can win," Garron said. "The casters, I mean. Not the noblemen."

I allowed my head to fall back and closed my eyes. A sign? What sign would inspire them? Another public hanging of one of their own?

"Blighted poxes on humanity," I mumbled under my breath.

Eadric's humor flared, but he wisely didn't comment on my colorful cursing. Darian's fingers dug deeper into the arch of my foot, and it helped me release some of the tension I held.

"What more of a sign do they need? Three of the queen's casting stones broke—quite visibly, mind you—in front of all the nobles gathered. Do they doubt their supporters' words?"

"We cannot ignore that Pogwid also lost her life after that bit of defiance," Eadric said. "The casters are afraid. As they should be."

His voice of reason didn't help abate my frustration.

"Two days," I reiterated. "Two days Edmund and Brandle have been in the queen's clutches. Do they still have their fingers and tongues? Pogwid lost hers in a matter of hours."

I felt their turbulent emotions at my words.

"We know," Daemon said quietly. "If we thought we could save them by storming the castle, we would have done so already. Waiting is anguish for us all. But without the casters, we have no hope and would lose our lives. Who will save Brandle and Edmund then?"

I tugged my foot from Darian's grasp and leaned forward to kiss him passionately.

Over the course of the last few days, I'd needed these spontaneous kisses with increasing frequency. My already questionable control was frayed to the point of breaking, and *that* we could not allow.

When Darian pulled back to look at me, I was breathing heavily and ready for more than kissing. He palmed my chest through my dress and pinched my nipple. Each morning and evening, one of them brought me to the height of pleasure, giving me the release I needed to reset the frustration. But never more than one of them and never more than once.

The desire I gathered from them never ceased now. They fed my well even when sitting in a room with boorish nobles, using pretty words to promise introductions to their casters but never appearing with them.

"I'm done waiting," I said. "Done."

Darian kissed my forehead. "What would you like to do?"

"Hunt them myself," I said. "Liam, I'll need your old clothes, please."

Eadric groaned, and I felt their collective resistance as I stood.

"Fetch them, or I start casting and let the queen come to me."

I meant every word. I was done—done with everything—the dinners, the fawning over my men…especially that.

One noble had had the audacity to think of pairing his niece with Liam. Of course, he didn't speak it, but he'd thought it *while kissing my hand*. It wasn't simply jealousy driving me. I'd had subtle hints of hidden agendas from all of the nobles. Nothing that aligned them with the queen, though. No, far from it. They were very eager to align themselves with the princes to win their favor. They wished for lavish gain.

Liam hurriedly slipped from the room as I fisted my hands in my skirts.

Eadric crossed the room and, without warning, swung me up onto his shoulder. His hand swatted my buttock with stinging strength. The pain was so shocking I couldn't even draw air.

"Um, Eadric, you might not want to do that," Daemon said. "She bites, remember?"

"I remember," he said. "But the kissing isn't working anymore."

He swatted my other buttock with the same stinging force.

His words and the pain cut through to the sensible part of my thoughts.

"Cease," I begged. "I am calmer now. I promise."

Eadric immediately righted me then hugged me.

"You can still bite me if you'd like."

I shook my head and hugged him in return.

"Unbelievable," Daemon whispered. "We would have broken noses if we spanked her like that."

Eadric chuckled and kissed the top of my head. "Thank you for not breaking my nose, Sparrow. I am a bit disappointed you didn't bite me in the arse. I saw the mark it left on Brandle and want one of my own."

I snorted and pulled away from him.

"You're ridiculous."

He shrugged and darted in for a quick kiss.

"Will you share your plan? Do you need a fellow miscreant to accompany you? I've been told I'm quite beggar-like in my old clothes."

I smoothed my hand over his handsomely tailored coat and slipped my hand inside to feel his fine linen shirt.

"The clothes don't make the man," I said. "It's his heart."

He pressed his hand over mine and kissed me more passionately. I was the one to step back from the distraction.

"Since I know that none of you wants me to go out alone, I will accept one person to accompany me. The choice is yours."

An hour later, Garron and I slipped out of the servants' door. With a hat pulled low over my brow and my hair tucked into it, I passed well enough for a man.

We weaved our way through the streets, once again avoiding the increased number of patrols. The route we chose didn't matter, though, since I meant to walk every street eventually.

"What are we looking for," Garron asked, noticing that we'd backtracked.

"A sense of wrongness like I felt when we turned onto Pogwid's street."

It took several hours before I found what I was looking for. The ever-present tingle of warning under my skin intensified when we turned down a street lined with well-kept homes.

A woman wove cloth in her side yard, humming to herself. A man sat on his front step and carved something. An older child turned the soil in a narrow strip beside her home.

And none of it was real.

I didn't know how I knew it since I could feel what they felt as they worked and saw the shadows they cast in the midday sun; I simply knew.

Stopping in front of the man, I watched him look up at me.

"Need something?" he asked gruffly.

"I do," I said. "Desperately."

He tilted his head, his expression full of suspicion.

"Well, speak already, boy. What do you need?"

I leaned in and whispered, "Your help to kill the queen."

The man swore and stood up abruptly, slamming his door in my face.

"Snow," Garron said in soft warning.

"Hush."

Focusing, I closed my eyes and told myself to see and feel the truth, not what the caster wanted me to see and feel. When I opened them again, the street looked much the same. All the homes were well-kept, but the people were missing, and only one home had smoke drifting from the chimney.

"There," I said, pointing.

The door opened at our approach as it had at Pogwid's.

Not waiting for an invitation, I walked inside and slowly peeled away the layers of the spell hiding what truly existed until I saw the older woman standing before me.

"You're the distant relative," she said a moment before I felt her attempt to touch my energy. I brushed it away and made no attempt to connect with hers.

"I am, and I am not, much like your neighbors and your home."

"So I see," the old woman said. "Then what are you?"

"The future queen," Garron said, speaking from behind me.

The old woman's gaze shifted to Garron, assessing.

"The sixth prince," the woman said. I liked her more for not fawning over him.

"I am," he acknowledged.

"And do you think that you'll take the throne over your brothers?" she asked.

Garron laughed, surprising me.

"My brothers and I will not fight each other for the throne once the queen is removed."

The woman's assessing gaze came back to me.

"What do you want from me? Help? You think the two of us can face the queen?" She scoffed, turned her back on me, and settled into a chair facing the fire.

Only...she didn't, not truly. The woman in the chair was the result of the subtle spell she'd been casting while speaking. What she did was walk around the room as if to leave the house.

I used a breeze to close the door before she reached it then cast a spell of my own. From nothing, I created two chairs and sat in one. Something that should have been complex was easier than anything I'd previously cast because I finally understood. The energy inside of me was whatever I needed it to be.

"I'd like a few moments of your time," I said, meeting the gaze of the real caster.

I could feel Garron's surprise and knew he'd been watching the woman at the fire.

"My name is Kellen. May I ask yours?"

"Getaina," the woman said. Her gaze shifted from me to the chair. "It's real?"

"Find out for yourself."

She shuffled forward, touched the chair, then sat facing me.

"You're the one Pogwid was protecting."

"She said I was dangerous because I lack control. Did you feel me when I cast just now?" I asked.

"No. Do you still lack control?"

"Yes."

"No," Garron said. "She doesn't lack control. She loses control when she experiences extreme emotions. There's a difference."

"True," Getaina said. "Were you at her hanging?"

"I was."

"Was it you who broke the queen's casting stones?"

"It was." I hesitated for a moment. "I couldn't save her. Pogwid. She wouldn't let me."

"I should think not. You have too much potential to waste like that." She folded her arms over her stomach and leaned back into the chair. "Do you know how to search people's minds?"

"I do."

"Good. You need to search mine. I have eighty years of

knowledge you need, and we have no time for me to teach you. Look into my mind."

"So you can look into mine?" I asked.

Her wide grin answered my question.

"You might be offended by what you see," I said.

"I'm old, girl, and you're dressed like a lad. I doubt anything I see will be offending."

Garron set his hand on my shoulder. "If I have a vote, I'm against this. We don't know her."

"Smart to be wary," Getaina said with a nod.

"You do have a vote, Garron," I said, patting his hand. "One for it, one against, and no tiebreakers other than the fact we're running out of time."

He gave my shoulder a squeeze and released me.

"Do not harm her," he said.

I knew his warning was meant for Getaina but found myself worrying regardless. The time I'd looked into Pogwid's mind, my abilities had still been caged by Maeve's spell. Joining with Liam had broken it, and understanding the true nature of energy had freed me even more.

When I carefully touched my energy to Getaina's well, it felt different. So very different. I could see everywhere with little effort and could control where she was looking in my mind. I let her see everything from my youth, fearing nothing found there, not even the trouble Eloise and I caused from time to time. However, I kept the intimate time with the princes hazy.

While she learned from me, I learned from her.

Everything. Her sad childhood, neglected by a father with too many children and a second wife fresh in the grave. Her first marriage when her powers were still growing. I watched her daughter marry then die in childbirth.

With each memory flooding me, so too did the emotions associated with them. They became my own. Tears trailed down my cheeks. I felt Getaina's terror over the last two decades and her heartbreak over all the innocent lives lost. So many children. So many wards she'd made that the queen always found a way around.

"Lend me your wisdom," I murmured. "Help me."

Spells—failures and successes—bloomed in my mind between one blink and the next.

CHAPTER 15

"Stop. Please. I beg you. I can't."

The words were a distant ripple in my mind.

The crack of Garron's hand across my face wasn't. I shot to my feet and struck his nose with the heel of my hand. He grunted and stumbled back a step.

"You were hurting her, Kellen," he said. "You weren't answering."

A chaotic storm of thoughts, not all my own, tumbled around in my head, making it ache and hard to understand what he was saying.

"The tea," Getaina said faintly.

A second later, a cup was pressed to my mouth. The rancid taste of the healing tea was familiar enough that I swallowed it despite the taste.

"I meant for me, you dolt," Getaina said.

"I know, but Kellen needed it more," Garron said, taking away the cup. "You saw what happens when she loses control."

The ache in my head eased, and my thoughts settled as he handed her the remaining tea. She drank it quickly.

"Do I owe you an apology?" I asked.

Her sharp gaze found mine, and I could feel her pain.

"You lack finesse, girl, but I can see what Pogwid saw. You ripped my entire life from my head within minutes. And look at you. Barely a headache. Can you feel the way my heart is pounding? My blood feels hot, close to boiling. And the way my head... It felt like I was dying."

"I'm sorry. I don't know—" I stopped because I *did* know. The knowledge of how to touch someone's mind without causing pain existed in my mind as if it had always existed...as if it was my own knowledge and not her memories.

"I don't understand what I did, but I know things. Spells. It feels like I've always known them."

She nodded. "It was knowledge freely given. Not the rest, though. I had to fight you for that." She looked at Garron. "You should thank me. If I'd let her have it all, your future bride would think she was me."

"Sincerely, I thank you," he said with a regal bow.

Getaina snorted. "Words are useless. Thank me by helping me live more comfortably. Help—one hour a day—from one of the princes for the rest of my life."

"Granted, except for when we travel, unless you wish to travel with us."

She waved away the offer and focused on me.

"Like Pogwid, the bulk of my strength now lies in my knowledge, which you now have. There's nothing more I can do for you, girl. Don't return until the queen is gone. Now, go."

She leaned back in her chair and waved us out.

When we emerged, the man once again sat on his doorstep, carving. He nodded at us and then went back to work.

I eyed the meager distance between the sun and the horizon as Garron and I walked down the road.

"We should return to the estate," I said softly.

The words barely left my mouth when I sensed a patrol coming. Grabbing Garron's hand, I pulled him in between the homes at the end of the road. I lifted my finger to my lips and listened, afraid I'd once again exposed another caster.

"Have you seen any men not from Adele?" the guard asked over a sudden pounding.

The fake man answered, "How am I to know who's not from Adele by looking at them? Do they look odd?"

The pounding ceased.

"Seven of them," the guard barked. "Three with a woman posing as their sister and four others posing as their cousins. All of an age ranging between sixteen and twenty-one."

"Nope. Can't say that I've seen a group of men passing by. No reason to on this street."

The guard began moving our way. With a thought, I bent the light in the air to show the space behind us as if we didn't exist, a simpler way to hide than the complex cast I would need to create an illusion such as Getaina had.

Garron remained silent as we watched the guard pass us. I felt his anxiousness when one man looked our way, but it faded once they left.

"The queen knows," I said softly.

He nodded, took my hand, and led me back to the street and saw the reason for the pounding. Sketches had been nailed to the side of one house. Seven of them. One rough sketch for each prince's face.

Garron swore.

"You better go back in," the fake man said. "You'll need to fix your face before you can leave."

The door to Getaina's swung open, and I pulled us back inside.

I CAPPED the last vial and wrapped them all in the cloth Getaina had provided.

"How is your head?" I asked.

"Good. The pain's almost gone. My knees don't hurt at all either." She stood and sat several times. "Hips too. Take care when you brew your healing tea. Too potent and the bones can mend before they're set in place."

"So I read. I didn't feel anything broken inside of you, though."

She tsked at me and nodded to Garron, who was staring at the muddy liquid in the cup I'd given him.

"I think he doubts your skills," she said.

"Not in the slightest," Garron said. "However, I am regretting my choice to slap her earlier and hope that hasn't influenced her choice in remaking my appearance."

"I promise you'll be fine, Garron. Just drink already. The sun has set, and your brothers are worriers. We can't afford them roaming the streets until they drink these."

He wrinkled his nose and tipped back the brew. His gag reflex reacted violently, which Getaina found vastly amusing.

"Keep it down, boy. Too many ingredients were used to waste it like that. There you go. Good. Just breathe through it."

As I watched, his face began to shift and bubble.

"Does it hurt?" I asked.

"No. It itches fiercely, though."

Getaina remained quiet, and I felt her growing concern. She'd never seen the spell work like that before. I glanced at her.

"I thought spells either worked or didn't work," I said. "Can I cast wrong? Can I hurt them?"

"Of course you can cast wrong. Who told you that nonsense about it either working or not working?"

I looked at Garron.

"You were too afraid, Snow, and we needed you to be fearless."

His face settled into a misshaped imitation of his former self, completely unrecognizable if one only had the sketch to evaluate and compare.

"Well, that certainly will work. Let's hope it's not permanent, or you'll have ugly babies. Would you like to see?" She held out a mirror, which I snatched from her hand.

"He would not," I said.

Then I crossed the room and kissed Garron on his twisted lips.

"It's temporary. I promise."

"I trust you," he said.

"Perhaps you shouldn't. I was trying to turn you into a woman."

Getaina hooted and slapped her knee. "If you'd been able to manage that, you wouldn't have needed to see me. You would have been able to defeat the queen on your own. I've only heard of one caster in our history able to change people into something other than themselves. I'm pretty sure she turned a man into a beast."

"A beast? From the Dark Forest?"

"No, girl. That corruption is from the original wars. This story is from after that. To the north. I can't remember the name." She sat, her expression conveying her deep thought. "It'll come to me. I wonder if she's still alive. Her story is likely why the queen is obsessed with finding a way to stay young."

"What do you mean?"

"Rumor says that the caster who changed the man into a beast doesn't age."

"And if one caster can do it, then so can another," I said in understanding.

"Exactly. The queen is trying everything: breeding babies with strong bloodlines and sacrificing them for their powers, blood magic of every kind. She even tried capturing the Hunter."

"The Hunter?"

"It's a beast in the Dark Forest," Garron said. "It's smart and hunts men who enter its domain. We always avoid that part of the forest."

"Why does the queen want a beast?" I asked.

"It's rumored that he's the original beast," Getaina said.

"Thank you for your help and for the information," I said.

"You're welcome. I'm glad there's something I can still share that you didn't already pull from me."

"Why didn't she?" Garron asked.

"Sometimes, the little details slip through," Getaina said. "But it's often the little details that matter. Don't forget that, Kellen."

"I won't."

We left with the vials and evaded everyone after dark since I feared Garron's face would draw too much attention. Arriving at the back door of Philip's estate, my suspicions were confirmed when Margret answered the door and screamed at the sight of him.

"It's us," I said, quickly covering her mouth. "Kellen and Garron."

She nodded and stepped back from my hand.

"Forgive me. I didn't…" Her gaze shifted to Garron. "Will he be all right?"

"The spell will only last a few hours," I said. "He will be fine. Where are the others?"

"In the dining room with this evening's guests." Her gaze flicked between Garron and me.

I took his hand. "I believe we'll join them."

She nodded and led the way. When we entered, the kitchen help was removing the dishes from the second course of their meal.

"Please add two more settings," I said as Garron pulled out a chair for me.

Daemon's attempt to smother his humor in his napkin failed, and I reached up to stroke Garron's face so he knew I didn't find him repulsive.

"I know they're next," he said softly with a twisted grin.

He took his seat beside me, and I felt the complete shock of the nobles in attendance, all of whom I'd previously met. Not so with the brothers. They didn't care that I was dressed like a lad in front of the nobles or that Garron's face wasn't as it should be. They radiated curiosity.

"I apologize for our late arrival," I said. "Business kept us a bit longer than we'd anticipated. Lord Hamill, we've met with Getaina already, so there's no need for you to persuade her. As soon as we're finished here, Garron and I will continue searching for the others on our own."

Liam's concern almost matched Garron's, but neither refuted my words.

A hint of outrage drifted from Lord Hamill, which I found interesting.

"What precisely offends you, Lord Hamill? That I lacked the patience to wait until it was convenient for you to provide what we needed or that I'm fully capable of finding them without needing your help? The latter does pose a problem, doesn't it? Much harder to gain the favor of the princes when you have nothing to provide them."

His anger grew while, outwardly, he smiled benevolently.

"Offended? Never. The princes are fortunate to have someone with skills of her own on which they can depend."

"That won't do," I said as if to myself but loud enough for all to hear. "I insist you speak what you truly think." I touched his mind with my intent.

He slammed his hands down on the table, showing his real feelings.

"How dare you approach what's mine. You may have the favor of the princes now, but it won't last long. Once the throne is empty, they will have no use for a second-rate harlot caster and look to the noble families for a real queen."

His mouth snapped shut. His outrage evaporated, replaced by disbelief, shame, and defeat.

"I see," I said. "And how many of you also feel this way?" As my gaze swept the table, I touched each noble and their wives with my intent, freeing them to speak the thoughts they kept hidden.

"Our daughter should marry Brandle, the true successor," one woman said.

Another noble's hand slammed on the table. "She's betrothed to my son!"

Chaos broke out as they argued amongst themselves. Lord Hammill didn't join in. His gaze remained fixated on the table, his tumultuous thoughts focused on finding a way to salvage his standing.

"Enough," I said, silencing them all. "The Foul Queen knows the princes have returned. Posters with drawings of them are being spread around Adele as we speak. While I hope that means she hasn't yet discovered Brandle and Edmund in her midst, I am not prepared to stake their lives on it.

"Yes, Lord Hamill, that means Brandle and Edmund have been taken. She has held them for the last two days as handsome men for her next breeding. Thank you for paying attention to the conversation again.

"The games to bid for the princes' favor end tonight. You have a simple choice to make. Fully support the princes without condition in removing the queen or watch the princes leave Adele to its fate."

"They will never leave their brothers to the queen," Lord Hamill said.

"Correct. But freeing their brothers needn't mean that they face the queen." I took Garron's hand and smiled at him. "I've always wanted to see the south. I've heard women there wear pants all the time. Their clothing is almost see-through, mind you. Quite scandalous."

"I think I would like to see you dress thusly," Darian said. "I vote yes to going south instead of helping people who have no wish to be helped."

"I vote yes, too," Daemon said.

"It's impossible to sneak into the castle," one noble said desperately.

"Not if you're a handsome man. I'm certain that, after visiting a few more casters, I will have the knowledge I need to change my appearance and win my way into the castle, free the princes, and leave Adele before the new day dawns."

"That does sound appealing," Eadric said. "We can be back in our cottage tomorrow night. Life was simpler—happier—there."

"Very true," Liam said.

I could feel their annoyance with the nobles and their hope that I was only saying what was necessary to sway them. Collectively, the princes didn't want me going anywhere near the castle, but they weren't opposed to the idea of returning to the cottage. None of them wanted to leave the people under the queen's rule, though. Or the nobles, for that matter, now that they'd revealed their hidden intents.

"Choose," Liam said to them. "Stand with us, or lose everything you hold dear."

The speed at which they summoned their footmen to send messages to their casters would have been entertaining if not for the time we'd already lost.

Hungry, I dug into the small fowl that was set before me for the next course, purposely ignoring all etiquette. The revulsion of the wives amused me greatly.

"I am beginning to see the trouble you and your sister might have caused in your youths," Garron said softly beside me.

I flashed a grin at him and continued eating with my fingers and teeth.

Eadric's desire wrapped around me when I licked my fingers. So I repeated the process. Daemon and Darian's desire flooded into my well. I connected to them all, even feeling Brandle and Edmund. Their love for me and their exhaustion.

The leg I'd been eating fell to my plate as I stared straight at the woman's wig across from me and focused on Brandle and Edmund.

"Snow?" Garron asked, touching my arm.

"Hush."

Edmund's frustration grew.

"Something is happening to them," I said. "They're tired. Edmund is frustrated."

I touched him with my love, and his answered. Just as his desire started to surge, a spark of energy burst into existence around him.

The queen. She was trying to do something to him.

"He is mine!" My hands slammed down on the table.

The woman across from me grabbed at her neck in shock, but I ignored her and focused on Edmund's energy as Garron's hand encircled my upper arm.

"Do not reveal where we are," he said urgently.

In my mind, I also heard Edmund's voice clearly.

Your love protects us. Go.

I felt it then. The spell I'd cast in the glade to bind me to them was protecting him. Barely.

Touching my well through its lid, I sent my energy surging toward Edmund. It easily slipped under the queen's power and joined the thin barrier already surrounding him.

My love and intent merged with what was already there. The barrier grew thicker and more impenetrable.

Withdrawing from him, I stood. "Edmund's with the queen. He's safe. For now."

"Where are you going?"

"To take a bath. I can still feel her touching him, trying to arouse him. She knows who he is and is trying to secure her right to the throne." I looked at the nobles. "Your delays may have already cost you the freedom to choose."

I started from the room.

"Eadric, you may attend me," I called over my shoulder.

His chair scraped against the floor in his rush to follow me.

I waited outside the dining room for him.

"Did I go too far?" I asked.

He grinned widely and swept me up into his arms. "You were perfect, Sparrow. The way you stood up to the nobles and put them in their place was very...regal."

"Do you think the casters will arrive soon?"

"Yes. And I don't think our guests will leave until that happens. Were you serious about turning yourself into a handsome man and entering the castle?"

"I was. I've seen the illusions that Pogwid and Getaina used. Complex spells that required a great deal of power to cast but very little to maintain. There are already potions to change a person's appearance. Simple things like adding moles or removing them. And I also know that I can cast to make something become something against its nature."

"Peas with thorns," he said in understanding.

"Precisely. In theory, if I can do all of that, I should be able to temporarily turn myself into a man."

"I would very much like to see you as a man," he said. "One that Edmund doesn't recognize. Then you can kiss him."

I laughed at Eadric's imagination and hugged him in gratitude for helping me see some light in an otherwise dark time.

When my humor faded, I confided, "I heard Edmund clearly in my mind. He told me that my love is protecting them."

"Makes sense. When you cast that spell to bind yourself to us, it felt like you were wrapping your arms around me. That feeling hasn't left."

"It hasn't?"

"No."

Relaxed from Eadric's very attentive care, I lounged in the bath and let him play with the wet strands of my hair trailing over his chest. Our thundering pulses gradually slowed.

"Was I too rough?" he asked.

"No. You were perfect."

He kissed my temple. "You're perfect, Sparrow."

Darian knocked on the door to my room. The ease with which I knew this no longer confused me. I was connected with them and had been before I'd cast that spell in the clearing.

"Enter," I called.

The worry he carried melted away when he walked in and saw me reclining in the bath.

"I think I could use one of those," he said.

"And you can have one…once I've met with the casters who've come."

His brows rose. "You know?"

"I do. I could feel you thinking about them. You're worried because they're all so old." I sat up so I could see both brothers. "Does it bother you that I can feel what you're thinking?"

"Never," they both answered.

"Will you tell me if that ever changes?"

"It won't," Eadric said.

"I agree," Darian said. "It won't change. However, *if* it does, we will immediately speak our minds if you don't already guess it."

"Thank you."

I extended my hand so Darian could help me out of the bath and combed my fingers through his hair as he knelt to dry my legs. While he worked, I drank in his desire.

"I look forward to our lives together," I said softly. "Days where I can wake up in a loving embrace and play and read and relax."

Darian stood quickly to kiss me.

"We will worship you for the rest of our lives and ensure you don't regret a moment of the help you've given us."

He kissed my forehead then helped me dress. Eadric finished at the same time, and the three of us rejoined the others.

Gataina was there, listening to Lord Hamill's whispered words. A hint of annoyance pulled at her expression until she saw me. Her wink was filled with humor.

"There you are, girl," she said. "About time you showed up. I heard you've been causing all the fine nobles of Adele some concern. No deference. Haven't you learned your place yet?"

"I'm hoping to. Perhaps you would be willing to put in a good word for me so I can learn a bit faster?"

Getaina chuckled and looked at her peers.

"If you let her in, keep a tight hold on what's yours, or she'll take it all, and we'll be the ones who have to work to undo it."

"Let her in?" one woman asked. "Why?"

"Her control is shite," Getaina said bluntly. "That and I think she's the powerful caster that the queen needs to achieve her dream. If she finds Kellen before Kellen can learn to protect herself, we'll have lost before we've begun."

"I don't believe you," a woman said.

A second later, I felt her attempt to connect with my energy. Rather than brushing her away, I *pulled* her in. She sank into my well. I waited for that moment of panic that Pogwid had experienced then connected with her.

"Hold onto yourself," I heard Getaina say as the woman's memories flooded me.

She came from a wealthy family and had connections to the royal bloodline. She hated the queen who sat on the throne yet secretly wished she'd been smart enough and powerful enough to take it for herself in her youth. Or, at least, that she'd found a way to endear herself to the prince at the time. Then she could have been Queen.

We would have been Queen.

I would have been—

A palm landed on my cheek with a resonating crack. At the same time, arms wrapped around me from behind.

Their love, fear, and determination not to lose me calmed me before I could lash out at them.

"Free her, Kellen," Getaina said.

"Not yet," I rasped. "Please, Ulva...willingly give me your knowledge. Please."

Held up between her peers, tears ran down the woman's slack face. Yet, I felt her agreement a moment before information flooded me.

CHAPTER 16

H ER SUBTLE RETREAT SIGNALED AN END, AND I WITHDREW MY energy. She sagged further between her peers and groaned. The pain in my head was merely a kernel of grain in a sack filled with them. She possessed the sack.

With barely a thought, I gathered the moisture in the air, created the necessary herbs from nothing, and heated it. A cup appeared next to hold it all. I clasped it in my hand, took a sip, then brought it to the woman's lips.

"Drink. It will ease the pain."

I could feel she wanted to but watched some of it dribble from the corners of her mouth in her attempt.

"Pogwid had a similar reaction when she attempted to connect with my well. She said she could feel herself falling into it but pulled back. I suggest no one else attempt to take more than what I offer, just as I promise not to take more than what you offer."

The others nodded. I could feel the fear behind their agreement, though.

"I am not the queen. You have a choice. I did not force Ulva to dive into my well. She did that on her own. I haven't swayed

Getaina to lure you here, and I have no desire to consume all that you are. Nor am I interested in stealing the throne from the princes. If I had a choice, I wouldn't be here at all."

Shock rippled through the pair that had been thinking those thoughts.

"Pogwid said I'm a danger because I have no control. Getaina believes I have the control but lack the knowledge to protect myself. Yes, I can do things that Garron and Pogwid have said other casters can't do. But I don't understand how; they just happen.

"My request—and it is only a request—is that you share what you know. Knowledge is power. With it, I can protect not only myself but the people of Turre as well. And no, that does not mean I am interested in overthrowing the queen to take her place in subjugating others. I am very willing to leave the kingdom once it's freed. Now, will you help me?"

"No," one of the quiet women said firmly. She turned on her heel and started for the door.

"May I ask why?" I called after her.

I gained the answer despite her silence. Despite my words, she still thought I was after the queen's casting stones stolen from all the casters she's taken over the years, even her daughter's. The door closed behind her.

"Those who have no wish to help me may leave," I said. "I have other casters to visit yet this night."

"She's resting in her room," Philip said, entering the sitting room. "Do you still plan to seek out others?"

Liam had put an end to the night's progress and sent Getaina to sleep in a guest room with the promise that I would wake her once I'd rested—a promise he'd given without consulting with me. But I'd been too focused on controlling my need to vomit to argue with him. Thankfully, that had eased with the healing tea I'd brewed for myself—not the headache, though.

"I would like to put it to a vote," Eadric said.

Feeling their collective worry, I waved away his suggestion.

"I already know you lot are against it, and my head aches too much to uselessly argue whether or not I can take any more knowledge without rest. So take me to bed, but know that the queen is actively with your brothers, attempting to seduce them while I sleep to ease your worries."

"Unfair, Love," Liam said softly.

"That's life, isn't it?"

"She's beginning to sound like them," Eadric said. "Getaina warned this may happen."

"To bed, then," Daemon said, plucking me off my chair.

I settled against his chest and struggled not to give in to the irritation clawing at me. Too many thoughts rattled around in my pain-filled head. Getaina had warned me of the dangers but hadn't stopped me from consuming the knowledge of her peers, one after another. No, rather than dissuade me, I'd felt her curiosity. She wanted to know my limit. And each person from which I'd learned had added to her growing hope that I could one day be strong enough to face the queen.

However, we didn't have time for "one day."

Opening myself, I reached for their desire.

"Be careful, Snow," Garron said softly, proving that he felt me.

As their desire flooded me, I felt Edmund. He was sleeping. Yet, even in his sleep, he responded to me. His yearning was bittersweet.

Brandle's desire evaded me, however. Regardless of where I searched for him, he wasn't there.

"Lamb?" Daemon called.

I realized I was gripping his shoulder tightly and loosened my hold, but not my reach for their desire. I pulled harder.

Daemon stumbled a step, and Darian was there to steady us. Garron cleared his throat twice.

"What are you doing?" he asked.

"I can't feel Brandle," I said, fighting against my panic.

"It's okay, Sparrow," Eadric said. "It'll be okay."

But it wasn't. Where Brandle should have been was an empty void. I couldn't feel him. He was gone.

Panic boiled inside. Pulsing. Demanding to run wild.

Hands cupped my face, tapping my cheeks, demanding a response I couldn't give. Where had Brandle gone?

In frantic silence, I pleaded for an answer and let my desperation free.

A mouth closed over mine, kissing me hungrily. The floor rumbled beneath our feet.

"Daemon, stop."

Our teeth clacked together when one of the others cuffed him. A moment later, I was stolen from his arms and pinned in Eadric's tight embrace.

"Don't lose control," he pleaded. "We cannot lose you too."

Garron hugged us from behind. Then Liam, Daemon, and Darian joined the hug. I felt their love wrapping me in a cocoon of protection.

"Brandle's not gone," Darian said. "The queen wouldn't be quiet if he was."

"He's right," Garron said. "She knows who he is and will use that to help herself gain control."

"If you want to help him, sleep, Lamb. Please."

I nodded, and they released me. Eadric led me to the bed and held me close until I succumbed to the need to sleep.

It helped.

When I opened my eyes to the light of a new day, the pain in my head was gone, and I once more felt my usual self.

"Is your head better?" Liam, my pillow, asked.

"It is. Where are the others?"

He brushed the hair back from my face.

"There is news. They've left to verify it."

"What news?" Even as I asked, I knew—news of Brandle and Edmund.

"Another public hanging," Liam said. "Two of the kingdom's princes. All the nobles are required to attend at midday."

My mask slipped into place, saving me from the crashing waves of despair that wanted to overwhelm me. Touching my well, I reached for them. The connections came easily. All of them, including Brandle. His anger matched Edmund's. They knew what she had planned but didn't fear for themselves. They feared for me.

"It's a trap then," I said softly. "Not for the other princes, though. For me."

"How do you know?"

"I can feel Edmund and Brandle. Brandle isn't worried for himself or Edmund or any of his brothers. He's strongly afraid for me."

"How can he remember you? The spell to forget you if he were taken should have erased all memory of you."

I thought back to how it felt when I'd connected with Edmund.

"I don't think it could. I think the spell I cast in the clearing ensured I could never leave you. Not even the memory of me."

"Then it makes sense you're his greatest concern. We promised to protect you. If they are there for breeding and not giving in to her demands because of the love that broke the curse, she will want to remove you." Liam nodded thoughtfully. "And the quickest way to flush out the game is to bait the trap."

"The queen got to where she is by being clever. However, I've survived this long by being the same. Come. There's much to do before midday and little time to do it."

He rose with me and watched me put on my simple spun dress.

"Have Philip tell his staff I will need the kitchen. Garron should join me when he returns."

I swept out of the room and found Margret waiting in the hallway.

"Come with me to the study," I said. "I have a list of supplies I need you to find."

A short while later, she left with my list and Adogen's name, the only caster I knew who Margret could visit without drawing suspicion.

When I went to the dining room, Philip was sitting at the table with Liam. He immediately rose and bowed to me.

"The staff has been told you require the kitchen. They are setting it to rights now. Would you care for something to eat before you set to work?"

I liked that he didn't ask what I would be casting.

"Thank you," I said, taking a seat and accepting the pastry that Liam passed to me.

"Would you happen to have a male staff member willing to sample a potion for me? It won't harm him. I promise."

"Of course, Princess," he said.

"Would you care to share your plan?" Liam asked.

"Yes. If the trap is for me, she likely already anticipates I won't be attending alone. However, your faces are now well-known."

"If we appear as Garron did, we will still draw attention."

"Which is why I need to perfect the spell before then."

"I see."

"*If* I'm able to, you will need to attend with another noble house, or it will be odd for Philip to have such a bounty of heretofore unknown family suddenly."

"And once we're in the courtyard?" Liam asked.

"We will remove her casting stones from her by any means necessary. Without them, she will not be able to stand against me."

"That is not a plan, Love. That is a desperate hope."

"Do you have a better suggestion, or do you plan on standing in the throng and watching your brothers swing?"

He exhaled slowly, and I knew he was struggling against the storm of emotions my statement had evoked.

"As you said, I think this is a trap," he said slowly. "She's attempting to bait us into acting. I don't believe she's truly intent on killing Edmund and Brandle."

"So do nothing? And what if you're wrong?"

His frustration and helplessness simmered just beneath the surface. Leaning forward, I placed my hand over his.

"I'm not one to do nothing, Liam, am I?"

The frustration climbed a little higher.

"We both agree that we should attend. And we both agree that you and your brothers are too recognizable as you are. Send Getaina to me. While she and I will work on perfecting the spell we need, you and Philip can attempt to unite the nobles to stand with you should we need to make a stand today. Do you agree to that much?"

He nodded and kissed my knuckles.

"You are the light in our otherwise dark existences, Kellen. Thank you."

I smiled, already thinking of how I might need to remind him of that in the hours to come.

When Getaina joined me, she walked into the kitchen with a surer step and a hint of amusement.

"The others have already sent letters of support this morning," she said. "They will join us in the courtyard with their supporting families."

"They will?" I asked in surprise. "I thought…" I trailed off, respecting Getaina and her vast knowledge too much to speak of her age as if I believed it was a deterrent. It had been her opinion, not mine.

"That tea you made did more than cure the aches from the spell. It lent me energy that I haven't felt in years. I slept soundly, girl. Not a single ache to wake me in the middle of the night. Not even from my bladder." She flexed her fingers, fisting the gnarled digits tightly. "I agree with Pogwid. Better to unite and face the end bravely. The others will be here soon. What do we need to do?"

"Perfect the spell I attempted the last time."

Getaina's brows rose. "I've already told you. It's impossible."

I went to the shelves and removed a pea from its bag. She watched me place it on the table. It sprouted and grew, first as a pea and then into a thick vine with thorns. Then into a tree whose branches netted out along the ceiling. Its leaves filled the room until not a hint of the ceiling remained. Its trunk bent and lengthened to the side, creating another work table. From the wood, I created several bowls and changed them from wood to stone.

"How can I make this all from a single pea seed? Is this not also against its nature? Simply because something has not yet been done does not mean it can never be done. Believe it until it becomes reality."

Getaina picked up the stone bowl and mortar, hefting its weight in her hands to verify its authenticity.

"You can do things I cannot," she conceded. "But that doesn't mean we will be able to perfect the spell in a matter of hours. Be determined, but also be realistic, girl."

"That's precisely what I am. Now, are you here to work or talk my ear off?"

Her bark of laughter filled the room.

"I can conjure the herbs I'm familiar with but have sent Margret for the ones I'm not," I said, beginning.

The other casters appeared throughout the morning as we worked. The initial spell failed with less spectacular effect than the one Garron drank. The footman's hair grew out in a cascade to trail behind him, but nothing more changed on his features.

"A worthy hair tonic," Getaina said, making notes.

One of the other casters managed to enhance his eyelashes and another his lips.

"We're getting closer," Getaina said when she caught me frowning.

"We have another hour. Closer isn't enough. The princes' faces are known. Hair and eyelashes won't disguise them."

Daemon's entrance timed perfectly with my growing vexation. His gaze found mine as he crossed the room.

"You look like you want to cosh someone upside the head, Lamb. Should I fetch Eadric for you?"

I snorted, amused, though I shouldn't have been.

"I cannot get this spell to work, and my temper feels akin to Edmund's at the moment."

"That won't do." Gripping my shoulders, he spun me and dipped me low to steal a kiss. Several of the other casters chuckled at his playful antics when he immediately righted me.

"Better?" he asked.

"Perhaps." I lifted a cup filled with the newest concoction. "Would you care to try it?"

"For another kiss, I'll drink anything." He kissed me thoroughly before I could react then stole the cup and drained it in one gulp.

"You have to kiss me again no matter what I look like," he said, even as his face started to change before my eyes. His hair grew, and his body shrank, thinning everywhere but in the hips and chest. I struggled not to squeal in delight as I stared at a feminine version of Daemon that also looked a bit like me.

"How?" one of the casters breathed.

"Look at 'em. See how he looks like her? It was the kiss. Her saliva mixed with his." Getaina spit in another cup filled with the brew.

Daemon's gaze lit with humor. "Please tell me that one's for Darian."

"Fetch your brothers," I said, not hiding my delighted smile.

"Margret, we'll need five dresses," I called. "Hurry."

Daemon returned with Liam and Darian. They accepted their cups from the casters, and Daemon placed his hand over my mouth to prevent me from warning them. I stomped on his toe, but he barely flinched, too eager to watch them down the brew.

Darian did not make a pretty woman but didn't seem to mind his face when he noted his buxom chest. Liam sighed heavily at his body's change and arched a brow at me.

"You're unrecognizable," I said.

Getaina chose that moment to spit into another cup.

Darian started to heave mightily.

"Perhaps another caster should contribute so no two look alike," I said.

"Not helpful," Darian said between gags.

Garron and Eadric entered and looked at their brothers-turned-sisters. Garron was clever about hiding his amusement. Eadric was not. He howled with laughter and almost spilled the brew that Getaina handed him. He drank every drop, and Darian sought his revenge by sharing the secret ingredient. However, neither Garron nor Eadric seemed to care.

"I've read spells that contain worse," Garron said with a shrug.

"I've had to wash your socks," Eadric said. "Nothing can make me heave anymore."

"We should go, then," Getaina said. "It's best I arrive with Lord Hamill. Watch for me in the crowd and know you have our support." She nodded to the princes and left with the rest.

"They're coming?" Liam asked.

"They are. I could feel their doubt, though. They don't believe the casters we have on our side will be enough. However, they know they have little choice if they wish to live out the remainder of their lives naturally." I clapped my hands together. "Now, let's get you suitably attired and send you off as well, shall we?"

PHILIP STATED our names to the guards and escorted me into the courtyard.

"We didn't need to provide our names last night," I said. "Just the estate."

"I believe they will look for anyone unknown to them." Philip patted my hand. "There will be many unknown to the crown, though. Worry not."

I nodded and scanned the crowd for the princes' changed faces. I spotted Eadric first, standing beside Getaina and Lord Hamill. He fidgeted noticeably until Getaina sharply whispered a reprimand. I could feel his humor.

Daemon and Darian stood near each other. Thanks to Margret's efforts with their coiffed hair, they presented a picture of refinement. Liam and Garron were on the opposite side of the courtyard. Both wore bonnets with simple braids.

They looked nothing like the posters of the princes. But I saw it. A bit in the eyes. A hint in the nose and mouth. Despite knowing that they were hidden, I didn't feel safe. At least, we were spread apart.

My gaze shifted to the scaffolding in the center of the court-yard that now had three ropes on it. I frowned at the number and nudged Philip.

"I am curious as well," he said softly.

Whatever the queen planned, I vowed it would not come to pass. Focusing on the ropes, I separated the fibers one by one. The tingle of warning under my skin grew stronger, alerting me to her imminent arrival.

Satisfied the ropes would hold no weight, I stopped. They looked completely unchanged and hung straight and unmoving in the non-existent breeze.

The door set in the long expanse of the white wall opened.

The man who'd announced Pogwid's crimes stepped out, leading a procession of seven young girls. They wore white, matching the towers. The youngest held the hand of the oldest.

Brandle and Edmund emerged behind them. Chains bound their hands and feet, restricting their steps. They wore nothing else. My temper ignited as women audibly gasped at the shocking sight.

Did the queen think to degrade them?

Edmund's gaze scanned the crowd and locked on Eadric. I felt his shock ripple out like waves. How he knew his twin, I did not know. If he stood beside Eadric, they would appear to be distant relatives at best to a discerning eye.

The tingle under my skin increased as Edmund's gaze continued its search and found Liam. Brandle spotted Darian and Daemon but didn't let his attention settle on the twins for more than a moment. With growing dread, he looked down at his feet and elbowed Edmund.

I recalled Pogwid's thoughts and how the queen had let her keep her eyes so she could look to the people who had helped her.

A pulse of energy crashed against my consciousness as the queen emerged near the end of the procession. Stronger than the last time. How? What had she done?

Her face shone beautifully without a single blemish. She radiated health and vitality, which pulsed stronger with each step. But it wasn't the only thing that pulsed.

Faint green threads of energy spread out from her, connecting to each of the young girls.

I knew those threads; I *knew* what they did.

One of the girls faltered, and another helped her right herself.

Fear flared with my anger. The ground trembled.

Philip squeezed my arm in warning, but I could do little to curb what I was feeling. The queen was slowly killing the children in front of us.

The girls lined up before the scaffolding as Brandle and Edmund climbed the steps, and the Cryer took his place.

"Ungrateful people of Adele, your attempt to usurp your rightful ruler has failed. Look upon the former princes and know that the rebellion stops here."

Another man roughly forced Edmund onto a stool and looped the rope around his neck. Brandle stepped up on his own with calm dignity.

The queen smirked.

I fisted my hands and reminded myself why I needed to remain in control. How close had I been to hurting the tracker who'd come for me? Though there was no glass nearby, there were towers tall enough to crush us, and too many innocent people stood within the confines of the courtyard.

A scuffle broke out in the crowd. Philip swore under his breath, and I turned to see Eadric captured between two guards. He fought mightily as he was dragged toward the front. Another scuffle broke out to the left, and I saw Daemon and Darian do the same.

"I know you are here," the queen called out. "Know that these maids will die."

She looked at Daemon, Darian, and Eadric. "Or perhaps you are one of these three. Speak now to spare the other two. If you are not among these three, I will know and begin killing every female present until you are found."

The crowd's emotions escalated, stifling the air as mothers wept and held their daughters, even as I felt relief that the queen had no notion of who her guards had claimed.

"If these men you believe are the rightful heirs truly cared about their kingdom, they would speak out, name their rescuer, and spare the innocent, would they not?" the queen demanded.

A crow flew overhead and settled on the wall. It tilted its head and scanned the crowd.

I touched my energy to it and asked for its help.

It took flight and swooped low toward the scaffolding.

"False Queen!" it cawed. "Foul Queen. Lies and death are what you bring."

It pulled out of the swoop to return to the wall.

The queen's hand flicked toward the bird. I saw the glint of a small knife before it fell from the sky. Several women screamed and cried. I touched them with my energy and calmed them.

"Do you think your tricks will impress me?" The queen's gaze swept the crowd and landed on Eadric, Darian, and Daemon, who had almost reached her. "Do you think lies will cause the people to rise up and save you?"

She laughed and flung her hand out toward Eadric.

Metal glinted.

Eadric's shock flared as the blade shot toward his heart.

CHAPTER 17

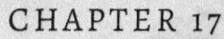

HE IS MINE!

Rage and fear roared out from my well, and the air in the courtyard exploded with multicolored particles. The knife remained locked in place, a scant breath from piercing Eadric's chest. One by one, I pried the guard's fingers from his arm.

The queen's gaze darted around the courtyard as people gasped and fell to their knees. Getaina and the other casters remained on their feet, along with several people too stunned to move.

"Where are you?" the queen yelled.

The green lines of energy connecting her to the girls flared. The children paled and staggered.

I sent my love and determination toward them along with my intent. *You've given enough. Let what was taken return twofold.*

The queen cried out as the lines of energy changed from green to a blinding white, seen by everyone present.

"No!" she howled.

I felt her reach for their energy and quickly added to my intent. *Let no spell touch you without your consent.* Her cast never touched them.

Eadric, seeing her distraction, barreled into her with his shoulder as if he were sparring with Edmund. The pair went down together, only Eadric was quick enough to roll to his feet again. Rather than dart away to make his escape, the fool grabbed the crown from her head and tossed it into the crowd.

One of the casters who'd vowed to help us caught it. "Your reign of terror and death is at an end!"

The queen laughed. The crazed sound echoed off the walls as she floated to her feet.

"An end, you say? I think not."

The old woman rose into the air, her mouth opening and closing in shock. Her face began to turn red.

"You have something that does not belong to you," the queen said.

I looked from the crown, laden with casting stones, to the queen. The remaining casting stones on her person pulsed with immense power. She'd wove spells of protection around them. Layers of energy preventing anything magic or otherwise from touching them.

But energy was energy. I connected with it easily, felt her intent, and whispered one word.

"No."

The protection fell aside. With a thought, I removed the stones from the queen's person. The chains holding them in place snapped as they floated away from her, shredding her gown and leaving her covered in rags that did little to conceal her body.

At the same time, I reshaped the ropes around Brandle and Edmund's necks, creating grand clothing fit for royal heirs.

The queen screamed her rage and grabbed for the knives she'd strapped to herself.

Darian punched the woman straight in the face before she could reach them. She barely staggered. Her gaze swung to him, and she hissed.

"You cannot best me!"

Without her stones, she had very little power. Yet, she still had some, which was something I could not allow.

I touched my energy to her well and delved into her thoughts, regardless of the pain it caused her. The horrors she'd unleashed onto Adele filled my mind. The children she'd birthed and sacrificed along with the fathers. Her fear of losing the power she'd gained. Cursing the heirs instead of killing them—she'd planned to have their children all along. The deaths of the King and Queen. The people she'd corrupted and persuaded to gain trust in the court. The innocent lives she'd taken to gain the energy she'd needed to start her coup.

Further and further back I went, learning who the queen was as tears tracked down my face.

I saw her childhood, raised by a caster obsessed with power. The queen's name was Spyra. She and four other girls—one named Maverene, also known as Meave—had been taken from their families and stolen in the middle of the night. They'd been trained, punished in the most brutal of ways, and pushed to claim the highest powers possible. They'd fought each other viciously for their foster mother's approval.

She was still alive, communicating with Spyra through a mirror. And Spyra feared her as much as she loved her. Memories of Spyra's real parents were buried so deeply that she no longer recalled them. But I found them and brought them forward. I showed her what real love was.

She screamed within her mind, unable to stop me, just as the other casters had been unable to stop me.

"Remember, Spyra. Remember who you were, and see the crimes you've committed through the loving eyes of your true parents," I said.

She fell to her knees, shaking and drooling as the memories took hold, and she saw her actions in a different light. She clawed at her face and screamed.

"Eadric, bind her hands," Brandle said.

I dove further into her well, leaving nothing untouched by my presence, then withdrew with a final thought. *You will never cast again. All magic is lost to you as if it had never been. You know nothing but the pain you brought.*

A hand settled on my shoulder.

"Come back, Kellen. Please."

I withdrew and found myself on my knees. My face hurt, and I realized I'd mirrored all of Spyra's actions.

Garron's tormented gaze swept over my face.

"I'll be fine," I said. "A bit of tea will fix me."

He nodded, looking unconvinced.

"I will be well. I promise."

"Can you stand?" Nodding, I accepted his help to my feet and turned to look at the dwindled crowd. Very few nobles remained.

"Most fled when Eadric knocked the queen—"

"Spyra," I said. "She was never a queen. Only a cruel tyrant."

"Right. When Eadric knocked her down, they ran."

"Is this a dream?" a woman asked, her hand reaching out to touch the dust still in the air. Nothing happened to her when she made contact.

"No," I said. "It's not."

"The queen? What happens to her now?" the woman asked. "Will she hang?"

"Look at her," I said, also turning to watch the woman. Though her hands were bound, she still pulled at her hair and wept in her madness. "Death would release her from the horror of her crimes. Does she deserve that mercy?"

The woman slowly shook her head. "She took my son. He was two. I never saw him again."

"I'm sorry," I said softly, feeling her grief.

Arms wrapped around me from behind. "Trouble, you damn near gave me a heart attack."

I turned in Edmund's arms and hugged him. "I felt you. I felt what she was trying to do. Are you all right?"

"I'm well. We both are. I'm curious why I have five sisters now, though."

Garron giggled then clapped a hand over his mouth.

"Please tell me this spell will wear off soon," he said from behind his hands.

"Before nightfall," I said.

Daemon made a sad sound and fondled his breasts.

"I thought it would have been Eadric in love with his breasts," Liam said.

"Nope," Eadric said, dusting off his backside. "Only Kellen's breasts mesmerize me."

Philip cleared his throat, reminding us of his presence.

"Perhaps that is a conversation best left for the privacy of your bed chamber?"

"Apologies," Brandle said.

"Think nothing of it, Your Highness."

"Your Highness?" the Cryer said with a hint of derision. "What gives you the right to the throne?"

"Their character and determination," I said before any of them could speak.

Then I touched my energy to his to search his intent. He'd needed very little persuading to follow the queen. He had craved the power and hurt people of his own free will. The maids in the palace hadn't been safe from his unwanted attention.

With a thought, I conjured chains and bound his hands.

"What right do you have?" he yelled.

"We will listen to the stories the maids have to tell about you and let your peers decide if you should be banished to the Dark Forest."

He paled and stuttered.

"Philip, assemble the nobles, please," Brandle said, offering me his arm. "Brothers, it's time we decide if we should return home."

I STOOD beside the other casters from the noble families and struggled with impatience as I listened to yet another nobleman expound on what he'd done for the kingdom during the Foul Queen's reign. Another scoffed and discounted several of the gentleman's self-claimed merits.

The desire to rule permeated the throne room, and many gazes drifted to the vacant throne with a lust for power. Thankfully, it was not an emotion shared by the casters around me, nor by the princes.

Another nobleman and noblewoman quietly entered the throne room unnoticed by most. I glanced at Philip, who was paying close attention to the attendees.

He met my gaze and nodded then intoned, "Each of the noble families is present."

"Finally," Liam said loud enough to be heard.

The speaking nobleman stopped abruptly and looked at Liam with distaste.

"Boarish ass," I whispered.

Getaina snorted beside me. "Each and every one of them."

Another caster nodded.

"You speak of what you've done to the kingdom as if the kingdom owes you compensation for your efforts," Brandle said, his voice ringing in the room. "That is what the Foul Queen thought too—that she was owed. The kingdom does not need another such ruler."

"And you think you're more suited to rule due to birthright?" a nobleman demanded. "You've been absent for almost two decades. You know nothing of Adele."

"You hid away in safety while the rest of us suffered," another called.

"Convenient that you appear just as the queen fell," a noble-woman added.

My impatience began to boil. While they argued, my sister waited. In what state? Was she safe?

"Squabbling children," I said lowly as I watched Eadric hold back Edmund from responding to the noblewoman's barb.

Getaina took my hand and patted it. "At times. At other times, they've protected those who couldn't protect themselves because they've suffered losses too. Children. Grandchildren. Husbands and wives."

"Generally, they aren't bad people," another caster whispered as Brandle faced the noblewoman who'd accused him of being an opportunist.

"Yes," another added. "They aren't opposed to one of the princes claiming the crown. Not truly. They're simply tired of living in subjugation."

"We all are," another said.

Yet, this meeting to determine who should rule Turre proved otherwise. With their level of desire for the throne, I doubted any of them would rule fairly for long.

"If the point of this debate is to convince the other houses whom they should support," Brandle said. "Then shouldn't we only speak truths?"

"Is it a lie that you only appeared at the end?" the noble-woman asked with an arched brow.

"Enough of this," I said under my breath. I touched every person in the room with my energy and my intent.

"Let those presenting themselves as the next king or queen step forward and speak truthfully about how they will rule if given the chance," I called out to the room.

A nobleman scowled at me. "You have no right to speak here, caster."

Getaina's disbelief rippled out from her. "No right? She is the one who brought the Foul Queen low. *She* is the one who locked away the Foul Queen's powers so she can never rise again. Kellen has every right."

"And with her power, she is also the most likely to take the Foul Queen's place," the man said. "I have no wish to grovel before another power-hungry mistress. When I am king, that will be my first ruling—all casters will be banished from Turre, just as they were wisely banished from Drisdall."

Gasps rang out in the room, along with a swell of indignation. Not all of it was from the casters standing with me.

"And what else would you do when you are king?" I asked.

His gaze swept over me. "Even with seven sons, the previous king wasn't able to hold his kingdom. I wouldn't stop until I'd sired twenty."

His wife, who'd stood supportively behind him, paled. I could feel her dawning understanding and anger since she'd passed her child-bearing years.

"Those in favor of banishing all casters from Turre and watching this man make mistresses out of any young miss who catches his fancy, say aye," I called.

Silence met my words, and the nobleman's face flushed scarlet.

"I dearly hope that we settle the matter of the crown today so I can sever my marriage to this unfaithful man," the woman said quietly. Her expression changed to shock, and I immediately soothed her as the man's face heated.

"You've spoken your intent truthfully, and your peers have rejected your proposal," Brandle said. "Let the next person step forward."

Five men spoke before they realized what had happened.

"You cursed us," one of them fumed.

"What you see as a curse, the people of Turre would see as a gift after being ruled over so harshly by a monarch with hidden intent. Who here wishes the spell to be lifted? Who here would rather not know the true intent of the next ruler?"

Again, silence answered Brandle's call.

"Then let us hear your truth," the nobleman demanded angrily. "How would you rule?"

"Preferably, not at all," Brandle said. "My brothers and I made a vow to return to Adele, remove the queen from the throne, and take her place. But since making the vow, we've gained something we want more than our birthright." He looked at me, and I felt his surge of love and adoration. "Kellen, the one who freed Adele, is looking for help to free her sister. Help I no longer believe she needs."

I realized he was right. With the knowledge I'd gained, I was certain I could face Maeve and lock away her powers as I'd done to her foster sister, Spyra.

"By Kellen's leave, we will return to her family and never return to Turre again."

Disbelief surged from the nobles as each of the princes moved to stand behind Brandle.

"You'd give up your birthright for a woman?" the first noble asked in disbelief.

"We would give up our lives for the woman we love," Eadric said.

"Without hesitation," Liam added.

My love for them welled out of me. Their desire flooded me in return.

"And if she did not wish to abandon Adele, how would you rule?" I asked, touching Brandle with the need to tell the truth, though I knew he would regardless.

"Equally," he said. "Eight thrones with an equal say in every decision. And we will not curry favor with the nobles but rather with all people. Anyone, regardless of birth, will be able to stand before the crown and be heard. Casters will not be turned away from our kingdom but welcomed and educated so they understand the responsibility of their gifts from the moment they emerge."

My heart ached for the picture he was painting. And I was not the only one. Getaina's pride in the princes swelled.

"Those in favor of the princes—"

"And Kellen," Garron said.

"—speak your favor now," Getaina called out.

Philip lifted his hand and said, "Aye." Lord Hamill followed. One by one, those who'd met with the princes agreed. So did many of the nobles who hadn't fled when Spyra had been knocked down.

"I witnessed the truth of the Foul Queen's fall," a noblewoman said when the room had gone quiet. "Kellen locked away the vile woman's power, and when I asked if she would hang for all the lives she'd taken—including my precious son's—Kellen asked if the queen deserved to be released from the horror of her crimes. The queen was dragged away screaming.

"I asked the Guard as we arrived, and one assured me she still weeps in her cell. She received a just judgment for her crimes from the just caster who freed us."

She knelt on the floor and bowed her head to me. "I pledge my loyalty to Kellen and the princes in an equal monarchy."

The rest of the room slowly followed suit. I met Brandle's remorseful gaze and shared the reluctance he and the other princes felt. Accepting the rule was a heavy burden—one we would not be able to walk away from until we assured the people that the kingdom was once again at peace.

Wait for me, Eloise, I thought.

I INHALED DEEPLY and patted the horse I'd ridden to the edge of the Dark Forest a farewell. How many days had passed since removing the Foul Queen? Seven? Twelve? I could no longer remember.

One of the guards led the horse away, and as I faced the forest, fear and regret consumed me.

The small bursts of multicolored particles that floated in the air gave away my inner turmoil. Arms wrapped around me from behind, and I leaned into Brandle's comforting embrace. He didn't speak or ask what troubled me. He already knew. They all did.

Over the last few days, our lives had fallen into a routine. I was never alone. One of the brothers remained with me at all times. And we shared everything—all our thoughts and fears. There were no secrets between us. We were one.

Garron had spent hours with me, poring over all the Foul Queen's gruesome spells, learning what she'd done to ensure anything that lingered could be undone. While we read, the others led with their presence. Edmund and Eadric had worked with the Guard, ensuring their loyalty and skill. Liam and Brandle had taken turns in the throne room, maintaining a presence throughout the day to hear any issues brought to the attention of the crown by nobles and the common people alike. Darian and Daemon had toured the city, speaking to merchants and tradesmen to learn what we needed and what we could offer other kingdoms. They purchased surplus from merchants using the gems from the caves and distributed what supplies they could to those in need.

The time we'd spent hadn't been in vain. We'd helped Adele and its people settle into a peaceful existence and had announced our intent to reestablish the trade route to Drisdall. It wasn't a lie, but it also wasn't our main reason for standing at the edge of the Dark Forest.

"Are you ready?" Liam asked, joining us and taking my hand.
"Very."
Brandle kissed the top of my head and released me.
"Then clear our path, Love," Liam said.
I opened myself to the forest. Each tree and bramble pulsed

with energy. With little effort, I consumed the energy of all plant life within the width of three wagons.

"Incredible," one of the guards breathed as I walked forward onto the sunlit bare earth.

Taking the energy I'd gained, I reformed the dirt into white cobbled stones. Embedded in the stones, I left my intent. No beast made of magic could walk this road.

My kings walked by my side on the path wide enough to accommodate us all. Step by step, we left the guards and Turre behind.

The trees disappeared before us, and cobbles appeared in our wake. Though we moved quietly, our presence attracted the beasts. They gathered in the shadows, watching...waiting. The soft sounds of their passage were broken with an occasional growl in the otherwise silent forest.

We paused midday to rest on the newly created road. Daemon held me in his lap while Eadric fed me.

"I like this," Liam said, watching me relax into Daemon's hold. "It's been so long since we could breathe easily."

"Do you regret it?" I asked. "Agreeing to rule?"

"Not yet."

I understood what he meant. He would regret it if accepting the crown cost me my father or my sister.

"Regardless of what we face in the future, I believe we made the right choice for the people of Turre," I said. "If there had been one decent noble interested in ruling, I would have supported them. Why didn't Philip offer?"

"Loyalty," Brandle said. "He cared for my parents and believed in how they ruled. He deeply believes the throne is ours by birthright."

"And you proved it was ours through your actions," Eadric said, giving me a quick kiss.

Daemon nudged him back with his foot. "Feed her or surrender her food to Darian."

Eadric made a face at Daemon and fed me my next bite.

"Are your feet weary, Princess?" Darian asked.

I rolled my eyes at him. "Deviant. Stay away from my feet."

"That's not what you were saying to him last night," Eadric said.

My core clenched at the memory of how the pair had put me to bed and how Brandle and Garron had woken me. Desire exploded from each of them in response to my need.

"Ah, Trouble," Edmund said, watching me. "Say the word, and I will bare myself on this road."

"Don't you dare." My gaze flicked to the trees even as I opened myself to search for the beasts. None of them pulsed with the energy of my father.

"We've made better time than I'd anticipated. Another hour and we'll be close to the cottage," Brandle said. "Or we can push through and reach Towdown by nightfall."

I thought about it and shook my head. "It would be wiser to arrive in daylight."

Once we finished our meal, I continued with the road until I felt my father to the North.

"He's still there," I breathed. "He's waiting."

"Then let us not keep him waiting any longer," Daemon said, taking my hand.

I opened myself wide, letting all that I was free into the world along with my intent of peaceful passage. The beasts snarled and snapped at the multicolored dust in the air but otherwise ignored the eight of us as we left the road I'd made.

My pace quickened the nearer we drew to the glade until I was jogging lightly to reach my father.

He waited at the edge of the trees where darkness met the lighter shadows. His tattered clothing was gone. Yet, when he turned his head at my approach, I saw the humanity still reflected in his gaze.

"Are you with me, Father?" I asked, not slowly.

In answer, he opened his arms.

Edmund cursed, and I felt his intent to stop me. The ability to manipulate the energy in everything, however, gave me the advantage, and I was wrapped in my father's embrace before Edmund could reach me.

My father's grief and regret weighed on him as his claws raked through my hair and settled at the back of my head.

"You're not alone," I whispered against his fur. "You will never be alone again. Now bear the pain, Father. For me and Eloise, you must bear it."

I touched my energy to his well, delving deep past his memories and into the spell that bound him. It was layered in hate and revenge—cast by a scorned lover who refused to let go. The spell demanded that the infected walk his remaining days alone, cursed to have a visage that reflected the beastly behavior shown to the original caster and cursed to destroy all that it might come to love.

Thanks to my spell, Father's hadn't yet settled into his very being. His lingering humanity protected him like a thin blanket of mist.

I set my hand on his cheek along with my intent. "This burden is not yours to bear. Shed it now and become what you truly believe you are. Between Father and Beast, the choice is yours."

Heat exploded between us and threw me backward. If not for Edmund's presence, I would have likely hurt myself. As it was, I simply used his body as a cushion, and he took the brunt of the impact with the ground.

"Kellen!"

Hands grabbed at me, helping me to my feet and blocking my view.

"Is he all right?"

"I'm fine," Edmund groaned.

"Not you. My father. Is he all right?"

CHAPTER 18

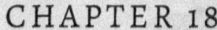

BRANDLE GLANCED OVER HIS SHOULDER THEN STRAIGHTENED abruptly.

"I believe we have some clothes that will fit you, sir," he said. "If you'd like to follow me to the cottage, I'll help you get settled; then you can speak with your daughter."

"No, I—"

"Let your father dress, Sparrow," Eadric said. "He's suffered enough injustice, don't you agree?"

I listened to their retreat as I shook out my dress and watched the others help Edmund to his feet.

"Are you unharmed?" I asked.

"All but my pride," he grumbled.

"Due to the fall or the fact I asked about my father first?"

Edmund scowled at me, and I knew it was the latter bothering him.

"I have been with you, by your side, for months but without my father. If your parents suddenly appeared, I would not begrudge you a moment spent caring for them so long as, at the end of the day, you returned to me."

"Very reasonable of you," Daemon said. "Don't you agree, brother?"

"I do," Darian said.

"We need to win over his favor, Edmund," Eadric said. "Earnestly and quickly. We cannot have him refusing us Sparrow's hand with our babe in her belly."

All motion and humor left them. Except for Eadric, the astute rogue.

I sighed and shook my head at him. "Your timing is deplorable."

"How so? I waited until we knew your father was right and well so as not to distract the rest from your goal or, worse, give them a reason to delay you. But I cannot, in good conscience, allow you to face another caster while carrying our child without warning them."

"Is it true, Trouble?" Edmund asked roughly.

"My monthlies may be a touch overdue," I said.

"And you told Eadric and kept it from the rest of us?" Darian asked, projecting his hurt.

"No, I told no one. Eadric apparently keeps better track of the passing days than I do."

"Nah," Eadric said with a smirk. "Your breasts are simply a bit swollen and more sensitive of late. That's how I knew."

"And you didn't *tell* us?" Garron demanded.

"Nope. I figured it was like that time you had her remove your memory. If we all knew, we would do foolish things that would result in upsetting Sparrow. I didn't want her or the babe to suffer, so I decided to wait until it was safe."

"Are you even our brother?" Daemon asked. "How could you keep such a thing from us?"

"He made the right decision," I said. "If you had tried to keep me from coming to my father, from casting the spell I just did, or anything between now and then, I'm not sure what my reaction would have been. You're an overprotective lot. While I love you so very much for it, I also know my control is still lacking, and I never again want to send any of you flying due to my anger."

"See?" Eadric said with a smile. "I was wise."

Garron cuffed him from the right and Daemon from the left. I kissed both his cheeks to make up for it then gave them all my saddest, most pitifully pleading gaze.

"Will you still dote on me when I'm swollen, round, and irritable?"

Edmund swore softly and reached for me. Too slowly, though. Daemon's hand on the back of my head turned me for his ravenous kiss. I melted under the onslaught and held on. Darian stole me from him when he started peppering my face with kisses. After Darian vowed to spoil me endlessly, Liam wrapped me in his arms and simply held me as I caught my breath. When he released me, Edmund picked me up and pinned me against a tree. His kiss was filled with a loving aggression that both confused and heated me.

"Don't you dare remove my dress," I said, breaking away from his kiss after feeling the direction of his thoughts.

His intense gaze held mine. "Tonight. I *will* see for myself if what Eadric noticed is true."

I felt what he wanted to do to me and shivered in anticipation. At the same time, I worried what my father would think if he heard us.

Eadric seemed to read my thoughts.

"Don't worry, Sparrow. Garron and I will be there to ensure you're quiet."

My anticipation and worry climbed, but I knew better than to deny either.

"Tonight then," I said. "But we will leave at first light. No delays like this morning."

They all quickly agreed.

Escorted by Edmund, we entered the clearing as my father left the cottage wearing a coarse tunic and pants that were a few inches too short for him. His hair was in a tangle, and his face was covered with dirt, but his eyes were clear and locked on me.

My smile grew with each step we drew nearer. I didn't release my hold on Edmund to get to Father. Not this time. This time, I needed my father to see that I'd found my place and chosen my path in life, just as he'd chosen his.

When I reached him, he surprised me by holding out his hand to Edmund.

"I saw what happened to you," he said. "Thank you."

After Edmund, he shook Liam's hand. "Thank you, and forgive me for not being able to do more to help keep her safe."

"It is us who should be asking your forgiveness, sir," Brandle said. "We—"

Father lifted his hand to stop Brandle from saying more, and I was grateful. I knew what Brandle wanted to apologize for and wasn't sure it was the right time to broach the subject of my relationship with them.

"I have eyes and ears, son. Some conversations are best left vague, so tell me simply, which of you will marry my daughter."

"All of us," Brandle said.

Father's gaze met mine, and I nodded without hesitation.

"I see. And do you plan to settle in Drisdall, Turre, or here, in between?"

"Father, perhaps an introduction is in order. These are the crown princes of Turre. Brandle, Edmund, Eadric, Darian, Daemon, Garron, and Liam." Each nodded to my father when I spoke their name.

"Princes? And you'll wed all of them? I don't recall that being..." He waved his hand as if shooing the thought away. "Whatever you decide, I will stand with you. I doubt very much anyone would be able to stand against you, regardless." His gaze and feelings conveyed his love and support until his thoughts turned toward Eloise. "Any news from your sister?"

"No. Only the hint that Maeve spoke when she was here. I'm grateful you didn't follow her, Father."

"And I'm grateful you were able to break the spell." He flushed as he spoke and cleared his throat. "When do we leave?"

"It's safest to stay here tonight and start out first thing in the morning," Brandle said.

"Morning?"

I could feel my father's need to reach Eloise.

"It will take half a day to reach Drisdall," I said.

"It's more dangerous once night falls," Liam said.

"And Kellen's been casting non-stop since we left this morning. She needs rest or risks hurting...herself."

That father didn't even flinch at the idea I could cast meant he'd been watching me from the trees before we'd left. However, Father's approval regarding my ability paled when I caught a hint of Brandle's growing worry. He'd caught Garron's hesitation and glanced at me.

"I'm fine," I said firmly. "Nothing I did tired me except for the long walk."

"Do you need a foot rub?" Darian asked.

"Hush," I said. "What we all need is a hearty dinner and an early bedtime so we can start out at first light."

"I'll light the fire," Edmund said.

"Garron and I will raid the cellar," Liam said.

"I'll set the table," Eadric said with a wink at me.

"Would you like to help me check the bedrolls, Lamb?" Daemon asked.

Brandle cuffed him. "Get the tub ready for Father."

I smiled as Daemon cast a sheepish look at my father and hurried inside.

"I'll show you around the place while you wait if you'd like, sir," Darian said.

"Thank you," Father said.

"I'll come too," I said, quickly tucking my hand around Father's arm. He smelled awful.

Father patted my hand, leaving behind dirt marks.

"I believe they'd like you to stay here and have a word with Brandle," Father said.

"Which is precisely why I'd prefer to stay with you," I said.

Father chuckled, and Brandle gently pried me away from him.

"Thank you, sir," Brandle said.

I watched Father walk away and looked up at Brandle. "Do you recall the time I clawed my way through the roof?"

"I do."

"And how did that end?"

"I believe I still carry your mark on my arse."

"It serves as a reminder to your brothers not to test me," I said primly.

"And me?"

"I doubt you and Edmund will ever stop testing me; however, I still have strong teeth when reminders are needed."

Brandle grinned and pulled me into his embrace.

"Is there a reason for this heavy warning?"

"I believe I'm pregnant," I said bluntly.

He froze briefly then tightened his grip on me.

"Oh, don't act so shocked. Since losing my maidenhead, I've only slept alone a handful of times. You had to know this would be the result of frequent f—"

His mouth covered mine in a hungry kiss that had me forgetting my words within moments. His hands cupped my face as he walked me backward. It wasn't until the bench hit the backs of my legs that he pulled back.

"Behave yourself, Kellen, or you will shock your poor father."

"Me? I wasn't the one who kissed—"

A throat cleared, and I saw Father standing near a grinning Darian.

"Kellen is my reserved daughter. Keep that in mind when you meet Eloise," Father said before going inside.

Brandle gave me a quizzical look.

"He means that *I'm* not the shocking daughter."

Brandle chuckled and stepped aside for Liam and Garron, who placed an array of roots and seeds on the table. The sun slowly descended as we worked together to fix a meal.

I never felt anyone's approach until an older woman leading an enormous, familiar pig by a rope emerged from the forest. The pig I knew. The woman, I did not. She didn't feel like Maeve, but she had power—more than any other caster I'd met—for when I opened myself to her energy, she had none. Not a drop.

"Dratted pig," the woman grumbled. "Walk faster."

I stood abruptly and focused all of my intent on my love for my family, sending out to surround them. Edmund cursed under his breath as I strode from the table and closed the distance between myself and the old woman.

"Kellen, let us free," he yelled.

She watched me rather than the pig, who was cowering at the end of its rope.

"Speak the purpose of your presence here," I said.

"My presence?" she looked up at the fading light in the sky. "I'm here to seek refuge from the beasts before nightfall. Are the men behind you so dangerous that you had to entrap them?"

"Don't feign innocence you no longer possess," I said.

The older woman barked out a laugh.

"You're a blunt one."

"So I've been told. Perhaps you will return the favor. Why are you here, caster?"

"Caster? Me?"

"Everything pulses with energy, even your pig, which isn't truly a pig, by the way...everything, except for *you*."

The woman glanced at the pig. "He's less of a pig than he was. That's for certain."

"I have no wish to harm you. If you do not speak your truth, I will find it myself."

"Oh? And how will you do that?"

Keeping the lid on my well-sealed tightly, I braced myself and touched my energy to hers as she touched mine.

Her recent memory of Eloise flashed in my mind, and I immediately withdrew my energy as I stepped forward and took her hand.

"My sister. Is she truly well?"

Rose's emotions vacillated between surprise, curiosity, and relief. Relief that I hadn't looked any deeper than I had and relief I was Eloise's twin who she'd come to find.

"You are not what I expected."

"My sister. Please," I begged.

"Eloise is well enough. She suffered much in your absence but does not hold you to blame. Those held to blame have been justly punished."

"Maeve is gone then?" I asked, hoping I understood correctly.

"She is. I felt you in my mind. You could have looked for more and seen for yourself. Why didn't you?"

"Eloise trusted you. That's enough for me. I have no wish to hurt anyone, especially not those who've helped my sister. Come, join us for dinner." As I spoke, I removed the shield from around my princes and father.

"Kellen Cartwright, if you ever do that again..." Edmund shouted.

"Excuse me," I said, turning quickly to intercept Edmund. However, it wasn't only Edmund storming my way. All seven of them were flushed with anger—even sweet Eadric.

I promptly and quite beautifully burst into tears and wailed, "Why are you yelling at me?"

Behind them, Father shook his head and smiled slightly.

Eloise might be the twin known for her theatrics to avoid punishment, but I was no novice myself.

All of their anger dissipated as they closed the distance between us. Edmund, who'd been in the lead, fell behind, unsure how to deal with my tears. Eadric and Daemon pulled ahead, but it was Brandle who wrapped me in a comforting hug.

"Hush, now. All is well. We apologize for yelling, don't we, Edmund?"

"Only moderately," Edmund said under his breath.

Someone cuffed him.

I hiccuped delicately and wiped my eyes as I looked up at Brandle. "If we are equals, each with our own strengths, is it not my duty to protect you when magic is involved and yours to protect me when strength is involved?"

"Kellen, you cannot risk yourself. Please," Brandle said gently. "Without you, what reason do we have to continue?"

"Am I to be your world but not allow you to be mine?" I asked.

Rose chuckled behind me, drawing his attention.

"This is Rose," I said, stepping back to make the introduction. "She is the caster Eloise sent to find me." I looked at my father, who'd slowly joined us. "Eloise is safe, and Maeve is gone. It's well past time for us to return home."

DESPITE EDMUND'S warning that he meant to have me that night, I slept undisturbed in his arms, with the exception of Eadric's palm on my breast all night.

Rose traveled with us through the trees, interested in seeing the road I was creating. When she did, she studied it and then me.

"I have yet to meet a caster so close to being my equal," Rose said. "I think I would like to accompany you to Drisdall."

I glanced at the woman who had changed from an older woman with unkempt, long grey hair and threadbare clothing that begged to be burned to a woman close to my mother's age with long, dark hair, a kind gaze, and a beautiful dress. The pig on the end of her lead, who had the energy of a human, remained unchanged.

"Who are you truly, Rose? A friend or a cruel caster?"

Her brows rose. "A friend, I would hope. Why do you believe me to be cruel?"

"I believe you changed his form as easily as you changed yours. Did he agree to be a pig?"

She laughed. "He chose his form with his actions. His greed for more saw him fed while others starved. He used his position to coerce sexual favor in return for food and went so far as to attempt to rape an innocent girl your age."

The pig let out a mournful squeal and promptly dropped to the ground.

"Rather than send him to the mines to die attempting labors he had no chance of surviving, I thought to reform him."

Eadric sniggered at her wit.

"I vow he has not been mistreated. In fact, your sister not only cared for him but helped him recover a shred of his humanity. As I said before, he's less of a pig than he was. However, he still has a long way to go." She met my gaze. "You are welcome to look if you'd like."

My other sense whispered she was safe. That I could touch her well and would find the truth.

"Have you, perchance, also changed a man into a beast?"

I felt her surprise. "I have. How did you know?"

"The caster who had been ruling Turre prior to our arrival was determined to master longevity because of rumors of yours." Though I was curious about Rose's age, I did not ask. Instead, I said, "Thank you for your explanation. You're welcome to travel with us. I would welcome the help creating the road."

As I spoke, I began to cast, absorbing the trees before us.

"I'm afraid I will not be much help. I'm unable to replenish what I'm using like you are. My well's running a bit low since I helped your sister."

"You shouldn't need to touch your well. It's a balanced cast," I said. "The trees provide what I need to make the road."

"Perhaps to make the stone, but not to embed the spell that's protecting it. That you're pulling from your well."

The worry of all seven men climbed.

"Consider carefully how you treat me when I am with child if you wish me to produce more than one heir," I said.

Rose chortled. Father muttered, "Child...heir..." and Garron flushed scarlet.

"Oh, this is going to be a lovely reunion," Rose said, walking on the road that erupted under our feet as we moved forward. "You're as likable as your sister, who I am quite fond of."

A hint of emotion drifted from her. Secrets and amusement. Rather than question her, I moved forward.

My kings demanded I take more frequent breaks, which proved mildly vexing until I stopped at a part of the old road that looked familiar.

"This is where I found the stone," I said to Edmund. "What a wicked caster I was then, was I not?"

He scoffed at me even as he hugged me. "Forgive me for being an arse."

"You weren't an arse. You were protecting yourself and your brothers. But I truly did find the stone here. I still question my luck in finding Father with a level of humanity remaining, finding the stone in the road when I needed it the most, and then your glade. Too much coincidence."

"You are right," Rose said. "It's not a coincidence but the powers you were touched with while still in the womb that guided you to where you were meant to be. Have you ever felt a whisper of warning? A tingle along the skin?"

"I have," I said.

She nodded. "You were guided. Energy doesn't disappear. It's reformed with the intent of the caster. I wonder at the caster's intent that touched you that both you and your sister have found princes to marry."

"Princes?" My father echoed.

"Yes, but only one for Eloise. And unlike this daughter, she cannot cast. That's for the best, perhaps," Rose said with a hint of amusement.

Father distracted me from it with a question. "Do you still have the stone, Kellen?"

"She does not. We took it from her so she wouldn't leave us."

"I thought you said because it was dangerous."

"It was. To us. We needed you, Kellen."

Father cleared his throat, and I stood, ready to continue on.

"If you have the stone, I would like it back, please," he said.

"Why?" I asked. "The road will keep you safe."

"Your mother gave it to me when Turre first fell."

"That sounds like a tale I would like to hear," I said.

While Father told the story, we moved closer to Eloise.

I DIDN'T STOP at creating the road to the edge of the trees but continued it all the way to the dirt road that led to Towdown. Walking on the dirt road wasn't as nice as the white cobble. Dust clung to the bottom of my skirt by the time we reached Towdown.

After one woman looked at us disdainfully, I removed all our travel dust with a simple thought. The woman's eyes rounded, and she ran off.

Rose chuckled, and I cringed.

"It's only been a few months, and I've already forgotten what it's like here," I said.

Rose took my hand and patted it. "Don't change who you are,

Kellen. Not for anyone. Only those with ill intent hide their true nature."

I glanced at Rose. "Did you not approach our glade in disguise?"

Rose smiled. "Perhaps this is my disguise. Who's to say?"

I could feel that Eadric found her funny. The others, however, including my father, did not.

We hadn't even reached the market when guards surrounded us. One of them attempted to touch me, which Edmund and Garron did not take kindly to, and I did not take kindly to the fists the guards threw in return for their accosting by my kings.

"Cease," I said.

All those fighting froze, even my men.

CHAPTER 19

"Trouble," Edmund growled.

"Had I not frozen you too, you would have hit him when he was unable to defend himself, and that wouldn't be fair. I want your word that you will not continue fighting when I release you."

"You have my word," Garron and Darian both said.

I glanced at Father and saw he, too, had jumped into the fray.

A sigh escaped me.

"Is this the way the kings of Turre wish to introduce themselves to the king of Drisdall?" I asked.

I felt the disbelief in the head guard, who I hadn't needed to freeze.

"Yes. Kings. Please send word to King Afton that Turre is no longer fallen. The road between our kingdoms has been repaired, and the kings are here to speak of a new trade agreement. And I am here to speak to my sister, Eloise Cartwright."

"Very well, come with me." The head guard's expression remained impassive as his disbelief continued. He meant to lead us toward the castle, but once there, he would ensure I was imprisoned for my open use of magic against the crown.

I snorted and released his guards.

"No more fighting, please," I said.

One of the guards moved to grab Edmund's arm, but his hand couldn't touch him. He tried several times before glancing at me.

"Please do not attempt to touch what is mine."

The guard looked to the head guard.

"At your leave, kind sir, I am ready to end this journey and see Eloise."

My feet, sore from the distance we'd already walked, ached fiercely by the time we reached the castle. When the head guard started to veer toward a side gate, I continued forward, straight toward the open main gate.

"Halt," the head guard cried.

"I understand you are only trying to do your duty. However, I promise my sister will not be pleased if you lead her sister and father to your dungeon. I'm sparing you a severe reprimanding, really."

Each attempt to stop us was met with failure due to the pocket of air I'd created around us like a barrier. It didn't close us off but simply prevented them from touching us.

The men truly tried. Their feet skidded along the stone as they braced against the barrier that moved with us. More guards were called before we reached the stairs, not that it did the lot any good.

"This is quite entertaining," Rose said, watching one take a tumble.

I quickly used air to cushion his fall and prevent him from cracking his head.

The emotions in my well were stirring dangerously with impatience and frustration, and I suddenly understood the temptation to turn people into the creatures they emulate.

By the time we reached the top step, the guards around us had started yelling to bar the castle doors.

"I have no wish to force my way in," I said, hesitating.

Rose chuckled. "I have no such qualms."

The doors froze, allowing just enough room for us to pass one at a time. Brandle went first, followed by Eadric then me, and finally Edmund and the others. Rose entered last, and the doors closed behind us, shutting out the guards who had gathered. They pounded on the doors; then suddenly, everything outside went quiet.

I breathed a sigh of relief as I looked at the stunned palace guards.

"Can you please let King Afton know that the Kings of Turre are here to see him about a new trade agreement and let Eloise Cartwright know that her father and sister are here to see her?"

The man slowly nodded and backed away a few steps before pivoting and hurrying away.

Beside me, I felt Rose's curiosity. She couldn't decide whether I was holding back what I could do out of politeness or if I lacked the knowledge.

"Since I just learned I was a caster a few months ago, it would be safe to presume I lack the knowledge to do whatever it is you think I should do," I said without taking my gaze from the far section of the grand entry where the guard had disappeared.

I felt Rose's surprise and glanced at her.

"I can't read thoughts but feel emotions. That's how I gain my energy, too. I thought you did the same when you said there was no source for you to replenish your well."

Her slow smile and growing amusement confused me. I was about to question her when I heard a familiar shout.

I looked down the hallway at my sister, who was running at me with her simple dress lifted high enough to show her stockings to the knee. Grinning through the sudden onslaught of my tears, I bolted for her.

We met in the middle, crashing into one another and falling to the floor—softly, thanks to Rose.

Eloise wrapped me in her arms, sobbing into my shoulder as I did almost the same but quieter.

"Should we at least pick them up?" I heard Darian ask.

"Give them a few moments," my father said.

At the sound of his voice, she released me and scrambled to her feet, only to leap the short distance to our father. As he always did, he caught her in his strong arms and held her tightly.

Liam and Darian helped me to my feet as I watched their reunion.

"Forgive me," Father whispered into her hair. "I wasn't myself."

She hugged him harder. "I know, Papa."

Tears tracked down his cheeks as he kissed the top of her head and released her.

When she faced me once more, I uttered my own apology. "I'm so sorry, El. Forgive me for taking so long."

She smiled. "You came back. It doesn't matter how long it took. You're here now." A sudden smile lifted her tear-stained cheeks.

"Would you like to meet my husband-to-be?"

Father and I both agreed. She wrapped her arms around both of ours and started towing us down the hall.

Edmund cleared his throat at the same time as Daemon and Liam.

We paused as I glanced back at them then flashed Eloise the crooked smile I only showed her when I was up to something truly mischievous.

"It's best I introduce you to mine first," I said. "They claim to have patience, but I've yet to see it. Eloise, I would like you to meet Brandle, Edmund, Eadric, Daemon, Darian, Garron, and Liam—the kings of Turre."

My twin released me as her gaze swept over them all.

"Mine?" she echoed. "All of them?"

"All of them," I confirmed.

Shock rolled through her, accompanied by her curiosity about whether Mr. Bentwell's books had influenced me. Sorrow followed.

"He died?" I asked.

She faced me and nodded.

"Maeve killed him when she searched for you. I got your clue. When I said you should leave, I didn't mean the Dark Forest, silly." She wrapped her arm around mine and hugged it. "Are you really marrying all seven of them?"

"She is," Brandle said.

I could feel their collective desire and determination at Brandle's words.

She glanced at my father.

He looked down, cleared his throat, and met my sister's gaze. "They are fine men, not due to their rather lofty titles but because of everything they've done to keep your sister safe. Also, have I ever refused either of you anything?"

A surge of hurt washed over Eloise, and I knew she'd recalled the time he had refused her—when she had asked him not to leave. However, we both knew it hadn't been his choice to leave. We'd suffered the effects of Maeve's curses firsthand.

I took her arm this time. "Do you still want to introduce me to your husband?"

"Of course."

She led us to the throne room, boldly walking through the doors and down the center aisle, straight toward the throne as if the throngs of noblemen and noblewomen standing on the outskirts of the room didn't matter.

The guard who'd left to announce us stood off to the side of the throne.

"That is the one, Your Majesty," the guard said.

"Princess Eloise," the King said in the hush, "I wasn't aware you were attending today's session. And with guests."

The man sitting to his right hadn't taken his eyes off of Eloise since she appeared. I could feel his love for her and also his concern. The guard had just claimed a powerful caster forced her way into the palace.

"Your Majesty," she said with a curtsey, "Greydon, I would like to present to you my sister, Kellen Cartwright, and my father, Atwell Cartwright."

I nodded in greeting to the King of Drisdall and felt shock ripple through the crowd.

"Your Majesty," my father said with a formal, low bow.

The king motioned for Father to rise, his gaze not leaving me. I could feel his speculation and hesitation, but anything more than that was difficult to guess. He was either adept at keeping his thoughts hidden or didn't know what to think of me.

"Are you a caster, child?" he asked bluntly.

I smiled slightly. "Allow me to introduce myself more thoroughly. I am Kellen Cartwright, betrothed to the Kings of Turre, who have come with welcome news."

Another ripple of shock and confusion swept through the crowd as I stepped aside and looked at Brandle.

"King Afton, almost two decades ago, a great evil slipped into Turre. The caster, Spyra Grimmoire, killed my parents, cursed my brothers and me, and took the throne. If not for your quick thinking to close the trade route between our two kingdoms, that evil might have spread.

"We've come for two reasons—three, actually. The first is to reunite Kellen with her sister, Eloise. The second is to personally tell you that the Foul Queen's reign has ended, all thanks to Kellen. Her determination to do whatever was necessary to return to her family led her down paths she never thought she would walk."

He took my hand, and I felt his love along with each of his brothers.

"And the third?" the King asked.

"We wish to reestablish our trade with Drisdall. Our kingdoms have been separated for too long. Though we have different views regarding casting, I believe we have more in common, such as our wish for prosperity and peace for our people."

The king stood, and his gaze drifted to the other six brothers before he descended the stairs. Greydon, the man Eloise had addressed, followed him and took my sister's hand.

"I still remember the gifts we sent for your birth, King Brandle," the king said. "For you and each of your brothers, truthfully. Your parents were fair rulers. I am sorry for your loss and that I could do no more for you than close the trade route. At the time, our kingdom also suffered an attack. Another Grimmoire—I believe a sister to the one who attacked your kingdom."

"Maeve and Spyra were stolen from their true families by a caster obsessed with power and raised as her own," I said. "They shared no blood relation, only the last name of the caster who twisted them to her purpose."

"She told you this?" the king asked, showing a hint of surprise.

I knew speaking of what I could do would not win me any favor, but Rose's words not to hide rang in my ears. I glanced back to look at the woman, but she wasn't there. Searching, I found the void of nothingness near the doors and needed to touch my well to see her. She once again looked like an old crone.

"Miss Cartwright," the king said, recalling my attention.

"Princess Kellen," Darian corrected.

I felt the king's annoyance as I reached into my bag, pulled out the edict my mother had kept in the attic, and handed it over to him. His eyes went wide as he read it.

"The road between Turre and Drisdall is wide enough for three wagons abreast and well-protected from the beasts who still linger in the forest," Liam said, stepping forward. "We have wool, cloth, grain from the north, and lumber in surplus. Our people are starved for vegetables and fruits we can't grow and for news of families who lived on this side of the forest."

The king shifted from the paper to me to Liam.

"You must be Prince Liam," he said.

"King Liam," Brandle corrected.

"You did not take the crown?" the king asked. I could feel that he'd already grasped the situation. However, he wanted us to clarify it here, in his court, for all of his subjects.

"What is it you fear?" I asked.

Surprise rippled through him and suspicion. A laugh escaped me as I understood.

"King Afton, you have no need to fear for your kingdom. Turre will need all seven of its Kings' full attention to repair what the Foul Queen broke during her reign. And by collectively marrying me—" gasps rang out, and several women fainted "—there won't be the passels of heirs hungry for our neighboring kingdom.

"We are only here for the reasons I stated." I looked at the older woman who'd been standing off to the side. "You are welcome to connect to my well and see for yourself if I am a person with ill intent."

The king glanced at the woman and nodded.

"That's Elspeth. The women from the letters," Eloise said quietly enough for her voice not to reach the nobles straining to hear. "She and Mother helped save the kingdom. That's why we have that letter."

I smiled at Elspeth.

"The books you left behind helped me understand what we faced. Thank you," I said.

She nodded to me and held out her hand.

"Hold onto who you are, Elspeth. I've been told my well is deep enough to lose oneself."

I felt her worry as I took her hand and let her in. While she searched me, I searched her and saw what history she allowed. When she withdrew, she was pale and shaky.

With a thought, I created a cup of healing tea and handed it to her. More gasps echoed.

"A few sips and you'll feel better," I said.

"By the bells, Kellen, just how powerful are you?" Eloise asked.

I smirked at my twin. "I figured out how to create a potion that can change a man into a woman. With the exception of the circumstance dictating its need, the results were quite amusing."

"Only for you, Princess," Darian said. "I still have nightmares."

A snort escaped me since I'd witnessed his dreams.

"I didn't mind it," Eadric said. "Wearing a skirt is quite freeing."

Someone laughed, easing the growing tension in the grand room.

"Your sister's power is immeasurable," Elspeth said after draining the cup. "If not for her warning, I doubt I would have…"

Taking the hand of the woman who had been like a mother to my mother, I shook my head. "Never. I would have never allowed anything to happen to you. Thank you for allowing me to see our past. It helped me understand why I am the way I am."

I looked at the king. "While protecting your pregnant queen from Maeve's attack so many years ago, I was deeply touched by that energy while my sister was only slightly touched. She has a sixth sense but nothing more."

"It's a fair trade," Eloise said. "You got all the magic, and I got all the height, what little of it there was for us."

Smiling, I returned my twin's wink. She laughed.

"Kellen, the cold," she scoffed. "If the boys from the market would see you now—" her gaze flicked to my kings. My father nudged her and shook his head.

"It seems we have much to discuss," the king said. He looked out at the nobles. "Out. This session is done."

Many of the nobles hurried for the door. A few lingered near the back. Families with daughters hoping to speak to the Kings of Turre. Including one who I recognized by their thoughts.

"Lord and Lady Thoning," I called. "You wished to speak?"

Lady Thoning's fear of me almost drowned her determination to gain the king's favor. Not her husband, though. He was all determination. And it wasn't solely centered on the king. Prince Greydon or my kings would do as well.

He strode forward with his wife and daughter, who was close to the age of Kellen and me.

My father didn't look at them, but I could feel his anger climbing.

"Your majesties," Lord Thoning said with a bow as his wife and daughter curtsied. "Pardon my forwardness. When I heard the name Cartwright, I knew I must speak."

"I agree, Lord Thoning," I said. "Speak, but know every word you utter will only be the truth...grandfather."

His disdain for me grew.

"Do not speak," he said. "You are beneath me, a wretched offspring from a disgraced daughter. You have no right to try to rise above your place."

"And where is my place?" I asked as his wife paled and tugged at his arm.

"In the gutter or swinging from a noose if what the guard said is true. All casters should die."

Edmund's ire exploded, and he punched Lord Thoning right in the mouth. The old man fell back like a toppled tree. I did not cushion him.

"You have no idea how much I've wanted to do that over the years," my father said, clapping Edmund on the back. "Thank you, Son."

Edmund's proud grin faded when he caught my stoic stare.

"Words, Edmund," I said.

With a signal from King Afton, the guards dragged Lord Thoning out, followed by a sniffling Lady Thoning. Their daughter wasn't crying, though. On the inside, she was laughing.

"Margaret," I called.

She paused to look back at me.

"You alone are welcome to visit me in Turre. The sister you've heard them whisper about was a great woman who also didn't want to be forced into a loveless marriage to elevate her parents' standing."

Lady Thoning grabbed her daughter and pulled her forcibly from the room.

"Those are our grandparents?" Eloise said in disbelief.

"They've never seen you as their granddaughters," Father said.

"Not even now, knowing who we are to wed," I said. "Margaret's different, though. She knew only rumors of the disgraced sister who's name she was given and was curious once she realized who we were."

"Perhaps I'll invite her to have tea with me," Eloise said.

"I like your sister," Eadric said.

I smiled at him.

"Perhaps we should retire to a quieter room," the king said. "I would very much like to speak to you about your daughter marrying my son now that you're here, Mr. Cartwright."

"While I am honored by your deference, in this situation, I believe it best to speak to Eloise regarding who she wishes to marry and when."

The king harrumphed. "After seeing your in-laws, I understand your hesitation. However, Eloise has already agreed. I wish to speak to you about..."

Their voices trailed off as they distanced themselves from us.

My sister gave me a quick hug and looked at my kings. "I am very much looking forward to getting to know my brothers. However, if I don't hurry, King Afton will have me in a room with twenty dressmakers and an etiquette teacher before the day is done."

Greydon bowed to me and allowed Eloise to pull him from the room.

I turned to my kings.

"Does this mean we're welcome?" Garron asked hesitantly.

"Yes and no. The king won't ask us to leave because of Eloise. However, my ability makes him uncomfortable, and my intent to wed all of you makes Greydon *very* uncomfortable. He's worried Eloise will get ideas."

I shifted my weight on my sore feet. They all noticed, but Daemon beat the rest to sweep me off my feet.

"My poor Lamb. Let's see if we can find a room to tend to you."

The agreement of the others wrapped around me, and I felt my hunger stir. It had been a very long walk from the cabin, and though I didn't feel depleted, I couldn't deny my need.

As we neared the door, I felt Rose.

"Thank you for watching over my sister," I said.

I felt her thanks in return and so much more.

By embracing everything that I was, I would help change both our kingdoms for the better. But before I traveled that exhausting path, I would need to replenish what I'd lost. My well was vast, but so too was the love my kings felt for me.

Be at peace and reign well, Kellen. Perhaps we will meet again in the future.

After that thought, I felt her leave.

EPILOGUE

I STOOD BEFORE THE LARGE MIRROR ON THE WALL AND GAZED AT Garron, who stood behind me.

"Do you think Greydon will allow the spell?" I asked.

"I doubt very much he could deny your sister anything," Garron said, wrapping his hands around my stomach to support its weight. I loved it when they did so. It was such a relief that I sighed and leaned back into him. He kissed my temple and then my neck.

"Your kisses are what keep me in this state," I said without any hint of rebuke.

I would be lost without their endless affection and attention. My thoughts turned to how Brandle had woken me with Edmund's help. The pair together often caused the air in the castle to shimmer with energy. Thankfully, it no longer caused a stir.

"Perhaps you should listen to Getaina after this one and take the brew for a time."

"Perhaps," I said, smiling slightly.

"I don't like when you smile like that," Garron said, frowning at me in the mirror. "It usually means you're about to do or say something we won't like."

I patted his arm. "You're paranoid. Do you think the rider was delayed? Or perhaps they had trouble finding a mirror?"

A knock echoed from the mirror before me, and I quickly pressed my hand against the glass.

My reflection with Garron disappeared, replaced by Eloise and Greydon standing in a similar pose. The moment Eloise saw me, she burst into tears.

"I miss you so much."

"Hush, sister. You'll upset your husband, and he'll take you away before we've had a proper talk. Where did you place your mirror?"

"Close to our bed chambers. I would have put it inside, but..."

"Mine is close as well. I'll have an attendant listening for a knock at all times. I promise."

Her gaze dipped to my rounded middle.

"I didn't realize we were so close."

I grinned. "We're not. I'm carrying twins."

Emotions surged through Garron, fear at the forefront.

"Twins? Truly?" Eloise asked. "Um, Garron looks like he paled."

"He probably did. I hadn't told them yet. I wanted you to know first before they locked me away for the remainder of this pregnancy."

"Do you have a good midwife attending you? Should I send mine?"

"I have the best midwives in Turre attending me. I'll be fine. And after these two are born, I'll take a brew for at least a year to ensure I'm fully healed."

"Good. We'll plan a visit then. I want our children to be as close as we were."

"Are," I said firmly. "These mirrors will help."

My twin made a face. "I can't say I like this. Even after all this time, the idea of using a mirror to communicate..."

"The past has passed. We cannot change it, but we can accept it and move on."

She nodded. "How is Father?"

"Good. He's teaching is Leedric how to ride and listening to Anna's heartfelt speech listing all the reasons she should be taught as well."

Eloise laughed. "Just like me, that one."

"She is," I agreed. "Much to Leedric's delight. The Prince and Princess keep their grandfather on his toes."

"Have you heard from Rose recently?"

I shook my head. "In her last correspondence, she said she was closer to discovering where Spyra and Maeve had hailed from."

"Do you truly believe there are more casters out there like that?" Eloise asked.

"It was in Spyra's memories before her mind broke. Three other girls were raised with them. And Spyra had been communicating with the woman until our return. As soon as I touched on where the woman was, though, everything vanished from her mind."

"You're a kinder person than I would have been in continuing to care for her," Eloise said with a hint of anger. I knew it wasn't aimed at me.

"She's no longer the person she was," I said. "Not a hint of evil intent lingers within her. Only a childlike innocence and fear. And, I will not lower myself to her level of cruelty to strike more fear into her heart when she can no longer understand why."

Eloise sighed and agreed. "Tell Father that I love him and miss him. He should visit me soon."

"We all will after your birth."

Garron made a sound of disagreement behind me, and I rolled my eyes. "Providing it will not bring any risk to me or the babes, we will greet the newest member of Drisdall's royal family once he or she arrives."

I saw the way Greydon flushed and smirked. It made him very uncomfortable when we visited. While I was unquestionably accepted as the queen to the seven Kings of Turre here in Adele, on the other side of the Dark Forest, Drisdall viewed the ruling family of Turre in a different light. Wanton. Immoral. Unnatural. Yet, I couldn't imagine living my life any other way.

"Just the two rooms, one for myself and my husbands and one for Father and the children will suffice again, Greydon," I said.

"Must you tease him so, sister?" Eloise asked with a grin.

"I must," I said. "I enjoy watching him squirm and wonder if my life choices appeal to you."

Eloise laughed and patted Greydon's hand resting on her stomach. "I'll assure him later that he's enough for me."

"And I will be busy assuring my own now that my secret is out. I love you, El. Thank you for being my sister."

"Thank you for coming back to me. My life wouldn't be the same without you in it. We'll talk again soon."

I touched the mirror and watched her image fade.

"Twins?" Garron echoed. "Truly?"

"Why are you so shocked? I'm a twin, and your brothers are twins. I imagine this won't be the last pair. Now, how do you propose I tell the others?"

"Naked. That's the only way you'll be able to distract them from their worry."

"The bathing pool then?"

I'd created a bathing pool large enough for us all to fit comfortably. It was my favorite place to be of late. It eased the ache in my back.

Garron hefted me into his arms and started walking. "Wait until we're there to call them to you."

I didn't wait. I let my need for them free and giggled when

Garron stumbled a step, unable to control his surge of desire for me.

"Woman, you will bring me to my knees one of these days."

"I dearly hope so," I said.

The others found us in the bath a short while later. Garron was indeed on his knees, and my head was thrown back in bliss.

Agreeing to give them each a piece of my heart was one of the best decisions I'd ever made. Embracing who I was meant to be and loving myself the way I was was another one.

AUTHOR'S NOTE

Dear Reader,

Thank you for reading the Tales of Snow!

I loved reimagining Snow White and Seven Dwarves set in the world I'd already created with the Beastly Tales. When I started thinking about writing a Cinderella story, I *knew* I was going to make her and Snow White twins. There were too many similarities in the classic versions not to. And I also *knew* I wanted Kellen to love the seven "dwarves." Don't get me wrong— I like the classic with the Prince at the end well enough, but I wanted something with more romance—more spice!

If you haven't yet read the Beastly Tales or the Tales of Cinder, you're missing out. If you have already read them and are hungry for more, that's a distinct possibility.

While writing about the Dark Forest, I had so many plot bunny thoughts about a Red Riding Hood retelling. And, obviously, based on the hints I dropped about more "evil" sisters, more than just the big bad wolf has been tumbling around in my head.

As always, though, I have more ideas than time. If you want to stay up to date on what I'm writing (or even to vote on what I write next), but sure to subscribe to my newsletter via my website mjhaag.melissahaag.com/subscribe so you can keep up on all my writing news. Since I only send monthly (or when there's a new release), I won't spam your inbox.

Be a dear, and if you love this book, please, please, please leave a review on a retailer of your choice AND tell your reader friends to "read. this. book." so I can write a Red Riding Hood one next. (It's no fun writing what no one is reading, you know?)

Until next time, happy reading!
Melissa
(a.k.a. Melissa Haag, M.J. Haag, Sage Alder, Melissa Nicole)

(If you're looking for more books by me, turn the page!)

THE
RESURRECTION CHRONICLES

Humor, romance, and sexy dark fey!

BOOK 1: DEMON EMBER

In a world going to hell, Mya must learn to accept help from her new-found demon protector in order to find her family as a zombie-like plague spreads.

BOOK 2: DEMON FLAMES

As hellhounds continue to roam and the zombie plague spreads, Drav leads Mya to the source of her troubles—Ernisi, an underground Atlantis and Drav's home. There Mya learns that the shadowy demons, who've helped devastate her world, are not what they seem.

BOOK 3: DEMON ASH

While in Ernisi, cites were been bombed and burned in an attempt to stop the plague. Now, Marauders, hellhounds, and the infected are doing their best to destroy what's left of the world. It's up to Mya and Drav to save it.

BOOK 4: DEMON ESCAPE

While running from zombies, hellhounds, and the people who kept her prisoner, Eden encounters a new creature. He claims he only wants to protect her. Eden must decide who the real devils are between man and demon, and choosing wrong could cost her life.

BOOK 5: DEMON DECEPTION

Grieving from the loss of her husband and youngest child, Cassie lives in fear of losing her remaining daughter. To gain protection, Cassie knows she needs to sleep with one of the dark fey and give him the one thing she isn't sure she can. Her heart.

THE
RESURRECTION
CHRONICLES

The apocalyptic adventure continues!

BOOK 6: DEMON NIGHT

Angel's growing weaker by the day and needs help. In exchange for food, she agrees to give Shax advice regarding how to win over Hannah. If Angel can help make that happen, just maybe she won't be kicked out when her fellow survivors find out she's pregnant.

BOOK 7: DEMON DAWN

In a post-apocalyptic world, Benna is faced with the choice of trading her body and heart to the dark fey in order to survive the infected.

BOOK 8: DEMON DISGRACE

Hannah is drinking away her life to stanch the bleeding pain from past trauma. Merdon, a dark fey with a violent history, relentlessly sets out to show her there's something worth living for.

BOOK 9: DEMON FALL

June never planned to fall in love. She had her eyes on the prize: a career and independence. Too bad the world ended and stole those options from her. Maybe falling in love had been the better choice after all.

THE BEASTLY TALES

Beauty and the Beast with seductively dark twists!

BOOK 1: DEPRAVITY

When impoverished, beautiful Benella is locked inside the dark and magical estate of the beast, she must bargain for her freedom if she wants to see her family again.

BOOK 2: DECEIT

Safely hidden within the estate's enchanted walls, Benella no longer has time to fear her tormentors. She's too preoccupied trying to determine what makes the beast so beastly. In order to gain her freedom, she must find a way to break the curse, but first, she must help him become a better man while protecting her heart.

BOOK 3: DEVASTATION

Abused and rejected, Benella strives to regain a purpose for her life, and finds herself returning to the last place she ever wanted to see. She must learn when it is right to forgive and when it is time to move on.

TALES OF CINDER

Becareful what you wish for...

PREQUEL: DISOWNED

In a world where the measure of a person rarely goes beneath the surface, Margaret Thoning refuses to play by its rules. She walks away from everything she's ever known to risk her heart and her life for the people who matter most.

BOOK 1: DEFIANT

When the sudden death of Eloise's mother points to forbidden magic, Eloise's life quickly goes from fairy tale to nightmare. Kaven, the prince's manservant, is Eloise's prime suspect. However, when dark magic is used, nothing is as simple as it seems.

BOOK 2: DISDAIN

Cursed to silence, Eloise is locked in the tattered remains of her once charming life. The smoldering spark of her anger burns for answers and revenge. However, games of magic can have dire consequences.

BOOK 3: DAMNATION

With the reason behind her mother's death revealed, Eloise must prevent her stepsisters from marrying the prince and exact her revenge. However, a secret of the royal court strikes a blow to her plans. Betrayed, Eloise will question how far she's willing to go for revenge.